The Broadview Anthology of
Victorian Short Stories

NATIONAL LIBRARY OF CANADA CATALOGUING IN PUBLICATION DATA

The Broadview anthology of Victorian short stories / edited by Dennis Denisoff.

Includes bibliographical references.

ISBN 1-55111-356-2

1. Short stories, English—19th century.   2. English fiction—19th century.
I. Denisoff, Dennis, 1961-

PR1304.B76 2004   823'.808   C2004-900727-0

BROADVIEW PRESS, LTD. is an independent, international publishing house, incorporated in 1985. Broadview believes in shared ownership, both with its employees and with the general public; since the year 2000 Broadview shares have traded publicly on the Toronto Venture Exchange under the symbol BDP.

We welcome comments and suggestions regarding any aspect of our publications–please feel free to contact us at the addresses below or at broadview@broadviewpress.com / www.broadviewpress.com.

North America
Post Office Box 1243,
Peterborough, Ontario, Canada K9J 7H5

3576 California Road,
Orchard Park, New York, USA 14127
TEL (705) 743-8990; FAX (705) 743-8353

E-MAIL customerservice@broadviewpress.com

United Kingdom and Europe
NBN Plymbridge.
Estover Road, Plymouth PL6 7PY, UK
TEL 44(0) 1752 202301
FAX 44 (0) 1752 202331
FAX ORDER LINE 44 (0) 1752 202333
CUST. SERVICE cservs@nbnplymbridge.com
ORDERS orders@nbnplymbridge.com

Australia & New Zealand
UNIREPS University of New South Wales
Sydney, NSW 2052
TEL 61 2 9664099; FAX 61 2 9664520
E-MAIL infopress@unsw.edu.au

BROADVIEW PRESS, LTD. gratefully acknowledges the financial support of the Government of Canada through the Book Publishing Industry Development Program for our publishing activities.

Cover design by Lisa Brawn.
Typeset by Liz Broes, Black Eye Design.

Printed in Canada

10 9 8 7 6 5 4 3

The Broadview Anthology of Victorian Short Stories

EDITED BY

Dennis Denisoff

broadview press

Contents

Acknowledgements

In the process of putting together this collection, I solicited advice from dozens of Victorianist scholars regarding which authors and works should be included, and why. I requested input from e-mail groups, solicited comments on stories from my students, casually wheedled opinions from colleagues in the hallways, and slyly turned dinner parties into brainstorming sessions on the Victorian short story: "Pretend you were being cast on a desert island ..." Not surprisingly, I lost track over the last three years of all the people who have been kind enough to help me in this regard, and I would like to take this moment to thank them collectively. I would like to note my particular gratitude to the members of the Victoria e-mail group, who consistently came through — both publicly and privately — with advice, suggestions, and leads. It is their advice that had the greatest impact on the selection process, and I apologize for not being able to include every worthy story they brought to my attention. My greatest debt is to my research assistants — Holly Crumpton, Jason Haslam, Alison Hilborn, Ruth Knechtel, Erin McDonald, and Scott Preston. They worked diligently on this project from the initial selection phase through to the final annotations and copy-editing. Their enthusiasm in the hunt for obscure references made this project inspiring, and at times a pleasure that verged on the giddy.

Gratitude is due as well to the staff at the Ryerson University Library, the British Library, Robarts Library at the University of Toronto, the Scott Library at York University, and the Dana Porter Library at the University of Waterloo. I would also like to acknowledge the crucial financial assistance given for this project by the Social Sciences and Humanities Research Council of Canada. The funding did not only allow me the necessary research travel and time to complete the project and share my findings, but it allowed me to benefit from the research efforts of four graduate students. Similarly, Ryerson University's funding for this project allowed me to share my work at various conferences and to hire a research assistant at the conclusion of the project when every tuck of an editorial loose end seemed to reveal a few more strands needing work. For this, I am most grateful.

I would like to end this note by thanking the one person who has worked with me throughout the project — my partner Morgan Holmes, whom I can never thank enough for his kindness, encyclopaedic knowledge, and zeal for literature.

Publication Sources

William Carleton. "Wildgoose Lodge." *Traits and Stories of the Irish Peasantry*. 1833. 4th ed. London: Baldwin and Cradock, 1836.

Mary Shelley. "The Mortal Immortal." *The Keepsake for 1834*. London: Longman, Rees, Orme, Brown, Green, and Longman, 1834.

Charles Dickens. "The Bloomsbury Christening." *The Monthly Magazine* XVII.100 (April 1834).

Thomas De Quincey. "The Vision of Sudden Death" and "The Dream-Fugue." *Blackwood's Edinburgh Magazine* LXVI.CCCCX (December 1849).

Wilkie Collins. "A Terribly Strange Bed." *Household Words* V.109 (24 April 1852).

Elizabeth Gaskell. "The Great Cranford Panic." *Household Words* VI.146 and VI.147 (8 and 15 January 1853).

Frances Browne. "The Story of Fairyfoot" 1857. *Granny's Wonderful Chair*. London: J.M. Dent, 1906.

Geraldine Jewsbury. "Agnes Lee." *Household Words* XVI.381 (11 July 1857).

Anthony Trollope. "George Walker at Suez." *Public Opinion* (28 December 1861).

Mary Elizabeth Braddon. "Eveline's Visitant." *Belgravia* I (January 1867).

Algernon Swinburne. "Dead Love." *Once a Week* (11 October 1862).

C.L. Dodgson. "Bruno's Revenge." *Aunt Judy's Magazine* IV (May 1867).

Sheridan Le Fanu. "Green Tea." *All The Year Round* 2.47–50 (23 October–13 November 1869).

Mary De Morgan. "A Toy Princess." *On a Pincushion and Other Tales*. London: Seeley, Jackson and Halliday, 1872.

Mary Beaumont. "The Revenge of Her Race." [1879?]. *A Ringby Lass and Other Stories*. New York: Macmillan, 1895.

Amelia Blanford Edwards. "Was it an Illusion? A Parson's Story." *Arrowsmith's Christmas Annual for 1881 — Thirteen at Dinner and What Came of It*. London: Griffith and Farren, 1881.

Thomas Hardy. "Interlopers at the Knap." *The English Illustrated Magazine 1883–1884*. London: Macmillan, 1884.

Robert Louis Stevenson. "Markheim." *The Broken Shaft: Unwin's Christmas Annual.* London: Fisher Unwin, 1886. Rpt. *The Merry Men and Other Tales and Fables*. London: Chatto & Windus, 1887.

Rudyard Kipling. "Lispeth." 1886. Rpt. *Plain Tales from the Hills*. Calcutta: Thacker, Spink, 1888. Reprinted by premission of A.P. Watt Ltd. on behalf of the National Trust for Places of Historic Interest or Natural Beauty.

Oscar Wilde. "The Happy Prince." *The Happy Prince and Other Tales*. London: David Nutt, 1888.

Arthur Conan Doyle. "A Scandal in Bohemia." *The Strand* II (July–December 1891).

George Egerton. "The Spell of the White Elf." *Keynotes*. London: Elkin Mathews and John Lane, 1893.

Evelyn Sharp. "In Dull Brown." *The Yellow Book* VIII (January 1896).

Ada Leverson. "The Quest of Sorrow." *The Yellow Book* VIII (January 1896).

H.G. Wells. "The Star." *The Graphic*. Christmas Number. (1897). Reprinted by premission of A.P. Watt Ltd. on behalf of the National Trust for Places of Historic Interest or Natural Beauty.

Israel Zangwill. "To Die in Jerusalem." *Ghetto Tragedies*. Philadelphia: Jewish Publication Society of America, 1899.

Edgar Allan Poe. Review of Nathaniel Hawthorne's *Twice-told Tales. Graham's magazine* (May 1842).

Charles Dickens. "Frauds on the Fairies." *Household Words* VIII.184 (1 October 1853).

Margaret Oliphant. "The ByWays of Literature: Reading for the Million." *Blackwood's Edinburgh Magazine* 84 (August 1858).

Frederick Wedmore. "The Short Story." *The Nineteenth Century* XLIII (March 1898).

Laura Marholm Hansson. "Neurotic Keynotes." *Six Modern Women: Psychological Sketches*. Trans. Hermione Ramsden. Boston: Roberts, 1896.

The publisher has made every effort to locate all copyright holders of the texts published in this book and would be pleased to hear from any party not duly acknowledged.

Introduction

Students do not need to be taught the importance and effectiveness of short stories — they have themselves been demonstrating their power for over a century.

Consider "The Priest and the Acolyte." Appearing anonymously in 1894 in the undergraduate journal *The Chameleon*, this short story was derivative of the Decadent literature already peaking in England at the time. The journal itself, edited by the student John Francis Bloxam, only lasted for a single issue, with a run of only 100 copies. Bloxam, it turns out, was also the author of "The Priest and the Acolyte." The likelihood was that this short story would become just one of the thousands that Victorians published, read, and forgot. Despite such unpromising origins, however, Bloxam's sympathetic depiction of a romantic relationship between a priest and his male assistant hit a nerve. The story caused something of a commotion in London and reviewers wrote bilious attacks based on the immorality of the subject. Oscar Wilde, the most famous participant in British Decadence, also criticized the piece, albeit on aesthetic grounds, finding that it lacked nuance.

Wilde had contributed "Phrases and Philosophies for the Use of the Young" to *The Chameleon*, but many attributed "The Priest and the Acolyte" to him as well. In fact, during the court trials between Wilde and the Marquess of Queensberry the following year, the prosecution turned to Bloxam's short story to attack the more famous writer's sexual interests. Even if Wilde was not the work's author, the fact that he had been published in the same periodical suggested guilt by association. Thus Wilde found himself, in one of the most famous court cases of the century, defending himself by discussing the merits of an undergraduate student's short story. Nobody could have expected that such a minor piece of fiction published anonymously in a short-lived, student journal would become a tool in a political event whose social repercussions continue to be felt to this day. In light of this history, we should probably be less surprised now of the impact that short stories can have.

Over 100 years after the scandal of "The Priest and the Acolyte," in 2002, a high school student in a town near Ottawa, Ontario, was asked to read his class assignment out loud. A fan of Stephen King, he had chosen to write on "fear," one of the topics suggested by the teacher. In his piece, "Twisted," a fictitious student blows up his school cafeteria in retaliation for having been bullied. In the background of this narrative was the 1999 massacre of 14 students in Columbine, Colorado, as well as the fact that the boy himself had recently been physically attacked by a number of students. After the assignment was presented, the police arrested the boy and then, ten days after that, also charged him with making additional death threats. Rumours about the writer having a hit list were never substantiated. Nor did he have a history of violence or crime. A night raid of his home came up with no weapons, explosions, or material used to make such things.

The arrest spurred a debate about free speech, with a key question being whether "Twisted" was proof of the student's earnest desire to hurt others or just a creative critique of society's blindness to bullying. Participants in the controversy included the police, the student's school, the Ontario Secondary School Teachers' Federation, Canada's Crown attorney, lawyers, psychologists, journalists, Internet chat groups, authors such as Margaret Atwood, Stephen King, and Michael Ondaatje, and writers' groups including the Canadian branch of PEN International, which campaigns on behalf of writers who have been imprisoned for their work. Seven students were eventually charged with assault in the bullying that had been a major catalyst in the creation of "Twisted." All the charges against the author, meanwhile, were withdrawn.

Although different in many ways, "The Priest and the Acolyte" and "Twisted" both demonstrate that not only individuals but also established social institutions such as the courts and schools have for over a century recognized and even fostered the influences that short stories and real-life politics have on each other. Notably, both pieces benefited from the fact that short fiction can be quickly and cheaply created and distributed — often orally. The genre thus offers unique opportunities for public commentary and influence. It helps give a voice to individuals who are often otherwise kept silent. Today, as in the Victorian age, one usually chooses to read short stories simply because they are well written and entertaining. As these two examples suggest, however, they are equally important for offering unique insights into the changing values, views, anxieties, and aspirations of both past eras and our own.

WHAT IS A VICTORIAN SHORT STORY?

In light of the variety of short fiction produced by the Victorians alone, it is not surprising that authors and scholars have yet to reach full agreement on what constitutes a short story.[1] Just as old types of writing such as diary entries have been gaining recognition as literature, new types such as the interactive hypertextual story continue to demand an expansion of valid defining criteria. Due to these ongoing changes, any definition can offer only a general starting point for understanding the genre. Recognizing this limitation, the genre of the short story can be broadly defined as relatively brief prose fiction with a plot (even if only implied).[2] While many scholars have noted that just because a piece of fiction is short does not mean it is a short story, length does make certain other characteristics common to the genre. The limit on words that was often imposed by periodical publishers encouraged authors to develop techniques of narrative economy that were not required in a longer genre such as the novel. As Mary Shelley, who often wrote her short stories for the popular annuals of the time, lamented: "When I write for them, I am worried to death to make my things shorter & shorter — till I fancy people think ideas can by conveyed by intuition" (245).[3] As Shelley suggests, elements such as allusion and concision are common to short stories and contribute to the argument that they differ from novels not only in size but also in kind — that is, in their inherent qualities or characteristics. The relative brevity results in short stories usually having only one or two main characters and focussing on one event. Moreover, objects included in a shorter narrative many times take on greater symbolic force and do so more readily.

---

1 Useful discussions of generic definitions can be found in Norman Friedman's "Recent Short Story Theories: Problems in Definition" (1989); Valerie Shaw's *The Short Story* (1983); and essays by Mary Louise Pratt, Allan H. Pasco, Robert F. Marler, and Wendell V. Harris in Charles E. May's collection *The New Short Story Theories* (1994).

2 Inevitably, even these few criteria are ambiguous. With regard to length, for example, it would be easiest to say that the genre be defined by some maximum number of words, but the task of selecting that number quickly demonstrates the randomness of the measure. In an 1842 essay, Edgar Allan Poe offered perhaps the first attempt at such a quantitative measure when he suggested that one should be able to read a "prose tale" comfortably in one sitting, roughly half an hour to two hours (see Appendix A). But degrees of literacy, speed of reading, level of education, familiarity with the genre, and other factors would all impact on Poe's measure.

3 As their name suggests, annuals were publications that came out once a year. Containing short stories, poetry, and engravings, they usually appeared for the Christmas season. Their popularity ran from the 1820s to the 1840s. Relatively elaborate and somewhat more expensive than other periodicals, annuals were envisioned as gifts, most often exchanged between middle-class women.

And yet, even though these traits can often be found in short stories, a piece need not display them in order to be an example of the genre.

The Victorian era is named after Queen Victoria's reign (1837–1901) but, because of the Reform Act of 1832 — which extended voting rights to the middle classes and drastically changed the power dynamics of the time — the Victorian era is often marked as beginning with this date.[1] This is the date that I have chosen as my starting point as well. The various works of short prose fiction that were finding an audience during this period reflect not only differences among writers and readers, but also a range of political and cultural influences. It is common to claim that British short fiction "matured" into the genre of the short story in the 1890s with pieces by authors such as Robert Louis Stevenson, Rudyard Kipling, and Joseph Conrad. Nevertheless, a comparison of these men's writings to each other, as well as to pieces such as "The Priest and the Acolyte" that appeared in more avant-garde periodicals, reveals that even in the last decade of the century short stories continued to take on such a diversity of forms that generic categorization would have been difficult, as it still is today. The situation is complicated even further when one realizes that Victorian authors themselves were never especially concerned with the categories into which their works were slotted. Some would even have questioned whether what they wrote constituted fiction at all. William Carleton, in Ireland, and Thomas Hardy, in England, for example, both felt it important that their short stories have roots in history, and they gathered the information that went into their works not only from written records but also from unofficial oral reports. Meanwhile, as Carleton's "Wildgoose Lodge" demonstrates, the choice of a historical basis for one's work does not necessarily deter embellishment.

Many people actually used terms like "story," "short story," "tale," and "sketch" interchangeably. Usually, the term "tale" is used to refer to a work that focuses primarily on the course and outcome of events. It is more interested in plot propulsion than evoking the aura of a moment. A sketch, meanwhile, is basically a work that captures relatively static scenes,

---

1   The Great Reform Act of 1832 marked the first official registration of voters and saw a massive increase in the proportion of voters who came from the rich middle classes. Despite their wishes, the working class remained excluded in large part. The 1832 act resulted in a stronger voting voice for people from Scotland and, to some degree, Ireland. It also extended parliamentary representation to major industrial towns such as Manchester and Birmingham.

   The Reform Act of 1867 roughly doubled the electorate, with a major segment of the added group coming from the industrial working class. It was not until 1918 that women were given the vote and, even then, only those over 30 (thus keeping them from holding a potential majority). Women over 21 received the vote in 1928.

and limits character and narrative development. The latter term was also used, however, to refer to any work that an author wished to suggest was a casual piece dashed off on the spur of the moment.[1] Elizabeth Gaskell, for example, referred to her tales about the town she called Cranford as sketches, probably to reflect the lightness with which she hoped readers would approach these humorous pieces. Gaskell's approach to the Cranford pieces illustrates the flexible approach that many authors took to short fiction. When she wrote the first sketch, she had no intention of creating more. Later, when she began writing additional pieces about the town, she would regret having killed off her central male character in the first one, because it meant she had to invent a new hero. It is not known when exactly she started to envision the pieces as functioning as a cohesive whole; however, the fifth of the eight sketches, "The Cranford Panic," shows that each also succeeds independently.

The image of Victorian stories prior to the 1890s as being predominantly quaint or sensationalist and unworthy of scholarly recognition did not arise from the popularity of the material or its importance to the culture and politics of the age. Rather, this view was the product primarily of authors from the first half of the twentieth century struggling to construct their own self-images as innovative and independent of past influences. The Modernist era (which dominated the cultural scene from roughly the 1900s to the 1940s) saw the prioritization of certain aesthetic values that nineteenth-century works, in retrospect, often failed to accommodate. For example, many Victorians felt that a story should offer a coherent, well-designed narrative with a beginning, middle, and end, as described by Aristotle.[2] Later writers and scholars, however, gave this convention a provincial connotation, preferring works that relied more on narratives blurred by suggestion and impressionistic nuance. Notably, this shift to a Modernist aesthetics actually arose in the Victorian age, as the stories in this collection by Kipling, George Egerton, Evelyn Sharp, and others confirm. Frederick Wedmore's view that "plot, or story proper" is not essential to a short story sounds distinctly post-Victorian, despite the fact that he made the statement in the 1890s and that (according to his essay included here as Appendix D) he began his study in the 1870s.

---

1   Extensive discussions of the ambiguities around terms like "short story," "tale," and "sketch" can be found in Ian Reid's *The Short Story* (1977) and Valerie Shaw's *The Short Story* (1983).

2   In his *Poetics*, Aristotle (384–322 BC) argues that coherence is crucial to a literary work. It is attained, he says, through a unified and interrelated plot structure with beginning, middle, and end. In many short stories, the beginning or even middle are often only alluded to, and sometimes they open with the climax which marks the end of the plot.

His description of the genre as including, among other things, works best described as episodes, panoramas, visions, and glimpses reflects both the variety that characterized nineteenth-century stories and the Modernist preference for vagueness and ambiguity.[1]

The short story is most often defined in contrast to the novel. This genre, which has been the short story's main competitor for readers, attained new heights of popularity during the Victorian period. Authors generally preferred writing novels because they were more lucrative and received higher critical respect. While many readers also favoured the novel and some enjoyed both types of writing, a large portion still preferred short prose works. There are a number of reasons for this. For starters, short stories were often aimed at a different, more specific audience than novels, such as young readers or those partial to a specific set of values. There was, for example, a relatively strong market for religious fiction at the beginning of the nineteenth century. Meanwhile, avant-garde magazines such as *The Chameleon*, *The Savoy*, and *The Yellow Book* proliferated during the *fin de siècle* as part of the Aesthetic Movement, whose participants included Egerton, Wilde, Algernon Swinburne, and Ada Leverson. In addition, readers who wanted a quick fix of excitement or sensationalism would have found that short stories fit the bill more readily than the more discursive novels. Meanwhile, people who were not strong readers would have found it more feasible to consume short fiction than a prolix novel. In fact, like short stories, many novels first appeared in periodicals in serial form; that is, they were themselves broken down into sections of short fiction. Novels were cheaper to access when published in periodicals, but generally speaking they were still overall more expensive than stories. Often novels were published as "three-deckers" — that is, in three volumes — to spread out the purchase price. One could also borrow these novels from lending libraries such as Mudie's Circulating Library, founded in 1842, for an even lower cost. This gave the libraries a virtual monopoly on the three-decker market, and also allowed them to dictate morals and values that reinforced the views of the growing middle class to which they catered. When the libraries concluded in 1894 that three-deckers were not cost-effective and stopped their publication, more

---

1   Even though Ian Reid's cogent overview *The Short Story* came out much later in 1977, it also recognizes the Modernist preference for allusion and fragmentation. Reid claims that modern writers eschew the "neat plot-making" and novelistic narrative techniques found in nineteenth-century stories in favour of poetic and dramatic qualities more readily located in writing *before* that time period (3–4). Despite his appreciation for Modernist qualities, Reid also maintains that the short story requires a narrative, offering a general definition of the genre as "any kind of fictitious prose narrative briefer than a novel" (9).

people turned to short stories. This shift contributed to making the 1890s the most popular decade of the century for the genre.

There were also practical reasons for some authors to write short stories. For one, they took less time and therefore could be more easily completed amid other work and responsibilities. Also, while novels were more profitable, it was easier to get a short piece published because of the reduced financial risk to the publisher should a work not prove popular. Many writers famous as novelists — such as Gaskell, William Makepeace Thackeray, and Wilkie Collins — were well known for their short stories. Some — such as Charles Dickens and Sheridan Le Fanu — were even editors of periodicals and encouraged other authors to write short prose pieces. To some degree, because such fiction was less lucrative, less respected, and less of a risk to publishers, it gave authors greater freedom to experiment. Despite the lower pay, it was also still possible to make a living as a short-story writer. Notably, Harold Orel's examples in *The Victorian Short Story* of relatively well-paid short-story writers — Stevenson, Kipling, Arthur Conan Doyle, and H.G. Wells — all wrote at the end of the century. The period that Orel suggests marks an increase in the monetary value of the short story was also the time at which authors, publishers, and the reading public began to recognize it as a serious literary genre. Prior to this date, the fact that short fiction was being consumed by millions from all classes, age groups, and literacy levels made it so common as to be invisible, and so popular as to be seen as unworthy of the exclusiveness associated with scholarly recognition. While such mass consumption continued through the end of the Victorian age and afterward, the increased effort to classify the genre fostered a hierarchization of only certain types of short fiction as worthy of generic consideration.

SOCIAL CHANGES AND SHIFTING SUBJECTS

While editing down my initial selection of the over 200 stories to the 26 that are in the final anthology, my aims have been to represent a range of popular subjects of the Victorian era and the ways in which the depiction of some of these subjects changed over time. In addition, I wished to reflect the stories' hybrid origins and disparate influences, as well as individual authors' unique imaginations and unconventional concerns and methods. In this collection, therefore, famous authors rub shoulders with some who are virtually unknown now. One can find examples of the comic, the gothic, the ghost story, experimental fantasy, adventure, science fiction, children's stories, "New Woman" writing, travel writing, Decadent works, realism, and colonialist literature.[1] Indeed, most of the stories fit into more than one of the above categories. Anthony Trollope's "George Walker at Suez," to offer one example, can be described as a comic, colonialist, travel tale.

I have also included a couple of pieces written early in the Victorian period. Though coming in large part from different traditions, the works by Mary Shelley and William Carleton both suggest the strong oral tradition that preceded the rise of the short story during the Victorian period. Their first-person narratives reflect the story-telling custom and encourage the stories to be delivered orally, thereby accommodating those members of society who were unable to read. It is this custom as well that fostered the creation of tales — with exciting narratives — more than sketches or the later, more psychological pieces. Part of the short story's formative history involved the genre's publication in periodicals that were usually shared by more than one person and often read aloud; this permitted even those members of the population who could not afford to buy literature or who could not read to develop a taste for written stories.

The number of consumers, meanwhile, was briskly increasing. Within 100 years, Britain's population more than tripled, reaching 42 million by 1900. A major demographic result of the Industrial Revolution was a shift in this growing population from rural areas to the city. One influence this had on the consumption of literature was that it made it easier to distribute material among more people.[2] Changes in legal and publishing procedures also had a major impact on this growing market's consumption of the short story. Due to a complex web of laws, publishers at the beginning of the nineteenth century found it most profitable to produce entertainment periodicals rather than newspapers. Walter Graham has noted that the start of the century marked a shift in the periodicals' emphasis from miscellanies of information to creative fiction. Improvements to paper-making and printing technology greatly reduced

---

1   The term "new woman" refers to a young, single, educated female who usually supported suffrage (women's right to vote), equality between genders, and the right to choose without condemnation a life not necessarily defined by traditional marital roles. Recent works among the notable wave of research on the topic include Ann Heilmann's *New Woman Fiction* (2000), Sally Ledger's *New Woman* (1997), and the collection *The New Woman in Fiction and in Fact* (2001) edited by Angelique Richardson and Chris Willis.

2   On the relationship between fiction and the Industrial Revolution, see Catherine Gallagher's *The Industrial Reformation of English Fiction 1832–1867* (1985).

the cost of production, thereby increasing competition and making written stories, which were a standard of periodicals, more affordable.[1] The repeal of the newspaper tax in 1855 only increased the profit margin for periodicals. Many publishers kept costs down further by paying their authors poorly. It was common for short stories to be written quickly by "hack" writers who were encouraged to emphasize exciting narratives while giving little attention to subtlety of language or depth of character. The cheapest and trashiest of these periodicals — as well as their contents — became known as "penny dreadfuls." They were published on inexpensive paper with simple, exciting stories and vivid illustrations seen to be as important as the written material.[2]

While literacy rates grew, readers' tastes did not become more discerning or exclusive, with a vast portion of the audience for fiction continuing to demand quick and easy entertainment. As Louis James explains, they wanted "anything to please for a few hours, and the less demands it made on the comprehension of the tired worker the better." Penny dreadfuls were aimed at these readers. According to Thomas Frost (*Forty Years*), the pulp publisher Edward Lloyd offered the following explanation of his strategy for success: "Our publications circulate among a class so different in education and social position from the readers of three-volume novels, that we sometimes distrust our judgement and place the manuscript in the hands of an illiterate person — servant or a machine boy for instance. If they pronounce favourably upon it, we think it will do" (90). Such stories may present overt moral messages, but these lurid, sometimes gory tales were aimed far more toward excitement than moral education or philosophical rumination.[3] Their

---

1   Louis James offers an overview of the lower-class market for short fiction during the early-Victorian period in *Fiction for the Working Man, 1830–1850* (1963).

2   John Camden Hotten's *Slang Dictionary* (1865) defined penny dreadfuls as "those penny publications which depend more upon sensationalism than upon merit, artistic or literary, for success." More information on and examples of stories from penny dreadfuls can be found in Michael Anglo's *Penny Dreadfuls and Other Victorian Horrors* (1977), Peter Haining's *The Penny Dreadful* (1975), and at my Web site *Victorian Pulp* <www.ryerson.ca/~denisoff>.

3   Even prior to the nineteenth century, the highly sensationalist *Newgate Calendar* stories describing the criminal exploits and eventual punishment of actual prisoners were popular among the lower and working classes. Springheel'd Jack, Tyburn Dick, and the other thieves, highwaymen, and murderers of these tales eventually found a home in the Victorian penny dreadfuls. Discussions of the *Newgate Calendar* and examples of these often gory stories can be found in Donald Thomas's *The Victorian Underworld* (1998) and at my Web site *Victorian Pulp*.

concentration on adventures, heroism, and fantastic scenarios position these works in the centuries-long tradition of romantic fiction.[1]

The Victorian short stories' attention to fear and suspense had major aesthetic roots in Romanticism and its emphasis on the emotions, feelings, and imagination of the individual. The Romantic Movement ran in England from roughly 1790 to 1830, and marked a major turn in artistic attention to individual expression, the imagination, and originality. These traits accord with the short story's own tendency to centre on a single character's experiences of an event. The focus on one emotional moment brings to mind Edgar Allan Poe's 1842 review of Nathaniel Hawthorne's *Twice-told Tales* (see Appendix A), which many see as offering the first important definition of what we now call the short story. Here, Poe argues that all the parts of a tale must contribute to attaining a unity of impression or effect. Although admired by authors such as Swinburne and Wilde, Poe's essay did not have a notable impact on the Victorian short story in general. Nevertheless, a similar aesthetic characteristic appears to have developed in Britain primarily through Romanticism.

The Romantic writers' interest in the individual's connection to the other-worldly also contributed to British society's increasing religious skepticism. As more and more Victorians stopped attending church on a regular basis, they developed greater interest in other unfamiliar or supernatural phenomena such as mesmerism, spiritualism, and the ability of the individual to communicate with the dead. Telepathy, Ouija boards, and table knocking were only some of the means of transmission. A number of people also acknowledged their belief in fairies, with some even claiming to have photographed them. Although Conan Doyle's character Sherlock Holmes relied heavily on logic, reasoning, and science to solve his crimes, the author himself asserted to have proof of life after death, felt he had the ability to communicate thoughts with his mind, and believed in fairies.[2] Such interests in the supernatural established a cultural context that

---

1   A related but less common subject of the short story that developed during this period was that of detective fiction. The American author Edgar Allan Poe is seen to have written the earliest examples with such pieces as "The Murders in the Rue Morgue" (1841) and "The Purloined Letter" (1845), although precursors exist. In Britain, authors of detective stories include Dickens, Mary Braddon, Collins, Le Fanu, and Conan Doyle. During the Victorian era, detective fiction appeared in the form of novels although the even more popular ghost stories often carried detective elements.

2   The most famous incident regarding belief in fairies is the case of the Cottingley Fairies. In 1917, two children — Elsie Wright and Frances Griffiths — cut some pictures of fairies out of their children's book *Princess Mary's Gift Book* and took pictures of themselves playing with the cutouts in nature. A huge number of people including Conan Doyle believed the photographs to show real fairies. One thing the Cottingley incident effectively demonstrates is the impact that fantasy has on everyday adult lives even after the Victorian era.

allowed the spectral to become one of the most popular topics in short fiction. It meant that ghost stories were not read simply as flights of fancy but as narratives of the paranormal tinged with the potential of fact. As "Twisted" has recently reminded us, a heightened sense of the possibility of something actually happening makes it even more disturbing.

The ghost stories' main precursor was the gothic, which began its rise to fame with Horace Walpole's 1764 novel *The Castle of Otranto* and waned around 1815. The genre is characterized by the isolated, frightening castle, evil male villain, and innocent, young heroine. The threat of sexual abuse was the major source of narrative, while the stories also allowed women — who made up a major portion of the writers and readers of these works — to represent and explore other gender-based concerns. The end of the nineteenth century saw the rise of what is now called the neo-gothic, which paid less attention to clearly delineated external threats in foreign (that is, non-English), isolated castles or monasteries and more to psychological disturbances or anxieties within local contexts. Le Fanu's "Green Tea" and Stevenson's "Markheim" are examples of this later form.[1]

Focussing on interactions between the living and the spirits of the dead, ghost stories usually combine frightening entertainment with a moral message.[2] In some works, such as Amelia B. Edwards's "Was it an Illusion?," the message is not simply a universalizing platitude but a pointed critique of particular views held by her society. The most famous example of this combination is Dickens's "A Christmas Carol." In this work, Scrooge learns a lesson not only about human kindness but also more specifically about economic exploitation and the superiority of the middle-class dream to either the extreme of poverty or that of wealth. In fact, Dickens was the major catalyst for the Victorian association of ghost stories with Christmas. It was common for periodicals to publish thicker issues for the festive period, when people were more likely to splurge on such entertainment (Altick, 363). As editor of the periodical *All the Year Round*, Dickens wrote and solicited ghost stories for these seasonal issues. It was their intense popularity that encouraged the spread of the practice until it became a festive tradition.

---

1   There have been many important and useful works written on the subject of the gothic, including William Patrick Day's *In the Circles of Fear and Desire* (1985); the collection of essays *The Female Gothic* (1983), edited by Juliann E. Fleenor; Sandra Gilbert and Susan Gubar's *The Madwoman in the Attic* (1979); and Fred Botting's *Gothic* (1996).

2   Both Michael Cox and R.A. Gilbert's introduction to *Victorian Ghost Stories* (1991) and J.A. Cuddon's introduction to *Penguin Book of Ghost Stories* (1986) give succinct summaries of the culture that gave rise to the ghost story.

In contrast to the gothic, the ghost story (like the neo-gothic that followed) had an aura of factuality attained in part by using local and domestic settings common to the average reader. Despite ghost stories' obviously fantastic elements, the presence of a strong vein of realism maximized the works' fear factor. M.H. Abrams offers the insightful description of realist fiction as being written "so as *to give the effect* that it represents life and the social world as it seems to the common reader" (174, emphasis added). Because realism is most easily evoked through an attention to detail, it requires length, which makes it more commonly a feature of novels than short stories. This is one of the reasons why Geraldine Jewsbury's "Agnes Lee" has the feel of a novel. Despite notable differences, Thomas Hardy's "Interlopers at the Knap" and Evelyn Sharp's "In Dull Brown" also demonstrate realist traits in their depiction of "ordinary" lower- or middle-class people and daily events with lifelike fidelity. Ghost stories could also accommodate these requirements. In Edwards's "Was it an Illusion?" realism has a special function. By making the over-all narrative feel more believable, it enhances the sense of the frightening events' probability, thereby encouraging her readers to question whether they might in some way be guilty of misdeeds similar to those depicted in the story.

Not surprisingly, ghost stories found an eager audience among children, as did the adventure narratives of the penny dreadfuls. At the same time, more and more children were learning how to read. In 1870, the Education Act established a system of schools for children up to the age of 12, and mandatory attendance was established 10 years later. By the 1880s, literacy rates had sky-rocketed. Many Victorians speculated (incorrectly) that the increase in education and reading competence would result in an increased market for realist literature, at the expense of the fantastic and romance fiction. Meanwhile, articles appeared arguing that sensationalist stories such as those found in penny dreadfuls were dangerous for children because they glorified crime. In 1874, James Greenwood published an essay entitled "A Short Way to Newgate" that attacked the "penny packets of poison" as "nasty-feeling, nasty-looking" trash that was dangerously seductive. As the main audience for the texts shifted from the lower and working classes in general toward adolescents and younger boys (thanks in large part to marketing), the fear that the material would encourage readers to commit similar crimes grew stronger.[1] By the end of the century, one had the

---

1   Peter Haining (1975) notes this shift in age-group as becoming marked in the 1860s (16). See also Edward Salmon's *Juvenile Literature As It Is* (1888) and Margaret Oliphant's "The ByWays of Literature: Reading for the Million" (1858). A selection of the latter is included here as Appendix C.

option of purchasing sanitized versions of these adventure stories that encouraged young male readers to develop traits such as bravery, honesty, and morality. The "nasty" narratives, however, did not go away. Rarely included in a consideration of children's literature, they were in fact the work that many young people preferred to devour.

When one thinks of Victorian children, one does not usually conjure up images of the many youngsters who read "nasty" short stories, let alone those who lived in dire poverty, turned to crime, were abandoned, or were forced to work in mines, factories, and workhouses. Rather, one probably first recalls the image favoured at the time of saucer-eyed, innocent darlings playing blissfully with kittens and ribbons. As Dickens's "The Bloomsbury Christening" and Egerton's "The Spell of the White Elf" reveal, however, not all people from the period bought into this image. In fact, many children's stories, while less daring than the dreadfuls, also questioned such false idealisation. Written fantasy stories began to gain popularity in Britain fairly early in the nineteenth century with the translations of such works as the Brothers Grimm's *German Popular Stories* in 1823 and later with Hans Christian Andersen's *Wonderful Stories for Children* in 1846. Less frightening than the tales on which they were based, Grimms' and Andersen's stories started a wave of such works. It was not until roughly the middle of the century that literature for youngsters became a mainstay of British culture, but it only took a few decades for the product to become homogenized and marketed as a reflection of the values of a bourgeois audience.

In his 1853 essay "Frauds on the Fairies" (Appendix B), Dickens warns authors not to rework tales in order to incorporate their own modern values, although he also praises fairy tales for endowing children with some rather specific traits — "forbearance, courtesy, consideration for the poor and aged, kind treatment of animals, the love of nature, [and] abhorrence of tyranny and brute force" (566). Less didactic than their precursors, most Victorian children's stories nevertheless do make suggestions for proper living. Frances Browne's "The Story of Fairyfoot" and C.L. Dodgson's "Bruno's Revenge" both reflect typical values of the Victorian children's story such as altruism and a strong work ethic. And yet, like most leading characters in such works, Fairyfoot and Bruno are depicted as marginalized misfits who struggle to gain a sense of self worth under society's critical gaze. As the pieces suggest, the stories are also open to symbolic interpretations intended for adults. Oscar Wilde had claimed that his own children's stories were "meant partly for children, and partly for those who have kept the childlike faculties of wonder and joy." Indeed, his "Happy Prince" seems aimed at adults more than children. The piece can be read, for example, as a critique of his society's materialism, its loss of spiritual values, or its narrow-minded parameters regarding love. Women writers also used children's literature to question normative models of love and conventions that supported gender imbalances. These topics are both addressed, for example, in Mary De Morgan's "A Toy Princess." Notably, in this story it is not just male characters who reinforce the tradition of male privilege. As Jack Zipes has argued, in a discussion of authors including Wilde and De Morgan, Victorian children's authors of both sexes often "created strong women characters and placed great emphasis on the fusion of female and male qualities and equality between men and women" (xxv). "The creation of fairy-tale worlds," Zipes explains, "allows the writers to deal symbolically with social taboos and to suggest alternatives to common English practice" (xxiv). Making full use of the symbolic potency that imbues the short story genre, children's tales are rarely intended only for the young.

While issues of gender bias and sexual discrimination can be found throughout the Victorian era, it was the final decade of the century that saw the "Woman Question" and women's rights become one of the most important subjects in short stories.[1] This was a reflection in part of the increased access to education that women received over the century. Queen's College and Bedford College for women were founded in 1848 and 1849 respectively. In 1869, the first women's college at Cambridge was established. Called Girton College, it gave rise to the term "Girton Girl," which was used to caricature young, educated women who appeared especially confident of their position in society and more demanding of gender equality. Meanwhile, the "Matrimonial Causes Act" (1857), the "Married Women's Property Act" (1870), and the second "Married Women's Property Act" (1882), while problematic, increased a woman's voice within marriage by, for example, making divorce easier and allowing women to hold property in their own name even after getting married. Women's suffrage became a key political issue for much of the final two decades of the century. As Sharp's story suggests, however, the notion that a woman may not be interested in marriage was still difficult for the majority of society to fathom. While literature depicted women having a much greater range of options from the time of Dickens's "Bloomsbury Christening" in

---

1   The "Woman Question" refers to the Victorian debate around the rights and responsibilities of women in society and in the home. For more information on the subject, see the essay collection *Victorian Women Writers and "The Woman Question"* (1999) edited by Nicola Thompson.

1834 to Egerton's "Spell of the White Elf" in 1893, the breadth of possibilities that they could actually realize remained narrow.

Restricted by employment opportunities, limited by laws on which they could not vote, and channelled by cultural expectations to take on extensive domestic responsibilities, women often had comparatively little time or money to write or publish fiction. It is amazing to see individuals such as Mary Braddon, who battled with poverty and later took responsibility for raising eleven children, produce the amount of work that they did. Although a number of female authors struggling under difficult conditions did succeed as novelists, women interested in literary careers would have been especially attracted to short stories, because of their brevity and comparative ease of publication. Speaking more generally, any writer who felt hindered by the status quo would have found the short story appealing not only because of its length but also because most critics and scholars did not yet recognize it as a genre worthy of scrutiny, qualification and constriction. This allusiveness resulted in a range of works reflecting a spirit of creativity, diversity, and disruption that undermines attempts at classification. Hopefully *The Broadview Anthology of Victorian Short Stories* will pass some of this spirit on to its readers.

WORKS CITED

Abrams, M.H. *A Glossary of Literary Terms*. 6th ed. Orlando, FL: Harcourt Brace, 1993.

Altick, Robert. *The English Common Reader: A Social History of the Mass Reading Public*. Chicago: U of Chicago P, 1957.

Anglo, Michael. *Penny Dreadfuls and Other Victorian Horrors*. London: Jupiter, 1977.

Aristotle. *The Poetics*. Oxford: Clarendon, 1968.

Bloxam, John Francis. "The Priest and the Acolyte." *The Chameleon* 1.1 (December 1894).

Botting, Fred. *Gothic*. London: Routledge, 1996.

Cox, Michael, and R.A. Gilbert, eds. *Victorian Ghost Stories: An Oxford Anthology*. Oxford: Oxford UP, 1991.

Cuddon, J.A. *The Penguin Book of Ghost Stories*. Harmondsworth, UK: Penguin, 1986.

Day, William Patrick. *In the Circles of Fear and Desire: A Study of Gothic Fantasy*. Chicago: U of Chicago P, 1985.

Denisoff, Dennis. *Victorian Pulp*. <www.ryerson.ca/~denisoff>.

Dickens, Charles. "Frauds on the Fairies." *Household Words* (October 1853).

Fleenor, Juliann E., ed. *The Female Gothic*. Montreal: Eden, 1983.

Friedman, Norman. "Recent Short Story Theories: Problems in Definition." *Short Story Theory at a Crossroads*. Ed. Susan Lohafer and Jo Ellyn Clarey. Baton Rouge: Louisiana UP, 1989. 13–32.

Frost, Thomas. *Forty Years' Recollections; Literary and Political*. London: Chatto and Windus, 1880.

Gallagher, Catherine. *The Industrial Reformation of English Fiction 1832–1867*. Chicago: U of Chicago P, 1985.

Gilbert, Sandra, and Susan Gubar. *The Madwoman in the Attic*. New Haven: Yale UP, 1979.

Greenwood, James. *Seven Curses of London*. Boston: Fields, Osgood, 1869.

Haining, Peter. "Introduction." *The Penny Dreadful, Or, Strange, Horrid and Sensational Tales!* Ed. Peter Haining. London: Victor Gollancz, 1975.

Heilmann, Ann. *New Woman Fiction: Women Writing First-Wave Feminism*. New York: St. Martin's, 2000.

Hotten, John Camden. *The Slang Dictionary*. London: Chatto and Windus, 1913.

James, Louis. *Fiction for the Working Man 1830–1850*. London: Oxford UP, 1963.

Ledger, Sally. *The New Woman: Fiction and Feminism at the Fin-de-siècle*. New York: Manchester UP, 1997.

May, Charles E., ed. *The New Short Story Theories*. Athens: Ohio UP, 1994.

Oliphant, Margaret. "The ByWays of Literature: Reading for the Million." *Blackwood's Edinburgh Magazine* 84 (August 1858): 200–16.

Orel, Harold. *The Victorian Short Story: Development and Triumph of a Literary Genre*. Cambridge: Cambridge UP, 1986.

Poe, Edgar Allan. Review of Nathaniel Hawthorne's *Twice-told Tales.* 1842.

Reid, Ian. *The Short Story.* London: Methuen, 1977.

Angelique Richardson, and Chris Willis, eds. *The New Woman in Fiction and in Fact: Fin de siècle Feminisms.* New York: Palgrave, 2001.

Salmon, Edward. *Juvenile Literature As It Is.* London: H.J. Drane, 1888.

Shaw, Valerie. *The Short Story.* London: Longman, 1983.

Shelley, Mary. *The Letters of Mary Wollstonecraft Shelley.* Ed. Betty T. Bennett. Vol. 2. Baltimore: Johns Hopkins UP, 1988.

Thomas, Donald. *The Victorian Underworld.* London: John Murray, 1998.

Thompson, Nicola, ed. *Victorian Women Writers and "The Woman Question."* Cambridge: Cambridge UP, 1999.

Zipes, Jack. "Introduction." *Victorian Fairy Tales: The Revolt of the Fairies and Elves.* Ed. Jack Zipes. New York: Routledge, 1987.

William Carleton

"Wildgoose Lodge" (1833)

[The Irish author William Carleton (1794–1869) grew up among the people depicted in his *Traits and Stories of the Irish Peasantry* (1830–35), a popular collection that includes the historically based "Wildgoose Lodge." An earlier version of the short story appeared in *The Dublin Literary Gazette* in 1830 as "Confessions of a Reformed Ribbonman." With an erratic formal education, Carleton attained his writing skills in part from occasional classes. After moving to Dublin, he converted to Protestantism, and his stories often offer strong anti-Catholic sentiments enhanced by a melodramatic style reflective of the pulp stories popular among many readers of the time. His work, which included novels, was admired by major authors such as Edgar Allan Poe and Alfred Tennyson.]

I had read the anonymous summons, but from its general import, I believed it to be one of those special meetings convened for some purpose affecting the usual objects and proceedings of the body; — at least the terms in which it was conveyed to me had nothing extraordinary or mysterious in them, beyond the simple fact, that it was not to be a general but a select meeting: this mark of confidence flattered me, and I determined to attend punctually. I was, it is true, desired to keep the circumstance entirely to myself, but there was nothing startling in this, for I had often received summonses of a similar nature. I therefore resolved to attend, according to the letter of my instructions, "on the next night, at the solemn hour of midnight, to deliberate and act upon such matters as should then and there be submitted to my consideration." The morning after I received this message, I arose and resumed my usual occupations; but, from whatever cause it may have proceeded, I felt a sense of approaching evil hang heavily upon me: the beats of my pulse were languid, and an undefinable feeling of anxiety pervaded my whole spirit; even my face was pale, and my eye so heavy, that my father and brothers concluded me to be ill; an opinion which I thought at the time to be correct, for I felt exactly that kind of depression which precedes a severe fever. I could not understand what I experienced, nor can I yet, except by supposing that there is in human nature some mysterious faculty, by which, in coming calamities, the dread of some fearful evil is anticipated, and that it is possible to catch a dark presentiment of the sensations which they subsequently produce. For my part I can neither analyze nor define it; but on that day I knew it by painful experience, and so have a thousand others in similar circumstances.

It was about the middle of winter. The day was gloomy and tempestuous almost beyond any other I remember: dark clouds rolled over the hills about me, and a close sleet-like rain fell in slanting drifts that chased each other rapidly towards the earth on the course of the blast. The outlying cattle sought the closest and calmest corners of the fields for shelter; the trees and young groves were tossed about, for the wind was so unusually high that it swept in hollow gusts through them, with that hoarse murmur which deepens so powerfully on the mind the sense of dreariness and desolation.

As the shades of night fell, the storm, if possible, increased. The moon was half gone, and only a few stars were visible by glimpses, as a rush of wind left a temporary opening in the sky. I had determined, if the storm should not abate, to incur any penalty rather than attend the meeting; but the appointed hour was distant, and I resolved to be decided by the future state of the night.

Ten o'clock came, but still there was no change; eleven passed, and on opening the door to observe if there were any likelihood of its clearing up, a blast of wind, mingled with rain, nearly blew me off my feet. At length it was approaching to the hour of midnight; and on examining a third time, I found it had calmed a little, and no longer rained.

I instantly got my oak stick, muffled myself in my great coat, strapped my hat about my ears, and, as the place of meeting was only a quarter of a mile distant, I presently set out.

The appearance of the heavens was lowering and angry, particularly in that point where the light of the moon fell against the clouds, from a seeming chasm in them, through which alone she was visible. The edges of this chasm were faintly bronzed, but the dense body of the masses that hung piled on each side of her, was black and impenetrable to sight. In no other point of the heavens was there any part of the sky visible; a deep veil of clouds overhung the horizon, yet was the light sufficient to give occasional glimpses of the rapid shifting which took place in this dark canopy, and of the tempestuous agitation with which the midnight storm swept to and fro beneath it.

At length I arrived at a long slated house, situated in a solitary part of the neighbourhood; a little below it ran a small stream, which was now swollen above its banks, and rushing with mimic roar over the flat meadows beside it. The appearance of the bare slated building in such a night was particularly sombre, and to those, like me, who knew the purpose to which it was usually devoted, it was or ought to have been, peculiarly so. There it stood, silent and gloomy, without any appearance of human life or enjoyment about or within it. As I approached the moon once more had broken out of the clouds, and shone dimly upon the wet, glittering slates and windows, with a death-like lustre, that gradually faded away as I left the point of observation, and entered the folding-door. It was the parish chapel.

The scene which presented itself here was in keeping not only with the external appearance of the house, but with the darkness, the storm, and the hour, which was now a little after midnight. About eighty persons were sitting in dead silence upon the circular steps of the altar. They did not seem to move; and as I entered and advanced, the echo of my footsteps rang through the building with a lonely distinctness, which added to the solemnity and mystery of the circumstances about me. The windows were secured with shutters on the inside, and on the altar a candle was lighted, which burned dimly amid the surrounding darkness, and lengthened the shadow of the altar itself, and those of six or seven persons who stood on its upper steps, until they mingled in the obscurity which shrouded the lower end of the chapel. The faces of the men who sat on the altar steps were not distinctly visible, yet their prominent and more characteristic features were in sufficient relief, and I observed, that some of the most malignant and reckless spirits in the parish were assembled. In the eyes of those who stood at the altar, and whom I knew to be invested with authority over the others, I could perceive gleams of some latent and ferocious purpose, kindled, as I soon observed, into a fiercer expression of vengeance, by the additional excitement of ardent spirits, with which they had stimulated themselves to a point of determination that mocked at the apprehension of all future responsibility, either in this world or the next.

The welcome which I received on joining them was far different from the boisterous good-humour that used to mark our greetings on other occasions: just a nod of the head from this or that person, on the part of those *who sat*, with a *ghud dhemur tha thu?*[1] in a suppressed voice, even

---

1 How are you? [Carleton's note].

below a common whisper: but from the standing group, who were evidently the projectors of the enterprise, I received a convulsive grasp of the hand, accompanied by a fierce and desperate look, that seemed to search my eye and countenance, to try if I were a person not likely to shrink from whatever they had resolved to execute. It is surprising to think of the powerful expression which a moment of intense interest or great danger is capable of giving to the eye, the features, and the slightest actions, especially in those whose station in society does not require them to constrain nature, by the force of social courtesies, into habits that conceal their natural emotions. None of the standing group spoke; but as each of them wrung my hand in silence, his eye was fixed on mine, with an expression of drunken confidence and secrecy, and an insolent determination not to be gainsayed without peril. If looks could be translated with certainty, they seemed to say, "we are bound upon a project of vengeance, and if you do not join us, remember that we *can* revenge." Along with this grasp, they did not forget to remind me of the common bond by which we were united, for each man gave me the secret grip of Ribbonism[1] in a manner that made the joints of my fingers ache for some minutes afterwards.

There was one present, however — the highest in authority — whose actions and demeanour were calm and unexcited. He seemed to labour under no unusual influence whatever, but evinced a serenity so placid and philosophical, that I attributed the silence of the sitting group, and the restraint which curbed in the out-breaking passions of those who *stood*, entirely to his presence. He was a schoolmaster, who taught his daily school in that chapel, and acted also, on Sunday, in the capacity of clerk to the priest — an excellent and amiable old man, who knew little of his illegal connexions and atrocious conduct.

When the ceremonies of brotherly recognition and friendship were past, the Captain (by which title I shall designate the last-mentioned person) stooped, and, raising a jar of whiskey on the corner of the altar, held a wine-glass to its neck, which he filled, and with a calm nod, handed it to me to drink. I shrunk back, with an instinctive horror, at the profaneness of such an act, in the house, and on the altar of God, and peremptorily refused to taste the proffered draught. He smiled mildly at what he considered my superstition, and added quietly, and in a low voice, "You'll be wantin' it, I'm thinkin', afther the wettin' you got."

"Wet or dry," said I, —

---

1 Principles of the Ribbon Society, a secret society made up of Irish Catholic nationalists.

"Stop man!" he replied, in the same tone; "spake low. But why wouldn't you take the whiskey? Sure there's as holy people to the fore as you: didn't they all take it? An' I wish we may never do worse nor dhrink a harmless glass o' whiskey, to keep the cowld out, any way."

"Well," said I, "I'll jist trust to God and the consequences, for the cowld, Paddy, ma bouchal;[1] but a blessed dhrop of it won't be crossin' my lips, avick;[2] so no more ghosther[3] about it; — dhrink it yourself, if you like. Maybe you want it as much as I do; wherein I've the patthern of a good big-coat upon me, so thick, your sowl, that if it was rainin' bullocks, a dhrop wouldn't get undher the nap of it."

He gave me a calm, but keen glance, as I spoke:

"Well, Jim," said he, "it's a good comrade you've got for the weather that's in it; but, in the mane time, to set you a dacent patthern, I'll just take this myself," — saying which, with the jar still upon its side, and the fore-finger of his left hand in its neck, he swallowed the spirits — "It's the first I dhrank to-night," he added, "nor would I dhrink it now, only to show you that I've heart an' spirit to do the thing that we're all bound an' sworn to, when the proper time comes;" after which he laid down the glass, and turned up the jar, with much coolness, upon the altar.

During our conversation, those who had been summoned to this mysterious meeting were pouring in fast; and as each person approached the altar, he received from one to two or three glasses of whiskey, according as he chose to limit himself; but, to do them justice, there were not a few of those present, who, in despite of their own desire, and the Captain's express invitation, refused to taste it in the house of God's worship. Such, however, as were scrupulous he afterwards recommended to take it on the outside of the chapel door, which they did, as, by that means, the sacrilege of the act was supposed to be evaded.

About one o'clock they were all assembled except six; at least so the Captain asserted, on looking at a written paper.

"Now, boys," said he, in the same low voice, "we are all present except the thraitors, whose names I am goin' to read to you; not that we are to count thim thraitors, till we know whether or not it was in their power to come. Any how, the night's terrible — but, boys, you're to know, that neither fire nor wather is to prevint yees, when duly summoned to attind a meeting — particularly whin the summons is widout a name, as you

---

1 (Irish) boy.

2 (Irish) my boy; my son.

3 (Irish) chatter.

have been told that there is always something of consequence to be done *thin*."

He then read out the names of those who were absent, in order that the real cause of their absence might be ascertained, declaring that they would be dealt with accordingly. After this, with his usual caution, he shut and bolted the door, and having put the key in his pocket, ascended the steps of the altar, and for some time traversed the little platform from which the priest usually addresses the congregation.

Until this night I had never contemplated the man's countenance with any particular interest; but as he walked the platform, I had an opportunity of observing him more closely. He was slight in person, apparently not thirty; and, on a first view, appeared to have nothing remarkable in his dress or features. I, however, was not the only person whose eyes were fixed upon him at that moment; in fact every one present observed him with equal interest, for hitherto he had kept the object of the meeting perfectly secret, and of course we all felt anxious to know it. It was while he traversed the platform that I scrutinized his features with a hope, if possible, to glean from them some evidence of what was passing within him. I could, however, mark but little, and that little was at first rather from the intelligence which seemed to subsist between him and those whom I have already mentioned as *standing* against the altar, than from any indication of his own. Their gleaming eyes were fixed upon him with an intensity of savage and demon-like hope, which blazed out in flashes of malignant triumph, as upon turning, he threw a cool but rapid glance at them, to intimate the progress he was making in the subject to which he devoted the undivided energies of his mind. But in the course of his meditation, I could observe, on one or two occasions, a dark shade come over his countenance, that contracted his brow into a deep furrow, and it was then, for the first time, that I saw the satanic expression of which his face, by a very slight motion of its muscles, was capable. His hands, during this silence, closed and opened convulsively; his eyes shot out two or three baleful glances, first to his confederates, and afterwards vacantly into the deep gloom of the lower part of the chapel; his teeth ground against each other, like those of a man whose revenge burns to reach a distant enemy, and finally, after having wound himself up to a certain determination, his features relapsed into their original calm and undisturbed expression.

At this moment a loud laugh, having something supernatural in it, rang out wildly from the darkness of the chapel; he stopped, and putting his open hand over his brows, peered down into the gloom, and said calmly in Irish, "*Bee dhu husth; ha nihl anam inh*: — hold your tongue, it is not yet the time."

Every eye was now directed to the same spot, but, in consequence of its distance from the dim light on the altar, none could perceive the person from whom the laugh proceeded. It was, by this time, near two o'clock in the morning.

He now stood for a few moments on the platform, and his chest heaved with a depth of anxiety equal to the difficulty of the design he wished to accomplish:

"Brothers," said he — "for we are all brothers — sworn upon all that's blessed an' holy, to obey whatever them that's over us, *manin' among ourselves*,[1] wishes us to do — are you now ready, in the name of God, upon whose althar I stand, to fulfil yer oaths?"

The words were scarcely uttered, when those who had *stood* beside the altar during the night, sprang from their places, and descending its steps rapidly, turned round, and raising their arms, exclaimed, "By all that's sacred an' holy, we're willin'."

In the mean time, those who *sat* upon the steps of the altar, instantly rose, and following the example of those who had just spoken, exclaimed after them, "To be sure — by all that's sacred an' holy, we're willin'."

"Now boys," said the Captain, "ar'nt yees big fools for your pains? an' one of yees doesn't know what I mane."

"You're our Captain," said one of those who had stood at the altar, "an' has yer ordhers from higher quarthers; of coorse, whatever ye command upon us we're bound to obey you in."

"Well," said he, smiling, "I only wanted to thry yees; an' by the oath yees tuck, there's not a captain in the county has as good a right to be proud of his min as I have. Well, yees won't rue it, maybe, when the right time comes; and for that same rason every one of yees must have a glass from the jar; thim that won't dhrink it *in* the chapel can dhrink it *widout*; an' here goes to open the door for them."

He then distributed another glass to every man who would accept it, and brought the jar afterwards to the chapel door, to satisfy the scruples of those who would not drink within. When this was performed, and all duly excited, he proceeded: —

"Now, brothers, you are solemnly sworn to obey me, and I'm sure there's no thraithur here that 'ud parjure himself for a thrifle; but *I'm* sworn

---

1   In opposition to the constituted authorities [Carleton's note].

to obay them that's above me, manin' still among ourselves; an' to show you that I don't scruple to do it, here goes!"

He then turned round, and taking the Missal[1] between his hands placed it upon the altar. Hitherto every word was uttered in a low precautionary tone; but on grasping the book, he again turned round, and looking upon his confederates with the same satanic expression which marked his countenance before, exclaimed, in a voice of deep determination:

"By this sacred an' holy book of God, I will perform the action which we have met this night to accomplish, be that what it may; an' this I swear upon God's book, an' God's althar!"

On concluding he struck the book violently with his open hand.

At this moment the candle which burned before him went suddenly out, and the chapel was wrapped in pitchy darkness; the sound as if of rushing wings fell upon our ears, and fifty voices dwelt upon the last words of his oath with wild and supernatural tones, that seemed to echo and to mock what he had sworn. There was a pause, and an exclamation of horror from all present: but the Captain was too cool and steady to be disconcerted. He immediately groped about until he got the candle, and proceeding calmly to a remote corner of the chapel, took up a half-burned turf[2] which lay there, and after some trouble, succeeded in lighting it again. He then explained what had taken place; which indeed was easily done, as the candle happened to be extinguished by a pigeon which sat directly above it. The chapel, I should have observed, was at this time, like many country chapels, unfinished inside, and the pigeons of a neighbouring dove-cote had built nests among the rafters of the unceiled roof; which circumstance also explained the rushing of the wings, for the birds had been affrighted by the sudden loudness of the noise. The mocking voices were nothing but the echoes, rendered naturally more awful by the scene, the mysterious object of the meeting, and the solemn hour of the night.

When the candle was again lighted, and these startling circumstances accounted for, the persons whose vengeance had been deepening more and more during the night, rushed to the altar in a body, where each, in a voice trembling with passionate eagerness, repeated the oath, and as every word was pronounced, the same echoes heightened the wildness of the horrible ceremony, by their long and unearthly tones. The countenances of these human tigers were livid with suppressed rage; their knit brows,

---

1   Book of prayers; or book containing the services for Mass for the full year.

2   Piece of peat used for fuel.

compressed lips, and kindled eyes, fell under the dim light of the taper, with an expression calculated to sicken any heart not absolutely diabolical.

As soon as this dreadful rite was completed, we were again startled by several loud bursts of laughter, which proceeded from the lower darkness of the chapel, and the captain, on hearing them, turned to the place, and reflecting for a moment, said in Irish, "*Gutsho nish, avohelhee —* come hither now, boys."

A rush immediately took place from the corner in which they had secreted themselves all the night; and seven men appeared, whom we instantly recognised as brothers and cousins of certain persons who had been convicted, some time before, for breaking into the house of an honest poor man in the neighbourhood, from whom, after having treated him with barbarous violence, they took away such fire-arms as he kept for his own protection.

It was evidently not the captain's intention to have produced these persons until the oath should have been generally taken, but the exulting mirth with which they enjoyed the success of his scheme betrayed them, and put him to the necessity of bringing them forward somewhat before the concerted moment.

The scene which now took place was beyond all power of description; peals of wild, fiend-like yells rang through the chapel, as the party which *stood* on the altar, and that which had crouched in the darkness, met; wringing of hands, leaping in triumph, striking of sticks and fire-arms against the ground and the altar itself, dancing and cracking of fingers, marked the triumph of some hellish determination. Even the Captain for a time was unable to restrain their fury; but, at length, he mounted the platform before the altar once more, and with a stamp of his foot, recalled their attention to himself and the matter in hand.

"Boys," said he, "enough of this, and too much; an' well for us it is that the chapel is in a lonely place, or our foolish noise might do us no good. Let thim that swore so manfully jist now, stand a one side, till the rest kiss the book one by one."

The proceedings, however, had by this time taken too fearful a shape for even the Captain to compel them to a blindfold oath; the first man he called, flatly refused to answer, until he should hear the nature of the service that was required. This was echoed by the remainder, who taking courage from the firmness of this person, declared generally, that until they first knew the business they were to execute, none of them would take the oath. The Captain's lip quivered slightly, and his brow again became knit with the same hellish expression, which I have remarked gave him so much the appearance of an embodied fiend; but this speedily passed away, and was succeeded by a malignant sneer, in which lurked, if there ever did in a sneer, "a laughing devil," calmly, determinedly atrocious.

"It wasn't worth yer whiles to refuse the oath," said he mildly, "for the truth is, I had next to nothing for yees to do. Not a hand, maybe, would have to *rise*, only jist to look on, an' if any resistance would be made, to show yourselves; yer numbers would soon make them see that resistance would be no use whatever in the present case. At all evints, the oath of *secresy must* be taken, or woe be to him that will refuse *that*; he won't know the day, nor the hour, nor the minute, when he'll be made a spatch-cock[1] ov."

He then turned round, and placing his right hand on the Missal, swore, "In the presence of God, and before his holy altar, that whatever might take place that night, he would keep secret, from man or mortal, except the priest, and that neither bribery, nor imprisonment, nor death, would wring it from his heart."

Having done this, he again struck the book violently, as if to confirm the energy with which he swore, and then calmly descending the steps, stood with a serene countenance, like a man conscious of having performed a good action. As this oath did not pledge those who refused to take the other to the perpetration of any specific crime, it was readily taken by all present. Preparations were then made to execute what was intended: the half-burned turf was placed in a little pot; another glass of whiskey was distributed; and the door being locked by the Captain, who kept the key as parish clerk and master, the crowd departed silently from the chapel.

The moment those who lay in the darkness during the night, made their appearance at the altar, we knew at once the persons we were to visit; for, as I said before, they were related to the miscreants whom one of those persons had convicted, in consequence of their midnight attack upon himself and his family. The Captain's object in keeping them unseen was, that those present, not being aware of the duty about to be imposed on them, might have less hesitation about swearing to its fulfilment. Our conjectures were correct, for on leaving the chapel we directed our steps to the house in which this devoted man resided.

The night was still stormy, but without rain; it was rather dark, too, though not so as to prevent us from seeing the clouds careering swiftly through the air. The dense curtain which had overhung and obscured the

---

1 Fowl that is split open and grilled.

horizon, was now broken, and large sections of the sky were clear, and thinly studded with stars that looked dim and watery, as did indeed the whole firmament; for in some places black clouds were still visible, threatening a continuance of tempestuous weather. The road appeared washed and gravelly; every dike was full of yellow water; and every little rivulet and larger stream dashed its hoarse music in our ears; every blast, too, was cold, fierce, and wintry, sometimes driving us back to a stand still, and again, when a turn in the road would bring it in our backs, whirling us along for a few steps with involuntary rapidity. At length the fated dwelling became visible, and a short consultation was held in a sheltered place, between the Captain and the two parties who seemed so eager for its destruction. Their fire-arms were now loaded, and their bayonets and short pikes, the latter shod and pointed with iron, were also got ready. The live coal which was brought in the small pot had become extinguished; but to remedy this, two or three persons from a remote part of the county entered a cabin on the wayside, and, under pretence of lighting their own and their comrades' pipes, procured a coal of fire, for so they called a lighted turf. From the time we left the chapel until this moment a profound silence had been maintained, a circumstance which, when I considered the number of persons present, and the mysterious and dreaded object of their journey, had a most appalling effect upon my spirits.

At length we arrived within fifty perches[1] of the house, walking in a compact body, and with as little noise as possible; but it seemed as if the very elements had conspired to frustrate our design, for on advancing within the shade of the farm-hedge, two or three persons found themselves up to the middle in water, and on stooping to ascertain more accurately the state of the place, we could see nothing but one immense sheet of it, — spread like a lake over the meadows which surrounded the spot we wished to reach.

Fatal night! The very recollection of it, when associated with the fearful tempests of the elements, grows, if that were possible, yet more wild and revolting. Had we been engaged in any innocent or benevolent enterprise, there was something in our situation just then that had a touch of interest in it to a mind imbued with a relish for the savage beauties of nature. There we stood, about a hundred and thirty in number, our dark forms bent forward, peering into the dusky expanse of water, with its dim gleams of reflected light, broken by the weltering of the mimic waves into ten thousand fragments, whilst the few stars that overhung it in the

---

1   Measurement of length; 50 perches equals 275 yards.

firmament, appeared to shoot through it in broken lines, and to be multiplied fifty-fold in the gloomy mirror on which we gazed.

Over us was a stormy sky, and around us a darkness through which we could only distinguish, in outline, the nearest objects, whilst the wild wind swept strongly and dismally upon us. When it was discovered that the common pathway to the house was inundated, we were about to abandon our object and return home. The Captain, however, stooped down low for a moment, and almost closing his eyes, looked along the surface of the waters, and then rising himself very calmly, said, in his usual quiet tone, "Yees needn't go back, boys, I've found a way; jist follow me."

He immediately took a more circuitous direction, by which we reached a causeway that had been raised for the purpose of giving a free passage to and from the house, during such inundations as the present. Along this we had advanced more than half way, when we discovered a breach in it, which, as afterwards appeared, had that night been made by the strength of the flood. This, by means of our sticks and pikes, we found to be about three feet deep, and eight yards broad. Again we were at a loss how to proceed, when the fertile brain of the Captain devised a method of crossing it.

"Boys," said he, "of coorse you've all played at leap-frog; very well, strip and go in, a dozen of you, lean one upon the back of another from this to the opposite bank, where one must stand facing the outside man, both their shoulders agin one another, that the outside man may be supported. Then *we* can creep over you, an' a dacent bridge you'll be, any way."

This was the work of only a few minutes, and in less than ten we were all safely over.

Merciful heaven! how I sicken at the recollection of what is to follow! On reaching the dry bank, we proceeded instantly, and in profound silence, to the house; the Captain divided us into companies, and then assigned to each division its proper station. The two parties who had been so vindictive all the night, he kept about himself; for of those who were present, they only were in his confidence, and knew his nefarious purpose; their number was about fifteen. Having made these dispositions, he, at the head of about five of them, approached the house on the windy side, for the fiend possessed a coolness which enabled him to seize upon every possible advantage. That he had combustibles about him was evident, for in less than fifteen minutes nearly one half of the house was enveloped in flames. On seeing this, the others rushed over to the spot where he and his gang were standing, and remonstrated earnestly, but in vain; the flames now burst forth with renewed violence, and as they flung their strong light upon the faces of the foremost group, I think hell itself could hardly present any thing more satanic than their countenances, now worked up into a paroxysm of infernal triumph, at their own revenge. The Captain's look had lost all its calmness, every feature started out into distinct malignity, the curve in his brow was deep, and ran up to the root of the hair, dividing his face into two segments, that did not seem to have been designed for each other. His lips were half open, and the corners of his mouth a little brought back on each side, like those of a man expressing intense hatred and triumph over an enemy who is in the death struggle under his grasp. His eyes blazed from beneath his knit eye-brows with a fire that seemed to be lighted up in the infernal pit itself. It is unnecessary, and only painful, to describe the rest of his gang; demons might have been proud of such horrible visages as they exhibited; for they worked under all the power of hatred, revenge, and joy; and these passions blended into one terrible scowl, enough almost to blast any human eye that would venture to look upon it.

When the others attempted to intercede for the lives of the inmates, there were at least fifteen guns and pistols levelled at them.

"Another word," said the Captain, "an' you're a corpse where you stand, or the first man who will dare to spake for them; no, no, it wasn't to spare them we came here. 'No mercy' is the pass-word for the night, an' by the sacred oath I swore beyant in the chapel, any one among yees that will attempt to show it, will find none at my hand. Surround the house, boys, I tell ye, I hear them stirring. 'No quarther — no mercy,' is the ordher of the night."

Such was his command over these misguided creatures, that in an instant there was a ring round the house to prevent the escape of the unhappy inmates, should the raging element give them time to attempt it; for none present durst withdraw themselves from the scene, not only from an apprehension of the Captain's present vengeance, or that of his gang, but because they knew that even had they then escaped, an early and certain death awaited them from a quarter against which they had no means of defence. The hour now was about half-past two o'clock. Scarcely had the last words escaped from the Captain's lips, when one of the windows of the house was broken, and a human head, having the hair in a blaze, was described, apparently a woman's, if one might judge by the profusion of burning tresses, and the softness of the tones, notwithstanding that it called, or rather shrieked, aloud, for help and mercy. The only reply to this was the whoop from the Captain and his gang, of "No mercy — no mercy!" and that instant the former, and one of the latter, rushed to the spot, and ere the action could be perceived, the head was transfixed with a bayonet and a pike, both having entered it together. The word mercy was divided in her mouth; a short silence ensued, the head hung down on the window, but was instantly tossed back into the flames!

This action occasioned a cry of horror from all present, except the *gang* and their leader, which startled and enraged the latter so much, that he ran towards one of them, and had his bayonet, now reeking with the blood of its innocent victim, raised to plunge it in his body, when, dropping the point, he said in a piercing whisper, that hissed in the ears of all: "It's no use *now*, you know; if one's to hang, all will hang; so our safest way, you persave, is to lave none of them to tell the story. Ye *may* go now, if you wish; but it won't save a hair of your heads. You cowardly set! I knew if I had tould yees the sport, that none of yees, except my *own* boys, would come, so I jist played a thrick upon you; but remimber what you are sworn to, and stand to the oath ye tuck."

Unhappily, notwithstanding the wetness of the preceding weather, the materials of the house were extremely combustible; the whole dwelling was now one body of glowing flame, yet the shouts and shrieks within rose awfully above its crackling and the voice of the storm, for the wind once more blew in gusts, and with great violence. The doors and windows were all torn open, and such of those within as had escaped the flames rushed towards them, for the purpose of further escape, and of claiming mercy at the hands of their destroyers; but whenever they appeared, the unearthly cry of "NO MERCY" rung upon their ears for a moment, and for a moment only, for they were flung back at the points of the weapons which the demons had brought with them to make the work of vengeance more certain.

As yet there were many persons in the house, whose cry for life was strong as despair, and who clung to it with all the awakened powers of reason and instinct. The ear of man could hear nothing so strongly calculated to stifle the demon of cruelty and revenge within him, as the long and wailing shrieks which rose beyond the elements, in tones that were carried off rapidly upon the blast, until they died away in the darkness that lay behind the surrounding hills. Had not the house been in a solitary situation, and the hour the dead of night, any person sleeping within a moderate distance must have heard them, for such a cry of sorrow rising into a yell of despair was almost sufficient to have awakened the dead. It was lost, however, upon the hearts and ears that heard it: to them, though in justice be it said, to only comparatively a few of them, it was as delightful as the tones of soft and entrancing music.

The claims of the surviving sufferers were now modified; they supplicated merely to suffer death *by the weapons of their enemies*; they were willing to bear that, provided they should be allowed to escape from the flames; but no — the horrors of the conflagration were calmly and malignantly gloried in by their merciless assassins, who deliberately flung them back into all their tortures. In the course of a few minutes a man appeared upon the side-wall of the house, nearly naked; his figure, as he stood against the sky in horrible relief, was so finished a picture of woebegone agony and supplication, that it is yet as distinct in my memory as if I were again present at the scene. Every muscle, now in motion by the powerful agitation of his sufferings, stood out upon his limbs and neck, giving him an appearance of desperate strength, to which by this time he must have been wrought up; the perspiration poured from his frame, and the veins and arteries of his neck were inflated to a surprising thickness. Every moment he looked down into the flames which were rising to where he stood; and as he looked, the indescribable horror which flitted over his features might have worked upon the devil himself to relent. His words were few: —

"My child," said he, "is still safe, she is an infant, a young crathur that never harmed you, nor any one — she is still safe. Your mothers, your wives, have young innocent childhre like it. Oh, spare her, think for a moment that it's one of your own: spare it, as you hope to meet a just God, or if you don't, in mercy shoot me first — put an end to me, before I see her burned!"

The Captain approached him coolly and deliberately. "You'll prosecute no one now, you bloody informer," said he: "you'll convict no more boys for takin' an ould gun an' pistol from you or for givin' you a neighbourly knock or two into the bargain."

Just then, from a window opposite him, proceeded the shrieks of a woman, who appeared at it, with the infant in her arms. She herself was almost scorched to death; but, with the presence of mind and humanity of her sex, she was about to put the little babe out of the window. The Captain noticed this, and, with characteristic atrocity, thrust, with a sharp bayonet, the little innocent, along with the person who endeavoured to rescue it, into the red flames, where they both perished. This was the work of an instant. Again he approached the man: "Your child is a coal now," said he, with deliberate mockery; "I pitched it in myself, on the point of this," — showing the weapon — "an' now is your turn," — saying which he clambered up, by the assistance of his gang, who stood with a front of pikes and bayonets bristling to receive the wretched man, should he attempt, in his despair, to throw himself from the wall. The Captain got up, and placing the point of his bayonet against his shoulder, flung him into the fiery element that raged behind him. He uttered one wild and terrific cry, as he fell back, and no more. After this nothing was heard but the crackling of the fire, and the rushing of the blast: all that had possessed life within were consumed, amounting either to eleven or fifteen persons.

When this was accomplished, those who took an active part in the murder, stood for some time about the conflagration; and as it threw its red light upon their fierce faces and rough persons, soiled as they now were with smoke and black streaks of ashes, the scene seemed to be changed to hell, the murderers to spirits of the damned, rejoicing over the arrival and the torture of some guilty soul. The faces of those who kept aloof from the slaughter were blanched to the whiteness of death: some of them fainted, and others were in such agitation that they were compelled to lean on their comrades. They became actually powerless with horror; yet to such a scene were they brought by the pernicious influence of Ribbonism.

It was only when the last victim went down, that the conflagration shot up into the air with most unbounded fury. The house was large, deeply thatched, and well furnished; and the broad red pyramid rose up with fearful magnificence towards the sky. Abstractedly it had sublimity, but now it was associated with nothing in my mind but blood and terror. It was not, however, without a purpose that the Captain and his gang stood to contemplate its effect. "Boys," said he, "we had betther be sartin that all's safe; who knows but there might be some of the sarpents crouchin' under a hape o' rubbish, to come out an' gibbet[1] us to-morrow or next day: we had betther wait a while, any how, if it was only to see the blaze."

Just then the flames rose majestically to a surprising height. Our eyes followed their direction; and we perceived, for the first time, that the dark clouds above, together with the intermediate air, appeared to reflect back, or rather to have caught the red hue of the fire. The hills and country about us appeared with an alarming distinctness; but the most picturesque part of it was the effect or reflection of the blaze on the floods that spread over the surrounding plains. These, in fact, appeared to be one broad mass of liquid copper, for the motion of the breaking waters caught from the blaze of the high waving column, as reflected in them, a glaring light, which eddied, and rose, and fluctuated, as if the flood itself had been a lake of molten fire.

---

1   Hang. Literally, an upright post with a projecting arm from which criminals were hung after execution.

Fire, however, destroys rapidly. In a short time the flames sank — became weak and flickering — by and by, they shot out only in fits — the crackling of the timbers died away — the surrounding darkness deepened — and, ere long, the faint light was overpowered by the thick volumes of smoke that rose from the ruins of the house, and its murdered inhabitants.

"Now, boys," said the Captain, "all is safe — we may go. Remember, every man of you, what you've sworn this night, on the book an' altar of God — not on a heretic Bible. If you perjure yourselves, you may hang us; but let me tell you, for your comfort, that if you do, there is them livin' that will take care the lase of your own lives will be but short."

After this we dispersed every man to his own home.

Reader, — not many months elapsed ere I saw the bodies of this Captain, whose name was Patrick Devann, and all those who were actively concerned in the perpetration of this deed of horror, withering in the wind, where they hung gibbetted, near the scene of their nefarious villany; and while I inwardly thanked heaven for my own narrow and almost undeserved escape, I thought in my heart how seldom, even in this world, justice fails to overtake the murderer, and to enforce the righteous judgment of God — that "whoso sheddeth man's blood, by man shall his blood be shed."

This tale of terror is, unfortunately, too true. The scene of hellish murder detailed in it, lies at Wildgoose Lodge, in the county of Louth, within about four miles of Carrickmacross, and nine of Dundalk. No such multitudinous murder has occurred, under similar circumstances, except the burning of the Sheas is the county of Tipperary. The name of the family burned in Wildgoose Lodge was Lynch. One of them had, shortly before this fatal night, prosecuted and convicted some of the neighbouring Ribbonmen, who visited him with severe marks of their displeasure, in consequence of his having refused to enrol himself as a member of their body.

The language of the story is partly fictitious; but the facts are pretty closely such as were developed during the trial of the murderers. Both parties were Roman Catholics. There were, if the author mistake not, either twenty-five or twenty-eight of those who took an active part in the burning, hanged and gibbetted in different parts of the county of Louth. Devann, the ringleader, hung for some months in chains, within about a hundred yards of his own house, and about half a mile from Wildgoose Lodge. His mother could neither go into nor out of her cabin, without seeing his body swinging from the gibbet. Her usual exclamation on looking at him was — "God be good to the sowl of my poor marthyr!" The peasantry, too, frequently exclaimed, on seeing him, "Poor Paddy!" A gloomy fact that speaks volumes!

Mary Shelley

"The Mortal Immortal" (1833)

[Mary Shelley (1797–1851) is best remembered as the author of *Frankenstein* (1818), considered by many to be the first example of science fiction. Not only does the novella offer an innovative revision of literary Gothic conventions but it also explores issues of ethics, science, sexuality, and oppression that have remained current since its publication. *Frankenstein* began as an exercise in writing a ghost story, and many of Shelley's short stories — including "The Mortal Immortal," which has remained one of her most popular — address similar issues. Daughter of the intellectuals Mary Wollstonecraft and William Godwin, and wife of the Romantic poet Percy Shelley, Mary Shelley turned full-time to a career writing short stories, essays, and novels only upon the death of her husband. Like "The Mortal Immortal," many of her shorter works were published in *The Keepsake*, one of many "annuals" so popular at the time. Annuals were collections of pictures and short, often sentimental pieces of fiction aimed primarily at a middle- to upper-class female audience.]

July 16, 1833. — This is a memorable anniversary for me; on it I complete my three hundred and twenty-third year!

The Wandering Jew?[1] — certainly not. More than eighteen centuries have passed over his head. In comparison with him, I am a very young Immortal.

Am I, then, immortal? This is a question which I have asked myself, by day and night, for now three hundred and three years, and yet cannot answer it. I detected a gray hair amidst my brown locks this very day — that surely signifies decay. Yet it may have remained concealed there for three hundred years — for some persons have become entirely white-headed before twenty years of age.

---

1 Legendary character doomed to wander the earth because he struck Christ on the day of the Crucifixion.

I will tell my story, and my reader shall judge for me. I will tell my story, and so contrive to pass some few hours of a long eternity, become so wearisome to me. For ever! Can it be? to live for ever! I have heard of enchantments, in which the victims were plunged into a deep sleep, to wake, after a hundred years, as fresh as ever: I have heard of the Seven Sleepers[1] — thus to be immortal would not be so burthensome: but, oh! the weight of never-ending time — the tedious passage of the still-succeeding hours! How happy was the fabled Nourjahad![2] — But to my task.

All the world has heard of Cornelius Agrippa.[3] His memory is as immortal as his arts have made me. All the world has also heard of his scholar, who, unawares, raised the foul fiend during his master's absence, and was destroyed by him. The report, true or false, of this accident, was attended with many inconveniences to the renowned philosopher. All his scholars at once deserted him — his servants disappeared. He had no one near him to put coals on his ever-burning fires while he slept, or to attend to the changeful colours of his medicines while he studied. Experiment after experiment failed, because one pair of hands was insufficient to complete them: the dark spirits laughed at him for not being able to retain a single mortal in his service.

I was then very young — very poor — and very much in love. I had been for about a year the pupil of Cornelius, though I was absent when this accident took place. On my return, my friends implored me not to return to the alchymist's abode. I trembled as I listened to the dire tale they told; I required no second warning; and when Cornelius came and offered me a purse of gold if I would remain under his roof, I felt as if Satan himself tempted me. My teeth chattered — my hair stood on end: — I ran off as fast as my trembling knees would permit.

My failing steps were directed whither for two years they had every evening been attracted, — a gently bubbling spring of pure living waters, beside which lingered a dark-haired girl, whose beaming eyes were fixed on the path I was accustomed each night to tread. I cannot remember the hour when I did not love Bertha; we had been neighbours and playmates from infancy — her parents, like mine, were of humble life, yet respectable

---

1   Seven martyrs who, by awakening after an extremely long sleep, reaffirmed the Roman Emperor Theodosius II's wavering faith.

2   *The Story of Nourjahad* (1767) by Frances Sheridan (1724–66) depicts the life of the character Nourjahad, who was tricked by Sultan Schemzeddin to believe that he had become immortal and that his nightly sleeps each lasted many years.

3   Heinrich Cornelius Agrippa of Nettesheim (1486–1534), scholar of alchemy, theology, and the occult sciences.

— our attachment had been a source of pleasure to them. In an evil hour, a malignant fever carried off both her father and mother, and Bertha became an orphan. She would have found a home beneath my paternal roof, but, unfortunately, the old lady of the near castle, rich, childless, and solitary, declared her intention to adopt her. Henceforth Bertha was clad in silk — inhabited a marble palace — and was looked on as being highly favoured by fortune. But in her new situation among her new associates, Bertha remained true to the friend of her humbler days; she often visited the cottage of my father, and when forbidden to go thither, she would stray towards the neighbouring wood, and meet me beside its shady fountain.

She often declared that she owed no duty to her new protectress equal in sanctity to that which bound us. Yet still I was too poor to marry, and she grew weary of being tormented on my account. She had a haughty but an impatient spirit, and grew angry at the obstacles that prevented our union. We met now after an absence, and she had been sorely beset while I was away; she complained bitterly, and almost reproached me for being poor. I replied hastily, —

"I am honest, if I am poor! — were I not, I might soon become rich!"

This exclamation produced a thousand questions. I feared to shock her by owning the truth, but she drew it from me; and then, casting a look of disdain on me, she said —

"You pretend to love, and you fear to face the Devil for my sake!"

I protested that I had only dreaded to offend her; — while she dwelt on the magnitude of the reward that I should receive. Thus encouraged — shamed by her — led on by love and hope, laughing at my late fears, with quick steps and a light heart, I returned to accept the offers of the alchymist, and was instantly installed in my office.

A year passed away. I became possessed of no insignificant sum of money. Custom had banished my fears. In spite of the most painful vigilance, I had never detected the trace of a cloven foot; nor was the studious silence of our abode ever disturbed by demoniac howls. I still continued my stolen interviews with Bertha, and Hope dawned on me — Hope — but not perfect joy; for Bertha fancied that love and security were enemies, and her pleasure was to divide them in my bosom. Though true of heart, she was somewhat of a coquette in manner; and I was jealous as a Turk. She slighted me in a thousand ways, yet would never acknowledge herself to be in the wrong. She would drive me mad with anger, and then force me to beg her pardon. Sometimes she fancied that I was not sufficiently submissive, and then she had some story of a rival, favoured by her protectress. She was surrounded by silk-clad youths — the rich and gay — What chance had the sad-robed scholar of Cornelius compared with these?

On one occasion, the philosopher made such large demands upon my time, that I was unable to meet her as I was wont. He was engaged in some mighty work, and I was forced to remain, day and night, feeding his furnaces and watching his chemical preparations. Bertha waited for me in vain at the fountain. Her haughty spirit fired at this neglect; and when at last I stole out during the few short minutes allotted to me for slumber, and hoped to be consoled by her, she received me with disdain, dismissed me in scorn, and vowed that any man should possess her hand rather than he who could not be in two places at once for her sake. She would be revenged! — And truly she was. In my dingy retreat I heard that she had been hunting, attended by Albert Hoffer. Albert Hoffer was favoured by her protectress, and the three passed in cavalcade before my smoky window. Methought that they mentioned my name — it was followed by a laugh of derision, as her dark eyes glanced contemptuously towards my abode.

Jealousy, with all its venom, and all its misery, entered my breast. Now I shed a torrent of tears, to think that I should never call her mine; and, anon, I imprecated a thousand curses on her inconstancy. Yet, still I must stir the fires of the alchymist, still attend on the changes of his unintelligible medicines.

Cornelius had watched for three days and nights, nor closed his eyes. The progress of his alembics[1] was slower than he expected: in spite of his anxiety, sleep weighed upon his eyelids. Again and again he threw off drowsiness with more than human energy; again and again it stole away his senses. He eyes his crucibles wistfully. "Not ready yet," he murmured; "will another night pass before the work is accomplished? Winzy, you are vigilant — you are faithful — you have slept, my boy — you slept last night. Look at that glass vessel. The liquid it contains is of a soft rose-colour: the moment it begins to change its hue, awaken me — till then I may close my eyes. First, it will turn white, and then emit golden flashes; but wait not till then; when the rose-colour fades, rouse me." I scarcely heard the last words, muttered, as they were, in sleep. Even then he did not quite yield to nature. "Winzy, my boy," he again said, "do not touch the vessel — do not put it to your lips; it is a philter — a philter to cure love; you would not cease to love your Bertha — beware to drink!"

---

1   An apparatus used in distilling.

And he slept. His venerable head sunk on his breast, and I scarce heard his regular breathing. For a few minutes I watched the vessel — the rosy hue of the liquid remained unchanged. Then my thoughts wandered — they visited the fountain, and dwelt on a thousand charming scenes never to be renewed — never! Serpents and adders were in my heart as the word "Never!" half formed itself on my lips. False girl! — false and cruel! Never more would she smile on me as that evening she smiled on Albert. Worthless, detested woman! I would not remain unrevenged — she should see Albert expire at her feet — she should die beneath my vengeance. She had smiled in disdain and triumph — she knew my wretchedness and her power. Yet what power had she? — the power of exciting my hate — my utter scorn — my — oh, all but indifference! Could I attain that — could I regard her with careless eyes, transferring my rejected love to one fairer and more true, that were indeed a victory!

A bright flash darted before my eyes. I had forgotten the medicine of the adept; I gazed on it with wonder: flashes of admirable beauty, more bright than those which the diamond emits when the sun's rays are on it, glanced from the surface of the liquid; an odour the most fragrant and grateful stole over my sense; the vessel seemed one globe of living radiance, lovely to the eye, and most inviting to the taste. The first thought, instinctively inspired by the grosser sense, was, I will — I must drink. I raised the vessel to my lips. "It will cure me of love — of torture!" Already I had quaffed half of the most delicious liquor ever tasted by the palate of man, when the philosopher stirred. I started — I dropped the glass — the fluid flamed and glanced along the floor, while I felt Cornelius's gripe[1] at my throat, as he shrieked aloud, "Wretch! you have destroyed the labour of my life!"

The philosopher was totally unaware that I had drunk any portion of his drug. His idea was, and I gave a tacit assent to it, that I had raised the vessel from curiosity, and that, frighted at its brightness, and the flashes of intense light it gave forth, I had let it fall. I never undeceived him. The fire of the medicine was quenched — the fragrance died away — he grew calm, as a philosopher should under the heaviest trials, and dismissed me to rest.

I will not attempt to describe the sleep of glory and bliss which bathed my soul in paradise during the remaining hours of that memorable night. Words would be faint and shallow types of my enjoyment, or of the gladness that possessed my bosom when I woke. I trod air — my thoughts

---

1 Grip.

were in heaven. Earth appeared heaven, and my inheritance upon it was to be one trance of delight. "This it is to be cured of love," I thought; "I will see Bertha this day, and she will find her lover cold and regardless; too happy to be disdainful, yet how utterly indifferent to her!"

The hours danced away. The philosopher, secure that he had once succeeded, and believing that he might again, began to concoct the same medicine once more. He was shut up with his books and drugs, and I had a holiday. I dressed myself with care; I looked in an old but polished shield, which served me for a mirror; methought my good looks had wonderfully improved. I hurried beyond the precincts of the town, joy in my soul, the beauty of heaven and earth around me. I turned my steps towards the castle — I could look on its lofty turrets with lightness of heart, for I was cured of love. My Bertha saw me afar off, as I came up the avenue. I know not what sudden impulse animated her bosom, but at the sight, she sprung with a light fawn-like bound down the marble steps, and was hastening towards me. But I had been perceived by another person. The old high-born hag, who called herself her protectress, and was her tyrant, had seen me, also; she hobbled, panting, up the terrace; a page, as ugly as herself, held up her train, and fanned her as she hurried along, and stopped my fair girl with a "How, now, my bold mistress? whither so fast? Back to your cage — hawks are abroad!"

Bertha clasped her hands — her eyes were still bent on my approaching figure. I saw the contest. How I abhorred the old crone who checked the kind impulses of my Bertha's softening heart. Hitherto, respect for her rank had caused me to avoid the lady of the castle; now I disdained such trivial considerations. I was cured of love, and lifted above all human fears; I hastened forwards, and soon reached the terrace. How lovely Bertha looked! her eyes flashing fire, her cheeks glowing with impatience and anger, she was a thousand times more graceful and charming than ever — I no longer loved — Oh! no, I adored — worshipped — idolized her!

She had that morning been persecuted, with more than usual vehemence, to consent to an immediate marriage with my rival. She was reproached with the encouragement that she had shown him — she was threatened with being turned out of doors with disgrace and shame. Her proud spirit rose in arms at the threat; but when she remembered the scorn that she had heaped upon me, and how, perhaps, she had thus lost one whom she now regarded as her only friend, she wept with remorse and rage. At that moment I appeared. "O, Winzy!" she exclaimed, "take me to your mother's cot; swiftly let me leave the detested luxuries and wretchedness of this noble dwelling — take me to poverty and happiness."

I clasped her in my arms with transport. The old lady was speechless with fury, and broke forth into invective only when we were far on our road to my natal cottage. My mother received the fair fugitive, escaped from a gilt cage to nature and liberty, with tenderness and joy; my father, who loved her, welcomed her heartily; it was a day of rejoicing, which did not need the addition of the celestial potion of the alchymist to steep me in delight.

Soon after this eventful day, I became the husband of Bertha. I ceased to be the scholar of Cornelius, but I continued his friend. I always felt grateful to him for having, unawares, procured me that delicious draught of a divine elixir, which, instead of curing me of love (sad cure! solitary and joyless remedy for evils which seem blessings to the memory), had inspired me with courage and resolution, thus winning for me an inestimable treasure in my Bertha.

I often called to mind that period of trance-like inebriation with wonder. The drink of Cornelius had not fulfilled the task for which he affirmed that it had been prepared, but its effects were more potent and blissful than words can express. They had faded by degrees, yet they lingered long — and painted life in hues of splendour. Bertha often wondered at my lightness of heart and unaccustomed gaiety; for, before, I had been rather serious, or even sad, in my disposition. She loved me the better for my cheerful temper, and our days were winged by joy.

Five years afterwards I was suddenly summoned to the bedside of the dying Cornelius. He had sent for me in haste, conjuring my instant presence. I found him stretched on his pallet, enfeebled even to death; all of life that yet remained animated his piercing eyes, and they were fixed on a glass vessel, full of a roseate liquid.

"Behold," he said, in a broken and inward voice, "the vanity of human wishes! a second time my hopes are about to be crowned, a second time they are destroyed. Look at that liquor — you remember five years ago I had prepared the same, with the same success; — then, as now, my thirsting lips expected to taste the immortal elixir — you dashed it from me! and at present it is too late."

He spoke with difficulty, and fell back on his pillow. I could not help saying, —

"How, revered master, can a cure for love restore you to life?"

A faint smile gleamed across his face as I listened earnestly to his scarcely intelligible answer.

"A cure for love and for all things — the Elixir of Immortality. Ah! if now I might drink, I should live for ever!"

As he spoke, a golden flash gleamed from the fluid; a well-remembered fragrance stole over the air; he raised himself, all weak as he was — strength seemed miraculously to re-enter his frame — he stretched forth his hand — a loud explosion startled me — a ray of fire shot up from the elixir, and the glass vessel which contained it was shivered to atoms! I turned my eyes towards the philosopher; he had fallen back — his eyes were glassy — his features rigid — he was dead!

But I lived, and was to live for ever! So said the unfortunate alchymist, and for a few days I believed his words. I remembered the glorious drunkenness that had followed my stolen draught. I reflected on the change I had felt in my frame — in my soul. The bounding elasticity of the one — the buoyant lightness of the other. I surveyed myself in a mirror, and could perceive no change in my features during the space of the five years which had elapsed. I remembered the radiant hues and grateful scent of that delicious beverage — worthy the gift it was capable of bestowing — I was, then, IMMORTAL!

A few days after I laughed at my credulity. The old proverb, that "a prophet is least regarded in his own country,"[1] was true with respect to me and my defunct master. I loved him as a man — I respected him as a sage — but I derided the notion that he could command the powers of darkness, and laughed at the superstitious fears with which he was regarded by the vulgar. He was a wise philosopher, but had no acquaintance with any spirits but those clad in flesh and blood. His science was simply human; and human science, I soon persuaded myself, could never conquer nature's laws so far as to imprison the soul for ever within its carnal habitation. Cornelius had brewed a soul-refreshing drink — more inebriating than wine — sweeter and more fragrant than any fruit: it possessed probably strong medicinal powers, imparting gladness to the heart and vigor to the limbs; but its effects would wear out; already were they diminished in my frame. I was a lucky fellow to have quaffed health and joyous spirits, and perhaps long life, at my master's hands; but my good fortune ended there: longevity was far different from immortality.

I continued to entertain this belief for many years. Sometimes a thought stole across me — Was the alchymist indeed deceived? But my habitual credence was, that I should meet the fate of all the children of Adam at my appointed time — a little late, but still at a natural age. Yet it was certain that I retained a wonderfully youthful look. I was laughed at for my

---

1   Variations on this phrase appears throughout the bible. See Matthew 13:57, Mark 6:4, Luke 4:23, Luke 4:24, and John 4:44.

vanity in consulting the mirror so often, but I consulted it in vain — my brow was untrenched — my cheeks — my eyes — my whole person continued as untarnished as in my twentieth year.

I was troubled. I looked at the faded beauty of Bertha — I seemed more like her son. By degrees our neighbours began to make similar observations, and I found at last that I went by the name of the Scholar bewitched. Bertha herself grew uneasy. She became jealous and peevish, and at length she began to question me. We had no children; we were all in all to each other; and though, as she grew older, her vivacious spirit became a little allied to ill-temper, and her beauty sadly diminished, I cherished her in my heart as the mistress I had idolized, the wife I had sought and won with such perfect love.

At last our situation became intolerable: Bertha was fifty — I twenty years of age. I had, in very shame, in some measure adopted the habits of a more advanced age; I no longer mingled in the dance among the young and gay, but my heart bounded along with them while I restrained my feet; and a sorry figure I cut among the Nestors[1] of our village. But before the time I mention, things were altered — we were universally shunned; we were — at least, I was — reported to have kept up an iniquitous acquaintance with some of my former master's supposed friends. Poor Bertha was pitied, but deserted. I was regarded with horror and detestation.

What was to be done? we sat by our winter fire — poverty had made itself felt, for none would buy the produce of my farm; and often I had been forced to journey twenty miles, to some place where I was not known, to dispose of our property. It is true we had saved something for an evil day — that day was come.

We sat by our lone fireside — the old-hearted youth and his antiquated wife. Again Bertha insisted on knowing the truth; she recapitulated all she had ever heard said about me, and added her own observations. She conjured me to cast off the spell; she described how much more comely gray hairs were than my chestnut locks; she descanted on the reverence and respect due to age — how preferable to the slight regard paid to mere children: could I imagine that the despicable gifts of youth and good looks outweighed disgrace, hatred, and scorn? Nay, in the end I should be burnt as a dealer in the black art, while she, to whom I had not deigned to communicate any portion of my good fortune, might be stoned as my accomplice. At length she insinuated that I must share my secret with her,

---

1 People of advanced age. The original reference is to an elder statesman of Greek myth who outlived two generations.

and bestow on her like benefits to those I myself enjoyed, or she would denounce me — and then she burst into tears.

Thus beset, methought it was the best way to tell the truth. I revealed it as tenderly as I could, and spoke, only of a *very long life*, not of immortality — which representation, indeed, coincided best with my own ideas. When I ended, I rose and said,

"And now, my Bertha, will you denounce the lover of your youth? — You will not, I know. But it is too hard, my poor wife, that you should suffer from my ill-luck and the accursed arts of Cornelius. I will leave you — you have wealth enough, and friends will return in my absence. I will go; young as I seem, and strong as I am, I can work and gain my bread among strangers, unsuspected and unknown. I loved you in youth; God is my witness that I would not desert you in age, but that your safety and happiness require it."

I took my cap and moved towards the door; in a moment Bertha's arms were round my neck, and her lips were pressed to mine. "No, my husband, my Winzy," she said, "you shall not go alone — take me with you; we will remove from this place, and, as you say, among strangers we shall be unsuspected and safe. I am not so very old as quite to shame you, my Winzy; and I dare say the charm will soon wear off and, with the blessing of God, you will become more elderly-looking, as is fitting; you shall not leave me."

I returned the good soul's embrace heartily. "I will not, my Bertha; but for your sake I had not thought of such a thing. I will be your true, faithful husband while you are spared to me, and do my duty by you to the last."

The next day we prepared secretly for our emigration. We were obliged to make great pecuniary sacrifices — it could not be helped. We realised a sum sufficient, at least, to maintain us while Bertha lived; and, without saying adieu to any one, quitted our native country to take refuge in a remote part of western France.

It was a cruel thing to transport poor Bertha from her native village, and the friends of her youth, to a new country, new language, new customs. The strange secret of my destiny rendered this removal immaterial to me; but I compassionated her deeply, and was glad to perceive that she found compensation for her misfortunes in a variety of little ridiculous circumstances. Away from all tell-tale chroniclers, she sought to decrease the apparent disparity of our ages by a thousand feminine arts — rouge, youthful dress, and assumed juvenility of manner. I could not be angry — Did not I myself wear a mask? Why quarrel with hers, because it was less successful? I grieved deeply when I remembered that this was my Bertha, whom I had loved so fondly, and won with such transport — the dark-eyed, dark-haired girl, with smiles of enchanting archness and a step like a fawn — this mincing, simpering, jealous old woman. I should have revered her gray locks and withered cheeks; but thus! — It was my work, I knew; but I did not the less deplore this type of human weakness.

Her jealousy never slept. Her chief occupation was to discover that, in spite of outward appearances, I was myself growing old. I verily believe that the poor soul loved me truly in her heart, but never had woman so tormenting a mode of displaying fondness. She would discern wrinkles in my face and decrepitude in my walk, while I bounded along in youthful vigour, the youngest looking of twenty youths. I never dared address another woman: on one occasion, fancying that the belle of the village regarded me with favouring eyes, she brought me a gray wig. Her constant discourse among her acquaintances was, that though I looked so young, there was ruin at work within my frame; and she affirmed that the worst symptom about me was my apparent health. My youth was a disease, she said, and I ought at all times to prepare, if not for a sudden and awful death, at least to awake some morning white-headed, and bowed down with all the marks of advanced years. I let her talk — I often joined in her conjectures. Her warnings chimed in with my never-ceasing speculations concerning my state, and I took an earnest, though painful, interest in listening to all that her quick wit and excited imagination could say on the subject.

Why dwell on these minute circumstances? We lived on for many long years. Bertha became bed-rid and paralytic: I nursed her as a mother might a child. She grew peevish, and still harped upon one string — of how long I should survive her. It has ever been a source of consolation to me, that I performed my duty scrupulously towards her. She had been mine in youth, she was mine in age, and at last, when I heaped the sod over her corpse, I wept to feel that I had lost all that really bound me to humanity.

Since then how many have been my cares and woes, how few and empty my enjoyments! I pause here in my history — I will pursue it no further. A sailor without rudder or compass, tossed on a stormy sea — a traveller lost on a widespread heath, without landmark or stone to guide him — such have I been: more lost, more hopeless than either. A nearing ship, a gleam from some far cot, may save them; but I have no beacon except the hope of death.

Death! mysterious, ill-visaged friend of weak humanity! Why alone of all mortals have you cast me from your sheltering fold? O, for the peace of the grave! the deep silence of the iron-bound tomb! that thought would cease to work in my brain, and my heart beat no more with emotions varied only by new forms of sadness!

Am I immortal? I return to my first question. In the first place, is it not more probable that the beverage of the alchymist was fraught rather with longevity than eternal life? Such is my hope. And then be it remembered, that I only drank *half* of the potion prepared by him. Was not the whole necessary to complete the charm? To have drained half the Elixir of Immortality is but to be half immortal — my For-ever is thus truncated and null.

But again, who shall number the years of the half of eternity? I often try to imagine by what rule the infinite may be divided. Sometimes I fancy age advancing upon me. One gray hair I have found. Fool! do I lament? Yes, the fear of age and death often creeps coldly into my heart; and the more I live, the more I dread death, even while I abhor life. Such an enigma is man — born to perish — when he wars, as I do, against the established laws of his nature.

But for this anomaly of feeling surely I might die: the medicine of the alchymist would not be proof against fire — sword — and the strangling waters. I have gazed upon the blue depths of many a placid lake, and the tumultuous rushing of many a mighty river, and have said, peace inhabits those waters; yet I have turned my steps away, to live yet another day. I have asked myself, whether suicide would be a crime in one to whom thus only the portals of the other world could be opened. I have done all, except presenting myself as a soldier or duelist, an object of destruction to my — no, *not* my fellow-mortals, and therefore I have shrunk away. They are not my fellows. The inextinguishable power of life in my frame, and their ephemeral existence, places us wide as the poles asunder. I could not raise a hand against the meanest or the most powerful among them.

Thus I have lived on for many a year — alone, and weary of myself — desirous of death, yet never dying — a mortal immortal. Neither ambition nor avarice can enter my mind, and the ardent love that gnaws at my heart, never to be returned — never to find an equal on which to expend itself — lives there only to torment me.

This very day I conceived a design by which I may end all — without self-slaughter, without making another man a Cain[1] — an expedition, which mortal frame can never survive, even endued with the youth and strength that inhabits mine. Thus I shall put my immortality to the test, and rest for ever — or return, the wonder and benefactor of the human species.

---

1   In the bible, Adam and Eve's first son and, after killing his brother Abel, the first murderer.

Before I go, a miserable vanity has caused me to pen these pages. I would not die, and leave no name behind. Three centuries have passed since I quaffed the fatal beverage: another year shall not elapse before, encountering gigantic dangers — warring with the powers of frost in their home — beset by famine, toil, and tempest — I yield this body, too tenacious a cage for a soul which thirsts for freedom, to the destructive elements of air and water — or, if I survive, my name shall be recorded as one of the most famous among the sons of men; and, my task achieved, I shall adopt more resolute means, and, by scattering and annihilating the atoms that compose my frame, set at liberty the life imprisoned within, and so cruelly prevented from soaring from this dim earth to a sphere more congenial to its immortal essence.

Charles Dickens

"The Bloomsbury Christening" (1834)

[Charles Dickens (1812–70) was born to a lower-middle-class family. At one point his father was even imprisoned for debt. Dickens began his career by writing stories and sketches on the courts and parliament, efforts that eventually lead to the novels for which he is now best known. Indeed, the first of his fourteen novels — *Pickwick Papers* (1836–37) — reads less like a novel and more like a string of connected stories. His short fiction — especially his Christmas pieces — were popular throughout his career. Like his novels, short stories such as "The Bloomsbury Christening" combine comedy with a sensitivity to the classism and corruption supported by the middle-class drive for wealth and status. In addition to being a writer, Dickens also encouraged others to write short stories through his role as editor for *Bentley's Miscellany*, *Household Words*, and *All the Year Round*.]

Mr. Nicodemus Dumps, or, as his acquaintance called him, "long Dumps," was a bachelor, six feet high, and fifty years old, — cross, cadaverous, odd, and ill-natured. He was never happy but when he was miserable (pardon the contradiction); and always miserable when he had the best reason to be happy. The only real comfort of his existence was to make everybody about him wretched — then he might be truly said to enjoy life. He was afflicted with a situation in the Bank worth five hundred a-year, and he rented a "first floor furnished" at Pentonville, which he originally took because it commanded a dismal prospect of an adjacent churchyard. He was familiar with the face of every tombstone, and the burial service seemed to excite his strongest sympathy. His friends said he was surly — he insisted he was nervous; they thought him a lucky dog, but he protested that he was "the most unfortunate man in the world." Cold as he was, and wretched as he declared himself to be, he was not wholly unsusceptible of attachments. He revered the memory of Hoyle,[1] as he was himself an admirable and imperturbable whist-player, and he chuckled with delight at a fretful and impatient adversary. He adored King Herod for his massacre of the innocents;[2] for if he hated one thing more than another, it was a child. However, he could hardly be said to hate any thing in particular, because he disliked every thing in general; but perhaps his greatest antipathies were cabs, old women, doors that would not shut, musical amateurs, and omnibus cads.[3] He subscribed to the Society for the Suppression of Vice[4] for the pleasure of putting a stop to any harmless amusements; and he contributed largely towards the support of two itinerant methodist[5] parsons, under the amiable hope that if circumstances rendered many happy in this world, they might perchance be rendered miserable by fears for the next.

Mr. Dumps had a nephew who had been married about a year, and who was somewhat of a favourite with his uncle, because he was an admirable subject to exercise his misery-creating powers upon. Mr. Charles Kitterbell was a small, sharp, spare man, with a very large head, and a broad good-humoured countenance. He looked like a faded giant, with the head and face partially restored; and he had a cast in his eye which rendered it quite impossible for any one with whom he conversed to know where he was looking. His eyes appeared fixed on the wall, and he was staring you out of countenance; in short, there was no catching his eye, and perhaps it is a merciful dispensation of Providence that such eyes are not catching. In addition to these characteristics, it may be added that Mr. Charles Kitterbell was one of the most credulous and matter-of-fact little personages that ever took *to* himself a wife, and *for* himself a house in Great Russell-street, Russell-square (Uncle Dumps always dropped the "Russell-square," and inserted in lieu thereof, the dreadful words "Tottenham-court-road").[6]

---

1   Edmond Hoyle (1672–1769), English authority on card games.

2   King Herod was the ruler of Judea at the time of the birth of Jesus. His ruthlessness is recounted in the Gospel of Matthew (2:16) when he orders the slaughter of all boys under the age of three after a prophesy warned him that a child in his kingdom would become the "King of the Jews."

3   The omnibus was a stagecoach taxi; cads were the drivers, notorious for their poor manners.

4   First instituted in London in 1802, its mandate was to suppress obscene literature and pictures, as well as lottery and policy gambling.

5   Belonging to the popular, lower middle-class, Protestant sect, which stressed bible reading, open-air meetings, and abstinence from drinking and gambling.

6   Russell Square was a prestigious area of London, while Tottenham-court road was a thoroughfare known for shops selling cheap linen products.

"No, but uncle, 'pon my life you must — you must promise to be god-father," said Mr. Kitterbell, as he sat in conversation with his respected relative one morning.

"I cannot, indeed I cannot," returned Dumps.

"Well, but why not? Jemima will think it very unkind. It's very little trouble."

"As to the trouble," rejoined the most unhappy man in existence, "I don't mind that; but my nerves are in that state — I cannot go through the ceremony. You know I don't like going out. — For God's sake, Charles, don't fidget with that stool so, you'll drive me mad." Mr. Kitterbell, quite regardless of his uncle's nerves, had occupied himself for some ten minutes in describing a circle on the floor with one leg of the office-stool on which he was seated, keeping the other three up in the air and holding fast on by the desk.

"I beg your pardon, uncle," said Kitterbell, quite abashed, suddenly releasing his hold of the desk, and bringing the three wandering legs back to the floor with a force sufficient to drive them throught it.

"But come, don't refuse. If it's a boy, you know, we must have two godfathers."

"*If* it's a boy!" said Dumps, "why can't you say at once whether it *is* a boy or not?"

"I should be very happy to tell you, but it's impossible I can undertake to say whether it's a girl or a boy if the child isn't born yet."

"Not born yet!" echoed Dumps, with a gleam of hope lighting up his lugubrious visage; "oh, well, it *may* be a girl, and then you won't want me, or if it is a boy, it *may* die before it's christened."

"I hope not," said the father that expected to be, looking very grave.

"I hope not," acquiesced Dumps, evidently pleased with the subject. He was beginning to get happy. "*I* hope not, but distressing cases frequently occur during the first two or three days of a child's life; fits I am told are exceedingly common, and alarming convulsions are almost matters of course."

"Lord, uncle!" ejaculated little Kitterbell, gasping for breath.

"Yes; my landlady was confined — let me see — last Tuesday: an uncommonly fine boy. On the Thursday night the nurse was sitting with him upon her knee before the fire, and he was as well as possible. Suddenly he became black in the face, and alarmingly spasmodic. The medical man was instantly sent for, and every remedy was tried, but —"

"How frightful!" interrupted the horror-stricken Kitterbell.

"The child died of course. However your child *may* not die, and if it should be a boy, and should *live* to be christened, why I suppose I must be one of the sponsors." Dumps was evidently good-natured on the faith of his anticipations.

"Thank you, uncle," said his agitated nephew, grasping his hand as warmly as if he had done him some essential service. "Perhaps I had better not tell Mrs. K. what you have mentioned."

"Why, if she's low spirited, perhaps you had better not mention the melancholy case to her," returned Dumps, who of course had invented the whole story, "though perhaps it would be but doing your duty as a husband to prepare her for the *worst*."

A day or two afterwards, as Dumps was perusing a morning paper at the chop-house which he regularly frequented, the following paragraph met his eye: —

"*Births.* — On Saturday the 18th inst., in Great Russell-street, the lady of Charles Kitterbell, Esq. of a son."

"It *is* a boy!" he exclaimed, dashing down the paper to the astonishment of the waiters. "It *is* a boy!" But he speedily regained his composure as his eye rested on a paragraph quoting the number of infant deaths from the bills of mortality.

Six weeks passed away, and as no communication had been received from the Kitterbells, Dumps was beginning to flatter himself that the child was dead, when the following note painfully resolved his doubts: —

"*Great Russell-street,*
"DEAR UNCLE: *Monday morning*
"You will be delighted to hear that my dear Jemima has left her room, and that your future godson is getting on capitally; he was very thin at first, but he is getting much larger, and nurse says he is filling out every day. He cries a good deal, and is a very singular colour, which made Jemima and me rather uncomfortable; but as nurse says it's natural, and as, of course, we know nothing about these things yet, we are quite satisfied with what nurse says. We think he will be a sharp child; and nurse says she's sure he will, because he never goes to sleep. You will readily believe that we are all very happy, only we're a little worn out for want of rest, as he keeps us awake all night; but this we must expect, nurse says, for the first six or eight months. He has been vaccinated, but in consequence of the operation being rather awkwardly performed, some small particles of

glass were introduced into the arm with the matter.[1] Perhaps this may in some degree account for his being rather fractious; at least, so nurse says. We propose to have him christened at twelve o'clock on Friday, at Saint George's church, in Hart-street, by the name of Frederick Charles William. Pray don't be later than a quarter before twelve. We shall have a very few friends in the evening, when, of course, we shall see you. I am sorry to say that the dear boy appears rather restless and uneasy to-day: the cause, I fear, is fever.

"Believe me, dear Uncle,
"Yours affectionately,
"CHARLES KITTERBELL."

"P.S. I open this note to say that we have just discovered the cause of little Frederick's restlessness. It is not fever, as I apprehended, but a small pin, which nurse accidentally stuck in his leg yesterday evening. We have taken it out, and he appears more composed, though he still sobs a good deal."

It is almost unnecessary to say that the perusal of the above interesting statement was no great relief to the mind of the hypochondriacal Dumps. It was impossible to recede, however, and so he put the best face — that is to say, an uncommonly miserable one — upon the matter; and purchased a handsome silver mug for the infant Kitterbell, upon which he ordered the initials "F.C.W.K.," with the customary untrained grape-vine-looking flourishes, and a large full stop, to be engraved forthwith.

Monday was a fine day, Tuesday was delightful, Wednesday was equal to either, and Thursday was finer than ever; four successive fine days in London! Hackney coachmen[2] became revolutionary, and crossing sweepers[3] began to doubt the existence of a First Cause.[4] The *Morning Herald* informed its readers that an old woman, in Camden Town, had been heard to say, that the fineness of the season was "unprecedented in the memory of the oldest inhabitant;" and Islington clerks, with large families and small salaries, left off their black gaiters, disdained to carry their once green cotton umbrellas, and walked to town in the conscious pride

1 In the vaccination process, the skin was first lightly punctured with glass to allow the vaccine to enter the blood system.

2 Drivers of a six-person coach available for hire.

3 People employed to sweep street intersections.

4 Origin of life or a prime mover, such as God.

of white stockings, and cleanly brushed Bluchers.[1] Dumps beheld all this with an eye of supreme contempt — his triumph was at hand. — He knew that if it had been fine for four weeks instead of four days, it would rain when he went out; he was lugubriously happy in the conviction that Friday would be a wretched day — and so it was. "I knew how it would be," said Dumps, as he turned round opposite the Mansion House at half-past eleven o'clock on the Friday morning. — "I knew how it would be, *I* am concerned, and that's enough;" — and certainly the appearance of the day was sufficient to depress the spirits of a much more buoyant-hearted individual than himself. It had rained, without a moment's cessation, since eight o'clock; everybody that passed up Cheapside, and down Cheapside, looked wet, cold, and dirty. All sorts of forgotten and long-concealed umbrellas had been put into requisition. Cabs whisked about, with the "fare" as carefully boxed up behind two glazed calico curtains, as any mysterious picture in any one of Mrs. Radcliffe's castles;[2] omnibus horses smoked like steam-engines; nobody thought of "standing up" under doorways or arches; they were painfully convinced it was a hopeless case; and so everybody went hastily along, jumbling and jostling, and swearing and perspiring, and slipping about, like amateur skaters behind wooden chairs on the Serpentine[3] on a frosty Sunday.

Dumps paused; he could not think of walking, being rather smart for the christening. If he took a cab he was sure to be spilt, and a hackney-coach was too expensive for his economical ideas. An omnibus was waiting at the opposite corner — it was a desperate case — he had never heard of an omnibus upsetting or running away, and if the cad did knock him down, he could "pull him up" in return.

"Now, Sir!" cried the young gentleman who officiated as "cad" to the "Lads of the Village," which was the name of the machine just noticed. Dumps crossed.

"This vay, sir!" shouted the driver of the "Hark away," pulling up his vehicle immediately across the door of the opposition — "This vay, sir — he's full." Dumps hesitated, whereupon the "Lads of the Village" commenced pouring out a torrent of abuse against the "Hark away;" but the conductor of the "Admiral Napier" settled the contest in a most satisfactory manner for all parties, by seizing Dumps round the waist, and

---

1   Strong leather half-boots or high shoes.

2   Ann Radcliffe (1764–1823), popular writer of Gothic literature of which frightening castles and peculiar portraits are staples.

3   Lake in Hyde Park, near central London, named for its winding shape.

thrusting him into the middle of his vehicle, which had just come up, and only wanted the sixteenth inside.

"All right," said the "Admiral," and off the thing thundered, like a fire-engine at full gallop, with the kidnapped customer inside, standing in the position of a half doubled up boot jack,[1] and falling about with every jerk of the machine, first on one side and then on the other, like a "Jack in the green," on May-day,[2] "setting" to the lady with the brass ladle.

"For God's sake, where am I to sit?" inquired the miserable man of an old gentleman, into whose stomach he had just fallen for the fourth time.

"Anywhere but on my *chest*, sir," replied the old gentleman, in a surly tone.

"Perhaps the *box*[3] would suit the gentleman better," suggested a very damp lawyer's clerk, in a pink shirt and a smirking countenance.

After a great deal of struggling and falling about, Dumps at last managed to squeeze himself into a seat, which, in addition to the slight disadvantage of being between a window that wouldn't shut, and a door that must be open, placed him in close contact with a passenger, who had been walking about all the morning without an umbrella, and who looked as if he had spent the day in a full water-butt — only wetter.

"Don't bang the door so," said Dumps to the conductor, as he shut it after letting out four of the passengers; "I am very nervous — it destroys me."

"Did any gen'lm'n say any think?" replied the cad, thrusting in his head, and trying to look as if he didn't understand the request.

"I told you not to bang the door so," repeated Dumps, with an expression of countenance, like the knave of clubs in convulsions.

"Oh! vy it's rayther a sing'ler circumstance about this here door, sir, that it von't shut without banging," replied the conductor; and he opened the door very wide, and shut it again with a terrific bang, in proof of the assertion.

"I beg your pardon, sir," said a little prim wheezing old gentleman, sitting opposite Dumps, "I beg your pardon; but have you ever observed, when you have been in an omnibus on a wet day, that four people out of five, always come in with large cotton umbrellas, without a handle at the top, or the brass spike at the bottom?"

---

1 Device used to remove boots.

2 May Day celebrations on May 1st often included a man dressed in a leaf-covered box — a Jack-in-the-green — who participated in the festivities by dancing, playing games, and so on.

3 Top of the coach, where the driver is seated.

"Why, sir," returned Dumps, as he heard the clock strike twelve, "it never struck me before; but now you mention it, I — Hollo! hollo!" — shouted the persecuted individual, as the omnibus dashed past Drury-lane, where he had directed to be set down. — "Where is the cad?"

"I think he's on the box, sir," said the young gentleman before noticed in the pink shirt, which looked like a white one ruled with red ink.

"I want to be set down!" said Dumps, in a faint voice, overcome by his previous efforts.

"I think these cads want to be *set down*,"[1] returned the attorney's clerk, chuckling at his sally.

"Hollo!" cried Dumps again.

"Hollo!" echoed the passengers; the omnibus passed St. Giles's church.

"Hold hard!" said the conductor, "I'm blowed if we ha'n't forgot the gen'lm'n as vas to be set down at Doory-lane. — Now, sir, make haste, if you please," he added, opening the door, and assisting Dumps out with as much coolness as if it was "all right." Dumps' indignation was for once getting the better of his cynical equanimity. "Drury-lane!" he gasped, with the voice of a boy in a cold-bath for the first time.

"Doory-lane, sir? — yes, sir, — third turning on the right hand side, sir."

Dumps' passion was paramount, he clutched his umbrella, and was striding off with the firm determination of not paying the fare. The cad, by a remarkable coincidence, happened to entertain a directly contrary opinion, and heaven knows how far the altercation would have proceeded if it had not been most ably and satisfactorily brought to a close by the driver.

"Hollo!" said that respectable person standing up on the box, and leaning with one hand on the roof of the omnibus. "Hollo, Tom! tell the gentleman if so be as he feels aggrieved, we will take him up to the Edge-er (Edgeware) Road for nothing, and set him down at Doory-lane when we comes back. He can't reject that anyhow."

The argument was irresistible; Dumps paid the disputed sixpence, and in a quarter of an hour was on the staircase of No. 14, Great Russell-street.

Every thing indicated that preparations were making for the reception of "a few friends" in the evening. Two dozen extra tumblers, and four ditto wine-glasses — looking anything but transparent, with little bits of straw in them — were on the slab in the passage, just arrived. There was a great smell of nutmeg, port wine, and almonds on the staircase; the covers were taken off the stair-carpet, and the figure of Venus on the first

---

1   To be let off a conveyance; but also to be humiliated or scolded.

landing looked as if she were ashamed of the composition-candle[1] in her right hand, which contrasted beautifully with the lamp-blacked[2] drapery of the goddess of love. The female servant (who looked very warm and bustling) ushered Dumps into a front drawing-room very prettily furnished with a plentiful sprinkling of little baskets, paper table-mats, china watchmen,[3] pink and gold albums, and rainbow-bound little books on the different tables.

"Ah, uncle!" said Mr. Kitterbell, "how d'ye do? allow me — Jemima, my dear — my uncle, — I think you've seen Jemima before, sir?"

"Have had the *pleasure*," returned big Dumps, his tone and look making it doubtful whether in his life he had ever experienced the sensation.

"I'm sure," said Mrs. Kitterbell with a languid smile, and a slight cough; "I'm sure — hem — any friend — of Charles's — hem — much less a relation is —"

"Knew you'd say so, my love," said little Kitterbell, who while he appeared to be gazing on the opposite houses, was looking at his wife with a most affectionate air; "bless you." The last two words were accompanied with an interesting simper, and a squeeze of the hand, which stirred up all Uncle Dumps' bile.

"Jane, tell nurse to bring down baby," said Mrs. Kitterbell, addressing the servant. Mrs. Kitterbell was a tall thin young lady with very light hair, and a particularly white face — one of those young women who almost invariably, though one hardly knows why, recall to one's mind the idea of a cold fillet of veal. Out went the servant, and in came the nurse, with a remarkably small parcel in her arms packed up in a blue mantle trimmed with white fur. — This was the baby.

"Now, uncle," said Mr. Kitterbell, lifting up that part of the mantle which covered the infant's face, with an air of great triumph, "*Who* do you think he's like?"

"He! he! Yes, who?" said Mrs. K. putting her arm through her husband's, and looking up into Dumps' face with an expression of as much interest as she was capable of displaying.

"Good God, how small he is!" cried the amiable uncle, starting back with well-feigned surprise; "*remarkably* small indeed."

"Do you think so?" inquired poor little Kitterbell rather alarmed. "He's a monster to what he was — an't he nurse?"

---

1 Candle made of various ingredients.

2 Stained black by the soot from the burning oil in lamps.

3 Sentinels or look-outs, but also used to refer to angels.

"He's a dear;" said the nurse squeezing the child, and evading the question — not because she scrupled to disguise the fact, but because she couldn't afford to throw away the chance of Dumps' half-crown.

"Well, but who is he like?" inquired little Kitterbell.

Dumps looked at the little pink heap before him, and only thought at the moment of the best mode of mortifying the youthful parents.

"I really don't know *who* he's like," he answered, very well knowing the reply expected of him.

"Don't you think he's like *me*?" inquired his nephew, with a knowing air.

"Oh, *decidedly* not!" returned Dumps, with an emphasis not to be misunderstood. "Decidedly not like you. — Oh, certainly not."

"Like Jemima?" asked Kitterbell faintly.

"Oh dear, no; not in the least. I'm no judge, of course, in such cases; but I really think he's more like one of those little interesting carved representations that one sometimes sees blowing a trumpet on a tombstone!" The nurse stooped down over the child, and with great difficulty prevented an explosion of mirth. Pa and ma looked almost as miserable as their amiable uncle.

"Well!" said the disappointed little father, "you'll be better able to tell what he's like by and bye. You shall see him this evening with his mantle off."

"Thank you," said Dumps, feeling particularly grateful.

"Now, my love," said Kitterbell to his wife, "it's time we were off. We're to meet the other godfather and the godmother at the church, uncle, — Mr. and Mrs. Wilson from over the way — uncommonly nice people. My love, are you well wrapped up?"

"Yes, dear."

"Are you sure you won't have another shawl?" inquired the anxious husband.

"No, sweet," returned the charming mother, accepting Dumps' proffered arm; and the little party entered the hackney-coach that was to take them to the church. Dumps amusing Mrs. Kitterbell by expatiating largely on the danger of measles, thrush, teeth-cutting, and other interesting diseases to which children are subject.

The ceremony (which occupied about five minutes) passed off without anything particular occurring. The clergyman had to dine some distance from town, and had got two churchings,[1] three christenings, and a funeral to perform in something less than an hour. The godfathers and godmother, therefore, promised to renounce the devil and all his works

---

1 The public appearance of women at church after childbirth.

— "and all that sort of thing," — as little Kitterbell said — "in less than no time;" and, with the exception of Dumps nearly letting the child fall into the font[1] when he handed it to the clergyman, the whole affair went off in the usual business-like and matter-of-course manner, and Dumps re-entered the Bank-gates at two o'clock with heavy heart, and the painful conviction that he was regularly booked for an evening party.

Evening came — and so did Dumps' pumps, black silk stockings, and white cravat which he had ordered to be forwarded, per boy, from Pentonville. The depressed godfather dressed himself at a friend's count-ing-house,[2] from whence, with his spirits fifty degrees below proof, he sal-lied forth — as the weather had cleared up, and the evening was tolerably fine — to walk to Great Russell-street. Slowly he paced up Cheapside, Newgate-street, down Snow Hill, and up Holborn ditto, looking as grim as the figure-head of a man-of-war,[3] and finding out fresh causes of misery at every step. As he was crossing the corner of Hatton Garden, a man, apparently intoxicated, rushed against him, and would have knocked him down had he not been providentially caught by a very genteel young man who happened to be close to him at the time. The shock so dis-arranged Dumps' nerves, as well as his dress, that he could hardly stand. The gentleman took his arm, and in the kindest manner walked with him as far as Furnival's Inn. Dumps, for about the first time in his life, felt grateful and polite; and he and the gentlemanly-looking young man parted with mutual expressions of good will.

"There are at least some well disposed men in the world," ruminated the misanthropical Dumps, as he proceeded towards his destination.

Rat–tat–ta-ra-ra-ra-ra-rat — knocked a hackney-coachman at Kitterbell's door, in imitation of a gentleman's servant, just as Dumps reached it, and out came an old lady in a large toque, and an old gentleman in a blue coat, and three female copies of the old lady in pink dresses, and shoes to match.

"It's a large party," sighed the unhappy godfather, wiping the perspi-ration from his forehead, and leaning against the area-railings. It was some time before the miserable man could muster up courage to knock at the door, and when he did, the smart appearance of a neighbouring green-grocer (who had been hired to wait for seven and sixpence, and whose calves alone were worth double the money), the lamp in the passage,

1 Baptismal fountain.

2 Building or office where a business does its book-keeping.

3 One of the navy's battleships.

and the Venus on the landing, added to the hum of many voices, and the sound of a harp and two violins, painfully convinced him that his surmises were but too well founded.

"How are you?" said little Kitterbell in a greater bustle than ever, bolting out of the little back parlour with a corkscrew in his hand, and various particles of saw-dust, looking like so many inverted commas, on his inexpressibles.[1]

"Good God!" said Dumps, turning into the aforesaid parlour to put his shoes on which he had brought in his coat-pocket, and still more appalled by the sight of seven fresh drawn corks, and a corresponding number of decanters. "How many people are there up stairs?"

"Oh, not above thirty-five. We've had the carpet taken up in the back drawing-room, and the piano, and the card-tables are in the front. Jemima thought we'd better have a regular sit down supper, in the front parlour, because of the speechifying, and all that. But, Lord! uncle, what's the matter?" continued the excited little man, as Dumps stood with one shoe on, rummaging his pockets with the most frightful distortion of visage. "What have you lost? Your pocket-book?"

"No," returned Dumps, diving first into one pocket and then into the other, and speaking in a voice like Desdemona[2] with the pillow over her mouth.

"Your card-case? snuff-box? the key of your lodgings?" continued Kitterbell, pouring question on question with the rapidity of lightning.

"No! no!" ejaculated Dumps, still diving eagerly into his empty pocket.

"Not — not — the *mug* you spoke of this morning?"

"Yes, the *mug*!" replied Dumps, sinking into a chair.

"How *could* you have done it?" inquired Kitterbell. "Are you sure you brought it out?"

"Yes! yes! I see it all;" said Dumps, starting up as the idea flashed across his mind; "miserable dog that I am — I was born to suffer. I see it all; it was the gentlemanly-looking young man!"

"Mr. Dumps!" shouted the green-grocer in a stentorian[3] voice, as he ushered the somewhat recovered godfather into the drawing-room half an hour after the above declaration. "Mr. Dumps!" — every body looked at the door, and in came Dumps, feeling about as much out of place as a salmon might be supposed to be on a gravel-walk.

---

1   Breeches or trousers.

2   In Shakespeare's *Othello* (1602/04), Othello suffocates his wife Desdemona with a pillow.

3   Booming, loud.

"Happy to see you again," said Mrs. Kitterbell, quite unconscious of the unfortunate man's confusion and misery; "you must allow me to introduce you to a few of our friends: — my mamma, Mr. Dumps — my papa and sisters." Dumps seized the hand of the mother as warmly as if she was his own parent, bowed *to* the young ladies, and *against* a gentleman behind him, and took no notice whatever of the father, who had been bowing incessantly for three minutes and a quarter.

"Uncle," said little Kitterbell, after Dumps had been introduced to a select dozen or two, "you must let me lead you to the other end of the room, to introduce you to my friend Danton. Such a splendid fellow! — I'm sure you'll like him — this way." — Dumps followed as tractably as a tame bear.

Mr. Danton was a young man of about five-and-twenty, with a considerable stock of impudence, and a very small share of ideas: he was a great favourite, especially with young ladies of from sixteen to twenty-six years of age, both inclusive. He could imitate the French horn to admiration, sang comic songs most inimitably, and had the most insinuating way of saying impertinent nothings to his doating female admirers. He had acquired, somehow or other, the reputation of being a great wit, and, accordingly, whenever he opened his mouth, everybody who knew him laughed very heartily.

The introduction took place in due form. Mr. Danton bowed and twirled a lady's handkerchief, which he held in his hand, in a most comic way. Everybody smiled.

"Very warm," said Dumps, feeling it necessary to say something.

"Yes. It was warmer yesterday," returned the brilliant Mr. Danton. — A general laugh.

"I have great pleasure in congratulating you on your first appearance in the character of a father, sir," he continued, addressing Dumps — "god-father, I mean." — The young ladies were convulsed, and the gentlemen in ecstasies.

A general hum of admiration interrupted the conversation and announced the entrance of nurse with the baby. A universal rush of the young ladies immediately took place. (Girls are always *so* fond of babies in company.)

"Oh, you dear!" said one.

"How sweet!" cried another, in a low tone of the most enthusiastic admiration.

"Heavenly!" added a third.

"Oh! what dear little arms!" said a fourth, holding up an arm and fist about the size and shape of the leg of a fowl cleanly picked.

"Did you ever" — said a little coquette with a large bustle, who looked like a French lithograph, appealing to a gentleman in three waistcoats — "Did you ever" —

"Never, in my life," returned her admirer, pulling up his collar.

"Oh, *do* let me take it, nurse," cried another young lady. "The love!"

"Can it open its eyes, nurse?" inquired another, affecting the utmost innocence. — Suffice it to say that the single ladies unanimously voted him an angel, and that the married ones, *nem. con.*,[1] agreed that he was decidedly the finest baby they had ever beheld — except their own.

The quadrilles were resumed with great spirit, Mr. Danton was universally admitted to be beyond himself, several young ladies enchanted the company and gained admirers by singing, "We met" — "I saw her at the Fancy Fair" — "Can I believe Love's Wreath will pain?" — and other equally sentimental and interesting ballads. "The young men," as Mrs. Kitterbell said, "made themselves very agreeable;" the girls did not lose their opportunity; and the evening promised to go off excellently. Dumps didn't mind it: he had devised a plan for himself — a little bit of fun in his own way — and he was almost happy! He played a rubber,[2] and lost every point. Mr. Danton said he could not have lost every point, because he made a point of losing: — everybody laughed tremendously. Dumps retorted with a better joke, and nobody smiled, with the exception of the host, who seemed to consider it his duty to laugh, till he was black in the face, at everything. There was only one drawback — the musicians did not play with quite as much spirit as could have been wished. The cause, however, was satisfactorily explained; for it appeared, on the testimony of a gentleman who had come up from Gravesend in the afternoon, that they had been engaged on board a steamer all day, and had played almost without cessation all the way to Gravesend, and all the way back again.

The "sit-down supper" was excellent; there were four barley-sugar temples[3] on the table, which would have looked beautiful if they had not melted away when the supper began; and a water-mill, whose only fault was, that instead of going round, it ran over the table-cloth. Then there were fowls, and tongue, and trifle, and sweets, and lobster salad, and potted beef — and everything. And little Kitterbell kept calling out for clean plates, and the clean plates didn't come; and then the gentlemen who

---

1   (Latin) unanimously.

2   A set of games such as cards where one tries to win most of the games in the set, such as three out of five.

3   Sweets made from sugar and boiled barley.

wanted the plates said they didn't mind, they'd take a lady's; and then Mrs. Kitterbell applauded their gallantry; and the green-grocer ran about till he thought his *7s. 6d.*[1] was very hardly earned; and the young ladies didn't eat much for fear it shouldn't look romantic, and the married ladies eat as much as possible for fear they shouldn't have enough; and a great deal of wine was drank, and everybody talked and laughed considerably.

"Hush! hush!" said Mr. Kitterbell, rising and looking very important. "My love (this was addressed to his wife at the other end of the table), take care of Mrs. Maxwell, and your mamma, and the rest of the married ladies; the gentlemen will persuade the young ladies to fill their glasses, I am sure."

"Ladies and gentlemen," said long Dumps, in a very sepulchral voice and rueful accent, rising from his chair like the ghost in Don Juan,[2] "will you have the kindness to charge your glasses? I am desirous of proposing a toast."

A dead silence ensued, and the glasses were filled — everybody looked serious — "from *gay* to *grave*, from lively to severe."

"Ladies and gentlemen," slowly continued the ominous Dumps, "I" — (Here Mr. Danton imitated two notes from the French-horn, in a very loud key, which electrified the nervous toast-proposer, and convulsed his audience).

"Order! order!" said little Kitterbell, endeavouring to suppress his laughter.

"Order!" said the gentlemen.

"Danton, be quiet," said a particular friend on the opposite side of the table.

"Ladies and gentlemen," resumed Dumps, somewhat recovered, and not much disconcerted, for he was always a pretty good hand at a speech — "In accordance with what is, I believe, the established usage on these occasions, I, as one of the godfathers of Master Frederick Charles William Kitterbell — (here the speaker's voice faltered, for he remembered the mug) — venture to rise to propose a toast. I need hardly say that it is the health and prosperity of that young gentleman, the particular event of whose early life we are here met to celebrate — (applause). Ladies and gentlemen, it is impossible to suppose that our friends here, whose sin-

1   Seven shillings and six pence, a fair sum of money in this context.

2   Spanish legend about a seducer (Juan) in which a statue comes to life and kills Juan. There have been many versions of the story, including Wolfgang Amadeus Mozart's well-known *Don Giovanni* (1786).

cere well-wishers we all are, can pass through life without some trials, considerable suffering, severe affliction, and heavy losses!" — Here the arch-traitor paused, and slowly drew forth a long, white pocket-handkerchief — his example was followed by several ladies. "That these trials may be long spared them, is my most earnest prayer, my most fervent wish (a distinct sob from the grandmother). I hope and trust, ladies and gentlemen, that the infant whose christening we have this evening met to celebrate, may not be removed from the arms of his parents by premature decay (several cambrics[1] were in requisition); that his young and now *apparently* healthy form, may not be wasted by lingering disease. (Here Dumps cast a sardonic glance around, for a great sensation was manifest among the married ladies.) You, I am sure, will concur with me in wishing that he may live to be a comfort and a blessing to his parents. ('Hear, hear!' and an audible sob from Mr. Kitterbell.) But should he not be what we could wish — should he forget, in after times, the duty which he owes to them — should they unhappily experience that distracting truth, 'how sharper than a serpent's tooth it is to have a thankless child'" — Here Mrs. Kitterbell, with her handkerchief to her eyes, and accompanied by several ladies, rushed from the room, and went into violent hysterics in the passage, leaving her better half in almost as bad a condition, and a general impression in Dumps' favour: for people like sentiment after all.

It need hardly be added that this occurrence quite put a stop to the harmony of the evening. Vinegar, hartshorn, and cold water were now as much in request as negus, rout cakes, and *bon-bons*[2] had been a short time before. Mrs. Kitterbell was immediately conveyed to her apartment, the musicians were silenced, flirting ceased, and the company slowly departed. Dumps left the house at the commencement of the bustle, and walked home with a light step, and (for him) a cheerful heart. His landlady, who slept in the next room, has offered to make oath that she heard him laugh, in his peculiar manner, after he had locked his door. The assertion, however, is so improbable, and bears on the face of it such strong evidence of untruth, that it has never obtained credence to this hour.

The family of Mr. Kitterbell has considerably increased since the period to which we have referred; he has now two sons and a daughter: and as he expects, at no distant period, to have another addition to his

---

1   Linen handkerchiefs.

2   Vinegar, hartshorn, and cold water were commonly used to revive or calm a distraught person, hartshorn being a medicine made from the shavings of deer's antlers. Negus is hot, sweetened wine mixed with water, and rout-cakes are small, rich cakes usually served on special occasions.

blooming progeny, he is anxious to secure an eligible godfather for the occasion. He is determined, however, to impose upon him two conditions: he must bind himself, by a solemn obligation, not to make any speech after supper; and it is indispensable that he should be in no way connected with "the most miserable man in the world."

Thomas De Quincey

"The Vision of Sudden Death" & "The Dream-Fugue" (1849)

[Thomas De Quincey (1785–1859) was born in Manchester and, after a scattered education mixed with travels around England, Ireland, and Wales, he studied philosophy as well as English and German literature at Oxford University. While there, he began taking opium for medicinal purposes, leading to his famous *Confessions of an Opium-Eater* (1821), which first appeared in serial form in the *London Magazine*. For the last two decades of his life, he lived in or near Edinburgh, Scotland, where he continued to write stories, essays, and reviews. One of his most skilled works from this time is the descriptive *English Mail-Coach* (1849), which combined the forms of the tale, the essay, and a more experimental model akin to the sketch. The two sections of this piece included here — "The Vision of Sudden Death" and "The Dream-Fugue" — reflect the protean state of short fiction in the early Victorian period and the experimental freedom this lack of generic formulation permitted.]

(The reader is to understand this present paper, in its two sections of *The Vision*, &c., and *The Dream-Fugue*, as connected with a previous paper on *The English Mail-Coach*, published in the Magazine for October. The ultimate object was the Dream-Fugue, as an attempt to wrestle with the utmost efforts of music in dealing with a colossal form of impassioned horror. The Vision of Sudden Death contains the mail-coach incident, which did really occur, and did really suggest the variations of the Dream, here taken up by the Fugue, as well as other variations not now recorded. Confluent with these impressions, from the terrific experience on the Manchester and Glasgow mail, were other and more general impressions, derived from long familiarity with the English mail, as developed in the former paper; impressions, for instance, of animal beauty and power, of rapid motion, at that time unprecedented, of connexion with the government and public business of a great nation, but, above all, of connexion with the national victories at an unexampled crisis, — the mail being the privileged organ for publishing and dispersing all news of that kind. From this function of the mail, arises naturally the introduction of Waterloo into the fourth variation of the Fugue; for the mail itself having been carried into the dreams by the incident in the Vision, naturally all the accessory circumstances of pomp and grandeur investing this national carriage followed in the train of the principal image.)

What is to be thought of sudden death? It is remarkable that, in different conditions of society, it has been variously regarded, as the consummation of an earthly career most fervently to be desired, and, on the other hand, as that consummation which is most of all to be deprecated. Cæsar the Dictator,[1] at his last dinner party, (*cœna*,[2]) and the very evening before his assassination, being questioned as to the mode of death which, in *his* opinion, might seem the most eligible, replied — "That which should be most sudden." On the other hand, the divine Litany of our English Church, when breathing forth supplications, as if in some representative character for the whole human race prostrate before God, places such a death in the very van of horrors. "From lightning and tempest; from plague, pestilence, and famine; from battle and murder, and from sudden death, — *Good Lord, deliver us.*" Sudden death is here made to crown the climax in a grand ascent of calamities; it is the last of curses; and yet, by the noblest of Romans, it was treated as the first of blessings. In that difference, most readers will see little more than the difference between Christianity and Paganism. But there I hesitate. The Christian church may be right in its estimate of sudden death; and it is a natural feeling, though after all it may also be an infirm one, to wish for a quiet dismissal from life — as that which *seems* most reconcilable with meditation, with penitential retrospects, and with the humilities of farewell prayer. There does not, however, occur to me any direct scriptural warrant for this earnest petition of the English Litany. It seems rather a petition indulged to human infirmity, than exacted from human piety. And, however *that* may be, two remarks suggest themselves as prudent restraints upon a doctrine, which else *may* wander, and *has* wandered, into an uncharitable superstition. The first is this: that many people are likely to exaggerate the horror of a sudden death, (I mean the *objective* horror to him who contemplates such a death, not the *subjective* horror to him who

---

1   Julius Caesar (100–44 BC), Roman general, statesman, and ruler.

2   (Latin) supper.

suffers it) from the false disposition to lay a stress upon words or acts, simply because by an accident they have become words or acts. If a man dies, for instance, by some sudden death when he happens to be intoxicated, such a death is falsely regarded with peculiar horror; as though the intoxication were suddenly exalted into a blasphemy. But *that* is unphilosophic. The man was, or he was not, *habitually* a drunkard. If not, if his intoxication were a solitary accident, there can be no reason at all for allowing special emphasis to this act, simply because through misfortune it became his final act. Nor, on the other hand, if it were no accident, but one of his *habitual* transgressions, will it be the more habitual or the more a transgression, because some sudden calamity, surprising him, has caused this habitual transgression to be also a final one? Could the man have had any reason even dimly to foresee his own sudden death, there would have been a new feature in his act of intemperance — a feature of presumption and irreverence, as in one that by possibility felt himself drawing near to the presence of God. But this is no part of the case supposed. And the only new element in the man's act is not any element of extra immorality, but simply of extra misfortune.

The other remark has reference to the meaning of the word *sudden*. And it is a strong illustration of the duty which for ever calls us to the stern valuation of words — that very possibly Cæsar and the Christian church do not differ in the way supposed; that is, do not differ by any difference of doctrine as between Pagan and Christian views of the moral temper appropriate to death, but that they are contemplating different cases. Both contemplate a violent death; a βιαθανατυς — death that is Βιαιος: but the difference is — that the Roman by the word "sudden" means an *unlingering* death: whereas the Christian litany by "sudden" means a death *without warning*, consequently without any available summons to religious preparation. The poor mutineer, who kneels down to gather into his heart the bullets from twelve firelocks[1] of his pitying comrades, dies by a most sudden death in Cæsar's sense: one shock, one mighty spasm, one (possibly *not* one) groan, and all is over. But, in the sense of the Litany, his death is far from sudden; his offence originally, his imprisonment, his trial, the interval between his sentence and its execution, having all furnished him with separate warnings of his fate — having all summoned him to meet it with solemn preparation.

Meantime, whatever may be thought of a sudden death as a mere variety in the modes of dying, where death in some shape is inevitable — a

---

1   Guns equipped with a lock that produces sparks for ignition.

question which, equally in the Roman and the Christian sense, will be variously answered according to each man's variety of temperament — certainly, upon one aspect of sudden death there can be no opening for doubt, that of all agonies incident to man it is the most frightful, that of all martyrdoms it is the most freezing to human sensibilities — namely, where it surprises a man under circumstances which offer (or which seem to offer) some hurried and inappreciable chance of evading it. Any effort, by which such an evasion can be accomplished, must be as sudden as the danger which it affronts. Even *that*, even the sickening necessity for hurrying in extremity where all hurry seems destined to be vain, self-baffled, and where the dreadful knell of *too late* is already sounding in the ears by anticipation — even that anguish is liable to a hideous exasperation in one particular case, namely, where the agonising appeal is made not exclusively to the instinct of self-preservation, but to the conscience, on behalf of another life besides your own, accidentally cast upon *your* protection. To fail, to collapse in a service merely your own, might seem comparatively venial; though, in fact, it is far from venial. But to fail in a case where Providence has suddenly thrown into your hands the final interests of another — of a fellow-creature shuddering between the gates of life and death; this, to a man of apprehensive conscience, would mingle the misery of an atrocious criminality with the misery of a bloody calamity. The man is called upon, too probably, to die; but to die at the very moment when, by any momentary collapse, he is self-denounced as a murderer. He had but the twinkling of an eye for his effort, and that effort might, at the best, have been unavailing; but from this shadow of a chance, small or great, how if he has recoiled by a treasonable *lâcheté*?[1] The effort *might* have been without hope; but to have risen to the level of that effort — would have rescued him, though not from dying, yet from dying as a traitor to his duties.

The situation here contemplated exposes a dreadful ulcer, lurking far down in the depths of human nature. It is not that men generally are summoned to face such awful trials. But potentially, and in shadowy outline, such a trial is moving subterraneously in perhaps all men's natures — muttering under ground in one world, to be realised perhaps in some other. Upon the secret mirror of our dreams such a trial is darkly projected at intervals, perhaps, to every one of us. That dream, so familiar to childhood, of meeting a lion, and, from languishing prostration in hope and vital energy, that constant sequel of lying down before him, publishes the secret frailty of human nature — reveals its deep-

---

1 (French) cowardice.

seated Pariah falsehood to itself — records its abysmal treachery. Perhaps not one of us escapes that dream; perhaps, as by some sorrowful doom of man, that dream repeats for every one of us, through every generation, the original temptation in Eden. Every one of us, in this dream, has a bait offered to the infirm places of his own individual will; once again a snare is made ready for leading him into captivity to a luxury of ruin; again, as in aboriginal Paradise, the man falls from innocence; once again, by infinite iteration, the ancient Earth groans to God, through her secret caves, over the weakness of her child; "Nature from her seat, sighing through all her works," again "gives signs of woe that all is lost;"[1] and again the counter sigh is repeated to the sorrowing heavens of the endless rebellion against God. Many people think that one man, the patriarch of our race,[2] could not in his single person execute this rebellion for all his race. Perhaps they are wrong. But, even if not, perhaps in the world of dreams every one of us ratifies for himself the original act. Our English rite of "Confirmation,"[3] by which, in years of awakened reason, we take upon us the engagements contracted for us in our slumbering infancy, — how sublime a rite is that! The little postern[4] gate, through which the baby in its cradle had been silently placed for a time within the glory of God's countenance, suddenly rises to the clouds as a triumphal arch, through which, with banners displayed and martial pomps, we make our second entry as crusading soldiers militant for God, by personal choice and by sacramental oath. Each man says in effect — "Lo! I rebaptise myself; and that which once was sworn on my behalf, now I swear for myself." Even so in dreams, perhaps, under some secret conflict of the midnight sleeper, lighted up to the consciousness at the time, but darkened to the memory as soon as all is finished, each several child of our mysterious race completes for himself the aboriginal fall.

As I drew near to the Manchester post-office, I found that it was considerably past midnight; but to my great relief, as it was important for me to be in Westmorland by the morning, I saw by the huge saucer eyes of the mail, blazing through the gloom of overhanging houses, that my

---

1 From John Milton's *Paradise Lost*, Book 9 (1783–84), the section describes Eve debating whether or not to eat the apple.

2 Adam.

3 Christian ceremony in which an adult is given full membership into the church after s/he confirms the promise to be a good Christian; also the promises made by the godparents at one's christening.

4 Back entrance.

chance was not yet lost. Past the time it was; but by some luck, very unusual in my experience, the mail was not even yet ready to start. I ascended to my seat on the box, where my cloak was still lying as it had lain at the Bridgewater Arms. I had left it there in imitation of a nautical discoverer, who leaves a bit of bunting on the shore of his discovery, by way of warning off the ground the whole human race, and signalising to the Christian and the heathen worlds, with his best compliments, that he has planted his throne for ever upon that virgin soil; henceforward claiming the *jus dominii*[1] to the top of the atmosphere above it, and also the right of driving shafts to the centre of the earth below it; so that all people found after this warning, either aloft in the atmosphere, or in the shafts, or squatting on the soil, will be treated as trespassers — that is, decapitated by their very faithful and obedient servant, the owner of the said bunting. Possibly my cloak might not have been respected, and the *jus gentium*[2] might have been cruelly violated in my person — for, in the dark, people commit deeds of darkness, gas being a great ally of morality — but it so happened that, on this night, there was no other outside passenger; and the crime, which else was but too probable, missed fire for want of a criminal. By the way, I may as well mention at this point, since a circumstantial accuracy is essential to the effect of my narrative, that there was no other person of any description whatever about the mail — the guard, the coachman, and myself being allowed for — except only one — a horrid creature of the class known to the world as insiders, but whom young Oxford called sometimes "Trojans," in opposition to our Grecian selves, and sometimes "vermin." A Turkish Effendi,[3] who piques himself on good-breeding, will never mention by name a pig. Yet it is but too often that he has reason to mention this animal; since constantly, in the streets of Stamboul, he has his trousers deranged or polluted by this vile creature running between his legs. But under any excess of hurry he is always careful, out of respect to the company he is dining with, to suppress the odious name, and to call the wretch "that other creature," as though all animal life beside formed one group, and this odious beast (to whom, as Chrysippus[4] observed, salt serves as an apology for a soul) formed another and alien group on the

---

1 Law of dominion.

2 International law.

3 Turkish title of respect.

4 Greek Stoic philosopher (c. 280–207 BC). Stoics believe that whatever happens is in accordance with divine reason and should therefore be accepted.

outside of creation. Now I, who am an English Effendi, that think myself to understand good-breeding as well as any son of Othman,[1] beg my reader's pardon for having mentioned an insider by his gross natural name. I shall do so no more: and, if I should have occasion to glance at so painful a subject, I shall always call him "that other creature." Let us hope, however, that no such distressing occasion will arise. But, by the way, an occasion arises at this moment; for the reader will be sure to ask, when we come to the story, "Was this other creature present?" He was *not*; or more correctly, perhaps, *it* was not. We dropped the creature — or the creature, by natural imbecility, dropped itself — within the first ten miles from Manchester. In the latter case, I wish to make a philosophic remark of a moral tendency. When I die, or when the reader dies, and by repute suppose of fever, it will never be known whether we died in reality of the fever or of the doctor. But this other creature, in the case of dropping out of the coach, will enjoy a coroner's inquest; consequently he will enjoy an epitaph. For I insist upon it, that the verdict of a coroner's jury makes the best of epitaphs. It is brief, so that the public all find time to read it; it is pithy, so that the surviving friends (if any *can* survive such a loss) remember it without fatigue; it is upon oath, so that rascals and Dr Johnsons[2] cannot pick holes in it. "Died through the visitation of intense stupidity, by impinging on a moonlight night against the off[3] hind wheel of the Glasgow mail! Deodand[4] upon the said wheel — two pence." What a simple lapidary inscription! Nobody much in the wrong but an off-wheel; and with few acquaintances; and if it were but rendered into choice Latin, though there would be a little bother in finding a Ciceronian[5] word for "off-wheel," Morcellus[6] himself, that great master of sepulchral eloquence, could not show a better. Why I call this little remark *moral*, is, from the compensation it points out. Here, by the supposition, is that other creature on the one side, the beast of the world; and he (or it) gets an epitaph. You and I, on the contrary, the pride of our friends, get none.

---

1   Citizen of the Ottoman Empire (which included Turkey).

2   Samuel Johnson (1709–84), author, best known for his *Dictionary of the English Language* (1755).

3   Right — as opposed to the "near" or left — wheel, which is on the side where the passengers and driver mount.

4   Personal possessions that are a direct cause of death and therefore sold by the Crown with the proceeds used for good, such as helping the poor.

5   Cicero (106–43 BC), Roman orator and statesman.

6   Stefano Antonio Morcelli (1737–1822), Italian author of *De Stilo Inscriptionum Latinarum* (1780).

But why linger on the subject of vermin? Having mounted the box, I took a small quantity of laudanum,[1] having already travelled two hundred and fifty miles — viz., from a point seventy miles beyond London, upon a simple breakfast. In the taking of laudanum there was nothing extraordinary. But by accident it drew upon me the special attention of my assessor on the box, the coachman. And in *that* there was nothing extraordinary. But by accident, and with great delight, it drew my attention to the fact that this coachman was a monster in point of size, and that he had but one eye. In fact he had been foretold by Virgil[2] as —

"Monstrum horrendum, informe, ingens,
    cui lumen ademptum."[3]

He answered in every point — a monster he was — dreadful, shapeless, huge, who had lost an eye. But why should *that* delight me? Had he been one of the Calendars in the Arabian Nights,[4] and had paid down his eye as the price of his criminal curiosity, what right had *I* to exult in his misfortune? I did *not* exult: I delighted in no man's punishment, though it were even merited. But these personal distinctions identified in an instant an old friend of mine, whom I had known in the south for some years as the most masterly of mail-coachmen. He was the man in all Europe that could best have undertaken to drive six-in-hand[5] full gallop over *Al Sirat*[6] — that famous bridge of Mahomet across the bottomless gulf, backing himself against the Prophet and twenty such fellows. I used to call him *Cyclops mastigophorus*, Cyclops the whip-bearer, until I observed that his skill made whips useless, except to fetch off an impertinent fly from a leader's head; upon which I changed his Grecian name to Cyclops *diphrélates* (Cyclops the charioter.) I, and others known to me, studied under him the diphrelatic art.[7] Excuse, reader, a word too elegant to be pedantic. And also take this remark from me, as a *gage d'amitié*[8] — that no word ever was or *can* be

---

1   Opium in a solution of alcohol, used medicinally.

2   Roman poet (70–19 BC) best known for the *Aeneid*. By the middle ages, his writings were used to predict the future.

3   (Latin) "Monster horrendous, misshapen, vast, and deprived of sight," from Virgil's *Aeneid*.

4   Princes disguised as begging dervishes, the subjects of tales in the *Arabian Nights*.

5   Carriage pulled by six horses.

6   In Muslim tradition, the bridge to Paradise, which only the good succeed in crossing.

7   Art of driving a chariot.

8   (French) token of friendship.

pedantic which, by supporting a distinction, supports the accuracy of logic; or which fills up a chasm for the understanding. As a pupil, though I paid extra fees, I cannot say that I stood high in his esteem. It showed his dogged honesty, (though, observe, not his discernment,) that he could not see my merits. Perhaps we ought to excuse his absurdity in this particular by remembering his want of an eye. *That* made him blind to my merits. Irritating as this blindness was, (surely it could not be envy?) he always courted my conversation, in which art I certainly had the whip-hand of him. On this occasion, great joy was at our meeting. But what was Cyclops doing here? Had the medical men recommended northern air, or how? I collected, from such explanations as he volunteered, that he had an interest at stake in a suit-at-law pending at Lancaster; so that probably he had got himself transferred to this station, for the purpose of connecting with his professional pursuits an instant readiness for the calls of his law-suit.

Meantime, what are we stopping for? Surely we've been waiting long enough. Oh, this procrastinating mail, and oh this procrastinating post-office! Can't they take a lesson upon that subject from *me*? Some people have called *me* procrastinating. Now you are witness, reader, that I was in time for *them*. But can *they* lay their hands on their hearts, and say that they were in time for me? I, during my life, have often had to wait for the post-office: the post-office never waited a minute for me. What are they about? The guard tells me that there is a large extra accumulation of foreign mails this night, owing to irregularities caused by war and by the packet-service, when as yet nothing is done by steam. For an *extra* hour, it seems, the post-office has been engaged in threshing out the pure wheaten correspondence of Glasgow, and winnowing it from the chaff of all baser intermediate towns. We can hear the flails going at this moment. But at last all is finished. Sound your horn, guard. Manchester, good bye; we've lost an hour by your criminal conduct at the post-office: which, however, though I do not mean to part with a serviceable ground of complaint, and one which really *is* such for the horses, to me secretly is an advantage, since it compels us to recover this last hour amongst the next eight or nine. Off we are at last, and at eleven miles an hour: and at first *I* detect no changes in the energy or in the skill of Cyclops.

From Manchester to Kendal, which virtually (though not in law) is the capital of Westmoreland, were at this time seven stages of eleven miles each. The first five of these, dated from Manchester, terminated in Lancaster, which was therefore fifty-five miles north of Manchester, and the same distance exactly from Liverpool. The first three terminated in Preston (called, by way of distinction from other towns of that name, *proud*

Preston,) at which place it was that the separate roads from Liverpool and from Manchester to the north became confluent. Within these first three stages lay the foundation, the progress, and termination of our night's adventure. During the first stage, I found out that Cyclops was mortal: he was liable to the shocking affection of sleep — a thing which I had never previously suspected. If a man is addicted to the vicious habit of sleeping, all the skill in aurigation of Apollo himself, with the horses of Aurora[1] to execute the motions of his will, avail him nothing. "Oh, Cyclops!" I exclaimed more than once, "Cyclops, my friend; thou art mortal. Thou snorest." Through this first eleven miles, however, he betrayed his infirmity — which I grieve to say he shared with the whole Pagan Pantheon[2] — only by short stretches. On waking up, he made an apology for himself, which, instead of mending the matter, laid an ominous foundation for coming disasters. The summer assizes[3] were now proceeding at Lancaster: in consequence of which, for three nights and three days, he had not lain down in a bed. During the day, he was waiting for his uncertain summons as a witness on the trial in which he was interested; or he was drinking with the other witnesses, under the vigilant surveillance of the attorneys. During the night, or that part of it when the least temptations existed to conviviality, he was driving. Throughout the second stage he grew more and more drowsy. In the second mile of the third stage, he surrendered himself finally and without a struggle to his perilous temptation. All his past resistance had but deepened the weight of this final oppression. Seven atmospheres of sleep seemed resting upon him; and, to consummate the case, our worthy guard, after singing "Love amongst the Roses," for the fiftieth or sixtieth time, without any invitation from Cyclops or myself, and without applause for his poor labours, had moodily resigned himself to slumber — not so deep doubtless as the coachman's, but deep enough for mischief; and having, probably, no similar excuse. And thus at last, about ten miles from Preston, I found myself left in charge of his Majesty's London and Glasgow mail then running about eleven miles an hour.

What made this negligence less criminal than else it must have been thought, was the condition of the roads at night during the assizes. At that time all the law business of populous Liverpool, and of populous

---

1   In Greek mythology, the horses of Aurora (goddess of the dawn) drew the chariot driven by Apollo (god of light) that carried the sun across the sky.

2   All of the ancient Greek or Roman gods and goddesses.

3   One of two yearly sessions when the justices of the peace tried cases outside the city of London.

Manchester, with its vast cincture of populous rural districts, was called up by ancient usage to the tribunal of Lilliputian[1] Lancaster. To break up this old traditional usage required a conflict with powerful established interests, a large system of new arrangements, and a new parliamentary statute. As things were at present, twice in the year so vast a body of business rolled northwards, from the southern quarter of the county, that a fortnight at least occupied the severe exertions of two judges for its despatch. The consequence of this was — that every horse available for such a service, along the whole line of road, was exhausted in carrying down the multitudes of people who were parties to the different suits. By sunset, therefore, it usually happened that, through utter exhaustion amongst men and horses, the roads were all silent. Except exhaustion in the vast adjacent county of York from a contested election, nothing like it was ordinarily witnessed in England.

On this occasion, the usual silence and solitude prevailed along the road. Not a hoof nor a wheel was to be heard. And to strengthen this false luxurious confidence in the noiseless roads, it happened also that the night was one of peculiar solemnity and peace. I myself, though slightly alive to the possibilities of peril, had so far yielded to the influence of the mighty calm as to sink into a profound reverie. The month was August, in which lay my own birth-day; a festival to every thoughtful man suggesting solemn and often sigh-born thoughts.[2] The county was my own native county — upon which, in its southern section, more than upon any equal area known to man past or present, had descended the original curse of labour in its heaviest form, not mastering the bodies of men only as of slaves, or criminals in mines, but working through the fiery will. Upon no equal space of earth, was, or ever had been, the same energy of human power put forth daily. At this particular season also of the assizes, that dreadful hurricane of flight and pursuit, as it might have seemed to a stranger, that swept to and from Lancaster all day long, hunting the county up and down, and regularly subsiding about sunset, united with the permanent distinction of Lancashire as the very metropolis and citadel of labour, to point the thoughts pathetically upon that counter vision of rest, of saintly repose from strife and sorrow, towards which, as to their secret haven, the profounder aspirations of man's heart are continually travelling. Obliquely we

---

1 Small (from Jonathan Swift's *Gulliver's Travels*).

2 "Sigh-born:" I owe the suggestion of this word to an obscure remembrance of a beautiful phrase in Giraldus Cambrensis, viz., *suspiriosæ cogitationes* [De Quincey's note]. Gerald of Wales (1145–?), churchman and author of seventeen books. In 1190, he attended the uncovering of a grave said to be King Arthur's and wrote an account of the event.

were nearing the sea upon our left, which also must, under the present circumstances, be repeating the general state of halcyon repose. The sea, the atmosphere, the light, bore an orchestral part in this universal lull. Moonlight, and the first timid tremblings of the dawn, were now blending; and the blendings were brought into a still more exquisite state of unity, by a slight silvery mist, motionless and dreamy, that covered the woods and fields, but with a veil of equable transparency. Except the feet of our own horses, which, running on a sandy margin of the road, made little disturbance, there was no sound abroad. In the clouds, and on the earth, prevailed the same majestic peace; and in spite of all that the villain of a schoolmaster has done for the ruin of our sublimer thoughts, which are the thoughts of our infancy, we still believe in no such nonsense as a limited atmosphere. Whatever we may swear with our false feigning lips, in our faithful hearts we still believe, and must for ever believe, in fields of air traversing the total gulf between earth and the central heavens. Still, in the confidence of children that tread without fear *every* chamber in their father's house, and to whom no door is closed, we, in that Sabbatic vision which sometimes is revealed for an hour upon nights like this, ascend with easy steps from the sorrow-stricken fields of earth, upwards to the sandals of God.

Suddenly from thoughts like these, I was awakened to a sullen sound, as of some motion on the distant road. It stole upon the air for a moment; I listened in awe; but then it died away. Once roused, however, I could not but observe with alarm the quickened motion of our horses. Ten years' experience had made my eye learned in the valuing of motion; and I saw that we were now running thirteen miles an hour. I pretend to no presence of mind. On the contrary, my fear is, that I am miserably and shamefully deficient in that quality as regards action. The palsy of doubt and distraction hangs like some guilty weight of dark unfathomed remembrances upon my energies, when the signal is flying for *action*. But, on the other hand, this accursed gift I have, as regards *thought*, that in the first step towards the possibility of a misfortune, I see its total evolution: in the radix,[1] I see too certainly and too instantly its entire expansion; in the first syllable of the dreadful sentence, I read already the last. It was not that I feared for ourselves. What could injure *us?* Our bulk and impetus charmed us against peril in any collision. And I had rode through too many hundreds of perils that were frightful to approach, that were matter of laughter as we looked back upon them, for any anxiety to rest upon *our* interests. The mail was not built, I felt assured, nor bespoke, that could betray *me*

---

1   Root, or origin.

who trusted to its protection. But any carriage that we could meet would be frail and light in comparison of ourselves. And I remarked this ominous accident of our situation. We were on the wrong side of the road. But then the other party, if other there was, might also be on the wrong side; and two wrongs might make a right. *That* was not likely. The same motive which had drawn *us* to the right-hand side of the road, viz., the soft beaten sand, as contrasted with the paved centre, would prove attractive to others. Our lamps, still lighted, would give the impression of vigilance on our part. And every creature that met us, would rely upon *us* for quartering.[1] All this, and if the separate links of the anticipation had been a thousand times more, I saw — not discursively or by effort — but as by one flash of horrid intuition.

Under this steady though rapid anticipation of the evil which *might* be gathering ahead, ah, reader! what a sullen mystery of fear, what a sigh of woe, seemed to steal upon the air, as again the far-off sound of a wheel was heard! A whisper it was — a whisper from, perhaps, four miles off — secretly announcing a ruin that, being foreseen, was not the less inevitable. What could be done — who was it that could do it — to check the storm-flight of these maniacal horses? What! could I not seize the reins from the grasp of the slumbering coachman? You, reader, think that it would have been in *your* power to do so. And I quarrel not with your estimate of yourself. But, from the way in which the coachman's hand was viced between his upper and lower thigh, this was impossible. The guard subsequently found it impossible, after this danger had passed. Not the grasp only, but also the position of this Polyphemus,[2] made the attempt impossible. You still think otherwise. See, then, that bronze equestrian statue. The cruel rider has kept the bit in his horse's mouth for two centuries. Unbridle him, for a minute, if you please, and wash his mouth with water. Or stay, reader, unhorse me that marble emperor: knock me those marble feet from those marble stirrups of Charlemagne.[3]

The sounds ahead strengthened, and were now too clearly the sounds of wheels. Who and what could it be? Was it industry in a taxed cart? — was it youthful gaiety in a gig? Whoever it was, something must be attempted to warn them. Upon the other party rests the active responsi-

---

1   "Quartering" — this is the technical word; and, I presume, derived from the French *cartayer*, to evade a rut or any obstacle [De Quincey's note].

2   A Cyclops (in Greek mythology, an evil one-eyed giant).

3   (742–814) King of the Franks from 768 and Holy Roman Emperor from 800. Through inheritance and conquest, he united most of Western Europe by 804.

bility, but upon *us* — and, woe is me! that *us* was my single self — rests the responsibility of warning. Yet, how should this be accomplished? Might I not seize the guard's horn? Already, on the first thought, I was making my way over the roof to the guard's seat. But this, from the foreign mails being piled upon the roof, was a difficult, and even dangerous attempt, to one cramped by nearly three hundred miles of outside travelling. And, fortunately, before I had lost much time in the attempt, our frantic horses swept round an angle of the road, which opened upon us the stage where the collision must be accomplished, the parties that seemed summoned to the trial, and the impossibility of saving them by any communication with the guard.

Before us lay an avenue, straight as an arrow, six hundred yards, perhaps, in length; and the umbrageous trees, which rose in a regular line from either side, meeting high overhead, gave to it the character of a cathedral aisle. These trees lent a deeper solemnity to the early light; but there was still light enough to perceive, at the further end of this gothic aisle, a light, reedy gig, in which were seated a young man, and, by his side, a young lady. Ah, young sir! what are you about? If it is necessary that you should whisper your communications to this young lady — though really I see nobody at this hour, and on this solitary road, likely to overhear your conversation — is it, therefore, necessary that you should carry your lips forward to hers? The little carriage is creeping on at one mile an hour; and the parties within it, being thus tenderly engaged, are naturally bending down their heads. Between them and eternity, to all human calculation, there is but a minute and a half. What is it that I shall do? Strange it is, and to a mere auditor of the tale, might seem laughable, that I should need a suggestion from the *Iliad*[1] to prompt the sole recourse that remained. But so it was. Suddenly I remembered the shout of Achilles, and its effect. But could I pretend to shout like the son of Peleus, aided by Pallas? No, certainly: but then I needed not the shout that should alarm all Asia militant; a shout would suffice, such as should carry terror into the hearts of two thoughtless young people, and one gig horse. I shouted — and the young man heard me not. A second time I shouted — and now he heard me, for now he raised his head.

Here, then, all had been done that, by me, *could* be done: more on *my* part was not possible. Mine had been the first step: the second was for the young man: the third was for God. If, said I, the stranger is a brave man, and if, indeed, he loves the young girl at his side — or, loving her not, if

---

1   Greek epic poem attributed to Homer. In one scene, just the shout of the hero Achilles sends fear into his enemies, the Trojans.

he feels the obligation pressing upon every man worthy to be called a man, of doing his utmost for a woman confided to his protection — he will at least make some effort to save her. If *that* fails, he will not perish the more, or by a death more cruel, for having made it; and he will die, as a brave man should, with his face to the danger, and with his arm about the woman that he sought in vain to save. But if he makes no effort, shrinking, without a struggle, from his duty, he himself will not the less certainly perish for this baseness of poltroonery. He will die no less: and why not? Wherefore should we grieve that there is one craven less in the world? No; *let* him perish, without a pitying thought of ours wasted upon him; and, in that case, all our grief will be reserved for the fate of the helpless girl, who, now, upon the least shadow of failure in *him*, must, by the fiercest of translations — must, without time for a prayer — must, within seventy seconds, stand before the judgment-seat of God.

But craven he was not: sudden had been the call upon him, and sudden was his answer to the call. He saw, he heard, he comprehended, the ruin that was coming down: already its gloomy shadow darkened above him; and already he was measuring his strength to deal with it. Ah! what a vulgar thing does courage seem, when we see nations buying it and selling it for a shilling a-day: ah! what a sublime thing does courage seem, when some fearful crisis on the great deeps of life carries a man, as if running before a hurricane, up to the giddy crest of some mountainous wave, from which, accordingly as he chooses his course, he descries two courses, and a voice says to him audibly — "This way lies hope; take the other way and mourn for ever!" Yet, even then, amidst the raving of the seas and the frenzy of the danger, the man is able to confront his situation — is able to retire for a moment into solitude with God, and to seek all his counsel from *him*! For seven seconds, it might be, of his seventy, the stranger settled his countenance steadfastly upon us, as if to search and value every element in the conflict before him. For five seconds more he sate immovably, like one that mused on some great purpose. For five he sate with eyes upraised, like one that prayed in sorrow, under some extremity of doubt, for wisdom to guide him towards the better choice. Then suddenly he rose; stood upright; and, by a sudden strain upon the reins, raising his horse's forefeet from the ground, he slewed him round on the pivot of his hind legs, so as to plant the little equipage in a position nearly at right-angles to ours. Thus far his condition was not improved; except as a first step had been taken towards the possibility of a second. If no more were done, nothing was done; for the little carriage still occupied the very centre of our path, though in an altered direction. Yet even now it may not be too late: fifteen of the twenty seconds may still be unexhausted; and one almighty bound forward may avail to clear the ground. Hurry then, hurry! for the flying moments — *they* hurry! Oh hurry, hurry, my brave young man! for the cruel hoofs of our horses — *they* also hurry! Fast are the flying moments, faster are the hoofs of our horses. Fear not for *him*, if human energy can suffice: faithful was he that drove, to his terrific duty; faithful was the horse to *his* command. One blow, one impulse given with voice and hand by the stranger, one rush from the horse, one bound as if in the act of rising to a fence, landed the docile creature's fore-feet upon the crown or arching centre of the road. The larger half of the little equipage had then cleared our over-towering shadow: *that* was evident even to my own agitated sight. But it mattered little that one wreck should float off in safety, if upon the wreck that perished were embarked the human freightage. The rear part of the carriage — was *that* certainly beyond the line of absolute ruin? What power could answer the question? Glance of eye, thought of man, wing of angel, which of these had speed enough to sweep between the question and the answer, and divide the one from the other? Light does not tread upon the steps of light more indivisibly, than did our all-conquering arrival upon the escaping efforts of the gig. *That* must the young man have felt too plainly. His back was now turned to us; not by sight could he any longer communicate with the peril; but by the dreadful rattle of our harness, too truly had his ear been instructed — that all was finished as regarded any further effort of *his*. Already in resignation he had rested from his struggle; and perhaps, in his heart he was whispering — "Father, which art above, do thou finish in heaven what I on earth have attempted." We ran past them faster than ever mill-race[1] in our inexorable flight. Oh, raving of hurricanes that must have sounded in their young ears at the moment of our transit! Either with the swingle-bar,[2] or with the haunch of our near leader, we had struck the off-wheel of the little gig, which stood rather obliquely and not quite so far advanced as to be accurately parallel with the near wheel. The blow, from the fury of our passage, resounded terrifically. I rose in horror, to look upon the ruins we might have caused. From my elevated station I looked down, and looked back upon the scene, which in a moment told its tale, and wrote all its records on my heart for ever.

The horse was planted immovably, with his fore-feet upon the paved crest of the central road. He of the whole party was alone untouched by the passion of death. The little cany carriage[3] — partly perhaps from the

---

1 The current of water that drives a mill-wheel.

2 The carriage crossbar, pivoted at the middle, to which the traces are tied.

3 Made of canes.

dreadful torsion of the wheels in its recent movement, partly from the thundering blow we had given to it — as if it sympathised with human horror, was all alive with tremblings and shiverings. The young man sat like a rock. He stirred not at all. But *his* was the steadiness of agitation frozen into rest by horror. As yet he dared not to look round; for he knew that, if anything remained to do, by him it could no longer be done. And as yet he knew not for certain if their safety were accomplished. But the lady —

But the lady —! Oh heavens! will that spectacle ever depart from my dreams, as she rose and sank upon her seat, sank and rose, threw up her arms wildly to heaven, clutched at some visionary object in the air, fainting, praying, raving, despairing! Figure to yourself, reader, the elements of the case; suffer me to recal before your mind the circumstances of the unparalleled situation. From the silence and deep peace of this saintly summer night, — from the pathetic blending of this sweet moonlight, dawnlight, dreamlight, — from the manly tenderness of this flattering, whispering, murmuring love, — suddenly as from the woods and fields, — suddenly as from the chambers of the air opening in revelation, — suddenly as from the ground yawning at her feet, leaped upon her, with the flashing of cataracts, Death the crownèd phantom, with all the equipage of his terrors, and the tiger roar of his voice.

The moments were numbered. In the twinkling of an eye our flying horses had carried us to the termination of the umbrageous aisle; at right-angles we wheeled into our former direction; the turn of the road carried the scene out of my eyes in an instant, and swept it into my dreams for ever.

DREAM-FUGUE.

ON THE ABOVE THEME OF SUDDEN DEATH.

"Whence the sound
Of instruments, that made melodious chime,
Was heard, of harp and organ; and who mov'd
Their stops and chords, was seen; his volant touch
Instinct through all proportions, low and high,
Fled and pursued transverse the resonant fugue."

Par. Lost, B. xi.[1]

Tumultuosissimamente.[2]

---

1   John Milton's epic poem *Paradise Lost* (1667) depicts the fall of humankind. De Quincey quotes part of a description of the vision of the future that Adam is shown by the archangel Michael just before being expelled from Paradise.

2   (Latin) mental confusion or disturbance.

Passion of Sudden Death! that once in youth I read and interpreted by the shadows of thy averted[1] signs; — Rapture of panic taking the shape, which amongst tombs in churches I have seen, of woman bursting her sepulchral bonds — of woman's Ionic[2] form bending forward from the ruins of her grave, with arching foot, with eyes upraised, with clasped adoring hands — waiting, watching, trembling, praying, for the trumpet's call to rise from dust for ever; — Ah, vision too fearful of shuddering humanity on the brink of abysses! vision that didst start back — that didst reel away — like a shrivelling scroll from before the wrath of fire racing on the wings of the wind! Epilepsy so brief of horror — wherefore is it that thou canst not die? Passing so suddenly into darkness, wherefore is it that still thou sheddest thy sad funeral blights upon the gorgeous mosaics of dreams? Fragment of music too stern, heard once and heard no more, what aileth thee that thy deep rolling chords come up at intervals through all the worlds of sleep, and after thirty years have lost no element of horror?

1.

Lo, it is summer, almighty summer! The everlasting gates of life and summer are thrown open wide; and on the ocean, tranquil and verdant as a savannah, the unknown lady from the dreadful vision and I myself are floating: she upon a fairy pinnace,[3] and I upon an English three-decker.[4] But both of us are wooing gales of festal happiness within the domain of our common country — within that ancient watery park — within that pathless chase where England takes her pleasure as a huntress through winter and summer, and which stretches from the rising to the setting sun. Ah! what a wilderness of floral beauty was hidden, or was suddenly revealed, upon the tropic islands through which the pinnace moved. And upon her deck what a bevy of human flowers — young women how lovely, young men how noble, that were dancing together, and slowly drifting towards *us* amidst music and incense, amidst blossoms from forests and

---

1   *"Averted* signs." — I read the course and changes of the lady's agony in the succession of her involuntary gestures; but let it be remembered that I read all this from the rear, never once catching the lady's full face, and even her profile imperfectly [De Quincey's note].

2   With scroll-like curves, echoing the columns popular in Greek architecture.

3   Small, light vessel which often functions as a scout for a larger vessel.

4   Ship with three decks.

gorgeous corymbi[1] from vintages, amidst natural caroling and the echoes of sweet girlish laughter. Slowly the pinnace nears us, gaily she hails us, and slowly she disappears beneath the shadow of our mighty bows. But then, as at some signal from heaven, the music and the carols, and the sweet echoing of girlish laughter — all are hushed. What evil has smitten the pinnace, meeting or overtaking her? Did ruin to our friends couch within our own dreadful shadow? Was our shadow the shadow of death? I looked over the bow for an answer; and, behold! the pinnace was dismantled; the revel and the revellers were found no more; the glory of the vintage was dust; and the forest was left without a witness to its beauty upon the seas. "But where," and I turned to our own crew — "where are the lovely women that danced beneath the awning of flowers and clustering corymbi? Whither have fled the noble young men that danced with *them*?" Answer there was none. But suddenly the man at the mast-head, whose countenance darkened with alarm, cried aloud — "Sail on the weather-beam! Down she comes upon us; in seventy seconds she will founder!"

2.

I looked to the weather-side, and the summer had departed. The sea was rocking, and shaken with gathering wrath. Upon its surface sate mighty mists, which grouped themselves into arches and long cathedral aisles. Down one of these, with the fiery pace of a quarrel from a crossbow, ran a frigate right athwart our course. "Are they mad?" some voice exclaimed from our deck. "Are they blind? Do they woo their ruin?" But in a moment, as she was close upon us, some impulse of a heady current or sudden vortex gave a wheeling bias to her course, and off she forged without a shock. As she ran past us, high aloft amongst the shrouds stood the lady of the pinnace. The deeps opened ahead in malice to receive her, towering surges of foam ran after her, the billows were fierce to catch her. But far away she was borne into desert spaces of the sea: whilst still by sight I followed her, as she ran before the howling gale, chased by angry sea-birds and by maddening billows; still I saw her, as at the moment when she ran past us, amongst the shrouds, with her white draperies streaming before the wind. There she stood with hair dishevelled, one hand clutched amongst the tackling — rising, sinking, fluttering, trembling, praying — there for leagues I saw her as she stood, raising at intervals one hand to

---

1   Cluster of ivy-berries or grapes.

heaven, amidst the fiery crests of the pursuing waves and the raving of the storm; until at last, upon a sound from afar of malicious laughter and mockery, all was hidden for ever in driving showers; and afterwards, but when I know not, and how I know not,

3.

Sweet funeral bells from some incalculable distance, wailing over the dead that die before the dawn, awakened me as I slept in a boat moored to some familiar shore. The morning twilight even then was breaking; and, by the dusky revelations which it spread, I saw a girl adorned with a garland of white roses about her head for some great festival, running along the solitary strand with extremity of haste. Her running was the running of panic; and often she looked back as to some dreadful enemy in the rear. But when I leaped ashore, and followed on her steps to warn her of a peril in front, alas! from me she fled as from another peril; and vainly I shouted to her of quicksands that lay ahead. Faster and faster she ran; round a promontory of rock she wheeled out of sight; in an instant I also wheeled round it, but only to see the treacherous sands gathering above her head. Already her person was buried; only the fair young head and the diadem of white roses around it were still visible to the pitying heavens; and, last of all, was visible one marble arm. I saw by the early twilight this fair young head, as it was sinking down to darkness — saw this marble arm, as it rose above her head and her treacherous grave, tossing, faultering, rising, clutching as at some false deceiving hand stretched out from the clouds — saw this marble arm uttering her dying hope, and then her dying despair. The head, the diadem, the arm, — these all had sunk; at last over these also the cruel quicksand had closed; and no memorial of the fair young girl remained on earth, except my own solitary tears, and the funeral bells from the desert seas, that, rising again more softly, sang a requiem over the grave of the buried child, and over her blighted dawn.

I sate, and wept in secret the tears that men have ever given to the memory of those that died before the dawn, and by the treachery of earth, our mother. But the tears and funeral bells were hushed suddenly by a shout as of many nations, and by a roar as from some great king's artillery advancing rapidly along the valleys, and heard afar by its echoes among the mountains. "Hush!" I said, as I bent my ear earthwards to listen — "hush! — this either is the very anarchy of strife, or else" — and then

I listened more profoundly, and said as I raised my head — "or else, oh heavens! it is *victory* that swallows up all strife."

4.

Immediately, in trance, I was carried over land and sea to some distant kingdom, and placed upon a triumphal car, amongst companions crowned with laurel. The darkness of gathering midnight, brooding over all the land, hid from us the mighty crowds that were weaving restlessly about our carriage as a centre — we heard them, but we saw them not. Tidings had arrived, within an hour, of a grandeur that measured itself against centuries; too full of pathos they were, too full of joy that acknowledged no fountain but God, to utter themselves by other language than by tears, by restless anthems, by reverberations rising from every choir, of the *Gloria in excelsis*.[1] These tidings we that sate upon the laurelled car had it for our privilege to publish amongst all nations. And already, by signs audible through the darkness, by snortings and tramplings, our angry horses, that knew no fear of fleshly weariness, upbraided us with delay. Wherefore *was* it that we delayed? We waited for a secret word, that should bear witness to the hope of nations, as now accomplished for ever. At midnight the secret word arrived; which word was — Waterloo and Recovered Christendom![2] The dreadful word shone by its own light; before us it went; high above our leaders' heads it rode, and spread a golden light over the paths which we traversed. Every city, at the presence of the secret word, threw open its gates to receive us. The rivers were silent as we crossed. All the infinite forests, as we ran along their margins, shivered in homage to the secret word. And the darkness comprehended it.

Two hours after midnight we reached a mighty minster. Its gates, which rose to the clouds, were closed. But when the dreadful word, that rode before us, reached them with its golden light, silently they moved back upon their hinges; and at a flying gallop our equipage entered the grand aisle of the cathedral. Headlong was our pace; and at every altar, in the little chapels and oratories to the right hand and left of our course, the lamps, dying or sickening, kindled anew in sympathy with the secret word that was flying past. Forty leagues we might have run in the cathe-

1   Medieval Christian Liturgy meaning "Glory to God in the highest" taken from Luke 2: 8–9; 13.

2   Reference to the Duke of Wellington's defeat of Napoleon at Waterloo in 1815, here used as a euphemism for "victory."

dral, and as yet no strength of morning light had reached us, when we saw before us the aërial galleries of the organ and the choir. Every pinnacle of the fret-work, every station of advantage amongst the traceries, was crested by white-robed choristers, that sang deliverance; that wept no more tears, as once their fathers had wept; but at intervals that sang together to the generations, saying —

"Chaunt the deliverer's praise in every tongue,"

and receiving answers from afar,

— "such as once in heaven and earth were sung."[1]

And of their chaunting was no end; of our headlong pace was neither pause nor remission.

Thus, as we ran like torrents — thus, as we swept with bridal rapture over the Campo Santo[2] of the cathedral graves — suddenly we became aware of a vast necropolis rising upon the far-off horizon — a city of sepulchres, built within the saintly cathedral for the warrior dead that rested from their feuds on earth. Of purple granite was the necropolis; yet, in the first minute, it lay like a purple stain upon the horizon — so mighty was the distance. In the second minute it trembled through many changes, growing into terraces and towers of wondrous altitude, so mighty was the pace. In the third minute already, with our dreadful gallop, we were entering its suburbs. Vast sarcophagi rose on every side, having towers and turrets that, upon the limits of the central aisle, strode forward with haughty intrusion, that ran back with mighty shadows into answering recesses. Every sarcophagus showed many bas-reliefs — bas-reliefs of battles — bas-reliefs of battle-fields; of battles from forgotten ages — of battles from yesterday — of battle-fields that, long since, nature had healed and reconciled to herself with the sweet oblivion of flowers — of battle-

---

1   From an 1816 poem by Filicaia Canzon.

2   *Campo Santo* — It is probable that most of my readers will be acquainted with the history of the Campo Santo at Pisa — composed of earth brought from Jerusalem for a bed of sanctity, as the highest prize which the noble piety of crusaders could ask or imagine. There is another Campo Santo at Naples, formed, however, (I presume,) on the example given by Pisa. Possibly the idea may have been more extensively copied. To readers who are unacquainted with England, or who (being English) are yet unacquainted with the cathedral cities of England, it may be right to mention that the graves within-side the cathedrals often form a flat pavement over which carriages and horses might roll; and perhaps a boyish remembrance of one particular cathedral, across which I had seen passengers walk and burdens carried, may have assisted my dream [De Quincey's note].

fields that were yet angry and crimson with carnage. Where the terraces ran, there did *we* run; where the towers curved, there did *we* curve. With the flight of swallows our horses swept round every angle. Like rivers in flood, wheeling round headlands; like hurricanes that ride into the secrets of forests; faster than ever light unwove the mazes of darkness, our flying equipage carried earthly passions — kindled warrior instincts — amongst the dust that lay around us; dust oftentimes of our noble fathers that had slept in God from Créci to Trafalgar.[1] And now had we reached the last sarcophagus, now were we abreast of the last bas-relief, already had we recovered the arrow-like flight of the illimitable central aisle, when coming up this aisle to meet us we beheld a female infant that rode in a carriage as frail as flowers. The mists, which went before her, hid the fawns that drew her, but could not hide the shells and tropic flowers with which she played — but could not hide the lovely smiles by which she uttered her trust in the mighty cathedral, and in the cherubim that looked down upon her from the topmost shafts of its pillars. Face to face she was meeting us; face to face she rode, as if danger there were none. "Oh baby!" I exclaimed, "shalt thou be the ransom for Waterloo? Must we, that carry tidings of great joy to every people, be messengers of ruin to thee?" In horror I rose at the thought; but then also, in horror at the thought, rose one that was sculptured on the bas-relief — a Dying Trumpeter. Solemnly from the field of battle he rose to his feet; and, unslinging his stony trumpet, carried it, in his dying anguish, to his stony lips — sounding once, and yet once again; proclamation that, in *thy* ears, oh baby! must have spoken from the battlements of death. Immediately deep shadows fell between us, and aboriginal silence. The choir had ceased to sing. The hoofs of our horses, the rattling of our harness, alarmed the graves no more. By horror the bas-relief had been unlocked into life. By horror we, that were so full of life, we men and our horses, with their fiery fore-legs rising in mid air to their everlasting gallop, were frozen to a bas-relief. Then a third time the trumpet sounded; the seals were taken off all pulses; life, and the frenzy of life, tore into their channels again; again the choir burst forth in sunny grandeur, as from the muffling of storms and darkness; again the thunderings of our horses carried temptation into the graves. One cry burst from our lips as the clouds, drawing off from the aisle, showed it empty before us — "Whither has the infant fled? — is the young child caught up to God?" Lo! afar off, in a vast recess, rose three mighty windows to the clouds; and on a level with their

---

1   Créci is an ancient battle. The Battle of Trafalgar in 1805 saw the British defeat the combined forces of the French and the Spanish.

summits, at height insuperable to man, rose an altar of purest alabaster. On its eastern face was trembling a crimson glory. Whence came *that*? Was it from the reddening dawn that now streamed *through* the windows? Was it from the crimson robes of the martyrs that were painted *on* the windows? Was it from the bloody bas-reliefs of earth? Whencesoever it were — there, within that crimson radiance, suddenly appeared a female head, and then a female figure. It was the child — now grown up to woman's height. Clinging to the horns of the altar, there she stood — sinking, rising, trembling, fainting — raving, despairing; and behind the volume of incense that, night and day, streamed upwards from the altar, was seen the fiery font, and dimly was descried the outline of the dreadful being that should baptise her with the baptism of death. But by her side was kneeling her better angel, that hid his face with wings; that wept and pleaded for *her*; that prayed when *she* could *not*; that fought with heaven by tears for *her* deliverance; which also, as he raised his immortal countenance from his wings, I saw, by the glory in his eye, that he had won at last.

5.

Then rose the agitation, spreading through the infinite cathedral, to its agony; then was completed the passion of the mighty fugue. The golden tubes of the organ, which as yet had but sobbed and muttered at intervals — gleaming amongst clouds and surges of incense — threw up, as from fountains unfathomable, columns of heart-shattering music. Choir and anti-choir[1] were filling fast with unknown voices. Thou also, Dying Trumpeter! — with thy love that was victorious, and thy anguish that was finishing, didst enter the tumult: trumpet and echo — farewell love, and farewell anguish — rang through the dreadful *sanctus*.[2] We, that spread flight before us, heard the tumult, as of flight, mustering behind us. In fear we looked round for the unknown steps that, in flight or in pursuit, were gathering upon our own. Who were these that followed? The faces, which no man could count — whence were *they*? "Oh, darkness of the grave!" I exclaimed, "that from the crimson altar and from the fiery font wert visited with secret light — that wert searched by the effulgence in the angel's eye — were these indeed thy children? Pomps of life, that, from the burials of centuries, rose again to the voice of perfect joy, could it be

---

1 Second choir singing in opposition to the first.

2 (Latin) holy; also the name of a hymn.

ye that had wrapped me in the reflux of panic?" What ailed me, that I should fear when the triumphs of earth were advancing? Ah! Pariah heart within me, that couldst never hear the sound of joy without sullen whispers of treachery in ambush; that, from six years old, didst never hear the promise of perfect love, without seeing aloft amongst the stars fingers as of a man's hand writing the secret legend — *"ashes to ashes, dust to dust!"*[1] — wherefore shouldst *thou* not fear, though all men should rejoice? Lo! as I looked back for seventy leagues through the mighty cathedral, and saw the quick and the dead that sang together to God, together that sang to the generations of man — ah! raving, as of torrents that opened on every side: trepidation, as of female and infant steps that fled — ah! rushing, as of wings that chased! But I heard a voice from heaven, which said — "Let there be no reflux of panic — let there be no more fear, and no more sudden death! Cover them with joy as the tides cover the shore!" *That* heard the children of the choir, *that* heard the children of the grave. All the hosts of jubilation made ready to move. Like armies that ride in pursuit, they moved with one step. Us, that, with laurelled heads, were passing from the cathedral through its eastern gates, they overtook, and, as with a garment, they wrapped us round with thunders that overpowered our own. As brothers we moved together; to the skies we rose — to the dawn that advanced — to the stars that fled: rendering thanks to God in the highest — that, having hid his face through one generation behind thick clouds of War, once again was ascending — was ascending from Waterloo — in the visions of Peace: — rendering thanks for thee, young girl! whom having overshadowed with his ineffable passion of Death — suddenly did God relent; suffered thy angel to turn aside his arm; and even in thee, sister unknown! shown to me for a moment only to be hidden for ever, found an occasion to glorify his goodness. A thousand times, amongst the phantoms of sleep, has he shown thee to me, standing before the golden dawn, and ready to enter its gates — with the dreadful Word going before thee — with the armies of the grave behind thee; shown thee to me, sinking, rising, fluttering, fainting, but then suddenly reconciled, adoring: a thousand times has he followed thee in the worlds of sleep — through storms; through desert seas; through the darkness of quicksands; through fugues and the persecution of fugues; through dreams, and the dreadful resurrections that are in dreams — only that at the last, with one motion of his victorious arm, he might record and emblazon the endless resurrections of his love!

---

1   From the English Burial Service, Genesis 3: 19.

Wilkie Collins

"A Terribly Strange Bed" (1852)

[After starting careers as a lawyer and painter, Wilkie Collins (1824–89) chose to become an author. He is now best known for his novels *The Woman in White* (1860) and *The Moonstone* (1868), although he published many other novels and stories as well. Collins found new ways of invigorating the gothic and horror motifs for which a keen audience had already been developed by authors such as Mary Shelley and William Carleton. His works were also formative in the development of a number of genres such as sensation fiction, the murder mystery, and detective fiction. The recognition of his importance is marked by the numerous translations of his work at the time and his hugely successful reading tour in Canada and the United States in 1873–74.]

The most difficult likeness I ever had to take, not even excepting my first attempt in the art of Portrait-painting, was a likeness of a gentleman named Faulkner. As far as drawing and colouring went, I had no particular fault to find with my picture; it was the *expression* of the sitter which I had failed in rendering — a failure quite as much his fault as mine. Mr. Faulkner, like many other persons by whom I have been employed, took it into his head that he must assume an expression, because he was sitting for his likeness; and, in consequence, contrived to look as unlike himself as possible, while I was painting him. I had tried to divert his attention from his own face, by talking with him on all sorts of topics. We had both travelled a great deal, and felt interested alike in many subjects connected with our wanderings over the same countries. Occasionally, while we were discussing our travelling experiences, the unlucky set-look left his countenance, and I began to work to some purpose; but it was always disastrously sure to return again, before I had made any great progress — or, in other words, just at the very time when I was most anxious that it should not re-appear. The obstacle thus thrown in the way of the satisfactory completion of my portrait, was the more to be deplored, because Mr. Faulkner's natural expression was a very remarkable one. I am not an author, so I cannot describe it. I ultimately succeeded in painting it, however; and this was the way in which I achieved my success: —

On the morning when my sitter was coming to me for the fourth time, I was looking at his portrait in no very agreeable mood — looking at it, in fact, with the disheartening conviction that the picture would be a perfect failure, unless the expression in the face represented were thoroughly altered and improved from nature. The only method of accomplishing this successfully, was to make Mr. Faulkner, somehow, insensibly forget that he was sitting for his picture. What topic could I lead him to talk on, which would entirely engross his attention while I was at work on his likeness? — I was still puzzling my brains to no purpose on this subject when Mr. Faulkner entered my studio; and, shortly afterwards, an accidental circumstance gained for me the very object which my own ingenuity had proved unequal to compass.

While I was "setting" my palette, my sitter amused himself by turning over some portfolios. He happened to select one for special notice, which contained several sketches that I had made in the streets of Paris. He turned over the first five views rapidly enough; but when he came to the sixth, I saw his face flush directly; and observed that he took the drawing out of the portfolio, carried it to the window, and remained silently absorbed in the contemplation of it for full five minutes. After that, he turned round to me; and asked very anxiously, if I had any objection to part with that sketch.

It was the least interesting drawing of the series — merely a view in one of the streets running by the backs of the houses in the Palais Royal.[1] Some four or five of these houses were comprised in the view, which was of no particular use to me in any way; and which was too valueless, as a work of Art, for me to think of *selling* it to my kind patron. I begged his acceptance of it, at once. He thanked me quite warmly; and then, seeing that I looked a little surprised at the odd selection he had made from my sketches, laughingly asked me if I could guess why he had been so anxious to become possessed of the view which I had given him?

"Probably" — I answered — "there is some remarkable historical association connected with that street at the back of the Palais Royal, of which I am ignorant."

1   The former residence of the King in Paris, and later the Duke of Orleans. Also the district surrounding the palace.

"No" — said Mr. Faulkner — "at least, none that *I* know of. The only association connected with the place in *my* mind, is a purely personal association. Look at this house in your drawing — the house with the water-pipe running down it from top to bottom. I once passed a night there — a night I shall never forget to the day of my death. I have had some awkward travelling adventures in my time; but *that* adventure —! Well, well! suppose we begin the sitting. I make but a bad return for your kindness in giving me the sketch, by thus wasting your time in mere talk."

He had not long occupied the sitter's chair (looking pale and thoughtful), when he returned — involuntarily, as it seemed — to the subject of the house in the back street. Without, I hope, showing any undue curiosity, I contrived to let him see that I felt a deep interest in everything he now said. After two or three preliminary hesitations, he at last, to my great joy, fairly started on the narrative of his adventure. In the interest of his subject he soon completely forgot that he was sitting for his portrait — the very expression that I wanted, came over his face — my picture proceeded towards completion, in the right direction, and to the best purpose. At every fresh touch, I felt more and more certain that I was now getting the better of my grand difficulty; and I enjoyed the additional gratification of having my work lightened by the recital of a true story, which possessed, in my estimation, all the excitement of the most exciting romance.

This, as nearly as I can recollect, is, word for word, how Mr. Faulkner told me the story: —

Shortly before the period when gambling-houses were suppressed by the French Government, I happened to be staying at Paris with an English friend. We were both young men then, and lived, I am afraid, a very dissipated life, in the very dissipated city of our sojourn. One night, we were idling about the neighbourhood of the Palais Royal, doubtful to what amusement we should next betake ourselves. My friend proposed a visit to Frascati's; but his suggestion was not to my taste. I knew Frascati's, as the French saying is, by heart; had lost and won plenty of five-franc pieces there, "merely for the fun of the thing," until it was "fun" no longer; and was thoroughly tired, in fact, of all the ghastly respectabilities of such a social anomaly as a respectable gambling-house. "For Heaven's sake" — said I to my friend — "let us go somewhere where we can see a little genuine, blackguard, poverty-stricken gaming, with no false gingerbread glitter thrown over it at all. Let us get away from fashionable Frascati's, to a house where they don't mind letting in a man with a ragged coat, or a man with no coat, ragged, or otherwise." — "Very well," said my friend, "we needn't go out of the Palais Royal to find the sort of company you want. Here's the place, just before us; as blackguard a place, by all report, as you could possibly wish to see." In another minute we arrived at the door, and entered the house, the back of which you have drawn in your sketch.

When we got up-stairs, and had left our hats and sticks with the door-keeper, we were admitted into the chief gambling-room. We did not find many people assembled there. But, few as the men were who looked up at us on our entrance, they were all types — miserable types — of their respective classes. We had come to see blackguards; but these men were something worse. There is a comic side, more or less appreciable, in all blackguardism — here, there was nothing but tragedy; mute, weird tragedy. The quiet in the room was horrible. The thin, haggard, long-haired young man, whose sunken eyes fiercely watched the turning up of the cards, never spoke; the flabby, fat-faced, pimply player, who pricked his piece of paste-board[1] perseveringly, to register how often black won, and how often red — never spoke; the dirty, wrinkled old man, with the vulture eyes, and the darned great coat, who had lost his last *sous*,[2] and still looked on desperately, after he could play no longer — never spoke. Even the voice of the croupier[3] sounded as if it were strangely dulled and thickened in the atmosphere of the room. I had entered the place to laugh; I felt that if I stood quietly looking on much longer, I should be more likely to weep. So, to excite myself out of the depression of spirits which was fast stealing over me, I unfortunately went to the table, and began to play. Still more unfortunately, as the event will show, I won — won prodigiously; won incredibly; won at such a rate, that the regular play-ers at the table crowded round me; and staring at my stakes with hungry, superstitious eyes, whispered to one another, that the English stranger was going to break the bank.

The game was *Rouge et Noir*. I had played at it in every city in Europe, without, however, the care or the wish to study the Theory of Chances — that philosopher's stone of all gamblers! And a gambler, in the strict sense of the word, I had never been. I was heart-whole from the corrod-ing passion for play. My gaming was a mere idle amusement. I never

---

1   Cheap material made by pasting together and compressing three or more sheets of paper. Slang: playing card, visiting card, or other hard piece of paper.

2   (French) small denomination of French currency.

3   One who rakes in money at a gaming table.

resorted to it by necessity, because I never knew what it was to want money. I never practised it so incessantly as to lose more than I could afford, or to gain more than I could coolly pocket without being thrown off my balance by my good luck. In short, I had hitherto frequented gambling-tables — just as I frequented ball-rooms and opera-houses — because they amused me, and because I had nothing better to do with my leisure hours.

But, on this occasion, it was very different — now, for the first time in my life, I felt what the passion for play really was. My success first bewildered, and then, in the most literal meaning of the word, intoxicated me. Incredible as it may appear, it is nevertheless true, that I only lost, when I attempted to estimate chances, and played according to previous calculation. If I left everything to luck, and staked without any care or consideration, I was sure to win — to win in the face of every recognised probability in favour of the bank. At first, some of the men present ventured their money safely enough on my colour; but I speedily increased my stakes to sums which they dared not risk. One after another they left off playing, and breathlessly looked on at my game. Still, time after time, I staked higher and higher; and still won. The excitement in the room rose to fever pitch. The silence was interrupted, by a deep, muttered chorus of oaths and exclamations in different languages, every time the gold was shovelled across to my side of the table — even the imperturbable croupier dashed his rake on the floor in a (French) fury of astonishment at my success. But one man present preserved his self-possession; and that man was my friend. He came to my side, and whispering in English, begged me to leave the place, satisfied with what I had already gained. I must do him the justice to say, that he repeated his warnings and entreaties several times; and only left me and went away, after I had rejected his advice (I was to all intents and purposes gambling-drunk) in terms which rendered it impossible for him to address me again that night.

Shortly after he had gone, a hoarse voice behind me cried: — "Permit me, my dear sir! — permit me to restore to their proper place two Napoleons[1] which you have dropped. Wonderful luck, sir! — I pledge you my word of honour as an old soldier, in the course of my long experience in this sort of thing, I never saw such luck as yours! — never! Go on, sir — *Sacré mille bombes!*[2] Go on boldly, and break the bank!"

---

1 French coins worth twenty francs each.

2 (French) expletive which translates literally to "A thousand sacred bombs."

I turned round and saw, nodding and smiling at me with inveterate civility, a tall man, dressed in a frogged and braided surtout.[1] If I had been in my senses, I should have considered him, personally, as being rather a suspicious specimen of an old soldier. He had goggling bloodshot eyes, mangy mustachios, and a broken nose. His voice betrayed a barrack-room intonation of the worst order, and he had the dirtiest pair of hands I ever saw — even in France. These little personal peculiarities exercised, however, no repelling influence on me. In the mad excitement, the reck-less triumph of that moment, I was ready to "fraternise" with anybody who encouraged me in my game. I accepted the old soldier's offered pinch of snuff; clapped him on the back, and swore he was the honestest fellow in the world; the most glorious relic of the Grand Army that I had ever met with. "Go on!" cried my military friend, snapping his fingers in ecstasy, — "Go on, and win! Break the bank — *Mille tonnerres!*[2] my gallant English comrade, break the bank!"

And I *did* go on — went on at such a rate, that in another quarter of an hour the croupier called out: "Gentlemen! the bank has discontinued for to-night." All the notes, and all the gold in that "bank," now lay in a heap under my hands; the whole floating capital of the gambling-house was waiting to pour into my pockets!

"Tie up the money in your pocket-handkerchief, my worthy sir," said the old soldier, as I wildly plunged my hands into my heap of gold. "Tie it up, as we used to tie up a bit of dinner in the Grand Army; your win-nings are too heavy for any breeches pockets that ever were sown. There! that's it! — shovel them in, notes and all! *Crediē!* what luck! — Stop! another Napoleon on the floor! *Ah! sacré petit polisson de Napoleon!*[3] have I found thee at last? Now then, sir — two tight double knots each way with your honourable permission, and the money's safe. Feel it! feel it, for-tunate sir! hard and round as a cannon ball — *Ah, bah!* if they had only fired such cannon balls at us, at Austerlitz — *nom d'une pipe!*[4] if they only had! And now, as an ancient grenadier, as an ex-brave of the French army, what remains for me to do? I ask what? Simply this: to entreat my valued English friend to drink a bottle of champagne with me, and toast the goddess Fortune in foaming goblets before we part!"

---

1 Military overcoat decorated with braids and fastenings.

2 (French) expletive, literally meaning "a thousand bolts of thunder."

3 (French) damned little devil of a Napoleon.

4 1805 battle at which Napoleon's army defeated the forces of Russia and Austria. (French) expletive "Heck!"

Excellent ex-brave! Convivial ancient grenadier! Champagne by all means! An English cheer for an old soldier! Hurrah! hurrah! Another English cheer for the goddess Fortune! Hurrah! Hurrah! Hurrah!

"Bravo! the Englishman; the amiable, gracious Englishman, in whose veins circulates the vivacious blood of France! Another glass? *Ah, bah!* — the bottle is empty! Never mind! *Vive le vin!*[1] I, the old soldier, order another bottle, and half-a-pound of *bon-bons* with it!"

No, no, ex-brave; never — ancient grenadier! *Your* bottle last time; *my* bottle this. Behold it! Toast away! The French Army! — the great Napoleon! — the present company! the croupier! the honest croupier's wife and daughters — if he has any! the Ladies generally! Everybody in the world!

By the time the second bottle of champagne was emptied, I felt as if I had been drinking liquid fire — my brain seemed all a-flame. No excess in wine had ever had this effect on me before in my life. Was it the result of a stimulant acting upon my system when I was in a highly-excited state? Was my stomach in a particularly disordered condition? Or was the champagne particularly strong?

"Ex-brave of the French Army!" cried I, in a mad state of exhilaration. "*I* am on fire! how are *you*? You have set me on fire! Do you hear; my hero of Austerlitz? Let us have a third bottle of champagne to put the flame out!" The old soldier wagged his head, rolled his goggle-eyes, until I expected to see them slip out of their sockets; placed his dirty forefinger by the side of his broken nose; solemnly ejaculated "Coffee!" and immediately ran off into an inner room.

The word pronounced by the eccentric veteran, seemed to have a magical effect on the rest of the company present. With one accord they all rose to depart. Probably they had expected to profit by my intoxication; but finding that my new friend was benevolently bent on preventing me from getting dead drunk, had now abandoned all hope of thriving pleasantly on my winnings. Whatever their motive might be, at any rate they went away in a body. When the old soldier returned, and sat down again opposite to me at the table, we had the room to ourselves. I could see the croupier, in a sort of vestibule which opened out of it, eating his supper in solitude. The silence was now deeper than ever.

A sudden change, too, had come over the "ex-brave." He assumed a portentously solemn look; and when he spoke to me again, his speech was

---

1   (French) Long live the wine!

ornamented by no oaths, enforced by no finger-snapping, enlivened by no apostrophes, or exclamations.

"Listen, my dear sir," said he, in mysteriously confidential tones — "listen to an old soldier's advice. I have been to the mistress of the house (a very charming woman, with a genius for cookery!) to impress on her the necessity of making us some particularly strong and good coffee. You must drink this coffee in order to get rid of your little amiable exaltation of spirits, before you think of going home — you *must*, my good and gracious friend! With all that money to take home to-night, it is a sacred duty to yourself to have your wits about you. You are known to be a winner to an enormous extent, by several gentlemen present to-night, who, in a certain point of view, are very worthy and excellent fellows; but they are mortal men, my dear sir, and they have their amiable weaknesses! Need I say more? Ah, no, no! you understand me! Now, this is what you must do — send for a cabriolet[1] when you feel quite well again — draw up all the windows when you get into it — and tell the driver to take you home only through the large and well-lighted thoroughfares. Do this; and you and your money will be safe. Do this; and to-morrow you will thank an old soldier for giving you a word of honest advice."

Just as the ex-brave ended his oration in very lachrymose tones, the coffee came in, ready poured out in two cups. My attentive friend handed me one of the cups, with a bow. I was parched with thirst, and drank it off at a draught. Almost instantly afterwards, I was seized with a fit of giddiness, and felt more completely intoxicated than ever. The room whirled round and round furiously; the old soldier seemed to be regularly bobbing up and down before me, like the piston of a steam-engine. I was half deafened by a violent singing in my ears; a feeling of utter bewilderment, helplessness, idiotcy, overcame me. I rose from my chair, holding on by the table to keep my balance; and stammered out, that I felt dreadfully unwell — so unwell, that I did not know how I was to get home.

"My dear friend," answered the old soldier; and even his voice seemed to be bobbing up and down, as he spoke — "My dear friend, it would be madness to go home, in *your* state. You would be sure to lose your money; you might be robbed and murdered with the greatest ease. *I* am going to sleep here: do *you* sleep here, too — they make up capital beds in this house — take one; sleep off the effects of the wine, and go home safely with your winnings, to-morrow — to-morrow, in broad daylight."

---

1   A light two-wheel carriage for hire; a "cab."

I had no power of thinking, no feeling of any kind, but the feeling that I must lie down somewhere, immediately, and fall off into a cool, refreshing, comfortable sleep. So I agreed eagerly to the proposal about the bed, and took the offered arms of the old soldier and the croupier — the latter having been summoned to show the way. They led me along some passages and up a short flight of stairs into the bedroom which I was to occupy. The ex-brave shook me warmly by the hand; proposed that we should breakfast together the next morning; and then, followed by the croupier, left me for the night.

I ran to the wash-hand-stand; drank some of the water in my jug; poured the rest out, and plunged my face into it — then sat down in a chair, and tried to compose myself. I soon felt better. The change for my lungs, from the fetid atmosphere of the gambling-room to the cool air of the apartment I now occupied; the almost equally refreshing change for my eyes, from the glaring gas-lights of the "Salon" to the dim, quiet flicker of one bed-room candle; aided wonderfully the restorative effects of cold water. The giddiness left me, and I began to feel a little like a reasonable being again. My first thought was of the risk of sleeping all night in a gambling-house; my second, of the still greater risk of trying to get out after the house was closed, and of going home alone at night, through the streets of Paris, with a large sum of money about me. I had slept in worse places than this, in the course of my travels; so I determined to lock, bolt, and barricade my door.

Accordingly, I secured myself against all intrusion; looked under the bed, and into the cupboard; tried the fastening of the window; and then, satisfied that I had taken every proper precaution, pulled off my upper clothing, put my light, which was a dim one, on the hearth among a feathery litter of wood ashes: and got into bed, with the handkerchief full of money under my pillow.

I soon felt, not only that I could not go to sleep, but that I could not even close my eyes. I was wide awake, and in a high fever. Every nerve in my body trembled — every one of my senses seemed to be preternaturally sharpened. I tossed, and rolled, and tried every kind of position, and perseveringly sought out the cold corners of the bed, and all to no purpose. Now, I thrust my arms over the clothes; now, I poked them under the clothes; now, I violently shot my legs straight out, down to the bottom of the bed; now, I convulsively coiled them up as near my chin as they would go; now, I shook out my crumpled pillow, changed it to the cool side, patted it flat, and lay down quietly on my back; now, I fiercely doubled it in two, set it up on end, thrust it against the board of the bed, and tried a sitting posture. Every effort was in vain; I groaned with vexation, as I felt that I was in for a sleepless night.

What could I do? I had no book to read. And yet, unless I found out some method of diverting my mind, I felt certain that I was in the condition to imagine all sorts of horrors; to rack my brains with forebodings of every possible and impossible danger; in short, to pass the night in suffering all conceivable varieties of nervous terror. I raised myself on my elbow, and looked about the room — which was brightened by a lovely moonlight pouring straight through the window — to see if it contained any pictures or ornaments, that I could at all clearly distinguish. While my eyes wandered from wall to wall, a remembrance of Le Maistre's[1] delightful little book, "Voyage autour de Ma Chambre," occurred to me. I resolved to imitate the French author, and find occupation and amusement enough to relieve the tedium of my wakefulness, by making a mental inventory of every article of furniture I could see, and by following up to their sources the multitude of associations which even a chair, a table, or a wash-hand-stand, may be made to call forth.

In the nervous unsettled state of my mind at that moment, I found it much easier to make my proposed inventory, than to make my proposed reflections, and soon gave up all hope of thinking in Le Maistre's fanciful track — or, indeed, thinking at all. I looked about the room at the different articles of furniture, and did nothing more. There was, first, the bed I was lying in — a four-post bed, of all things in the world to meet with in Paris! — yes, a thorough clumsy British four-poster, with the regular top lined with chintz — the regular fringed valance all round — the regular stifling, unwholesome curtains, which I remembered having mechanically drawn back against the posts, without particularly noticing the bed when I first got into the room. Then, there was the marble-topped wash-hand-stand, from which the water I had spilt, in my hurry to pour it out, was still dripping, slowly and more slowly, on to the brick floor. Then, two small chairs, with my coat, waistcoat, and trousers flung on them. Then, a large elbow chair covered with dirty-white dimity:[2] with my cravat and shirt-collar thrown over the back. Then, a chest of drawers, with two of the brass handles off, and a tawdry, broken china inkstand placed on it by way of ornament for the top. Then, the dressing-table, adorned by a very small looking-glass, and a very large pincushion. Then, the window — an unusually large window. Then, a dark old picture, which the feeble candle

---

1 French author Xavier comte de Maistre (1763–1852) wrote *Voyage autour de ma chambre* in 1794.

2 Kind of cotton usually used for wall hangings and dresses.

dimly showed me. It was the picture of a fellow in a high Spanish hat, crowned with a plume of towering feathers. A swarthy sinister ruffian, looking upward; shading his eyes with his hand, and looking intently upward — it might be at some tall gallows at which he was going to be hanged. At any rate he had the appearance of thoroughly deserving it.

This picture put a kind of constraint upon me to look upward too — at the top of the bed. It was a gloomy and not an interesting object, and I looked back at the picture. I counted the feathers in the man's hat; they stood out in relief; three, white; two, green. I observed the crown of his hat, which was of a conical shape, according to the fashion supposed to have been favoured by Guido Fawkes.[1] I wondered what he was looking up at. It couldn't be at the stars; such a desperado was neither astrologer nor astronomer. It must be at the high gallows, and he was going to be hanged presently. Would the executioner come into possession of his conical crowned hat, and plume of feathers? I counted the feathers again; three, white; two, green.

While I still lingered over this very improving and intellectual employment, my thoughts insensibly began to wander. The moonlight shining into the room reminded me of a certain moonlight night in England — the night after a pic-nic party in a Welsh valley. Every incident of the drive homeward through lovely scenery, which the moonlight made lovelier than ever, came back to my remembrance, though I had never given the pic-nic a thought for years; though, if I had *tried* to recollect it, I could certainly have recalled little or nothing of that scene long past. Of all the wonderful faculties that help to tell us we are immortal, which speaks the sublime truth more eloquently than memory? Here was I, in a strange house of the most suspicious character, in a situation of uncertainty, and even of peril, which might seem to make the cool exercise of my recollection almost out of the question; nevertheless remembering, quite involuntarily, places, people, conversations, minute circumstances of every kind, which I had thought forgotten for ever, which I could not possibly have recalled at will, even under the most favourable auspices. And what cause had produced in a moment the whole of this strange, complicated, mysterious effect? Nothing but some rays of moonlight shining in at my bedroom window.

I was still thinking of the pic-nic; of our merriment on the drive home; of the sentimental young lady who *would* quote Childe Harold,[2] because

---

1   Guy Fawkes (1570–1606), Englishman who was executed for his part in the failed Gunpowder Plot of 1605 to blow up the Houses of Parliament.

2   *Childe Harold's Pilgrimage* (1812–18), poem by Lord Byron (1788–1824).

it was moonlight. I was absorbed by these past scenes and past amusements, when, in an instant, the thread on which my memories hung,
snapped asunder; my attention immediately came back to present things,
more vividly than ever, and I found myself, I neither knew why nor
wherefore, looking hard at the picture again.

Looking for what? Good God, the man had pulled his hat down on his
brows! — No! The hat itself was gone! Where was the conical crown?
Where the feathers; three, white; two, green? Not there! In place of the
hat and feathers, what dusky object was it that now hid his forehead —
his eyes — his shading hand? Was the bed moving?

I turned on my back, and looked up. Was I mad? drunk? dreaming?
giddy again? or, was the top of the bed really moving down — sinking
slowly, regularly, silently, horribly, right down throughout the whole of
its length and breadth — right down upon Me, as I lay underneath?

My blood seemed to stand still; a deadly, paralysing coldness stole all
over me, as I turned my head round on the pillow, and determined to test
whether the bed-top was really moving, or not, by keeping my eye on the
man in the picture. The next look in that direction was enough. The dull,
black, frowsy outline of the valance above me was within an inch of being
parallel with his waist. I still looked breathlessly. And steadily, and slowly
— very slowly — I saw the figure, and the line of frame below the figure,
vanish, as the valance moved down before it.

I am, constitutionally, anything but timid. I have been, on more than
one occasion, in peril of my life, and have not lost my self-possession for
an instant; but, when the conviction first settled on my mind that the bed-
top was really moving, was steadily and continuously sinking down upon
me, I looked up for one awful minute, or more, shuddering, helpless,
panic-stricken, beneath the hideous machinery for murder, which was
advancing closer and closer to suffocate me where I lay.

Then the instinct of self-preservation came, and nerved me to save my
life, while there was yet time. I got out of bed very quietly, and quickly
dressed myself again in my upper clothing. The candle, fully spent, went
out. I sat down in the arm-chair that stood near, and watched the bed-
top slowly descending. I was literally spell-bound by it. If I had heard footsteps behind me, I could not have turned round; if a means of escape had
been miraculously provided for me, I could not have moved to take
advantage of it. The whole life in me, was, at that moment, concentrated in my eyes.

It descended — the whole canopy, with the fringe round it, came
down — down — close down; so close that there was not room now to

squeeze my finger between the bed-top and the bed. I felt at the sides, and discovered that what had appeared to me, from beneath, to be the ordinary light canopy of a four-post bed was in reality a thick, broad mattress, the substance of which was concealed by the valance and its fringe. I looked up, and saw the four posts rising hideously bare. In the middle of the bed-top was a huge wooden screw that had evidently worked it down through a hole in the ceiling, just as ordinary presses are worked down on the substance selected for compression. The frightful apparatus moved without making the faintest noise. There had been no creaking as it came down; there was now not the faintest sound from the room above. Amid a dead and awful silence I beheld before me — in the nineteenth century, and in the civilised capital of France — such a machine for secret murder by suffocation, as might have existed in the worst days of the Inquisition,[1] in the lonely Inns among the Hartz Mountains, in the mysterious tribunals of Westphalia! Still, as I looked on it, I could not move; I could hardly breathe; but I began to recover the power of thinking; and, in a moment, I discovered the murderous conspiracy framed against me, in all its horror.

My cup of coffee had been drugged, and drugged too strongly. I had been saved from being smothered, by having taken an overdose of some narcotic. How I had chafed and fretted at the fever-fit which had preserved my life by keeping me awake! How recklessly I had confided myself to the two wretches who had led me into this room, determined, for the sake of my winnings, to kill me in my sleep, by the surest and most horrible contrivance for secretly accomplishing my destruction! How many men, winners like me, had slept, as I had proposed to sleep, in that bed; and never been seen or heard of more! I shuddered as I thought of it.

But, erelong, all thought was again suspended by the sight of the murderous canopy moving once more. After it had remained on the bed — as nearly as I could guess — about ten minutes, it began to move up again. The villains, who worked it from above, evidently believed that their purpose was now accomplished. Slowly and silently, as it had descended, that horrible bed-top rose towards its former place. When it reached the upper extremities of the four posts, it reached the ceiling too. Neither hole nor screw could be seen — the bed became, in appearance, an ordinary bed again, the canopy, an ordinary canopy, even to the most suspicious eyes.

---

1   Tribunal of the Roman Catholic Church established in 1233 to suppress heresy by torture and other means. It was active in Westphalia (part of Germany) and the Hartz Mountains (known as a centre of witchcraft).

Now, for the first time, I was able to move, to rise from my chair, to consider of how I should escape. If I betrayed, by the smallest noise, that the attempt to suffocate me had failed, I was certain to be murdered. Had I made any noise already? I listened intently, looking towards the door. No! no footsteps in the passage outside; no sound of a tread, light or heavy, in the room above — absolute silence everywhere. Besides locking and bolting my door, I had moved an old wooden chest against it, which I had found under the bed. To remove this chest (my blood ran cold, as I thought what its contents *might* be!) without making some disturbance, was impossible; and, moreover, to think of escaping through the house, now barred-up for the night, was sheer insanity. Only one chance was left me — the window. I stole to it on tiptoe.

My bedroom was on the first floor, above an *entresol*,[1] and looked into the back street, which you have sketched in your view. I raised my hand to open the window, knowing that on that action hung, by the merest hair's-breadth, my chance of safety. They keep vigilant watch in a House of Murder — if any part of the frame cracked, if the hinge creaked, I was, perhaps, a lost man! It must have occupied me at least five minutes, reckoning by time — five *hours*, reckoning by suspense — to open that window. I succeeded in doing it silently, in doing it with all the dexterity of a house-breaker: and then looked down into the street. To leap the distance beneath me, would be almost certain destruction! Next, I looked round at the sides of the house. Down the left side, ran the thick water-pipe which you have drawn — it passed close by the outer edge of the window. The moment I saw the pipe, I knew I was saved; my breath came and went freely for the first time since I had seen the canopy of the bed moving down upon me!

To some men, the means of escape which I had discovered might have seemed difficult and dangerous enough — to *me*, the prospect of slipping down the pipe into the street did not suggest even a thought of peril. I had always been accustomed, by the practice of gymnastics, to keep up my schoolboy powers as a daring and expert climber; and knew that my head, hands, and feet would serve me faithfully in any hazards of ascent or descent. I had already got one leg over the window-sill, when I remembered the handkerchief, filled with money, under my pillow. I could well have afforded to leave it behind me; but I was revengefully determined that the miscreants of the gambling-house should miss their plunder as well as their victim. So I went back to the bed, and tied the

---

1   Mezzanine (between ground floor and first floor).

heavy handkerchief at my back by my cravat. Just as I had made it tight, and fixed it in a comfortable place, I thought I heard a sound of breathing outside the door. The chill feeling of horror ran through me again as I listened. No! dead silence still in the passage — I had only heard the night air blowing softly into the room. The next moment I was on the window-sill — and the next, I had a firm grip on the water-pipe with my hands and knees.

I slid down into the street easily and quietly, as I thought I should, and immediately set off, at the top of my speed, to a branch "Prefecture" of Police,[1] which I knew was situated in the immediate neighbourhood. A "Sub-Prefect"[2] and several picked men among his subordinates, happened to be up, maturing, I believe, some scheme for discovering the perpetrator of a mysterious murder, which all Paris was talking of just then. When I began my story, in a breathless hurry and in very bad French, I could see that the Sub-Prefect suspected me of being a drunken Englishman, who had robbed somebody, but he soon altered his opinion, as I went on; and before I had anything like concluded, he shoved all the papers before him into a drawer, put on his hat, supplied me with another (for I was bare-headed), ordered a file of soldiers, desired his expert followers to get ready all sorts of tools for breaking open doors and ripping-up brick-flooring, and took my arm, in the most friendly and familiar manner possible, to lead me with him out of the house. I will venture to say, that when the Sub-Prefect was a little boy, and was taken for the first time to the Play, he was not half as much pleased as he was now at the job in prospect for him at the "Gambling-House!"

Away we went through the streets, the Sub-Prefect cross-examining and congratulating me in the same breath, as we marched at the head of our formidable *posse comitatus*.[3] Sentinels were placed at the back and front of the gambling-house the moment we got to it; a tremendous battery of knocks was directed against the door; a light appeared at a window; I waited to conceal myself behind the police — then came more knocks, and a cry of "Open in the name of the law!" At that terrible summons, bolts and locks gave way before an invisible hand, and the moment after, the Sub-Prefect was in the passage, confronting a waiter, half-dressed and ghastly pale. This was the short dialogue which immediately took place.

---

1   A police station headed by a superintendent.

2   Assistant to the superintendent.

3   (Latin) power of the county, or citizens who may be called on to assist in enforcing the law; a "posse."

"We want to see the Englishman who is sleeping in this house?"

"He went away hours ago."

"He did no such thing. His friend went away; *he* remained. Show us to his bedroom!"

"I swear to you, Monsieur le Sous-Prefet, he is not here! he —"

"I swear to you, Monsieur le Garçon, he is. He slept here — he didn't find your bed comfortable — he came to us to complain of it — here he is, among my men — and here am I, ready to look for a flea or two in his bedstead. Picard! (calling to one of the subordinates, and pointing to the waiter) collar that man, and tie his hands behind him. Now, then, gentlemen, let us walk up stairs!"

Every man and woman in the house was secured — the "Old Soldier," the first. Then I identified the bed in which I had slept; and then we went into the room above. No object that was at all extraordinary appeared in any part of it. The Sub-Prefect looked round the place, commanded everybody to be silent, stamped twice on the floor, called for a candle, looked attentively at the spot he had stamped on, and ordered the flooring there to be carefully taken up. This was done in no time. Lights were produced, and we saw a deep raftered cavity between the floor of this room and the ceiling of the room beneath. Through this cavity there ran perpendicularly a sort of case of iron, thickly greased; and inside the case, appeared the screw, which communicated with the bed-top below. Extra lengths of screw, freshly oiled — levers covered with felt — all the complete upper works of a heavy press, constructed with infernal ingenuity so as to join the fixtures below — and, when taken to pieces again, to go into the smallest possible compass, were next discovered, and pulled out on the floor. After some little difficulty, the Sub-Prefect succeeded in putting the machinery together, and, leaving his men to work it, descended with me to the bedroom. The smothering canopy was then lowered, but not so noiselessly as I had seen it lowered. When I mentioned this to the Sub-Prefect, his answer, simple as it was, had a terrible significance. "My men," said he, "are working down the bed-top for the first time — the men whose money you won, were in better practice."

We left the house in the sole possession of two police agents — every one of the inmates being removed to prison on the spot. The Sub-Prefect, after taking down my "*procès-verbal*"[1] in his office, returned with me to my hotel to get my passport. "Do you think," I asked, as I gave it to him, "that any men have really been smothered in that bed, as they tried to smother *me*?"

---

1   Statement.

"I have seen dozens of drowned men laid out at the Morgue," answered the Sub-Prefect, "in whose pocket-books were found letters, stating that they had committed suicide in the Seine, because they had lost everything at the gaming-table. Do I know how many of those men entered the same gambling-house that *you* entered? won as *you* won? took that bed as *you* took it? slept in it? were smothered in it? and were privately thrown into the river, with a letter of explanation written by the murderers and placed in their pocket-books? No man can say how many, or how few, have suffered the fate from which you have escaped. The people of the gambling-house kept their bedstead machinery a secret from *us* — even from the police! The dead kept the rest of the secret for them. Good night, or rather good morning, Monsieur Faulkner! Be at my office again at nine o'clock — in the meantime, *au revoir!*"

The rest of my story is soon told. I was examined, and re-examined; the gambling-house was strictly searched all through, from top to bottom; the prisoners were separately interrogated; and two of the less guilty among them made a confession. *I* discovered that the Old Soldier was the master of the gambling-house —*justice* discovered that he had been drummed out of the army, as a vagabond, years ago; that he had been guilty of all sorts of villanies since; that he was in possession of stolen property, which the owners identified; and that he, the croupier, another accomplice, and the woman who had made my cup of coffee, were all in the secret of the bedstead. There appeared some reason to doubt whether the inferior persons attached to the house knew anything of the suffocating machinery; and they received the benefit of that doubt, by being treated simply as thieves and vagabonds. As for the Old Soldier and his two head-myrmidons,[1] they went to the galleys; the woman who had drugged my coffee was imprisoned for I forget how many years; the regular attendants at the gambling-house were considered "suspicious," and placed under "surveillance;" and I became, for one whole week (which is a long time), the head "lion" in Parisian society. My adventure was dramatised by three illustrious playmakers, but never saw theatrical daylight; for the censorship forbade the introduction on the stage of a correct copy of the gambling-house bedstead.

Two good results were produced by my adventure, which any censorship must have approved. In the first place, it helped to justify the Government in forthwith carrying out their determination to put down all gambling-houses; in the second place, it cured me of ever again trying

---

1 Unscrupulous helpers.

"Rouge et Noir" as an amusement. The sight of a green cloth, with packs of cards and heaps of money on it, will henceforth be for ever associated in my mind with the sight of a bed-canopy descending to suffocate me, in the silence and darkness of the night."

Just as Mr. Faulkner pronounced the last words, he started in his chair, and assumed a stiff, dignified position, in a great hurry. "Bless my soul!" cried he — with a comic look of astonishment and vexation — "while I have been telling you what is the real secret of my interest in the sketch you have so kindly given to me, I have altogether forgotten that I came here to sit for my portrait. For the last hour, or more, I must have been the worst model you ever had to paint from!"

"On the contrary, you have been the best," said I. "I have been painting from your expression; and, while telling your story, you have unconsciously shown me the natural expression I wanted."

Elizabeth Gaskell

"The Great Cranford Panic" (1853)

["The art of telling a story" wrote Elizabeth Gaskell (1810–65) in the magazine *Household Words* in May 1854, "is born with some people, and these have it to perfection." The deftness of Gaskell's writing suggests that she was one such person. It was the novel *Mary Barton* (1848) and its depiction of the plight of Manchester factory workers that first brought literary success to the London-born author. She was later equally praised for *Cranford* (1851–53), a collection of comic sketches — including the following — that sympathetically portray changing small-town customs and values. Gaskell's short fiction ranges from these gently satiric pieces to tales that are more morally earnest. She also developed the genre of the novella (or long short story), examples of which include *The Moorland Cottage* (1850) and *Cousin Phillis* (1863–64).]

CHAPTER THE FIRST.

Soon after the events of which I gave an account in my last paper, I was summoned home by my father's illness; and for a time I forgot, in anxiety about him, to wonder how my dear friends at Cranford were getting on, or how Lady Glenmire could reconcile herself to the dulness of the long visit which she was still paying to her sister-in-law, Mrs. Jamieson. When my father grew a little stronger I accompanied him to the sea-side, so that altogether I seemed banished from Cranford, and was deprived of the opportunity of hearing any chance intelligence of the dear little town for the greater part of that year. Late in November — when we had returned home again, and my father was once more in good health — I received a letter from Miss Matey; and a very mysterious letter it was. She began many sentences without ending them, running them one into another, in much the same confused sort of way in which written words run together on blotting-paper. All I could make out was, that if my father was better (which she hoped he was), and would take warning and wear a great coat from Michaelmas to Lady-day,[1] if turbans were in fashion, could I tell her? such a piece of gaiety was going to happen as had not been seen or known of since Wombwell's lions came,[2] when one of them ate a little child's arm; and she was, perhaps, too old to care about dress, but a new cap she must have; and, having heard that turbans were worn, and some of the county families likely to come, she would like to look tidy, if I would bring her a cap from the milliner I employed; and oh, dear! how careless of her to forget that she wrote to beg I would come and pay her a visit next Tuesday; when she hoped to have something to offer me in the way of amusement, which she would not now more particularly describe, only sea-green was her favourite colour. So she ended her letter; but in a P.S. she added, she thought she might as well tell me what was the peculiar attraction to Cranford just now; Signor Brunoni was going to exhibit his wonderful magic in the Cranford Assembly Rooms, on Wednesday and Friday evening in the following week.

I was very glad to accept the invitation from my dear Miss Matey, independently of the conjuror; and most particularly anxious to prevent her from disfiguring her small gentle mousey face with a great Saracen's[3] head turban; and, accordingly, I bought her a pretty, neat, middle-aged cap, which, however, was rather a disappointment to her when, on my arrival, she followed me into my bed-room, ostensibly to poke the fire, but in reality, I do believe, to see if the sea-green turban was not inside the cap-box with which I had travelled. It was in vain that I twirled the cap round on my hand to exhibit back and side fronts; her heart had been set upon a turban, and all she could do was to say, with resignation in her look and voice:

"I am sure you did your best, my dear. It is just like the caps all the ladies in Cranford are wearing, and they have had theirs for a year, I dare say. I should have liked something newer, I confess — something more like the turbans Miss Betty Barker tells me Queen Adelaide[4] wears; but it is very pretty, my dear. And I dare say lavender will wear better than sea-green. Well, after all, what is dress that we should care about it! You'll tell me if you want anything, my dear. Here is the bell. I suppose turbans have not got down to Drumble yet?"

So saying, the dear old lady gently bemoaned herself out of the room, leaving me to dress for the evening, when, as she informed me, she

---

1　September 29 to March 25.

2　George Wombwell (1778–1850), owner of a travelling circus.

3　Arab or Turk; more generally, a non-Christian heathen.

4　(1792–1849) Wife of British King William IV, on the throne from 1830–37.

expected Miss Pole and Mrs. Forrester, and she hoped I should not feel myself too much tired to join the party. Of course I should not; and I made some haste to unpack and arrange my dress; but, with all my speed, I heard the arrivals and the buzz of conversation in the next room before I was ready. Just as I opened the door, I caught the words — "I was foolish to expect anything very genteel out of the Drumble shops — poor girl! she did her best, I've no doubt." But for all that, I had rather that she blamed Drumble and me than disfigured herself with a turban. Miss Pole was always the person, in the trio of Cranford ladies now assembled, to have had adventures. She was in the habit of spending the morning in rambling from shop to shop; not to purchase anything (except an occasional reel of cotton, or a piece of tape), but to see the new articles and report upon them, and to collect all the stray pieces of intelligence in the town. She had a way, too, of demurely popping hither and thither into all sorts of places to gratify her curiosity on any point; a way which, if she had not looked so very genteel and prim, might have been considered impertinent. And now, by the expressive way in which she cleared her throat, and waited for all minor subjects (such as caps and turbans) to be cleared off the course, we knew she had something very particular to relate, when the due pause came — and I defy any people, possessed of common modesty, to keep up a conversation long, where one among them sits up aloft in silence, looking down upon all the things they chance to say as trivial and contemptible compared to what they could disclose, if properly entreated. Miss Pole began:

"As I was stepping out of Gordon's shop, to-day, I chanced to go into the George (my Betty has a second-cousin who is chambermaid there, and I thought Betty would like to hear how she was), and, not seeing any one about, I strolled up the staircase, and found myself in the passage leading to the Assembly Room (you and I remember the Assembly Room, I am sure, Miss Matey! and the *minuets de la cour!*[1]); so I went on, not thinking of what I was about, when, all at once, I perceived that I was in the middle of the preparations for to-morrow night — room being divided with great clothes-maids, over which Crosby's men were tacking red flannel — very dark and odd it seemed; it quite bewildered me, and I was going on behind the screens, in my absence of mind, when a gentleman (quite the gentleman, I can assure you,) stepped forwards and asked if I had any business he could arrange for me. He spoke such pretty broken English, I could not help thinking of Thaddeus of Warsaw and

---

1 (French) courtly minuets, a minuet being a formal dance.

the Hungarian Brothers, and Santo Sebastiani;[1] and while I was busy picturing his past life to myself, he had bowed me out of the room. But wait a minute! You have not heard half my story yet! I was going downstairs, when who should I meet but Betty's second cousin. So, of course, I stopped to speak to her for Betty's sake; and she told me that I had really seen the conjurer; the gentleman who spoke broken English was Signor Brunoni himself. Just at this moment he passed us on the stairs, making such a graceful bow, in reply to which I dropped a curtsey — all foreigners have such polite manners, one catches something of it. But when he had gone downstairs, I bethought me that I had dropped my glove in the Assembly Room (it was safe in my muff all the time, but I never found it till afterwards); so I went back, and, just as I was creeping up the passage left on one side of the great screen that goes nearly across the room, who should I see but the very same gentleman that had met me before, and passed me on the stairs, coming now forwards from the inner part of the room, to which there is no entrance — you remember, Miss Matey! — and just repeating, in his pretty broken English, the inquiry if I had any business there — I don't mean that he put it quite so bluntly, but he seemed very determined that I should not pass the screen — so, of course, I explained about my glove, which, curiously enough, I found at that very moment."

Miss Pole then had seen the conjuror — the real live conjuror! and numerous were the questions we all asked her: "Had he a beard? Was he young or old? Fair or dark? Did he look" — (unable to shape my question prudently, I put it in another form) — "How did he look?" In short, Miss Pole was the heroine of the evening, owing to her morning's encounter. If she was not the rose (that is to say the conjuror), she had been near it.

Conjuration, sleight of hand, magic, witchcraft were the subjects of the evening. Miss Pole was slightly sceptical, and inclined to think there might be a scientific solution found for even the proceedings of the Witch of Endor.[2] Mrs. Forrester believed everything, from ghosts to death-watches. Miss Matey ranged between the two — always convinced by the last speaker. I think she was naturally more inclined to Mrs. Forrester's side, but a desire of proving herself a worthy sister to Miss Jenkyns kept her equally balanced — Miss Jenkyns, who would never

1 Heros of popular romances by Jane Porter (1776), Anna Maria Porter (1780) and Catherine Cuthbertson (1806) respectively.

2 In the bible, she is asked by Saul to call up the spirit of Samuel.

allow a servant to call the little rolls of tallow that formed themselves round candles, "winding-sheets,"[1] but insisted on their being spoken of as "roly-poleys!" A sister of hers to be superstitious! It would never do.

After tea, I was despatched downstairs into the dining-parlour for that volume of the old encyclopedia which contained the nouns beginning with C, in order that Miss Pole might prime herself with scientific explanations for the tricks of the following evening. It spoilt the pool at Preference[2] which Miss Matey and Mrs. Forrester had been looking forward to, for Miss Pole became so much absorbed in her subject, and the plates by which it was illustrated, that we felt it would be cruel to disturb her, otherwise than by one or two well-timed yawns, which I threw in now and then, for I was really touched by the meek way in which the two ladies were bearing their disappointment. But Miss Pole only read the more zealously, imparting to us no more interesting information than this: —

"Ah! I see; I comprehend perfectly. A represents the ball. Put A between B and D — no! between C and F, and turn the second joint of the third finger of your left hand over the wrist of your right H. Very clear indeed! My dear Mrs. Forrester, conjuring and witchcraft is a mere affair of the alphabet. Do let me read you this one passage?"

Mrs. Forrester implored Miss Pole to spare her, saying, from a child upwards, she never could understand being read aloud to; and I dropped the pack of cards, which I had been shuffling very audibly; and by this discreet movement, I obliged Miss Pole to perceive that Preference was to have been the order of the evening, and to propose, rather unwillingly, that the pool should commence. The pleasant brightness that stole over the other two ladies' faces on this! Miss Matey had one or two twinges of self-reproach for having interrupted Miss Pole in her studies; and did not remember her cards well, or give her full attention to the game, until she had soothed her conscience by offering to lend the volume of the Encyclopædia to Miss Pole, who accepted it thankfully, and said Betty should take it home when she came with the lantern.

The next evening we were all in a little gentle flutter at the idea of the gaiety before us. Miss Matey went up to dress betimes, and hurried me until I was ready, when we found we had an hour and a half to wait before the "doors opened at seven, precisely." And we had only twenty yards to go! However, as Miss Matey said, it would not do to get too much absorbed in anything, and forget the time; so, she thought we had better

---

1   Grave clothing used to wrap corpses.

2   Card game, the pool being the combined bidding contributions of the players.

sit quietly, without lighting the candles, till five minutes to seven. So Miss Matey dozed, and I knitted.

At length we set off; and at the door, under the carriage-way at the George, we met Mrs. Forrester and Miss Pole: the latter was discussing the subject of the evening with more vehemence than ever, and throwing As and Bs at our heads like hail-stones. She had even copied one or two of the "receipts" — as she called them — for the different tricks, on backs of letters, ready to explain and to detect Signor Brunoni's arts. We went into the cloak-room adjoining the Assembly Room; Miss Matey gave a sigh or two to her departed youth, and the remembrance of the last time she had been there, as she adjusted her pretty new cap before the strange, quaint old mirror in the cloak-room. The Assembly Room had been added to the inn about a hundred years before, by the different county families, who met together there once a month during the winter, to dance and play at cards. Many a county beauty had first swam through the minuet that she afterwards danced before Queen Charlotte,[1] in this very room. It was said that one of the Gunnings[2] had graced the apartment with her beauty; it was certain that a rich and beautiful widow, Lady Williams, had here been smitten with the noble figure of a young artist, who was staying with some family in the neighbourhood for professional purposes, and accompanied his patrons to the Cranford Assembly. And a pretty bargain poor Lady Williams had of her handsome husband, if all tales were true! Now, no beauty blushed and dimpled along the sides of the Cranford Assembly Room; no handsome artist won hearts by his bow, *chapeau bras*[3] in hand: the old room was dingy; the salmon-coloured paint had faded into a drab; great pieces of plaster had chipped off from the white wreaths and festoons on its walls; but still a mouldy odour of aristocracy lingered about the place, and a dusty recollection of the days that were gone made Miss Matey and Mrs. Forrester bridle up as they entered, and walk mincingly up the room as if there were a number of genteel observers, instead of two little boys, with a stick of toffy between them with which to beguile the time.

We stopped short at the second front row; I could hardly understand why, until I heard Miss Pole ask a stray waiter if any of the County families were expected; and when he shook his head, and believed not, Mrs. Forrester and Miss Matey moved forwards, and our party represented a conversational square. The front row was soon augmented and enriched

---

1   (d. 1818), consort of King George III.

2   Famous eighteenth-century beauties Maria (1733–60) and Elizabeth (1734–90) Gunning.

3   Three-cornered silk hat that could be folded and carried under one arm.

by Lady Glenmire and Mrs. Jamieson. We six occupied the two front rows, and our aristocratic seclusion was respected by the groups of shop-keepers who strayed in from time to time, and huddled together on the back benches. At least I conjectured so, from the noise they made, and the sonorous bumps they gave in sitting down; but when, in weariness of the obstinate green curtain, that would not draw up, but would stare at me with two odd eyes, seen through holes, as in the old tapestry story, I would fain have looked round at the merry chattering people behind me, Miss Pole clutched my arm, and begged me not to turn, for "it was not the thing." What "the thing" was I never could find out, but it must have been something eminently dull and tiresome. However, we all sat eyes right, square front, gazing at the tantalizing curtain, and hardly speaking intelligibly, we were so afraid of being caught in the vulgarity of making any noise in a place of public amusement. Mrs. Jamieson was the most for-tunate, for she fell asleep. At length the eyes disappeared — the curtain quivered — one side went up before the other, which stuck fast; it was dropped again, and, with a fresh effort, and a vigorous pull from some unseen hand, it flew up, revealing to our sight a magnificent gentleman in the Turkish costume, seated before a little table, gazing at us (I should have said with the same eyes that I had last seen through the hole in the curtain) with calm and condescending dignity, "like a being of another sphere," as I heard a sentimental voice ejaculate behind me.

"That's not Signor Brunoni!" said Miss Pole decidedly, and so audi-bly that I am sure he heard, for he glanced down over his flowing beard at our party with an air of mute reproach. "Signor Brunoni had no beard — but perhaps he'll come soon." So she lulled herself into patience. Meanwhile, Miss Matey had reconnoitred through her eye-glass; wiped it, and looked again. Then she turned round, and said to me, in a kind, mild, sorrowful tone: —

"You see, my dear, turbans *are* worn."

But we had no time for more conversation. The Grand Turk, as Miss Pole chose to call him, arose and announced himself as Signor Brunoni.

"I don't believe him!" exclaimed Miss Pole, in a defiant manner. He looked at her again, with the same dignified upbraiding in his counte-nance. "I don't!" she repeated, more positively than ever. "Signor Brunoni had not got that muffy sort of thing about his chin, but looked like a close-shaved Christian gentleman."

Miss Pole's energetic speeches had the good effect of wakening up Mrs. Jamieson, who opened her eyes wide in sign of the deepest atten-tion, a proceeding which silenced Miss Pole, and encouraged the Grand

Turk to proceed, which he did in very broken English — so broken that there was no cohesion between the parts of his sentences; a fact which he himself perceived at last, and so left off speaking and proceeded to action.

Now we *were* astonished. How he did his tricks I could not imagine; no, not even when Miss Pole pulled out her pieces of paper and began reading aloud — or at least in a very audible whisper — the separate "receipts" for the most common of his tricks. If ever I saw a man frown, and look enraged, I saw the Grand Turk frown at Miss Pole; but, as she said, what could be expected but unchristian looks from a Mussulman?[1] If Miss Pole was sceptical, and more engrossed with her receipts and diagrams than with his tricks, Miss Matey and Mrs. Forrester were mystified and perplexed to the highest degree. Mrs. Jamieson kept taking her spectacles off and wiping them, as if she thought it was something defective in them which made the legerdemain;[2] and Lady Glenmire, who had seen many curious sights in Edinburgh, was very much struck with the tricks, and would not at all agree with Miss Pole, who declared that anybody could do them with a little practice — and that she would, herself, undertake to do all he did, with two hours given to study the Encyclopædia, and make her third finger flexible.

At last, Miss Matey and Mrs. Forrester became perfectly awe-struck. They whispered together. I sat just behind them, so I could not help hearing what they were saying. Miss Matey asked Mrs. Forrester, "if she thought it was quite right to have come to see such things? She could not help fearing they were lending encouragement to something that was not quite —" a little shake of the head filled up the blank. Mrs. Forrester replied, that the same thought had crossed her mind; she, too, was feeling very uncomfortable; it was so very strange. She was quite certain that it was her pocket-handkerchief which was in that loaf just now; and it had been in her own hand not five minutes before. She wondered who had furnished the bread? She was sure it could not be Dabine because he was the churchwarden. Suddenly, Miss Matey half turned towards me: —

"Will you look, my dear — you are a stranger in the town, and it won't give rise to unpleasant reports — will you just look round and see if the rector is here? If he is, I think we may conclude that this wonderful man is sanctioned by the Church, and that will be a great relief to my mind."

---

1 Muslim, usually Turk or Persian.

2 (French) sleight of hand.

I looked, and I saw the tall, thin, dry dusty rector sitting, surrounded by National School boys,[1] guarded by troops of his own sex from an approach of the many Cranford spinsters. His kind face was all agape with broad smiles, and the boys around him were in chinks of laughing. I told Miss Matey that the Church was smiling approval, which set her mind at ease. I have never named Mr. Hayter, the rector, because I, as a well-to-do and happy young woman, never came in contact with him. He was an old bachelor, but as afraid of matrimonial reports getting abroad about him as any girl of eighteen: and he would rush into a shop, or dive down an entry, sooner than encounter any of the Cranford ladies in the street; and, as for the Preference parties, I did not wonder at his not accepting invitations to them. To tell the truth, I always suspected Miss Pole of having given very vigorous chase to Mr. Hayter when he first came to Cranford; and not the less, because now she appeared to share so vividly in his dread lest her name should ever be coupled with his. He found all his interests among the poor and helpless; he had treated the National School boys this very night to the performance; and virtue was for once its own reward, for they guarded him right and left, and clung round him as if he had been the queen bee, and they the swarm. He felt so safe in their environment that he could even afford to give our party a bow as we filed out. Miss Pole ignored his presence, and pretended to be absorbed in convincing us that we had been cheated, and had not seen Signor Brunoni after all.

I think a series of circumstances dated from Signor Brunoni's visit to Cranford, which seemed at the time connected in our minds with him, though I don't know that he had anything really to do with them. All at once all sorts of uncomfortable rumours got afloat in the town. There were one or two robberies — real bonâ fide robberies; men had up before the magistrates and committed for trial; and that seemed to make us all afraid of being robbed; and for a long time at Miss Matey's, I know, we used to make a regular expedition all round the kitchens and cellars every night, Miss Matey leading the way, armed with the poker, I following with the hearth-brush, and Martha carrying the shovel and fire-irons with which to sound the alarm; and by the accidental hitting together of them she often frightened us so much that we bolted ourselves up, all three together, in the back kitchen, or store-room, or wherever we happened to be, till, when our affright was over, we recollected ourselves, and set out afresh with double valiance. By day we heard strange stories from the

---

1   Arising in 1816, it was the first major move toward a national education system.

shopkeepers and cottagers, of carts that went about in the dead of night, drawn by horses shod with felt, and guarded by men in dark clothes, going round the town, no doubt, in search of some unwatched house or some unfastened door. Miss Pole, who affected great bravery herself, was the principal person to collect and arrange these reports, so as to make them assume their most fearful aspect. But we discovered that she had begged one of Mr. Hoggins' worn-out hats to hang up in her lobby, and we (at least I) had my doubts as to whether she really would enjoy the little adventure of having her house broken into, as she protested she should. Miss Matey made no secret of being an arrant coward; but she went regularly through her house-keeper's duty of inspection, only the hour for this became earlier and earlier, till at last we went the rounds at half-past six, and Miss Matey adjourned to bed soon after seven, "in order to get the night over the sooner."

Cranford had so long piqued itself on being an honest and moral town, that it had grown to fancy itself too genteel and well-bred to be otherwise, and felt the stain upon its character at this time doubly. But we comforted ourselves with the assurance which we gave to each other, that the robberies could never have been committed by any Cranford person; it must have been a stranger or strangers, who brought this disgrace upon the town, and occasioned as many precautions as if we were living among the Red Indians or the French. This last comparison of our nightly state of defence and fortification, was made by Mrs. Forrester, whose father had served under General Burgoyne[1] in the American war, and whose husband had fought the French in Spain. She indeed inclined to the idea that, in some way, the French were connected with the small thefts, which were ascertained facts, and the burglaries and highway robberies, which were rumours. She had been deeply impressed with the idea of French spies, at some time in her life; and the notion could never be fairly eradicated, but sprung up again from time to time. And now her theory was this: the Cranford people respected themselves too much, and were too grateful to the aristocracy who were so kind as to live near the town, ever to disgrace their bringing up by being dishonest or immoral; therefore, we must believe that the robbers were strangers — if strangers, why not foreigners? — if foreigners, who so likely as the French? Signor Brunoni spoke broken English like a Frenchman, and, though he wore a turban like a Turk, Mrs. Forrester had seen a print of Madame de Staël[2]

---

1   American general (1722–92).

2   French writer (1766–1817) and critic of Napoleon.

with a turban on, and another of Mr. Denon[1] in just such a dress as that in which the conjurer had made his appearance; showing clearly that the French, as well as the Turks, wore turbans: there could be no doubt Signor Brunoni was a Frenchman — a French spy, come to discover the weak and undefended places of England; and, doubtless, he had his accomplices; for her part, she, Mrs. Forrester, had always had her own opinion of Miss Pole's adventure at the George Inn — seeing two men where only one was believed to be. French people had ways and means, which she was thankful to say the English knew nothing about; and she had never felt quite easy in her mind about going to see that conjurer; it was rather too much like a forbidden thing, though the rector was there. In short, Mrs. Forrester grew more excited than we had ever known her before; and, being an officer's daughter and widow, we looked up to her opinion, of course. Really I do not know how much was true or false in the reports which flew about like wildfire just at this time; but it seemed to me then that there was every reason to believe that at Mardon (a small town about eight miles from Cranford) houses and shops were entered by holes made in the walls, the bricks being silently carried away in the dead of the night, and all done so quietly, that no sound was heard either in or out of the house. Miss Matey gave it up in despair when she heard of this. "What was the use," said she, "of locks and bolts, and bells at the windows, and going round the house every night? That last trick was fit for a conjuror. Now she did believe that Signor Brunoni was at the bottom of it."

One afternoon, about five o'clock, we were startled by a hasty knock at the door. Miss Matey bade me run and tell Martha on no account to open the door till she (Miss Matey) had reconnoitred through the window; and she armed herself with a footstool to drop down on the head of the visitor, in case he should show a face covered with black crape, as he looked up in answer to her inquiry of who was there. But it was nobody but Miss Pole and Betty. The former came upstairs, carrying a little hand-basket, and she was evidently in a state of great agitation.

"Take care of that!" said she to me, as I offered to relieve her of her basket. "It's my plate.[2] I am sure there is a plan to rob my house to-night. I am come to throw myself on your hospitality, Miss Matey. Betty is going to sleep with her cousin at the George. I can sit up here all

---

1   Baron Dominique-Vivant Denon (1747–1825), French archaeologist and writer who accompanied Napoleon on his Egyptian campaign.

2   Silverware.

night, if you will allow me; but my house is so far from any neighbours; and I don't believe we could be heard if we screamed ever so!"

"But," said Miss Matey, "what has alarmed you so much? Have you seen any men lurking about the house?"

"Oh yes!" answered Miss Pole. "Two very bad-looking men have gone three times past the house, very slowly; and an Irish beggar-woman came not half an hour ago, and all but forced herself in past Betty, saying her children were starving, and she must speak to the mistress; you see, she said 'mistress,' though there was a hat hanging up in the hall, and it would have been more natural to have said 'master.' But Betty shut the door in her face, and came up to me, and we got the spoons[1] together, and sat in the parlour-window watching, till we saw Thomas Jones going from his work, when we called to him and asked him to take care of us into the town."

We might have triumphed over Miss Pole, who had professed such bravery until she was frightened; but we were too glad to perceive that she shared in the weaknesses of humanity to exult over her; and I gave up my room to her very willingly, and shared Miss Matey's bed for the night. But before we retired, the two ladies rummaged up, out of the recesses of their memory, such horrid stories of robbery and murder, that I quite quaked in my shoes. Miss Pole was evidently anxious to prove that such terrible events had occurred within her experience that she was justified in her sudden panic; and Miss Matey did not like to be outdone, and capped every story with one yet more horrible, till it reminded me, oddly enough, of an old story I had read somewhere, of a nightingale and a musician, who strove one against the other which could produce the most admirable music, till poor Philomel[2] dropped down dead.

One of the stories that haunted me for a long time afterwards, was of a girl, who was left in charge of a great old house in Cumberland, on some particular fair day, when the other servants all went off to the gaieties. The family were away in London, and a pedlar came by, and asked to leave his large and heavy pack in the kitchen, saying, he would call for it again at night; and the girl (a gamekeeper's daughter) roaming about in search of amusement, chanced to hit upon a gun hanging up in the hall, and took it down to look at the chasing; and it went off through the open kitchen door, hit the pack, and a slow dark thread of blood came oozing out. (How Miss Pole enjoyed this part of the story, dwelling on each

---

1   Silverware.

2   Character in Ovid's *Metamorphoses* who was eventually turned into a nightingale.

word as if she loved it!) She rather hurried over the further account of the girl's bravery, and I have but a confused idea that, somehow, she baffled the robbers with Italian irons, heated red hot, and then restored to blackness by being dipped in grease. We parted for the night with an awe-struck wonder as to what we should hear of in the morning — and, on my part, with a vehement desire for the night to be over and gone: I was so afraid lest the robbers should have seen, from some dark lurking-place, that Miss Pole had carried off her plate, and thus have a double motive for attacking our house.

But, until Lady Glenmire came to call next day, we heard of nothing unusual. The kitchen fire-irons were in exactly the same position against the back door, as when Martha and I had skilfully piled them up like spillikins,[1] ready to fall with an awful clatter, if only a cat had touched the outside panels. I had wondered what we should all do if thus awakened and alarmed, and had proposed to Miss Matey that we should cover up our faces under the bed-clothes, so that there should be no danger of the robbers thinking that we could identify them; but Miss Matey, who was trembling very much, scouted this idea, and said we owed it to society to apprehend them, and that she should certainly do her best to lay hold of them, and lock them up in the garret till morning.

When Lady Glenmire came, we almost felt jealous of her. Mrs. Jamieson's house had really been attacked; at least there were men's footsteps to be seen on the flower-borders, underneath the kitchen windows, "where nae men should be;" and Carlo had barked all through the night as if strangers were abroad. Mrs. Jamieson had been awakened by Lady Glenmire, and they had rung the bell which communicated with Mr. Mulliner's room, in the third story, and when his night-capped head had appeared over the bannisters, in answer to the summons, they had told him of their alarm, and the reasons for it; whereupon he retreated into his bed-room, and locked the door (for fear of draughts, as he informed them in the morning), and opened the window, and called out valiantly to say, if the supposed robbers would come to him he would fight them; but, as Lady Glenmire observed, that was but poor comfort, since they would have to pass by Mrs. Jamieson's room and her own, before they could reach him, and must be of a very pugnacious disposition indeed, if they neglected the opportunities of robbery presented by the unguarded lower stories to go up to a garret, and there force a door in order to get at the champion of the house. Lady Glenmire, after waiting and listen-

---

2   Splinters of wood, bone or ivory used in a children's game with the same name.

ing for some time in the drawing-room, had proposed to Mrs. Jamieson that they should go to bed; but that lady said she should not feel comfortable unless she sat up and watched; and, accordingly, she packed herself warmly up on the sofa, where she was found by the housemaid, when she came into the room at six o'clock, fast asleep; but Lady Glenmire went to bed, and kept awake all night.

When Miss Pole heard of this, she nodded her head in great satisfaction. She had been sure we should hear of something happening in Cranford that night; and we had heard. It was clear enough they had first proposed to attack her house; but when they saw that she and Betty were on their guard, and had carried off the plate, they had changed their tactics and gone to Mrs. Jamieson's, and no one knew what might have happened if Carlo had not barked, like a good dog as he was! Poor Carlo! his barking days were nearly over. Whether the gang who infested the neighbourhood were afraid of him; or whether they were revengeful enough for the way in which he had baffled them on the night in question to poison him; or whether, as some among the more uneducated people thought, he died of apoplexy, brought on by too much feeding and too little exercise; at any rate, it is certain that two days after this eventful night Carlo was found dead, with his poor little legs stretched out stiff in the attitude of running, as if by such unusual exertion he could escape the fell pursuer, Death. We were all sorry for Carlo, the old familiar friend who had snapped at us for so many years; and the mysterious mode of his death made us very uncomfortable. Could Signor Brunoni be at the bottom of this? He had apparently killed a canary with only a word of command; his will seemed of deadly force; who knew but what he might yet be lingering in the neighbourhood willing all sorts of awful things! We whispered these fancies among ourselves in the evenings; but in the mornings our courage came back with the daylight, and in a week's time we had got over the shock of Carlo's death; all but Mrs. Jamieson. She, poor thing, felt it as she had felt no event since her husband's death; indeed, Miss Pole said, that as the Honourable Mr. Jamieson drank a good deal, and occasioned her much uneasiness, it was possible that Carlo's death might be the greater affliction. But there was always a tinge of cynicism in Miss Pole's remarks. However, one thing was clear and certain; it was necessary for Mrs. Jamieson to have some change of scene; and Mr. Mulliner was very impressive on this point, shaking his head whenever we inquired after his mistress, and speaking of her loss of appetite and bad nights very ominously; and with justice too, for if she had two characteristics in her natural state of health, they were a facility of eating and sleeping. If she could neither eat nor sleep, she must be indeed out of spirits and out of health. Lady Glenmire (who had evidently taken very kindly to Cranford), did not like the idea of Mrs. Jamieson's going to Cheltenham, and more than once insinuated pretty plainly that it was Mr. Mulliner's doing, who had been much alarmed on the occasion of the house being attacked, and since had said, more than once, that he felt it a very responsible charge to have to defend so many women. However, Mrs. Jamieson went to Cheltenham, escorted by Mr. Mulliner; and Lady Glenmire remained in possession of the house, her ostensible office being to take care that the maid-servants did not pick up followers. She made a very pleasant-looking dragon: and, as soon as it was arranged for her to stay in Cranford, she found out that Mrs. Jamieson's visit to Cheltenham was just the best thing in the world. She had let her house in Edinburgh, and was for the time houseless, so the charge of her sister-in-law's comfortable abode was very convenient and acceptable.

CHAPTER THE SECOND.

Miss Pole was very much inclined to install herself as a heroine, because of the decided steps she had taken in flying from the two men and one woman, whom she entitled "that murderous gang." She described their appearance in glowing colours, and I noticed that every time she went over the story, some fresh trait of villany was added to their appearance. One was tall — he grew to be gigantic in height before we had done with him — he of course had black hair; and by and bye, it hung in elf-locks over his forehead and down his back. The other was short and broad, and a hump sprouted out on his shoulder before we heard the last of him; he had red hair, which deepened to carrotty, and she was almost sure he had a cast in his eye — a decided squint. As for the woman, her eyes glared, and she was masculine-looking; a perfect virago, most probably a man dressed in woman's clothes: afterwards, we heard of a beard on her chin, and a manly voice and a stride. If Miss Pole was delighted to recount the events of that afternoon to all inquirers, others were not so proud of their adventures in the robbery line. Mr. Hoggins, the surgeon, had been attacked at his own door by two ruffians, who were concealed in the shadow of the porch, and so effectually silenced him, that he was robbed in the interval between ringing his bell and the servant's answering it. Miss Pole was sure it would turn out that this robbery had been committed by "her men," and went the very day she heard of the report to have her teeth examined, and to question Mr.

Hoggins. She came to us afterwards; so we heard what she had heard, straight and direct from the source, while we were yet in the excitement and flutter of the agitation caused by the first intelligence; for the event had only occurred the night before.

"Well!" said Miss Pole, sitting down with the decision of a person who has made up her mind as to the nature of life and the world, (and such people never tread lightly, or seat themselves without a bump) — "Well, Miss Matey! men will be men. Every mother's son of them wishes to be considered Samson and Solomon[1] rolled into one — too strong ever to be beaten or discomfited, too wise ever to be outwitted. If you will notice, they have always foreseen events, though they never tell one for one's warning before the events happen; my father was a man, and I know the sex pretty well."

She had talked herself out of breath, and we should have been very glad to fill up the necessary pause as chorus, but we did not exactly know what to say, or which man had suggested this diatribe against the sex; so we only joined in generally, with a grave shake of the head, and a soft murmur of "They are very incomprehensible, certainly!"

"Now only think," said she. "There I have undergone the risk of having one of my remaining teeth drawn (for one is terribly at the mercy of any surgeon-dentist; and I, for one, always speak them fair till I have got my mouth out of their clutches), and after all, Mr. Hoggins is too much of a man to own that he was robbed last night."

"Not robbed!" exclaimed the chorus.

"Don't tell me!" Miss Pole exclaimed, angry that we could be for a moment imposed upon. "I believe he was robbed, just as Betty told me, and he is ashamed to own it: and, to be sure, it was very silly of him to be robbed just at his own door; I dare say, he feels that such a thing won't raise him in the eyes of Cranford society, and is anxious to conceal it — but he need not have tried to impose upon me, by saying I must have heard an exaggerated account of some petty theft of a neck of mutton, which, it seems, was stolen out of the safe in his yard last week; he had the impertinence to add, he believed that that was taken by the cat. I have no doubt, if I could get to the bottom of it, it was that Irishman dressed up in woman's clothes, who came spying about my house, with the story about the starving children."

After we had duly condemned the want of candour which Mr. Hoggins had evinced, and abused men in general, taking him for the representa-

---

1 Biblical heroes, known for their strength and wisdom respectively.

tive and type, we got round to the subject about which we had been talking when Miss Pole came in, namely, how far, in the present disturbed state of the country, we could venture to accept an invitation which Miss Matey had just received from Mrs. Forrester, to come as usual and keep the anniversary of her wedding-day, by drinking tea with her at five o'clock, and playing a quiet pool afterwards. Mrs. Forrester had said, that she asked us with some diffidence, because the roads were, she feared, very unsafe. But she suggested that, perhaps, one of us would not object to take the sedan;[1] and that the others, by walking briskly, might keep up with the long trot of the chairmen, and so we might all arrive safely at Over Place, a suburb of the town. (No. That is too large an expression: a small cluster of houses separated from Cranford by about two hundred yards of a dark and lonely lane.) There was no doubt but that a similar note was awaiting Miss Pole at home; so her call was a very fortunate affair, as it enabled us to consult together. We would all much rather have declined this invitation; but we felt that it would not be quite kind to Mrs. Forrester, who would otherwise be left to a solitary retrospect of her not very happy or fortunate life. Miss Matey and Miss Pole had been visitors on this occasion for many years; and now they gallantly determined to nail their colours to the mast, and to go through Darkness Lane rather than fail in loyalty to their friend.

But when the evening came, Miss Matey (for it was she who was voted into the chair, as she had a cold), before being shut down in the sedan like jack-in-a-box, implored the chairmen, whatever might befall, not to run away and leave her fastened up there, to be murdered; and even after they had promised, I saw her tighten her features into the stern determination of a martyr, and she gave me a melancholy and ominous shake of the head through the glass. However, we got there safely, only rather out of breath, for it was who could trot hardest through Darkness Lane, and I am afraid poor Miss Matey was sadly jolted.

Mrs. Forrester had made extra preparations in acknowledgment of our exertion in coming to see her through such dangers. The usual forms of genteel ignorance as to what her servants might send up were all gone through; and harmony and Preference seemed likely to be the order of the evening, but for an interesting conversation that began I don't know how, but which had relation, of course, to the robbers who infested the neighbourhood of Cranford. Having braved the dangers of Darkness Lane, and thus having a little stock of reputation for courage to fall back

---

1 Ornate chair used to transport passengers and carried usually by two men.

upon; and also, I dare say, desirous of proving ourselves superior to men (*videlicet*[1] Mr. Hoggins), in the article of candour, we began to relate our individual fears, and the private precautions we each of us took. I owned that my pet apprehension was eyes — eyes looking at me, and watching me, glittering out from some dull flat woollen surface; and that if I dared to go up to my looking-glass when I was panic-stricken, I should certainly turn it round, with its back towards me, for fear of seeing eyes behind me looking out of the darkness. I saw Miss Matey nerving herself up for a confession; and at last out it came. She owned that, ever since she had been a girl, she had dreaded being caught by her last leg, just as she was getting into bed, by some one concealed under the bed. She said, when she was younger and more active, she used to take a flying leap from a distance, and so bring both her legs up safely into bed at once; but that this had always annoyed Deborah, who piqued herself upon getting into bed gracefully, and she had given it up in consequence. But now the old terror would often come over her, especially since Miss Pole's house had been attacked (we had got quite to believe in the fact of the attack having taken place), and yet it was very unpleasant to think of looking under a bed, and seeing a man concealed, with a great fierce face staring out at you; so she had bethought herself of something — perhaps I had noticed that she had told Martha to buy her a penny ball, such as children play with — and now she rolled this ball under the bed every night; if it came out on the other side, well and good; if not, she always took care to have her hand on the bell-rope, and meant to call out John and Harry, just as if she expected men-servants to answer her ring.

We all applauded this ingenious contrivance, and Miss Matey sank back into satisfied silence, with a look at Mrs. Forrester as if to ask for *her* private weakness.

Mrs. Forrester looked askance at Miss Pole, and tried to change the subject a little, by telling us that she had borrowed a boy from one of the neighbouring cottages, and promised his parents a hundred weight of coal at Christmas, and his supper every evening, for the loan of him at nights. She had instructed him in his possible duties when he first came; and, finding him sensible, she had given him the major's sword (the major was her late husband), and desired him to put it very carefully behind his pillow at night, turning the edge towards the head of the pillow. He was a sharp lad, she was sure; for, spying out the major's cocked hat,[2] he had said, if

---

1   (Latin) namely.

2   Type of hat with brim turned upward, worn as part of army and navy uniforms.

he might have that to wear he was sure he could frighten two Englishmen, or four Frenchmen, any day. But she had impressed upon him anew that he was to lose no time in putting on hats or anything else; but, if he heard any noise, he was to run at it with his drawn sword. On my suggesting that some accident might occur from such slaughterous and indiscriminate directions, and that he might rush on Jenny getting up to wash, and have spitted her before he had discovered that she was not a Frenchman, Mrs. Forrester said she did not think that that was likely, for he was a very sound sleeper, and generally had to be well shaken, or cold-pigged[1] in a morning before they could rouse him. She sometimes thought such dead sleep must be owing to the hearty suppers the poor lad ate, for he was half-starved at home, and she told Jenny to see that he got a good meal at night.

Still this was no confession of Mrs. Forrester's peculiar timidity, and we urged her to tell us what she thought would frighten her more than anything. She paused, and stirred the fire, and snuffed the candles, and then she said, in a sounding whisper,

"Ghosts!"

She looked at Miss Pole, as much as to say she had declared it, and would stand by it. Such a look was a challenge in itself. Miss Pole came down upon her with indigestion, spectral illusions, optical delusions, and a great deal out of Dr. Ferrier and Dr. Hibbert[2] besides. Miss Matey had rather a leaning to ghosts, as I have said before, and what little she did say, was all on Mrs. Forrester's side, who, emboldened by sympathy, protested that ghosts were a part of her religion; that surely she, the widow of a major in the army, knew what to be frightened at, and what not; in short, I never saw Mrs. Forrester so warm either before or since, for she was a gentle, meek, enduring old lady in most things. Not all the elder-wine that ever was mulled, could this night wash out the remembrance of this difference between Miss Pole and her hostess. Indeed, when the elder-wine was brought in, it gave rise to a new burst of discussion: for Jenny, the little maiden who staggered under the tray, had to give evidence of having seen a ghost with her own eyes, not so many nights ago, in Darkness Lane — the very lane we were to go through on our way home. In spite of the uncomfortable feeling which this last consideration gave me, I could not help being amused at Jenny's position, which was exceedingly like that of a witness being examined and cross-

---

1   Doused with water, "pig" being slang for pitcher.

2   Dr. Ferrier (1761–1815) and Dr. Hibbert (1782–1848) were authorities on apparitions.

examined by two counsel who are not at all scrupulous about asking
leading questions. The conclusion I arrived at was, that Jenny had certainly seen something beyond what a fit of indigestion would have
caused. A lady all in white, and without her head, was what she deposed
and adhered to, supported by a consciousness of the secret sympathy of
her mistress under the withering scorn with which Miss Pole regarded
her. And not only she, but many others had seen this headless lady,
who sat by the roadside wringing her hands as in deep grief. Mrs.
Forrester looked at us from time to time, with an air of conscious triumph; but then she had not to pass through Darkness Lane before she
could bury herself beneath her own familiar bed-clothes.

We preserved a discreet silence as to the headless lady while we were
putting on our things to go home, for there was no knowing how near the
ghostly head and ears might be, or what spiritual connexion they might
be keeping up with the unhappy body in Darkness Lane; and therefore,
even Miss Pole felt that it was as well not to speak lightly on such subjects, for fear of vexing or insulting that woe-begone trunk. At least, so
I conjecture; for, instead of the busy clatter usual in the operation, we tied
on our cloaks as sadly as mutes at a funeral. Miss Matey drew the curtains
round the windows of the chair to shut out disagreeable sights; and the
men (either because they were in spirits that their labours were so nearly
ended, or because they were going down hill) set off at such a round and
merry pace, that it was all Miss Pole and I could do to keep up with
them. She had breath for nothing beyond an imploring "Don't leave
me!" uttered as she clutched my arm so tightly that I could not have
quitted her, ghost or no ghost. What a relief it was when the men, weary
of their burden and their quick trot, stopped just where Headingley-
causeway branches off from Darkness Lane! Miss Pole unloosed me and
caught at one of the men.

"Could not you — could not you take Miss Matey round by
Headingley-causeway, — the pavement in Darkness Lane jolts so, and she
is not very strong?"

A smothered voice was heard from the inside of the chair —

"Oh! pray go on! what is the matter? What is the matter? I will give you
six-pence more to go on very fast; pray don't stop here." — "And I'll give
you a shilling," said Miss Pole with tremulous dignity, "if you'll go by
Headingley-causeway."

The two men grunted acquiescence and took up the chair and went
along the causeway, which certainly answered Miss Pole's kind purpose
of saving Miss Matey's bones; for it was covered with soft thick mud, and

even a fall there would have been easy, till the getting up came, when there might have been some difficulty in extrication.

The next morning I met Lady Glenmire and Miss Pole, setting out on a long walk to find some old woman who was famous in the neighbourhood for her skill in knitting woollen stockings. Miss Pole said to me, with a smile half kindly and half contemptuous upon her countenance, "I have been just telling Lady Glenmire of our poor friend Mrs. Forrester, and her terror of ghosts. It comes from living so much alone, and listening to the bug-a-boo stories of that Jenny of hers." She was so calm and so much above superstitious fears herself, that I was almost ashamed to say how glad I had been of her Headingley-causeway proposition the night before, and turned off the conversation to something else.

In the afternoon Miss Pole called on Miss Matey to tell her of the adventure — the real adventure they had met with on their morning's walk. They had been perplexed about the exact path which they were to take across the fields, in order to find the knitting old woman, and had stopped to inquire at a little way-side public-house, standing on the high road to London, about three miles from Cranford. The good woman had asked them to sit down and rest themselves, while she fetched her husband, who could direct them better than she could; and, while they were sitting in the sanded parlour, a little girl came in. They thought that she belonged to the landlady, and began some trifling conversation with her; but, on Mrs. Roberts' return, she told them that the little thing was the only child of a couple who were staying in the house. And then she began a long story, out of which Lady Glenmire and Miss Pole could only gather one or two decided facts, which were that, about six weeks ago, a light spring-cart had broken down just before their door, in which there were two men, one woman, and this child. One of the men was seriously hurt — no bones broken, only "shaken," the landlady called it; but he had probably sustained some severe internal injury, for he had languished in their house ever since, attended by his wife, the mother of this little girl. Miss Pole had asked what he was, what he looked like. And Mrs. Roberts had made answer that he was not like a gentleman, nor yet like a common person; if it had not been that he and his wife were such decent quiet people, she could almost have thought he was a mountebank,[1] or something of that kind, for they had a great box in the cart, full of she did not know what. She had helped to unpack it, and take out their linen and clothes, when the other man — his twin brother, she believed he was — had gone off with the horse and cart.

---

1   One who falsely boasts to specialized knowledge or skill.

Miss Pole had begun to have her suspicions at this point, and expressed her idea that it was rather strange that the box and cart and horse and all should have disappeared; but good Mrs. Roberts seemed to have become quite indignant at Miss Pole's implied suggestion; in fact, Miss Pole said, she was as angry as if Miss Pole had told her that she herself was a swindler. As the best way of convincing the ladies, she bethought her of begging them to see the wife; and, as Miss Pole said, there was no doubting the honest, worn, bronzed face of the woman, who, at the first tender word from Lady Glenmire, burst into tears, which she was too weak to check, until some word from the landlady made her swallow down her sobs, in order that she might testify to the Christian kindness shown by Mr. and Mrs. Roberts. Miss Pole came round with a swing to as vehement a belief in the sorrowful tale as she had been sceptical before; and, as a proof of this, her energy in the poor sufferer's behalf was nothing daunted when she found out that he, and no other, was our Signor Brunoni, to whom all Cranford had been attributing all manner of evil this six weeks past! Yes! his wife said his proper name was Samuel Brown — "Sam," she called him — but to the last we preferred calling him "the Signor," it sounded so much better.

The end of their conversation with the Signora Brunoni was, that it was agreed that he should be placed under medical advice, and for any expense incurred in procuring this Lady Glenmire promised to hold herself responsible; and had accordingly gone to Mr. Hoggins to beg him to ride over to the Rising Sun that very afternoon, and examine into the Signor's real state; and as Miss Pole said, if it was desirable to remove him to Cranford to be more immediately under Mr. Hoggins's eye, she would undertake to see for lodgings, and arrange about the rent. Mrs. Roberts had been as kind as could be all throughout; but it was evident that their long residence there had been a slight inconvenience. Before Miss Pole left us, Miss Matey and I were as full of the morning's adventure as she was. We talked about it all the evening, turning it in every possible light, and we went to bed anxious for the morning, when we should surely hear from some one what Mr. Hoggins thought and recommended. For, as Miss Matey observed, though Mr. Hoggins did say "Jack's up," "a fig for his heels,"[1] and call Preference "Pref," she believed he was a very worthy man, and a very clever surgeon. Indeed, we were rather proud of our doctor at Cranford, as a doctor.

---

1 Expressions from cribbage.

We often wished, when we heard of Queen Adelaide or the Duke of Wellington[1] being ill, that they would send for Mr. Hoggins; but on consideration we were rather glad they did not, for if we were ailing, what should we do if Mr. Hoggins had been appointed physician-in-ordinary to the Royal Family? As a surgeon, we were proud of him; but as a man — or rather, I should say, as a gentleman — we could only shake our heads over his name and himself, and wish that he had read Lord Chesterfield's Letters[2] in the days when his manners were susceptible of improvement. Nevertheless, we all regarded his dictum in the Signor's case as infallible; and when he said, that with care and attention he might rally, we had no more fear for him.

But although we had no more fear, everybody did as much as if there was great cause for anxiety — as indeed there was, until Mr. Hoggins took charge of him. Miss Pole looked out clean and comfortable, if homely, lodgings; Miss Matey sent the sedan-chair for him; and Martha and I aired it well before it left Cranford, by holding a warming-pan[3] full of red hot coals in it, and then shutting it up close, smoke and all, until the time when he should get into it at the Rising Sun. Lady Glenmire undertook the medical department under Mr. Hoggins' directions; and rummaged up all Mrs. Jamieson's medicine glasses, and spoons, and bed-tables, in a free and easy way, that made Miss Matey feel a little anxious as to what that lady and Mr. Mulliner might say, if they knew. Mrs. Forrester made some of the bread-jelly, for which she was so famous, to have ready as a refreshment in the lodgings when he should arrive. A present of this bread-jelly was the highest mark of favour dear Mrs. Forrester could confer. Miss Pole had once asked her for the receipt, but she had met with a very decided rebuff; that lady told her that she could not part with it to any one during her life, and that after her death it was bequeathed, as her executors would find, to Miss Matey. What Miss Matey — or, as Mrs. Forrester called her (remembering the clause in her will, and the dignity of the occasion) Miss Matilda Jenkyns — might choose to do with the receipt when it came into her possession — whether to make it public, or to hand it down as an heir-loom — she did not know, nor would she dictate. And a mould of this admirable, digestible, unique bread-jelly was sent by Mrs. Forrester to our poor sick conjurer. Who says that the aristocracy

---

1   Arthur Wellesley (1769–1852), Prime Minister of Great Britain and Ireland, defeated Napoleon at Waterloo.

2   Published 1774, Chesterfield's letters featured advice on behaviour and manners.

3   A pan heated in the fireplace and used to warm a bed.

are proud? Here was a lady, by birth a Tyrrell, and descended from the great Sir Walter that shot King Rufus, and in whose veins ran the blood of him who murdered the little Princes in the Tower,[1] going every day to see what dainty dishes she could prepare for Samuel Brown, a mountebank! But, indeed, it was wonderful to see what kind feelings were called out by this poor man's coming amongst us. And also wonderful to see how the great Cranford panic, which had been occasioned by his first coming in his Turkish dress, melted away into thin air on his second coming — pale and feeble, and with his heavy filmy eyes that only brightened a very little when they fell upon the countenance of his faithful wife, or their pale and sorrowful little girl.

Somehow, we all forgot to be afraid. I dare say it was, that finding out that he, who had first excited our love of the marvellous by his unprecedented arts, had not sufficient every-day gifts to manage a shying horse, made us feel as if we were ourselves again. Miss Pole came with her little basket at all hours of the evening, as if her lonely house, and the unfrequented road to it, had never been infested by that "murderous gang;" Mrs. Forrester said, she thought that neither Jenny nor she need mind the headless lady who wept and wailed in Darkness Lane, for surely the power was never given to such beings to harm those who went about to try and do what little good was in their power; to which Jenny tremblingly assented; but her mistress's theory had little effect on the maid's practice, until she had sewed two pieces of red flannel, in the shape of a cross, on her inner garment.

I found Miss Matey covering her penny ball — the ball that she used to roll under her bed — with gay-coloured worsted[2] in rainbow stripes.

"My dear," said she, "my heart is sad for that little care-worn child. Although her father is a conjurer, she looks as if she had never had a good game of play in her life. I used to make very pretty balls in this way when I was a girl, and I thought I would try if I could not make this one smart and take it to Phœbe this afternoon. I think 'the gang' must have left the neighbourhood, for one does not hear any more of their violence and robbery now."

We were all of us far too full of the Signor's precarious state to talk about either robbers or ghosts. Indeed, Lady Glenmire said, she never

---

1 Walter Tyrrell reputedly shot the arrow that killed William Rufus, King of England (1087–1100). Sir James Tyrrell was beheaded in 1502 after confessing to murdering the legitimate heirs to the English throne, who were being kept prisoner in the Tower of London by their uncle Duke Richard of York (later King Richard III).

2 Woolen material — made in Worsted in Norfolk.

had heard of any actual robberies; except that two little boys had stolen some apples from Farmer Benson's orchard, and that some eggs had been missed on a market-day off Widow Hayward's stall. But that was expecting too much of us; we could not acknowledge that we had only had this small foundation for all our panic. Miss Pole drew herself up at this remark of Lady Glenmire's; and said "that she wished she could agree with her as to the very small reason we had had for alarm; but, with the recollection of the man disguised as a woman, who had endeavoured to force himself into her house, while his confederates waited outside; with the knowledge, gained from Lady Glenmire herself, of the foot-prints seen on Mrs. Jamieson's flower-borders; with the fact before her of the audacious robbery committed on Mr. Hoggins at his own door —" But here Lady Glenmire broke in with a very strong expression of doubt as to whether this last story was not an entire fabrication, founded upon the theft of a cat; she grew so red while she was saying all this, that I was not surprised at Miss Pole's manner of bridling up, and I am certain, if Lady Glenmire had not been "her ladyship," we should have had a more emphatic contradiction than the "Well, to be sure!" and similar fragmentary ejaculations, which were all that she ventured upon in my lady's presence. But when she was gone, Miss Pole began a long congratulation to Miss Matey that, so far, they had escaped marriage, which she noticed always made people credulous to the last degree; indeed, she thought it argued great natural credulity in a woman if she could not keep herself from being married; and in what Lady Glenmire had said about Mr. Hoggins's robbery, we had a specimen of what people came to, if they gave way to such a weakness; evidently, Lady Glenmire would swallow anything, if she could believe the poor vamped-up story about a neck of mutton and a pussy, with which he had tried to impose on Miss Pole, only she had always been on her guard against believing too much of what men said.

We were thankful, as Miss Pole desired us to be, that we had never been married; but I think, of the two, we were even more thankful that the robbers had left Cranford; at least I judge so from a speech of Miss Matey's that evening, as we sat over the fire, in which she evidently looked upon a husband as a great protector against thieves, burglars, and ghosts; and said that she did not think that she should dare to be always warning young people of matrimony, as Miss Pole did continually; to be sure, marriage was a risk, as she saw now she had had some experience; but she remembered the time when she had looked forward to being married as much as any one.

"Not to any particular person, my dear," said she, hastily checking herself up as if she were afraid of having admitted too much; "only the old story, you know, of ladies always saying 'When I marry,' and gentlemen, 'If I marry.'" It was a joke spoken in rather a sad tone, and I doubt if either of us smiled; but I could not see Miss Matey's face by the flickering firelight. In a little while she continued:

"But, after all, I have not told you the truth; it is so long ago, and no one ever knew how much I thought of it at the time, unless, indeed, my dear mother guessed; but I may say that there was a time when I did not think I should have been only Miss Matey Jenkyns all my life; for even if I did meet with any one who wished to marry me now (and, as Miss Pole says, one is never too safe), I could not take him — I hope he would not take it too much to heart, but I could *not* take him — or any one but the person I once thought I should be married to, and he is dead and gone, and he never knew how it all came about that I said 'no,' when I had thought many and many a time — Well, it's no matter what I thought. God ordains it all, and I am very happy, my dear. No one has such kind friends as I," continued she, taking my hand and holding it in hers. If I had never known of Mr. Holbrook, I could have said something in this pause, but as I had, I could not think of anything that would come in naturally, and so we both kept silence for a little time.

"My father once made us," she began, "keep a diary in two columns; on one side we were to put down in the morning what we thought would be the course and events of the coming day, and at night we were to put down on the other side what really had happened. It would be to some people rather a sad way of telling their lives" — a tear dropped upon my hand at these words — "I don't mean that mine has been sad, only so very different to what I expected. I remember, one winter's evening, sitting over our bedroom fire with Deborah, I remember it as if it were yesterday, and we were planning our future lives — both of us were planning, though only she talked about it. She said she should like to marry an archdeacon, and write his charges; and you know, my dear, she never was married, and, for aught I know, she never spoke to an unmarried archdeacon in her life. I never was ambitious, nor could I have written charges, but I thought I could manage a house (my mother used to call me her right hand), and I was always so fond of little children — the shyest babies would stretch out their little arms to come to me when I was a girl, I was half my leisure time nursing in the neighbouring cottages — but I don't know how it was, when I grew sad and grave — which I did a year or two after this time — the little things drew back from me, and I am afraid I lost the knack, though I am just as fond of children as ever, and have a strange yearning at my heart whenever I see a mother with her baby in her arms. Nay, my dear," — and by a sudden blaze which sprang up from a fall of the unstirred coals, I saw that her eyes were full of tears, gazing intently on some vision of what might have been — "do you know, I dream sometimes that I have a little child — always the same — a little girl of about two years old, she never grows older, though I have dreamt about her for many years. I don't think I ever dream of any words or sounds she makes; she is very noiseless and still, but she comes to me when she is very sorry or very glad, and I have wakened with the clasp of her dear little arms round my neck. Only last night — perhaps because I had gone to sleep, thinking of this ball for Phœbe — my little darling came in my dream, and put up her mouth to be kissed, just as I have seen real babies do to real mothers before going to bed. But all this is nonsense, dear! only don't be frightened by Miss Pole from being married. I can fancy it may be a very happy state, and a little credulity helps one on through life very smoothly, better than always doubting and doubting, and seeing difficulties and disagreeables in everything."

If I had been inclined to be daunted from matrimony, it would not have been Miss Pole to do it; it would have been the lot of poor Signor Brunoni and his wife. And yet again, it was an encouragement to see how, through all their cares and sorrows, they thought of each other and not of themselves; and how keen were their joys, if they only passed through each other, or through the little Phœbe. The Signora told me, one day, a good deal about their lives up to this period. It began by my asking her whether Miss Pole's story of the twin-brothers was true; it sounded so wonderful a likeness, that I should have had my doubts, if Miss Pole had been unmarried. But the Signora, or (as we found out she preferred to be called) Mrs. Brown, said it was quite true; that her brother-in-law was by many taken for her husband, which was of great assistance to them in their profession; "though," she continued, "How people can mistake Thomas for the real Signor Brunoni, I can't conceive; but he says they do; so I suppose I must believe him. Not but what he is a very good man; I am sure I don't know how we should have paid our bill at the Rising Sun, but for the money he sends; but people must know very little about art, if they can take him for my husband. Why, Miss, in the ball trick, where my husband spreads his fingers wide, and throws out his little finger with quite an air and a grace, Thomas just clumps up his hand like a fist, and might have ever so many balls hidden in it. Besides, he has never been in India, and knows nothing of the proper sit of a turban."

"Have you been in India?" said I, rather astonished.

"Oh yes! many a year, ma'am. Sam was a serjeant in the 31st; and when the regiment was ordered to India, I drew a lot to go, and I was more thankful than I can tell; for it seemed as if it would only be a slow death to me to part from my husband. But, indeed, ma'am, if I had known all, I don't know whether I would not rather have died there and then, than gone through what I have done since. To be sure, I've been able to comfort Sam, and to be with him; but, ma'am, I've lost six children," said she, looking up at me with those strange eyes, that I have never noticed but in mothers of dead children — with a kind of wild look in them, as if seeking for what they never more might find; — "Yes! Six children died off, like little buds nipped untimely, in that cruel India. I thought, as each died, I never could — I never would — love a child again; and when the next came, it had not only its own love, but the deeper love that came from the thoughts of its little dead brothers and sisters. And when Phœbe was coming, I said to my husband, 'Sam, when the child is born, and I am strong, I shall leave you; it will cut my heart cruel; but if this baby dies too, I shall go mad. The madness is in me now; but if you let me go down to Calcutta, carrying my baby step by step, it will may-be work itself off; and I will save, and I will hoard, and I will beg, — and I will die, to get a passage home to England, where our baby may live!' God bless him! He said I might go; and he saved up his pay, and I saved every pice[1] I could get for washing or any way; and when Phœbe came, and I grew strong again, I set off. It was very lonely; through the thick forests, dark again with their heavy trees — along by the rivers' side — (but I had been brought up near the Avon in Warwickshire, so that flowing noise sounded like home), from station to station, from Indian village to village, I went along, carrying my child. I had seen one of the officer's ladies with a little picture, ma'am, done by a Catholic foreigner, ma'am, of the Virgin and the little Saviour, ma'am. She had him on her arm, and her form was softly curled round him, and their cheeks touched. Well, when I went to bid good-bye to this lady, for whom I had washed, she cried sadly; for she, too, had lost her children, but she had not another to save, like me; and I was bold enough to ask her would she give me that print? And she cried the more, and said *her* children were with that little blessed Jesus; and gave it me, and told me she had heard it had been painted on the bottom of a cask, which made it have that round shape. And when my body was very weary, and my heart was sick, (for there were times when I misdoubted

---

1 An Indian coin.

if I could ever reach my home, and there were times when I thought of my husband; and one time when I thought my baby was dying) I took out that picture and looked at it, till I could have thought the mother spoke to me, and comforted me. And the natives were very kind. We could not understand one another; but they saw my baby on my breast, and they came out to me, and brought me rice and milk, and sometimes flowers — I have got some of the flowers dried. Then the next morning I was so tired; and they wanted me to stay with them — I could tell that — and tried to frighten me from going into the deep woods, which, indeed, looked very strange and dark; but it seemed to me as if Death was following me to take my baby away from me; and as if I must go on, and on — and I thought how God had cared for mothers ever since the world was made, and would care for me; so I bade them good-bye, and set off afresh. And once when my baby was ill, and both she and I needed rest, He led me to a place where I found a kind Englishman lived, right in the midst of the natives."

"And you reached Calcutta safely at last!"

"Yes! safely. Oh! when I knew I had only two days' journey more before me, I could not help it, ma'am — it might be idolatry, I cannot tell — but I was near one of the native temples, and I went in it with my baby to thank God for his great mercy; for it seemed to me, that where others had prayed before to their God, in their joy or in their agony, was of itself a sacred place. And I got as servant to an invalid lady, who grew quite fond of my baby aboard-ship; and, in two years' time, Sam earned his discharge, and came home to me, and to our child. Then he had to fix on a trade; but he knew of none; and, once, once upon a time, he had learnt some tricks from an Indian juggler, so he set up conjuring, and it answered so well that he took Thomas to help him — as his man, you know, not as another conjuror, though Thomas has set it up now on his own hook. But it has been a great help to us that likeness between the twins, and made a good many tricks go off well that they made up together. And Thomas is a good brother, only he has not the fine carriage of my husband, so that I can't think how he can be taken for Signor Brunoni himself, as he says he is."

"Poor little Phœbe!" said I, my thoughts going back to the baby she carried all those hundred miles.

"Ah! you may say so! I never thought I should have reared her, though, when she fell ill at Chunderabaddad; but that good, kind Aga Jenkyns took us in, which I believe was the very saving of her."

"Jenkyns!" said I.

"Yes! Jenkyns. I shall think all people of that name are kind; for here is that nice old lady who comes every day to take Phœbe a walk!"

But an idea had flashed through my head. Could the Aga Jenkyns be the lost Peter? True he was reported by many to be dead. But, equally true, some had said that he had arrived at the dignity of great Lama of Thibet. Miss Matey thought he was alive. I would make further inquiry.

Frances Browne

"The Story of Fairyfoot" (1857)

[When only one and a half years old, Frances Browne (1816–79) suffered a case of smallpox that left her permanently blind. Born in Ireland, the seventh of twelve children, Browne never received a formal education, learning from her older siblings. She began her career by writing poetry, with her first collection *The Star of Atteghei* appearing in 1844. Her poetry ranges from children's verse within an Irish tradition to serious pieces about the famine in her home county of Donegal. Browne moved to Edinburgh in 1847 where she made a living writing for periodicals. Five years later, she moved to London. In 1857, she published her most famous work for children, *Granny's Wonderful Chair*. A series of stories embedded within a frame narrative of a woman telling the tales to her grandchildren, the collection vividly captures the idyllic image of childhood popular among Victorians at the time. The stories, including "The Story of Fairyfoot," had a notable influence on the genre of fairy stories — which peaked in the Victorian era — and have remained popular to this day, making early editions of her works highly collectable. Note that the following story is narrated entirely by the character of Granny.]

"Once upon a time there stood far away in the west country a town called Stumpinghame. It contained seven windmills, a royal palace, a market place, and a prison, with every other convenience befitting the capital of a kingdom. A capital city was Stumpinghame, and its inhabitants thought it the only one in the world. It stood in the midst of a great plain, which for three leagues round its walls was covered with corn, flax, and orchards. Beyond that lay a great circle of pasture land, seven leagues in breadth, and it was bounded on all sides by a forest so thick and old that no man in Stumpinghame knew its extent; and the opinion of the learned was that it reached to the end of the world.

"There were strong reasons for this opinion. First, that forest was known to be inhabited time out of mind by the fairies, and no hunter cared

153

to go beyond its borders — so all the west country believed it to be solidly full of old trees to the heart. Secondly, the people of Stumpinghame were no travellers — man, woman, and child had feet so large and heavy that it was by no means convenient to carry them far. Whether it was the nature of the place or the people, I cannot tell, but great feet had been the fashion there time immemorial, and the higher the family the larger were they. It was, therefore, the aim of everybody above the degree of shepherds, and such-like rustics, to swell out and enlarge their feet by way of gentility; and so successful were they in these undertakings that, on a pinch, respectable people's slippers would have served for panniers.[1]

"Stumpinghame had a king of its own, and his name was Stiffstep; his family was very ancient and large-footed. His subjects called him Lord of the World, and he made a speech to them every year concerning the grandeur of his mighty empire. His queen, Hammerheel, was the greatest beauty in Stumpinghame. Her majesty's shoe was not much less than a fishing-boat; their six children promised to be quite as handsome, and all went well with them till the birth of their seventh son.

"For a long time nobody about the palace could understand what was the matter — the ladies-in-waiting looked so astonished, and the king so vexed; but at last it was whispered through the city that the queen's seventh child had been born with such miserably small feet that they resembled nothing ever heard of in Stumpinghame, except the feet of the fairies.

"The chronicles furnished no example of such an affliction ever before happening in the royal family. The common people thought it portended some great calamity to the city; the learned men began to write books about it; and all the relations of the king and queen assembled at the palace to mourn with them over their singular misfortune. The whole court and most of the citizens helped in this mourning, but when it had lasted seven days they all found out it was of no use. So the relations went to their homes, and the people took to their work. If the learned men's books were written, nobody ever read them; and to cheer up the queen's spirits, the young prince was sent privately out to the pasture lands, to be nursed among the shepherds.

"The chief man there was called Fleecefold, and his wife's name was Rough Ruddy. They lived in a snug cottage with their son Blackthorn and their daughter Brownberry, and were thought great people, because they kept the king's sheep. Moreover, Fleecefold's family were known to be ancient; and Rough Ruddy boasted that she had the largest feet in all the

---

1 Baskets.

pastures. The shepherds held them in high respect, and it grew still higher when the news spread that the king's seventh son had been sent to their cottage. People came from all quarters to see the young prince, and great were the lamentations over his misfortune in having such small feet.

"The king and queen had given him fourteen names, beginning with Augustus — such being the fashion in that royal family; but the honest country people could not remember so many; besides, his feet were the most remarkable thing about the child, so with one accord they called him Fairyfoot. At first it was feared this might be high-treason, but when no notice was taken by the king or his ministers, the shepherds concluded it was no harm, and the boy never had another name throughout the pastures. At court it was not thought polite to speak of him at all. They did not keep his birthday, and he was never sent for at Christmas, because the queen and her ladies could not bear the sight. Once a year the undermost scullion was sent to see how he did, with a bundle of his next brother's cast-off clothes; and, as the king grew old and cross, it was said he had thoughts of disowning him.

"So Fairyfoot grew in Fleecefold's cottage. Perhaps the country air made him fair and rosy — for all agreed that he would have been a handsome boy but for his small feet, with which nevertheless he learned to walk, and in time to run and to jump, thereby amazing everybody, for such doings were not known among the children of Stumpinghame. The news of court, however, travelled to the shepherds, and Fairyfoot was despised among them. The old people thought him unlucky; the children refused to play with him. Fleecefold was ashamed to have him in his cottage, but he durst not disobey the king's orders. Moreover, Blackthorn wore most of the clothes brought by the scullion. At last, Rough Ruddy found out that the sight of such horrid jumping would make her children vulgar; and, as soon as he was old enough, she sent Fairyfoot every day to watch some sickly sheep that grazed on a wild, weedy pasture, hard by the forest.

"Poor Fairyfoot was often lonely and sorrowful; many a time he wished his feet would grow larger, or that people wouldn't notice them so much; and all the comfort he had was running and jumping by himself in the wild pasture, and thinking that none of the shepherds' children could do the like, for all their pride of their great feet.

"Tired of this sport, he was lying in the shadow of a mossy rock one warm summer's noon, with the sheep feeding around, when a robin, pursued by a great hawk, flew into the old velvet cap which lay on the ground beside him. Fairyfoot covered it up, and the hawk, frightened by his shout, flew away.

"'Now you may go, poor robin!' he said, opening the cap: but instead of the bird, out sprang a little man dressed in russet-brown, and looking as if he were an hundred years old. Fairyfoot could not speak for astonishment, but the little man said —

"'Thank you for your shelter, and be sure I will do as much for you. Call on me if you are ever in trouble, my name is Robin Goodfellow;' and darting off, he was out of sight in an instant. For days the boy wondered who that little man could be, but he told nobody, for the little man's feet were as small as his own, and it was clear he would be no favourite in Stumpinghame. Fairyfoot kept the story to himself, and at last midsummer came. That evening was a feast among the shepherds. There were bonfires on the hills, and fun in the villages. But Fairyfoot sat alone beside his sheepfold, for the children of his village had refused to let him dance with them about the bonfire, and he had gone there to bewail the size of his feet, which came between him and so many good things. Fairyfoot had never felt so lonely in all his life, and remembering the little man, he plucked up spirit, and cried —

"'Ho! Robin Goodfellow!'

"'Here I am,' said a shrill voice at his elbow; and there stood the little man himself.

"'I am very lonely, and no one will play with me, because my feet are not large enough,' said Fairyfoot.

"'Come then and play with us,' said the little man. 'We lead the merriest lives in the world, and care for nobody's feet; but all companies have their own manners, and there are two things you must mind among us: first, do as you see the rest doing; and secondly, never speak of anything you may hear or see, for we and the people of this country have had no friendship ever since large feet came in fashion.'

"'I will do that, and anything more you like,' said Fairyfoot; and the little man taking his hand, led him over the pasture into the forest, and along a mossy path among old trees wreathed with ivy (he never knew how far), till they heard the sound of music, and came upon a meadow where the moon shone as bright as day, and all the flowers of the year — snowdrops, violets, primroses, and cowslips — bloomed together in the thick grass. There were a crowd of little men and women, some clad in russet colour, but far more in green, dancing round a little well as clear as crystal. And under great rose-trees which grew here and there in the meadow, companies were sitting round low tables covered with cups of milk, dishes of honey, and carved wooden flagons filled with clear red wine. The little man led Fairyfoot up to the nearest table, handed him one of the flagons, and said —

"'Drink to the good company!'

"Wine was not very common among the shepherds of Stumpinghame, and the boy had never tasted such drink as that before; for scarcely had it gone down, when he forgot all his troubles — how Blackthorn and Brownberry wore his clothes, how Rough Ruddy sent him to keep the sickly sheep, and the children would not dance with him: in short, he forgot the whole misfortune of his feet, and it seemed to his mind that he was a king's son, and all was well with him. All the little people about the well cried —

"'Welcome! welcome!' and everyone said — 'Come and dance with me!' So Fairyfoot was as happy as a prince, and drank milk and ate honey till the moon was low in the sky, and then the little man took him by the hand, and never stopped nor stayed till he was at his own bed of straw in the cottage corner.

"Next morning Fairyfoot was not tired for all his dancing. Nobody in the cottage had missed him, and he went out with the sheep as usual; but every night all that summer, when the shepherds were safe in bed, the little man came and took him away to dance in the forest. Now he did not care to play with the shepherds' children, nor grieve that his father and mother had forgotten him, but watched the sheep all day singing to himself or plaiting rushes; and when the sun went down, Fairyfoot's heart rejoiced at the thought of meeting that merry company.

"The wonder was that he was never tired nor sleepy, as people are apt to be who dance all night; but before the summer was ended Fairyfoot found out the reason. One night, when the moon was full and the last of the ripe corn rustling in the fields, Robin Goodfellow came for him as usual, and away they went to the flowery green. The fun there was high, and Robin was in haste. So he only pointed to the carved cup from which Fairyfoot every night drank the clear red wine.

"'I am not thirsty, and there is no use losing time,' thought the boy to himself, and he joined the dance; but never in all his life did Fairyfoot find such hard work as to keep pace with the company. Their feet seemed to move like lightning; the swallows did not fly so fast or turn so quickly. Fairyfoot did his best, for he never gave in easily, but at length, his breath and strength being spent, the boy was glad to steal away, and sit down behind a mossy oak, where his eyes closed for very weariness. When he awoke the dance was nearly over, but two little ladies clad in green talked beside him.

"'What a beautiful boy!' said one of them. 'He is worthy to be a king's son. Only see what handsome feet he has!'

"'Yes,' said the other, with a laugh that sounded spiteful; 'they are just like the feet Princess Maybloom had before she washed them in the Growing Well. Her father has sent far and wide throughout the whole country searching for a doctor to make them small again, but nothing in this world can do it except the water of the Fair Fountain, and none but I and the nightingales know where it is.'

"'One would not care to let the like be known,' said the first little lady: 'there would come such crowds of these great coarse creatures of mankind, nobody would have peace for leagues round. But you will surely send word to the sweet princess! — she was so kind to our birds and butterflies, and danced so like one of ourselves!'

"'Not I, indeed!' said the spiteful fairy. 'Her old skinflint of a father cut down the cedar which I loved best in the whole forest, and made a chest of it to hold his money in; besides, I never liked the princess — everybody praised her so. But come, we shall be too late for the last dance.'

"When they were gone, Fairyfoot could sleep no more with astonishment. He did not wonder at the fairies admiring his feet, because their own were much the same; but it amazed him that Princess Maybloom's father should be troubled at hers growing large. Moreover, he wished to see that same princess and her country, since there were really other places in the world than Stumpinghame.

"When Robin Goodfellow came to take him home as usual he durst not let him know that he had overheard anything; but never was the boy so unwilling to get up as on that morning, and all day he was so weary that in the afternoon Fairyfoot fell asleep, with his head on a clump of rushes. It was seldom that anyone thought of looking after him and the sickly sheep; but it so happened that towards evening the old shepherd, Fleecefold, thought he would see how things went on in the pastures. The shepherd had a bad temper and a thick staff, and no sooner did he catch sight of Fairyfoot sleeping, and his flock straying away, than shouting all the ill names he could remember, in a voice which woke up the boy, he ran after him as fast as his great feet would allow; while Fairyfoot, seeing no other shelter from his fury, fled into the forest, and never stopped nor stayed till he reached the banks of a little stream.

"Thinking it might lead him to the fairies' dancing-ground, he followed that stream for many an hour, but it wound away into the heart of the forest, flowing through dells, falling over mossy rocks and at last leading Fairyfoot, when he was tired and the night had fallen, to a grove of great rose-trees, with the moon shining on it as bright as day, and thousands of nightingales singing in the branches. In the midst of that grove was a clear spring, bordered with banks of lilies, and Fairyfoot sat down by it to rest himself and listen. The singing was so sweet he could have listened for ever, but as he sat the nightingales left off their songs, and began to talk together in the silence of the night —

"'What boy is that,' said one on a branch above him, 'who sits so lonely by the Fair Fountain? He cannot have come from Stumpinghame with such small and handsome feet.'

"'No, I'll warrant you,' said another, 'he has come from the west country. How in the world did he find the way?'

"'How simple you are!' said a third nightingale. 'What had he to do but follow the ground-ivy which grows over height and hollow, bank and bush, from the lowest gate of the king's kitchen garden to the root of this rose-tree? He looks a wise boy, and I hope he will keep the secret, or we shall have all the west country here, dabbling in our fountain, and leaving us no rest to either talk or sing.'

"Fairyfoot sat in great astonishment at this discourse, but by and by, when the talk ceased and the songs began, he thought it might be as well for him to follow the ground-ivy, and see the Princess Maybloom, not to speak of getting rid of Rough Ruddy, the sickly sheep, and the crusty old shepherd. It was a long journey; but he went on, eating wild berries by day, sleeping in the hollows of old trees by night, and never losing sight of the ground-ivy, which led him over height and hollow, bank and bush, out of the forest, and along a noble high road, with fields and villages on every side, to a great city, and a low old-fashioned gate of the king's kitchen-garden, which was thought too mean for the scullions, and had not been opened for seven years.

"There was no use knocking — the gate was overgrown with tall weeds and moss; so, being an active boy, he climbed over, and walked through the garden, till a white fawn came frisking by, and he heard a soft voice saying sorrowfully —

"'Come back, come back, my fawn! I cannot run and play with you now, my feet have grown so heavy;' and looking round he saw the loveliest young princess in the world, dressed in snow-white, and wearing a wreath of roses on her golden hair; but walking slowly, as the great people did in Stumpinghame, for her feet were as large as the best of them.

"After her came six young ladies, dressed in white and walking slowly, for they could not go before the princess; but Fairyfoot was amazed to see that their feet were as small as his own. At once he guessed that this must be the Princess Maybloom, and made her an humble bow, saying —

"'Royal princess, I have heard of your trouble because your feet have grown large: in my country that's all the fashion. For seven years past I have been wondering what would make mine grow, to no purpose; but I know of a certain fountain that will make yours smaller and finer than ever they were, if the king, your father, gives you leave to come with me, accompanied by two of your maids that are the least given to talking, and the most prudent officer in all his household; for it would grievously offend the fairies and the nightingales to make that fountain known.'

"When the princess heard that, she danced for joy in spite of her large feet, and she and her six maids brought Fairyfoot before the king and queen, where they sat in their palace hall, with all the courtiers paying their morning compliments. The lords were very much astonished to see a ragged, bare-footed boy brought in among them, and the ladies thought Princess Maybloom must have gone mad; but Fairyfoot, making an humble reverence, told his message to the king and queen, and offered to set out with the princess that very day. At first the king would not believe that there could be any use in his offer, because so many great physicians had failed to give any relief. The courtiers laughed Fairyfoot to scorn, the pages wanted to turn him out for an impudent impostor, and the prime-minister said he ought to be put to death for high-treason.

"Fairyfoot wished himself safe in the forest again, or even keeping the sickly sheep; but the queen, being a prudent woman, said —

"'I pray your majesty to notice what fine feet this boy has. There may be some truth in his story. For the sake of our only daughter, I will choose two maids who talk the least of all our train, and my chamberlain, who is the most discreet officer in our household. Let them go with the princess: who knows but our sorrow may be lessened?'

"After some persuasion the king consented, though all his councillors advised the contrary. So the two silent maids, the discreet chamberlain, and her fawn, which would not stay behind, were sent with Princess Maybloom, and they all set out after dinner. Fairyfoot had hard work guiding them along the track of the ground-ivy. The maids and the chamberlain did not like the brambles and rough roots of the forest — they thought it hard to eat berries and sleep in hollow trees; but the princess went on with good courage, and at last they reached the grove of rose-trees, and the spring bordered with lilies.

"The chamberlain washed — and though his hair had been grey, and his face wrinkled, the young courtiers envied his beauty for years after. The maids washed — and from that day they were esteemed the fairest in all the palace. Lastly, the princess washed also — it could make her no fairer, but the moment her feet touched the water they grew less, and when she had washed and dried them three times, they were as small and finely shaped as Fairyfoot's own. There was great joy among them, but the boy said sorrowfully —

"'Oh, if there had been a well in the world to make my feet large, my father and mother would not have cast me off, nor sent me to live among the shepherds.'

"'Cheer up your heart,' said the Princess Maybloom; 'if you want large feet, there is a well in this forest that will do it. Last summer time, I came with my father and his foresters to see a great cedar cut down, of which he meant to make a money chest. While they were busy with the cedar, I saw a bramble branch covered with berries. Some were ripe and some were green, but it was the longest bramble that ever grew; for the sake of the berries, I went on and on to its root, which grew hard by a muddy-looking well, with banks of dark green moss, in the deepest part of the forest. The day was warm and dry, and my feet were sore with the rough ground, so I took off my scarlet shoes, and washed my feet in the well; but as I washed they grew larger every minute, and nothing could ever make them less again. I have seen the bramble this day; it is not far off, and as you have shown me the Fair Fountain, I will show you the Growing Well.'

"Up rose Fairyfoot and Princess Maybloom, and went together till they found the bramble, and came to where its root grew, hard by the muddy-looking well, with banks of dark green moss in the deepest dell of the forest. Fairyfoot sat down to wash, but at that minute he heard a sound of music, and knew it was the fairies going to their dancing ground.

"'If my feet grow large,' said the boy to himself, 'how shall I dance with them?' So, rising quickly, he took the Princess Maybloom by the hand. The fawn followed them; the maids and the chamberlain followed it, and all followed the music through the forest. At last they came to the flowery green. Robin Goodfellow welcomed the company for Fairyfoot's sake, and gave every one a drink of the fairies' wine. So they danced there from sunset till the grey morning, and nobody was tired; but before the lark sang, Robin Goodfellow took them all safe home, as he used to take Fairyfoot.

"There was great joy that day in the palace because Princess Maybloom's feet were made small again. The king gave Fairyfoot all manner of fine clothes and rich jewels; and when they heard his wonderful story, he and the queen asked him to live with them and be their son. In process of time Fairyfoot and Princess Maybloom were married, and still live happily. When they go to visit at Stumpinghame, they always wash their feet in the Growing Well, lest the royal family might think them a disgrace, but when they come back, they make haste to the Fair Fountain; and the fairies and the nightingales are great friends to them, as well as the maids and the chamberlain, because they have told nobody about it, and there is peace and quiet yet in the grove of rose-trees."

Geraldine Jewsbury

"Agnes Lee" (1857)

["It is no good your getting up a theory about me," Geraldine Jewsbury (1812–80) once wrote to her close friend Jane Carlyle, "I was born to drive theories and rules to distraction." It is perhaps the fact that Jewsbury has always been difficult to categorize that has lead to her not attaining a high degree of fame or recognition. That said, she was a distinguished participant in the literary culture of her day. She did not only write short stories and novels, but published pieces in Douglas Jerrold's *Shilling Magazine* and worked as a reviewer of novels for the *Athenaeum* for 30 years. In addition, she worked as a reader for the publishers Hurst and Blackett, as well as Richard Bentley, a career which (in combination with her other literary involvements) made her one of the most influential women in the literary culture of the time. An on-going subject in works such as "Agnes Lee" is "the woman question" — the rights and roles of women in society, especially regarding education and employment. Jewsbury gradually became more conservative in her views, often criticizing works for a sensationalism that can be found in her own early novels such as *Zoe* (1845) and *The Half-Sisters* (1848).]

CHAPTER THE FIRST.

Mrs. Warren was a charming woman — as like the popular notion of a perfect angel as anybody could hope to find, if they took the longest summer day for the search. She was an Irishwoman, the widow of an English gentleman of large fortune, who had left her endowed with an ample jointure and a handsome manor-house in Staffordshire. She was young, bright, fascinating, and thoroughly good-natured; she enjoyed nothing so much as making people happy, and would sacrifice her own pleasure or convenience even, for an entire stranger, provided the necessities of the case had been brought before her with sufficient eloquence or emphasis. She did everything in the easiest and most graceful manner, and had the virtue of forgetting all about it herself, as soon as the occasion had passed away. She was devoted to her friends, and loved them dearly, so long as they were there to assist themselves; but, if they went away, she never thought of them till the next time she saw them, when she was again as fond of them as ever. With all her generosity, however, her tradespeople complained that she did not pay her bills; that she did very shabby things, and that she drove dreadfully hard bargains. A poor woman whom she had employed to do some plain work,[1] declared contemptuously that she would sooner work for Jews than for charitable ladies: they screwed down so in the price, and kept folks waiting so long for their money.

It was not difficult for Mrs. Warren to be an angel: she had no domestic discipline to test her virtues too severely, nor to ruffle the bird of paradise beauty of her wings. Husbands are daily stumbling-blocks in the path of female perfection; they have the faculty of taking the shine out of the most dazzling appearances. It is easier to be an angel than to be an average good woman under domestic difficulties.

Mrs. Huxley was the wife of the hard-working clergyman in whose parish Mrs. Warren's manor-house was situated. She had a cross husband, who did not adore her, but who (chiefly from the force of habit) found fault with everything she did; nothing but the purest gold could have stood the constant outpouring of so much sulphuric acid. Yet Mrs. Huxley went on in the even tenor of her way, struggling with straitened means, delicate health, recurring washing-days, and her husband's temper. Her economical feebleness, and the difficulties of keeping her weekly bills in a state of liquidation, were greatly complicated in consequence of all the poor people in the parish coming to her as to a sort of earthly Providence, to supply all they lacked in the shape of food, physic, raiment, and good advice. Strangers said that Mrs. Huxley looked fretful, and that it was a pity a clergyman's wife should have such unattractive manners; that it must be a trial to such a pleasant genial man as her husband to have a partner so unlike himself, and all that. The recording angel might have given a different verdict; the poor of her parish knew her value.

The family at the Rectory consisted of one daughter, named Miriam, and an orphan niece of Mr. Huxley's, whom they had adopted. Mr. Huxley had made many difficulties when this plan was first proposed. He objected to the expense, and wished the girl to be sent as an articled pupil to some cheap school, where she might qualify herself to become a nursery governess, or to wait on young ladies. This he said on the plea that,

---

1   Needlework or sewing, distinct from fancy embroidery.

as they would not be able to give her any fortune, it would be cruel to give her a taste for comforts she could not hereafter expect; that it was best to accustom her betimes to the hardships of her lot. Mrs. Huxley did not often contradict her husband; but, on this occasion, she exerted her powers of speech; she was a mother, and acted as she would have wished another to act by her own Miriam. Mr. Huxley graciously allowed himself to be persuaded, and Agnes Lee, the child of his favourite sister, was adopted into the Rectory nursery on a perfect equality with her cousin. It somehow got to be reported abroad, that Mrs. Huxley had greatly opposed her husband's generosity, and had wished the little orphan to be sent to the workhouse.[1]

The two children grew up together, and were as fond of each other as sisters usually are; but Agnes Lee had the strongest will and the most energy. So it was she who settled the plays and polity of doll-land, and who took the lead in all matters of "books, and work, and needle-play." Agnes was twelve, and Miriam fourteen, when the fascinating Mrs. Warren came to live at the Great House.

She took up the Rectory people most warmly, and threw herself with enthusiasm into all manner of benevolent schemes for the benefit of the parish. To the two girls she seemed like a good fairy. She had them constantly to her beautiful house, she gave them lessons in singing, and taught them to dance; her French maid manufactured their bonnets and dresses; she lavished gifts upon them, she made pets of them, and was never weary of inventing schemes for giving them pleasure. It was delightful to see their enjoyment and to receive their gratitude, and she never suspected the delicate unobtrusive care with which poor cold, stiff, Mrs. Huxley contrived that the two girls should never fall too heavily upon the hands of their beautiful patroness. She also tried to inspire them with a portion of her own reserve; but that was not so easy. Miriam — a mild, shy, undemonstrative girl — felt an admiration of Mrs. Warren that approached to idolatry. It took the place of a first love. Mrs. Warren liked the excitement of being loved with enthusiasm; but she never calculated the responsibility it brought along with it, and omitted nothing that could stimulate Miriam's passionate attachment. Agnes was less impressionable. She had a precocious amount of common sense, and Mrs. Warren's fascinations did not take too much hold upon her. The Rector was almost as much bewitched as his daughter by the fair widow. She talked gaily to him, and obliged him

---

1   Publicly supported institution which provided people food and shelter in exchange for their labour. After 1834, they were deliberately made unpleasant so as to deter people from relying on them.

to rub up his ancient gallantry, which had fallen into rusty disuse. She dressed all the children of his school in green gowns and red ribbons. She subscribed a painted window to the church. She talked over two refractory churchwardens, who had been the torment of his life: above all, she admired his sermons; and, as she was in correspondence with a lord bishop, he had sanguine hopes that her admiration might lead to something better. Mrs. Huxley was the only person who refused to be charmed. She did not contradict the raptures expressed by her husband and daughter, but she heard them in silence.

When Miriam was sixteen, she fell into delicate health; a slight accident developed a spinal affection. A London physician, who with his wife was on a short visit to Mrs. Warren, saw Miriam at her request, and gave little hope that she would ever be anything but a life-long invalid. She was ordered to keep as much as possible in a recumbent position. Mrs. Warren was on the point of departing for London. Nothing could exceed her sympathy and generosity. At first she declared she would postpone her journey, to assist Mrs. Huxley to nurse her sweet Miriam; but she easily gave up that idea when Mrs. Huxley declared, rather dryly, "that there was not the least occasion; for, as the case was likely to be tedious, it was better to begin as they could go on." Mrs. Warren, however, loaded Miriam with presents. She made Miriam promise to write to her all she read and thought; and, for this purpose, she gave her a supply of fairy-like paper and a gold pen. Miriam, on her side, promised to write twice a-week at least, and to tell Mrs. Warren everything that could amuse her. Mrs. Warren gave orders to her gardener to supply the Rectory with fruit, flowers, and vegetables; but either Mrs. Warren's directions were not clear, or the gardener did not choose to act upon them. He charged for everything that he sent down, and gave as his reason that his mistress paid him no wages in her absence, but let him pick up what he could.

After Mrs. Warren's departure, she wrote for a month; after that, her letters ceased. Newspapers supplied their place; and, it appeared from the notices of fashionable life, that Mrs. Warren had taken her place amongst the gayest. At last the newspapers ceased; the last that came contained the announcement that Mrs. Warren had left town for Paris. After this, no more news reached the Rectory. The Manor House remained shut up, and the lodge-keeper said "that the Missis was spending the winter at Bath."

At first Miriam wrote in all the enthusiasm and good faith of youthful adoration. Mrs. Warren had begged she would not count with her letter for letter, but have trust in her unalterable attachment, &c., &c.; and Miriam went on writing, long after all answers had ceased. Everything earthly has its limit; and, when reciprocity is all on one side, the term is reached rather earlier than it might otherwise have been. Poor Miriam lay on her couch, and went through all the heart-sickening process of disenchantment about the friendship which she had made the light of her life. She rejoiced moodily in her physical sufferings, and hoped that she should soon die, as she could not endure such misery long. The young believe in the eternity of all they feel.

She was roused from this sorrow of sentiment by a real affliction. Scarlet fever broke out in the parish. Mr. Huxley caught it, and died, after a fortnight's illness. A life insurance for a thousand pounds, and a few hundreds painfully saved and laid by in the Bank of England, was all the provision that remained to his family.

A fortnight after the funeral, Mrs. Huxley and Agnes were sitting sadly before the fire, which had burned low, on a dull, chill November evening. Miriam lay on her couch, and could scarcely be discerned in the deepening shadow. The dusk was gathering thick, the curtains were not drawn; both without and within, the world looked equally desolate to these three women. The silence was broken only by the sighs of poor Mrs. Huxley; the dull firelight showed her widow's cap, and the glaze of tears upon her pale clay-like cheeks. At length Agnes roused herself. She had taken the lead in the house since the family troubles, and now moved briskly about the room, endeavouring to impart something like comfort. She replenished the fire, trimmed the lamp; and made the old servant bring in tea.

Agnes threw in an extra spoonful of green,[1] spread a tempting slice of toast, and placed a small table between Mrs. Huxley and Miriam, who both began insensibly to be influenced by the change she had produced. When tea was over, they became almost cheerful. After tea, Mrs. Huxley took out her knitting, and Agnes brought out her work-basket.

"Now listen, dear aunt; for I have schemed a scheme, which only needs your approval."

"That will go a very little way towards doing good," sighed Mrs. Huxley.

"Oh, it will go further than you think!" said Agnes, cheerfully. "I was up at the Green this morning, and I heard that Sam Blacksmith is going to leave his cottage for another that is nearer to his smithy. It struck me that the one he is leaving would just suit you, and Miriam, and old Mary. There is a garden; and the cottage in your hands will be charming. This

---

1 Unprocessed tea.

furniture will look to more advantage there than it does here; and, when I have seen you comfortably settled, I shall leave you, to seek my fortune."

"My dear, you are so rash, and you talk so fast, I don't hear one word you say," said Mrs. Huxley, querulously.

"I was talking, aunt, about a cottage I had seen this morning," said Agnes, gently. "I thought it would just suit us."

"I am sure I shall not like it. It will have stone floors, which will not do for Miriam. You talk so wildly of going to seek your fortune. I am sure I don't know what is to become of us. You are so sanguine: no good ever comes of it. You were all so set up with Mrs. Warren, and you see what came of it."

"Well, aunt, my belief is, that Mrs. Warren would be as good as ever, if she only saw us; but she cannot recollect people out of sight."

"She loves flattery, and she likes fresh people," said Miriam, bitterly.

Agnes went to the piano, and began to play some old hymn tunes very softly.

"Agnes, my dear, I cannot bear music. Do come back and sit still," said her aunt.

The next morning Agnes persuaded her aunt to go with her to the Green, to look at the cottage; and, after some objections, Mrs. Huxley agreed that it might be made to do.

Whilst making arrangements for the removal, Agnes thought seriously how she was to obtain a situation of some kind, and anxiously examined what she was qualified to undertake. She knew that she had only herself to depend upon. A few days afterwards the postman brought a letter with a foreign postmark. It was Mrs. Warren's handwriting. Agnes bounded with it into the parlour, exclaiming, "See! who was right about Mrs. Warren? It is for you."

Miriam turned aside her head. Mrs. Huxley put on her spectacles; and, after turning the letter over half-a-dozen times, opened it. A bank-note for twenty pounds fell out. The letter was written in the kindest tone. She had just seen the mention of Mr. Huxley's death, and wrote on the spur of the moment. She was full of self-reproach for her neglect; begged them to believe she loved them as much as ever; spoke of Miriam with great kindness, but without any speciality; begged to be informed of their plans for the future; and, in a hasty postscript, said, that the enclosure was towards erecting a tablet to the memory of her dear friend, or for any other purpose they preferred.

Nothing could be kinder or more delicate; but Miriam was nearly choked with bitter feelings. The letter showed her how completely she had faded away from Mrs. Warren's affection. She vehemently urged her mother and cousin to send back the money.

Agnes undertook to answer the letter; which she did with great judgment. Even Miriam was satisfied. She mentioned her own desire to find a situation as preparatory governess, and asked Mrs. Warren if she had it in her power to recommend her.

As soon as could reasonably be expected, the answer came, addressed to Mrs. Huxley, begging that Agnes might at once join the writer in Paris, where, she had not the least doubt, she would be able to place her advantageously. Minute directions were given for the journey. On arriving in Paris, Agnes was to proceed at once to the Hotel Raymond, where Mrs. Warren was staying.

"How kind! how very kind!" exclaimed Agnes. "You see her heart is in the right place after all!"

"It is certainly very kind; but I do not like you to take so long a journey alone, you are too young. I cannot feel it either right or prudent," said Mrs. Huxley.

"My dear Agnes," said Miriam, "you shall not be trusted to the mercy of that woman. She cares for nothing but excitement. She has no notion of obligation, and will be as likely as not to have left Paris by the time you arrive, if the fancy has taken her for visiting Egypt or Mexico. I know what she is, and you shall not go."

"My dear aunt, as I am to make my own way in the world, the sooner I begin the better. I am to take charge of others, and I must learn to take care of myself. My dear Miriam, you are unjust. I place very little dependence on the stability of Mrs. Warren's emotions; but she always likes people when they are with her. It is an opening I am not likely to have again, and the sooner I avail myself of it the better."

"Agnes, be warned, I entreat you. No good will ever come out of that woman's random benefits. They are no better than snares. Have nothing to do with her."

Agnes would not be warned. She wished to go out into the world, to make her own way. She had no fears for herself. She argued and persuaded, and at last her aunt consented. Miriam was over-ruled, and a grateful acceptance was written to Mrs. Warren, fixing that day three weeks for her departure.

"The die is cast now!" said Agnes, when she returned from carrying the letter to the post, "I wonder what my future lot will be!"

CHAPTER THE SECOND.

The diligence[1] rolled heavily into the Court of the Messageries Royal in Paris, towards the middle of a keen bright day in the last week of December. A fair, elegant English girl, in deep mourning, looked anxiously out of the window of the coupé,[2] in search of some one to claim her.

"Is there any one waiting for you, Ma'mselle?" asked the good-natured conductor. "Will it please you to alight?"

"I see no one," said Agnes, who was bewildered with the noise and bustle. "I must have a coach to go to this address, please."

"Mrs. Warren, Hotel Raymond," read the conductor, looking at her keenly. "You want to go there, do you? Well, I will see. Your friends ought not to have left you to arrive alone. But the English are so droll!"

In a few minutes he returned.

"Now, Ma'mselle, here is a coach. The driver is my friend; he will see you safe. You may trust him. I would go with you myself, but —"

"You have been very kind to me," said Agnes, gratefully. Her command of French was very limited, and she said this in English; but the look that accompanied it spoke the language which needs no interpreter.

"Pardon. No thanks; it is my duty. Ma'mselle is too generous! There is no occasion." And the gallant conductor put back the five-franc piece that Agnes tendered with some embarrassment; for, during the journey he had shown her kindness that she felt could not be repaid in money. She took from her purse a half-crown piece English money. This the conductor put into his left waistcoat-pocket, as he said "for a remembrance of Ma'mselle."

The hackney-coach soon arrived at Raymond's. A grand-looking servant came to the door of the coach, and inquired her pleasure, with an elaborate politeness that would have been overwhelming at any other time; but Agnes scarcely noticed him. She eagerly handed him Mrs. Warren's card; but what little French she could command had entirely departed, and she could not utter a word. The garçon took the card, looked at it with a slight gesture of surprise, and returned to the house. In the meantime the coachman dismounted, took down the modest luggage, and demanded his fare. Agnes alighted, gave the man what he asked, and he had just driven away, when the garçon returned, accompanied by another.

---

1   A heavy French stagecoach.

2   Four-wheeled carriage.

"Ma'mselle is under a meestake," said the new comer, who evidently believed that he spoke English like a native. "Madame Warren is no more here — she departed two days since for Marseilles."

Agnes looked stupidly at him. She had heard what he said perfectly, and she was quite calm; but it was the calmness that makes the heart stand still, and turns the life within to stone.

"She told me to come here. She knew I was to come." Agnes spoke with stiffened lips and a voice that did not seem her own.

"She may have left some message — some letter for Ma'mselle," suggested the first garçon. "I will inquire."

Agnes sat down upon her trunk. She felt convinced that Mrs. Warren had gone and left no directions about her. She had just five francs and half a guinea left of money. Her position presented itself to her with perfect lucidity; but she felt no alarm, only a horrible stillness and paralysis of all emotion.

The garçon returned: he had a letter in his hand. Madame Warren had departed for Marseilles, en route for Sicily. She had left no message or direction. That letter had arrived a few hours after her departure, but they did not know where to forward it.

Agnes looked at the letter. It was her own, stating the time she would arrive in Paris, and requesting to be met. She gave it back to the garçon without speaking, and rested her head dreamily and wearily upon her hand.

The sight of a young and extremely pretty English girl in deep mourning and sitting upon her trunk, had by this time attracted a group of curious spectators. The fate of Agnes Lee was trembling in the balance. Already, a man, no longer young, who had lost his front teeth, and who looked as if he had no bones in his body, and a woman with a hard, insolent, determined face, varnished with cajolery, approached her. The woman addressed her in passably good English, but Agnes seemed not to hear. At this crisis a grave, middle-aged man made his way from the street. He looked round with surprise at the persons crowding in the court, and his eye fell on Agnes. He went up to her. The man and woman both shrank back from his glance.

"What is the meaning of all this, my child? How came you here, and what do you want?"

He spoke with a certain benevolent austerity. His tone roused Agnes; she looked up and passed her hand in a bewildered way over her forehead; but she could not recollect or explain her story. Mechanically she gave him Mrs. Warren's letter directing her to the Hotel Raymond, and looked acutely at him as his eye glanced over it.

"My poor child, you cannot remain here. They ought not to have left you here for a moment. You must come in and speak to my wife. We will see what can be done."

The loiterers dispersed — the new-comer was the proprietor of the hotel. Desiring a porter to take up her trunk, he led her into a private office, where a pleasant-looking woman of about forty sat at a desk surrounded by account-books and ledgers. She looked up from her writing as they entered. He spoke to her in a low voice, and gave her the letter to read.

"Mais c'est une infamie!"[1] said she, vehemently, when she had read it. You have done well to bring her in — it was worthy of you, my friend. Heavens! she is stupefied with cold and fear!"

Agnes stood still, apparently unconscious of what was passing; she heard, but she could give no sign. At length sight and sound became confused, and she fell.

When she recovered, she was lying in bed, and a pleasant-looking nurse was sitting beside her, dressed in a tall white Normandy cap and striped jacket. She nodded and smiled, and showed her white teeth, when Agnes opened her eyes, shook her head, and jabbered something that Agnes could not comprehend. The girl felt too weak and too dreamy to attempt to unravel the mystery of where she was and how she came there. In a short time, the lady she had seen sitting in the office amongst the daybooks and ledgers came in. She laid her hand gently on her forehead, saying, in a cheerful voice, "You are better now. You are with friends. You shall tell us your story when you are stronger. You must not agitate yourself."

Agnes endeavoured to rise, but sank back; the long journey and the severe shock she had received had made her seriously ill. The doctor who had been called to revive her from her long trance-like swoon ordered the profoundest quiet, and, thanks to the Samaritan kindness of her new friends, Agnes was enabled to follow the doctor's directions: for two days she lay in a delightful state of repose, between waking and dreaming. Everything she needed was brought to her, as by some friendly magic, at precisely the right moment. On the third day she felt almost well, and expressed a wish to get up and dress. Her hostess took her down to a pleasant parlour beyond the office. There were books, and prints, and newspapers; she was desired to amuse herself, and not to trouble her head with any anxiety about the future: she was a visitor.

M. Raymond, the proprietor, came in. Agnes had not seen him since the day he brought her into his house. He was a grave sensible man. To

---

1   (French) "But, it's absolutely scandalous!"

him she told her whole story, and gave him Mrs. Warren's letters to read. "My good young lady," said he, as he returned them, "we have only a little strength, and should not waste it in superfluities; we need it all to do our simple duty. This lady was too fond of the luxury of doing good, as it is called; but I cannot understand her thoughtlessness. There must be some mistake; though, after incurring the responsibility of sending for you, no mistake ought to have been possible."

Agnes tried to express all the gratitude she felt; but M. Raymond interrupted her. She was far from realising all the danger she had escaped; she knew it in after years. "I shall write home," she said; "my aunt and cousin will be anxious until they hear."

"Let them be uneasy a little longer, till you can tell them something definite about your prospects. Anything you could say now would only alarm them."

Two days afterwards M. Raymond came to her and said, "Do not think we want to get rid of you; but, if it suits you, I have heard of a situation. Madame Tremordyn wants a companion — a young lady who will be to her as like a daughter as can be got for money. She is a good woman, but proud and peculiar; and, so long as her son does not fall in love with you, she will treat you well. The son is with his regiment in Algiers just now; so you are safe. I will take you to her this afternoon."

They went accordingly. Madame Tremordyn — an old Bréton lady, stately with grey hair and flashing dark grey eyes, dressed in stiff black silk — received her with stately urbanity, explained the duties of her situation, and expressed her wish that Agnes should engage with her. The salary was liberal, and Agnes thankfully accepted the offer. It was settled that she should come the next morning. "Recollect your home is with us," said M. Raymond. "Come back to us if you are unhappy."

That night Agnes wrote to her aunt the history of all that had befallen her, and the friends who had been raised up to her, and the home that had offered in a land of strangers. But, with all this cause for thankfulness, Agnes cried herself to sleep that night. She realised for the first time that she was alone in her life, and belonged to nobody.

CHAPTER THE THIRD.

All who have had to live under the dynasty of a peculiar temper, know that it can neither be defined nor calculated upon. It is the knot in the wood that prevents the material from ever being turned to any good account. Madame Tremordyn always declared that she was the least exacting person in existence; and, so long as Agnes was always in the room with her, always on the alert watching her eye for anything she might need — so long Madame was quite satisfied. Madame Tremordyn had a passion for everything English. She would be read aloud to at all hours of the day or night. Agnes slept upon a bed in her room, whence she might be roused, if Madame Tremordyn herself could not rest; and woe to Agnes if her attention flagged, and if she did not seem to feel interest and enjoyment in whatever the book in hand might be — whether it were the History of Miss Betty Thoughtless, or the Economy of Human Life.[1] Madame Tremordyn took the life of Agnes, and crumbled it away: she used it up like a choice condiment, to give a flavour to her own.

Yet, with all this exigence, Agnes was nothing to Madame Tremordyn, who considered her much as she did the gown she wore, or the dinner she ate. She was one of the many comforts with which she had surrounded herself; she gave Agnes no more regard or confidence, notwithstanding their close intercourse, than she granted to her arm-chair, or to the little dog that stood on its hind legs. Yet, Agnes had no material hardship to complain of; she only felt as if the breath were being drawn out of her, and she were slowly suffocating. But where else could she go? what could she do? At length, Madame Tremordyn fell really ill, and required constant nursing and tending. Agnes had sleepless nights, as well as watchful days, but it was a more defined state of existence. Agnes was a capital nurse; the old lady was human, after all, and was touched by skill and kindness. She declared that Agnes seemed to nurse her as if she liked it.

Henceforth Agnes had not to live in a state of moral starvation. The old lady treated her like a human being, and really felt an interest in her. She asked her questions about home, and about her aunt and cousin; also, she told Agnes about herself, about her son, and about her late husband. She spoke of her own affairs and of her own experiences. It was egotism certainly; but egotism that asks for sympathy is the one touch of nature which makes the whole world kin. Agnes grew less unhappy as she felt she became more necessary to the strange exacting old woman with whom her

---

1   Works by Eliza Haywood (1693–1756) and Robert Dodsley (1703–64) respectively.

lot was cast. She had the pleasure of sending remittances to her aunt and cousin — proofs of her material well-being; and she always wrote cheerfully to them. Occasionally, but very rarely, she was allowed to go and visit her friends the Raymonds.

No news ever came of Mrs. Warren. She might have been a myth; so completely had she passed away. There had been an admixture of accident in her neglect; but it was accident that rather aggravated than excused her conduct. The day after she wrote so warmly to Agnes to come to her in Paris, Sir Edward Destrayes came to her, and entreated her to go to his mother, who was ill; and Mrs. Warren was her most intimate friend: indeed, they were strangers in Paris, and Mrs. Warren was nearly the only person they knew. Lady Destrayes was ordered to the South of France — would dear, kind Mrs. Warren go with her? It would be the greatest kindness in the world! Mrs. Warren spoke French so beautifully, and neither mother nor son spoke it at all. Sir Edward Destrayes was some years younger than Mrs. Warren. The world, if it had been ill-natured, might have said he was a mere boy to her; nevertheless, Mrs. Warren was in love with him, and she hoped it was nothing but his bashfulness that hindered him from declaring himself in love with her. Gladly would she have agreed to the proposed journey; but there was that invitation to Agnes. She must await her answer. Agnes, as we have seen, accepted the offer, which Mrs. Warren felt to be provoking enough — Lady Destrayes needed her so much! What was to be done? A certain Madame de Brissac, to whom she confided her dilemma, offered to take Agnes into her own nursery (without salary) until a better place could be found. Mrs. Warren was enchanted: nothing could be better. She wrote a note to Agnes, telling her she had found her a situation with Madame de Brissac; where she hoped she would be happy, and enclosed her some money, along with Madame de Brissac's address. The preparations for departure were hurried; for the party set out some days earlier than was intended. Agnes and her concerns passed entirely from Mrs. Warren's mind. Six weeks afterwards, searching her portfolio, a letter fell out with the seal unbroken; it was her own letter to Agnes. The sight of it turned her sick. She did not dare to think of what might have happened. She sat for a few moments stupified, and then hastily flung the accusing letter into the fire, without a thought for the money inside. She tried not to think of Agnes. She did not dare to write to Mrs. Huxley to inquire what had become of her. Mrs. Huxley and Miriam never heard from her again; the Manor House was sold, and Mrs. Warren passed away like a dream. Meantime she married Sir Edward Destrayes against his mother's wishes. It is to be presumed that he did not find her the angel she was reputed to be; for, at the end of a year, they separated. She always got on better alone; but, as she had married without settlement, she had not the wherewith to be so much of an angel in her latter days as in the beginning.

Agnes wondered and speculated what could have become of her. Madame Tremordyn grimly smiled, and said nobody ever made such mischief in life as those who did at once too much and too little. "If you begin an act of benevolence, you are no longer free to lay it down in the middle. So, my dear, don't go off into benevolence. You never know where it will lead you."

When Agnes had been with Madame Tremordyn a little more than a year, Madame Tremordyn's son came home from Africa. He was a handsome, soldierly young man; but grave and melancholy; poetical, dreamy, gentle as a woman; but proud and sensitive. Agnes was nineteen, extremely lovely, with golden hair, blue eyes, and a delicate wild-rose complexion; a little too firmly set in figure for her height, but that seemed characteristic. She had learned to be self-reliant, and had been obliged to keep all her thoughts and emotions to herself. At first Madame Tremordyn was proud to show off her son. She insisted that Agnes should admire him, and was never weary of talking about him. Agnes had been trained to be a good listener. Madame liked her son to sit with her, and he showed himself remarkably tractable — a model for sons. He did not seem to care in the least for going out. He preferred sitting and watching Agnes — listening to her as she read — whilst he pretended to be writing or reading. In a little while Madame Tremordyn opened her eyes to the fact that her son was in love with Agnes — Agnes, a portionless orphan, with few friends and no connexions. But Agnes was a mortal maiden, and she loved M. Achille Tremordyn, who might have aspired to the hand of an heiress with a shield full of quarterings.[1]

M. Achille Tremordyn opened his heart to his mother, and begged her blessing and consent to his marrying Agnes. Madame Tremordyn was very indignant. She accused Agnes of the blackest ingratitude, and desired her son, if he valued her blessing in the least, not to think of her, but dutifully to turn his eyes to the young lady she destined for him, and with whose parents she had, indeed, opened a negotiation. M. Achille declared that he would have his own way; Agnes only wept. The storm of dame

---

1   Denotes someone who not only is noble but also has alliances with other noble families so that the coat-of-arms must be divided to represent the various coats.

Tremordyn's wrath fell heaviest upon her, she being the weakest, and best able to hear it without reply. The result was, that Agnes was sent away in disgrace.

The Raymonds gladly received her, and entered warmly into her case. Madame Raymond declared it was unheard-of barbarism and pride, and that the old lady would find it come home to her. M. Achille Tremordyn left home to join his regiment, first having had an interview with Agnes. He vowed eternal constancy, and all the passionate things that to lovers make the world, for the time being, look like enchantment. It was the first ray of romance that had gilded Agnes's life. She loved as she did everything else, — thoroughly, steadfastly, and with her whole heart; but refused to marry, or to hold a correspondence with her lover, until his mother gave her consent. She would, however, wait, even if it were for life.

After her son was gone, Madame Tremordyn felt very cross and miserable. She did not, for one moment, believe she had done wrong; but it was very provoking that neither her son nor Agnes could be made to confess that she had done right.

Agnes remained with the Raymonds, wrapped round with a sense of happiness she had never known before. She assisted Madame Raymond to keep the books; for they would not hear of her leaving them. Madame Tremordyn felt herself aggrieved. She had engaged a young person in the room of Agnes, with whom no man was likely to be attracted; but, unluckily, Madame Tremordyn found her as unpleasant and unattractive as the rest of the world did. She missed Agnes sorely. At length she fairly fretted and fumed herself into a nervous fever. Mademoiselle Bichat, her companion, became doubly insupportable. Madame wrote a note to Agnes, reproaching her with cruelty for leaving her, and bidding her come back. She signed herself The Mother of Achille. There was nothing for it but to go; and Agnes went, hoping that the difficulties that lay between her and happiness were soluble, and had begun to melt away. The demoiselle Bichat was discarded, and Agnes re-installed in her old place. The old lady was not the least more amiable or reasonable for being ill. She talked incessantly about her son, and reproached Agnes with having stolen his heart away from her, his mother; yet, with curious contradiction, she loved Agnes all the more for the very attachment she so bitterly deprecated. If Agnes could only have loved him in a humble, despairing way, she would have been allowed to be miserable to her heart's content. But to be loved in return! To aspire to marry him! That was the offence.

Two years passed over. At the end of them Achille returned on sick-leave. He had had a fever, which had left him in a low, desponding state.

Madame Tremordyn would not spare Agnes, — she could not do without her. She told her she would never consent to her marriage with her son, and that she must submit to her lot like a Christian, and nurse Achille like a sister; which she had no objection to consider her. The sight of Achille, gaunt and worn with illness, made Agnes thankful to stop on any terms.

Achille was greatly changed; he was irritable, nervous, and full of strange fancies. He clung to Agnes as a child to its mother. Her calm and tender gentleness soothed him, and she could rouse him from the fits of gloom and depression to which he was subject. His mother lamented over the wreck he had become; but the love of Agnes became stronger and deeper. The nature of it had changed, but his need of her had a more touching charm than when, in his brilliant days, she had looked up to him as a something more than mortal, and wondered, in her humility, what he saw in her to attract him. Gradually he seemed to recover his health. The shadow that lay upon him was lifted off, and he became like his old self. He was not, however, able to return to the army. He retired, with the grade of captain and the decoration of the Legion of Honour.[1]

Madame Tremordyn's fortune was small, and consisted in a life-rent.[2] There would be little or nothing at her death for her son. It was necessary he should find some employment. Through the influence of some relatives, he obtained a situation in the Customs.[3] The salary was modest, but it was enough to live upon in tolerable comfort. He again announced to his mother his intention of marrying Agnes; and, this time, he met with no opposition — it would have been useless. Agnes was presented to friends and relatives of the clan Tremordyn as the betrothed of Achille. It was half settled that Agnes should pay a visit to her aunt and cousin whom she had not seen for near four years; but Mrs. Tremordyn fell ill, and could not spare her. The visit was postponed till she could go with her husband; and, in the meanwhile, letters of love and congratulation came from them. The whole Tremordyn tribe expressed their gracious approbation of the young English girl their kinsman had chosen, and made liberal offerings of marriage gifts. The good Raymonds furnished the trousseau, and Agnes could scarcely believe in the happiness that arose upon her life. Once or twice she perceived a strangeness in Achille. It was no coldness or estrangement, for he could not bear her out of his sight. He was quite well in health, and, at times, in extravagantly good

---

1   French order of distinction, conferred for civil or military services.

2   Right to use and enjoy a property during one's life.

3   Custom-house or office at which taxes are paid on goods going to market.

spirits. Yet he was unlike himself: he appeared conscious that she perceived something, and was restless and annoyed if she looked at him. The peculiarity passed off, and she tried to think it was her own fancy.

The wedding-day came. The wedding guests were assembled in Madame Raymond's best salon; for Agnes was their adopted daughter, and was to be married from their house. Neither Achille nor his mother had arrived. Agnes, looking lovely in her white dress and veil, sat in her room until she should be summoned. The time passed on — some of the guests looked at their watches — a carriage drove up. Madame Tremordyn, dressed magnificently, but looking pale and terror-stricken, came into the room, her usual stately step was now tottering and eager.

"Is my son, is Achille here?" she asked in an imperious but hollow voice. No one replied. A thrill of undefined terror passed through all assembled. "Is he here, I ask? He left home two hours ago."

"He has not been here. We have not seen him," replied the eldest member of the family. "Calm yourself, my cousin, doubtless he will be here soon."

There was an uneasy silence, broken by the rustling of dresses, and the restless moving of people afraid to stir; feeling, as it were under a spell. The eldest kinsman spoke again.

"Let some one go in search of him."

Three or four rose at this suggestion. Madame Tremordyn bowed her head, and said "Go!" It was all she had the force to articulate. The guests who remained looked at each other with gloomy forebodings, and knew not what to do. At last the door opened and Agnes entered. A large shawl was wrapped over her bridal dress, but she was without either veil or ornaments; her face was pale, her eyes dilated.

"What is all this? Let me know the worst — what has happened?" She looked from one to the other, but none answered her. She went up to Madame Tremordyn, and said, "Tell me, mother."

But, Madame Tremordyn put her aside, and said:

"You are the cause of whatever ill has befallen him."

A murmur rose from the company; but the poor mother looked so stricken and miserable that no one had the heart to blame her unreason. Everybody felt the position too irksome to endure longer; and, one after another, they glided noiselessly away; leaving only Agnes, Madame Tremordyn, and the good Raymonds. The hours passed on, and still no tidings. The suspense became intolerable. M. Raymond went out to seek for information, and also to put the police in motion. Agnes, who had sat all this while still and calm, without uttering a word or shedding a tear, rose and beckoned Madame Raymond to come out of hearing.

"I must change this dress and go home with her; we must be at home when he is brought back."

"But you cannot go there my child — it would be unheard of."

"They will both need me — there is no one who can fill my place — let me go."

She spoke gently, but resolutely. Madame Raymond saw that it was no case for remonstrance. In a few moments Agnes returned in her walking-dress. She laid her hand on Madame Tremordyn, and said:

"Let us go home."

The poor mother, looking ten years older than on the previous day, rose, and leaning upon Agnes walked feebly to the door. Madame Raymond supported her on the other side; she would have gone with them, but Agnes shook her head and kissed her silently. Arrived at home Agnes resumed her old position. She busied herself about Madame Tremordyn. She made her take some nourishment, chafed her hands and feet, and tried to keep some warmth and life within her; but little speech passed between them.

The weary hours passed on, and no tidings; about midnight a strangely sounding footstep was heard upon the stair. The door of the room opened, and Achille, with his dress disordered and torn, and covered with mud, stood before them. He stopped short at seeing them, and evidently did not recognise them. He did not speak. There was a wild glare in his eye, — he was quite mad.

Madame Tremordyn, in extreme terror, shrank back in her arm-chair, trying to hide herself. Agnes placed herself before her; looking steadily at Achille, she said quietly,

"Make no noise, your mother is ill."

He sat down slowly, and with apparent reluctance, upon the chair she indicated. She kept her eye fixed upon him, and he moved uneasily under its influence. It was like being with an uncaged wild beast; and, what was to be the end, she did not know. At length he rose stealthily and backed towards the door, which remained open. The instant he gained the landing-place he sprang down stairs with a yell. The house door was closed with violence, and he was heard running furiously up the street; his yells and shouts ringing through the air. Agnes drew a deep breath, and turned to Madame Tremordyn, who lay back in her chair speechless; her face was dreadfully distorted. She had been struck with paralysis.

CHAPTER THE FOURTH.

Agnes roused the domestics for medical assistance, and got Madame Tremordyn to bed, as speedily as possible. Her strength and calmness seemed little less than supernatural. The medical man remained in attendance the rest of the night; but no change for the better took place. Madame Tremordyn lay still speechless, distorted, yet not altogether insensible, as might be seen by her eyes, which followed Agnes wistfully. No tidings came of Achille, until the next day at noon, when Mrs. Tremordyn's kinsman came with the news that Achille had been conveyed to the Bicêtre,[1] a furious maniac. He spoke low, but Mrs. Tremordyn heard him; a gleam of terrible anguish shone from her eyes, but she was powerless to move.

"We must leave him there," said the kinsman. "He will be better attended to than he could be elsewhere. I will make inquiries to-morrow about him, and send you tidings. The physician says it has been coming on for some time. How fortunate, dear girl, that it was before the marriage instead of after: what a frightful fate you have escaped!"

"Do you think so?" said Agnes, sadly. "I must regret it always; for, if I had been his wife I should have had the right to be with him ill or well."

"You could do him no good. I doubt whether he would know you; but you are romantic."

Day after day passed slowly on without any change. The accounts of Achille were that he continued dangerous and ungovernable; that his was one of the worst cases in the house. Mrs. Tremordyn lay helpless and speechless. The guests who had assembled at the ill-omened wedding, had departed to their different abodes; most of them had come up from distant parts of the country for the occasion; none of them resided permanently in Paris. The old kinsman alone remained until Madame Tremordyn's state declared itself one way or other.

One night, about a fortnight after her seizure, Madame Tremordyn recovered her speech so far as to be intelligible. She spoke lucidly to Agnes, who was watching beside her, and began to give her some directions about her affairs; but her mind was too much weakened. She blessed her for all her attention and goodness; bade her be the good angel of her son; and, while speaking, a stupor benumbed her, and she never awoke from it.

The kinsman assumed the direction of affairs, took possession of her effects, broke up her establishment, made Agnes a present, and a handsome

---

1   Famous hospital in Paris, used as a lunatic asylum.

speech, and evidently considered her connection with the family at an end. Agnes went back to the Raymonds to consider what she would do.

The first thing needful, was to recruit her strength. She felt bitterly the severance of the tie between her and the rest of Achille's family. They had made up their minds that he was never to get better; but, to her, the idea of leaving him to his fate was too painful to contemplate. As soon as she had sufficiently recovered she asked M. Raymond to take her to the Bicêtre. There she had an interview with the head physician; who said that Achille's case, if not hopeless, would be of long duration. Agnes entreated to be allowed to see him — of course she was refused; but her importunity was not to be put by; and, at last, she was conducted to his cell. He received her calmly, and declared he knew she would come, and that he had been expecting her since the day before. He seemed quite rational and collected, and entreated her to take him away as it drove him mad to be there. The physician spoke, but Achille did not heed him. He kept his eyes fixed on Agnes, with a look of touching entreaty. Agnes looked wistfully at the physician, who said to Achille, "It depends entirely on yourself. You shall go the moment you render it possible for us to send you away."

Achille put his hand to his forehead, as though endeavouring to follow out an idea. At last he said, "I understand. I will obey."

He gravely kissed Agnes's hand, and attended her to the door of the cell, as though it had been a drawing-room.

"You have wonderful power over that patient, Mademoiselle," said the physician, "are you accustomed to mad persons?"

Agnes shook her head.

"Although he looks so quiet now, I would not be left alone with him for a thousand pounds," said he.

During their ride home, Agnes never spoke; she was maturing a plan in her mind. She asked the Raymonds to procure her some out-of-door teaching. They entreated her to remain with them as their daughter, and to live with them; but she steadily refused their kindness, and they were obliged to desist. They procured her some pupils, whom she was to instruct in music, drawing, and English. She still further distressed the Raymonds by withdrawing from their house, and establishing herself in a modest lodging near the Bicêtre; she attended her pupils, and visited Achille whenever the authorities permitted. As for Achille, from the first day she came, a great change had come over him. He was still mad, but seemed by superhuman effort, to control all outward manifestations of his madness. His delusions were as grave as ever, — sometimes he was betrayed into speaking of them, and he never renounced them — but all his actions were sane and collected. If Agnes were a day beyond her time he grew restless and desponding. In her personal habits Agnes exercised an almost sordid parsimony — she laid by nearly the whole of her earnings — her clientèle increased — she had more work than she could do. Her story excited interest wherever it was known, and her own manners and appearance confirmed it. She received many handsome presents, and was in the receipt of a comfortable income: still she confined herself to the barest necessaries of life. The Raymonds seldom saw her, and they were hurt that she took them so little into her confidence.

A year passed, and Agnes made a formal demand to have Achille discharged from the hospital, and given over to her care. There were many difficulties raised, and a great deal of opposition. M. Achille Tremordyn was not recovered; he was liable to a dangerous outbreak at any moment; it was not a fit charge for a young woman, and much besides; but Agnes was gifted with the power of bearing down all opposition. She argued and entreated, and finally prevailed.

Great was the astonishment of Monsieur Raymond, to see her thus accompanied, drive up to his door: that of Madame Raymond, of course was not less, but the surprise of both reached its height, when Agnes gravely, and without any embarrassment requested him to come with them to the Mairie[1] to see her married. Achille stood by, perfectly calm, but the imprisoned madness lurked in his eyes, and looked out as on the watch to spring forth. He spoke, however, with grave and graceful courtesy, and said that M. and Madame Raymond must perceive that Agnes was his good angel who had procured his deliverance, and that it was necessary she should give him the right to remain with her and protect her. He could not leave her — it was necessary to fulfill their old contract. He said this in a subdued, measured way; but with a suppressed impatience, as if a very little opposition would make him break out into violence. M. Raymond took her apart, and represented everything that common sense and friendship could suggest. Agnes was immovable. Her sole reply was, "He will never get well there; if he comes to me I will cure him." In the end, M. Raymond had to give way as the doctors had done. He and Madame Raymond went with them to the Mairie, and saw them married.

They went home with them afterwards. Agnes had arranged her modest ménage with cheerfulness and good taste. A sensible good-looking, middle-aged woman was the only domestic.

---

1 City hall.

"I have known her long," said Agnes, "she lived with Madame Tremordyn in Normandie, and she knew Achille as a boy, and is quite willing to share my task."

"I believe you are a rational lunatic, Agnes," said M. Raymond. "However, if you fail, you will come to us at once."

They remained to partake of an English tea which Agnes had got up, Achille performed his part, as host, with simple dignity. M. Raymond was almost re-assured. Nevertheless he led her aside, and said, "My dear girl, I stand here as your father. Are you sure you are not afraid to remain with this man?"

"Afraid? oh, no. How can one feel afraid of a person we love?" said she, looking up at him with a smile. And then she tried to utter her thanks for all his goodness to her; but her voice choked, and she burst into tears.

"There, there, my child, do not agitate yourself. You know we look on you as our daughter — we love you."

And tears dropped upon the golden curls as he kissed them. Poor Madame Raymond sobbed audibly, as she held Agnes in her arms, and would not let her go. Achille stood by, looking on.

"Why do you weep?" he asked, gently; "are you afraid that I shall hurt your friend? You need not fear, — she is my one blessing. I will make her great — I will!"

He seemed to recollect himself, and stopped, drawing himself up haughtily. Agnes disengaged herself gently from the embrace of Madame Raymond, and Achille attended them courteously to their coach.

There was a dangerous glare in his eyes when he came back. "Now Agnes, those people are gone. They shall never come back. If they had stayed a moment longer I would have killed them!"

After that evening, the Raymonds did not see Agnes for many months. Whatever were the secrets of her home, no eye saw them; she struggled with her lot alone. She attended her pupils regularly, and none of them saw any signs of weakness or anxiety. Her face was stern and grave; but her duties were punctually fulfilled, and no plea of illness or complaint, of any kind, escaped her. It was understood that her husband was an invalid, and that she did not go into company — that was all the world knew of her affairs.

The old servant died, and her place was never filled up. Agnes went to market and managed all her household affairs before she went to her pupils. Her husband was seen sometimes working in the garden or sitting — if the weather was warm — in the sunny arbour, shaded with climbing plants; but, he never left the house except with his wife.

At the end of three years, the hope to which Agnes had clung with such passionate steadfastness was fulfilled. Her husband entirely recovered his reason; but, in this hope realised there was mixed a great despair. With recovered sanity came the consciousness of all that his wife had done for him, and he had not breadth of magnanimity to accept it. It may be that the habits of rule and self-reliance which had been forced upon her by her position did not exactly suit the changed position of things — people must brave the defects of their qualities. This trial was the hardest she had endured; but she hid suffering bravely. Her husband respected her — honoured her — was always gentle and courteous — did everything except love her; but she loved him, and it is more blessed to give than to receive. It is the love we give to others, not the love they give us, that fills our heart.

Six years after marriage Achille Tremordyn died. He expressed eloquently and even tenderly his sense of all he owed to his wife, and his high opinion of her many virtues, and regretted all she had suffered for him. It was not the farewell that a woman and a wife would wish for; but she loved him, and did not cavil at his words.

After his death she went to live near the Raymonds. She still continued to teach, though no longer from necessity; but, after she had somewhat recovered from the blankness which had fallen on her life, she devoted herself to finding out friendless young girls, and providing them with homes and the means of gaining a living. For this purpose she worked, and to it she devoted all her earnings: recollecting the aunt who had adopted her when she arrived in Paris, and found herself abandoned. The good Raymonds left her a fortune, with which she built a house, and was the mother in it; and many were the daughters who had cause to bless her. She lived to an advanced age, and died quite recently.

Anthony Trollope

"George Walker at Suez" (1861)

[Anthony Trollope (1815–82), the son of the writer Frances Trollope, worked for the post office much of his adult life both in Ireland and England. His job took him on official business to Egypt, the West Indies and the United States, and he also travelled in Australia, New Zealand, and South Africa. In 1865, toward the end of his postal career, he founded the magazine *Fortnightly Review*, after which he served as editor for the *Pall Mall Gazette* and *St. Paul's Magazine*. Trollope, who was extremely prolific, viewed fiction writing as a trade. According to his calculations, he wrote 3000 words before he breakfasted and left to work each day. He is now best known for his affectionate *Barchester* books (1855 to 1867), which chronicle life in a small town. Generally viewed as novels, the beauty and charm of the books rest less on any over-arching narrative or cumulative purpose than on their attention to everyday characters and incidents. "His great, his inestimable merit," Henry James would write, "was his complete appreciation of the usual." The story "George Walker at Suez," which was published after his return from Egypt, reveals not only this quality but also the author's interest in the politics of nation and identity.]

Of all the spots on the world's surface that I, George Walker, of Friday-street, London, have ever visited, Suez, in Egypt, at the head of the Red Sea, is by far the vilest, the most unpleasant, and the least interesting. There are no women there, no water, and no vegetation. It is surrounded, and, indeed, often filled, by a world of sand. A scorching sun is always overhead, and one is domiciled in a huge, cavernous hotel, which seems to have been made purposely destitute of all the comforts of civilised life. Nevertheless, in looking back upon the week of my life which I spent there, I always enjoy a certain sort of triumph — or, rather, upon one day of that week, which lends a sort of halo, not only to my sojourn at Suez, but to the whole period of my residence in Egypt.

I am free to confess that I am not a great man, and that, at any rate in the earlier part of my career, I had a hankering after the homage which is paid to greatness. I would fain have been a popular orator, feeding myself on the incense tendered to me by thousands, or, failing that, a man born to power, whom those around him were compelled to respect, and perhaps to fear. I am not ashamed to acknowledge this, and I believe that most of my neighbours in Friday-street would own as much were they as candid and open-hearted as myself.

It is now nearly ten years since I was recommended to pass the four first months of the year in Cairo, because I had a sore throat. The doctor may have been right, but I shall never divest myself of the idea that my partners wished to be rid of me while they made certain changes in the management of the firm. They would not otherwise have shown such interest every time I blew my nose or relieved my huskiness by a slight cough; they would not have been so intimate with that surgeon from St. Bartholomew's, who dined with them thrice at the Albion; nor would they have gone to work directly that my back was turned, and have done those very things which they could not have done had I remained at home. Be that as it may, I was frightened and went to Cairo, and while there I made a trip to Suez for a week.

I was not happy at Cairo, for I knew nobody there, and the people at the hotel were, as I thought, uncivil. It seemed to me as though I were allowed to go in and out merely by sufferance; and yet I paid my bill regularly every week. The house was full of company, but the company was made up of parties of two and threes, and they all seemed to have their own friends. I did make attempts to overcome that terrible British exclusiveness — that *noli me tangere*[1] with which an Englishman arms himself, and in which he thinks it necessary to envelop his wife; but it was in vain; and I found myself sitting down to breakfast and dinner, day after day, as much alone as I should do if I called for a chop at a separate table in the Cathedral Coffee-house. And yet, at breakfast and at dinner, I made one of an assemblage of thirty or forty people. That I thought dull.

But as I stood one morning on the steps before the hotel, bethinking myself that my throat was as well as ever I remembered it to be, I was suddenly slapped on the back. Never in my life did I feel a more pleasant sensation, or turn round with more unaffected delight to return a friend's greeting. It was as though a cup of water had been handed to me in the

---

1 (Latin) "touch me not," Christ's words to Mary Magdalene after the Resurrection (John 20: 11-17).

desert. I knew that a cargo of passengers for Australia had reached Cairo that morning, and were to be passed on to Suez as soon as the railway would take them, and did not, therefore, expect that the greeting had come from any sojourner in Egypt. I should, perhaps, have explained that the even tenour of our life at the hotel was disturbed, some four times a month, by a flight through Cairo of a flock of travellers, who, like locusts, eat up all that there was eatable at the inn for the day. They sat down at the same tables with us, never mixing with us, having their own separate interests and hopes, and being often, as I thought, somewhat loud and almost selfish in their expression of them. These flocks consisted of passengers passing and repassing by the overland route to and from India and Australia; and had I nothing else to tell, I should delight to describe all that I watched of their habits and manners — the outwardbound being so different in their traits from their brethren on their return. But I have to tell of my own triumph at Suez, and must, therefore, hasten on to say, that on turning round quickly with my outstretched hand, I found it clasped by John Robinson.

"Well, Robinson, is this you?"

"Halloo, Walker, what are you doing here?"

That, of course, was the style of greeting. Elsewhere I should not have cared much to meet John Robinson, for he was a man who had never done well in the world; he had been in business, and connected with a fairly good house[1] in Size-lane; but he had married early, and things had not exactly gone well with him. I don't think the house broke — but he did; and so he was driven to take himself and five children off to Australia. Elsewhere I should not have cared to come across him; but I was positively glad to be slapped on the back by anybody on that landing-place in front of Shepheard's hotel at Cairo.

I soon learned that Robinson, with his wife and children, and, indeed, with all the rest of the Australian cargo, was to be passed on to Suez that afternoon; and after a while I agreed to accompany the party. I had made up my mind, on coming out from England, that I would see all the wonders of Egypt, and hitherto I had seen nothing. I did ride, on one day, some fifteen miles on a donkey to see the petrified forest; but the guide, who called himself a dragoman,[2] took me wrong or cheated me in some way. We rode on, half the day, over a stony, sandy plain, seeing nothing, with a terrible wind that filled my mouth with hot grit; and at last the drago-

---

1   Business establishment.

2   Guide and interpreter in countries where Arabic, Turkish, or Persian is spoken.

man got off. "Dere ," said he, picking up a small bit of stone, "dis is de forest made of stone. Carry dat home." Then we turned around and rode back to Cairo. My chief observation, as to the country, was this — that whichever way we went, the wind blew right into our teeth. The day's work cost me five-and-twenty shillings; and since that, I had not as yet made any other expedition. I was, therefore, glad of an opportunity of going to Suez, and of making the journey in company with an acquaintance.

At that time the railway was open, as far as I remember, nearly half the way from Cairo to Suez. It did not run four or five times a day as railways do in other countries, but four or five times a month. In fact it only carried passengers, on the arrival of these flocks camping between England and her Eastern possessions. There were trains passing backwards and forwards constantly, as I perceived in walking to and from the station, but, as I learned, they carried nothing but the labourers working on the line, and the water sent into the desert for their use. It struck me forcibly at the time that I should not have liked to have money in that investment.

Well, I went with Robinson to Suez. The journey, like everything else in Egypt, was sandy, hot, and unpleasant. The railway carriages were pretty fair, and we had room enough, but even in them the dust was a great nuisance. We travelled about ten miles an hour, and stopped about half an hour at every ten miles. This was tedious, but we had cigars with us and a trifle of brandy-and-water, and in this manner the railway journey wore itself away. In the middle of the night, however, we were moved from the railway carriages into omnibuses, as they were called, and then I was not comfortable. These omnibuses were wooden boxes, placed each upon a pair of wheels, and supposed to be capable of carrying six passengers. I was thrust into one with Robinson, his wife, and five children, and immediately began to repent of my good nature in accompanying them. To each vehicle were attached four horses or mules, and I must acknowledge, that as on the railway they went as slow as possible, so now in these conveyances dragged through the sand, they went as fast as the beasts could be made to gallop. I remember the Fox Tally-ho coach on the Birmingham road, when Boyce drove it, but, as regards pace, the Fox Tally-ho was nothing to these machines in Egypt. On the first going off I was jolted right on to Mrs. R. and her infant; and for a long time that lady thought that the child had been squeezed out of its proper shape; but at last we arrived at Suez and the baby seemed to me to be all right when it was handed down into the boat at the quay.

The Robinsons were allowed time to breakfast at that cavernous hotel — which looked to me like a scheme to save the expense of the passengers' meal on board the ship — and then they were off. I shook hands with him heartily as I parted with him at the quay, and wished him well through all his troubles. A man who takes a wife and five young children out into a colony, and that with his pockets but indifferently lined, certainly has his troubles before him. So he has at home, no doubt, but, judging for myself, I should always prefer sticking to the old ship as long as there is a bag of biscuits in the locker. Poor Robinson! I have never heard a word of him or his since that day, and sincerely trust that the baby was none the worse for the little accident in the box.

And now I had the prospect of a week before me at Suez, and the Robinsons had not been gone half an hour, before I began to feel that I should have been better off even at Cairo. I secured a bedroom at the hotel — I might have secured sixty bedrooms had I wanted them — and then went out and stood at the front door, or gate. It is a huge house, built round a quadrangle, looking with one front towards the head of the Red Sea, and with the other into an arid, or a sandy, dead-looking open square. There I stood for ten minutes, and, finding that it was too hot to go forth, returned to the long cavernous room in which we had all breakfasted. In that long cavernous room I was destined to eat all my meals alone for the next six days. Now, at Cairo, I could at any rate see my fellow creatures at their food. So I lit a cigar, and began to wonder whether I could survive the week. It was now clear to me that I had done a very rash thing in coming to Suez with the Robinsons.

Somebody about the place had asked me my name, and I had told it plainly — George Walker. I never was ashamed of my name yet, and never had cause to be. I believe at this day it will go as far in Friday-street as any other. A man may be popular, or he may not. That depends mostly on circumstances, which are in themselves trifling. But the value of his name depends on the way in which he is known at his bank. I have never dealt in tea-spoons or gravy-spoons,[1] but my name will go, I believe, as far as another man's. "George Walker," I answered, therefore, in a tone of some little authority, to the man who asked me, and who sat inside the gate of the hotel in an old dressing-gown and slippers.

That was a melancholy day with me, and twenty times before dinner did I wish myself back at Cairo. I had been travelling all night, and therefore hoped that I might get through some time in sleeping, but the mosquitoes attacked me the moment I had laid myself down. In other places mosquitoes torment you only at night, but at Suez they buzz around you

---

1   Been extremely exact.

without ceasing at all hours. A scorching sun was blazing overhead, and absolutely forbade me to leave the house. I stood for a while in the verandah, looking down at the few small vessels which were moored to the quay, but there was no life in them; not a sail was set, not a boatman or sailor was to be seen, and the very water looked as though it were hot. I could fancy that the glare of the sun was cracking the paint on the gunwales of the boats. I was the only visitor in the house, and during all the long hours of the morning it seemed as though the servants had deserted it.

I dined at four; not that I chose that hour, but because no choice was given to me. At the hotels in Egypt, one has to dine at an hour fixed by the landlord, and no entreaties will suffice to obtain a meal at any other. So at four I dined, and after dinner was again reduced to despair.

I was sitting in the cavernous chamber, almost mad at the prospect of the week before me, when I heard a noise as of various feet in the passage leading from the quadrangle. Was it possible that other human beings were coming into the hotel — Christian human beings at whom I could look, whose voices I could hear, whose words I could understand, and with whom I might possibly associate? I did not move, however, for I was still hot, and I knew that my chances might be better if I did not show myself over eager for companionship at the first moment. The door, however, was soon opened, and I saw that at least in one respect, I was destined to be disappointed. The strangers who were entering the room were not Christians, if I might judge by the nature of the garments in which they were clothed.

The door had been opened by the man in an old dressing-gown and slippers, whom I had seen sitting inside the gate. He was the Arab porter of the hotel, and as he marshalled the new visitors into the room, I heard him pronounce some sound similar to my own name, and perceived that he pointed me out to the most prominent person of those who then entered the apartment. This was a stout portly man, dressed from head to foot in Eastern costume of the brightest colours. He wore, not only the red fez cap which everybody wears — even I myself had accustomed myself to a fez cap — but a turban round it, of which the voluminous folds were snowy white. His face was fat, but not the less grave, and the lower part of it was enveloped in a magnificent beard which projected round it on all sides, and touched his breast as he walked. It was a grand grizzled beard, and I acknowledged at a moment that it added a singular dignity to the appearance of the stranger. His flowing robe was of bright colours, and the under garment, which fitted close round his breast and then descended, becoming beneath his sash a pair of the loosest pantaloons — I might perhaps better describe them as bags– of a rich tawny silk. These loose pantaloons were tied close round his leg above the ankle, and over a pair of scrupulously white stockings, and on his feet he wore a pair of yellow slippers. It was manifest to me at a glance that the Arab gentleman was got up in his best raiment, and that no expense had been spared on the suit.

And here I cannot but make a remark on the personal bearing of these Arabs. Whether they be Arabs, or Turks, or Copts,[1] it is always the same. They are a mean, false, cowardly race, I believe. They will bear blows, and respect the man who gives them. Fear goes farther with them than love, and between man and man they understand nothing of forebearance. He who does not exact from them all that he can exact is simply a fool in their estimation, to the extent of that which he loses. In all this they are immeasurably inferior to us, who have Christian teaching. But in one thing they beat us — they always know how to maintain their personal dignity.

Look at my friend and partner Judkins, as he stands with his hands in his trousers pockets at the door of our house in Friday-street. What can be meaner than his appearance? He is a stumpy, short, podgy man; but then so also was my Arab friend at Suez. Judkins is always dressed from head to foot in a decent black cloth suit; his coat is ever a dress coat, and is neither old nor shabby. On his head he carries a shining new silk hat, such as fashion in our metropolis demands. Judkins is rather a dandy than otherwise, piquing himself somewhat on his apparel. And yet how mean is his appearance as compared with the appearance of that Arab! how mean also is his gait, how ignoble his step! Judkins could buy that Arab out five times over and hardly feel the loss; and yet, were they to enter a room together, Judkins would know and acknowledge by his look that he was the inferior personage. Not the less, should a personal quarrel arise between them, would Judkins punch the Arab's head; ay, and reduce him to utter ignominy at his feet. Judkins would break his heart in despair rather than not return a blow, whereas the Arab would put up with any indignity of that sort. Nevertheless, Judkins is altogether deficient in personal dignity. I often thought, as the hours hung heavy on my hands in Egypt, whether it might not be practicable to introduce an Oriental costume into Friday-street.

At this moment, as the Arab gentleman entered the cavernous coffee-room, I felt that I was greatly the inferior personage. He was followed by four or five others dressed somewhat as himself — though by no means

---

1   Descendents of the ancient Egyptians who converted to Christianity in the first century.

in such magnificent colours — and by one gentleman in a coat and trousers. The gentleman in the coat and trousers came last, and I could see that he was one of the least of the number. As for myself I felt almost overawed by the dignity of the stout party in the turban, and seeing that he came directly across the room to the place where I was seated, I got up on my legs, and made to him some sign of Christian obeisance. I am a little man, and not podgy as is Judkins, and I flatter myself that I showed more deportment at any rare than he would have exhibited.

I made, as I have said, some Christian obeisance — I bobbed my head, that is, rubbing my hands together the while, and expressed an opinion that it was a fine day. But if I was civil, as I hope I was, the Arab was much more so. He advanced till he was about six paces from me, then placed his right hand open upon his silken breast, and, inclining forward with his whole body, made to me a bow which Judkins never could accomplish. The turban and flowing robe might be passable in Friday-street, but of what avail would be the outer garments and mere symbols, if the inner sentiment of personal dignity were wanting? I have often since tried it when alone, but I could never accomplish anything like that bow. The Arab with the flowing robe bowed, and then the other Arabs all bowed also; and after that the Christian gentleman with the coat and trousers made a leg.[1] I made a leg also, rubbed my hands again, and added to my former remarks that it was rather hot.

"Dat berry true," said the porter in the dirty dressing-gown, who stood by. I could see at a glance that the manner of that porter towards me was greatly altered, and I began to feel comforted in my wretchedness. Perhaps a Christian from Friday-street, with plenty of money in his pockets, would stand in higher esteem at Suez than at Cairo. If so, that alone would go far to atone for the apparent wretchedness of the place. At Cairo I had not received that attention which had certainly been due to me as the second partner in the flourishing Manchester house of Grimes, Walker, and Judkins.

But now, as my friend with the beard again bowed to me, I felt that this deficiency was to be made up. It was clear, however, that this new acquaintance, though I liked the manner of it, would be attended with considerable inconvenience, for the Arab gentleman commenced an address to me in French. It has always been to me a source of sorrow that my parents did not teach me the French language; and the deficiency on my part has given rise to an incredible amount of supercilious overbearing pre-

---

1   Made a bow by drawing back one leg and bending the other.

tension on the part of Judkins, who, after all, can hardly do more than translate a correspondent's letter. I do not believe that he could have understood a word of that Arab's oration; but, at any rate, I did not. He went on to the end, however, speaking for some three or four minutes, and then again he bowed. If I could only have learned that bow, I might still have been greater than Judkins, with all his French.

"I am very sorry," said I, "but I don't exactly follow the French language — when it is spoken."

"Ah! no French!" said the Arab, in very broken English; "dat is one sorrow." How is it that these fellows learn all languages under the sun? I afterwards found that this man could talk Italian, and Turkish, and Armenian fluently, and say a few words in German, as he could also in English. I could not ask for my dinner in any other language than English, if it were to save me from starvation. Then he called to the Christian gentleman in the pantaloons, and, as far as I could understand, made over to him the duty of interpreting between us. There seemed, however, one difficulty in the way of this being carried on with efficiency — the Christian gentleman could not speak English himself. He knew of it, perhaps, something more than did the Arab, but by no means enough to enable us to have a fluent conversation. And, indeed, had the interpreter — who turned out to be an Italian from Trieste, attached to the Austrian Consulate at Alexandria — had the interpreter spoken English with the greatest ease, I should have had considerable difficulty in understanding and digesting, in all its bearings, the splendid proposition that was made to me. But before I proceed to the proposition, I must describe a ceremony which took place previous to its discussion. I had hardly observed, when first the procession entered the room, that one of my friend's followers — my friend's name, as I learned afterwards, was Mahmoud al Ackbar, and I will therefore call him Mahmoud — that one of Mahmoud's followers bore in his arms a bundle of long sticks, and that another carried an iron pot and a tray. Such was the case; and now these followers came forward to perform their services, while I, having been literally pressed down on to the sofa by Mahmoud, watched them in their progress. Mahmoud also sat down, and not a word was spoken while the ceremony went on. The man with the sticks first placed on the ground two little pans, one at my feet, and then one at the feet of his master. After that he loosed an ornamental bag which he carried round his neck, and producing from it tobacco, proceeded to fill two pipes. This he did with the utmost gravity, and apparently with very peculiar ease. The pipes had been already fixed to one end of the sticks, and to the other end the man had fastened two large yellow balls. These, as I afterwards perceived, were mouthpieces made of amber. Then he lit the pipes, drawing up the difficult smoke by long painful suckings at the mouthpieces; and then, when the work had become apparently easy, he handed one pipe to me and the other to his master. The bowls he had first placed in the little pans on the ground.

During all this time no word was spoken and I was left altogether in the dark as to the cause which had produced this extraordinary courtesy. There was a stationary sofa — they called it there a divan — which was fixed into the corner of the room; and on one side of the angle sat Mahmoud al Ackbar, with his feet turned in under him, while I sat on the other. The remainder of the party stood around, and I felt so little master of the occasion that I did not know whether it would become me to bid them be seated. I was not the master of the entertainment — they were not my pipes; nor was it my coffee which I saw one of the followers preparing in a distant part of the room. And, indeed, I was much confused as to the management of the stick and amber mouthpiece with which I had been presented. With a cigar I am as much at home as any man in the City; I can nibble off the end of it, and smoke it to the last ash, when I am three parts asleep. But I had never before been invited to regale myself with such an instrument as this. What was I to do with that huge yellow ball? So I watched my friend closely.

It had manifestly been a part of his urbanity not to commence till I had done so, but seeing my difficulty, he at last raised the ball to his mouth and sucked it. I looked at him, and envied the gravity of his countenance and the dignity of his demeanour. I sucked also, but I made a sputtering noise, and must confess that I did not enjoy it. The smoke curled gracefully from his mouth and nostrils as he sat there in mute composure. I was mute also, as regarded speech, but I coughed as the smoke came from me in convulsive puffs. And then the attendant brought us coffee in little tin cups — black coffee, without sugar and full of grit, of which the berries had been only bruised and not ground. I took the cup and swallowed the mixture, for I could not refuse; but I wished that I might have asked for some milk and sugar. Nevertheless, there was something very pleasing in the whole ceremony, and at last I began to find myself more at home with my pipe.

When Mahmoud had exhausted his tobacco, and perceived that I also had ceased to puff forth smoke, he spoke in Italian to the interpreter, and the interpreter forthwith proceeded to explain to me the purport of their visit. This was done with much difficulty, for the interpreter's stock of English was very scanty; but after a while I understood, or thought that I understood, as follows: — At some previous period of my existence, I had done some deed which had given infinite satisfaction to Mahmoud al Ackbar. Whether, however, I had done it myself or whether my father had done it, was not quite clear to me. My father, then some time deceased, had been a wharfinger[1] at Liverpool, and it was quite possible that Mahmoud might have found himself at the port. Mahmoud had heard of my arrival in Egypt, and had been given to understand that I was coming to Suez, to carry myself away in the ship, as the interpreter phrased it. This I could not understand, but I let it pass. Having heard these agreeable tidings — and Mahmoud, sitting in the corner, bowed low to me as this was said — he had prepared for my acceptance a slight refection for the morrow, hoping that I would not carry myself away in the ship till this had been eaten. On this subject I soon made him quite at ease, and he then proceeded to explain that as there was no point of interest at Suez, Mahmoud was anxious that I should partake of the refection, somewhat in the guise of a picnic, at the well of Moses,[2] over in Asia, on the other side of the head of the Red Sea. Mahmoud would provide a boat to take across the party in the morning, and camels on which we would return after sunset; or else we would go and return on camels, or go on camels and return in the boat. Indeed, any arrangement could be made that I preferred. If I was afraid of the heat, and disliked the open boat, I could be carried round in a litter. The provisions had already been sent over to the well of Moses, in the anticipation that I would not refuse this little request.

I did not refuse it. Nothing could have been more agreeable to me than this plan of seeing something of the sights and wonders of this land, and of thus seeing them in good company. I had not heard of the well of Moses before; but now that I learned that it was in Asia, in another quarter of the globe — to be reached by a transit of the Red Sea — and be returned from by a journey on camels' backs, I burned with anxiety to visit its waters. What a story would this be for Judkins! This was, no doubt, the point at which the Israelites had passed; of these waters had they drunk. I almost felt that I had already found one of Pharaoh's chariot wheels.[3] I readily gave my assent, and then with much ceremony and many low salaams Mahmoud and his attendants left me. "I am very glad that I came to Suez," said I to myself.

---

1   Someone who owns or runs a wharf.

2   Where Moses made camp following the parting of the waters and miraculously brought forth water from the sands. A pilgrimage destination.

3   The Pharaoh's army of chariots drowned in the Red Sea while pursuing the Israelites as they fled Egypt. Finding a wheel would provide proof of the biblical story.

I did not sleep much that night, for the mosquitoes of Suez are very persevering; but I was saved from the agonising despair which these animals so frequently produce by my agreeable thoughts as to Mahmoud al Ackbar. I will put it to any of my readers who have travelled whether it is not a painful thing to find oneself regarded among strangers without any kindness or ceremonious courtesy. I had on this account been wretched at Cairo, but all this was to be made up to me at Suez. Nothing could be more pleasant than the whole conduct of Mahmoud al Ackbar, and I determined to take full advantage of it, not caring overmuch what might be the nature of those previous favours to which he had alluded. That was his affair, and if he was satisfied, why should not I be also?

On the following morning I was dressed at six, and looking out of my bed-room, I saw the boat in which we were to be wafted over into Asia, being brought up to the quay close under my window. It had been arranged that we should start early, so as to avoid the mid-day sun, breakfast in the boat — Mahmoud having in this way engaged to provide me with two refections — take our rest at noon in a pavilion which had been built close upon the well of the patriarch, then eat our dinner, and return, riding upon camels, in the cool of the evening. Nothing could sound more pleasant than such a plan, and knowing, as I did, that the hampers of provisions had already been sent over, I did not doubt that the table arrangements would be excellent. Even now, standing at my window, I could see a basket laden with long-necked bottles, going into the boat, and became aware that we should not depend altogether for our morning repasts on that gritty coffee which my friend Mahmoud's follower prepared.

I had promised to be ready at six, and having carefully completed my toilet, and put a clean collar and comb into my pocket, ready for dinner, I descended to the great gateway and walked slowly round to the quay. As I passed out the porter greeted me with a low obeisance, and walking on, I felt that I stepped the ground with a sort of dignity of which I had before been ignorant. It is not, as a rule, the man who gives grace and honour to the position, but the position which confers the grace and honour upon the man. I have often envied the solemn gravity and grand demeanour of the Lord Chancellor,[1] as I have seen him on the bench, but I doubt whether even Judkins would not look grave and dignified under such a wig. Mahmoud al Ackbar had called upon me and done me honour, and

---

1   Most powerful member of the legal profession in England, outranked only by the royal family and the archbishop of Canterbury.

I felt myself personally capable of sustaining, before the people of Suez, the honour which he had done me.

As I walked forth with a proud step from beneath the portal, I perceived, looking down from the square along the street, that there was already some commotion in the town. I saw the flowing robes of many Arabs, with their backs turned towards me, and I thought that I observed the identical gown and turban of my friend Mahmoud on the back and head of a stout, short man, who was hurrying round a corner in the distance. I felt sure that it was Mahmoud. Some of his servants must have failed in their preparations, I said to myself, as I made my way round to the water's edge. This was only another testimony how anxious he was to do me honour.

I stood for a while on the edge of the quay, looking into the boat, and admiring the comfortable cushions which were luxuriously arranged round the seats. The men who were at work did not know me, and I was unnoticed, but I should soon take my place upon the softest of those cushions. I walked slowly backwards and forwards on the quay, listening to a hum of voices that came to me from a distance. There was clearly something stirring in the town, and I felt certain that all the movement and all those distant voices were connected in some way with my expedition to the well of Moses. At last there came a lad upon the walk, dressed in Frank costume,[1] and I asked what was in the wind. He was a clerk, attached to an English warehouse, and he told me that there had been an arrival from Cairo. He knew no more than that, but he had heard that the omnibuses had just come in. Could it be possible that Mahmoud al Ackbar had heard of another old acquaintance, and had gone to welcome him also?

At first my ideas on the subject were altogether pleasant. I by no means wished to monopolise the delights of all those cushions, nor would it be to me a cause of sorrow that there should be someone to share with me the conversational powers of that interpreter. Should another guest be found, he might also be an Englishman, and I might thus form an acquaintance, which would be desirable. Thinking of these things, I walked on the quay for some minutes in a happy frame of mind; but by degrees I became impatient, and by degrees also disturbed in my spirit. I observed that one of the Arab boatmen walked round from the vessel to the front of the hotel, and that on his return he looked at me, as I thought, not with courteous eyes. Then also I saw, or rather heard someone in the verandah of the

---

1   French-styled clothing.

hotel above me, and was conscious that I was being viewed from thence. I walked and walked, and nobody came to me, and I perceived by my watch that it was seven o'clock. The noise, too, had come nearer and nearer, and I was now aware that wheels had been drawn up before the front door of the hotel, and that many voices were speaking there. It might be well that Mahmoud should wait for some other friend, but why did he not send someone to inform me? And then, as I made a sudden turn at the end of the quay, I caught sight of the retreating legs of the Austrian interpreter, and I became aware that he had been sent down, and had gone away, afraid to speak to me. "What can I do?" said I to myself; "I can but keep my ground." I own that I feared to go round to the front of the hotel; so I still walked slowly up and down the length of the quay, and began to whistle to show that I was not uneasy. The Arab sailors looked at me uncomfortably, and from time to time someone peered at me round the corner. It was now fully half-past seven, and the sun was becoming hot in the heavens. Why did we not hasten to place ourselves beneath the awning in the boat?

I had just made up my mind that I would go round to the front, and penetrate this mystery, when, on turning, I saw approaching to me a man dressed at any rate like an English gentleman. As he came near to me, he raised his hat, and accosted me in my own language.

"Mr. George Walker, I believe?" said he.

"Yes," said I, with some little attempt at a high demeanour; "of the firm of Grimes, Walker, and Judkins, Friday-street, London."

"A most respectable house, I am sure," said he; "I'm afraid there has been a little mistake here."

"No mistake as to the respectability of that house," said I. I felt that I was again alone in the world, and that it was necessary that I should support myself. Mahmoud al Ackbar had separated himself from me forever. Of that I had no longer a doubt.

"Oh, none at all," said he. "But about this little expedition over the water" — and he pointed contemptuously to the boat — "there has been a mistake about that. Mr. Walker, I happen to be the English Vice-Consul[1] here."

I took off my hat and bowed. It was the first time I had ever been addressed civilly by any British Consular authority.

"And they have made me get out of bed to come down and explain all this to you."

"All what?" said I.

---

1   Deputy sent by the Consul to a foreign nation to protect England's citizens and trade interests.

"You are a man of the world, I know, and I'll just tell it you plainly. My old friend Mahmoud al Ackbar has mistaken you for Sir George Walker, the new Lieutenant-Governor of Pegu.[1] Sir George Walker is now here; he has come this morning, and Mahmoud does not know how to get him into the boat, because he is ashamed to face you after what has occurred. If you won't object to withdraw with me into the hotel, I'll explain it all."

I felt as though a thunderbolt had fallen, and I must say that even up to this day I think that the Consul might have been a little less abrupt.

"We can get in here," said he, evidently in a hurry, and pointing to a small door which opened out from one corner of the house to the quay. What could I do but follow him? I did follow him, and in a few words learned the remainder of the story. When he had once withdrawn me from the public walk, he seemed but little anxious about the rest, and soon left me again alone. The facts, as far as I could learn them, were simply these:

Sir George Walker, who was now going out to Pegu as governor, had been in India in former years, commanding an army there. I had never heard of him, and had made no attempt to pass myself off as his relative. Nobody could have been more innocent than I was, or have received worse usage. I have as much right to the name as he has. Well; when he was in India before, he had taken the city of Begum after a terrible siege, — Begum, I think the Consul called it; and Mahmoud had been there, having been, as it seemed, a great man at Begum, and Sir George had spared him and his money. In this way the whole thing had come to pass. There was no further explanation than that. The rest of it was all transparent. Mahmoud, having heard my name from the porter, had hurried down to invite me to his party. So far, so good. But why had he been afraid to face me in the morning? And, seeing that the fault had all been his, why had he not asked me to join his expedition? Sir George and I may, after all, be cousins. But, coward as he was, he had been afraid of me. When they found that I was on the quay, they had not dared to face me. I wish that I had kept the quay all day, and faced them one by one as they entered the boat. But I was down in the mouth, and when the Consul left me I crept wearily back to my bedroom.

And the Consul did leave me almost immediately. A faint hope had at one time come upon me that he would have asked me to breakfast. Had he done so, I should have felt it as some compensation for what I had suffered. I am not an exacting man; but I own that I like civility. In Friday-street I can command it, and in Friday-street for the rest of my life will

1   British governor of southern Burma.

I remain. From this Consul I received no civility. As soon as he had got me out of the way, and spoken the few words which he had to say, he again raised his hat and left me; I also again raised mine, and then crept up to my bedroom.

From my window, standing a little behind the white curtain, I could see the whole embarcation. There was Mahmoud al Ackbar, looking, indeed, a little hot, but still going through his work with all that excellence of deportment which had graced him on the preceding evening. Had his foot slipped, and had he fallen backwards into that shallow water, my spirit would, I confess, have been relieved; but, on the contrary, everything went well with him. There was the real Sir George, my namesake, and, perhaps, my cousin, as fresh as paint, cool from the bath which he had been taking while I had been walking on that terrace. How is it that these governors and commanders-in-chief go through such heavy work without fagging?[1] It was not yet two hours since he was jolting about in that omnibus-box; and there he had been all night! I could not have gone off to the well of Moses immediately on my arrival. It's the dignity of the position that does it. I have long known that the head of a firm must never count on a mere clerk to get through as much work as he can do himself. It's the interest in the matter that supports the man.

There they went; and Sir George, as I was well assured, had never heard a word about me. Had he done so, is it not probable that he would have requested my attendance? But Mahmoud and his followers, no doubt, kept their own counsel as to that little mistake. There they went; and the gentle, rippling breeze filled their sail pleasantly as the boat moved away into the bay. I felt no spite against any of them but Mahmoud. Why had he avoided me with such cowardice? I could still see them when the morning tchibouk[2] was handed to Sir George; and though I wished him no harm, I did envy him, as he lay there reclining luxuriously upon the cushions.

A more wretched day than that I never spent in my life. As I went in and out the porter at the gate absolutely scoffed at me. Once I made up my mind to complain within the house; but what could I have said of the dirty Arab? They would have told me that it was his religion, or a national observance, or meant for a courtesy. What can a man do in a strange country, when he is told that a native spits in his face by way of civility? I bore it. I bore it — like a man; and sighed for the comforts of Friday-street.

---

1 Tiring.

2 Long Turkish tobacco-pipe.

As to one matter I made up my mind on that day, and I fully carried out my purpose on the next. I would go across to the well of Moses in a boat. I would visit the coasts of Asia, and I would ride back into Africa on a camel. Though I did it alone, I would have my day's pleasuring. I had money in my pocket, and though it might cost me twenty pounds, I would see all that my namesake had seen. It did cost me the best part of twenty pounds, and as for the pleasuring I can't say much for it.

I went to bed early that night, having concluded my bargain for the morrow with a rapacious Arab who spoke English. I went to bed early in order to escape the returning party, and was again on the quay at six the next morning. On this occasion I stept boldly into the boat the very moment that I came along the shore. It was my boat. There is nothing in the world like paying for what you use. I served myself to the bottle of brandy, and the cold meat, and acknowledged that a cigar out of my case would suit me better than that long stick. The long stick might do very well for a Governor of Pegu, but would be highly inconvenient in Friday-street. Well, I am not going to give an account of my day's journey here, though, perhaps, I may do so some day. I did go to the well of Moses, if a small dirty pool of salt water, lying high above the sands, can be called a well. I did eat my dinner in the miserable ruined cottage which they graced by the name of a pavilion; and, alas, for my poor bones, I did ride home upon a camel. If Sir George did so also, and started for Pegu early the next morning — and I was informed that such was the fact — he must indeed have been made of iron. I lay in bed the whole day, suffering grievously; but I was told that on such a journey I should have slackened my thirst with oranges, and not with brandy.

I survived those four terrible days which remained to me at Suez, and after another month was once again in Friday-street. I suffered greatly on the occasion; but it is some consolation to me to reflect that I did smoke a pipe with Mahmoud al Ackbar; that I saw the hero of Begum, while journeying out to new triumphs at Pegu; that I sailed into Asia in my own yacht — hired for the occasion; and that I rode back into Africa on a camel. Nor can Judkins, with all his ill-nature, rob me of those remembrances.

Mary Elizabeth Braddon

"Eveline's Visitant" (1862)

[Mary Elizabeth Braddon (1837–1915) is best known as the author of sensation novels. She turned to writing for the money, after spending three years supporting herself and her mother as an actress. She also worked as the editor of *Belgravia*, *Temple Bar*, and other magazines. In 1874 she married the publisher John Maxwell, who had been giving her moral support for many years. "Eveline's Visitant" was published in the same year as her hugely successful sensation novel *Lady Audley's Secret* (1862) and, like the novel, it reveals the descriptive style, romantic notions of love, and sinister narrative that made Braddon's work so popular. These same traits lead critics such as Margaret Oliphant to question the author's morality.]

It was at a masked ball at the Palais Royal that my fatal quarrel with my first cousin André de Brissac began. The quarrel was about a woman. The women who followed the footsteps of Philip of Orleans[1] were the causes of many such disputes; and there was scarcely one fair head in all that glittering throng which, to a man versed in social histories and mysteries, might not have seemed bedabbled with blood.

I shall not record the name of her for love of whom André de Brissac and I crossed one of the bridges, in the dim August dawn on our way to the waste ground beyond the church of Saint-Germain des Prés.

There were many beautiful vipers in those days, and she was one of them. I can feel the chill breath of that August morning blowing in my face, as I sit in my dismal chamber at my château of Puy Verdun to-night, alone in the stillness, writing the strange story of my life. I can see the white mist rising from the river, the grim outline of the Châtelet, and the square towers of Notre Dame[2] black against the pale-grey sky. Even

---

1   Ruler of France as regent from 1715 to 1723, at which point Louis XV was old enough to take the throne as king.

2   Notre Dame cathedral, major landmark in Paris, built from 1163 to approximately 1345.

more vividly can I recall André's fair young face, as he stood opposite to me with his two friends — scoundrels both, and alike eager for that unnatural fray. We were a strange group to be seen in a summer sunrise, all of us fresh from the heat and clamour of the Regent's saloons — André in a quaint hunting-dress copied from a family portrait at Puy Verdun, I costumed as one of Law's Mississippi Indians;[1] the other men in like garish frippery, adorned with broideries and jewels that looked wan in the pale light of dawn.

Our quarrel had been a fierce one — a quarrel which could have but one result, and that the direst. I had struck him; and the welt raised by my open hand was crimson upon his fair womanish face as he stood opposite to me. The eastern sun shone on the face presently, and dyed the cruel mark with a deeper red; but the sting of my own wrongs was fresh, and I had not yet learned to despise myself for that brutal outrage.

To André de Brissac such an insult was most terrible. He was the favourite of Fortune, the favourite of women; and I was nothing, — a rough soldier who had done my country good service, but in the boudoir of a Parabère[2] a mannerless boor.

We fought, and I wounded him mortally. Life had been very sweet for him; and I think that a frenzy of despair took possession of him when he felt the life-blood ebbing away. He beckoned me to him as he lay on the ground. I went, and knelt at his side.

"Forgive me, André!" I murmured.

He took no more heed of my words than if that piteous entreaty had been the idle ripple of the river near at hand.

"Listen to me, Hector de Brissac," he said. "I am not one who believes that a man has done with earth because his eyes glaze and his jaw stiffens. They will bury me in the old vault at Puy Verdun; and you will be master of the château. Ah, I know how lightly they take things in these days, and how Dubois will laugh when he hears that *Ça* has been killed in a duel. They will bury me, and sing masses for my soul; but you and I have not finished our affair yet, my cousin. I will be with you when you least look to see me, — I, with this ugly scar upon the face that women have praised and loved. I will come to you when your life seems brightest. I will come between you and all that you hold fairest and dearest. My ghostly hand shall

---

1 John Law (see note 5 on page 208) assisted the Duke of Orleans to form the West India Company, which gave the French king sovereignty over the Mississippi valley.

2 Euphemism for a beautiful and licentious woman; the reference is to Marie-Madeleine de Vieuville, countess of Parabère, a mistress of Philip of Orleans.

drop a poison in your cup of joy. My shadowy form shall shut the sunlight from your life. Men with such iron will as mine can do what they please, Hector de Brissac. It is my will to haunt you when I am dead."

All this in short broken sentences he whispered into my ear. I had need to bend my ear close to his dying lips; but the iron will of André de Brissac was strong enough to do battle with Death, and I believe he said all he wished to say before his head fell back upon the velvet cloak they had spread beneath him, never to be lifted again.

As he lay there, you would have fancied him a fragile stripling, too fair and frail for the struggle called life; but there are those who remember the brief manhood of André de Brissac, and who can bear witness to the terrible force of that proud nature.

I stood looking down at the young face with that foul mark upon it, and God knows I was sorry for what I had done.

Of those blasphemous threats which he had whispered in my ear I took no heed. I was a soldier, and a believer. There was nothing absolutely dreadful to me in the thought that I had killed this man. I had killed many men on the battlefield; and this one had done me cruel wrong.

My friends would have had me cross the frontier to escape the consequences of my act; but I was ready to face those consequences, and I remained in France. I kept aloof from the court, and received a hint that I had best confine myself to my own province. Many masses were chanted in the little chapel of Puy Verdun, for the soul of my dead cousin, and his coffin filled a niche in the vault of our ancestors.

His death had made me a rich man; and the thought that it was so made my newly-acquired wealth very hateful to me. I lived a lonely existence in the old château, where I rarely held converse with any but the servants of the household, all of whom had served my cousin, and none of whom liked me.

It was a hard and bitter life. It galled me, when I rode through the village, to see the peasant-children shrink away from me. I have seen old women cross themselves stealthily as I passed them by. Strange reports had gone forth about me; and there were those who whispered that I had given my soul to the Evil One as the price of my cousin's heritage. From my boyhood I had been dark of visage and stern of manner; and hence, perhaps, no woman's love had ever been mine. I remembered my mother's face in all its changes of expression; but I can remember no look of affection that ever shone on me. That other woman, beneath whose feet I laid my heart, was pleased to accept my homage, but she never loved me; and the end was treachery.

I had grown hateful to myself, and had well-nigh begun to hate my fellow-creatures, when a feverish desire seized upon me, and I pined to be back in the press and throng of the busy world once again. I went back to Paris, where I kept myself aloof from the court, and where an angel took compassion upon me.

She was the daughter of an old comrade, a man whose merits had been neglected, whose achievements had been ignored, and who sulked in his shabby lodging like a rat in a hole, while all Paris went mad with the Scotch Financier,[1] and gentlemen and lacqueys were trampling one another to death in the Rue Quincampoix. The only child of this little cross-grained old captain of dragoons was an incarnate sunbeam, whose mortal name was Eveline Duchalet.

She loved me. The richest blessings of our lives are often those which cost us least. I wasted the best years of my youth in the worship of a wicked woman, who jilted and cheated me at last.

I gave this meek angel but a few courteous words — a little fraternal tenderness — and lo, she loved me. The life which had been so dark and desolate grew bright beneath her influence; and I went back to Puy Verdun with a fair young bride for my companion.

Ah, how sweet a change there was in my life and in my home! The village children no longer shrank appalled as the dark horseman rode by, the village crones no longer crossed themselves; for a woman rode by his side — a woman whose charities had won the love of all those ignorant creatures, and whose companionship had transformed the gloomy lord of the château into a loving husband and a gentle master. The old retainers forgot the untimely fate of my cousin, and served me with cordial willingness, for love of their young mistress.

There are no words which can tell the pure and perfect happiness of that time. I felt like a traveller who had traversed the frozen seas of an arctic region, remote from human love or human companionship, to find himself on a sudden in the bosom of a verdant valley, in the sweet atmosphere of home. The change seemed too bright to be real; and I strove in vain to put away from my mind the vague suspicion that my new life was but some fantastic dream.

So brief were those halcyon hours, that, looking back on them now, it is scarcely strange if I am still half inclined to fancy the first days of my married life could have been no more than a dream.

---

1   John Law (1671–1729), a Scot who helped the French Duke of Orleans out of bankruptcy and established a bank dealing in paper currency whose success resulted in sky-rocketing inflation followed by the bank's collapse in 1720.

Neither in my days of gloom nor in my days of happiness had I been troubled by the recollection of André's blasphemous oath.

The words which with his last breath he had whispered in my ear were vain and meaningless to me. He had vented his rage in those idle threats, as he might have vented it in idle execrations.

That he will haunt the footsteps of his enemy after death is the one revenge which a dying man can promise himself; and if men had power thus to avenge themselves, the earth would be peopled with phantoms.

I had lived for three years at Puy Verdun; sitting alone in the solemn midnight by the hearth where he had sat, pacing the corridors that had echoed his footfall; and in all that time my fancy had never so played me false as to shape the shadow of the dead. Is it strange, then, if I had forgotten André's horrible promise? There was no portrait of my cousin at Puy Verdun. It was the age of boudoir art, and a miniature set in the lid of a gold bonbonnière, or hidden artfully in a massive bracelet, was more fashionable than a clumsy life-size image, fit only to hang on the gloomy walls of a provincial chateau rarely visited by its owner. My cousin's fair face had adorned more than one bonbonnière, and had been concealed in more than one bracelet; but it was not among the faces that looked down from the panelled walls of Puy Verdun.

In the library I found a picture which awoke painful associations. It was the portrait of a de Brissac, who had flourished in the time of Francis the First;[1] and it was from this picture that my cousin André had copied the quaint hunting-dress he wore at the Regent's ball. The library was a room in which I spent a good deal of my life; and I ordered a curtain to be hung before this picture.

We had been married three months, when Eveline one day asked, "Who is the lord of the château nearest to this?"

I looked with her in astonishment.

"My dearest," I answered, "do you not know that there is no other château within forty miles of Puy Verdun?"

"Indeed!" she said; "that is strange."

I asked her why the fact seemed strange to her; and after much entreaty I obtained from her the reason of her surprise.

In her walks about the park and woods during the last month, she had met a man who, by his dress and bearing, was obviously of noble rank. She had imagined that he occupied some château near at hand, and that his estate adjoined ours. I was at a loss to imagine who this stranger could be;

---

1   Probably Francis I (1494–1547), King of France from 1515–47.

for my estate of Puy Verdun lay in the heart of a desolate region, and unless when some traveller's coach went lumbering and jingling through the village, one had little more chance of encountering a gentleman than of meeting a demigod.

"Have you seen this man often, Eveline?" I asked.

She answered, in a tone which had a touch of sadness, "I see him every day."

"Where, dearest?"

"Sometimes in the park, sometimes in the wood. You know the little cascade, Hector, where there is some old neglected rock-work that forms a kind of cavern. I have taken a fancy to that spot, and have spent many mornings there reading. Of late I have seen the stranger there every morning."

"He has never dared to address you?"

"Never. I have looked up from my book, and have seen him standing at a little distance, watching me silently. I have continued reading; and when I have raised my eyes again I have found him gone. He must approach and depart with a stealthy tread, for I never hear his footfall.

Sometimes I have almost wished that he would speak to me. It is so terrible to see him standing silently there."

"He is some insolent peasant who seeks to frighten you."

My wife shook her head.

"He is no peasant," she answered. "It is not by his dress alone I judge, for that is strange to me.

He has an air of nobility which it is impossible to mistake."

"Is he young or old?"

"He is young and handsome."

I was much disturbed by the idea of this stranger's intrusion on my wife's solitude; and I went straight to the village to inquire if any stranger had been seen there. I could hear of no one. I questioned the servants closely, but without result. Then I determined to accompany my wife in her walks, and to judge for myself of the rank of the stranger.

For a week I devoted all my mornings to rustic rambles with Eveline in the park and woods; and in all that week we saw no one but an occasional peasant in sabots, or one of our own house-hold returning from a neighbouring farm.

I was a man of studious habits, and those summer rambles disturbed the even current of my life. My wife perceived this, and entreated me to trouble myself no further.

"I will spend my mornings in the pleasaunce,[1] Hector," she said; "the stranger cannot intrude upon me there."

"I begin to think the stranger is only a phantasm of your own romantic brain," I replied, smiling at the earnest face lifted to mine. "A châtelaine[2] who is always reading romances may well meet handsome cavaliers in the woodlands. I daresay I have Mdlle. Scuderi[3] to thank for this noble stranger, and that he is only the great Cyrus[4] in modern costume."

"Ah, that is the point which mystifies me, Hector," she said. "The stranger's costume is not modern. He looks as an old picture might look if it could descend from its frame."

Her words pained me, for they reminded me of that hidden picture in the library, and the quaint hunting costume of orange and purple, which André de Brissac wore at the Regent's ball.

After this my wife confined her walks to the pleasaunce; and for many weeks I heard no more of the nameless stranger. I dismissed all thought of him from my mind, for a graver and heavier care had come upon me. My wife's health began to droop. The change in her was so gradual as to be almost imperceptible to those who watched her day by day. It was only when she put on a rich gala dress which she had not worn for months that I saw how wasted the form must be on which the embroidered bodice hung so loosely, and how wan and dim were the eyes which had once been brilliant as the jewels she wore in her hair.

I sent a messenger to Paris to summon one of the court physicians; but I knew that many days must needs elapse before he could arrive at Puy Verdun.

In the interval I watched my wife with unutterable fear.

It was not her health only that had declined. The change was more painful to behold than any physical alteration. The bright and sunny spirit had vanished, and in the place of my joyous young bride I beheld a woman weighed down by rooted melancholy. In vain I sought to fathom the cause of my darling's sadness. She assured me that she had no reason for sorrow or discontent, and that if she seemed sad without a motive, I must forgive her sadness, and consider it as a misfortune rather than a fault.

I told her that the court physician would speedily find some cure for her despondency, which must needs arise from physical causes, since she

---

1   Pleasure-ground; park-like enclosure.

2   Mistress of an estate or large house.

3   Madeleine de Scudéry (1607–91), French author of heroic romances.

4   First Achaemenian Emperor of Persia who, according to the bible, was raised as a shepherd.

had no real ground for sorrow. But although she said nothing, I could see she had no hope or belief in the healing powers of medicine.

One day, when I wished to beguile her from that pensive silence in which she was wont to sit an hour at a time, I told her, laughing, that she appeared to have forgotten her mysterious cavalier of the wood, and it seemed also as if he had forgotten her.

To my wonderment, her pale face became of a sudden crimson; and from crimson changed to pale again in a breath.

"You have never seen him since you deserted your woodland grotto?" I said.

She turned to me with a heart-rending look.

"Hector," she cried," I see him every day; and it is that which is killing me."

She burst into a passion of tears when she had said this. I took her in my arms as if she had been a frightened child, and tried to comfort her.

"My darling, this is madness," I said. "You know that no stranger can come to you in the pleasaunce. The moat is ten feet wide and always full of water, and the gates are kept locked day and night by old Massou. The châtelaine of a mediæval fortress need fear no intruder in her antique garden."

My wife shook her head sadly.

"I see him every day," she said.

On this I believed that my wife was mad. I shrank from questioning her more closely concerning her mysterious visitant. It would be ill, I thought, to give a form and substance to the shadow that tormented her by too close inquiry about its look and manner, its coming and going.

I took care to assure myself that no stranger to the household could by any possibility penetrate to the pleasaunce. Having done this, I was fain to await the coming of the physician.

He came at last. I revealed to him the conviction which was my misery. I told him that I believed my wife to be mad. He saw her — spent an hour alone with her, and then came to me. To my unspeakable relief he assured me of her sanity.

"It is just possible that she may be affected by one delusion," he said; "but she is so reasonable upon all other points, that I can scarcely bring myself to believe her the subject of a monomania.

I am rather inclined to think that she really sees the person of whom she speaks. She described him to me with a perfect minuteness. The descriptions of scenes or individuals given by patients afflicted with monomania are always more or less disjointed; but your wife spoke to me as clearly and calmly as I am now speaking to you. Are you sure there is no one who can approach her in that garden where she walks?"

"I am quite sure."

"Is there any kinsman of your steward, or hanger-on of your household, — a young man with a fair womanish face, very pale and rendered remarkable by a crimson scar, which looks like the mark of a blow?"

"My God!" I cried, as the light broke in upon me all at once. "And the dress — the strange old-fashioned dress?"

"The man wears a hunting costume of purple and orange," answered the doctor.

I knew then that André de Brissac had kept his word, and that in the hour when my life was brightest his shadow had come between me and happiness.

I showed my wife the picture in the library, for I would fain assure myself that there was some error in my fancy about my cousin. She shook like a leaf when she beheld it, and clung to me convulsively.

"This is witchcraft, Hector," she said. "The dress in that picture is the dress of the man I see in the pleasaunce; but the face is not his."

Then she described to me the face of the stranger; and it was my cousin's face line for line — André de Brissac, whom she had never seen in the flesh. Most vividly of all did she describe the cruel mark upon his face, the trace of a fierce blow from an open hand.

After this I carried my wife away from Puy Verdun. We wandered far — through the southern provinces, and into the very heart of Switzerland. I thought to distance the ghastly phantom, and I fondly hoped that change of scene would bring peace to my wife.

It was not so. Go where we would, the ghost of André de Brissac followed us. To my eyes that fatal shadow never revealed itself. That would have been too poor a vengeance. It was my wife's innocent heart which André made the instrument of his revenge. The unholy presence destroyed her life. My constant companionship could not shield her from the horrible intruder. In vain did I watch her; in vain did I strive to comfort her.

"He will not let me be at peace," she said; "he comes between us, Hector. He is standing between us now. I can see his face with the red mark upon it plainer that I see yours."

One fair moonlight night, when we were together in a mountain village in the Tyrol, my wife cast herself at my feet, and told me she was the worst and vilest of women. "I have confessed all to my director," she said; "from the first I have not hidden my sin from Heaven. But I feel that death is near me; and before I die I would fain reveal my sin to you."

"What sin, my sweet one?"

"When first the stranger came to me in the forest, his presence bewildered and distressed me, and I shrank from him as from something strange and terrible. He came again and again; by and by I found myself thinking of him, and watching for his coming. His image haunted me perpetually; I strove in vain to shut his face out of my mind. Then followed an interval in which I did not see him; and, to my shame and anguish, I found that life seemed dreary and desolate without him. After that came the time in which he haunted the pleasaunce; and — O, Hector, kill me if you will, for I deserve no mercy at your hands! — I grew in those days to count the hours that must elapse before his coming, to take no pleasure save in the sight of that pale face with the red brand upon it. He plucked all old familiar joys out of my heart, and left in it but one weird unholy pleasure — the delight of his presence. For a year I have lived but to see him. And now curse me, Hector; for this is my sin. Whether it comes of the baseness of my own heart, or is the work of witchcraft, I know not; but I know that I have striven against this wickedness in vain.

I took my wife to my breast, and forgave her. In sooth, what had I to forgive? Was the fatality that overshadowed us any work of hers? On the next night she died, with her hand in mine; and at the very last she told me, sobbing and affrighted, that he was by her side.

Algernon Swinburne

"Dead Love" (1862)

[It is said that Algernon Swinburne's (1837–1909) work displays the widest vocabulary among all English authors. With his elfish image and unruly mass of wavy red hair, he first began to gain notice at Eton and Oxford University where he learnt, among other things, the aesthetic views of the Pre-Raphaelites and the pleasures of flagellation. He is best known for poems such as "Atalanta in Calydon" (1865) and the collection *Poems and Ballads* (1866). His poetry received notoriety for depicting lesbianism, necrophilia, and other less common forms of desire. His prose output, although extensive, never attained equal attention, in part because — as "Dead Love" demonstrates — it demands to be read like poetry, savoured word for word. Some of the short pieces move toward the category of the prose poem, a newly developed genre that was receiving greater attention in France. Swinburne's style itself influenced a number of other writers, including Oscar Wilde.]

About the time of the great troubles in France, that fell out between the parties of Armagnac and of Burgundy, there was slain in a fight in Paris a follower of the Duke John, who was a good knight called Messire Jacques d'Aspremont. This Jacques was a very fair and strong man, hardy of his hands, and before he was slain he did many things wonderful and of great courage, and forty of the folk of the other party he slew, and many of these were great captains, of whom the chief and the worthiest was Messire Olivier de Bois-Percé; but at last he was shot in the neck with an arrow, so that between the nape and the apple the flesh was cleanly cloven in twain. And when he was dead his men drew forth his body of the fierce battle, and covered it with a fair woven cloak. Then the people of Armagnac, taking good heart because of his death, fell the more heavily upon his followers, and slew very many of them. And a certain soldier, named Amaury de Jacqueville, whom they called Courtebarbe, did best of all that party; for, crying out with a great noise, "Sus, sus!" he brought up the men after him, and threw them forward into the hot part of the fighting, where there was a sharp clamour; and this Amaury, laughing and crying out as a man that took a great delight in such matters of war, made of himself more noise with smiting and with shouting than any ten, and they of Burgundy were astonished and beaten down. And when he was weary, and his men had got the upper hand of those of Burgundy, he left off slaying, and beheld where Messire d'Aspremont was covered up with his cloak; and he lay just across the door of Messire Olivier, whom the said Jacques had slain, who was also a cousin of Amaury's. Then said Amaury:

"Take up now the body of this dead fellow, and carry it into the house; for my cousin Madame Yolande shall have great delight to behold the face of the fellow dead by whom her husband has got his end, and it shall make the tiding sweeter to her."

So they took up this dead knight Messire Jacques, and carried him into a fair chamber lighted with broad windows, and herein sat the wife of Olivier, who was called Yolande de Craon, and she was akin far off to Pierre de Craon, who would have slain the Constable. And Amaury said to her:

"Fair and dear cousin, and my good lady, we give you for your husband slain the body of him that slew my cousin; make the best cheer that you may, and comfort yourself that he has found a good death and a good friend to do justice on his slayer; for this man was a good knight, and I that have revenged him account myself none of the worst."

And with this Amaury and his people took leave of her. Then Yolande, being left alone, began at first to weep grievously, and so much that she was heavy and weary; and afterward she looked upon the face of Jacques d'Aspremont, and held one of his hands with hers, and said:

"Ah, false thief and coward! it is great pity thou wert not hung on a gallows, who hast slain by treachery the most noble knight of the world, and to me the most loving and the faithfulest man alive, and that never did any discourtesy to any man, and was the most single and pure lover that ever a married lady had to be her knight, and never said any word to me but sweet words. Ah, false coward! there was never such a knight of thy kin."

Then, considering his face earnestly, she saw that it was a fair face enough, and by seeming the face of a good knight; and she repented of her bitter words, saying with herself:

"Certainly this one, too, was a good man and valiant," and was sorry for his death.

And she pulled out the arrow-head that was broken, and closed up the wound of his neck with ointments. And then beholding his dead open eyes, she fell into a great torrent of weeping, so that her tears fell all over his face and throat. And all the time of this bitter sorrow she thought how goodly a man this Jacques must have been in his life, who being dead had such power upon her pity. And for compassion of his great beauty she wept so exceedingly and long that she fell down upon his body in a swoon, embracing him, and so lay the space of two hours with her face against his; and being awaked she had no other desire but only to behold him again, and so all that day neither ate nor slept at all, but for the most part lay and wept. And afterward, out of her love, she caused the body of this knight to be preserved with spice, and made him a golden coffin open at the top, and clothed him with the fairest clothes she could get, and had this coffin always by her bed in her chamber. And when this was done she sat down over against him and held his arms about her neck, weeping, and she said:

"Ah, Jacques! although alive I was not worthy, so that I never saw the beauty and goodness of your living body with my sorrowful eyes, yet now being dead, I thank God that I have this grace to behold you. Alas, Jacques! you have no sight now to discern what things are beautiful, therefore you may now love me as well as another, for with dead men there is no difference of women. But, truly, although I were the fairest of all Christian women that now is, I were in nowise worthy to love you; nevertheless, have compassion upon me that for your sake have forgotten the most noble husband of the world."

And this Yolande, that made such complaining of love to a dead man, was one of the fairest ladies of all that time, and of great reputation; and there were many good men that loved her greatly, and would fain have had some favour at her hands; of whom she made no account, saying always, that her dead lover was better than many lovers living. Then certain people said that she was bewitched; and one of these was Amaury. And they would have taken the body to burn it, that the charm might be brought to an end; for they said that a demon had entered in and taken it in possession; which she hearing fell into extreme rage, and said that if her lover were alive, there was not so good a knight among them, that he should undertake the charge of that saying; at which speech of hers there was great laughter. And upon a night there came into her house Amaury and certain others, that were minded to see this matter for themselves. And no man kept the doors; for all her people had gone away, saving only a damsel that remained with her; and the doors stood open, as in a house where there is no man. And they stood in the doorway of her chamber, and heard her say this that ensues: —

"O most fair and perfect knight, the best that ever was in any time of battle, or in any company of ladies, and the most courteous man, have pity upon me, most sorrowful woman and handmaid. For in your life you had some other lady to love you, and were to her a most true and good lover; but now you have none other but me only, and I am not worthy that you should so much as kiss me on my sad lips, wherein is all this lamentation. And though your own lady were the fairer and the more worthy, yet consider, for God's pity and mine, how she has forgotten the love of your body and the kindness of your espousals, and lives easily with some other man, and is wedded to him with all honour; but I have neither ease nor honour, and yet I am your true maiden and servant."

And then she embraced and kissed him many times. And Amaury was very wroth, but he refrained himself: and his friends were troubled and full of wonder. Then they beheld how she held his body between her arms, and kissed him in the neck with all her strength; and after a certain time it seemed to them that the body of Jacques moved and sat up; and she was no whit amazed, but rose up with him, embracing him. And Jacques said to her:

"I beseech you, now that you would make a covenant with me, to love me always."

And she bowed her head suddenly, and said nothing.

Then said Jacques:

"Seeing you have done so much for love of me, we twain shall never go in sunder: and for this reason has God given back to me the life of my mortal body."

And after this they had the greatest joy together, and the most perfect solace that may be imagined: and she sat and beheld him, and many times fell into a little quick laughter for her great pleasure and delight.

Then came Amaury suddenly into the chamber, and caught his sword into his hand, and said to her:

"Ah, wicked leman,[1] now at length is come the end of thy horrible love and of thy life at once;" and smote her through the two sides with his sword, so that she fell down, and with a great sigh full unwillingly delivered up her spirit, which was no sooner fled out of her perishing body, but immediately the soul departed also out of the body of her lover, and he became as one that had been all those days dead. And the next day the people caused their two bodies to be burned openly in the place where witches were used to be burned: and it is reported by some that an evil

---

1   Lover, or mistress.

spirit was seen to come out of the mouth of Jacques d'Aspremont, with a most pitiful cry, like the cry of a hurt beast. By which thing all men knew that the soul of this woman, for the folly of her sinful and most strange affection, was thus evidently given over to the delusion of the evil one and the pains of condemnation.

C.L. Dodgson [Lewis Carroll]

"Bruno's Revenge" (1867)

[C(harles) L(utwidge) Dodgson (pseud. Lewis Carroll; 1832–98) is the Victorian era's best known children's author. After his education at Oxford University, Dodgson taught mathematics there. He published scholarly books on algebra and logic, created board games intended to instruct children on the same, and became a skilled portrait photographer, specializing in photographs of girls such as Alice Liddell, the inspiration for the heroine of *Alice's Adventures in Wonderland* (1865). The story "Bruno's Revenge" — which he wrote in the same year as he began work on *Through the Looking Glass* — shows the author at the peak of his form and marks the beginning of his last children's novels *Sylvie and Bruno* (1889) and *Sylvie and Bruno Concluded* (1893). These books differ from *Alice* most notably in their more serious tone and stronger moral thread.]

It was a very hot afternoon — too hot to go for a walk or do anything — or else it wouldn't have happened, I believe.

In the first place, I want to know why fairies should always be teaching *us* to do our duty, and lecturing *us* when we go wrong, and we should never teach *them* anything? You can't mean to say that fairies are never greedy, or selfish, or cross, or deceitful, because that would be nonsense, you know. Well then, don't you agree with me that they might be all the better for a little scolding and punishing now and then?

I really don't see why it shouldn't be tried, and I'm almost sure (only *please* don't repeat this loud in the woods) that if you could only catch a fairy, and put it in the corner, and give it nothing but bread and water for a day or two, you'd find it quite an improved character — it would take down its conceit a little, at all events.

The next question is, what is the best time for seeing fairies? I believe I can tell you all about that.

The first rule is, that it must be a *very* hot day — that we may consider as settled: and you must be just a *little* sleepy — but not too sleepy to keep your eyes open, mind. Well, and you ought to feel a little — what one may call "fairyish" — the Scotch call it "eerie," and perhaps that's a prettier word; if you don't know what it means, I'm afraid I can hardly explain it; you must wait till you meet a fairy, and then you'll know.

And the last rule is, that the crickets shouldn't be chirping. I can't stop to explain that rule just now — you must take it on trust for the present.

So, if all these things happen together, you've a good chance of seeing a fairy — or at least a much better chance than if they didn't.

The one I'm going to tell you about was a real, naughty little fairy. Properly speaking, there were two of them, and one was naughty and one was good, but perhaps you would have found that out for yourself.

Now we really *are* going to begin the story.

It was Tuesday afternoon, about half past three — it's always best to be particular as to dates — and I had wandered down into the wood by the lake, partly because I had nothing to do, and that seemed to be a good place to do it in, and partly (as I said at first) because it was too hot to be comfortable anywhere, except under trees.

The first thing I noticed, as I went lazily along through an open place in the wood, was a large beetle lying struggling on its back, and I went down directly on one knee to help the poor thing on its feet again. In some things, you know, you can't be quite sure what an insect would like: for instance, I never could quite settle, supposing I were a moth, whether I would rather be kept out of the candle, or be allowed to fly straight in and get burnt — or again, supposing I were a spider, I'm not sure if I should be *quite* pleased to have my web torn down, and the fly let loose — but I feel quite certain that, if I were a beetle and had rolled over on my back, I should always be glad to be helped up again.

So, as I was saying, I had gone down on one knee, and was just reaching out a little stick to turn the beetle over, when I saw a sight that made me draw back hastily and hold my breath, for fear of making any noise and frightening the little creature away.

Not that she looked as if she would be easily frightened: she seemed so good and gentle that I'm sure she would never expect that any one could wish to hurt her. She was only a few inches high, and was dressed in green, so that you really would hardly have noticed her among the long grass; and she was so delicate and graceful that she quite seemed to belong to the place, almost as if she were one of the flowers. I may tell you, besides, that she had no wings (I don't believe in fairies with wings), and that she had quantities of long brown hair and large earnest brown eyes, and then I shall have done all I can to give you an idea of what she was like.

Sylvie (I found out her name afterwards) had knelt down, just as I was doing, to help the beetle; but it needed more than a little stick for *her* to get it on its legs again; it was as much as she could do, with both arms, to roll the heavy thing over; and all the while she was talking to it, half scolding and half comforting, as a nurse might do with a child that had fallen down.

"There, there! You needn't cry so much about it; you're not killed yet — though if you were, you couldn't cry, you know, and so it's a general rule against crying, my dear! And how did you come to tumble over? But I can see well enough how it was — I needn't ask you that — walking over sand-pits with your chin in the air, as usual. Of course if you go among sand-pits like that, you must expect to tumble; you should look."

The beetle murmured something that sounded like "I *did* look," and Sylvie went on again:

"But I know you didn't! You never do! You always walk with your chin up — you're so dreadfully conceited. Well, let's see how many legs are broken this time. Why, none of them, I declare! though that's certainly more than you deserve. And what's the good of having six legs, my dear, if you can only kick them all about in the air when you tumble? Legs are meant to walk with, you know. Now don't be cross about it, and don't begin putting out your wings yet; I've some more to say. Go down to the frog that lives behind that buttercup — give him my compliments — Sylvie's compliments — can you say 'compliments'?"

The beetle tried and, I suppose, succeeded.

"Yes, that's right. And tell him he's to give you some of that salve I left with him yesterday. And you'd better get him to rub it in for you; he's got rather cold hands, but you mustn't mind that."

I think the beetle must have shuddered at this idea, for Sylvie went on in a graver tone — "Now you needn't pretend to be so particular as all that, as if you were too grand to be rubbed by a frog. The fact is, you ought to be very much obliged to him. Suppose you could get nobody but a toad to do it, how would you like that?"

There was a little pause, and then Sylvie added, "Now you may go. Be a good beetle, and don't keep your chin in the air." And then began one of those performances of humming, and whizzing, and restless banging about, such as a beetle indulges in when it has decided on flying, but hasn't quite made up its mind which way to go. At last, in one of its awkward zigzags, it managed to fly right into my face, and by the time I had recovered from the shock, the little fairy was gone.

I looked about in all directions for the little creature, but there was no trace of her — and my "eerie" feeling was quite gone off, and the crickets were chirping again merrily — so I knew she was really gone.

And now I've got time to tell you the rule about the crickets. They always leave off chirping when a fairy goes by — because a fairy's a kind of queen over them, I suppose — at all events it's a much grander thing than a cricket — so whenever you're walking out, and the crickets suddenly leave off chirping, you may be sure that either they see a fairy, or else they're frightened at your coming so near.

I walked on sadly enough, you may be sure. However, I comforted myself with thinking "It's been a very wonderful afternoon, so far — I'll just go quietly on and look about me, and I shouldn't wonder if I come across another fairy somewhere."

Peering about in this way, I happened to notice a plant with rounded leaves, and with queer little holes cut out in the middle of several of them. "Ah! The leafcutter bee," I carelessly remarked — you know I am very learned in natural history (for instance, I can always tell kittens from chickens at one glance) — and I was passing on, when a sudden thought made me stoop down and examine the leaves more carefully.

Then a little thrill of delight ran through me — for I noticed that the holes were all arranged so as to form letters; there were three leaves side by side, with "B," "R," and "U" marked on them, and after some search I found two more, which contained an "N" and an "O."

By this time the "eerie" feeling had all come back again, and I suddenly observed that no crickets were chirping; so I felt quite sure that "Bruno" was a fairy, and that he was somewhere very near.

And so indeed he was — so near that I had very nearly walked over him without seeing him; which would have been dreadful, always supposing that fairies *can* be walked over — my own belief is that they are something of the nature of will-o'-the-wisps,[1] and there's no walking over *them*.

Think of any pretty little boy you know, rather fat, with rosy cheeks, large dark eyes, and tangled brown hair, and then fancy him made small enough to go comfortably into a coffee-cup, and you'll have a very fair idea of what the little creature was like.

"What's your name, little fellow?" I began, in as soft a voice as I could manage. And, by the way, that's another of the curious things in life that I never could quite understand — why we always begin by asking little children their names; is it because we fancy there isn't quite enough of them,

---

1 Anything allusive that leads one astray.

and a name will help to make them a little bigger? You never thought of asking a real large man his name, now, did you? But, however that may be, I felt it quite necessary to know *his* name; so, as he didn't answer my question, I asked it again a little louder. "What's your name, my little man?"

"What's yours?" he said, without looking up.

"My name's Lewis Carroll," I said, quite gently, for he was much too small to be angry with for answering so uncivilly.

"Duke of Anything?" he asked, just looking at me for a moment, and then going on with his work.

"Not Duke at all," I said, a little ashamed of having to confess it.

"You're big enough to be two Dukes," said the little creature; "I suppose you're Sir Something, then?"

"No," I said, feeling more and more ashamed. "I haven't got any title."

The fairy seemed to think that in that case I really wasn't worth the trouble of talking to, for he quietly went on digging, and tearing the flowers to pieces as fast as he got them out of the ground.

After a few minutes I tried again. "*Please* tell me what your name is."

"B'uno," the little fellow answered, very readily: "why didn't you say 'please' before?"

"That's something like what we used to be taught in the nursery," I thought to myself, looking back through the long years (about a hundred and fifty of them) to the time when I used to be a little child myself. And here an idea came into my head, and I asked him "Aren't you one of the fairies that teach children to be good?"

"Well, we have to do that sometimes," said Bruno, "and a d'eadful bother it is." As he said this, he savagely tore a heartsease in two, and trampled on the pieces.

"What *are* you doing there, Bruno?" I said.

"Spoiling Sylvie's garden," was all the answer Bruno would give at first. But, as he went on tearing up the flowers, he muttered to himself "The nasty c'oss thing — wouldn't let me go and play this morning, though I wanted to ever so much — said I must finish my lessons first — lessons, indeed! — I'll vex her finely, though!"

"Oh, Bruno, you shouldn't do that!" I cried. "Don't you know that's revenge? And revenge is a wicked, cruel, dangerous thing!"

"River-edge?" said Bruno. "What a funny word! I suppose you call it c'ooel and dangerous because if you went too far and tumbled in, you'd get d'owned."

"No, not river-edge," I explained: "rev-enge" (saying the word very slowly and distinctly). But I couldn't help thinking that Bruno's explanation did very well for either word.

"Oh!" said Bruno, opening his eyes very wide, but without attempting to repeat the word.

"Come! Try and pronounce it, Bruno!" I said, cheerfully. "Rev-enge, rev-enge."

But Bruno only tossed his little head, and said he couldn't; that his mouth wasn't the right shape for words of that kind. And the more I laughed, the more sulky the little fellow got about it.

"Well, never mind, little man!" I said. "Shall I help you with the job you've got there?"

"Yes, please," Bruno said, quite pacified. "Only I wish I could think of something to vex her more than this. You don't know how hard it is to make her ang'y!"

"Now listen to me, Bruno, and I'll teach you quite a splendid kind of revenge!"

"Something that'll vex her finely?" Bruno asked with gleaming eyes.

"Something that'll vex her finely. First, we'll get up all the weeds in her garden. See, there are a good many at this end — quite hiding the flowers."

"But *that* won't vex her," said Bruno, looking rather puzzled.

"After that," I said, without noticing the remark, "we'll water this highest bed — up here. You see it's getting quite dry and dusty."

Bruno looked at me inquisitively, but he said nothing this time.

"Then after that," I went on, "the walks want sweeping a bit; and I think you might cut down that tall nettle — it's so close to the garden that it's quite in the way —"

"What *are* you talking about?" Bruno impatiently interrupted me. "All that won't vex her a bit!"

"Won't it?" I said, innocently. "Then, after that, suppose we put in some of these coloured pebbles — just to mark the divisions between the different kinds of flowers, you know. That'll have a very pretty effect."

Bruno turned round and had another good stare at me. At last there came an odd little twinkle in his eye, and he said, with quite a new meaning in his voice, "Ve'y well — let's put 'em in rows — all the 'ed together, and all the blue together."

"That'll do capitally," I said; "and then — what kind of flowers does Sylvie like best in her garden?"

Bruno had to put his thumb in his mouth and consider a little before he could answer. "Violets," he said, at last.

"There's a beautiful bed of violets down by the lake —"

"Oh, let's fetch 'em!" cried Bruno, giving a little skip into the air. "Here! Catch hold of my hand, and I'll help you along. The g'ass is rather thick down that way."

I couldn't help laughing at his having so entirely forgotten what a big creature he was talking to. "No, not yet, Bruno," I said; "we must consider what's the right thing to do first. You see we've got quite a business before us."

"Yes, let's consider," said Bruno, putting his thumb into his mouth again, and sitting down upon a dead mouse.

"What do you keep that mouse for?" I said. "You should bury it, or throw it into the lake."

"Why, it's to measure with!" cried Bruno. "How ever would you do a garden without one? We make each bed th'ee mouses and a half long, and two mouses wide."

I stopped him, as he was dragging it off by the tail to show me how it was used, for I was half afraid the "eerie" feeling might go off before we had finished the garden, and in that case I should see no more of him or Sylvie. "I think the best way will be for *you* to weed the beds, while *I* sort out these pebbles, ready to mark the walks with."

"That's it!" cried Bruno. "And I'll tell you about the caterpillars while we work."

"Ah, let's hear about the caterpillars," I said, as I drew the pebbles together into a heap, and began dividing them into colours.

And Bruno went on in a low, rapid tone, more as if he were talking to himself. "Yesterday I saw two little caterpillars, when I was sitting by the brook, just where you go into the wood. They were quite g'een, and they had yellow eyes, and they didn't see *me*. And one of them had got a moth's wing to carry — a g'eat b'own moth's wing, you know, all d'y, with feathers. So he couldn't want it to eat, I should think — perhaps he meant to make a cloak for the winter?"

"Perhaps," I said, for Bruno had twisted up the last word into a sort of question, and was looking at me for an answer.

One word was quite enough for the little fellow, and he went on merrily. "Well, and so he didn't want the other caterpillar to see the moth's wing, you know — so what must he do but t'y to carry it with all his left legs, and he t'ied to walk on the other set. Of course he toppled over after that."

"After what?" I said, catching at the last word, for, to tell the truth, I hadn't been attending much.

"He toppled over," Bruno repeated, very gravely, "and if *you* ever saw a caterpillar topple over, you'd know it's a serious thing, and not sit g'inning like that — and I shan't tell you any more."

"Indeed and indeed, Bruno, I, didn't mean to grin. See, I'm quite grave again now."

But Bruno only folded his arms, and said "Don't tell *me*. I see a little twinkle in one of your eyes — just like the moon."

"Am *I* like the moon, Bruno?" I asked.

"Your face is large and round like the moon," Bruno answered, looking at me thoughtfully. "It doesn't shine quite so bright — but it's cleaner."

I couldn't help smiling at this. "You know I wash *my* face, Bruno. The moon never does that."

"Oh, doesn't she though!" cried Bruno; and he leant forwards and added in a solemn whisper "The moon's face gets dirtier and dirtier every night, till it's black all ac'oss. And then, when it's dirty all over — *so* —" (he passed his hand across his own rosy cheeks as he spoke) "then she washes it."

"And then it's all clean again, isn't it?"

"Not all in a moment," said Bruno. "What a deal of teaching you want! She washes it little by little — only she begins at the other edge."

By this time he was sitting quietly on the dead mouse with his arms folded, and the weeding wasn't getting on a bit: so I was obliged to say "Work first and pleasure afterwards — no more talking till that bed's finished."

After that we had a few minutes of silence, while I sorted out the pebbles, and amused myself with watching Bruno's plan of gardening. It was quite a new plan to me: he always measured each bed before he weeded it, as if he was afraid the weeding would make it shrink; and once, when it came out longer than he wished, he set to work to thump the mouse with his tiny fist, crying out "There now! It's all 'ong again! Why don't you keep your tail st'aight when I tell you!"

"I'll tell you what I'll do," Bruno said in a half-whisper, as we worked: "I'll get you an invitation to the king's dinner-party. I know one of the head-waiters."

I couldn't help laughing at this idea. "Do the waiters invite the guests?" I asked.

"Oh, not *to sit down!*" Bruno hastily replied. "But to help, you know. You'd like that, wouldn't you? To hand about plates, and so on."

"Well, but that's not so nice as sitting at the table, is it?"

"Of course it isn't," Bruno said, in a tone as if he rather pitied my ignorance; "but if you're not even Sir Anything, you can't expect to be allowed to sit at the table, you know."

I said, as meekly as I could, that I didn't expect it, but it was the only way of going to a dinner-party that I really enjoyed. And Bruno tossed his head, and said, in a rather offended tone, that I might do as I pleased — there were many he knew that would give their ears to go.

"Have you ever been yourself, Bruno?"

"They invited me once last year," Bruno said, very gravely. "It was to wash up the soup-plates — no, the cheese-plates I mean — that was g'and enough. But the g'andest thing of all was, *I* fetched the Duke of Dandelion a glass of cider!"

"That *was* grand!" I said, biting my lip to keep myself from laughing.

"Wasn't it?" said Bruno, very earnestly. "You know it isn't every one that's had such an honour as *that*!"

This set me thinking of the various queer things we call "an honour" in this world, which, after all, haven't a bit more honour in them than what the dear little Bruno enjoyed (by the way, I hope you're beginning to like him a little, naughty as he was?) when he took the Duke of Dandelion a glass of cider.

I don't know how long I might have dreamed on in this way, if Bruno hadn't suddenly roused me. "Oh, come here quick!" he cried, in a state of the wildest excitement. "Catch hold of his other horn! I can't hold him more than a minute!"

He was struggling desperately with a great snail, clinging to one of its horns, and nearly breaking his poor little back in his efforts to drag it over a blade of grass.

I saw we should have no more gardening if I let this sort of thing go on, so I quietly took the snail away, and put it on a bank where he could-n't reach it. "We'll hunt it afterwards, Bruno," I said, "if you really want to catch it. But what's the use of it when you've got it?"

"What's the use of a fox when you've got it?" said Bruno. "I know you big things hunt foxes."

I tried to think of some good reason why "big things" should hunt foxes, and he shouldn't hunt snails, but none came into my head: so I said at last "Well, I suppose one's as good as the other. I'll go snail-hunting myself some day."

"I should think you wouldn't be so silly," said Bruno, "as to go snail-hunting all by yourself. Why, you'd never get the snail along, if you hadn't somebody to hold on to his other horn!"

"Of course I shan't go alone," I said, quite gravely. "By the way, is that the best kind to hunt, or do you recommend the ones without shells?"

"Oh no, we never hunt the ones without shells," Bruno said, with a little shudder at the thought of it. "They're always so c'oss about it; and then, if you tumble over them, they're ever so sticky!"

By this time we had nearly finished the garden. I had fetched some violets, and Bruno was just helping me to put in the last, when he suddenly stopped and said, "I'm tired."

"Rest, then," I said: "I can go on without you."

Bruno needed no second invitation: he at once began arranging the dead mouse as a kind of sofa. "And I'll sing you a little song," he said as he rolled it about.

"Do," said I: "there's nothing I should like better."

"Which song will you choose?" Bruno said, as he dragged the mouse into a place where he could got a good view of me. "'Ting, ting, ting,' is the nicest."

There was no resisting such a strong hint as this: however, I pretended to think about it for a moment, and then said "Well, I like 'Ting, ting, ting' best of all."

"That shows you're a good judge of music," Bruno said, with a pleased look. "How many blue-bells would you like?" And he put his thumb into his mouth to help me to consider.

As there was only one blue-bell within easy reach, I said very gravely that I thought one would do *this* time, and I picked it and gave it to him. Bruno ran his hand once or twice up and down the flowers, like a musician trying an instrument, producing a most delicious delicate tinkling as he did so. I had never heard flower-music before — I don't think one can, unless one's in the "eerie" state — and I don't know quite how to give you an idea of what it was like, except by saying that it sounded like a peal of bells a thousand miles off. When he had satisfied himself that the flowers were in tune, he seated himself on the dead mouse (he never seemed really comfortable anywhere else), and, looking up at me with a merry twinkle in his eyes, he began. By the way, the tune was rather a curious one, and you might like to try it for yourself, so here are the notes.

> "Rise, oh, rise! The daylight dies:
>   The owls are hooting, ting, ting, ting!
> Wake, oh, wake! Beside the lake
>   The elves are fluting, ting, ting, ting!
> Welcoming our fairy king
>   We sing, sing, sing."

He sang the first four lines briskly and merrily, making the blue-bells chime in time with the music; but the last two he sang quite slowly and gently, and merely waved the flowers backwards and forwards above his head. And when he had finished the first verse, he left off to explain. "The name of our fairy king is Obberwon"(he meant "Oberon,"[1] I believe), "and he lives over the lake — *there* — and now and then he comes in a little boat — and then we go and meet him — and then we sing this song, you know."

"And then you go and dine with him?" I said, mischievously.

"You shouldn't talk," Bruno hastily said: "it interrupts the song so."

I said I wouldn't do it again.

"I never talk myself when I'm singing," he went on very gravely; "so you shouldn't either." Then he tuned the blue-bells once more, and sang.

> "Hear, oh, hear! From far and near
>   A music stealing, ting, ting, ting!
> Fairy bells adown the dells
>   Are merrily pealing, ting, ting, ting!
> Welcoming our fairy king
>   We ring, ring, ring.

> "See, oh, see! On every tree
>   What lamps are shining, ting, ting, ting!

---

1   King of the fairies, made famous through Shakespeare's play *A Midsummer Night's Dream*.

They are eyes of fiery flies
    To light our dining, ting, ting, ting!
Welcoming our fairy king
    They swing, swing, swing.

"Haste, oh, haste! to take and taste
    The dainties waiting, ting, ting, ting!
Honey-dew is stored —"

"Hush, Bruno!" I interrupted, in a warning whisper. "She's coming!"

Bruno checked his song only just in time for Sylvie not to hear him, and then, catching sight of her as she slowly made her way through the long grass, he suddenly rushed out headlong at her like a little bull, shouting "Look the other way! Look the other way!"

"Which way?" Sylvie asked, in rather a frightened tone, as she looked round in all directions to see where the danger could be.

"*That* way!" said Bruno, carefully turning her round with her face to the wood. "Now, walk backwards — walk gently — don't be f'ightened: you shan't t'ip!"

But Sylvie did "t'ip" notwithstanding: in fact he led her, in his hurry, across so many little sticks and stones, that it was really a wonder the poor child could keep on her feet at all. But he was far too much excited to think of what he was doing.

I silently pointed out to Bruno the best place to lead her to, so as to get a view of the whole garden at once: it was a little rising ground, about the height of a potato; and, when they had mounted it, I drew back into the shade, that Sylvie mightn't see me.

I heard Bruno cry out triumphantly "*Now* you may look!" and then followed a great clapping of hands, but it was all done by Bruno himself. Sylvie was quite silent — she only stood and gazed with her hands clasped tightly together, and I was half afraid she didn't like it after all.

Bruno too was watching her anxiously, and when she jumped down off the mound, and began wandering up and down the little walks, he cautiously followed her about, evidently anxious that she should form her own opinion of it all, without any hint from him. And when at last she drew a long breath, and gave her verdict — in a hurried whisper, and without the slightest regard to grammar — "It's the loveliest thing as I never saw in all my life before!" the little fellow looked as well pleased as if it had been given by all the judges and juries in England put together.

"And did you really do it all by yourself, Bruno?" said Sylvie. "And all for me?"

"I was helped a bit," Bruno began, with a merry little laugh at her surprise. "We've been at it all the afternoon — I thought you'd like —" and here the poor little fellow's lip began to quiver, and all in a moment he burst out crying, and running up to Sylvie he flung his arms passionately round her neck, and hid his face on her shoulder.

There was a little quiver in Sylvie's voice too, as she whispered "Why, what's the matter, darling?" and tried to lift up his head and kiss him.

But Bruno only clung to her, sobbing, and wouldn't be comforted till he had confessed all. "I tried — to spoil your garden — first — but — I'll never — never —" and then came another burst of tears, which drowned the rest of the sentence. At last be got out the words "I liked — putting in the flowers — for *you*, Sylvie — and I never was so happy before —" and the rosy little face came up at last to be kissed, all wet with tears as it was.

Sylvie was crying too by this time, and she said nothing but "Bruno dear!" and "*I* never was so happy before —" though why two children who had never been so happy before should both be crying, was a great mystery to me.

I felt very happy too, but of course I didn't cry: "big things" never do, you know — we leave all that to the fairies. Only I think it must have been raining a little just then, for I found a drop or two on my cheeks.

After that they went through the whole garden again, flower by flower, as if it were a long sentence they were spelling out, with kisses for commas, and a great hug by way of a full-stop when they got to the end.

"Do you know, that was my river-edge, Sylvie?" Bruno began, looking solemnly at her.

Sylvie laughed merrily. "What *do* you mean?" she said; and she pushed back her heavy brown hair with both hands, and looked at him with dancing eyes in which the big tear-drops were still glittering.

Bruno drew in a long breath, and made up his mouth for a great effort. "I mean rev-enge," he said: "now you under'tand." And he looked so happy and proud at having said the word right at last, that I quite envied him. I rather think Sylvie didn't "under'tand" at all; but she gave him a little kiss on each cheek, which seemed to do just as well.

So they wandered off lovingly together, in among the buttercups, each with an arm twined round the other, whispering and laughing as they went, and never so much as once looked back at poor me. Yes, once, just before I quite lost sight of them, Bruno half turned his head, and nodded me a saucy little good-bye over one shoulder. And that was all the thanks I got for *my* trouble.

I know you're sorry the story's come to an end — aren't you? — so I'll just tell you one thing more. The very last thing I saw of them was this — Sylvie was stooping down with her arms round Bruno's neck, and saying coaxingly in his ear "Do you know, Bruno, I've quite forgotten that hard word — do say it once more. Come! Only this once, dear!"

But Bruno wouldn't try it again.

Sheridan Le Fanu

"Green Tea"[1] (1869)

["The master of us all" — so had the famous twentieth-century ghost story writer M.R. James described Joseph Sheridan Le Fanu (1814–1873). Born in Dublin to an upper-class Protestant family, Le Fanu made full use of Irish folklore and ghost stories such as those William Carleton made popular to develop his own haunting and horrific works. Le Fanu also wrote poetry and essays and edited a number of Irish periodicals, including the influential *Dublin University Magazine* (in which his earliest stories had been published beginning in 1838). By mid-century, he was one of the best selling English-language authors due to his well-honed gothic fiction and, more precisely, his shift of the genre away from the aim of simply shocking or frightening readers and toward a psychological horror that encouraged readers to question their society's cultural, spiritual, and political assumptions. Many scholars view Le Fanu's short fiction as more subtly crafted than his novels, of which *Uncle Silas* (1864) is the best known. His most famous collection of stories is *In a Glass Darkly* (1872), which includes the following psychological thriller.]

A CASE REPORTED BY MARTIN HESSELIUS, THE
GERMAN PHYSICIAN
In Ten Chapters. Preface.

Though carefully educated in medicine and surgery, I have never practised either. The study of each continues, nevertheless, to interest me profoundly. Neither idleness nor caprice caused my secession from the honourable profession which I had just entered. The cause was a very trifling scratch inflicted by a dissecting-knife. This trifle cost me the loss of two fingers, amputated promptly, and the more painful loss of my health,

---

1 Unfermented tea.

for I have never been quite well since, and have seldom been twelve months together in the same place.

In my wanderings I became acquainted with Dr. Martin Hesselius, a wanderer like myself, like me a physician, and like me an enthusiast in his profession. Unlike me in this, that his wanderings were voluntary, and he a man, if not of fortune, as we estimate fortune in England, at least in what our forefathers used to term "easy circumstances."

In Dr. Martin Hesselius I found my master. His knowledge was immense, his grasp of a case was an intuition. He was the very man to inspire a young enthusiast, like me, with awe and delight. My admiration has stood the test of time and survived the separation of death. I am sure it was well-founded.

For nearly twenty years I acted as his medical secretary. His immense collection of papers he has left in my care, to be arranged, indexed, and bound. His treatment of some of these cases is curious. He writes in two distinct characters. He describes what he saw and heard as an intelligent layman might, and when in this style of narrative he has seen the patient either through his own hall-door, to the light of day, or through the gates of darkness to the caverns of the dead, he returns upon the narrative, and in the terms of his art, and with all the force and originality of genius, proceeds to the work of analysis, diagnosis, and illustration.

Here and there a case strikes me as of a kind to amuse or horrify a lay reader with an interest quite different from the peculiar one which it may possess for an expert. With slight modifications, chiefly of language, and of course a change of names, I copy the following. The narrator is Dr. Martin Hesselius. I find it among the voluminous notes of cases which he made during a tour in England about fifty-four years ago.

It is related in a series of letters to his friend Professor Van Loo of Leyden. The professor was not a physician, but a chemist, and a man who read history and metaphysics and medicine, and had, in his day, written a play.

The narrative is therefore, if somewhat less valuable as a medical record, necessarily written in a manner more likely to interest an unlearned reader.

These letters, from a memorandum attached, appear to have been returned on the death of the professor, in 1819, to Dr. Hesselius. They are written, some in English, some in French, but the greater part in German. I am a faithful, though I am conscious, by no means a graceful, translator, and although, here and there, I omit some passages, and shorten others, and disguise names, I have interpolated nothing.

CHAPTER 1
Dr. Hesselius Relates How He Met the Rev. Mr. Jennings.

The Rev. Mr. Jennings is tall and thin. He is middle-aged, and dresses with a natty, old-fashioned, high-church[1] precision. He is naturally a little stately, but not at all stiff. His features, without being handsome, are well formed, and their expression extremely kind, but also shy.

I met him one evening at Lady Mary Heyduke's. The modesty and benevolence of his countenance are extremely prepossessing.

We were but a small party, and he joined agreeably enough in the conversation. He seems to enjoy listening very much more than contributing to the talk; but what he says is always to the purpose and well said. He is a great favourite of Lady Mary's, who, it seems, consults him upon many things, and thinks him the most happy and blessed person on earth. Little knows she about him.

The Rev. Mr. Jennings is a bachelor, and has, they say, sixty thousand pounds in the funds. He is a charitable man. He is most anxious to be actively employed in his sacred profession, and yet, though always tolerably well elsewhere, when be goes down to his vicarage in Warwickshire, to engage in the active duties of his sacred calling, his health soon fails him, and in a very strange way. So says Lady Mary.

There is no doubt that Mr. Jennings's health does break down in, generally, a sudden and mysterious way, sometimes in the very act of officiating in his old and pretty church at Kenlis. It may be his heart, it may be his brain. But so it has happened three or four times, or oftener, that after proceeding a certain way in the service, he has on a sudden stopped short, and after a silence, apparently quite unable to resume, he has fallen into solitary, inaudible prayer, his hands and eyes uplifted, and then pale as death, and in the agitation of a strange shame and horror, descended trembling, got into the vestry-room, and left his congregation, without explanation, to themselves. This occurred when his curate was absent. When he goes down to Kenlis, now, he always takes care to provide a clergyman to share his duty, and to supply his place on the instant, should he become thus suddenly incapacitated.

When Mr. Jennings breaks down quite, and beats a retreat from the vicarage, and returns to London, where, in a dark street off Piccadilly, he inhabits a very narrow house, Lady Mary says that he is always perfectly

---

1   In this temporal context, the term refers to being devoted to the established ways of the Church of England.

well. I have my own opinion about that. There are degrees of course. We shall see.

Mr. Jennings is a perfectly gentleman-like man. People, however, remark something odd. There is an impression a little ambiguous. One thing which certainly contributes to it, people, I think, don't remember — perhaps, distinctly remark. But I did, almost immediately. Mr. Jennings has a way of looking sidelong upon the carpet, as if his eye followed the movements of something there. This, of course, is not always. It occurs only now and then. But often enough to give a certain oddity as I have said to his manner, and in this glance travelling along the floor, there is something both shy and anxious.

A medical philosopher, as you are good enough to call me, elaborating theories by the aid of cases sought out by himself, and by him watched and scrutinised with more time at command, and consequently infinitely more minuteness than the ordinary practitioner can afford, falls insensibly into habits of observation which accompany him everywhere, and are exercised, as some people would say, impertinently, upon every subject that presents itself with the least likelihood of rewarding inquiry.

There was a promise of this kind in this slight, timid, kindly, but reserved gentleman, whom I met for the first time at this agreeable little evening gathering. I observed, of course, more than I here set down; but I reserve all that borders on the technical for a strictly scientific paper.

I may remark, that when I here speak of medical science, I do so as I hope some day to see it more generally understood, in a much more comprehensive sense than its generally material treatment would warrant. I believe that the entire natural world is but the ultimate expression of that spiritual world from which, and in which alone, it has its life. I believe that the essential man is a spirit, that the spirit is an organised substance, but as different in point of material from what we ordinarily understand by matter, as light or electricity is; that the material body is, in the most literal sense, a vesture,[1] and death consequently no interruption of the living man's existence, but simply his extrication from the natural body — a process which commences at the moment of what we term death, and the completion of which, at furthest, a few days later, is the resurrection "in power."

The person who weighs the consequences of these positions will probably see their practical bearing upon medical science. This is, however, by no means the proper place for displaying the proofs and discussing the consequences of this too generally unrecognised state of facts.

---

1   Something that covers or cloaks like a piece of clothing.

In pursuance of my habit, I was covertly observing Mr. Jennings, with all my caution — I think he perceived it — and I saw plainly that he was as cautiously observing me. Lady Mary happening to address me by my name, as Dr. Hesselius, I saw that he glanced at me more sharply, and then became thoughtful for a few minutes.

After this, as I conversed with a gentleman at the other end of the room, I saw him look at me more steadily, and with an interest which I thought I understood. I then saw him take an opportunity of chatting with Lady Mary, and was, as one always is, perfectly aware of being the subject of a distant inquiry and answer.

This tall clergyman approached me by-and-by: and in a little time we had got into conversation. When two people, who like reading, and know books and places, having travelled, wish to converse, it is very strange if they can't find topics. It was not accident that brought him near me, and led him into conversation. He knew German, and had read my Essays on Metaphysical Medicine, which suggest more than they actually say.

This courteous man, gentle, shy, plainly a man of thought and reading, who moving and talking among us, was not altogether of us, and whom I already suspected of leading a life whose transactions and alarms were carefully concealed, with an impenetrable reserve from, not only the world, but his best beloved friends — was cautiously weighing in his own mind the idea of taking a certain step with regard to me.

I penetrated his thoughts without his being aware of it, and was careful to say nothing which could betray to his sensitive vigilance my suspicions respecting his position, or my surmises about his plans respecting myself.

We chatted upon indifferent subjects for a time; but at last he said:

"I was very much interested by some papers of yours, Dr. Hesselius, upon what you term Metaphysical Medicine — I read them in German, ten or twelve years ago — have they been translated?"

"No, I'm sure they have not — I should have heard. They would have asked my leave, I think."

"I asked the publishers here, a few months ago, to get the book for me in the original German; but they tell me it is out of print."

"So it is, and has been for some years; but it flatters me as an author to find that you have not forgotten my little book, although," I added, laughing, "ten or twelve years is a considerable time to have managed without it; but I suppose you have been turning the subject over again in your mind, or something has happened lately to revive your interest in it."

At this remark, accompanied by a glance of inquiry, a sudden embarrassment disturbed Mr. Jennings, analogous to that which makes a young lady blush and look foolish. He dropped his eyes, and folded his hands together uneasily, and looked oddly, and you would have said, guilty for a moment.

I helped him out of his awkwardness in the best way, by appearing not to observe it, and going straight on, I said: "Those revivals of interest in a subject happen to me often; one book suggests another, and often sends me back [on] a wild-goose chase over an interval of twenty years. But if you still care to possess a copy, I shall be only too happy to provide you; I have still got two or three by me — and if you allow me to present one I shall be very much honoured."

"You are very good indeed," he said, quite at his ease again, in a moment: "I almost despaired — I don't know how to thank you."

"Pray don't say a word; the thing is really so little worth that I am only ashamed of having offered it, and if you thank me any more I shall throw it into the fire in a fit of modesty."

Mr. Jennings laughed. He inquired where I was staying in London, and after a little more conversation on a variety of subjects, he took his departure.

CHAPTER II
The Doctor Questions Lady Mary, and She Answers.

"I like your vicar so much, Lady Mary," said I, so soon as he was gone. "He has read, travelled, and thought, and having also suffered, he ought to be an accomplished companion."

"So he is, and, better still, he is a really good man," said she. "His advice is invaluable about my schools, and all my little undertakings at Dawlbridge, and he's so painstaking, he takes so much trouble — you have no idea — wherever he thinks he can be of use: he's so good-natured and so sensible."

"It is pleasant to hear so good an account of his neighbourly virtues. I can only testify to his being an agreeable and gentle companion, and in addition to what you have told me, I think I can tell you two or three things about him," said I.

"Really!"

"Yes, to begin with, he's unmarried.'"

"Yes, that's right, — go on."

"He has been writing, that is he *was*, but for two or three years, perhaps, he has not gone on with his work, and the book was upon some rather abstract subject — perhaps theology."

"Well, he was writing a book, as you say; I'm not quite sure what it was about, but only that it was nothing that I cared for, very likely you are right, and he certainly did stop — yes."

"And although he only drank a little coffee here to-night, he likes tea, at least, did like it, extravagantly."

"Yes; that's *quite* true."

"He drank green tea, a good deal, didn't he?" I pursued.

"Well, that's very odd! Green tea was a subject on which we used almost to quarrel."

"But he has quite given that up," I continued.

"So he has."

"And, now, one more fact. His mother, or his father, did you know them?"

"Yes, both; his father is only ten years dead, and their place is near Dawlbridge. We knew them very well," she answered.

"Well, either his mother or his father — I should rather think his father — saw a ghost," said I.

"Well, you really are a conjurer, Doctor Hesselius."

"Conjurer or no, haven't I said right?" I answered, merrily.

"You certainly have, and it *was* his father: he was a silent, whimsical man, and he used to bore my father about his dreams, and at last he told him a story about a ghost he had seen and talked with, and a very odd story it was. I remember it particularly because I was so afraid of him. This story was long before he died — when I was quite a child — and his ways were so silent and moping, and he used to drop in, sometimes, in the dusk, when I was alone in the drawing-room, and I used to fancy there were ghosts about him."

I smiled and nodded.

"And now having established my character as a conjurer I think I must say good-night," said I.

"But how *did* you find it out?"

"By the planets of course, as the gipsies do," I answered, and so, gaily, we said good-night.

Next morning I sent the little book he had been inquiring after, and a note to Mr. Jennings, and on returning late that evening, I found that he had called and left his card. He asked whether I was at home, and asked at what hour he would be most likely to find me.

Does he intend opening his case, and consulting me "professionally," as they say? I hope so. I have already conceived a theory about him. It is supported by Lady Mary's answers to my parting questions. I should like much to ascertain from his own lips. But what can I do consistently with good breeding to invite a confession? Nothing. I rather think he meditates one. At all events, my dear Van L., I shan't make myself difficult of access; I mean to return his visit tomorrow. It will be only civil in return for his politeness, to ask to see him. Perhaps something may come of it. Whether much, little, or nothing, my dear Van L., you shall hear.

CHAPTER III
Dr. Hesselius Picks Up Something In Latin Books.

Well, I have called at Blank-street.

On inquiring at the door, the servant told me that Mr. Jennings was engaged very particularly with a gentleman, a clergyman from Kenlis, his parish in the country. Intending to reserve my privilege and to call again, I merely intimated that I should try another time, and had turned to go, when the servant begged my pardon, and asked me, looking at me a little more attentively than well-bred persons of his order usually do, whether I was Dr. Hesselius, and, on learning that I was, he said, "Perhaps then, sir, you would allow me to mention it to Mr. Jennings, for I am sure he wishes to see you."

The servant returned in a moment, with a message from Mr. Jennings, asking me to go into his study, which was in effect his back drawing-room, promising to be with me in a very few minutes.

This was really a study — almost a library. The room was lofty, with two tall slender windows, and rich dark curtains. It was much larger than I had expected, and stored with books on every side, from the floor to the ceiling. The upper carpet — for to my tread it felt that there were two or three — was a Turkey carpet. My steps fell noiselessly. The book-cases standing out, placed the windows, particularly narrow ones, in deep recesses. The effect of the room was, although extremely comfortable, and even luxurious, decidedly gloomy, and aided by the silence, almost oppressive. Perhaps, however, I ought to have allowed something for association. My mind had connected peculiar ideas with Mr. Jennings. I stepped into this perfectly silent room, of a very silent house, with a peculiar foreboding; and its darkness, and solemn clothing of books, for except where two narrow looking-glasses were set in the wall, they were everywhere, helped this sombre feeling.

While awaiting Mr. Jennings's arrival, I amused myself by looking into some of the books with which his shelves were laden. Not among these, but immediately under them, with their backs upward, on the floor, I lighted upon a complete set of Swedenborg's Arcana Cælestia,[1] in the original Latin, a very fine folio set, bound in the natty livery which theology affects, pure vellum, namely, gold letters, and carmine edges. There were paper markers in several of these volumes. I raised and placed them, one after the other, upon the table, and opening where these papers were placed, I read in the solemn Latin phraseology, a series of sentences indicated by pencilled line at the margin. Of these I copy here a few, translating them into English.

"When man's interior sight is opened, which is that of his spirit, then there appear the things of another life, which cannot possibly be made visible to the bodily sight." ....

"By the internal sight it has been granted me to see the things that are in the other life, more clearly than I see those that are in the world. From these considerations, it is evident that external vision exists from interior vision, and this from a vision still more interior, and so on." ....

"There are with every man at least two evil spirits." ....

"With wicked genii there is also a fluent speech, but harsh and grating. There is also among them, a speech which is not fluent, wherein the dissent of the thoughts is perceived as something secretly creeping along within it." ....

"The evil spirits associated with man are, indeed, from the hells, but when with man they are not then in hell, but are taken out thence. The place where they then are is in the midst between heaven and hell, and is called the world of spirits — when the evil spirits who are with man, are in that world, they are not in any infernal torment, but in every thought and affection of the man, and so, in all that the man himself enjoys. But when they are remitted into their hell, they return to their former state." ....

"If evil spirits could perceive that they were associated with man, and yet that they were spirits separate from him, and if they could flow in into the things of his body, they would attempt by a thousand means to destroy him; for they hate man with a deadly hatred." ....

"Knowing, therefore, that I was a man in the body, they were continually striving to destroy me, not as to the body only, but especially as to the soul; for to destroy any man or spirit is the very delight of the life of all who are in hell; but I have been continually protected by the Lord.

---

1   Emanuel Swedenborg (1688-1772), Swedish theologian and philosopher. His study *Arcana Caelestia* (1749-46) (Latin for "Heavenly Secrets") argues that the bible embodies through symbols a law of correspondences that can give humans a sense of the spiritual realm.

Hence it appears how dangerous it is for man to be in a living consort with spirits, unless he be in the good of faith." ....

"Nothing is more carefully guarded from the knowledge of associate spirits than their being thus conjoint with a man, for if they knew it they would speak to him, with the intention to destroy him." ....

"The delight of hell is to do evil to man, and to hasten his eternal ruin."

A long note, written with a very sharp and fine pencil, in Mr. Jennings's neat hand, at the foot of the page, caught my eye. Expecting his criticism upon the text, I read a word or two, and stopped, for it was something quite different, and began with these words, Deus misereatur mei — "May God compassionate me." Thus warned of its private nature, I averted my eyes, and shut the book, replacing all the volumes as I had found them, except one which interested me, and in which, as men studious and solitary in their habits will do, I grew so absorbed as to take no cognisance of the outer world, nor to remember where I was.

I was reading some pages which refer to "representatives" and "correspondents," in the technical language of Swedenborg, and had arrived at a passage, the substance of which is, that evil spirits, when seen by other eyes than those of their infernal associates, present themselves, by "correspondence," in the shape of the beast (fera) which represents their particular lust and life in aspect direful and atrocious. This is a long passage, and particularises a number of those bestial forms.

CHAPTER IV
Four Eyes Were Reading The Passage.

I was running the head of my pencil-case along the line as I read it, and something caused me to raise my eyes.

Directly before me was one of the mirrors I have mentioned, in which I saw reflected the tall shape of my friend Mr. Jennings leaning over my shoulder, and reading the page at which I was busy, and with a face so dark and wild that I should hardly have known him.

I turned and rose. He stood erect also, and with an effort laughed a little, saying:

"I came in and asked you how you did, but without succeeding in awaking you from your book; so I could not restrain my curiosity, and very impertinently, I'm afraid, peeped over your shoulder. This is not your first time of looking into those pages. You have looked into Swedenborg, no doubt, long ago?"

"Oh dear, yes! I owe Swedenborg a great deal; you will discover traces of him in the little book on Metaphysical Medicine, which you were so good as to remember."

Although my friend affected a gaiety of manner, there was a slight flush in his face, and I could perceive that he was inwardly much perturbed.

"I'm scarcely yet qualified, I know so little of Swedenborg. I've only had them a fortnight," he answered, "and I think they are rather likely to make a solitary man nervous — that is, judging from the very little I have read — I don't say that they have made me so," he laughed; "and I'm so very much obliged for the book. I hope you got my note?"

I made all proper acknowledgments and modest disclaimers.

"I never read a book that I go with so entirely as that of yours," he continued.

"I saw at once there is more in it than is quite unfolded. Do you know Dr. Harley?" he asked, rather abruptly.

In passing, the editor remarks that the physician here named was one of the most eminent who ever practised in England.

I did, having had letters to him, and had experienced from him great courtesy and considerable assistance during my visit to England.

"I think that man one of the very greatest fools I ever met in my life," said Mr. Jennings.

This was the first time I had ever heard him say a sharp thing of anybody, and such a term applied to so high a name a little startled me.

"Really! and in what way?" I asked. "In his profession," he answered.

I smiled.

"I mean this," he said: "he seems to me, one half, blind — I mean one half of all he looks at is dark — preternaturally bright and vivid all the rest; and the worst of it is, it seems *wilful*. I can't get him — I mean he won't — I've had some experience of him as a physician, but I look on him as, in that sense, no better than a paralytic mind, an intellect half dead. I'll tell you — I know I shall some time — all about it," he said, with a little agitation. "You stay some months longer in England. If I should be out of town during your stay for a little time, would you allow me to trouble you with a letter?"

"I should be only too happy," I assured him.

"Very good of you. I am so utterly dissatisfied with Harley."

"A little leaning to the materialistic school," I said.

"A *mere* materialist," he corrected me; "you can't think how that sort of thing worries one who knows better. You won't tell any one — any of my friends you know — that I am hippish;[1] now, for instance, no one

---

1 Melancholy.

knows — not even Lady Mary — that I have seen Dr. Harley, or any other doctor. So pray don't mention it; and, if I should have any threatening of an attack, you'll kindly let me write, or, should I be in town, have a little talk with you."

I was full of conjecture, and unconsciously I found I had fixed my eyes gravely on him, for he lowered his for a moment, and he said:

"I see you think I might as well tell you now, or else you are forming a conjecture; but you may as well give it up. If you were guessing all the rest of your life, you will never hit on it."

He shook his head smiling, and over that wintry sunshine a black cloud suddenly came down, and he drew his breath in through his teeth, as men do in pain.

"Sorry, of course, to learn that you apprehend occasion to consult any of us; but, command me when and how you like, and I need not assure you that your confidence is sacred."

He then talked of quite other things, and in a comparatively cheerful way; and, after a little time, I took my leave.

CHAPTER V
Doctor Hesselius Is Summoned To Richmond.

We parted cheerfully, but he was not cheerful, nor was I. There are certain expressions of that powerful organ of spirit — the human face — which, although I have seen them often, and possess a doctor's nerve, yet disturb me profoundly. One look of Mr. Jennings haunted me. It had seized my imagination with so dismal a power that I changed my plans for the evening, and went to the opera, feeling that I wanted a change of ideas.

I heard nothing of or from him for two or three days, when a note in his hand reached me. It was cheerful, and full of hope. He said that he had been for some little time so much better — quite well, in fact — that he was going to make a little experiment, and run down for a month or so to his parish, to try whether a little work might not quite set him up. There was in it a fervent religious expression of gratitude for his restoration, as he now almost hoped he might call it.

A day or two later I saw Lady Mary, who repeated what his note had announced, and told me that he was actually in Warwickshire, having resumed his clerical duties at Kenlis; and she added, "I begin to think that he is really perfectly well, and that there never was anything the matter, more than nerves and fancy; we are all nervous, but I fancy there is nothing like a little hard work for that kind of weakness, and he has made up his mind to try it. I should not be surprised if he did not come back for a year."

Notwithstanding all this confidence, only two days later I had this note, dated from his house off Piccadilly:

"Dear sir. I have returned disappointed. If I should feel at all able to see you, I shall write to ask you kindly to call. At present I am too low, and, in fact, simply unable to say all I wish to say. Pray don't mention my name to my friends. I can see no one. By-and-by, please God, you shall hear from me. I mean to take a run into Shropshire, where some of my people are. God bless you! May we, on my return, meet more happily than I can now write."

About a week after this I saw Lady Mary at her own house, the last person, she said, left in town, and just on the wing for Brighton, for the London season was quite over. She told me that she had heard from Mr. Jennings's niece, Martha, in Shropshire. There was nothing to be gathered from her letter, more than that he was low and nervous. In those words, of which healthy people think so lightly, what a world of suffering is sometimes hidden!

Nearly five weeks passed without any further news of Mr. Jennings. At the end of that time I received a note from him. He wrote:

"I have been in the country, and have had change of air, change of scene, change of faces, change of everything and in everything — but *myself*. I have made up my mind, so far as the most irresolute creature on earth can do it, to tell my case fully to you. If your engagements will permit, pray come to me to-day, to-morrow, or the next day; but, pray defer as little as possible. You know not how much I need help. I have a quiet house at Richmond, where I now am. Perhaps you can manage to come to dinner, or to luncheon, or even to tea. You shall have no trouble in finding me out. The servant at Blank-street, who takes this note, will have a carriage at your door at any hour you please; and I am always to be found. You will say that I ought not to be alone. I have tried everything. Come and see."

I called up the servant, and decided on going out the same evening, which accordingly I did.

He would have been much better in a lodging-house, or a hotel, I thought, as I drove up through a short double row of sombre elms to a very old-fashioned brick house, darkened by the foliage of these trees, which over-topped, and nearly surrounded it. It was a perverse choice, for nothing could be imagined more triste[1] and silent. The house, I found, belonged to him. He had stayed for a day or two in town, and, finding it for some cause insupportable, had come out here, probably because being furnished and his own, he was relieved of the thought and delay of selection, by coming here.

The sun had already set, and the red reflected light of the western sky illuminated the scene with the peculiar effect with which we are all familiar. The hall seemed very dark, but, getting to the back drawing-room, whose windows command the west, I was again in the same dusky light. I sat down, looking out upon the richly-wooded landscape that glowed in the grand and melancholy light which was every moment fading. The corners of the room were already dark; all was growing dim, and the gloom was insensibly toning my mind, already prepared for what was sinister. I was waiting alone for his arrival, which soon took place. The door communicating with the front room opened, and the tall figure of Mr. Jennings, faintly seen in the ruddy twilight, came, with quiet stealthy steps, into the room.

We shook hands, and, taking a chair to the window, where there was still light enough to enable us to see each other's faces, he sat down beside me, and, placing his hand upon my arm, with scarcely a word of preface, began his narrative.

CHAPTER VI
How Mr. Jennings Met His Companion.

The faint glow of the west, the pomp of the then lonely woods of Richmond, were before us, behind and about us the darkening room, and on the stony face of the sufferer — for the character of his face, though still gentle and secret, was changed — rested that dim, odd glow which seems to descend and produce, where it touches, lights, sudden though faint, which are lost, almost without gradation, in darkness. The silence, too, was utter; not a distant wheel, or bark, or whistle from without; and within the depressing stillness of an invalid bachelor's house.

I guessed well the nature, though not even vaguely the particulars, of the revelations I was about to receive, from that fixed face of suffering that, so oddly flushed, stood out, like a portrait of Schalken's,[2] before its background of darkness.

---

1   Sad.

2   Godfried Schalken (1643–1703), Dutch painter best known for his technique with shadow and light.

"It began," he said, "on the 15th of October, three years and eleven weeks ago, and two days — I keep very accurate count, for every day is torment. If I leave anywhere a chasm in my narrative tell me.

"About four years ago I began a work, which had cost me very much thought and reading. It was upon the religious metaphysics of the ancients."

"I know," said I; "the actual religion of educated and thinking paganism, quite apart from symbolic worship? A wide and very interesting field."

"Yes; but not good for the mind — the Christian mind, I mean. Paganism is all bound together in essential unity, and, with evil sympathy, their religion involves their art, and both their manners, and the subject is a degrading fascination and the nemesis sure. God forgive me!

"I wrote a great deal; I wrote late at night. I was always thinking on the subject, walking about, wherever I was, everywhere. It thoroughly infected me. You are to remember that all the material ideas connected with it were more or less of the beautiful, the subject itself delightfully interesting, and I, then, without a care."

He sighed heavily.

"I believe that every one who sets about writing in earnest does his work, as a friend of mine phrased it, *on* something — tea, or coffee, or tobacco. I suppose there is a material waste that must be hourly supplied in such occupations, or that we should grow too abstracted, and the mind, as it were, pass out of the body, unless it were reminded often of the connexion by actual sensation. At all events, I felt the want, and I supplied it. Tea was my companion — at first the ordinary black tea, made in the usual way, not too strong; but I drank a great deal, and increased its strength as I went on. I never experienced an uncomfortable symptom from it. I began to take a little green tea. I found the effect pleasanter, it cleared and intensified the power of thought so. I had come to take it frequently, but not stronger than one might take it for pleasure. I wrote a great deal out here, it was so quiet, and in this room. I used to sit up very late, and it became a habit with me to sip my tea — green tea — every now and then as my work proceeded. I had a little kettle on my table, that swung over a lamp, and made tea two or three times between eleven o'clock and two or three in the morning, my hours of going to bed. I used to go into town every day. I was not a monk, and, although I often spent an hour or two in a library, hunting up authorities and looking out lights upon my theme, I was in no morbid state, so far as I can judge. I met my friends pretty much as usual, and enjoyed their society, and, on the whole, existence had never been, I think, so pleasant before.

"I had met with a man who had some odd old books, German editions in mediæval Latin, and I was only too happy to be permitted access to them. This obliging person's books were in the City, a very out-of-the-way part of it. I had rather out-stayed my intended hour, and, on coming out, seeing no cab near, I was tempted to get into the omnibus which used to drive past this house. It was darker than this by the time the 'bus had reached an old house, you may have remarked, with four poplars at each side of the door, and there the last passenger but myself got out. We drove along rather faster. It was twilight now. I leaned back in my corner next the door ruminating pleasantly.

"The interior of the omnibus was nearly dark. I had observed in the corner opposite to me at the other side, and at the end next the horses, two small circular reflections, as it seemed to me, of a reddish light. They were about two inches apart, and about the size of those small brass buttons that yachting men used to put upon their jackets. I began to speculate, as listless men will, upon this trifle, as it seemed. From what centre did that faint but deep red light come, and from what — glass beads, buttons, toy decorations — was it reflected? We were lumbering along gently, having nearly a mile still to go. I had not solved the puzzle, and it became in another minute more odd, for these two luminous points, with a sudden jerk, descended nearer the floor, keeping still their relative distance and horizontal position, and then, as suddenly, they rose to the level of the seat on which I was sitting, and I saw them no more.

"My curiosity was now really excited, and, before I had time to think, I saw again these two dull lamps, again together near the floor; again they disappeared, and again in their old corner I saw them.

"So, keeping my eyes upon them, I edged quietly up my own side, towards the end at which I still saw these tiny discs of red.

"There was very little light in the 'bus. It was nearly dark. I leaned forward to aid my endeavour to discover what these little circles really were. They shifted their position a little as I did so. I began now to perceive an outline of something black, and I soon saw with tolerable distinctness the outline of a small black monkey, pushing its face forward in mimicry to meet mine; those were its eyes, and I now dimly saw its teeth grinning at me.

"I drew back, not knowing whether it might not meditate a spring. I fancied that one of the passengers had forgot this ugly pet, and wishing to ascertain something of its temper, though not caring to trust my fingers to it, I poked my umbrella softly towards it. It remained immovable — up to it — *through* it! For through it, and back and forward, it passed, without the slightest resistance.

"I can't, in the least, convey to you the kind of horror that I felt. When I had ascertained that the thing was an illusion, as I then supposed, there came a misgiving about myself and a terror that fascinated me in impotence to remove my gaze from the eyes of the brute for some moments. As I looked, it made a little skip back, quite into the corner, and I, in a panic, found myself at the door, having put my head out, drawing deep breaths of the outer air, and staring at the lights and trees we were passing, too glad to reassure myself of reality.

"I stopped the 'bus, and got out. I perceived the man look oddly at me as I paid him. I dare say there was something unusual in my looks and manner, for I had never felt so strangely before."

CHAPTER VII
The Journey: First Stage.

"When the omnibus drove on, and I was alone upon the road, I looked carefully round to ascertain whether the monkey had followed me. To my indescribable relief I saw it nowhere. I can't describe easily what a shock I had received, and my sense of genuine gratitude on finding myself, as I supposed, quite rid of it.

"I had got out a little before we reached this house, two or three hundred steps away. A brick wall runs along the footpath, and inside the wall is a hedge of yew or some dark evergreen of that kind, and within that again the row of fine trees which you may have remarked as you came.

"This brick wall is about as high as my shoulder, and happening to raise my eyes I saw the monkey, with that stooping gait, on all fours, walking or creeping, close beside me on top of the wall. I stopped looking at it with a feeling of loathing and horror. As I stopped so did it. It sat up on the wall with its long hands on its knees looking at me. There was not light enough to see it much more than in outline, nor was it dark enough to bring the peculiar light of its eyes into strong relief. I still saw, however, that red foggy light plainly enough. It did not show its teeth, nor exhibit any sign of irritation, but seemed jaded and sulky, and was observing me steadily.

"I drew back into the middle of the road. It was an unconscious recoil, and there I stood, still looking at it. It did not move.

"With an instinctive determination to try something — anything, I turned about and walked briskly towards town with a scaunce look, all the time watching the movements of the beast. It crept swiftly along the wall, at exactly my pace.

"Where the wall ends, near the turn of the road, it came down and with a wiry spring or two brought itself close to my feet, and continued to keep up to me, as I quickened my pace. It was at my left side, so close to my leg that I felt every moment as if I should tread upon it.

"The road was quite deserted and silent, and it was darker every moment. I stopped dismayed and bewildered, turning as I did so, the other way — I mean, towards this house, away from which I had been walking. When I stood still, the monkey drew back to a distance of, I suppose, about five or six yards, and remained stationary, watching me.

"I had been more agitated than I have said. I had read, of course, as every one has, something about 'spectral illusions,' as you physicians term the phenomena of such cases. I considered my situation and looked my misfortune in the face.

"These affections, I had read, are sometimes transitory and sometimes obstinate. I had read of cases in which the appearance, at first harmless, had, step by step, degenerated into something direful and insupportable, and ended by wearing its victim out. Still as I stood there, but for my bestial companion, quite alone, I tried to comfort myself by repeating again and again the assurance, 'the thing is purely disease, a well-known physical affection, as distinctly as small-pox or neuralgia.[1] Doctors are all agreed on that, philosophy demonstrates it. I must not be a fool. I've been sitting up too late, and I dare say my digestion is quite wrong, and with God's help, I shall be all right, and this is but a symptom of nervous dyspepsia.' Did I believe all this? Not one word of it, no more than any other miserable being ever did who is once seized and riveted in this satanic captivity. Against my convictions, I might say my knowledge, I was simply bullying myself into a false courage.

"I now walked homeward. I had only a few hundred yards to go. I had forced myself into a sort of resignation, but I had not got over the sickening shock and the flurry of the first certainty of my misfortune.

"I made up my mind to pass the night at home. The brute moved close beside me, and I fancied there was the sort of anxious drawing toward the house, which one sees in tired horses or dogs, sometimes as they come toward home.

"I was afraid to go into town — I was afraid of any one's seeing and recognising me. I was conscious of an irrepressible agitation in my manner.

---

1 Disease the symptoms of which include sharp pain extending along a nerve or nerves.

Also, I was afraid of any violent change in my habits, such as going to a place of amusement, or walking from home in order to fatigue myself. At the hall-door it waited till I mounted the steps, and when the door was opened entered with me.

"I drank no tea that night. I got cigars and some brandy-and-water. My idea was that I should act upon my material system, and by living for a while in sensation apart from thought, send myself forcibly, as it were, into a new groove. I came up here to this drawing-room. I sat just here. The monkey got upon a small table that then stood *there*. It looked dazed and languid. An irrepressible uneasiness as to its movements kept my eyes always upon it. Its eyes were half-closed, but I could see them glow. It was looking steadily at me. In all situations, at all hours, it is awake and looking at me. That never changes.

"I shall not continue in detail my narrative of this particular night. I shall describe, rather, the phenomena of the first year, which never varied, collectively. I shall describe the monkey as it appeared in daylight. In the dark, as you shall presently hear, there are peculiarities. It is a small monkey, perfectly black. It had only one peculiarity — a character of malignity — unfathomable malignity. During the first year it looked sullen and sick. But this character of intense malice and vigilance was always underlying that surly languor. During all that time it acted as if on a plan of giving me as little trouble as was consistent with watching me. Its eyes were never off me. I have never lost sight of it, except in my sleep, light or dark, day or night, since it came here, excepting when it withdraws for some weeks at a time, unaccountably.

"In total dark it is visible as in daylight. I do not mean merely its eyes. It is *all* visible distinctly in a halo that resembles a glow of red embers, and which accompanies it in all its movements.

"When it leaves me for a time, it is always at night, in the dark, and in the same way. It grows at first uneasy, and then furious, and then advances towards me, grinning and shaking its paws clenched, and, at the same time, there comes the appearance of fire in the grate. I never have any fire, I can't sleep in the room where there is any, and it draws nearer and nearer to the chimney, quivering, it seems, with rage, and when its fury rises to the highest pitch, it springs into the grate, and up the chimney, and I see it no more.

"When first this happened I thought I was released. I was a new man. A day passed — a night — and no return, and a blessed week — a week — another week — I was always on my knees, Dr. Hesselius, always, thanking

God and praying. A whole month passed of liberty, but on a sudden, it was with me again."

CHAPTER VIII
The Second Stage.

"It was with me, and the malice which before was torpid under a sullen exterior, was now active. It was perfectly unchanged in every other respect. This new energy was apparent in its activity and its looks, and soon in other ways.

"For a time, you will understand, the change was shown only in an increased vivacity, and an air of menace, as if it was always brooding over some atrocious plan. Its eyes, as before, were never off me."

"Is it here now?" I asked.

"No," he replied, "it has been absent exactly a fortnight and a day — fifteen days. It has sometimes been away so long as nearly two months, once for three. Its absence always exceeds a fortnight, although it may be but by a single day. Fifteen days having past since I saw it last, it may return now at any moment."

"Is its return," I asked, "accompanied by any peculiar manifestation?"

"Nothing — no," he said. "It is simply with me again. On lifting my eyes from a book, or turning my head, I see it, as usual, looking at me, and then it remains, as before, for its appointed time. I have never told so much and so minutely before to any one."

I perceived that he was agitated, and looking like death, and he repeatedly applied his handkerchief to his forehead, and I suggested that he might be tired, and told him that I would call, with pleasure, in the morning, but he said:

"No, if you don't mind hearing it all now. I have got so far, and I should prefer making one effort of it. When I spoke to Dr. Harley, I had nothing like so much to tell. You are a philosophic physician. You give spirit its proper rank. If this thing is real —"

He paused, looking at me with agitated inquiry.

"We can discuss it by-and-by, and very fully. I will give you all I think," I answered, after an interval.

"Well — very well. If it is anything real, I say, it is prevailing, little by little, and drawing me more interiorly into hell. Optic nerves, he talked of. Ah! well — there are other nerves of communication. May God Almighty help me! You shall hear.

"Its power of action, I tell you, had increased. Its malice became, in a way, aggressive. About two years ago, some questions that were pending between me and the bishop, having been settled, I went down to my parish in Warwickshire, anxious to find occupation in my profession. I was not prepared for what happened, although I have since thought I might have apprehended something like it. The reason of my saying so, is this —"

He was beginning to speak with a great deal more effort and reluctance, and sighed often, and seemed at times nearly overcome. But at this time his manner was not agitated. It was more like that of a sinking patient, who has given himself up.

"Yes, but I will first tell you about Kenlis, my parish.

"It was with me when I left this for Dawlbridge. It was my silent traveling companion, and it remained with me at the vicarage. When I entered on the discharge of my duties, another change took place. The thing exhibited an atrocious determination to thwart me. It was with me in the church — in the reading-desk — in the pulpit — within the communion-rails. At last, it reached this extremity, that while I was reading to the congregation, it would spring upon the open book and squat there, so that I was unable to see the page. This happened more than once.

"I left Dawlbridge for a time. I placed myself in Dr. Harley's hands. I did everything he told me. He gave my case a great deal of thought. It interested him, I think. He seemed successful. For nearly three months I was perfectly free from a return. I began to think I was safe. With his full assent I returned to Dawlbridge.

"I travelled in a chaise. I was in good spirits. I was more — I was happy and grateful. I was returning, as I thought, delivered from a dreadful hallucination, to the scene of duties which I longed to enter upon. It was a beautiful sunny evening, everything looked serene and cheerful, and I was delighted. I remember looking out of the window to see the spire of my church at Kenlis among the trees, at the point where one has the earliest view of it. It is exactly where the little stream that bounds the parish, passes under the road by a culvert, and where it emerges at the road-side, a stone with an old inscription is placed. As we passed this point, I drew my head in and sat down, and in the corner of the chaise was the monkey.

"For a moment I felt faint, and then quite wild with despair and horror. I called to the driver, and got out, and sat down at the road-side, and prayed to God silently for mercy. A despairing resignation supervened. My companion was with me as I re-entered the vicarage. The same persecution followed. After a short struggle I submitted, and soon I left the place.

"I told you," he said "that the beast has before this become in certain ways aggressive. I will explain a little. It seemed to be actuated by intense and increasing fury, whenever I said my prayers, or even meditated prayer. It amounted at last to a dreadful interruption. You will ask, how could a silent immaterial phantom effect that? It was thus, whenever I meditated praying; it was always before me, and nearer and nearer.

"It used to spring on a table, on the back of a chair, on the chimney-piece, and slowly to swing itself from side to side, looking at me all the time. There is in its motion an indefinable power to dissipate thought, and to contract one's attention to that monotony, till the ideas shrink, as it were, to a point, and at last to nothing — and unless I had started up, and shook off the catalepsy I have felt as if my mind were on the point of losing itself. There are other ways," he sighed heavily; "thus, for instance, while I pray with my eyes closed, it comes closer and closer, and I see it. I know it is not to be accounted for physically, but I do actually see it, though my lids are closed, and so it rocks my mind, as it were, and overpowers me, and I am obliged to rise from my knees. If you had ever yourself known this, you would be acquainted with desperation."

CHAPTER IX
The Third Stage.

"I see, Dr. Hesselius, that you don't lose one word of my statement. I need not ask you to listen specially to what I am now going to tell you. They talk of the optic nerves, and of spectral illusions, as if the organ of sight was the only point assailable by the influences that have fastened upon me — I know better. For two years in my direful case that limitation prevailed. But as food is taken in softly at the lips, and then brought under the teeth, as the tip of the little finger caught in a mill-crank will draw in the hand, and the arm, and the whole body, so the miserable mortal who has been once caught firmly by the end of the finest fibre of his nerve, is drawn in and in, by the enormous machinery of hell, until he is as I am. Yes, doctor, as *I* am, for while I talk to you, and implore relief, I feel that my prayer is for the impossible, and my pleading with the inexorable."

I endeavoured to calm his visibly increasing agitation, and told him that he must not despair.

While we talked the night had overtaken us. The filmy moonlight was wide over the scene which the window commanded, and I said:

"Perhaps you would prefer having candles. This light, you know, is odd. I should wish you, as much as possible, under your usual conditions while I make my diagnosis, shall I call it — otherwise I don't care."

"All lights are the same to me," he said: "except when I read or write, I care not if night were perpetual. I am going to tell you what happened about a year ago. The thing began to speak to me."

"Speak! How do you mean — speak as a man does, do you mean?"

"Yes; speak in words and consecutive sentences, with perfect coherence and articulation; but there is a peculiarity. It is not like the tone of a human voice. It is not by my ears it reaches me — it comes like a singing through my head.

"This faculty, the power of speaking to me, will be my undoing. It won't let me pray, it interrupts me with dreadful blasphemies. I dare not go on, I could not. Oh! doctor, can the skill, and thought, and prayers of man avail me nothing!"

"You must promise me, my dear sir, not to trouble yourself with unnecessarily exciting thoughts; confine yourself strictly to the narrative of *facts*; and recollect, above all, that even if the thing that infests you be as you seem to suppose, a reality with an actual independent life and will, yet it can have no power to hurt you, unless it be given from above: its access to your senses depends mainly upon your physical condition — this is, under God, your comfort and reliance: we are all alike environed. It is only that in your case, the 'paries,'[1] the veil of the flesh, the screen, is a little out of repair, and sights and sounds are transmitted. We must enter on a new course, sir — be encouraged. I'll give to-night to the careful consideration of the whole case."

"You are very good, sir; you think it worth trying, you don't give me quite up; but, sir, you don't know, it is gaining such an influence over me: it orders me about, it is such a tyrant, and I'm growing so helpless. May God deliver me!"

"It orders you about — of course you mean by speech?"

"Yes, yes; it is always urging me to crimes, to injure others, or myself. You see, doctor, the situation is urgent, it is indeed. When I was in Shropshire, a few weeks ago" (Mr. Jennings was speaking rapidly and trembling now, holding my arm with one hand, and looking in my face), "I went out one day with a party of friends for a walk: my persecutor, I tell you, was with me at the time. I lagged behind the rest: the country near the Dee, you know, is beautiful. Our path happened to lie near a coal

---

1   (Latin) wall.

mine, and at the verge of the wood is a perpendicular shaft, they say, a hundred and fifty feet deep. My niece had remained behind with me — she knows, of course, nothing of the nature of my sufferings. She knew, however, that I had been ill, and was low, and she remained to prevent my being quite alone. As we loitered slowly on together the brute that accompanied me was urging me to throw myself down the shaft. I tell you now — oh, sir, think of it! — the one consideration that saved me from that hideous death was the fear lest the shock of witnessing the occurrence should be too much for the poor girl. I asked her to go on and take her walk with her friends, saying that I could go no further. She made excuses, and the more I urged her the firmer she became. She looked doubtful and frightened. I suppose there was something in my looks or manner that alarmed her; but she would not go, and that literally saved me. You had no idea, sir, that a living man could be made so abject a slave of Satan," he said, with a ghastly groan and a shudder.

There was a pause here, and I said, "You *were* preserved nevertheless. It was the act of God. You are in his hands and in the power of no other being: be therefore confident for the future."

CHAPTER X
Home.

I made him have candles lighted, and saw the room looking cheery and inhabited before I left him. I told him that he must regard his illness strictly as one dependent on physical, though *subtle* physical, causes. I told him that he had evidence of God's care and love in the deliverance which he had just described, and that I had perceived with pain that he seemed to regard its peculiar features as indicating that he had been delivered over to spiritual reprobation. Than such a conclusion nothing could be, I insisted, less warranted; and not only so, but more contrary to facts, as disclosed in his mysterious deliverance from that murderous influence during his Shropshire excursion. First, his niece had been retained by his side without his intending to keep her near him; and, secondly, there had been infused into his mind an irresistible repugnance to execute the dreadful suggestion in her presence.

As I reasoned this point with him, Mr. Jennings wept. He seemed comforted. One promise I exacted, which was that should the monkey at any time return, I should be sent for immediately; and, repeating my assurance that I would give neither time nor thought to any other subject until I had thoroughly investigated his case, and that to-morrow he should hear the result, I took my leave.

Before getting into the carriage I told the servant that his master was far from well, and that he should make a point of frequently looking into his room.

My own arrangements I made with a view to being quite secure from interruption.

I merely called at my lodgings, and, with a travelling-desk and carpet-bag, set off in a hackney-carriage for an inn about two miles out of town, called The Horns, a very quiet and comfortable house, with good thick walls. And there I resolved, without the possibility of intrusion or distraction, to devote some hours of the night, in my comfortable sitting-room, to Mr. Jennings's case, and so much of the morning as it might require.

(There occurs here a careful note of Dr. Hesselius's opinion upon the case, and of the habits, dietary, and medicines which he prescribed. It is curious — some people would say mystical. But on the whole I doubt whether it would sufficiently interest a reader of the kind I am likely to meet with to warrant its being here reprinted. This whole letter was plainly written at the inn in which he had hid himself for the occasion. The next letter is dated from his town lodgings.)

I left town for the inn where I slept last night at half-past nine, and did not arrive at my room in town until one o'clock this afternoon. I found a letter in Mr. Jennings's hand upon my table. It had not come by post, and on inquiry, I learned that Mr. Jennings's servant had brought it, and on learning that I was not to return until to-day, and that no one could tell him my address, he seemed very uncomfortable, and said that his orders from his master were that he was not to return without an answer.

I opened the letter, and read:

"Dear Dr. Hesselius. It is here. You had not been an hour gone when it returned. It is speaking. It knows all that has happened. It knows everything — it knows you, and is frantic and atrocious. It reviles. I send you this. It knows every word I have written — I write. This I promised, and I therefore write, but I fear very confused, very incoherently. I am so interrupted, disturbed.

"Ever yours, sincerely yours,
"Robert Lynder Jennings."

"When did this come?" I asked.

"About eleven last night; the man was here again, and has been here three times to-day. The last time is about an hour since."

Thus answered, and with the notes I had made upon his case in my pocket, I was, in a few minutes, driving out to Richmond, to see Mr. Jennings.

I by no means, as you perceive, despaired of Mr. Jennings's case. He had himself remembered and applied, though quite in a mistaken way, the principle which I lay down in my Metaphysical Medicine, and which governs all such cases. I was about to apply it in earnest. I was profoundly interested, and very anxious to see and examine him while the "enemy" was actually present.

I drove up to the sombre house, and ran up the steps, and knocked. The door, in a little time, was opened by a tall woman in black silk. She looked ill, and as if she had been crying. She curtseyed, and heard my question, but she did not answer. She turned her face away, extending her hand hurriedly towards two men who were coming down-stairs; and thus having, as it were, tacitly made me over to them, she passed through a side-door hastily and shut it.

The man who was nearest the hall, I at once accosted, but being now close to him, I was shocked to see that both his hands were covered with blood.

I drew back a little, and the man passing down-stairs merely said in a low tone, "Here's the servant, sir."

The servant had stopped on the stairs, confounded and dumb at seeing me. He was rubbing his hands in a handkerchief, and it was steeped in blood.

"Jones, what is it, what has happened?" I asked, while a sickening suspicion overpowered me.

The man asked me to come up to the lobby. I was beside him in a moment, and frowning and pallid, with contracted eyes, he told me the horror which I already half guessed.

His master had made away with himself.

I went up-stairs with him to the room — what I saw there I won't tell you. He had cut his throat with his razor. It was a frightful gash. The two men had laid him upon the bed and composed his limbs. It had happened, as the immense pool of blood on the floor declared, at some distance between the bed and the window. There was carpet round his bed, and a carpet under his dressing-table, but none on the rest of the floor, for the man said he did not like carpet on his bedroom. In this sombre, and now terrible room, one of the great elms that darkened the house was slowly moving the shadow of one of its great boughs upon this dreadful floor.

I beckoned to the servant and we went down-stairs together. I turned, off the hall, into an old-fashioned panelled room, and there standing, I heard all the servant had to tell. It was not a great deal.

"I concluded, sir, from your words, and looks, sir, as you left last night, that you thought my master seriously ill. I thought it might be that you were afraid of a fit, or something. So I attended very close to your directions. He sat up late, till past three o'clock. He was not writing or reading. He was talking a great deal to himself, but that was nothing unusual. At about that hour I assisted him to undress, and left him in his slippers and dressing-gown. I went back softly in about half an hour. He was in his bed, quite undressed, and a pair of candles lighted on the table beside his bed. He was leaning on his elbow and looking out at the other side of the bed when I came in. I asked him if he wanted anything, and he said no.

"I don't know whether it was what you said to me, sir, or something a little unusual about him, but I was uneasy, uncommon uneasy, about him last night.

"In another half hour, or it might be a little more, I went up again. I did not hear him talking as before. I opened the door a little. The candles were both out, which was not usual. I had a bedroom candle, and I let the light in, a little bit, looking softly round. I saw him sitting in that chair beside the dressing-table with his clothes on again. He turned round and looked at me. I thought it strange he should get up and dress, and put out the candles to sit in the dark, that way. But I only asked him again if I could do anything for him. He said, no, rather sharp, I thought. I asked if I might light the candles, and he said, 'Do as you like, Jones.' So I lighted them, and I lingered a little about the room, and he said, 'Tell me truth, Jones, why did you come again — you did not hear any one cursing?' 'No, sir,' I said, wondering what he could mean.

"'No,' said he, after me, 'of course, no;' and I said to him, 'Wouldn't it be well, sir, you went to bed? It's just five o'clock;' and he said nothing but, 'Very likely: good-night, Jones.' So I went, sir, but in less than an hour I came again. The door was fast, and he heard me, and called as I thought from the bed to know what I wanted, and he desired me not to disturb him again. I lay down and slept for a little. It must have been between six and seven when I went up again. The door was still fast, and he made no answer, so I did not like to disturb him, and thinking he was asleep, I left him till nine. It was his custom to ring when he wished me to come, and I had no particular hour for calling him. I tapped very gently, and getting no answer, I stayed away a good while, supposing he was getting some rest then. It was not till eleven o'clock I grew really uncomfortable about him — for at the latest he was never, that I could remember, later than half-past ten. I got no answer. I knocked and called, and still no answer. So not being able to force the door, I called Thomas from the stables, and together we forced it, and found him in the shocking way you saw."

Jones had no more to tell. Poor Mr. Jennings was very gentle, and very kind. All his people were fond of him. I could see that the servant was very much moved.

So, dejected and agitated, I passed from that terrible house, and its dark canopy of elms, and I hope I shall never see it more. While I write to you I feel like a man who has but half waked from a frightful and monotonous dream. My memory rejects the picture with incredulity and horror. Yet I know it is true. It is the story of the process of a poison, a poison which excites the reciprocal action of spirit and nerve, and paralyses the tissue that separates those cognate functions of the senses, the external and the interior. Thus we find strange bed-fellows, and the mortal and immortal prematurely make acquaintance.

CONCLUSION
A Word For Those Who Suffer.

My dear Van L., you have suffered from an affection similar to that which I have just described. You twice complained of a return of it.

Who, under God, cured you? Your humble servant, Martin Hesselius. Let me rather adopt the more emphasised piety of a certain good old French surgeon of three hundred years ago: "I treated, and God cured you."

Come, my friend, you are not to be hippish. Let me tell you a fact.

I have met with, and treated, as my book shows, fifty-seven cases of this kind of vision, which I term indifferently "sublimated," "precocious," and "interior."

There is another class of affections which are truly termed — though commonly confounded with those which I describe — spectral illusions. These latter I look upon as being no less simply curable than a cold in the head or a trifling dyspepsia.

It is those which rank in the first category that test our promptitude of thought. Fifty-seven such cases have I encountered, neither more nor less. And in how many of these have I failed? In no one single instance.

There is no one affliction of mortality more easily and certainly reducible, with a little patience, and a rational confidence in the physician. With these simple conditions, I look upon the cure as absolutely certain.

You are to remember that I had not even commenced to treat Mr. Jennings's case. I have not any doubt that I should have cured him perfectly in eighteen months, or possibly it might have extended to two years. Some cases are very rapidly curable, others extremely tedious. Every intelligent physician who will give thought and diligence to the task, will effect a cure.

You know my tract on The Cardinal Functions of the Brain. I there, by the evidence of innumerable facts, prove, as I think, the high probability of a circulation arterial and venous in its mechanism, through the nerves. Of this system, thus considered, the brain is the heart. The fluid, which is propagated hence through one class of nerves, returns in an altered state through another, and the nature of that fluid is spiritual, though not immaterial, any more than, as I before remarked, light or electricity are so.

By various abuses, among which the habitual use of such agents as green tea is one, this fluid may be affected as to its quality, but it is more frequently disturbed as to equilibrium. This fluid being that which we have in common with spirits, a congestion found upon the masses of brain or nerve, connected with the interior sense, forms a surface unduly exposed, on which disembodied spirits may operate: communication is thus more or less effectually established. Between this brain circulation and the heart circulation there is an intimate sympathy. The seat, or rather the instrument of exterior vision, is the eye. The seat of interior vision is the nervous tissue and brain, immediately about and above the eyebrow. You remember how effectually I dissipated your pictures by the simple application of iced eau-de-cologne. Few cases, however, can be treated exactly alike with anything like rapid success. Cold acts powerfully as a repellant of the nervous fluid. Long enough continued it will even produce that permanent insensibility which we call numbness, and a little longer, muscular as well as sensational paralysis.

I have not, I repeat, the slightest doubt that I should have first dimmed and ultimately sealed that inner eye which Mr. Jennings had inadvertently opened. The same senses are opened in delirium tremens,[1] and entirely shut up again when the over-action of the cerebral heart, and the prodi-

---

1   State that appears in people who are going through withdrawal, usually from alcohol. It can consist of agitation, shaking and hallucinations.

gious nervous congestions that attend it, are terminated by a decided change in the state of the body. It is by acting steadily upon the body, by a simple process, that this result is produced — and inevitably produced — I have never yet failed.

Poor Mr. Jennings made away with himself. But that catastrophe was the result of a totally different malady, which, as it were, projected itself upon that disease which was established. His case was in the distinctive manner a complication, and the complaint under which he really succumbed, was hereditary suicidal mania. Poor Mr. Jennings I cannot call a patient of mine, for I had not even begun to treat his case, and he had not yet given me, I am convinced, his full and unreserved confidence. If the patient do not array himself on the side of the disease, his cure is certain.

Mary De Morgan

"A Toy Princess" (1877)

[Mary De Morgan's (1850–1907) mother was herself an author while Mary's brother, William De Morgan, was an author and illustrator. The two siblings eventually shared a house in Chelsea, turning it into a meeting place for artists and literary figures of the day. Through her parents, De Morgan met such important artists and writers as Edward Burne-Jones, William Morris, and Dante Gabriel Rossetti. The woodcuts that her brother did for her first collection of tales, *On a Pincushion and Other Tales* (1877), reflect this Pre-Raphaelite influence. Her other two collections of children's stories were *The Necklace of Princess Fiorimonde* (1880) and *The Windfairies* (1900). De Morgan is known to have repeatedly practised her stories on a live audience as a means of revising, before publishing them in written form. One of her audience members was Rudyard Kipling. Due to health reasons, she eventually moved to Cairo, where she managed a children's reformatory until her death. "A Toy Princess" has been one of De Morgan's most popular works, but it also stands out for its effective combination of entertainment and education; in this instance, it is De Morgan's concerns regarding women's rights and agency that come forward.]

More than a thousand years ago, in a country quite on the other side of the world, it fell out that the people all grew so very polite that they hardly ever spoke to each other. And they never said more than was quite necessary, as "Just so," "Yes indeed," "Thank you," and "If you please." And it was thought to be the rudest thing in the world for any one to say they liked or disliked, or loved or hated, or were happy or miserable. No one ever laughed aloud, and if any one had been seen to cry they would at once have been avoided by their friends.

The King of this country married a Princess from a neighbouring land, who was very good and beautiful, but the people in her own home were as unlike her husband's people as it was possible to be. They laughed and talked, and were noisy and merry when they were happy, and cried and lamented if they were sad. In fact, whatever they felt they showed at once, and the Princess was just like them.

So when she came to her new home, she could not at all understand her subjects, or make out why there was no shouting and cheering to welcome her, and why every one was so distant and formal. After a time, when she found they never changed, but were always the same, just as stiff and quiet, she wept, and began to pine for her own old home.

Every day she grew thinner and paler. The courtiers were much too polite to notice how ill their young Queen looked, but she knew it herself, and she believed she was going to die.

Now she had a fairy godmother, named Taboret, whom she loved dearly, and who was always kind to her. When she knew her end was drawing near she sent for her godmother, and when she came had a long talk with her quite alone.

No one knew what was said, and soon afterwards a little Princess was born, and the Queen died. Of course all the courtiers were sorry for the poor Queen's death, but it would have been thought rude to say so. So, although there was a grand funeral, and the court put on mourning, everything else went on much as it had done before.

The little baby was christened Ursula, and given to some court ladies to be taken charge of. Poor little Princess! *She* cried hard enough, and nothing could stop her.

All her ladies were frightened, and said that they had not heard such a dreadful noise for a long time. But, till she was about two years old, nothing could stop her crying when she was cold or hungry, or crowing when she was pleased.

After that she began to understand a little what was meant when her nurses told her, in cold, polite tones, that she was being naughty, and she grew much quieter.

She was a pretty little girl, with a round baby face and big merry blue eyes; but as she grew older, her eyes grew less and less merry and bright, and her fat little face grew thin and pale. She was not allowed to play with any other children, lest she might learn bad manners; and she was not taught any games or given any toys. So she passed most of her time, when she was not at her lessons, looking out of the window at the birds flying against the clear blue sky; and sometimes she would give a sad little sigh when her ladies were not listening.

One day the old fairy Taboret made herself invisible, and flew over to the King's palace to see how things were going on there. She went straight up to the nursery, where she found poor little Ursula sitting by the window, with her head leaning on her hand.

It was a very grand room, but there were no toys or dolls about, and when the fairy saw this, she frowned to herself and shook her head.

"Your Royal Highness's dinner is now ready," said the head nurse to Ursula.

"I don't want any dinner," said Ursula, without turning her head.

"I think I have told your Royal Highness before that it is not polite to say you don't want anything, or that you don't like it," said the nurse. "We are waiting for your Royal Highness."

So the Princess got up and went to the dinner-table, and Taboret watched them all the time. When she saw how pale little Ursula was, and how little she ate, and that there was no talking or laughing allowed, she sighed and frowned even more than before, and then she flew back to her fairy home, where she sat for some hours in deep thought.

At last she rose, and went out to pay a visit to the largest shop in Fairyland.

It was a queer sort of shop. It was neither a grocer's, nor a draper's, nor a hatter's. Yet it contained sugar, and dresses, and hats. But the sugar was magic sugar, which transformed any liquid into which it was put; the dresses each had some special charm, and the hats were wishing-caps. It was, in fact, a shop where every sort of spell or charm was sold.

Into this shop Taboret flew; and as she was well known there as a good customer, the master of the shop came forward to meet her at once, and bowing, begged to know what he could get for her.

"I want," said Taboret, "a Princess."

"A Princess!" said the shopman, who was in reality an old wizard. "What size do you want it? I have one or two in stock."

"It must look now about six years old. But it must grow."

"I can make you one," said the wizard, "but it'll come rather expensive."

"I don't mind that," said Taboret. "See! I want it to look exactly like this," and so saying she took a portrait of Ursula out of her bosom and gave it to the old man, who examined it carefully.

"I'll get it for you," he said. "When will you want it?"

"As soon as possible," said Taboret. "By to-morrow evening if possible. How much will it cost?"

"It'll come to a good deal," said the wizard, thoughtfully. "I have such difficulty in getting these things properly made in these days. What sort of a voice is it to have?"

"It need not be at all talkative," said Taboret, "so that won't add much to the price. It need only say, 'If you please,' 'No, thank you,' 'Certainly,' and 'Just so.'"

"Well, under those circumstances," said the wizard, "I will do it for four cats' footfalls, two fishes' screams, and two swans' songs."

"It is too much," cried Taboret. "I'll give you the footfalls and the screams, but to ask for swans' songs!"

She did not really think it dear, but she always made a point of trying to beat tradesmen down.

"I can't do it for less," said the wizard, "and if you think it too much, you'd better try another shop."

"As I am really in a hurry for it, and cannot spend time in searching about, I suppose I must have it," said Taboret; "but I consider the price very high. When will it be ready?"

"By to-morrow evening."

"Very well, then, be sure it is ready for me by the time I call for it, and whatever you do, don't make it at all noisy or rough in its ways"; and Taboret swept out of the shop and returned to her home.

Next evening she returned and asked if her job was done.

"I will fetch it, and I am sure you will like it," said the wizard, leaving the shop as he spoke. Presently he came back, leading by the hand a pretty little girl of about six years old — a little girl so like the Princess Ursula that no one could have told them apart.

"Well," said Taboret, "it looks well enough. But are you sure that it's a good piece of workmanship, and won't give way anywhere?"

"It's as good a piece of work as ever was done," said the wizard, proudly, striking the child on the back as he spoke. "Look at it! Examine it all over, and see if you find a flaw anywhere. There's not one fairy in twenty who could tell it from the real thing, and no mortal could."

"It seems to be fairly made," said Taboret, approvingly, as she turned the little girl round. "Now I'll pay you and then will be off"; with which she raised her wand in the air and waved it three times, and there arose a series of strange sounds.

The first was a low tramping, the second shrill and piercing screams, the third voices of wonderful beauty, singing a very sorrowful song.

The wizard caught all the sounds and pocketed them at once, and Taboret, without ceremony, picked up the child, took her head downwards under her arm, and flew away.

At court that night the little Princess had been naughty, and had refused to go to bed. It was a long time before her ladies could get her into her crib, and when she was there, she did not really go to sleep, only lay still and pretended, till every one went away; then she got up and stole noiselessly to the window, and sat down on the window-seat all curled up in a little bunch, while she looked out wistfully at the moon. She was such a pretty soft thing, with all her warm bright hair falling over her shoulders, that it would have been hard for most people to be angry with her. She leaned her chin on her tiny white hands, and as she gazed out, the tears rose to her great blue eyes; but remembering that her ladies would call this naughty, she wiped them hastily away with her nightgown sleeve.

"Ah moon, pretty bright moon!" she said to herself, "I wonder if they let you cry when you want to. I think I'd like to go up there and live with you; I'm sure it would be nicer than being here."

"Would you like to go away with me?" said a voice close beside her; and looking up she saw a funny old woman in a red cloak, standing near to her. She was not frightened, for the old woman had a kind smile and bright black eyes, though her nose was hooked and her chin long.

"Where would you take me?" said the little Princess, sucking her thumb, and staring with all her might.

"I'd take you to the sea-shore, where you'd be able to play about on the sands, and where you'd have some little boys and girls to play with, and no one to tell you not to make a noise."

"I'll go," said Ursula, springing up at once.

"Come along," said the old woman, taking her tenderly in her arms and folding her in her warm red cloak. Then they rose up in the air, and flew out of the window, right away over the tops of the houses.

The night air was sharp, and Ursula soon fell asleep; but still they kept flying on, on, over hill and dale, for miles and miles, away from the palace, towards the sea.

Far away from the court and the palace, in a tiny fishing village, on the sea, was a little hut where a fisherman named Mark lived with his wife and three children He was a poor man, and lived on the fish he caught in his little boat. The children, Oliver, Philip, and little Bell, were rosy-cheeked and bright-eyed. They played all day long on the shore, and shouted till they were hoarse. To this village the fairy bore the still sleeping Ursula, and gently placed her on the door-step of Mark's cottage; then she kissed her cheeks, and with one gust blew the door open, and disappeared before any one could come to see who it was.

The fisherman and his wife were sitting quietly within. She was making the children clothes, and he was mending his net, when without any noise the door opened and the cold night air blew in.

"Wife," said the fisherman, "just see who's at the door."

The wife got up and went to the door, and there lay Ursula, still sleeping soundly, in her little white nightdress.

The woman gave a little scream at sight of the child, and called to her husband.

"Husband, see, here's a little girl!" and so saying she lifted her in her arms, and carried her into the cottage. When she was brought into the warmth and light, Ursula awoke, and sitting up, stared about her in fright. She did not cry, as another child might have done, but she trembled very much, and was almost too frightened to speak.

Oddly enough, she had forgotten all about her strange flight through the air, and could remember nothing to tell the fisherman and his wife, but that she was the Princess Ursula; and, on hearing this, the good man and woman thought the poor little girl must be a trifle mad. However, when they examined her little nightdress, made of white fine linen and embroidery, with a crown worked in one corner, they agreed that she must belong to very grand people. They said it would be cruel to send the poor little thing away on such a cold night, and they must of course keep her till she was claimed. So the woman gave her some warm bread-and-milk, and put her to bed with their own little girl.

In the morning, when the court ladies came to wake Princess Ursula, they found her sleeping as usual in her little bed, and little did they think it was not she, but a toy Princess placed there in her stead. Indeed the ladies were much pleased; for when they said, "It is time for your Royal Highness to arise," she only answered, "Certainly," and let herself be dressed without another word. And as the time passed, and she was never naughty, and scarcely ever spoke, all said she was vastly improved, and she grew to be a great favourite.

The ladies all said that the young Princess bid fair to have the most elegant manners in the country, and the King smiled and noticed her with pleasure.

In the meantime, in the fisherman's cottage far away, the real Ursula grew tall and straight as an alder, and merry and light-hearted as a bird.

No one came to claim her, so the good fisherman and his wife kept her and brought her up among their own little ones. She played with them on the beach, and learned her lessons with them at school, and her old life had become like a dream she barely remembered.

But sometimes the mother would take out the little embroidered nightgown and show it to her, and wonder whence she came, and to whom she belonged.

"I don't care who I belong to," said Ursula; "they won't come and take me from you, and that's all I care about." So she grew tall and fair, and as she grew, the toy Princess, in her place at the court, grew too, and always was just like her, only that whereas Ursula's face was sunburnt and her cheeks red, the face of the toy Princess was pale, with only a very slight tint in her cheeks.

Years passed, and Ursula at the cottage was a tall young woman, and Ursula at the court was thought to be the most beautiful there, and every one admired her manners, though she never said anything but "If you please," "No, thank you," "Certainly," and "Just so."

The King was now an old man, and the fisherman Mark and his wife were grey-headed. Most of their fishing was now done by their eldest son Oliver, who was their great pride. Ursula waited on them, and cleaned the house, and did the needlework, and was so useful that they could not have done without her. The fairy Taboret had come to the cottage from time to time, unseen by anyone, to see Ursula, and always finding her healthy and merry, was pleased to think of how she had saved her from a dreadful life. But one evening when she paid them a visit, not having been there for some time, she saw something which made her pause and consider. Oliver and Ursula were standing together watching the waves, and Taboret stopped to hear what they said, —

"When we are married," said Oliver, softly, "we will live in that little cottage yonder, so that we can come and see them every day. But that will not be till little Bell is old enough to take your place, for how would my mother do without you?"

"And we had better not tell them," said Ursula, "that we mean to marry, or else the thought that they are preventing us will make them unhappy."

When Taboret heard this she became grave, and pondered for a long time. At last she flew back to the court to see how things were going on there. She found the King in the middle of a state council. On seeing this, she at once made herself visible, when the King begged her to be seated near him, as he was always glad of her help and advice.

"You find us," said his Majesty, "just about to resign our sceptre into younger and more vigorous hands; in fact, we think we are growing too old to reign, and mean to abdicate in favour of our dear daughter, who will reign in our stead."

"Before you do any such thing," said Taboret, "just let me have a little private conversation with you"; and she led the King into a corner, much to his surprise and alarm.

In about half an hour he returned to the council, looking very white, and with a dreadful expression on his face, whilst he held a handkerchief to his eyes.

"My lords," he faltered, "pray pardon our apparently extraordinary behaviour. We have just received a dreadful blow; we hear on authority, which we cannot doubt, that our dear, dear daughter" — here sobs choked his voice, and he was almost unable to proceed — "is — is — in fact, not our daughter at all, and only a *sham*." Here the King sank back in his chair, overpowered with grief, and the fairy Taboret, stepping to the front, told the courtiers the whole story; how she had stolen the real Princess, because she feared they were spoiling her, and how she had placed a toy Princess in her place. The courtiers looked from one to another in surprise, but it was evident they did not believe her.

"The Princess is a truly charming young lady," said the Prime Minister.

"Has your Majesty any reason to complain of her Royal Highness's conduct?" asked the old Chancellor.

"None whatever," sobbed the King; "she was ever an excellent daughter."

"Then I don't see," said the Chancellor, "what reason your Majesty can have for paying any attention to what this — this person says."

"If you don't believe me, you old idiots," cried Taboret, "call the Princess here, and I'll soon prove my words."

"By all means," cried they.

So the King commanded that her Royal Highness should be summoned.

In a few minutes she came, attended by her ladies. She said nothing, but then she never did speak till she was spoken to. So she entered, and stood in the middle of the room silently.

"We have desired that your presence be requested," the King was beginning, but Taboret without any ceremony advanced towards her, and struck her lightly on the head with her wand. In a moment the head rolled on the floor, leaving the body standing motionless as before, and showing that it was but an empty shell. "Just so," said the head, as it rolled towards the King, and he and the courtiers nearly swooned with fear.

When they were a little recovered, the King spoke again. "The fairy tells me," he said, "that there is somewhere a real Princess whom she wishes us to adopt as our daughter. And in the meantime let her Royal Highness be carefully placed in a cupboard, and a general mourning be proclaimed for this dire event."

So saying he glanced tenderly at the body and head, and turned weeping away.

So it was settled that Taboret was to fetch Princess Ursula, and the King and council were to be assembled to meet her.

That evening the fairy flew to Mark's cottage, and told them the truth about Ursula, and that they must part from her.

Loud were their lamentations, and great their grief, when they heard she must leave them. Poor Ursula herself sobbed bitterly.

"Never mind," she cried after a time, "if I am really a great Princess, I will have you all to live with me. I am sure the King, my father, will wish it, when he hears how good you have been to me."

On the appointed day, Taboret came for Ursula in a grand coach and four, and drove her away to the court. It was a long, long drive; and she stopped on the way and had the Princess dressed in a splendid white silk dress trimmed with gold, and put pearls round her neck and in her hair, that she might appear properly at court.

The King and all the council were assembled with great pomp, to greet their new Princess, and all looked grave and anxious. At last the door opened, and Taboret appeared, leading the young girl by the hand.

"That is your father!" said she to Ursula, pointing to the King; and on this, Ursula, needing no other bidding, ran at once to him, and putting her arms round his neck, gave him a sounding kiss.

His Majesty almost swooned, and all the courtiers shut their eyes and shivered.

"This is really!" said one.

"This is truly!" said another.

"What have I done?" cried Ursula, looking from one to another, and seeing that something was wrong, but not knowing what. "Have I kissed the *wrong person*?" On hearing which every one groaned.

"Come now," cried Taboret, "if you don't like her, I shall take her away to those who do. I'll give you a week, and then I'll come back and see how you're treating her. She's a great deal too good for any of you." So saying she flew away on her wand, leaving Ursula to get on with her new friends as best she might. But Ursula could not get on with them at all, as she soon began to see.

If she spoke or moved they looked shocked, and at last she was so frightened and troubled by them that she burst into tears, at which they were more shocked still.

"This is indeed a change after our sweet Princess," said one lady to another.

"Yes, indeed," was the answer, "when one remembers how even after her head was struck off she behaved so beautifully, and only said, 'Just so.'"

And all the ladies disliked poor Ursula, and soon showed her their dislike. Before the end of the week, when Taboret was to return, she had grown quite thin and pale, and seemed afraid of speaking above a whisper.

"Why, what is wrong?" cried Taboret, when she returned and saw how much poor Ursula had changed. "Don't you like being here? Aren't they kind to you?"

"Take me back, dear Taboret," cried Ursula, weeping. "Take me back to Oliver, and Philip, and Bell. As for these people, I *hate* them."

And she wept again.

Taboret only smiled and patted her head, and then went in to the King and courtiers.

"Now, how is it," she cried, "I find the Princess Ursula in tears? and I am sure you are making her unhappy. When you had that bit of wood-and-leather Princess, you could behave well enough to it, but now that you have a real flesh-and-blood woman, you none of you care for her."

"Our late dear daughter —" began the King, when the fairy interrupted him.

"I do believe," she said, "that you would like to have the doll back again. Now I will give you your choice. Which will you have — my Princess Ursula, the real one, or your Princess Ursula, the sham?"

The King sank back into his chair. "I am not equal to this," he said: "summon the council, and let them settle it by vote." So the council were summoned, and the fairy explained to them why they were wanted.

"Let both Princesses be fetched," she said; and the toy Princess was brought in with great care from her cupboard, and her head stood on the table beside her, and the real Princess came in with her eyes still red from crying and her bosom heaving.

"I should think there could be no doubt which one would prefer," said the Prime Minister to the Chancellor.

"I should think not either," answered the Chancellor.

"Then vote," said Taboret; and they all voted, and every vote was for the sham Ursula, and not one for the real one. Taboret only laughed.

"You are a pack of sillies and idiots," she said, "but you shall have what you want"; and she picked up the head, and with a wave of her wand stuck it on to the body, and it moved round slowly and said, "Certainly," just in its old voice; and on hearing this, all the courtiers gave something as like a cheer as they thought polite, whilst the old King could not speak for joy.

"We will," he cried, "at once make our arrangements for abdicating and leaving the government in the hands of our dear daughter"; and on hearing this the courtiers all applauded again.

But Taboret laughed scornfully, and taking up the real Ursula in her arms, flew back with her to Mark's cottage.

In the evening the city was illuminated and there were great rejoicings at the recovery of the Princess, but Ursula remained in the cottage and married Oliver, and lived happily with him for the rest of her life.

Mary Beaumont

"The Revenge of Her Race" (1879?)

[Mary Beaumont (pseud. 1849–1910) was born in Halifax, Yorkshire, the daughter of Caroline and Enoch Mellor, a minister. In his 1912 introduction to Beaumont's novel *Joan Seaton* (1896), her friend Robert Horton remarked on her "elevated sweetness of temper, that bright humour, that unfailing idealism, [and] that charm of manner and expression." Her family life was characterized by a combination of piety and intellectual discovery. An author of prose and poetry, her earliest publications appeared in *Sunday Magazine*. Due to weak health, however, she put off her literary work. Eventually she published the well-received short story collection *A Ringby Lass* (1895), which included the following story, probably the one work by her that has recently received the most attention. *Joan Seaton* was also well received, although other publications garnered less attention.]

The low hedge, where the creepers climbed, divided the lawn and its magnificent Wellingtonias from the meadow. There was little grass to be seen, for it was at this time one vast profusion of delicate ixias of every bright and tender shade.

— The evening was still, and the air heavy with scent. In a room opening upon the verandah, wreathed with white and scarlet passion-flowers, where she could see the garden and the meadow, and, beyond all, the Mountain Beautiful, lay a sick woman. Her dark face was lovely as an autumn leaf is lovely — hectic with the passing life. Her eyes wandered to the upper snows of the mountain, from time to time resting upon the brown-haired English girl who sat on a low stool by her side, holding the frail hand in her cool, firm clasp.

The invalid was speaking; her voice was curiously sweet, and there was a peculiarity about the "s," and an occasional turn of the sentence, which told the listener that her English was an acquired language.

"I am glad he is not here," she said slowly. "I do not want him to have pain."

"But perhaps, Mrs. Denison, you will be much better in a day or two, and able to welcome him when he comes back."

"No, I shall not be here when he comes back, and it is just as it should be. I asked him to turn round as he left the garden, and I could see him, oh, so well. He looked kind and so beautiful, and he waved to me his hand. Now he will come back, and he will be sad. He did not want to leave me, but the Governor sent for him. He will be sad, and he will remember that I loved him, and some day he will be glad again." She smiled into the troubled face near her.

The girl stroked the thick dark hair lovingly.

"Don't," she implored, "it hurts me. You are better to-night, and the children are coming in." Mrs. Denison closed her eyes, and with her left hand she covered her face.

"No, not the children," she whispered, "not my darlings. I cannot bear it, I must see them no more." She pressed her companion's hand with a sudden, close pressure. "But you will help them, Alice; you will make them English like you — like him. We will not pretend to-night, it is not long that I shall speak to you. I ask you to promise me to help them to be English."

"Dear," the girl urged, "they are such a delicious mixture of England and New Zealand — prettier, sweeter than any mere English child could ever be. They are enchanting." But into the dying woman's eyes leapt an eager flame.

"They must be all English, no Maori!"[1] she cried. A violent fit of coughing interrupted her, and, when the paroxysm was over, she was too exhausted to speak. The English nurse, Mrs. Bentley, an elderly Yorkshire woman, who had been with Mrs. Denison since her first baby came six years ago, and who had, in fact, been Horace Denison's own nurse-maid, came in and sent the agitated girl into the garden.

"For you haven't had a breath of fresh air to-day," she said. At the door Alice turned. The large eyes were resting upon her with an intent and solemn regard, in which lay a message. "What was it?" she thought, as she passed through the wide hall sweet with flowers. "She wanted to say something; I am sure she did. To-morrow I will ask her." But before the morrow came she knew. Mrs. Denison had said *Good-bye*.

The funeral was over. Mr. Denison, who had looked unaccountably ill and weary for months, had been sent home by Dr. Danby for at least a year's change and rest, and the doctor's young sister had yielded to var-

---

1 Indigenous people of New Zealand.

ious pressure, and promised to stay with the children until he returned. There was every reason for it. She had loved and been loved by the gentle Maori mother, she delighted in the dark beauty and sweetness of the children. And they, on their side, clung to her as to an adorable fairy relative, dowered with love and the fruits of love, tales and new games and tender ways. Best reason of all, in a sense, Mrs. Bentley that kind autocrat, entreated her to stay, "as the happiest thing for the children, and to please that poor lamb we laid yonder, who fair longed that you should! She was mightily taken up with you, Miss Danby, and you've your brother and his wife near, so that you won't be lonesome, and if there's aught I can do to make you comfortable, you've only to speak, Miss." As for Mr. Denison, he was pathetically grateful and relieved when Alice promised to remain.

After the evening romp, and the last goodnight, when the two elder children, Ben and Marie, called after her mother, Maritana, had given her their last injunctions to be sure and come for them "her very own self" on her way down to breakfast in the morning, she usually rode down between the cabbage-trees, down by the old Rata,[1] fired last autumn. Away through the grass lands to the doctor's house, a few miles nearer Rochester, or he and his wife would ride out to chat with her. But there were many evenings when she preferred the quiet of the airy house and the garden. The colonial life was new to her, everything had its charm, and in the colonies there is always a letter to write to those at home, the mail-bag is never satisfied. On such evenings it was her custom to cross the meadow to the copse of feathery trees beyond, where, sung to by the brook and the Tui,[2] the children's mother slept. And from the high presence of the Mountain Beautiful, there fell a dew of peace.

She would often ask Mrs. Bentley to sit with her until bed-time, and revel in the shrewd North-country woman's experiences, and her impressions of the new land to which love had brought her. Each woman grew to have a sincere and trustful affection for the other, and one night, seven or eight months after Mrs. Denison's death, Mrs. Bentley told a story which explained what had frequently puzzled Alice, the patient sorrow in Mrs. Denison's eyes, and Mr. Denison's harassed and dejected manner. "But for your goodness to the children," said the old woman, "and the way that precious baby takes to you, I don't think I should be willing to say what I am going to do, Miss. Though my dear mistress wished it, and said,

---

1   Tree used by the Maoris for paddles and other tools.

2   The parson bird [Beaumont's note].

the very last night, 'You must tell her all about it, someday, Nana' — and I promised, to quiet her, — I don't think I could bring myself to it if I hadn't lived with you and known you." And then the good nurse told her strange and moving tale.

She described how her master had come out young and careless-hearted to New Zealand in the service of the Government. And how scandalised and angry his father and mother, the old Tory Squire and his wife, had been to receive from him, after a year or two, letters brimming with a boyish love for his "beautiful Maori princess," whom he described as having "the sweetest heart, and the loveliest eyes in the world." It gave them little comfort to hear that her father was one of the wealthiest Maori in the island, and that, though but half-civilised himself, he had had his daughter well educated in the "Bishop's" and other English schools. To them she was a savage. There was no threat of disinheritance, for there was nothing for him to inherit. There was little money, and the estate was entailed on the elder brother. But all that could be done to intimidate him was done, and in vain. Then silence fell between the parents and the son.

But one spring day came the news of a grandson, called Benjamin, after his grandfather, and an urgent letter from their boy himself, enclosing a prettily and humbly-worded note from the new strange daughter, begging for an English nurse. She told them that she had now no father and no mother, for they had died before the baby came, and if she might love her husband's parents a little she would be glad.

"My lady read the letters to me herself," Mrs. Bentley said, "I'd taken the housekeeper's place a bit before, and she asked me to find her a sensible young woman. Well, I tried, but there wasn't a girl in the place that was fit to nurse Master Horace's child. And the end of it was, I came myself, for Master Horace had been like my own when he was a little lad. My lady pretended to be vexed with me, but the day I sailed she thanked me in words I never thought to hear from her, for she was a bit proud always." The faithful servant's voice trembled. She leaned back in her chair, and forgot for the moment the new house, and the new duties. She was back again in the old nursery with the fair-haired child playing about her knees. But Alice's face recalled her, and she continued the story. She had, she said, dreaded the meeting with her new mistress, and was prepared to find her "a sort of a heathen woman, who'd pull down Mr. Horace till he couldn't call himself a gentleman."

But when she saw the graceful creature who received her with gentle words and gestures of kindliness, and when she found her young master not only content, but happy, and when she took in her arms the laughing healthy baby, she felt — though she regretted its dark eyes and hair — more at home than she could have believed possible. The nurseries were so large and comfortable, and so much consideration was shown to her, that she confessed, "I should have been more ungrateful than a cat if I hadn't settled comfortable."

Then came nearly five happy years, during which time her young mistress had found a warm and secure place in the good Yorkshire heart. "She was that loving and that kind, that Dick Burdas the groom used to say that he believed she was an angel as had took up with them dark folks, to show 'em what an angel was like." Mrs. Bentley went on —

"She wasn't always quite happy, and I wondered what brought the shadow into her face, and why she would at times sigh that deep that I could have cried. After a bit I knew what it was. It was the Maori in her. She told me one night that she was a wicked woman, and ought never to have married Mr. Horace, for she got tired sometimes of the English house and its ways, and longed for her father's 'wharé'; that's a native hut, Miss. She grieved something awful one day when she had been to see old Tim, the Maori who lives behind the stables. She called herself a bad and ungrateful woman, and thought there must be some evil spirit in her tempting her into the old ways, because, when she saw Tim eating, and you know what bad stuff they eat, she had fair longed to join him. She gave me a fright I didn't get over for nigh a week. She leaned her bonnie head against my knee, and I stroked her cheek and hummed some silly nursery tune — for she was all of a tremble and like a child — and she fell asleep just where she was."

"Poor thing," said Alice, softly.

"Eh, but it's what's coming that upsets me ma'am. Eh, what suffering for my pretty lamb, and her that wouldn't have hurt a worm! Baby would be about six months old when she came in one day with him in her arms, and they *were a* picture. His little hand was fast in her hair. She always walked as if she'd wheels in her feet, that gliding and graceful. She had on a sort of sheeny yellow silk, and her cheeks were like them damask roses at home, and her eyes fair shone like stars. 'Isn't he a beauty, Nana?' she asked me, 'If only he had blue eyes, and that hair of gold like my husband's, and not these ugly eyes of mine!' And as she spoke she sighed as I dreaded to hear. Then she told me to help her to unpack her new dress from Paris, which she was to wear at the Rochester races the next day. Mr. Horace always chose her dresses, and he was right proud of her in them. And next morning he came into the nursery with her, and she was all in pale red, and that beautiful! 'Isn't she scrumptious, Nana?' he said in his boyish way, 'don't spoil her dress, children. How like her Marie grows!" Those two little ones, they had got her on her knees on the ground, and were hugging her as if they couldn't let her go. But when he said that, she got up very still and white —

'I am sorry,' she said, they must never be like me.'

' They can't be like any one better, can they, baby?' he answered her, and he tossed the child nearly up to the ceiling. But he looked worried as he went out. I saw them drive away, and they seemed happy enough. And, oh Miss, I saw them come back. We were in the porch, me and the children. Master Horace lifted her down, and I heard him say, 'Never mind, Marie.' But she never looked his way nor ours; she walked straight in and upstairs to her room, past my bonnie darling with his arms stretched out to her, and past Miss Marie, who was jumping up and down, and shouting 'Muvver,' and I heard her door shut. Then Master Horace took baby from me.

'Go up to her,' he said, and I could scarce hear him. His face was all drawn-like, but I felt that silly and stupid that I could say nothing, and just went upstairs." Mrs. Bentley put her knitting down, and throwing her apron over her head sobbed aloud —

"O, Nurse, what was it?" cried Alice, and the colour left her cheeks, "do tell me, I am so sorry for them, what was it?" It was several minutes before the good woman could recover herself, then she began —

"She told me, and Dick Burdas he told me, and it was like this. When they got to the race-course, — it was the first races they'd had in Rochester, — all the gentry was there, and those that knew her always made a deal of her, she had such half-shy winning ways! And she seemed very bright, Dick said, talking with the governor's lady, who is full of fun and sparkle. The carriages were all together, and Major Beaumont, a kind old gentleman who's always been a good friend to Master Horace, would have them in his carriage for luncheon, or whatever it was. Dick says he was thinking that she was the prettiest lady there when his eye was caught by two or three parties of Maories setting themselves right in front of the carriages. There were four or five in each lot, and they were mostly old. They got out their sharks' flesh and that bad corn they eat, and began to make their meal of them. Near Mrs. Denison there was one old man with a better sort of face, and Dick heard her say to Master, 'Isn't he like my father?' What Master Horace answered he didn't hear, he says he never saw anything like her face, so sad and wild, and working for all the world as if something were fighting her within. Then all in a minute she ran out and slipped down in her beautiful dress, close by the old

Maori in his dirty rags, and was rubbing her face against his, as them folks do when they meet. She had just taken a mouthful of the raw fish, when Master Horace missed her. He hadn't noticed her slip away. But in a moment he seemed to understand what it meant. He saw the Maori come out strong in her face, and he knew the Maori had got the better of every-thing, husband and friends and all. He gave a little cry, and in a minute he had her on her feet and was bringing her back to the carriage. Some folks thought Dick Burdas a rough hard man, and I know he was a shocker of a lad, he was fra Whitby, but that night he cried like a baby when he tell't me," and Mrs. Bentley fell for a moment into the dialect of her youth.

"He said," she continued, "that she looked like a poor stricken thing condemned, and let herself be led back as submissive as a child, and Mr. Horace's face was like the dead. He didn't think anyone but the Major and Dr. Danby saw her go, all was done in a minute, but it was done. And some few had seen, and it got out, and things were said that wasn't true. Not the doctor! No, miss, you needn't tell me that, he's told none, that I'll warrant. He's faithful and he's close."

"O, Mrs. Bentley, how dreadful for her, how dreadful!" and the girl went down on her knees by the old woman, her tears flowing fast.

"That's it, miss, you understand. I feel like that. It was bad enough for Master Horace with the future before him, and his children to think of, but for her it was desperate cruel. Eh, ma'am, what she went through! She loved more than you'd have thought us poor human beings could. And after all, the nature was in her, she didn't put it there. I've had a deal to do to keep down sinful thoughts since then, there's a lot of things that's wrong in this world, ma'am."

"What did she do?" Alice whispered.

"She! She was for going away and leaving everything, she felt herself the worst woman in the world. It was only by begging and praying of her on my knees that I got her to stay in the house that night, for she was so far English, and had such a fancy, that she saw everything blacker than any English-woman would, even the partick'lerest. Afterwards Master Horace was that good and gentle, and she loved him so much, that he per-suaded her to say nothing more about it, and to try to live as if it hadn't been. And so she seemed to do, outward-like, to other people. But it wasn't ever the same again. Something had broken in them both, with him it was his trust and his pride, but in her it was her heart."

"But the children — surely they comforted her."

"Eh, Miss, that was the worst. Poor lamb, poor lamb, — never after that day, though they were more to her nor children ever were to a mother before, would she have them with her. Just a morning and a good-night kiss, and a quarter of an hour at most, and I must take them away. She watched them play in the garden from her window, or the little hill there, and when they were asleep she would sit by them for hours, saying how bonnie they were and how good they were growing. And she looked after their clothes and their food and every little toy and pleasure, but never came in for a romp and a chat any more."

"Dear, brave heart," murmured the girl.

"Yes, ma'am, you feel for her, I know. She was fair terrified of them turning Maori and shaming their father. That was it. You didn't notice? No, after you came she was too ill to bear them about, and it seemed natural, I daresay. The Maoris are a fearful delicate set of folks. A bad cold takes them off into consumption directly. And with her there was the sorrow as well as the cold. It was wonderful that she lived so long." Alice threw her arms round Mrs. Bentley's neck.

"Oh, nurse, it is all so dreadful and sad. Couldn't we have somehow kept her with us and made her happy?"

The old woman held her close. "Nay, my dear bairn, never after that happened. It, or worse, might have come again. It's something stronger in them than we know, it's the very blood, I'm thinking. But she's gone to be the angel that Dick always said she was."

Alice looked away over the starlit garden to where the plumy trees stirred in the night-wind. "No," she said fervently, "not 'gone to be,' nurse dear, she was an angel always. Dick was right."

Amelia B. Edwards

"Was it an Illusion?
A Parson's Story" (1881)

[Amelia B(landford) Edwards (1831–92) was born in London and eventually supported her parents by writing short stories for *Household Words*, *All the Year Round*, and other magazines. She also published eight novels. Although not well known today, she was an extremely popular ghost story writer in her time and, as "Was it an Illusion?" reflects, her works move beyond simply entertaining through terror or horror to fusing these elements with social critique. Her main passion, however, was ancient history. In 1873, a trip to Egypt lead to her eventually becoming the most important British Egyptologist of the century. Her Egyptian collection can be seen at University College, London. Her most famous work is the book *A Thousand Miles Up the Nile*. She is now generally recognized as one of the best Victorian authors of ghost stories.]

The facts which I am about to relate happened to myself some sixteen or eighteen years ago, at which time I served Her Majesty as an Inspector of Schools. Now, the Provincial Inspector is perpetually on the move; and I was still young enough to enjoy a life of constant travelling. There are, indeed, many less agreeable ways in which an unbeneficed parson may contrive to scorn delights and live laborious days. In remote places where strangers are scarce, his annual visit is an important event; and though at the close of a long day's work he would sometimes prefer the quiet of a country inn, he generally finds himself the destined guest of the rector or the squire. It rests with himself to turn these opportunities to account. If he makes himself pleasant, he forms agreeable friendships and sees English home-life under one of its most attractive aspects; and sometimes, even in these days of universal common-placeness, he may have the luck to meet with an adventure.

My first appointment was to a West of England district largely peopled with my personal friends and connections. It was, therefore, much to my annoyance that I found myself, after a couple of years of very pleasant work, transferred to what a policeman would call 'a new beat,' up in the North. Unfortunately for me, my new beat — a rambling, thinly populated area of something under 1,800 square miles — was three times as large as the old one, and more than proportionately unmanageable. Intersected at right angles by two ranges of barren hills and cut off to a large extent from the main lines of railway, it united about every inconvenience that a district could possess. The villages lay wide apart, often separated by long tracts of moorland; and in place of the well-warmed railway compartment and the frequent manor-house, I now spent half my time in hired vehicles and lonely country inns.

I had been in possession of this district for some three months or so, and winter was near at hand, when I paid my first visit of inspection to Pit End, an outlying hamlet in the most northerly corner of my county, just twenty-two miles from the nearest station. Having slept overnight at a place called Drumley, and inspected Drumley schools in the morning, I started for Pit End, with fourteen miles of railway and twenty-two of hilly cross-roads between myself and my journey's end. I made, of course, all the enquiries I could think of before leaving; but neither the Drumley schoolmaster nor the landlord of the Drumley 'Feathers' knew much more of Pit End than its name. My predecessor, it seemed, had been in the habit of taking Pit End 'from the other side', the roads, though longer, being less hilly that way. That the place boasted some kind of inn was certain; but it was an inn unknown to fame, and to mine host of the 'Feathers'. Be it good or bad, however, I should have to put up at it.

Upon this scant information I started. My fourteen miles of railway journey soon ended at a place called Bramsford Road, whence an omnibus conveyed passengers to a dull little town called Bramsford Market. Here I found a horse and 'trap' to carry me on to my destination; the horse being a raw-boned grey with a profile like a camel, and the trap a rickety high gig which had probably done commercial travelling in the days of its youth. From Bramsford Market the way lay over a succession of long hills, rising to a barren, high-level plateau. It was a dull, raw afternoon of mid-November, growing duller and more raw as the day waned and the east wind blew keener.

'How much further now, driver?' I asked, as we alighted at the foot of a longer and a stiffer hill than any we had yet passed over.

He turned a straw in his mouth, and grunted something about 'fower or foive mile by the rooad'.

And then I learned that by turning off at a point which he described as 't'owld tollus', and taking a certain footpath across the fields, this distance might be considerably shortened. I decided, therefore, to walk the rest of the way; and, setting off at a good pace, I soon left driver and trap behind. At the top of the hill I lost sight of them, and coming presently to a little road-side ruin which I at once recognized as the old toll-house, I found the footpath without difficulty. It led me across a barren slope divided by stone fences, with here and there a group of shattered sheds, a tall chimney, and a blackened cinder-mound, marking the site of a deserted mine. A light fog, meanwhile, was creeping up from the east, and the dusk was gathering fast.

Now, to lose one's way in such a place and at such an hour would be dis-agreeable enough, and the footpath — a trodden track already half oblit-erated — would be indistinguishable in the course of another ten minutes. Looking anxiously ahead, therefore, in the hope of seeing some sign of habitation, I hastened on, scaling one stone stile after another, till I all at once found myself skirting a line of park-palings.[1] Following these, with bare boughs branching out overhead and dead leaves rustling underfoot, I came presently to a point where the path divided; here continuing to skirt the enclosure, and striking off yonder across a space of open meadow.

Which should I take?

By following the fence, I should be sure to arrive at a lodge where I could enquire my way to Pit End; but then the park might be of any extent, and I might have a long distance to go before I came to the near-est lodge. Again, the meadow-path, instead of leading to Pit End, might take me in a totally opposite direction. But there was no time to be lost in hesitation; so I chose the meadow, the further end of which was lost to sight in a fleecy bank of fog.

Up to this moment I had not met a living soul of whom to ask my way; it was, therefore, with no little sense of relief that I saw a man emerging from the fog and coming along the path. As we neared each other — I advancing rapidly; he slowly — I observed that he dragged the left foot, limping as he walked. It was, however, so dark and so misty, that not till we were within half a dozen yards of each other could I see that he wore a dark suit and an Anglican felt hat, and looked something like a dis-senting[2] minister. As soon as we were within speaking distance, I addressed him.

'Can you tell me', I said, 'if I am right for Pit End, and how far I have to go?'

---

1   Wood fencing.

2   Protestant.

He came on, looking straight before him; taking no notice of my question; apparently not hearing it.

'I beg your pardon,' I said, raising my voice; 'but will this path take me to Pit End, and if so' —

He had passed on without pausing; without looking at me; I could almost have believed, without seeing me!

I stopped, with the words on my lips; then turned to look after — perhaps, to follow — him.

But instead of following, I stood bewildered.

What had become of him? And what lad was that going up the path by which I had just come — that tall lad, half-running, half-walking, with a fishing-rod over his shoulder? I could have taken my oath that I had neither met nor passed him. Where then had he come from? And where was the man to whom I had spoken not three seconds ago, and who, at his limping pace, could not have made more than a couple of yards in the time?

My stupefaction was such that I stood quite still, looking after the lad with the fishing-rod till he disappeared in the gloom under the park-palings.

Was I dreaming?

Darkness, meanwhile, had closed in apace, and, dreaming or not dreaming, I must push on, or find myself benighted. So I hurried forward, turning my back on the last gleam of daylight, and plunging deeper into the fog at every step. I was, however, close upon my journey's end. The path ended at a turnstile; the turnstile opened upon a steep lane; and at the bottom of the lane, down which I stumbled among stones and ruts, I came in sight of the welcome glare of a blacksmith's forge.

Here, then, was Pit End. I found my trap standing at the door of the village inn; the raw-boned grey stabled for the night; the landlord watching for my arrival.

The 'Greyhound' was a hostelry of modest pretensions, and I shared its little parlour with a couple of small farmers and a young man who informed me that he 'travelled in' Thorley's Food for Cattle. Here I dined, wrote my letters, chatted awhile with the landlord, and picked up such scraps of local news as fell in my way.

There was, it seemed, no resident parson at Pit End; the incumbent being a pluralist with three small livings, the duties of which, by the help of a rotatory curate,[1] he discharged in a somewhat easy fashion. Pit End,

---

1   A curate is generally an assistant to a parson (or clergymen). Here, "rotatory curate" refers to one who rotates services among parishes. A pluralist is somebody who holds more than one office simultaneously.

as the smallest and furthest off, came in for but one service each Sunday, and was almost wholly relegated to the curate. The squire was a more confirmed absentee than even the vicar. He lived chiefly in Paris, spending abroad the wealth of his Pit End coal-fields. He happened to be at home just now, the landlord said, after five years' absence; but he would be off again next week, and another five years might probably elapse before they should again see him at Blackwater Chase.

Blackwater Chase! — the name was not new to me; yet I could not remember where I had heard it. When, however, mine host went on to say that, despite his absenteeism, Mr Wolstenholme was 'a pleasant gentleman and a good landlord', and that, after all, Blackwater Chase was 'a lonesome sort of world-end place for a young man to bury himself in', then I at once remembered Phil Wolstenholme of Balliol,[1] who, in his grand way, had once upon a time given me a general invitation to the shooting at Blackwater Chase. That was twelve years ago, when I was reading hard at Wadham,[2] and Wolstenholme — the idol of a clique to which I did not belong — was boating, betting, writing poetry, and giving wine parties at Balliol.

Yes; I remembered all about him — his handsome face, his luxurious rooms, his boyish prodigality, his utter indolence, and the blind faith of his worshippers, who believed that he had only 'to pull himself together' in order to carry off every honour which the University had to bestow. He did take the Newdigate;[3] but it was his first and last achievement, and he left college with the reputation of having narrowly escaped a plucking. How vividly it all came back upon my memory — the old college life, the college friendships, the pleasant time that could never come again! It was but twelve years ago; yet it seemed like half a century. And now, after these twelve years, here were Wolstenholme and I as near neighbours as in our Oxford days! I wondered if he was much changed, and whether, if changed, it were for the better or the worse. Had his generous impulses developed into sterling virtues, or had his follies hardened into vices? Should I let him know where I was, and so judge for myself? Nothing would be easier than to pencil a line upon a card tomorrow morning, and send it up to the big house. Yet, merely to satisfy a purposeless curiosity, was it worthwhile to reopen the acquaintanceship?

---

1   College at Oxford University.

2   College at Oxford University.

3   The Newdigate Prize for poetry, given at Oxford University.

Thus musing, I sat late over the fire, and by the time I went to bed, I had well nigh forgotten my adventure with the man who vanished so mysteriously and the boy who seemed to come from nowhere.

Next morning, finding I had abundant time at my disposal, I did pencil that line upon my card — a mere line, saying that I believed we had known each other at Oxford, and that I should be inspecting the National Schools from nine till about eleven. And then, having dispatched it by one of my landlord's sons, I went off to my work. The day was brilliantly fine. The wind had shifted round to the north, the sun shone clear and cold, and the smoke-grimed hamlet, and the gaunt buildings clustered at the mouths of the coalpits round about, looked as bright as they could look at any time of the year. The village was built up a long hill-side; the church and schools being at the top, and the 'Greyhound' at the bottom. Looking vainly for the lane by which I had come the night before, I climbed the one rambling street, followed a path that skirted the church-yard, and found myself at the schools. These, with the teachers' dwellings, formed three sides of a quadrangle; the fourth side consisting of an iron railing and a gate. An inscribed tablet over the main entrance-door recorded how 'These school-houses were re-built by Philip Wolstenholme, Esquire: AD 18—.'

'Mr Wolstenholme, sir, is the Lord of the Manor,' said a soft, obsequious voice.

I turned, and found the speaker at my elbow, a square-built, sallow man, all in black, with a bundle of copy-books under his arm.

'You are the — the schoolmaster?' I said; unable to remember his name, and puzzled by a vague recollection of his face.

'Just so, sir. I conclude I have the honour of addressing Mr Frazer?'

It was a singular face, very pallid and anxious-looking. The eyes, too, had a watchful, almost a startled, look in them, which struck me as peculiarly unpleasant.

'Yes,' I replied, still wondering where and when I had seen him. 'My name is Frazer. Yours, I believe, is — is —,' and I put my hand into my pocket for my examination papers.

'Skelton — Ebenezer Skelton. Will you please to take the boys first, sir?'

The words were commonplace enough, but the man's manner was studiously, disagreeably deferential; his very name being given, as it were, under protest, as if too insignificant to be mentioned.

I said I would begin with the boys; and so moved on. Then, for we had stood still till now, I saw that the schoolmaster was lame. In that moment I remembered him. He was the man I met in the fog.

'I met you yesterday afternoon, Mr Skelton,' I said, as we went into the school-room.

'Yesterday afternoon, sir?' he repeated.

'You did not seem to observe me,' I said, carelessly. 'I spoke to you, in fact; but you did not reply to me.'

'But — indeed, I beg your pardon, sir — it must have been someone else,' said the schoolmaster. 'I did not go out yesterday afternoon.'

How could this be anything but a falsehood? I might have been mistaken as to the man's face; though it was such a singular face, and I had seen it quite plainly. But how could I be mistaken as to his lameness? Besides, that curious trailing of the right foot, as if the ankle was broken, was not an ordinary lameness.

I suppose I looked incredulous, for he added, hastily:

'Even if I had not been preparing the boys for inspection, sir, I should not have gone out yesterday afternoon. It was too damp and foggy. I am obliged to be careful — I have a very delicate chest.'

My dislike to the man increased with every word he uttered. I did not ask myself with what motive he went on heaping lie upon lie; it was enough that, to serve his own ends, whatever those ends might be, he did lie with unparalleled audacity.

'We will proceed to the examination, Mr Skelton,' I said, contemptuously.

He turned, if possible, a shade paler than before, bent his head silently, and called up the scholars in their order.

I soon found that, whatever his shortcomings as to veracity, Mr Ebenezer Skelton was a capital schoolmaster. His boys were uncommonly well taught, and as regarded attendance, good conduct, and the like, left nothing to be desired. When, therefore, at the end of the examination, he said he hoped I would recommend the Pit End Boys' School for the Government grant, I at once assented. And now I thought I had done with Mr Skelton for, at all events, the space of one year. Not so, however. When I came out from the Girls' School, I found him waiting at the door.

Profusely apologizing, he begged leave to occupy five minutes of my valuable time. He wished, under correction, to suggest a little improvement. The boys, he said, were allowed to play in the quadrangle, which was too small, and in various ways inconvenient; but round at the back there was a piece of waste land, half an acre of which, if enclosed, would admirably answer the purpose. So saying, he led the way to the back of the building, and I followed him.

'To whom does this ground belong?' I asked.

'To Mr Wolstenholme, sir.'

'Then why not apply to Mr Wolstenholme? He gave the schools, and I dare say he would be equally willing to give the ground.'

'I beg your pardon, sir. Mr Wolstenholme has not been over here since his return, and it is quite possible that he may leave Pit End without honouring us with a visit. I could not take the liberty of writing to him, sir.'

'Neither could I in my report suggest that the Government should offer to purchase a portion of Mr Wolstenholme's land for a play-ground to schools of Mr Wolstenholme's own building.' I replied. 'Under other circumstances'...

I stopped and looked round.

The schoolmaster repeated my last words.

'You were saying, sir — under other circumstances?' —

I looked round again.

'It seemed to me that there was someone here,' I said; 'some third person, not a moment ago.'

'I beg your pardon, sir — a third person?'

'I saw his shadow on the ground, between yours and mine.'

The schools faced due north, and we were standing immediately behind the buildings, with our backs to the sun. The place was bare, and open, and high; and our shadows, sharply defined, lay stretched before our feet.

'A — a shadow?' he faltered. 'Impossible.'

There was not a bush or a tree within half a mile. There was not a cloud in the sky. There was nothing, absolutely nothing, that could have cast a shadow.

I admitted that it was impossible, and that I must have fancied it; and so went back to the matter of the playground.

'Should you see Mr Wolstenholme,' I said, 'you are at liberty to say that I thought it a desirable improvement.'

'I am much obliged to you, sir. Thank you — thank you very much,' he said, cringing at every word. 'But — but I had hoped that you might perhaps use your influence' —

'Look there!' I interrupted. 'Is *that* fancy?'

We were now close under the blank wall of the boys' schoolroom. On this wall, lying to the full sunlight, our shadows — mine and the schoolmaster's — were projected. And there, too — no longer between his and mine, but a little way apart, as if the intruder were standing back — there, as sharply defined as if cast by lime-light on a prepared background, I again distinctly saw, though but for a moment, that third shadow. As I spoke, as I looked round, it was gone!

'Did you not see it?' I asked.

He shook his head.

'I — I saw nothing,' he said, faintly. 'What was it?'

His lips were white. He seemed scarcely able to stand.

'But you *must* have seen it!' I exclaimed. 'It fell just there — where that bit of ivy grows. There must be some boy hiding — it was a boy's shadow, I am confident.'

'A boy's shadow!' he echoed, looking round in a wild, frightened way. 'There is no place — for a boy — to hide.'

'Place or no place,' I said, angrily, 'if I catch him, he shall feel the weight of my cane!'

I searched backwards and forwards in every direction, the schoolmaster, with his scared face, limping at my heels; but, rough and irregular as the ground was, there was not a hole in it big enough to shelter a rabbit.

'But what was it?' I said, impatiently.

'An — an illusion. Begging your pardon, sir — an illusion.'

He looked so like a beaten hound, so frightened, so fawning, that I felt I could with lively satisfaction have transferred the threatened caning to his own shoulders.

'But you saw it?' I said again.

'No, sir. Upon my honour, no, sir. I saw nothing — nothing whatever.'

His looks belied his words. I felt positive that he had not only seen the shadow, but that he knew more about it than he chose to tell. I was by this time really angry. To be made the object of a boyish trick, and to be hoodwinked by the connivance of the schoolmaster, was too much. It was an insult to myself and my office.

I scarcely knew what I said; something short and stern at all events. Then, having said it, I turned my back upon Mr Skelton and the schools, and walked rapidly back to the village.

As I neared the bottom of the hill, a dog-cart drawn by a high-stepping chestnut dashed up to the door of the 'Greyhound', and the next moment I was shaking hands with Wolstenholme, of Balliol. Wolstenholme, of Balliol, as handsome as ever, dressed with the same careless dandyism, looking not a day older than when I last saw him at Oxford! He gripped me by both hands, vowed that I was his guest for the next three days, and insisted on carrying me off at once to Blackwater Chase. In vain I urged that I had two schools to inspect tomorrow ten miles the other side of Drumley; that I had a horse and trap waiting; and that my room was ordered at the 'Feathers'. Wolstenholme laughed away my objections.

'My dear fellow,' he said, 'you will simply send your horse and trap back with a message to the "Feathers", and a couple of telegrams to be dispatched to the two schools from Drumley station. Unforeseen circumstances compel you to defer those inspections till next week!'

And with this, in his masterful way, he shouted to the landlord to send my portmanteau up to the manor-house, pushed me up before him into the dog-cart, gave the chestnut his head, and rattled me off to Blackwater Chase.

It was a gloomy old barrack of a place, standing high in the midst of a sombre deer-park some six or seven miles in circumference. An avenue of oaks, now leafless, led up to the house; and a mournful heron-haunted tarn in the loneliest part of the park gave to the estate its name of Blackwater Chase. The place, in fact, was more like a border fastness[1] than an English north-country mansion. Wolstenholme took me through the picture gallery and reception rooms after luncheon, and then for a canter round the park; and in the evening we dined at the upper end of a great oak hall hung with antlers, and armour, and antiquated weapons of warfare and sport.

'Now, tomorrow,' said my host, as we sat over our claret in front of a blazing log-fire; 'tomorrow, if we have decent weather, you shall have a day's shooting on the moors; and on Friday, if you will but be persuaded to stay a day longer, I will drive you over to Broomhead and give you a run with the Duke's hounds. Not hunt? My dear fellow, what nonsense! All our parsons hunt in this part of the world. By the way, have you ever been down a coal pit? No? Then a new experience awaits you. I'll take you down Carshalton shaft, and show you the home of the gnomes and trolls.'

'Is Carshalton one of your own mines?' I asked.

'All these pits are mine,' he replied. 'I am king of Hades,[2] and rule the under world as well as the upper. There is coal everywhere underlying these moors. The whole place is honeycombed with shafts and galleries. One of our richest seams runs under this house, and there are upwards of forty men at work in it a quarter of a mile below our feet here every day. Another leads right away under the park, heaven only knows how far! My father began working it five-and-twenty years ago, and we have gone on working it ever since; yet it shows no sign of failing.'

---

1 A stronghold, fortress.

2 In Greek mythology, the underworld where the spirits of the dead live, later conflated with the Christian notion of hell.

'You must be as rich as a prince with a fairy godmother!'

He shrugged his shoulders.

'Well,' he said, lightly, 'I am rich enough to commit what follies I please; and that is saying a good deal. But then, to be always squandering money — always rambling about the world — always gratifying the impulse of the moment — is that happiness? I have been trying the experiment for the last ten years; and with what result? Would you like to see?'

He snatched up a lamp and led the way through a long suite of unfurnished rooms, the floors of which were piled high with packing cases of all sizes and shapes, labelled with the names of various foreign ports and the addresses of foreign agents innumerable. What did they contain? Precious marbles from Italy and Greece and Asia Minor; priceless paintings by old and modern masters; antiquities from the Nile, the Tigris, and the Euphrates; enamels from Persia, porcelain from China, bronzes from Japan, strange sculptures from Peru; arms, mosaics, ivories, wood-carvings, skins, tapestries, old Italian cabinets, painted bride-chests, Etruscan terracottas; treasures of all countries, of all ages, never even unpacked since they crossed that threshold which the master's foot had crossed but twice during the ten years it had taken to buy them! Should he ever open them, ever arrange them, ever enjoy them? Perhaps — if he became weary of wandering — if he married — if he built a gallery to receive them. If not — well, he might found and endow a museum; or leave the things to the nation. What did it matter? Collecting was like fox-hunting; the pleasure was in the pursuit, and ended with it!

We sat up late that first night, I can hardly say conversing, for Wolstenholme did the talking, while I, willing to be amused, led him on to tell me something of his wanderings by land and sea. So the time passed in stories of adventure, of perilous peaks ascended, of deserts traversed, of unknown ruins explored, of 'hairbreadth 'scapes' from icebergs and earthquakes and storms; and when at last he flung the end of his cigar into the fire and discovered that it was time to go to bed, the clock on the mantel-shelf pointed far on among the small hours of the morning.

Next day, according to the programme made out for my entertainment, we did some seven hours' partridge-shooting on the moors; and the day next following I was to go down Carshalton shaft before breakfast, and after breakfast ride over to a place some fifteen miles distant called Picts' Camp, there to see a stone circle[1] and the ruins of a prehistoric fort.

---

1   Ring of stones which past communities build for as-yet unestablished purposes. The Picts were one of an ancient people of northern Britain.

Unused to field sports, I slept heavily after those seven hours with the guns, and was slow to wake when Wolstenholme's valet came next morning to my bedside with the waterproof suit in which I was to effect my descent into Hades.

'Mr Wolstenholme says, sir, that you had better not take your bath till you come back,' said this gentlemanly vassal, disposing the ungainly garments across the back of a chair as artistically as if he were laying out my best evening suit. 'And you will be pleased to dress warmly underneath the waterproofs, for it is very chilly in the mine.'

I surveyed the garments with reluctance. The morning was frosty, and the prospect of being lowered into the bowels of the earth, cold, fasting, and unwashed, was anything but attractive. Should I send word that I would rather not go? I hesitated; but while I was hesitating, the gentlemanly valet vanished, and my opportunity was lost. Grumbling and shivering, I got up, donned the cold and shiny suit, and went downstairs.

A murmur of voices met my ear as I drew near the breakfast-room. Going in, I found some ten or a dozen stalwart colliers grouped near the door, and Wolstenholme, looking somewhat serious, standing with his back to the fire.

'Look here, Frazer,' he said, with a short laugh, 'here's a pleasant piece of news. A fissure has opened in the bed of Blackwater Tarn; the lake has disappeared in the night; and the mine is flooded! No Carshalton shaft for you today!'

'Seven foot o' wayter in Jukes's seam, an' eight in th' owd north and south galleries,' growled a huge red-headed fellow, who seemed to be the spokesman.

'An' it's the Lord's own marcy a' happened o' noight-time, or we'd be dead men all,' added another.

'That's true, my man,' said Wolstenholme, answering the last speaker. 'It might have drowned you like rats in a trap; so we may thank our stars it's no worse. And now, to work with the pumps! Lucky for us that we know what to do, and how to do it.'

So saying, he dismissed the men with a good-humoured nod, and an order for unlimited ale.

I listened in blank amazement. The tarn vanished! I could not believe it. Wolstenholme assured me, however, that it was by no means a solitary phenomenon. Rivers had been known to disappear before now, in mining districts; and sometimes, instead of merely cracking, the ground would cave in, burying not merely houses, but whole hamlets in one common ruin. The foundations of such houses were, however, generally known to be insecure long enough before the crash came; and these accidents were not therefore often followed by loss of life.

'And now,' he said, lightly, 'you may doff your fancy costume; for I shall have time this morning for nothing but business. It is not every day that one loses a lake, and has to pump it up again!'

Breakfast over, we went round to the mouth of the pit, and saw the men fixing the pumps. Later on, when the work was fairly in train, we started off across the park to view the scene of the catastrophe. Our way lay far from the house across a wooded upland, beyond which we followed a broad glade leading to the tarn. Just as we entered this glade — Wolstenholme rattling on and turning the whole affair into jest — a tall, slender lad, with a fishing-rod across his shoulder, came out from one of the side paths to the right, crossed the open at a long slant, and disappeared among the tree-trunks on the opposite side. I recognized him instantly. It was the boy whom I saw the other day, just after meeting the schoolmaster in the meadow.

'If that boy thinks he is going to fish in your tarn,' I said, 'he will find out his mistake.'

'What boy?' asked Wolstenholme, looking back.

'That boy who crossed over yonder, a minute ago.'

'Yonder! — in front of us?'

'Certainly. You must have seen him?'

'Not I.'

'You did not see him? — a tall, thin boy, in a grey suit, with a fishing-rod over his shoulder. He disappeared behind those Scotch firs.'

Wolstenholme looked at me with surprise.

'You are dreaming!' he said. 'No living thing — not even a rabbit — has crossed our path since we entered the park gates.'

'I am not in the habit of dreaming with my eyes open,' I replied, quickly.

He laughed, and put his arm through mine.

'Eyes or no eyes,' he said, 'you are under an illusion this time!'

An illusion — the very word made use of by the schoolmaster! What did it mean? Could I, in truth, no longer rely upon the testimony of my senses? A thousand half-formed apprehensions flashed across me in a moment. I remembered the illusions of Nicolini, the bookseller, and other similar cases of visual hallucination, and I asked myself if I had suddenly become afflicted in like manner.

'By Jove! this *is* a queer sight!' exclaimed Wolstenholme.

And then I found that we had emerged from the glade, and were looking down upon the bed of what yesterday was Blackwater Tarn.

It was indeed a queer sight — an oblong, irregular basin of blackest slime, with here and there a sullen pool, and round the margin an irregular fringe of bulrushes. At some little distance along the bank — less than a quarter of a mile from where we were standing — a gaping crowd had gathered. All Pit End, except the men at the pumps, seemed to have turned out to stare at the bed of the vanished tarn.

Hats were pulled off and curtsies dropped at Wolstenholme's approach. He, meanwhile, came up smiling, with a pleasant word for everyone.

'Well,' he said, 'are you looking for the lake, my friends? You'll have to go down Carshalton shaft to find it! It's an ugly sight you've come to see, anyhow!'

'Tes an ugly soight, squoire,' replied a stalwart blacksmith in a leathern apron; 'but thar's summat uglier, mebbe, than the mud, ow'r yonder.'

'Something uglier than the mud?' Wolstenholme repeated.

'Wull yo be pleased to stan' this way, squoire, an' look strite across at yon little tump o' bulrashes — doan't yo see nothin'?'

'I see a log of rotten timber sticking half in and half out of the mud,' said Wolstenholme; 'and something — a long reed, apparently … by Jove! I believe it's a fishing rod!'

'It *is* a fishin' rod, squoire,' said the blacksmith with rough earnestness; 'an' if yon rotten timber bayn't an unburied corpse, mun I never stroike hammer on anvil agin!'

There was a buzz of acquiescence from the bystanders. 'Twas an unburied corpse, sure enough. Nobody doubted it.

Wolstenholme made a funnel with his hands, and looked through it long and steadfastly.

'It must come out, whatever it is,' he said presently. 'Five feet of mud, do you say? Then here's a sovereign apiece for the first two fellows who wade through it and bring that object to land!'

The blacksmith and another pulled off their shoes and stockings, turned up their trousers, and went in at once.

They were over their ankles at the first plunge, and, sounding their way with sticks, went deeper at every tread. As they sank, our excitement rose. Presently they were visible from only the waist upwards. We could see their chests heaving, and the muscular efforts by which each step was gained. They were yet full twenty yards from the goal when the mud mounted to their armpits … a few feet more, and only their heads would remain above the surface!

An uneasy movement ran through the crowd.

'Call 'em back, vor God's sake!' cried a woman's voice.

But at this moment — having reached a point where the ground gradually sloped upwards — they began to rise above the mud as rapidly as they had sunk into it. And now, black with clotted slime, they emerge waist-high … now they are within three or four yards of the spot … and now … now they are there!

They part the reeds — they stoop low above the shapeless object on which all eyes are turned — they half-lift it from its bed of mud — they hesitate — lay it down again — decide, apparently, to leave it there; and turn their faces shorewards. Having come a few paces, the blacksmith remembers the fishing-rod; turns back; disengages the tangled line with some difficulty, and brings it over his shoulder.

They had not much to tell — standing, all mud from head to heel, on dry land again — but that little was conclusive. It was, in truth, an unburied corpse; part of the trunk only above the surface. They tried to lift it; but it had been so long under water, and was in so advanced a stage of decomposition, that to bring it to shore without a shutter was impossible. Being cross-questioned, they thought, from the slenderness of the form, that it must be the body of a boy.

'Thar's the poor chap's rod, anyhow,' said the blacksmith, laying it gently down upon the turf.

I have thus far related events as I witnessed them. Here, however, my responsibility ceases. I give the rest of my story at second-hand, briefly, as I received it some weeks later, in the following letter from Philip Wolstenholme:

'Blackwater Chase, Dec. 20th, 18—.

Dear Frazer, My promised letter has been a long time on the road, but I did not see the use of writing till I had something definite to tell you. I think, however, we have now found out all that we are ever likely to know about the tragedy in the tarn; and it seems that — but, no; I will begin at the beginning. That is to say, with the day you left the Chase, which was the day following the discovery of the body.

You were but just gone when a police inspector arrived from Drumley (you will remember that I had immediately sent a man over to the sitting magistrate); but neither the inspector nor anyone else could do anything till the remains were brought to shore, and it took us the best part of a week to accomplish this difficult operation. We had to sink no end of big stones in order to make a rough and ready causeway across the mud. This done, the body was brought over decently upon a shutter. It proved to be the corpse of a boy of perhaps fourteen or fifteen years of age. There was a fracture three inches long at the back of the skull, evidently fatal. This might, of course, have been an accidental injury; but when the body came to be raised from where it lay, it was found to be pinned down by a pitchfork, the handle of which had been afterwards whittled off, so as not to show above the water, a discovery tantamount to evidence of murder. The features of the victim were decomposed beyond recognition; but enough of the hair remained to show that it had been short and sandy. As for the clothing, it was a mere mass of rotten shreds; but on being subjected to some chemical process, proved to have once been a suit of lightish grey cloth.

A crowd of witnesses came forward at this stage of the inquiry — for I am now giving you the main facts as they came out at the coroner's inquest — to prove that about a year or thirteen months ago, Skelton the schoolmaster had staying with him a lad whom he called his nephew, and to whom it was supposed that he was not particularly kind. This lad was described as tall, thin, and sandy-haired. He habitually wore a suit corresponding in colour and texture to the shreds of clothing discovered on the body in the tarn; and he was much addicted to angling about the pools and streams, wherever he might have the chance of a nibble.

And now one thing led quickly on to another. Our Pit End shoemaker identified the boy's boots as being a pair of his own making and selling. Other witnesses testified to angry scenes between the uncle and nephew. Finally, Skelton gave himself up to justice, confessed the deed, and was duly committed to Drumley gaol for wilful murder.

And the motive? Well, the motive is the strangest part of my story. The wretched lad was, after all, not Skelton's nephew, but Skelton's own illegitimate son. The mother was dead, and the boy lived with his maternal grandmother in a remote part of Cumberland. The old woman was poor, and the schoolmaster made her an annual allowance for his son's keep and clothing. He had not seen the boy for some years, when he sent for him to come over on a visit to Pit End. Perhaps he was weary of the tax upon his purse. Perhaps, as he himself puts it in his confession, he was disappointed to find the boy, if not actually half-witted, stupid, wilful, and ill brought-up. He at all events took a dislike to the poor brute, which dislike by and by developed into positive hatred. Some amount of provocation there would seem to have been. The boy was as backward as a child of five years old. That Skelton put him into the Boys' School, and could do nothing with him; that he defied discipline, had a passion for fishing, and was continually wandering about the country with his rod and line, are facts borne out by the independent testimony of various witnesses. Having hidden his fishing-tackle, he was in the habit of slipping away at school-hours, and showed himself the more cunning and obstinate the more he was punished.

At last there came a day when Skelton tracked him to the place where his rod was concealed, and thence across the meadows into the park, and as far as the tarn. His (Skelton's) account of what followed is wandering and confused. He owns to having beaten the miserable lad about the head and arms with a heavy stick that he had brought with him for the purpose; but denies that he intended to murder him. When his son fell insensible and ceased to breathe, he for the first time realized the force of the blows he had dealt. He admits that his first impulse was one, not of remorse for the deed, but of fear for his own safety. He dragged the body in among the bulrushes by the water's edge, and there concealed it as well as he could. At night, when the neighbours were in bed and asleep, he stole out by starlight, taking with him a pitchfork, a coil of rope, a couple of old iron-bars, and a knife. Thus laden, he struck out across the moor, and entered the park by a stile and footpath on the Stoneleigh side; so making a circuit of between three and four miles. A rotten old punt used at that time to be kept on the tarn. He loosed this punt from its moorings, brought it round, hauled in the body, and paddled his ghastly burden out into the middle of the lake as far as a certain clump of reeds which he had noted as a likely spot for his purpose. Here he weighted and sunk the corpse, and pinned it down by the neck with his pitchfork. He then cut away the handle of the fork; hid the fishing-rod among the reeds; and believed, as murderers always believe, that discovery was impossible. As regarded the Pit End folk, he simply gave out that his nephew had gone back to Cumberland; and no one doubted it. Now, however, he says that accident has only anticipated him; and that he was on the point of voluntarily confessing his crime. His dreadful secret had of late become intolerable. He was haunted by an invisible Presence. That Presence sat with him at table, followed him in his walks, stood behind him in the school-room, and watched by his bedside. He never saw it; but he felt that it was always there. Sometimes he raves of a shadow on the wall of his cell. The gaol authorities are of opinion that he is of unsound mind.

I have now told you all that there is at present to tell. The trial will not take place till the spring assizes. In the meanwhile I am off tomorrow to

Paris, and thence, in about ten days, on to Nice, where letters will find me at the Hotel des Empereurs.

Always, dear Frazer,
Yours, &c., &c.,
P.W.

P.S. — Since writing the above, I have received a telegram from Drumley to say that Skelton has committed suicide. No particulars given. So ends this strange eventful history.

By the way, that was a curious illusion of yours the other day when we were crossing the park; and I have thought of it many times. Was it an illusion? — that is the question.'

Ay, indeed! that *is* the question; and it is a question which I have never yet been able to answer. Certain things I undoubtedly saw — with my mind's eye, perhaps — and as I saw them, I have described them; withholding nothing, adding nothing, explaining nothing. Let those solve the mystery who can. For myself, I but echo Wolstenholme's question: Was it an illusion?

Thomas Hardy

"Interlopers at the Knap" (1884)

[Thomas Hardy (1840–1928) left school at sixteen to become an architect's apprentice. Gradually, however, he turned to writing, producing stories and poems, as well as the novels for which he is most famous. He always saw poetry as a superior art form to fiction and, in 1895, he gave up writing prose almost entirely. His best known collection of stories is *Wessex Tales* (1888). He grouped the collection with his "novels of character and environment," as opposed to "romances and fantasies" or "novels of ingenuity." Hardy's categorization of *Wessex Tales* as a novel points to the novelistic qualities found in stories like "Interlopers at the Knap." In the case of the short stories, the complex narrative of love and pain and the characters' psychological and emotional details often only come across through suggestion, a trait that connects Hardy's work to the rise of Modernism.]

I.

The north-west road from Casterbridge is tedious and lonely, especially in winter time. Along a part of its course it is called Holloway Lane, a monotonous track without a village or hamlet for many miles, and with very seldom a turning. Unapprised wayfarers who are too old, or too young, or in other respects too weak for the distance to be traversed, but who, nevertheless, have to walk it, say, as they look wistfully ahead, "Once at the top of that hill, and I must surely see the end of Holloway Lane!" But they reach the hill-top, and Holloway Lane stretches in front as mercilessly as before.

Some few years ago a certain farmer was riding through this lane in the gloom of a winter evening. The farmer's friend, a dairyman, was riding beside him. A few paces in the rear rode the farmer's man. All three were well horsed on strong, round-barrelled cobs;[1] and to be well horsed

---

1   Small, sturdy horses.

was to be in better spirits about Holloway Lane than poor pedestrians could attain to during its passage.

But the farmer did not talk much to his friend as he rode along. The enterprise which had brought him there filled his mind; for in truth it was important. Not altogether so important was it, perhaps, when estimated by its value to society at large; but if the true measure of a deed be proportionate to the space it occupies in the heart of him who undertakes it, Farmer Charles Darton's business to-night could hold its own with the business of kings.

He was a large farmer. His turnover, as it is called, was probably thirty thousand pounds a year. He had a great many draught horses, a great many milch cows, and of sheep a multitude. This comfortable position was, however, none of his own making. It had been created by his father, a man of a very different stamp from the present representative of the line.

Darton, the father, had been a one-idea'd character, with a buttoned-up pocket and a chink-like eye brimming with commercial subtlety. In Darton the son, this trade subtlety had become transmuted into emotional, and the harshness had disappeared; he would have been called a sad man but for his constant care not to divide himself from lively friends by piping notes out of harmony with theirs. Contemplative, he allowed his mind to be a quiet meeting-place for memories and hopes. So that, naturally enough, since succeeding to the agricultural calling, and up to his present age of thirty-two, he had neither advanced nor receded as a capitalist — a stationary result which did not agitate one of his unambitious unstrategic nature, since he had all that he desired. The motive of his expedition to-night showed the same absence of anxious regard for number one.

The party rode on in the slow, safe trot proper to night-time and bad roads, Farmer Darton's head jigging rather unromantically up and down against the sky, and his motions being repeated with bolder emphasis by his friend Japheth Johns; while those of the latter were travestied in jerks still less softened by art in the person of the lad who attended them. A pair of whitish objects hung one on each side of the latter, bumping against him at each step, and still further spoiling the grace of his seat. On close inspection they might have been perceived to be open rush baskets — one containing a turkey, and the other some bottles of wine.

"D'ye feel ye can meet your fate like a man, neighbour Darton?" asked Johns, breaking a silence which had lasted while five-and-twenty hedgerow trees had glided by.

Mr. Darton with a half laugh murmured, "Ay — call it my fate! Hanging and wiving go by destiny." And then they were silent again.

The darkness thickened rapidly, at intervals shutting down on the land in a perceptible flap like the wave of a wing. The customary close of day was accelerated by a simultaneous blurring of the air. With the fall of night had come a mist just damp enough to incommode, but not sufficient to saturate them. Countrymen as they were — born, as may be said, with only an open door between them and the four seasons — they regarded the mist but as an added obscuration, and ignored its humid quality.

They were travelling in a direction that was enlivened by no modern current of traffic, the place of Darton's pilgrimage being the old-fashioned village of Hintocks Abbas, where the people make the best cider and cider-wine in all Wessex, and where the dunghills smell of pomace[1] instead of stable refuse as elsewhere. The lane was sometimes so narrow that the brambles of the hedge, which hung forward like anglers' rods over a stream, scratched their hats and curry-combed their whiskers as they passed. Yet this neglected lane had been a highway to Queen Elizabeth's court, and other cavalcades of the past. But its day was over now, and its history as a national artery done for ever.

"Why I have decided to marry her," resumed Darton (in a measured musical voice of confidence which revealed a good deal of his composition) as he glanced round to see that the lad was not too near, "is not only that I like her, but that I can do no better, even from a fairly practical point of view. That I might ha' looked higher is possibly true, though it is really all nonsense. I have had experience enough in looking above me. 'No more superior women for me,' said I — you know when. Sally is a comely, independent, simple character, with no make-up about her, who'll think me as much a superior to her as I used to think — you know who I mean — was to me."

"Ay," said Johns. "However, I shouldn't call Sally Hall simple. Primary, because no Sally is; secondary, because if some could be this one wouldn't. 'Tis a wrong denomination to apply to a woman, Charles, and affects me, as your best man, like cold water. 'Tis like recommending a stage play by saying there's neither murder, villany, nor harm of any sort in it, when that's what you've paid your half-crown to see."

"Well; may your opinion do you good. Mine's a different one." And turning the conversation from the philosophical to the practical, Darton expressed a hope that the said Sally had received what he'd sent on by the carrier that day.

Johns wanted to know what that was.

---

1 Mashed apples remaining after producing cider.

"It is a dress," said Darton. "Not exactly a wedding dress, though she may use it as one if she likes. It is rather serviceable than showy — suitable for the winter weather."

"Good," said Johns. "Serviceable is a wise word in a bridegroom. I commend ye, Charles."

"For," said Darton, "why should a woman dress up like a rope-dancer because she's going to do the most solemn deed of her life except dying?"

"Faith, why? But she will because she will, I suppose," said Dairyman Johns.

"H'm," said Darton.

The lane they followed had been nearly straight for several miles, but it now took a turn, and winding uncertainly for some distance forked into two. By night country roads are apt to reveal ungainly qualities which pass without observation during day; and though Darton had travelled this way before, he had not done so frequently, Sally having been wooed at the house of a relative near his own. He never remembered seeing at this spot a pair of alternative ways looking so equally probable as these two did now. Johns rode on a few steps.

"Don't be out of heart, sonny," he cried. "Here's a handpost. Enoch — come and climb this post, and tell us the way."

The lad dismounted, and jumped into the hedge where the post stood under a tree.

"Unstrap the baskets, or you'll smash up that wine!" cried Darton, as the young man began spasmodically to climb the post, baskets and all.

"Was there ever less head in a brainless world?" said Johns. "Here, simple Nocky, I'll do it." He leapt off, and with much puffing climbed the post, striking a match when he reached the top, and moving the light along the arm, the lad standing and gazing at the spectacle.

"I have faced tantalisation these twenty years with a temper as mild as milk!" said Japheth; "but such things as this don't come short of devilry!" And flinging the match away, he slipped down to the ground.

"What's the matter?" asked Darton.

"Not a letter, sacred or heathen — not so much as would tell us the way to the great fireplace — ever I should sin to say it! Either the moss and mildew have eat away the words, or we have arrived in a land where no traveller has planted the art of writing, and should have brought our compass like Christopher Columbus."

"Let us take the straightest road," said Darton placidly; "I sha'n't be sorry to get there — 'tis a tiresome ride. I would have driven if I had known."

"Nor I neither, sir," said Enoch. "These straps plough my shoulder like a zull.[1] If 'tis much further to your lady's home, Maister Darton, I shall ask to be let carry half of these good things in my innerds — hee, hee!"

"Don't you be such a reforming radical, Enoch," said Johns sternly. "Here, I'll take the turkey."

This being done, they went forward by the right-hand lane, which ascended a hill, the left winding away under a plantation. The pit-a-pat of their horses' hoofs lessened up the slope; and the ironical directing-post stood in solitude as before, holding out its blank arms to the raw breeze, which brought a snore from the wood as if Skrymir the Giant[2] were sleeping there.

II.

Three miles to the left of the travellers, along the road they had not followed, rose an old house with mullioned windows of Ham-hill stone, and chimneys of lavish solidity. It stood at the top of a slope beside Hintock village street; and immediately in front of it grew a large sycamore-tree, whose bared roots formed a convenient staircase from the road below to the front door of the dwelling. Its situation gave the house what little distinctive name it possessed, namely, "The Knap." Some forty yards off a brook dribbled past, which, for its size, made a great deal of noise. At the back was a dairy barton,[3] accessible for vehicles and live-stock by a side 'drong.' Thus much only of the character of the homestead could be divined out of doors at this shady evening-time.

But within there was plenty of light to see by, as plenty was construed at Hintock. Beside a Tudor fireplace, whose moulded four-centred arch was nearly hidden by a figured blue-cloth blower, were seated two women — mother and daughter — Mrs. Hall, and Sarah, or Sally; for this was a part of the world where the latter modification had not as yet been effaced as a vulgarity by the march of intellect. The owner of the name was the young woman by whose means Mr. Darton proposed to put an end to his bachelor condition on the approaching day.

The mother's bereavement had been so long ago as not to leave much mark of its occurrence upon her now, either in face or clothes. She had

---

1   Plough.

2   Mythological character who travelled with the god Thor.

3   Farmyard.

resumed the mob-cap of her early married life, enlivening its whiteness by a few rose-du-Barry[1] ribbons. Sally required no such aids to pinkness. Roseate good-nature lit up her gaze; her features showed curves of decision and judgment; and she might have been regarded without much mistake as a warm-hearted, quick-spirited, handsome girl.

She did most of the talking, her mother listening with a half absent air, as she picked up fragments of red-hot wood ember with the tongs, and piled them upon the brands. But the number of speeches that passed was very small in proportion to the meanings exchanged. Long experience together often enabled them to see the course of thought in each other's minds without a word being spoken. Behind them, in the centre of the room, the table was spread for supper, certain whiffs of air laden with fat vapours, which ever and anon entered from the kitchen, denoting its preparation there.

"The new gown he was going to send you stays about on the way like himself," Sally's mother was saying.

"Yes, not finished, I dare say," cried Sally independently. "Lord, I shouldn't be amazed if it didn't come at all! Young men make such kind promises when they are near you, and forget 'em when they go away. But he doesn't intend it as a wedding-dress — he gives it to me merely as a dress to wear when I like — a travelling-dress is what it would be called in great circles. Come rathe or come late it don't much matter, as I have a dress of my own to fall back upon. But what time is it?"

She went to the family clock and opened the glass, for the hour was not otherwise discernible by night, and indeed at all times was rather a thing to be investigated than beheld, so much more wall than window was there in the apartment. "It is nearly eight," said she.

"Eight o'clock, and neither dress nor man," said Mrs. Hall.

"Mother, if you think to tantalise me by talking like that, you are much mistaken. Let him be as late as he will — or stay away altogether — I don't care," said Sally. But a tender minute quaver in the negation showed that there was something forced in that statement.

Mrs. Hall perceived it, and drily observed that she was not so sure about Sally not caring. "But perhaps you don't care so much as I do, after all," she said. 'For I see what you don't, that it is a good and flourishing match for ye; a very honourable offer in Mr. Darton. And I think I see a kind husband in him. So pray God 'twill go smooth, and wind up well."

---

1 Soft shade of pink.

Sally would not listen to misgivings. Of course it would go smoothly, she asserted. "How you are up and down, mother!" she went on. "At this moment, whatever hinders him, we are not so anxious to see him as he is to be here, and his thought runs on before him, and settles down upon us like the star in the east. Hark!" she exclaimed, with a breath of relief, her eyes sparkling. "I heard something. Yes — here they are!"

The next moment her mother's slower ear also distinguished the familiar reverberation occasioned by footsteps clambering up the roots of the sycamore.

"Yes, it sounds like them at last," she said. "Well, it is not so very late after all, considering the distance."

The footfall ceased, and they rose, expecting a knock. They began to think it might have been, after all, some neighbouring villager under Bacchic influence,[1] giving the centre of the road a wide berth, when their doubts were dispelled by the newcomer's entry into the passage. The door of the room was gently opened, and there appeared, not the pair of travellers with whom we have already made acquaintance, but a pale-faced man in the garb of extreme poverty — almost in rags.

"Oh, it's a tramp — gracious me!" said Sally, starting back.

His cheeks and eye-orbits were deep concaves — rather, it might be, from natural weakness of constitution than irregular living, though there were indications that he had led no careful life. He gazed at the two women fixedly for a moment; then with an abashed, humiliated demeanour, dropped his glance to the floor, and sank into a chair without uttering a word.

Sally was in advance of her mother, who had remained standing by the fire. She now tried to discern the visitor across the candles.

"Why — mother," said Sally faintly, turning back to Mrs. Hall. "It is Phil, from Australia!"

Mrs. Hall started, and grew pale, and a fit of coughing seized the man with the ragged clothes. "To come home like this!" she said. "Oh, Philip — are you ill?"

"No, no, mother," replied he, impatiently, as soon as he could speak.

"But for God's sake how do you come here — and just now too?"

"Well — I am here," said the man. "How it is I hardly know. I've come home, mother, because I was driven to it. Things were against me out there, and went from bad to worse."

---

1 Drunk (Bacchus being the Roman god of wine).

"Then why didn't you let us know? — you've not writ a line for the last two or three years.

The son admitted sadly that he had not. He said that he had hoped and thought he might fetch up again, and be able to send good news. Then he had been obliged to abandon that hope, and had finally come home from sheer necessity — previous to making a new start. "Yes, things are very bad with me," he repeated, perceiving their commiserating glances at his clothes.

They brought him nearer the fire, took his hat from his thin hand, which was so small and smooth as to show that his attempts to fetch up again had not been in a manual direction. His mother resumed her inquiries, and dubiously asked if he had chosen to come that particular night for any special reason.

For no reason, he told her. His arrival had been quite at random. Then Philip Hall looked round the room, and saw for the first time that the table was laid somewhat luxuriously, and for a larger number than themselves; and that an air of festivity pervaded their dress. He asked quickly what was going on.

"Sally is going to be married in a day or two," replied the mother; and she explained how Mr. Darton, Sally's intended husband, was coming there that night with the bridesman, Mr. Johns, and other details. "We thought it must be their step when we heard you," said Mrs. Hall.

The seedy wanderer looked again on the floor. "I see — I see," he murmured. "Why, indeed, should I have come to-night! Such folk as I are not wanted here at these times, naturally. And I have no business here — spoiling other people's happiness."

"Phil," said his mother, with a tear in her eye, but with a thinness of lip and severity of manner which were presumably not more than past events justified, "since you speak like that to me, I'll speak honestly to you. For these three years you have taken no thought for us. You left home with a good supply of money, and strength and education, and you ought to have made good use of it all. But you come back like a beggar; and that you come in a very awkward time for us cannot be denied. Your return to-night may do us much harm. But mind — you are welcome to this home as long as it is mine. I don't wish to turn you adrift. We will make the best of a bad job; and I hope you are not seriously ill?"

"Oh, no. I have only this infernal cough."

She looked at him anxiously. "I think you had better go to bed at once," she said.

"Well — I shall be out of the way there," said the son, wearily. "Having ruined myself, don't let me ruin you by being seen in these togs, for Heaven's sake. Who do you say Sally is going to be married to — a Farmer Darton?"

"Yes — a gentleman-farmer — quite a wealthy man. Far better in station than she could have expected. It is a good thing, altogether."

"Well done, little Sal!" said her brother, brightening and looking up at her with a smile. "I ought to have written; but perhaps I have thought of you all the more. But let me get out of sight. I would rather go and jump into the river than be seen here. But have you anything I can drink? I am confoundedly thirsty with my long tramp."

"Yes, yes; we will bring something up stairs to you," said Sally, with grief in her face.

"Ay, that will do nicely. But, Sally and mother —" He stopped, and they waited. "Mother, I have not told you all," he resumed slowly, still looking on the floor between his knees. "Sad as what you see of me is, there's worse behind."

His mother gazed upon him in grieved suspense, and Sally went and leant upon the bureau, listening for every sound, and sighing. Suddenly she turned round, saying, "Let them come, I don't care! Philip, tell the worst, and take your time."

"Well then," said the unhappy Phil, "I am not the only one in this mess. Would to Heaven I were! But — I have a wife as destitute as I."

"A wife?" said his mother.

"Unhappily."

"A wife! Yes, that is the way with sons!"

"And besides —" said he.

"Besides! O, Philip, surely —"

"I have two little children."

"Wife and children!" whispered Mrs. Hall to herself.

"Poor little things!" said Sally, involuntarily.

His mother turned again to him. "I suppose these helpless beings are left in Australia?"

"No. They are in England."

"Well, I can only hope you've left them in a respectable place."

"I have not left them at all. They are here — within a few yards of us. In short, they are in the stable. I did not like to bring them indoors till I had seen you, mother, and broken the bad news a bit to you. They were very tired, and are resting out there on some straw."

Mrs. Hall's fortitude visibly broke down. She had been brought up not without refinement, and was even more moved by such a collapse of genteel aims as this than a substantial dairyman's widow would in ordinary have been moved. "Well, it must be borne," she said, in a low voice, with her hands tightly joined. "A starving son, a starving wife, starving children. Let it be. But why is this come to us now, to-day, to-night! Could no other misfortune happen to helpless women than this, which will quite upset my poor girl's chance of a happy life? Why have you done us this wrong, Philip? What respectable man will come here, and marry open-eyed into a family of vagabonds!"

"Nonsense, mother!" said Sally, vehemently, while her face flushed. "Charley isn't the man to desert me! But if he should be, and won't marry me because Phil's come, let him go and marry elsewhere. I won't be ashamed of my own flesh and blood for any man in England — not I!" And then Sally turned away and burst into tears.

"Wait till you are twenty years older and you will tell a different tale," replied her mother.

The son stood up. "Mother," he said, "as I have come, so I will go. All I ask of you is that you will allow me and mine to lie in your stable to-night. I give you my word that we'll be gone by break of day, and trouble you no further."

Mrs. Hall, the mother, changed at that. "Oh, no," she answered, hastily "never shall it be said that I sent any of my own family from my door. Bring 'em in, Philip, or take me out to them."

"We will put 'em all into the large bedroom," said Sally, brightening, "and make up a large fire. Let's go and help them in, and call Susannah." (Susannah was the woman who assisted at the dairy and housework; she lived in a cottage hard by with her husband who attended to the cows.)

Sally went to fetch a lantern from the back kitchen, but her brother said, "You won't want a light. I lit the lantern that was hanging there."

"What must we call your wife?" asked Mrs. Hall.

"Helena," said Philip.

With shawls over their heads they proceeded towards the back door.

"One minute before you go," interrupted Philip. "I — I haven't confessed all."

"Then Heaven help us!" said Mrs. Hall, pushing to the door in calm despair.

"We passed through Verton as we came," he continued, "and I just looked in at the *Dog* to see if old Mike still kept on there as usual. The carrier had come in from Casterbridge at that moment, and guessing that I was bound for this place — for I think he knew me — he asked me to bring on a dressmaker's parcel for Sally that was marked 'immediate.' My wife had walked on with the children. 'Twas a flimsy parcel, and the paper was torn, and I found on looking at it that it was a thick warm gown. I didn't wish you to see poor Helena in a shabby state. I was ashamed that you should — 'twas not what she was born to. I untied the parcel in the road, took it on to her where she was waiting in the Abbot's Barn, and told her I had managed to get it for her, and that she was to ask no question. She, poor thing, must have supposed I obtained it on trust, through having reached a place where I was known, for she put it on gladly enough. She has it on now. Sally has other gowns, I dare say."

Sally looked at her mother, speechless.

"You have others, I dare say," repeated Phil, with a sick man's impatience. "I thought to myself, 'Better Sally cry than Helena freeze.' Well, is the dress of great consequence? 'Twas nothing very ornamental, as far as I could see."

"No — no; not of consequence" returned Sally, sadly, adding in a gentle voice, "You will not mind if I lend her another instead of that one, will you?"

Philip's agitation at the confession had brought on another attack of the cough, which seemed to shake him to pieces. He was so obviously unfit to sit in a chair that they helped him up stairs at once; and having hastily given him a cordial and kindled the bedroom fire, they descended to fetch their unhappy new relations.

III.

It was with strange feelings that the girl and her mother, lately so cheerful, passed out of the back door into the open air of the barton, laden with hay scents and the herby breath of cows. A fine sleet had begun to fall, and they trotted across the yard quickly. The stable door was open; a light shone from it — from the lantern which always hung there, and which Philip had lit, as he said. Softly nearing the door, Mrs. Hall pronounced the name "Helena?"

There was no answer for the moment. Looking in she was taken by surprise. Two people appeared before her. For one, instead of the drabbish woman she had expected, Mrs. Hall saw a pale, dark-eyed, lady-like creature, whose personality ruled her attire rather than was ruled by it. She was in a new and handsome gown, of course, and an old bonnet. She was standing up, agitated; her hand was held by her companion — none else than Sally's affianced, Farmer Charles Darton, upon whose fine figure the pale stranger's eyes were fixed, as his were fixed upon her. His other hand held the rein of his horse, which was standing saddled as if just led in.

At sight of Mrs. Hall they both turned, looking at her in a way neither quite conscious nor unconscious, and without seeming to recollect that words were necessary as a solution to the scene. In another moment Sally entered also, when Mr. Darton dropped his companion's hand, led the horse aside, and came to greet his betrothed and Mrs. Hall.

"Ah!" he said, smiling — with something like forced composure — "this is a roundabout way of arriving you will say, my dear Mrs. Hall. But I saw a light here, and led in my horse at once — my friend Johns and my man have gone back to the *Sheaf of Arrows* with theirs, not to crowd you too much. No sooner had I entered than I saw that this lady had taken temporary shelter here — and found I was intruding."

"She is my daughter-in-law," said Mrs. Hall calmly. "My son, too, is in the house, but he has gone to bed unwell."

Sally had stood staring wonderingly at the scene until this moment, hardly recognizing Darton's shake of the hand. The spell that bound her was broken by her perceiving the two little children seated on a heap of hay. She suddenly went forward, spoke to them, and took one on her arm and the other in her hand.

"And two children?" said Mr. Darton, showing thus that he had not been there long enough as yet to understand the situation.

"My grandchildren," said Mrs. Hall, with as much affected ease as before.

Philip Hall's wife, in spite of this interruption to her first rencontre, seemed scarcely so much affected by it as to feel any one's presence in addition to Mr. Darton's. However, arousing herself by a quick reflection, she threw a sudden critical glance of her sad eyes upon Mrs. Hall; and, apparently finding her satisfactory, advanced to her in a meek initiative. Then Sally and the stranger spoke some friendly words to each other, and Sally went on with the children into the house. Mrs. Hall and Helena followed, and Mr. Darton followed these, looking at Helena's dress and outline, and listening to her voice like a man in a dream.

By the time the others reached the house Sally had already gone up stairs with the tired children. She rapped against the wall for Susannah to come in and help to attend to them, Susannah's house being a little "spit-and-dab" cabin leaning against the substantial stonework of Mrs. Hall's taller erection. When she came a bed was made up for the little ones, and some supper given to them. On descending the stairs after seeing this done, Sally went to the sitting-room. Young Mrs. Hall entered it just in advance of her, having in the interim retired with her mother-in-law to take off her bonnet, and otherwise make herself presentable. Hence it was evident that no further communication could have passed between her and Mr. Darton since their brief interview in the stable.

Mr. Japheth Johns now opportunely arrived, and broke up the restraint of the company, after a few orthodox meteorological commentaries had passed between him and Mrs. Hall by way of introduction. They at once sat down to supper, the present of wine and turkey not being produced for consumption to-night, lest the premature display of those gifts should seem to throw doubt on Mrs. Hall's capacities as a provider.

"Drink bold, Mr. Johns — drink bold," said that matron, magnanimously. "Such as it is there's plenty of. But perhaps cider-wine is not to your taste? — though there's body in it."

"Quite the contrary, ma'am — quite the contrary," said the dairyman. "For though I inherit the malt-liquor principle from my father, I am a cider-drinker on my mother's side. She came from these parts, you know. And there's this to be said for't — 'tis a more peaceful liquor, and don't lie about a man like your hotter drinks. With care, one may live on it a twelvemonth without knocking down a neighbour, or getting a black eye from an old acquaintance."

The general conversation thus begun was continued briskly, though it was in the main restricted to Mrs. Hall and Japheth, who in truth required but little help from anybody. There being slight call upon Sally's tongue she had ample leisure to do what her heart most desired, namely, watch her intended husband and her sister-in-law with a view of elucidating the strange momentary scene in which her mother and herself had surprised them in the stable. If that scene meant anything, it meant, at least, that they had met before. That there had been no time for explanation Sally could see, for their manner was still one of suppressed amazement at each other's presence there. Darton's eyes, too, fell continually on the dress worn by Helena, as if this were an added riddle to his perplexity; though to Sally it was the one feature in the case which was no mystery. He seemed to feel that fate had impishly changed his *vis-à-vis* in the lover's jig he was about to tread; that while the gown had been expected to inclose a Sally, a Helena's face looked out from the bodice; that some long lost hand met his own from the sleeves.

Sally could see that whatever Helena might know of Darton, she knew nothing of how the dress entered into his embarrassment. And at moments the young girl would have persuaded herself that Darton's looks at her sister-in-law were entirely the fruit of the clothes query. But surely at other times a more extensive range of speculation and sentiment was expressed by her lover's eye than that which the changed dress would account for.

Sally's independence made her one of the least jealous of women. But there was something in the relations of these two visitors which ought to be explained.

Japheth Johns continued to converse in his well known style, interspersing his talk with some private reflections on the position of Darton and Sally, which, though the sparkle in his eye showed them to be highly entertaining to himself, were apparently not quite communicable to the company. At last he withdrew for the night, going off to the *Sheaf of Arrows*, whither Darton promised to follow him in a few minutes.

Half an hour passed, and then Mr. Darton also rose to leave, Sally and her sister-in-law simultaneously wishing him good-night as they retired up stairs to their rooms. But on his arriving at the front door with Mrs. Hall a sharp shower of rain began to come down, when the widow suggested that he should return to the fireside till the storm ceased.

Darton accepted her proposal, but insisted that, as it was getting late, and she was obviously tired, she should not sit up on his account, since he could let himself out of the house, and would quite enjoy smoking a pipe by the hearth alone. Mrs. Hall assented; and Darton was left by himself. He spread his knees to the brands, lit up his tobacco as he had said, and sat gazing into the fire and at the notches of the chimney crook which hung above.

An occasional drop of rain rolled down the chimney with a hiss, and still he smoked on; but not like a man whose mind was at rest. In the long run, however, despite his meditations, early hours afield and a long ride in the open air produced their natural result. He began to doze.

How long he remained in this half unconscious state he did not know. He suddenly opened his eyes. The back-brand had burnt itself in two, and ceased to flame; the light which he had placed on the mantelpiece had nearly gone out. But in spite of these deficiencies there was a light in the apartment, and it came from elsewhere. Turning his head, he saw Philip Hall's wife standing at the entrance of the room with a bed candle in one hand, a small brass tea-kettle in the other, and *his* dress, as it certainly seemed, still upon her.

"Helena!" said Darton, starting up.

Her countenance expressed dismay, and her first words were an apology. "I — did not know you were here, Mr. Darton," she said, while a blush flashed to her cheek. "I thought every one had retired — I was coming to make a little water boil; my husband seems to be worse. But perhaps the kitchen fire can be lighted up again."

"Don't go on my account. By all means put it on here as you intended," said Darton. "Allow me to help you." He went forward to take the kettle from her hand, but she did not allow him, and placed it on the fire herself.

They stood some way apart, one on each side of the fireplace, waiting till the water should boil, the candle on the mantel between them, and Helena with her eyes on the kettle. Darton was the first to break the silence. "Shall I call Sally?" he said.

"Oh, no," she quickly returned. "We have given trouble enough already. We have no right here. But we are the sport of fate, and were obliged to come."

"No right here!" said he in surprise.

"None. I can't explain it now," answered Helena. "This kettle is very slow."

There was another pause; the proverbial dilatoriness of watched pots was never more clearly exemplified.

Helena's face was of that sort which seems to ask for assistance without the owner's knowledge — the very antipodes of Sally's, which was self-reliance expressed. Darton's eyes travelled from the kettle to Helena's face, then back to the kettle, then to the face for rather a longer time. "So I am not to know anything of the mystery that has distracted me all the evening?" he said. "How is it that a woman, who refused me because (as I supposed) my position was not good enough for her taste, is found to be the wife of a man who certainly seems to be worse off than I?"

"He had the prior claim," said she.

"What! you knew him at that time?"

"Yes, yes. Please say no more," she implored. "Whatever my errors I have paid for them during the last five years."

The heart of Darton was subject to sudden overflowings. He was kind to a fault. "I am sorry from my soul," he said, involuntarily approaching her. Helena withdrew a step or two, at which he became conscious of his movement, and quickly took his former place. Here he stood without speaking, and the little kettle began to sing.

"Well, you might have been my wife if you had chosen," he said at last. "But that's all past and gone. However, if you are in any trouble or poverty

I shall be glad to be of service, and as your relative by marriage I shall have a right to be. Does your uncle know of your distress?"

"My uncle is dead. He left me without a farthing. And now we have two children to maintain."

"What, left you nothing? How could he be so cruel as that?"

"I disgraced myself in his eyes."

"Now," said Darton earnestly, "let me take care of the children, at least while you are so unsettled. *You* belong to another, so I cannot take care of you."

"Yes you can," said a voice; and suddenly a third figure stood beside them. It was Sally. "You can, since you seem to wish to," she repeated. "She no longer belongs to another … My poor brother is dead!"

Her face was red, her eyes sparkled, and all the woman came to the front. "I have heard it!" she went on to him passionately. "You can protect her now as well as the children!" She turned then to her agitated sister-in-law. "I heard something," said Sally (in a gentle murmur, differing much from her previous passionate words), "and I went into his room. It must have been the moment you left. He went off so quickly, and weakly, and it was so unexpected, that I couldn't leave even to call you."

Darton was just able to gather from the confused discourse which followed that, during his sleep by the fire, this brother whom he had never seen had become worse; and that during Helena's absence for water the end had unexpectedly come. The two young women hastened up stairs, and he was again left alone.

After standing there a short time he went to the front door and looked out; till, softly closing it behind him, he advanced and stood under the large sycamore tree. The stars were flickering coldly, and the dampness which had just descended upon the earth in rain now sent up a chill from it. Darton was in a strange position, and he felt it. The unexpected appearance, in deep poverty, of Helena — a young lady, daughter of a deceased naval officer, who had been brought up by her uncle, a solicitor, and had refused Darton in marriage years ago — the passionate, almost angry demeanour of Sally at discovering them, the abrupt announcement that Helena was a widow; all this coming together was a conjuncture difficult to cope with in a moment, and made him question whether he ought to leave the house or offer assistance. But for Sally's manner he would unhesitatingly have done the latter.

He was still standing under the tree when the door in front of him opened, and Mrs. Hall came out. She went round to the garden-gate at the side without seeing him. Darton followed her intending to speak.

Pausing outside, as if in thought, she proceeded to a spot where the sun came earliest in spring-time, and where the north wind never blew; it was where the row of beehives stood under the wall. Discerning her object, he waited till she had accomplished it.

It was the universal custom thereabout to wake the bees by tapping at their hives whenever a death occurred in the household, under the belief that if this were not done the bees themselves would pine away and perish during the ensuing year. As soon as an interior buzzing responded to her tap at the first hive Mrs. Hall went on to the second, and thus passed down the row. As soon as she came back he met her.

"What can I do in this trouble, Mrs. Hall?" he said.

"Oh — nothing, thank you, nothing," she said in a tearful voice, now just perceiving him. "We have called Susannah and her husband, and they will do everything necessary." She told him in a few words the particulars of her son's arrival, broken in health — indeed, at death's very door, though they did not suspect it — and suggested, as the result of a conversation between her and her daughter, that the wedding should be postponed.

"Yes, of course," said Darton. "I think now to go straight to the inn and tell Johns what has happened." It was not till after he had shaken hands with her that he turned hesitatingly and added, "Will you tell the mother of his children that, as they are now left fatherless, I shall be glad to take the eldest of them, if it would be any convenience to her and to you?"

Mrs. Hall promised that her son's widow should he told of the offer, and they parted. He retired down the rooty slope and disappeared in the direction of the *Sheaf of Arrows*, where he informed Johns of the circumstances. Meanwhile Mrs. Hall had entered the house. Sally was down stairs in the sitting-room alone, and her mother explained to her that Darton had readily assented to the postponement.

"No doubt he has," said Sally, with sad emphasis. "It is not put off for a week, or a month, or a year. I shall never marry him, and she will."

IV.

Time passed, and the household on the Knap became again serene under the composing influences of daily routine. A desultory, very desultory, correspondence, dragged on between Sally Hall and Darton, who, not quite knowing how to take her petulant words on the night of her brother's death, had continued passive thus long. Helena and her children lived on at the dairy-house, almost of necessity, and Darton therefore deemed it advisable to stay away.

One day, seven months later on, when Mr. Darton was as usual at his farm, twenty miles from Hintock, a note reached him from Helena. She thanked him for his kind offer about her children, which her mother-in-law had duly communicated, and stated that she would be glad to accept it as regarded the eldest, the boy. Helena had, in truth, good need to do so, for her uncle had left her penniless, and all application to some relatives in India had failed. There was, besides, as she said, no good school near Hintock to which she could send the child.

On a fine summer day the boy came. He was accompanied half-way by Sally and his mother — to the *Pack Horse*, a roadside inn — where he was handed over to Darton's bailiff in a shining spring-cart, who met them there.

He was entered as a day-scholar at a popular school at Casterbridge, three or four miles from Darton's, having first been taught by Darton to ride a forest-pony, on which he cantered to and from the aforesaid fount of knowledge, and (as Darton hoped) brought away a promising headful of the same at each diurnal expedition. The thoughtful taciturnity into which Darton had latterly fallen was quite dissipated by the presence of this boy.

When the Christmas holidays came it was arranged that he should spend them with his mother. The journey was, for some reason or other, performed in two stages, as at his coming, except that Darton in person took the place of the bailiff, and that the boy and himself rode on horseback.

Reaching the renowned *Pack Horse*, Darton inquired if Miss and young Mrs. Hall were there to meet little Philip (as they had agreed to be). He was answered by the appearance of Helena alone at the door.

"At the last moment Sally would not come," she faltered.

That meeting practically settled the point towards which these long-severed persons were converging. But nothing was broached about it for some time yet. Sally Hall had, in fact, imparted the first decisive motion to events by refusing to accompany Helena. She soon gave them a second move by writing the following note: —

[*Private.*]
"Dear Charles,

"Living here so long and intimately with Helena, I have naturally learnt her history, especially that of it which refers to you. I am sure she would accept you as a husband at the proper time, and I think you ought to give her the opportunity. You inquire in an old note if I am sorry that

I showed temper (which it *wasn't*) that night when I heard you talking to her. No, Charles, I am not sorry at all for what I said then.

"Yours sincerely,
"Sally Hall."

Thus set in train the transfer of Darton's heart back to its original quarters proceeded by mere lapse of time. In the following July Darton went to his friend Japheth to ask him at last to fulfil the bridal office which had been in abeyance since the previous January twelvemonths.

"With all my heart, man o' constancy!" said Dairyman Johns, warmly. "I've lost most of my genteel fair complexion haymaking this hot weather, 'tis true, but I'll do your business as well as them that look better. There be scents and good hair-oil in the world yet, thank God, and they'll take off the roughest o' my edge. I'll compliment her. 'Better late than never, Sally Hall,' I'll say."

"It is not Sally," said Darton, hurriedly. "It is young Mrs. Hall."

Japheth's face, as soon as he really comprehended, became a picture of reproachful dismay. "Not Sally?" he said. "Why not Sally? I can't believe it! Young Mrs. Hall! Well, well — where's your wisdom!"

Darton shortly explained particulars; but Johns would not be reconciled. "She was a woman worth having if ever woman was," he cried. "And now to let her go!"

"But I suppose I can marry where I like," said Darton.

"H'm," replied the dairyman, lifting his eyebrows expressively. "This don't become you, Charles — it really do not. If I had done such a thing you would have sworn I was a d— no'thern fool to be drawn off the scent by such a red-herring doll-oll-oll."

Farmer Darton responded in such sharp terms to this laconic opinion that the two friends finally parted in a way they had never parted before. Johns was to be no groomsman to Darton after all. He had flatly declined. Darton went off sorry, and even unhappy, particularly as Japheth was about to leave that side of the county, so that the words which had divided them were not likely to be explained away or softened down.

A short time after the interview Darton was united to Helena at a simple matter-of-fact wedding; and she and her little girl joined the boy who had already grown to look on Darton's house as home.

For some months the farmer experienced an unprecedented happiness and satisfaction. There had been a flaw in his life, and it was as neatly mended as was humanly possible. But after a season the stream of events followed less clearly, and there were shades in his reveries. Helena was a fragile woman, of little staying power, physically or morally, and since the time that he had originally known her — eight or ten years before — she had been severely tried. She had loved herself out, in short, and was now occasionally given to moping. Sometimes she spoke regretfully of the gentilities of her early life, and instead of comparing her present state with her condition as the wife of the unlucky Hall, she mused rather on what it had been before she took the first fatal step of clandestinely marrying him. She did not care to please such people as those with whom she was thrown as a thriving farmer's wife. She allowed the pretty trifles of agricultural domesticity to glide by her as sorry details, and had it not been for the children Darton's house would have seemed but little brighter than it had been before.

This led to occasional unpleasantness, until Darton sometimes declared to himself that such endeavours as his to rectify early deviations of the heart by harking back to the old point mostly failed of success. "Perhaps Johns was right," he would say. "I should have gone on with Sally. Better go with the tide and make the best of its course than stem it at the risk of a capsize." But he kept these unmelodious thoughts to himself, and was outwardly considerate and kind.

This somewhat barren tract of his life had extended to less than a year and half when his ponderings were cut short by the loss of the woman they concerned. When she was in her grave he thought better of her than when she had been alive; the farm was a worse place without her than with her, after all. No woman short of divine could have gone through such an experience as hers with her first husband without becoming a little soured. Her stagnant sympathies, her sometimes unreasonable manner, had covered a heart frank and well-meaning, and originally hopeful and warm. She left him a tiny red infant in white wrappings. To make life as easy as possible to this touching object became at once his care.

As this child learnt to walk and talk Darton learnt to see feasibility in a scheme which pleased him. Revolving the experiment which he had hitherto made upon life, he fancied he had gained wisdom from his mistakes and caution from his miscarriages.

What the scheme was needs no penetration to discover. Once more he had opportunity to recast and rectify his ill-wrought situations by returning to Sally Hall, who still lived quietly on under her mother's roof at Hintock Abbas. Helena had been a woman to lend pathos and refinement to a home; Sally was the woman to brighten it. She would not, as Helena did, despise the rural simplicities of a farmer's fireside. Moreover, she had a pre-eminent qualification for Darton's household; no other woman could make so desirable a mother to her brother's two children and Darton's one as Sally — while Darton, now that Helena had gone, was a more promising husband for Sally than he had ever been when liable to reminders from an uncured sentimental wound.

Darton was not a man to act rapidly, and the working out of his reparative designs might have been delayed for some time. But there came a winter evening precisely like the one which had darkened over that former ride to Hintock Abbas, and he asked himself why he should postpone longer, when the very landscape called for a repetition of that attempt.

He told his man to saddle the mare, booted and spurred himself with a younger horseman's nicety, kissed the two youngest children, and rode off. To make the journey a complete parallel to the first, he would fain have had his old acquaintance Japheth Johns with him. But Johns, alas, was missing. His removal to the other side of the county had left unrepaired the breach which had arisen between him and Darton; and though Darton had forgiven him a hundred times, as Johns had probably forgiven Darton, the effort of reunion in present circumstances was one not likely to be made.

He screwed himself up to as cheerful a pitch as he could without his former crony, and became content with his own thoughts as he rode, instead of the words of a companion. The sun went down; the boughs appeared scratched in like an etching against the sky; old crooked men with faggots at their backs said "Good-night, sir," and Darton replied "Good-night" right heartily.

By the time he reached the forking roads it was getting as dark as it had been on the occasion when Johns climbed the directing-post. Darton made no mistake this time. "Nor shall I be able to mistake, thank Heaven, when I arrive," he murmured. It gave him peculiar satisfaction to think that the proposed marriage, like his first, was of the nature of setting in order things long awry, and not a momentary freak of fancy.

Nothing hindered the smoothness of his journey, which seemed not half its former length. Though dark, it was only between five and six o'clock when the bulky chimneys of Mrs. Hall's residence appeared in view behind the sycamore tree. He put up at the *Sheaf of Arrows* as in former time; and when he had plumed himself before the inn mirror, called for a glass of negus,[1] and smoothed out the incipient wrinkles of care, he walked on to the Knap with a quick step.

---

1 Drink made of sugar, water, and sherry or port.

V.

That evening Sally was making "pinners"[1] for the milkers, who were now increased by two, for her mother and herself no longer joined in milking the cows themselves. But upon the whole there was little change in the household economy, and not much in its appearance, beyond such minor particulars as that the crack over the window, which had been a hundred years coming, was a trifle wider; that the beams were a shade blacker; that the influence of modernism had supplanted the open chimney corner by a grate; that Susannah, who had worn a cap when she had plenty of hair, had left it off now she had scarce any, because it was reported that caps were not fashionable; and that Sally's face had naturally assumed a more womanly and experienced cast.

Mrs. Hall was actually lifting coals with the tongs, as she had used to do.

"Five years ago this very night, if I am not mistaken —" she said laying on an ember.

"Not this very night — though 'twas one night this week," said the correct Sally.

"Well, 'tis near enough. Five years ago Mr. Darton came to marry you, and my poor boy Phil came home to die." She sighed. "Ah, Sally," she presently said, "if you had managed well Mr. Darton would have had you, Helena, or none."

"Don't be sentimental about that mother," begged Sally. "I didn't care to manage well in such a case. Though I liked him, I wasn't so anxious. I would never have married the man in the midst of such a hitch as that was," she added with decision; "and I don't think I would if he were to ask me now."

"I am not so sure about that, unless you have another in your eye."

"I wouldn't; and I'll tell you why. I could hardly marry him for love at this time o' day. And as we've quite enough to live on if we give up the dairy to-morrow, I should have no need to marry for any meaner reason. ... I am quite happy enough as I am, and there's an end o't."

Now it was not long after this dialogue that there came a mild rap at the door, and in a moment there entered Susannah, looking as though a ghost had arrived. The fact was that that accomplished skimmer and churner (now a resident in the house) had overheard the desultory observations between mother and daughter, and on opening the door to Mr. Darton thought the coincidence must have a grisly meaning in it. Mrs.

---

1 Pinafores.

Hall welcomed the farmer with warm surprise, as did Sally, and for a moment they rather wanted words.

"Can you push up the chimney-crook[1] for me, Mr Darton? the notches hitch," said the matron. He did it, and the homely little act bridged over the awkward consciousness that he had been a stranger for four years.

Mrs. Hall soon saw what he had come for, and left the principals together while she went to prepare him a late tea, smiling at Sally's late hasty assertions of indifference, when she saw how civil Sally was. When tea was ready she joined them. She fancied that Darton did not look so confident as when he had arrived; but Sally was quite light-hearted, and the meal passed pleasantly.

About seven he took his leave of them. Mrs. Hall went as far as the door to light him down the slope. On the doorstep he said frankly:

"I came to ask your daughter to marry me; chose the night and everything, with an eye to a favourable answer. But she won't."

"Then she's a very ungrateful girl," emphatically said Mrs. Hall.

Darton paused to shape his sentence, and asked, "I — I suppose there's nobody else more favoured?"

"I can't say that there is, or that there isn't," answered Mrs. Hall. "She's private in some things. I'm on your side, however, Mr. Darton, and I'll talk to her."

"Thank ye, thank ye," said the farmer in a gayer accent; and with this assurance the not very satisfactory visit came to an end. Darton descended the roots of the sycamore, the light was withdrawn, and the door closed. At the bottom of the slope he nearly ran against a man about to ascend.

"Can a jack-o'-lent[2] believe his few senses on such a dark night, or can't he?" exclaimed one whose utterance Darton recognizes in a moment, despite its unexpectedness. "I dare not swear he can, though I fain would!" The speaker was Johns.

Darton said he was glad of this opportunity, bad as it was, of putting an end to the silence of years, and asked the dairyman what he was travelling that way for.

Japheth showed the old jovial confidence in a moment. "I'm going to see your — relations — as they always seem to me," he said — "Mrs. Hall and Sally. Well, Charles, the fact is I find the natural barbarousness of

---

1   A device used for hanging food or a pot over a chimney fire.

2   A sort of scarecrow or dummy set up in each community during the religious festival of Lent.

man is much increased by a bachelor life, and, as your leavings were always good enough for me, I'm trying civilisation here." He nodded towards the house.

"Not with Sally — to marry her?" said Darton, feeling something like a rill of ice water between his shoulders.

"Yes, by the help of Providence and my personal charms. And I think I shall get her. I am this road every week — my present dairy is only four miles off, you know, and I see her through the window. 'Tis rather odd that I was going to speak practical to-night to her for the first time. You've just called?"

"Yes, for a short while. But she didn't say a word about you."

"A good sign, a good sign. Now that decides me. I'll sling the mallet[1] and get her answer this very night as I planned."

A few more remarks and Darton, wishing his friend joy of Sally in a slightly hollow tone of jocularity, bade him good-bye. Johns promised to write particulars, and ascended, and was lost in the shade of the house and tree. A rectangle of light appeared when Johns was admitted, and all was dark again.

"Happy Japheth!" said Darton. "This, then, is the explanation!"

He determined to return home that night. In a quarter of an hour he passed out of the village, and the next day went about his swede-lifting and storing as if nothing had occurred.

He waited and waited to hear from Johns whether the wedding-day was fixed: but no letter came. He learnt not a single particular till, meeting Johns one day at a horse auction, Darton exclaimed genially — rather more genially than he felt — "When is the joyful day to be?"

To his great surprise a reciprocity of gladness was not conspicuous in Johns. "Not at all," he said, in a very subdued tone. "'Tis a bad job; she won't have me."

Darton held his breath till he said with treacherous solicitude, "Try again — 'tis coyness."

"Oh, no," said Johns decisively. "There's been none of that. We talked it over dozens of times in the most fair and square way. She tells me plainly, I don't suit her. 'Twould be simply annoying her to ask her again. Ah, Charles, you threw a prize away when you let her slip five years ago."

"I did — I did," said Darton.

---

1 Euphemism for "demand action."

He returned from that auction with a new set of feelings in play. He had certainly made a surprising mistake in thinking Johns his successful rival. It really seemed as if he might hope for Sally after all.

This time, being rather pressed by business, Darton had recourse to pen and ink, and wrote her as manly and straightforward a proposal as any woman could wish to receive. The reply came promptly: —

"Dear Mr. Darton,

"I am as sensible as any woman can be of the goodness that leads you to make me this offer a second time. Better women than I would be proud of the honour, for when I read your nice long speeches on mangold-wurzel,[1] and such like topics, at the Casterbridge Farmers' Club, I do feel it an honour, I assure you. But my answer is just the same as before. I will not try to explain what, in truth, I cannot explain — my reasons; I will simply say that I must decline to be married to you. With good wishes as in former times, I am,

"Your faithful friend,
"Sally Hall."

Darton dropped the letter hopelessly. Beyond the negative, there was just a possibility of sarcasm in it — "nice long speeches on mangold-wurzel" had a suspicious sound. However, sarcasm or none, there was the answer, and he had to be content.

He proceeded to seek relief in a business which at this time engrossed much of his attention — that of clearing up a curious mistake just current in the county, that he had been nearly ruined by the recent failure of a local bank. A farmer named Darton had lost heavily, and the similarity of name had probably led to the error. Belief in it was so persistent that it demanded several days of letter-writing to set matters straight, and persuade the world that he was as solvent as ever he had been in his life. He had hardly concluded this worrying task when, to his delight, another letter arrived in the handwriting of Sally.

Darton tore it open; it was very short.

"Dear Mr. Darton,

"We have been so alarmed these last few days by the report that you were ruined by the stoppage of — 's Bank, that now it is contradicted, I hasten, by my mother's wish, to say how truly glad we are to find there is

---

1   Root-crop used as winter food for livestock.

no foundation for the report. After your kindness to my poor brother's children, I can do no less than write at such a moment. We had a letter from each of them a few days ago.

> "Your faithful friend,
> "Sally Hall."

"Mercenary little woman!" said Darton to himself with a smile. "Then that's the secret of her refusal this time — she thought I was ruined."

Now, such was Darton, that as hours went on he could not help feeling too generously towards Sally to condemn her in this. What did he want in a wife, he asked himself. Love and integrity. What next? Worldly wisdom. And was there really more than worldly wisdom in her refusal to go aboard a sinking ship? "Begad," he said, "I'll try her again."

The fact was he had so set his heart upon Sally, and Sally alone, that nothing was to be allowed to baulk him; and his reasoning was purely formal.

Anniversaries having been unpropitious he waited on till a bright day late in May — a day when all animate nature was fancying, in its trusting, foolish way, that it was going to bask out of doors for evermore. As he rode through Holloway Lane it was scarce recognisable as the track of his two winter journeys. No mistake could be made now, even with his eyes shut. The cuckoo's note was at its best between April tentativeness and Midsummer decrepitude, and the reptiles in the sun behaved as winningly as kittens on a hearth. Though afternoon, and about the same time as on the last occasion, it was broad day and sunshine when he entered Hintock Abbas, and the details of the Knap dairy-house were visible far up the road. He saw Sally in the garden, and was set vibrating. He had first intended to go on to the inn; but "No," he said; "I'll tie my horse to the garden gate. If all goes well it can soon be taken round: if not, I mount and ride away."

The tall shade of the horseman darkened the room in which Mrs. Hall sat, and made her start, for he had ridden by a side path to the top of the slope, where riders seldom came. In a few seconds he was in the garden with Sally.

Five — ay, three minutes — did the business at the back of that row of bees. Though spring had come, and heavenly blue consecrated the scene, Darton succeeded not. "No," said Sally firmly. "I will never, never marry you, Mr. Darton. I would have once; but now I never can."

"But" — implored Mr. Darton. And with a burst of real eloquence he went on to declare all sorts of things that he would do for her. He would drive her to see her mother every week — take her to London — settle so much money upon her — Heaven knows what he did not promise, suggest, and tempt her with. But it availed nothing. She interposed with a stout negative, which closed the course of his argument like an iron gate across a highway. Darton paused.

"Then," said he, simply, "you hadn't heard of my supposed failure when you declined last time?"

"I had not," she said. "But if I had 'twould have been all the same."

"And 'tis not because of any soreness from my slighting you years ago?"

"No. That soreness is long past."

"Ah — then you despise me, Sally!"

"No," she slowly answered. "I don't altogether despise you. I don't think you quite such a hero as I once did — that's all. The truth is, I am happy enough as I am; and I don't mean to marry at all. Now, may *I* ask a favour, sir?" She spoke with an ineffable charm which, whenever he thought of it, made him curse his loss of her as long as he lived.

"To any extent."

"Please do not put this question to me any more. Friends as long as you like, but lovers and married never."

"I never will," said Darton. "Not if I live a hundred years."

And he never did. That he had worn out his welcome in her heart was only too plain.

When his step-children had grown up, and were placed out in life, all communication between Darton and the Hall family ceased. It was only by chance that, years after, he learnt that Sally, notwithstanding the solicitations her attractions drew down upon her, had refused several offers of marriage, and steadily adhered to her purpose of leading a single life.

Robert Louis Stevenson

"Markheim" (1885)

[The inhabitants of Samoa called him "Tusitala" — the Storyteller. Born in Edinburgh, Robert Louis Stevenson (1850–1894) has become the best known Victorian writer of adventure stories. His focus on action over character echoes the strategy of the pulp fiction that preceded his work, and fostered a huge audience, especially among children and young adults. His image as an author of young adult fiction, however, obscured his complex explorations into psychology, sexuality, morality, and consumerism. *Treasure Island* (1883), *Kidnapped* (1886), *The Strange Case of Dr. Jekyll and Mr. Hyde* (1886) — all of his most famous works imbue the adventure and suspense with an analysis of mental conflict and ethical deviations. The combination can also be found in many of his shorter prose works, including the story "Markheim," in which the allegory and the psychological combat are both more engaging than the limited action. Stevenson also published a number of works describing his extensive travels, conducted in large part for health reasons. He eventually settled in Samoa, where he died in 1894.]

'Yes,' said the dealer, 'our windfalls are of various kinds. Some customers are ignorant, and then I touch a dividend on my superior knowledge. Some are dishonest,' and here he held up the candle, so that the light fell strongly on his visitor, 'and in that case,' he continued, 'I profit by my virtue.'

Markheim had but just entered from the daylight streets, and his eyes had not yet grown familiar with the mingled shine and darkness in the shop. At these pointed words, and before the near presence of the flame, he blinked painfully and looked aside.

The dealer chuckled. 'You come to me on Christmas Day,' he resumed, 'when you know that I am alone in my house, put up my shutters, and make a point of refusing business. Well, you will have to pay for that; you will have to pay for my loss of time, when I should be balancing my books; you will have to pay, besides, for a kind of manner that I remark

in you to-day very strongly. I am the essence of discretion, and ask no awkward questions; but when a customer cannot look me in the eye, he has
to pay for it.' The dealer once more chuckled; and then, changing to his
usual business voice, though still with a note of irony, 'You can give, as
usual, a clear account of how you came into the possession of the object?'
he continued. 'Still your uncle's cabinet? A remarkable collector, sir!'

And the little pale, round-shouldered dealer stood almost on tip-toe,
looking over the top of his gold spectacles, and nodding his head with
every mark of disbelief. Markheim returned his gaze with one of infinite
pity, and a touch of horror.

'This time,' said he, 'you are in error. I have not come to sell, but to buy.
I have no curios to dispose of; my uncle's cabinet is bare to the wainscot;
even were it still intact, I have done well on the Stock Exchange, and
should more likely add to it than otherwise, and my errand to-day is
simplicity itself. I seek a Christmas present for a lady,' he continued,
waxing more fluent as he struck into the speech he had prepared; 'and certainly I owe you every excuse for thus disturbing you upon so small a
matter. But the thing was neglected yesterday; I must produce my little
compliment at dinner; and, as you very well know, a rich marriage is not
a thing to be neglected.'

There followed a pause, during which the dealer seemed to weigh
this statement incredulously. The ticking of many clocks among the curious lumber of the shop, and the faint rushing of the cabs in a near thoroughfare, filled up the interval of silence.

'Well, sir,' said the dealer, 'be it so. You are an old customer after all;
and if, as you say, you have the chance of a good marriage, far be it from
me to be an obstacle. Here is a nice thing for a lady now,' he went on, 'this
hand glass — fifteenth century, warranted; comes from a good collection,
too; but I reserve the name, in the interests of my customer, who was just
like yourself, my dear sir, the nephew and sole heir of a remarkable collector.'

The dealer, while he thus ran on in his dry and biting voice, had
stopped to take the object from its place; and, as he had done so, a shock
had passed through Markheim, a start both of hand and foot, a sudden
leap of many tumultuous passions to the face. It passed as swiftly as it
came, and left no trace beyond a certain trembling of the hand that now
received the glass.

'A glass,' he said hoarsely, and then paused, and repeated it more
clearly. 'A glass? For Christmas? Surely not?'

'And why not?' cried the dealer. 'Why not a glass?'

Markheim was looking upon him with an indefinable expression. 'You ask me why not?' he said. 'Why, look here — look in it — look at yourself! Do you like to see it? No! nor I — nor any man.'

The little man had jumped back when Markheim had so suddenly confronted him with the mirror; but now, perceiving there was nothing worse on hand, he chuckled. 'Your future lady, sir, must be pretty hard favoured,' said he.

'I ask you,' said Markheim, 'for a Christmas present, and you give me this — this damned reminder of years, and sins and follies — this hand-conscience! Did you mean it? Had you a thought in your mind? Tell me. It will be better for you if you do. Come, tell me about yourself. I hazard a guess now, that you are in secret a very charitable man?'

The dealer looked closely at his companion. It was very odd, Markheim did not appear to be laughing; there was something in his face like an eager sparkle of hope, but nothing of mirth.

'What are you driving at?' the dealer asked.

'Not charitable?' returned the other, gloomily. 'Not charitable; not pious; not scrupulous; unloving, unbeloved; a hand to get money, a safe to keep it. Is that all? Dear God, man, is that all?'

'I will tell you what it is,' began the dealer, with some sharpness, and then broke off again into a chuckle. 'But I see this is a love match of yours, and you have been drinking the lady's health.'

'Ah!' cried Markheim, with a strange curiosity. 'Ah, have you been in love? Tell me about that.'

'I,' cried the dealer. 'I in love! I never had the time, nor have I the time to-day for all this nonsense. Will you take the glass?'

'Where is the hurry?' returned Markheim. 'It is very pleasant to stand here talking; and life is so short and insecure that I would not hurry away from any pleasure — no, not even from so mild a one as this. We should rather cling, cling to what little we can get, like a man at a cliff's edge. Every second is a cliff, if you think upon it — a cliff a mile high — high enough, if we fall, to dash us out of every feature of humanity. Hence it is best to talk pleasantly. Let us talk of each other: why should we wear this mask? Let us be confidential. Who knows, we might become friends?'

'I have just one word to say to you,' said the dealer. 'Either make your purchase, or walk out of my shop!'

'True, true,' said Markheim. 'Enough fooling. To business. Show me something else.'

The dealer stooped once more, this time to replace the glass upon the shelf, his thin blond hair falling over his eyes as he did so. Markheim moved a little nearer, with one hand in the pocket of his greatcoat; he drew himself up and filled his lungs; at the same time many different emotions were depicted together on his face — terror, horror, and resolve, fascination and a physical repulsion; and through a haggard lift of his upper lip, his teeth looked out.

'This, perhaps, may suit,' observed the dealer: and then, as he began to re-arise, Markheim bounded from behind upon his victim. The long, skewerlike dagger flashed and fell. The dealer struggled like a hen, striking his temple on the shelf, and then tumbled on the floor in a heap.

Time had some score of small voices in that shop, some stately and slow as was becoming to their great age; others garrulous and hurried. All these told out the seconds in an intricate chorus of tickings. Then the passage of a lad's feet, heavily running on the pavement, broke in upon these smaller voices and startled Markheim into the consciousness of his surroundings. He looked about him awfully. The candle stood on the counter, its flame solemnly wagging in a draught; and by that inconsiderable movement, the whole room was filled with noiseless bustle and kept heaving like a sea: the tall shadows nodding, the gross blots of darkness swelling and dwindling as with respiration, the faces of the portraits and the china gods changing and wavering like images in water. The inner door stood ajar, and peered into that leaguer of shadows with a long slit of daylight like a pointing finger.

From these fear-stricken rovings, Markheim's eyes returned to the body of his victim, where it lay both humped and sprawling, incredibly small and strangely meaner than in life. In these poor, miserly clothes, in that ungainly attitude, the dealer lay like so much sawdust. Markheim had feared to see it, and lo! it was nothing. And yet, as he gazed, this bundle of old clothes and pool of blood began to find eloquent voices. There it must lie; there was none to work the cunning hinges or direct the miracle of locomotion — there it must lie till it was found. Found! ay, and then? Then would this dead flesh lift up a cry that would ring over England, and fill the world with the echoes of pursuit. Ay, dead or not, this was still the enemy. 'Time was that when the brains were out,' he thought; and the first word struck into his mind. Time, now that the deed was accomplished — time, which had closed for the victim, had become instant and momentous for the slayer.

The thought was yet in his mind, when, first one and then another, with every variety of pace and voice — one deep as the bell from a cathedral turret, another ringing on its treble notes the prelude of a waltz — the clocks began to strike the hour of three in the afternoon.

The sudden outbreak of so many tongues in that dumb chamber staggered him. He began to bestir himself, going to and fro with the candle, beleaguered by moving shadows, and startled to the soul by chance reflections. In many rich mirrors, some of home design, some from Venice or Amsterdam, he saw his face repeated and repeated, as it were an army of spies; his own eyes met and detected him; and the sound of his own steps, lightly as they fell, vexed the surrounding quiet. And still, as he continued to fill his pockets, his mind accused him with a sickening iteration, of the thousand faults of his design. He should have chosen a more quiet hour; he should have prepared an alibi; he should not have used a knife; he should have been more cautious, and only bound and gagged the dealer, and not killed him; he should have been more bold, and killed the servant also; he should have done all things otherwise: poignant regrets, weary, incessant toiling of the mind to change what was unchangeable, to plan what was now useless, to be the architect of the irrevocable past. Meanwhile, and behind all this activity, brute terrors, like the scurrying of rats in a deserted attic, filled the more remote chambers of his brain with riot; the hand of the constable would fall heavy on his shoulder, and his nerves would jerk like a hooked fish; or he beheld, in galloping defile, the dock, the prison, the gallows, and the black coffin.

Terror of the people in the street sat down before his mind like a besieging army. It was impossible, he thought, but that some rumour of the struggle must have reached their ears and set on edge their curiosity; and now, in all the neighbouring houses, he divined them sitting motionless and with uplifted ear — solitary people, condemned to spend Christmas dwelling alone on memories of the past, and now startingly recalled from that tender exercise; happy family parties, struck into silence round the table, the mother still with raised finger: every degree and age and humour, but all, by their own hearths, prying and hearkening and weaving the rope that was to hang him. Sometimes it seemed to him he could not move too softly; the clink of the tall Bohemian goblets rang out loudly like a bell; and alarmed by the bigness of the ticking, he was tempted to stop the clocks. And then, again, with a swift transition of his terrors, the very silence of the place appeared a source of peril, and a thing to strike and freeze the passer-by; and he would step more boldly, and bustle aloud among the contents of the shop, and imitate, with elaborate bravado, the movements of a busy man at ease in his own house.

But he was now so pulled about by different alarms that, while one portion of his mind was still alert and cunning, another trembled on the brink of lunacy. One hallucination in particular took a strong hold on his credulity. The neighbour hearkening with white face beside his window, the passer-by arrested by a horrible surmise on the pavement — these could at worst suspect, they could not know; through the brick walls and shuttered windows only sounds could penetrate. But here, within the house, was he alone? He knew he was; he had watched the servant set forth sweet-hearting, in her poor best, 'out for the day' written in every ribbon and smile. Yes, he was alone, of course; and yet, in the bulk of empty house above him, he could surely hear a stir of delicate footing — he was surely conscious, inexplicably conscious of some presence. Ay, surely; to every room and corner of the house his imagination followed it; and now it was a faceless thing, and yet had eyes to see with; and again it was a shadow of himself; and yet again behold the image of the dead dealer, reinspired with cunning and hatred.

At times, with a strong effort, he would glance at the open door which still seemed to repel his eyes. The house was tall, the skylight small and dirty, the day blind with fog; and the light that filtered down to the ground story was exceedingly faint, and showed dimly on the threshold of the shop. And yet, in that strip of doubtful brightness, did there not hang wavering a shadow?

Suddenly, from the street outside, a very jovial gentleman began to beat with a staff on the shop-door, accompanying his blows with shouts and railleries in which the dealer was continually called upon by name. Markheim, smitten into ice, glanced at the dead man. But no! he lay quite still; he was fled away far beyond earshot of these blows and shoutings; he was sunk beneath seas of silence; and his name, which would once have caught his notice above the howling of a storm, had become an empty sound. And presently the jovial gentleman desisted from his knocking and departed.

Here was a broad hint to hurry what remained to be done, to get forth from this accusing neighbourhood, to plunge into a bath of London multitudes, and to reach, on the other side of day, that haven of safety and apparent innocence — his bed. One visitor had come: at any moment another might follow and be more obstinate. To have done the deed, and yet not to reap the profit, would be too abhorrent a failure. The money, that was now Markheim's concern; and as a means to that, the keys.

He glanced over his shoulder at the open door, where the shadow was still lingering and shivering; and with no conscious repugnance of the mind, yet with a tremor of the belly, he drew near the body of his victim. The human character had quite departed. Like a suit half-stuffed with bran, the limbs lay scattered, the trunk doubled, on the floor; and yet the thing repelled him. Although so dingy and inconsiderable to the eye, he feared it might have more significance to the touch. He took the body by the shoulders and turned it on its back. It was strangely light and supple, and the limbs, as if they had been broken, fell into the oddest postures. The face was robbed of all expression; but it was as pale as wax, and shockingly smeared with blood about one temple. That was, for Markheim, the one displeasing circumstance. It carried him back, upon the instant, to a certain fair-day in a fishers' village: a gray day, a piping wind, a crowd upon the street, the blare of brasses, the booming of drums, the nasal voice of a ballad singer; and a boy going to and fro, buried over head in the crowd and divided between interest and fear, until, coming out upon the chief place of concourse, he beheld a booth and a great screen with pictures, dismally designed, garishly coloured: Brownrigg with her apprentice; the Mannings with their murdered guest; Weare in the death-grip of Thurtell;[1] and a score besides of famous crimes. The thing was as clear as an illusion; he was once again that little boy; he was looking once again, and with the same sense of physical revolt, at these vile pictures; he was still stunned by the thumping of the drums. A bar of that day's music returned upon his memory; and at that, for the first time, a qualm came over him, a breath of nausea, a sudden weakness of the joints, which he must instantly resist and conquer.

He judged it more prudent to confront than to flee from these considerations; looking the more hardily in the dead face, bending his mind to realise the nature and greatness of his crime. So little a while ago that face had moved with every change of sentiment, that pale mouth had spoken, that body had been all on fire with governable energies; and now, and by his act, that piece of life had been arrested, as the horologist,[2] with interjected finger, arrests the beating of the clock. So he reasoned in vain; he could rise to no more remorseful consciousness; the same heart which had shuddered before the painted effigies of crime, looked on its reality unmoved. At best, he felt a gleam of pity for one who had been endowed in vain with all those faculties that can make the world a garden of enchantment, one who had never lived and who was now dead. But of penitence, no, not a tremor.

With that, shaking himself clear of these considerations, he found the keys and advanced towards the open door of the shop. Outside, it had begun to rain smartly; and the sound of the shower upon the roof had ban-

---

1   Prisoners of Newgate prison whose stories where made popular when published in the *Newgate Calender*.

2   Expert in the science of measuring time.

ished silence. Like some dripping cavern, the chambers of the house were haunted by an incessant echoing, which filled the ear and mingled with the ticking of the clocks. And, as Markheim approached the door, he seemed to hear, in answer to his own cautious tread, the steps of another foot withdrawing up the stair. The shadow still palpitated loosely on the threshold. He threw a ton's weight of resolve upon his muscles, and drew back the door.

The faint, foggy daylight glimmered dimly on the bare floor and stairs; on the bright suit of armour posted, halbert[1] in hand, upon the landing; and on the dark wood-carvings, and framed pictures that hung against the yellow panels of the wainscot. So loud was the beating of the rain through all the house, that, in Markheim's ears, it began to be distinguished into many different sounds. Footsteps and sighs, the tread of regiments marching in the distance, the chink of money in the counting, and the creaking of doors held stealthily ajar, appeared to mingle with the patter of the drops upon the cupola and the gushing of the water in the pipes. The sense that he was not alone grew upon him to the verge of madness. On every side he was haunted and begirt by presences. He heard them moving in the upper chambers; from the shop, he heard the dead man getting to his legs; and as he began with a great effort to mount the stairs, feet fled quietly before him and followed stealthily behind. If he were but deaf, he thought, how tranquilly he would possess his soul! And then again, and hearkening with ever fresh attention, he blessed himself for that unresting sense which held the outposts and stood a trusty sentinel upon his life. His head turned continually on his neck; his eyes, which seemed starting from their orbits, scouted on every side, and on every side were half-rewarded as with the tail of something nameless vanishing. The four-and-twenty steps to the first floor were four-and-twenty agonies.

On that first storey, the doors stood ajar, three of them like three ambushes, shaking his nerves like the throats of cannon. He could never again, he felt, be sufficiently immured and fortified from men's observing eyes; he longed to be home, girt in by walls, buried among bedclothes, and invisible to all but God. And at that thought he wondered a little, recollecting tales of other murderers and the fear they were said to entertain of heavenly avengers. It was not so, at least, with him. He feared the laws of nature, lest, in their callous and immutable procedure, they should preserve some damning evidence of his crime. He feared

---

1 Weapon of the fifteenth and sixteenth centuries with an axe-like blade and steel spike on a long shaft.

tenfold more, with a slavish, superstitious terror, some scission in the continuity of man's experience, some willful illegality of nature. He played a game of skill, depending on the rules, calculating consequence from cause; and what if nature, as the defeated tyrant overthrew the chessboard, should break the mould of their succession? The like had befallen Napoleon (so writers said) when the winter changed the time of its appearance. The like might befall Markheim: the solid walls might become transparent and reveal his doings like those of bees in a glass hive; the stout planks might yield under his foot like quicksands and detain him in their clutch; ay, and there were soberer accidents that might destroy him: if, for instance, the house should fall and imprison him beside the body of his victim; or the house next door should fly on fire, and the firemen invade him from all sides. These things he feared; and, in a sense, these things might be called the hands of God reached forth against sin. But about God himself he was at ease; his act was doubtless exceptional, but so were his excuses, which God knew; it was there, and not among men, that he felt sure of justice.

When he had got safe into the drawing-room, and shut the door behind him, he was aware of a respite from alarms. The room was quite dismantled, uncarpeted besides, and strewn with packing cases and incongruous furniture; several great pier-glasses,[1] in which he beheld himself at various angles, like an actor on a stage; many pictures, framed and unframed, standing, with their faces to the wall; a fine Sheraton sideboard, a cabinet of marquetry, and a great old bed, with tapestry hangings. The windows opened to the floor; but by great good fortune the lower part of the shutters had been closed, and this concealed him from the neighbours. Here, then, Markheim drew in a packing case before the cabinet, and began to search among the keys. It was a long business, for there were many; and it was irksome, besides; for, after all, there might be nothing in the cabinet, and time was on the wing. But the closeness of the occupation sobered him. With the tail of his eye he saw the door — even glanced at it from time to time directly, like a besieged commander pleased to verify the good estate of his defences. But in truth he was at peace. The rain falling in the street sounded natural and pleasant. Presently, on the other side, the notes of a piano were wakened to the music of a hymn, and the voices of many children took up the air and words. How stately, how comfortable was the melody! How fresh the youthful voices! Markheim gave ear to it smilingly, as he sorted out the

---

1   Long mirrors placed between two windows.

keys; and his mind was thronged with answerable ideas and images; church-going children and the pealing of the high organ; children afield, bathers by the brookside, ramblers on the brambly common, kite-flyers in the windy and cloud-navigated sky; and then, at another cadence of the hymn, back again to church, and the somnolence of summer Sundays, and the high genteel voice of the parson (which he smiled a little to recall) and the painted Jacobean[1] tombs, and the dim lettering of the Ten Commandments in the chancel.

And as he sat thus, at once busy and absent, he was startled to his feet. A flash of ice, a flash of fire, a bursting gush of blood, went over him, and then he stood transfixed and thrilling. A step mounted the stair slowly and steadily, and presently a hand was laid upon the knob, and the lock clicked, and the door opened.

Fear held Markheim in a vice. What to expect he knew not, whether the dead man walking, or the official ministers of human justice, or some chance witness blindly stumbling in to consign him to the gallows. But when a face was thrust into the aperture, glanced round the room, looked at him, nodded and smiled as if in friendly recognition, and then withdrew again, and the door closed behind it, his fear broke loose from his control in a hoarse cry. At the sound of this the visitant returned.

'Did you call me?' he asked, pleasantly, and with that he entered the room and closed the door behind him.

Markheim stood and gazed at him with all his eyes. Perhaps there was a film upon his sight, but the outlines of the new comer seemed to change and waver like those of the idols in the wavering candlelight of the shop; and at times he thought he knew him; and at times he thought he bore a likeness to himself; and always, like a lump of living terror, there lay in his bosom the conviction that this thing was not of the earth and not of God.

And yet the creature had a strange air of the commonplace, as he stood looking on Markheim with a smile; and when he added: 'You are looking for the money, I believe?' it was in the tones of everyday politeness.

Markheim made no answer.

'I should warn you,' resumed the other, 'that the maid has left her sweetheart earlier than usual and will soon be here. If Mr. Markheim be found in this house, I need not describe to him the consequences.'

'You know me?' cried the murderer.

The visitor smiled. 'You have long been a favourite of mine,' he said; 'and I have long observed and often sought to help you.'

---

1 From the reign of King James I (1603–25).

'What are you?' cried Markheim: 'the devil?'

'What I may be,' returned the other, 'cannot affect the service I propose to render you.'

'It can,' cried Markheim, 'it does! Be helped by you? No, never; not by you! You do not know me yet; thank God, you do not know me!'

'I know you,' replied the visitant, with a sort of kind severity or rather firmness. 'I know you to the soul.'

'Know me!' cried Markheim. 'Who can do so? My life is but a travesty and slander on myself. I have lived to belie my nature. All men do; all men are better than this disguise that grows about and stifles them. You see each dragged away by life, like one whom bravos[1] have seized and muffled in a cloak. If they had their own control — if you could see their faces, they would be altogether different, they would shine out for heroes and saints! I am worse than most; myself is more overlaid; my excuse is known to me and God. But, had I the time, I could disclose myself.'

'To me?' inquired the visitant.

'To you before all,' returned the murderer. 'I supposed you were intelligent. I thought — since you exist — you would prove a reader of the heart. And yet you would propose to judge me by my acts! Think of it; my acts! I was born and I have lived in a land of giants; giants have dragged me by the wrists since I was born out of my mother — the giants of circumstance. And you would judge me by my acts! But can you not look within? Can you not understand that evil is hateful to me? Can you not see within me the clear writing of conscience, never blurred by any wilful sophistry, although too often disregarded? Can you not read me for a thing that surely must be common as humanity — the unwilling sinner?

'All this is very feelingly expressed,' was the reply, 'but it regards me not. These points of consistency are beyond my province, and I care not in the least by what compulsion you may have been dragged away, so as you are but carried in the right direction. But time flies; the servant delays, looking in the faces of the crowd and at the pictures on the hoardings,[2] but still she keeps moving nearer; and remember, it is as if the gallows itself was striding towards you through the Christmas streets! Shall I help you; I, who know all? Shall I tell you where to find the money?'

'For what price?' asked Markheim.

'I offer you the service for a Christmas gift,' returned the other.

---

1   Villains; hired murderers.

2   Temporary fencing around buildings.

Markheim could not refrain from smiling with a kind of bitter triumph. 'No,' said he, 'I will take nothing at your hands; if I were dying of thirst, and it was your hand that put the pitcher to my lips, I should find the courage to refuse. It may be credulous, but I will do nothing to commit myself to evil.'

'I have no objection to a death-bed repentance,' observed the visitant.

'Because you disbelieve their efficacy!' Markheim cried.

'I do not say so,' returned the other; 'but I look on these things from a different side, and when the life is done my interest falls. The man has lived to serve me, to spread black looks under colour of religion, or to sow tares[1] in the wheat-field, as you do, in a course of weak compliance with desire. Now that he draws so near to his deliverance, he can add but one act of service — to repent, to die smiling, and thus to build up in confidence and hope the more timorous of my surviving followers. I am not so hard a master. Try me. Accept my help. Please yourself in life as you have done hitherto; please yourself more amply, spread your elbows at the board; and when the night begins to fall and the curtains to be drawn, I tell you, for your greater comfort, that you will find it even easy to compound your quarrel with your conscience, and to make a truckling peace with God. I came but now from such a deathbed, and the room was full of sincere mourners, listening to the man's last words: and when I looked into that face, which had been set as a flint against mercy, I found it smiling with hope.'

'And do you, then, suppose me such a creature?' asked Markheim. 'Do you think I have no more generous aspirations than to sin, and sin, and sin, and, at the last, sneak into heaven? My heart rises at the thought. Is this, then, your experience of mankind? or is it because you find me with red hands that you presume such baseness? and is this crime of murder indeed so impious as to dry up the very springs of good?'

'Murder is to me no special category,' replied the other. 'All sins are murder, even as all life is war. I behold your race, like starving mariners on a raft, plucking crusts out of the hands of famine and feeding on each other's lives. I follow sins beyond the moment of their acting; I find in all that the last consequence is death; and to my eyes, the pretty maid who thwarts her mother with such taking graces on a question of a ball, drips no less visibly with human gore than such a murderer as yourself. Do I say that I follow sins? I follow virtues also; they differ not by the thickness of a nail, they are both scythes for the reaping angel of

---

1 Corn-weed.

Death. Evil, for which I live, consists not in action but in character. The bad man is dear to me; not the bad act, whose fruits, if we could follow them far enough down the hurtling cataract of the ages, might yet be found more blessed than those of the rarest virtues. And it is not because you have killed a dealer, but because you are Markheim, that I offer to forward your escape.'

'I will lay my heart open to you,' answered Markheim. 'This crime on which you find me is my last. On my way to it I have learned many lessons; itself is a lesson, a momentous lesson. Hitherto I have been driven with revolt to what I would not; I was a bond-slave to poverty, driven and scourged. There are robust virtues that can stand in these temptations; mine was not so: I had a thirst of pleasure. But to-day, and out of this deed, I pluck both warning and riches — both the power and a fresh resolve to be myself. I become in all things a free actor in the world; I begin to see myself all changed, these hands the agents of good, this heart at peace. Something comes over me out of the past; something of what I have dreamed on Sabbath evenings to the sound of the church organ, of what I forecast when I shed tears over noble books, or talked, an inno-cent child, with my mother. There lies my life; I have wandered a few years, but now I see once more my city of destination.'

'You are to use this money on the Stock Exchange, I think?' remarked the visitor; 'and there, if I mistake not, you have already lost some thousands?'

'Ah,' said Markheim, 'but this time I have a sure thing.'

'This time, again, you will lose,' replied the visitor quietly.

'Ah, but I keep back the half!' cried Markheim.

'That also you will lose,' said the other.

The sweat started upon Markheim's brow. 'Well, then, what matter?' he exclaimed. 'Say it be lost, say I am plunged again in poverty, shall one part of me, and that the worst, continue until the end to override the better? Evil and good run strong in me, haling me both ways. I do not love the one thing, I love all. I can conceive great deeds, renunciations, mar-tyrdoms; and though I be fallen to such a crime as murder, pity is no stranger to my thoughts. I pity the poor; who knows their trials better than myself? I pity and help them; I prize love, I love honest laughter; there is no good thing nor true thing on earth but I love it from my heart. And are my vices only to direct my life, and my virtues to lie without effect, like some passive lumber of the mind? Not so; good, also, is a spring of acts.'

But the visitant raised his finger. 'For six-and-thirty years that you have been in this world,' said he, 'through many changes of fortune and varieties of humour, I have watched you steadily fall. Fifteen years ago you would have started at a theft. Three years back you would have blenched at the name of murder. Is there any crime, is there any cruelty or meanness, from which you still recoil? — five years from now I shall detect you in the fact! Downward, downward, lies your way; nor can anything but death avail to stop you.'

'It is true,' Markheim said huskily, 'I have in some degree complied with evil. But it is so with all; the very saints, in the mere exercise of living, grow less dainty, and take on the tone of their surroundings.'

'I will propound to you one simple question,' said the other; 'and as you answer, I shall read to you your moral horoscope. You have grown in many things more lax; possibly you do right to be so; and at any account, it is the same with all men. But granting that, are you in any one particular, however trifling, more difficult to please with your own conduct, or do you go in all things with a looser rein?'

'In any one?' repeated Markheim, with an anguish of consideration. 'No,' he added, with despair, 'in none! I have gone down in all.'

'Then,' said the visitor, 'content yourself with what you are, for you will never change; and the words of your part on this stage are irrevocably written down.'

Markheim stood for a long while silent, and indeed it was the visitor who first broke the silence. 'That being so,' he said, 'shall I show you the money?'

'And grace?' cried Markheim.

'Have you not tried it?' returned the other. 'Two or three years ago, did I not see you on the platform of revival meetings, and was not your voice the loudest in the hymn?'

'It is true,' said Markheim; 'and I see clearly what remains for me by way of duty. I thank you for these lessons from my soul; my eyes are opened, and I behold myself at last for what I am.'

At this moment, the sharp note of the door-bell rang through the house; and the visitant, as though this were some concerted signal for which he had been waiting, changed at once in his demeanour.

'The maid!' he cried. 'She has returned, as I forewarned you, and there is now before you one more difficult passage. Her master, you must say, is ill; you must let her in, with an assured but rather serious countenance — no smiles, no overacting, and I promise you success! Once the girl within, and the door closed, the same dexterity that has already rid you of the dealer will relieve you of this last danger in your path. Thenceforward you have the whole evening — the whole night, if needful — to ransack the treasures of the house and to make good your safety.

This is help that comes to you with the mask of danger. Up!' he cried, 'up, friend; your life hangs trembling in the scales: up, and act!'

Markheim steadily regarded his counsellor. 'If I be condemned to evil acts,' he said, 'there is still one door of freedom open — I can cease from action. If my life be an ill thing, I can lay it down. Though I be, as you say truly, at the beck of every small temptation, I can yet, by one decisive gesture, place myself beyond the reach of all. My love of good is damned to barrenness; it may, and let it be! But I have still my hatred of evil; and from that, to your galling disappointment, you shall see that I can draw both energy and courage.'

The features of the visitor began to undergo a wonderful and lovely change; they brightened and softened with a tender triumph, and, even as they brightened, faded and dislimned. But Markheim did not pause to watch or understand the transformation. He opened the door and went downstairs very slowly, thinking to himself. His past went soberly before him; he beheld it as it was, ugly and strenuous like a dream, random as chance-medley — a scene of defeat. Life, as he thus reviewed it, tempted him no longer; but on the further side he perceived a quiet haven for his bark. He paused in the passage, and looked into the shop, where the candle still burned by the dead body. It was strangely silent. Thoughts of the dealer swarmed into his mind, as he stood gazing. And then the bell once more broke out into impatient clamour.

He confronted the maid upon the threshold with something like a smile.

'You had better go for the police,' said he: 'I have killed your master.'

Rudyard Kipling

"Lispeth" (1886)

[The stories in works such as *Plain Tales from the Hills* (1888) and *The Jungle Book* series (1894; 1895), as well as his novel *Kim* (1901), suggest that Rudyard Kipling (1865–1936) spent most of his life in India. In fact, soon after his birth in Bombay, he was sent to England for his education. It was not until he was a young man that he returned to India to work as a journalist for an English-language newspaper. His early, often satiric stories about "the white man's burden" (as he dubbed the British military's presence in India at the time) found a large audience back in Britain, to which he returned in 1889. During the next decade, England's imperialist image would begin to crumble, and the reputation of Kipling's writing — which had always met with some criticism for its "might makes right" approach to cross-cultural relations — suffered along with it. His oeuvre, however, offers more than sheer jingoism, with many of his stories focussing not on a grand political agenda but, like "Lispeth," on the minutiae of daily experience and emotion felt both by locals and foreigners. Many view Kipling as the greatest English short story writer ever and, in 1907, he became the first English writer to be awarded the Nobel Prize.]

Look, you have cast out Love! What Gods are these,
    You bid me please?
The Three in One, the One in Three? Not so!
    To my own Gods I go.
It may be they shall give me greater ease
Than your cold Christ and tangled Trinities.

        The Convert.

She was the daughter of Sonoo a Hill man, and Jadéh his wife. One year their maize failed, and two bears spent the night in their only poppy-field just above the Sutlej Valley, on the Kotgarh side;[1] so, next season, they turned Christian, and brought their baby to the Mission to be baptised. The Kotgarh Chaplain christened her Elizabeth, and "Lispeth" is the Hill or *pahari*[2] way of pronouncing it.

After a while, cholera came into the Kotgarh Valley, and carried off Sonoo and Jadéh, and Lispeth became half servant, half companion, to the wife of the then Chaplain of Kotgarh. This was after the time of the Moravian missionaries,[3] but before Kotgarh had quite forgotten her title of "Mistress of the Northern Hills."

Whether Christianity improved Lispeth, or whether the Gods of her own people would have done as much for her under any circumstances, I do not know; but she grew very lovely. When a Hill girl grows lovely, she is worth travelling fifty miles over bad ground to see. Lispeth had a Greek face — one of those faces people paint so often, and see so seldom. She was of a pale ivory colour and, for her race, extremely tall. Also, she possessed eyes that were wonderful; and, had she not been dressed in the abominable print-cloths affected by Missions, you would, meeting her on a hill side unexpectedly, have taken her for the original Diana[4] of the Romans, going out to slay.

Lispeth took to Christianity readily, and did not fall out of it when she reached womanhood, as do some Hill girls. Her own people hated her, because she had, they said, become a *memsahib*,[5] and washed herself daily; and the Chaplain's wife did not know what to do with her. Somehow, one can't ask a stately goddess, five foot ten in her shoes, to clean plates and dishes. She played with the Chaplain's children and took classes in the Sunday School, and read all the books in the house and grew more and more beautiful, like the Princesses in fairy tales. The Chaplain's wife said that the girl ought to take service in Simla as a nurse or something "genteel." But Lispeth did not want to take service. She was very happy where she was.

When travellers from Simla came in to Kotgarh, — there were not many in those days, — Lispeth used to lock herself into her own room for fear they might take her away to Simla or somewhere out into the unknown world.

One day, a few months after she was seventeen years old, Lispeth went out for a walk. She did not walk like English ladies — a mile and

---

1   The Sutlej Valley is in the Himalayas, Kotgarth having become a British territory in 1815.

2   Language and people who live in India and Pakistan and practice the Hindu religion.

3   Missionaries belonging to a Protestant sect from Saxony, founded in the eighteenth century.

4   Roman goddess of hunting and virginity.

5   Indian name for a European wife living in India.

a half out, and a ride back again. She covered between twenty and thirty miles a day in her little constitutionals, all about and about, between Kotgarh and Narkunda. This time, she came back at full dusk, stepping down the break-neck descent into Kotgarh with something heavy in her arms. The Chaplain's wife was dozing in the drawing-room when Lispeth came in, breathing hard, and very exhausted with her burden. Lispeth put it down on the sofa, and said simply: — "This is my husband. I found him on the Bagi Road. He has hurt himself. We will nurse him, and, when he is well, your husband shall marry him to me."

This was the first mention Lispeth had ever made of her matrimonial views, and the Chaplain's wife shrieked with horror. However, the man on the sofa needed attention first. He was a young Englishman, and his head had been cut to the bone by something jagged. Lispeth said she had found him down the *khud*,[1] so she had brought him in. He was breathing queerly, and was unconscious.

He was put to bed, and looked after by the Chaplain, who knew something of medicine; and Lispeth waited outside the door, in case she could be useful. She explained to the Chaplain that this was the man she meant to marry; and the Chaplain and his wife lectured her severely on the impropriety of her conduct. Lispeth listened quietly, and repeated what she had first said. It takes a great deal of Christianity to wipe out uncivilized Eastern instincts, such as falling in love at first sight. Lispeth, having found the man she worshipped, did not see why she should keep silent as to her choice. She had no intention of being sent away either. She was going to nurse that Englishman until he was well enough to marry her. This was her little programme.

After a fortnight of slight fever and inflammation, the Englishman recovered and thanked the Chaplain, and his wife, and Lispeth — especially Lispeth — for their kindness. He was a traveller in the East he said — they never talked about "globe-trotters" in those days, when the P. & O. fleet[2] was young and small — and had come from Dehra Dun to go touring among the Simla hills, hunting for plants and butterflies. No one at Simla, therefore, knew anything of him. He fancied he must have fallen over the cliff after a fern on a rotten tree-trunk, and that his coolies[3] must have stolen his baggage and fled. He thought he would go back to Simla when he was a little stronger. He wanted no more mountaineering.

---

1   Ravine or extremely steep hill.

2   Peninsular and Orient fleet.

3   East Indians, Chinese or Japanese people transported to provide labour in another country.

He made no haste to go away, and got his strength back very slowly. Lispeth objected to being advised either by the Chaplain or his wife; so the latter spoke to the Englishman and told him how matters stood in Lispeth's heart. He laughed a good deal, and said it was very pretty and romantic, a perfect idyl of the Himalayas; but, as he was engaged to a girl at Home, he fancied that nothing would happen. Certainly he would behave himself with discretion. He did that, but, still he found it very pleasant to talk to Lispeth, and walk with Lispeth, and say nice things to her, and call her pet names while he was getting strong enough to go away. It meant nothing at all to him, but everything in the world to Lispeth. She was very happy while the fortnight lasted; because she had found a man to love.

Now, being a savage by birth, she took no trouble to hide her feelings; and the Englishman was amused. When he went away, back to Simla, Lispeth went with him up the hill as far as Narkunda, very troubled and very miserable. The Chaplain's wife being a good Christian, and disliking anything in the shape of fuss or scandal, — Lispeth was beyond her management entirely, — had told the Englishman to tell Lispeth that he was coming back to marry her. "She is but a child you know, and I fear at heart a heathen," said the Chaplain's wife. So, all the twelve miles up hill, the Englishman, with his arm round Lispeth's waist, was assuring the girl that he would come back and marry her, and Lispeth made him promise over and over again; and she cried on the Narkunda Ridge till he had passed out of sight along the Muttiani path.

Then she dried her tears and went in to Kotgarh again, and said to the Chaplain's wife: — "He will come back and marry me. He has gone to his own people to tell them so." And the Chaplain's wife soothed Lispeth and said: — "He will come back." At the end of two months, Lispeth grew impatient, and was told that the Englishman had gone over the seas to England. She knew where England was, because she had read little geography primers; but, of course, she had no conception of the nature of the sea, being a Hill girl. There was an old puzzle-map of the World in the house. Lispeth had played with it when she was a child. She unearthed it again, and used to put it together of evenings and cry to herself, and try to imagine where her Englishman was. As she had no ideas of distance, or steamboats, her notions were somewhat erroneous. It would not have made the least difference had she been perfectly correct; for the Englishman had no intention of coming back to marry a Hill girl. He forgot all about her by the time he was butterfly-hunting in Assam. He wrote a book on the East afterwards; and Lispeth's name did not appear in it.

At the end of three months, Lispeth made a daily pilgrimage to Narkunda, to see if her Englishman was coming along the road. It gave her comfort, and the Chaplain's wife, finding her happier, thought she was getting over her "barbarous and most indelicate folly." A little later the walks ceased to help Lispeth, and her temper grew very bad. The Chaplain's wife thought this a profitable time to let her know the real state of affairs — that the Englishman had only promised to keep her quiet; that he had never meant anything; and that it was most "wrong and improper" of Lispeth to think of marriage with an Englishman, who was of a different clay, besides being promised in marriage to a girl of his own people. Lispeth said that all this was clearly impossible, because he had said he loved her, and the Chaplain's wife had, with her own lips, asserted that the Englishman was coming back. "How can what he and you said be untrue?" asked Lispeth. "We said it as an excuse to keep you quiet, child," said the Chaplain's wife. "Then you have lied to me," said Lispeth; "you and he?" The Chaplain's wife bowed her head, and said nothing. Lispeth was silent, too, for a little time; then she went out down the valley, and came back in the dress of a Hill girl — infamously dirty, but without the nose and ear rings. She had had her hair braided into the long pigtail helped out with black thread, that Hill women wear.

"I am going back to my own people," said she. "You have killed Lispeth — there is only old Jadéh's daughter left — the daughter of a *pahari*, and the servant of *Tarka Devi*.[1] You are all liars, you English." By the time that the Chaplain's wife had recovered from the shock of the announcement that Lispeth had returned to her mother's gods, the girl had gone; and she never came back.

She took to her own unclean people savagely, as if to make up the arrears of the life she had stepped out of; and in a little time she married a wood-cutter who beat her, after the manner of *paharis*, and her beauty faded very soon.

"There is no law whereby you can account for the vagaries of the heathen" said the Chaplain's wife, "and I believe that Lispeth was always at heart an infidel." Seeing she had been taken into the Church of England at the mature age of five weeks, this statement does not do credit to the Chaplain's wife.

Lispeth was a very old woman when she died. She always had a perfect command of English; and, when she was sufficiently drunk, could sometimes be induced to tell the story of her first love affair. It was hard

---

1   Goddess of the Dawn.

then to realise that the wrinkled, unclean creature, very much of the texture and appearance of charred rag, could ever have been "Lispeth of the Kotgarh Mission."

Oscar Wilde

"The Happy Prince" (1888)

[After studying at Trinity College, Dublin, and Oxford University, Dublin-born Oscar Wilde (1854–1900) quite quickly became the leader of the Aesthetic Movement. As a writer, he succeeded in every genre he attempted, but has been most admired in his time and throughout the following century for his wit and eloquence. His essays, poems, plays, and his one novel *The Picture of Dorian Gray* (1890; 1891) have all been acknowledged as exemplary works, and his short stories have been translated into numerous languages. Following a period of inattention received because of the notoriety from the court cases in the mid-1890s surrounding his homosexuality, Wilde's work has steadily gained attention and respect. Marking the centenary of his death, a statue was unveiled in London and a stained-glass window was hung in Westminster Abbey. The artifice and excess of his writing style did not only entertain adults but also fit effectively with the English tradition of children's literature. Wilde made use of the genre and its fantastic elements to explore issues such as sexuality, morality, and materialism. He often orated his philosophical positions to friends as stories; "The Happy Prince," for example, was told to students at Cambridge University before it was published.]

High above the city, on a tall column, stood the statue of the Happy Prince. He was gilded all over with thin leaves of fine gold, for eyes he had two bright sapphires, and a large red ruby glowed on his sword-hilt.

He was very much admired indeed. "He is as beautiful as a weather-cock," remarked one of the Town Councillors who wished to gain a reputation for having artistic tastes; "only not quite so useful," he added, fearing lest people should think him unpractical, which he really was not.

"Why can't you be like the Happy Prince?" asked a sensible mother of her little boy who was crying for the moon. "The Happy Prince never dreams of crying for anything."

"I am glad there is some one in the world who is quite happy," muttered a disappointed man as he gazed at the wonderful statue.

"He looks just like an angel," said the Charity Children[1] as they came out of the cathedral in their bright scarlet cloaks, and their clean white pinafores.

"How do you know?" said the Mathematical Master, "you have never seen one."

"Ah! but we have, in our dreams," answered the children; and the Mathematical Master frowned and looked very severe, for he did not approve of children dreaming.

One night there flew over the city a little Swallow. His friends had gone away to Egypt six weeks before, but he had stayed behind, for he was in love with the most beautiful Reed. He had met her early in the spring as he was flying down the river after a big yellow moth, and had been so attracted by her slender waist that he had stopped to talk to her.

"Shall I love you?" said the Swallow, who liked to come to the point at once, and the Reed made him a low bow. So he flew round and round her, touching the water with his wings, and making silver ripples. This was his courtship, and it lasted all through the summer.

"It is a ridiculous attachment," twittered the other Swallows, "she has no money, and far too many relations;" and indeed the river was quite full of Reeds. Then, when the autumn came, they all flew away.

After they had gone he felt lonely, and began to tire of his lady-love. "She has no conversation," he said, "and I am afraid that she is a coquette, for she is always flirting with the wind." And certainly, whenever the wind blew, the Reed made the most graceful curtsies. "I admit that she is domestic," he continued, "but I love travelling, and my wife, consequently, should love travelling also."

"Will you come away with me?" he said finally to her; but the Reed shook her head, she was so attached to her home.

"You have been trifling with me," he cried, "I am off to the Pyramids. Good-bye!" and he flew away.

All day long he flew, and at night-time he arrived at the city. "Where shall I put up?" he said; "I hope the town has made preparations."

Then he saw the statue on the tall column. "I will put up there," he cried; "it is a fine position with plenty of fresh air." So he alighted just between the feet of the Happy Prince.

---

1   Children attending a school founded by a private benefactor. These children wore badges indicating their status.

"I have a golden bedroom," he said softly to himself as he looked round, and he prepared to go to sleep; but just as he was putting his head under his wing a large drop of water fell on him. "What a curious thing!" he cried, "there is not a single cloud in the sky, the stars are quite clear and bright, and yet it is raining. The climate in the north of Europe is really dreadful. The Reed used to like the rain, but that was merely her selfishness."

Then another drop fell.

"What is the use of a statue if it cannot keep the rain off?" he said; "I must look for a good chimney-pot," and he determined to fly away.

But before he had opened his wings, a third drop fell, and he looked up, and saw — Ah! what did he see?

The eyes of the Happy Prince were filled with tears, and tears were running down his golden cheeks. His face was so beautiful in the moonlight that the little Swallow was filled with pity.

"Who are you?" he said.

"I am the Happy Prince."

"Why are you weeping then?" asked the Swallow; "you have quite drenched me."

"When I was alive and had a human heart," answered the statue, "I did not know what tears were, for I lived in the Palace of Sans-Souci,[1] where sorrow is not allowed to enter. In the daytime I played with my companions in the garden, and in the evening I led the dance in the Great Hall. Round the garden ran a very lofty wall, but I never cared to ask what lay beyond it, everything about me was so beautiful. My courtiers called me the Happy Prince, and happy indeed I was, if pleasure be happiness. So I lived, and so I died. And now that I am dead they have set me up here so high that I can see all the ugliness and all the misery of my city, and though my heart is made of lead yet I cannot choose but weep."

"What, is he not solid gold?" said the Swallow to himself. He was too polite to make any personal remarks out loud.

"Far away," continued the statue in a low musical voice, "far away in a little street there is a poor house. One of the windows is open, and through it I can see a woman seated at a table. Her face is thin and worn, and she has coarse, red hands, all pricked by the needle, for she is a seamstress. She is embroidering passion-flowers on a satin gown for the loveliest of the Queen's maids-of-honour to wear at the next Court-ball.

---

1   Palaces with this name were built in both Germany and Haiti. Sans-Souci is French for "without care."

In a bed in the corner of the room her little boy is lying ill. He has a fever, and is asking for oranges. His mother has nothing to give him but river water, so he is crying. Swallow, Swallow, little Swallow, will you not bring her the ruby out of my sword-hilt? My feet are fastened to this pedestal and I cannot move."

"I am waited for in Egypt," said the Swallow. "My friends are flying up and down the Nile, and talking to the large lotus-flowers. Soon they will go to sleep in the tomb of the great King. The King is there himself in his painted coffin. He is wrapped in yellow linen, and embalmed with spices. Round his neck is a chain of pale green jade, and his hands are like withered leaves."

"Swallow, Swallow, little Swallow," said the Prince, "will you not stay with me for one night, and be my messenger? The boy is so thirsty, and the mother so sad."

"I don't think I like boys," answered the Swallow. "Last summer, when I was staying on the river, there were two rude boys, the miller's sons, who were always throwing stones at me. They never hit me, of course; we swallows fly far too well for that, and besides, I come of a family famous for its agility; but still, it was a mark of disrespect."

But the Happy Prince looked so sad that the little Swallow was sorry. "It is very cold here," he said; "but I will stay with you for one night, and be your messenger."

"Thank you, little Swallow," said the Prince.

So the Swallow picked out the great ruby from the Prince's sword, and flew away with it in his beak over the roofs of the town.

He passed by the cathedral tower, where the white marble angels were sculptured. He passed by the palace and heard the sound of dancing. A beautiful girl came out on the balcony with her lover. "How wonderful the stars are," he said to her, "and how wonderful is the power of love!" "I hope my dress will be ready in time for the State-ball," she answered; "I have ordered passion-flowers to be embroidered on it; but the seamstresses are so lazy."

He passed over the river, and saw the lanterns hanging to the masts of the ships. He passed over the Ghetto, and saw the old Jews bargaining with each other, and weighing out money in copper scales. At last he came to the poor house and looked in. The boy was tossing feverishly on his bed, and the mother had fallen asleep, she was so tired. In he hopped, and laid the great ruby on the table beside the woman's thimble. Then he flew gently round the bed, fanning the boy's forehead with his wings. "How cool I feel," said the boy, "I must be getting better;" and he sank into a delicious slumber.

Then the Swallow flew back to the Happy Prince, and told him what he had done. "It is curious," he remarked, "but I feel quite warm now, although it is so cold."

"That is because you have done a good action," said the Prince. And the little Swallow began to think, and then he fell asleep. Thinking always made him sleepy.

When day broke he flew down to the river and had a bath. "What a remarkable phenomenon," said the Professor of Ornithology[1] as he was passing over the bridge. "A swallow in winter!" And he wrote a long letter about it to the local newspaper. Every one quoted it, it was full of so many words that they could not understand.

"To-night I go to Egypt," said the Swallow, and he was in high spirits at the prospect. He visited all the public monuments, and sat a long time on top of the church steeple. Wherever he went the Sparrows chirruped, and said to each other, "What a distinguished stranger!" so he enjoyed himself very much.

When the moon rose he flew back to the Happy Prince. "Have you any commissions for Egypt?" he cried; "I am just starting."

"Swallow, Swallow, little Swallow," said the Prince, "will you not stay with me one night longer?"

"I am waited for in Egypt," answered the Swallow. "To-morrow my friends will fly up to the Second Cataract. The river-horse[2] couches there among the bulrushes, and on a great granite throne sits the God Memnon.[3] All night long he watches the stars, and when the morning star shines he utters one cry of joy, and then he is silent. At noon the yellow lions come down to the water's edge to drink. They have eyes like green beryls, and their roar is louder than the roar of the cataract."

"Swallow, Swallow, little Swallow," said the Prince, "far away across the city I see a young man in a garret. He is leaning over a desk covered with papers, and in a tumbler by his side there is a bunch of withered violets. His hair is brown and crisp, and his lips are red as a pomegranate, and he has large and dreamy eyes. He is trying to finish a play for the Director of the Theatre, but he is too cold to write any more. There is no fire in the grate, and hunger has made him faint."

---

1   Study of birds.

2   Hippopotamus.

3   Son of Aurora (goddess of the dawn) and god of the morning sun.

"I will wait with you one night longer," said the Swallow, who really had a good heart. "Shall I take him another ruby?"

"Alas! I have no ruby now," said the Prince; "my eyes are all that I have left. They are made of rare sapphires, which were brought out of India a thousand years ago. Pluck out one of them and take it to him. He will sell it to the jeweller, and buy food and firewood, and finish his play."

"Dear Prince," said the Swallow, "I cannot do that;" and he began to weep.

"Swallow, Swallow, little Swallow," said the Prince, "do as I command you."

So the Swallow plucked out the Prince's eye, and flew away to the student's garret. It was easy enough to get in, as there was a hole in the roof. Through this he darted, and came into the room. The young man had his head buried in his hands, so he did not hear the flutter of the bird's wings, and when he looked up he found the beautiful sapphire lying on the withered violets.

"I am beginning to be appreciated," he cried; "this is from some great admirer. Now I can finish my play," and he looked quite happy.

The next day the Swallow flew down to the harbour. He sat on the mast of a large vessel and watched the sailors hauling big chests out of the hold with ropes. "Heave a-hoy!" they shouted as each chest came up. "I am going to Egypt!" cried the Swallow, but nobody minded, and when the moon rose he flew back to the Happy Prince.

"I am come to bid you good-bye," he cried.

"Swallow, Swallow little Swallow," said the Prince, "will you not stay with me one night longer?"

"It is winter," answered the Swallow, "and the chill snow will soon be here. In Egypt the sun is warm on the green palm-trees, and the crocodiles lie in the mud and look lazily about them. My companions are building a nest in the Temple of Baalbec,[1] and the pink and white doves are watching them, and cooing to each other. Dear Prince, I must leave you, but I will never forget you, and next spring I will bring you back two beautiful jewels in place of those you have given away. The ruby shall be redder than a red rose, and the sapphire shall be as blue as the great sea."

"In the square below," said the Happy Prince, "there stands a little match-girl. She has let her matches fall in the gutter, and they are all spoiled. Her father will beat her if she does not bring home some money,

---

1 Ancient city in Syria famous for its Temple of the Sun. The city was destroyed in 1759 by an earthquake and its ruins were a popular subject for Victorian painters.

and she is crying. She has no shoes or stockings, and her little head is bare. Pluck out my other eye, and give it to her, and her father will not beat her."

"I will stay with you one night longer," said the Swallow, "but I cannot pluck out your eye. You would be quite blind then."

"Swallow, Swallow, little Swallow," said the Prince, "do as I command you."

So he plucked out the Prince's other eye, and darted down with it. He swooped past the match-girl, and slipped the jewel into the palm of her hand. "What a lovely bit of glass," cried the little girl; and she ran home, laughing.

Then the Swallow came back to the Prince. "You are blind now," he said, "so I will stay with you always."

"No, little Swallow," said the poor Prince, "you must go away to Egypt."

"I will stay with you always," said the Swallow, and he slept at the Prince's feet.

All the next day he sat on the Prince's shoulder, and told him stories of what he had seen in strange lands. He told him of the red ibises,[1] who stand in long rows on the banks of the Nile, and catch gold fish in their beaks; of the Sphinx, who is as old as the world itself, and lives in the desert, and knows everything; of the merchants, who walk slowly by the side of their camels, and carry amber beads in their hands; of the King of the Mountains of the Moon, who is as black as ebony, and worships a large crystal; of the great green snake that sleeps in a palm-tree, and has twenty priests to feed it with honey-cakes; and of the pygmies who sail over a big lake on large flat leaves, and are always at war with the butterflies.

"Dear little Swallow," said the Prince, "you tell me of marvellous things, but more marvellous than anything is the suffering of men and of women. There is no Mystery so great as Misery. Fly over my city, little Swallow, and tell me what you see there."

So the Swallow flew over the great city, and saw the rich making merry in their beautiful houses, while the beggars were sitting at the gates. He flew into dark lanes, and saw the white faces of starving children looking out listlessly at the black streets. Under the archway of a bridge two little boys were lying in one another's arms to try and keep themselves warm. "How hungry we are!" they said. "You must not lie here," shouted the Watchman, and they wandered out into the rain.

Then he flew back and told the Prince what he had seen.

---

1 Tropical birds related to flamingos and storks.

"I am covered with fine gold," said the Prince, "you must take it off, leaf by leaf, and give it to my poor; the living always think that gold can make them happy."

Leaf after leaf of the fine gold the Swallow picked off, till the Happy Prince looked quite dull and grey. Leaf after leaf of the fine gold he brought to the poor, and the children's faces grew rosier, and they laughed and played games in the street. "We have bread now!" they cried.

Then the snow came, and after the snow came the frost. The streets looked as if they were made of silver, they were so bright and glistening; long icicles like crystal daggers hung down from the eaves of the houses, everybody went about in furs, and the little boys wore scarlet caps and skated on the ice.

The poor little Swallow grew colder and colder, but he would not leave the Prince, he loved him too well. He picked up crumbs outside the baker's door when the baker was not looking, and tried to keep himself warm by flapping his wings.

But at last he knew that he was going to die. He had just strength to fly up to the Prince's shoulder once more. "Good-bye, dear Prince!" he murmured, "will you let me kiss your hand?"

"I am glad that you are going to Egypt at last, little Swallow," said the Prince, "you have stayed too long here; but you must kiss me on the lips, for I love you."

"It is not to Egypt that I am going," said the Swallow. "I am going to the House of Death. Death is the brother of Sleep, is he not?"

And he kissed the Happy Prince on the lips, and fell down dead at his feet.

At that moment a curious crack sounded inside the statue, as if something had broken. The fact is that the leaden heart had snapped right in two. It certainly was a dreadfully hard frost.

Early the next morning the Mayor was walking in the square below in company with the Town Councillors. As they passed the column he looked up at the statue: "Dear me! how shabby the Happy Prince looks!" he said.

"How shabby indeed!" cried the Town Councillors, who always agreed with the Mayor, and they went up to look at it.

"The ruby has fallen out of his sword, his eyes are gone, and he is golden no longer," said the Mayor; "in fact, he is little better than a beggar!"

"Little better than a beggar," said the Town Councillors.

"And here is actually a dead bird at his feet!" continued the Mayor. "We must really issue a proclamation that birds are not to be allowed to die here." And the Town Clerk made a note of the suggestion.

So they pulled down the statue of the Happy Prince. "As he is no longer beautiful he is no longer useful," said the Art Professor at the University.

Then they melted the statue in a furnace, and the Mayor held a meeting of the Corporation to decide what was to be done with the metal. "We must have another statue, of course," he said, "and it shall be a statue of myself."

"Of myself," said each of the Town Councillors, and they quarrelled. When I last heard of them they were quarrelling still.

"What a strange thing!" said the overseer of the workmen at the foundry. "This broken lead heart will not melt in the furnace. We must throw it away." So they threw it on a dust-heap where the dead Swallow was also lying.

"Bring me the two most precious things in the city," said God to one of His Angels; and the Angel brought Him the leaden heart and the dead bird.

"You have rightly chosen," said God, "for in my garden of Paradise this little bird shall sing for evermore, and in my city of gold the Happy Prince shall praise me."

Arthur Conan Doyle

"A Scandal in Bohemia" (1891)

["Elementary, my dear Watson." Arthur Conan Doyle's (1859–1930) character Sherlock Holmes has become so famous that, for many, he overshadows his Scottish-born creator. Although Doyle wrote novels, political works, and other material, he remains best known for his plot-driven short stories about Holmes and Watson. Doyle's education at the medical school at the University of Edinburgh led to his career as a doctor. It also gave him the minute details that allowed his detective to demonstrate his skills of ratiocination. Many scholars, however, rank as one of Doyle's greatest inventions in the detective tradition Holmes's weaknesses and potential for failure, as displayed in the following story. The inadequacies and secrets of a man whose identity is rooted in facts, fairness, and morality can be read as the personification of Britain — a country that was strongly questioning its own position of authority and its reliance on biases such as those of race, ethnicity, class, and gender.]

To Sherlock Holmes she is always *the* woman. I have seldom heard him mention her under any other name. In his eyes she eclipses and predominates the whole of her sex. It was not that he felt any emotion akin to love for Irene Adler. All emotions, and that one particularly, were abhorrent to his cold, precise, but admirably balanced mind. He was, I take it, the most perfect reasoning and observing machine that the world has seen; but, as a lover, he would have placed himself in a false position. He never spoke of the softer passions, save with a gibe and a sneer. They were admirable things for the observer — excellent for drawing the veil from men's motives and actions. But for the trained reasoner to admit such intrusions into his own delicate and finely adjusted temperament was to introduce a distracting factor which might throw a doubt upon all his mental results. Grit in a sensitive instrument, or a crack in one of his own high-power lenses, would not be more disturbing than a strong emotion in a nature such as his. And yet there was but one woman to him, and that woman was the late Irene Adler, of dubious and questionable memory.

I had seen little of Holmes lately. My marriage had drifted us away from each other. My own complete happiness, and the home-centred interests which rise up around the man who first finds himself master of his own establishment, were sufficient to absorb all my attention; while Holmes, who loathed every form of society with his whole Bohemian soul, remained in our lodgings in Baker-street, buried among his old books, and alternating from week to week between cocaine and ambition, the drowsiness of the drug, and the fierce energy of his own keen nature. He was still, as ever, deeply attracted by the study of crime, and occupied his immense faculties and extraordinary powers of observation in following out those clues, and clearing up those mysteries, which had been abandoned as hopeless by the official police. From time to time I heard some vague account of his doings: of his summons to Odessa in the case of the Trepoff murder, of his clearing up of the singular tragedy of the Atkinson brothers at Trincomalee, and finally of the mission which he had accomplished so delicately and successfully for the reigning family of Holland. Beyond these signs of his activity, however, which I merely shared with all the readers of the daily press, I knew little of my former friend and companion.

One night — it was on the 20th of March, 1888 — I was returning from a journey to a patient (for I had now returned to civil practice), when my way led me through Baker-street. As I passed the well-remembered door, which must always be associated in my mind with my wooing, and with the dark incidents of the Study in Scarlet,[1] I was seized with a keen desire to see Holmes again, and to know how he was employing his extraordinary powers. His rooms were brilliantly lit, and, even as I looked up, I saw his tall spare figure pass twice in a dark silhouette against the blind. He was pacing the room swiftly, eagerly, with his head sunk upon his chest, and his hands clasped behind him. To me, who knew his every mood and habit, his attitude and manner told their own story. He was at work again. He had risen out of his drug-created dreams, and was hot upon the scent of some new problem. I rang the bell, and was shown up to the chamber which had formerly been in part my own.

His manner was not effusive. It seldom was; but he was glad, I think, to see me. With hardly a word spoken, but with a kindly eye, he waved me to an armchair, threw across his case of cigars, and indicated a spirit

---

1 Another "Sherlock Holmes" story by Doyle, published in 1881.

case and a gasogene[1] in the corner. Then he stood before the fire, and looked me over in his singular introspective fashion.

"Wedlock suits you," he remarked. "I think, Watson, that you have put on seven and a half pounds since I saw you."

"Seven," I answered.

"Indeed, I should have thought a little more. Just a trifle more, I fancy, Watson. And in practice again, I observe. You did not tell me that you intended to go into harness."

"Then, how do you know?"

"I see it, I deduce it. How do I know that you have been getting yourself very wet lately, and that you have a most clumsy and careless servant girl?"

"My dear Holmes," said I, "this is too much. You would certainly have been burned, had you lived a few centuries ago. It is true that I had a country walk on Thursday and came home in a dreadful mess; but, as I have changed my clothes, I can't imagine how you deduce it. As to Mary Jane, she is incorrigible, and my wife has given her notice; but there again I fail to see how you work it out."

He chuckled to himself and rubbed his long nervous hands together.

"It is simplicity itself," said he; "my eyes tell me that on the inside of your left shoe, just where the firelight strikes it, the leather is scored by six almost parallel cuts. Obviously they have been caused by someone who has very carelessly scraped round the edges of the sole in order to remove crusted mud from it. Hence, you see, my double deduction that you had been out in vile weather, and that you had a particularly malignant boot-slitting specimen of the London slavey.[2] As to your practice, if a gentleman walks into my rooms smelling of iodoform,[3] with a black mark of nitrate of silver[4] upon his right fore-finger, and a bulge on the side of his top-hat to show where he has secreted his stethoscope, I must be dull indeed, if I do not pronounce him to be an active member of the medical profession."

I could not help laughing at the ease with which he explained his process of deduction. "When I hear you give your reasons," I remarked, "the thing always appears to me to be so ridiculously simple that I could

---

1   Apparatus used for aerating liquids.

2   Servant.

3   Crystalline iodine compound used as an antiseptic.

4   Salt produced by combining nitric acid and silver, used in developing photographs.

easily do it myself, though at each successive instance of your reasoning I am baffled, until you explain your process. And yet I believe that my eyes are as good as yours."

"Quite so," he answered, lighting a cigarette, and throwing himself down into an armchair. "You see, but you do not observe. The distinction is clear. For example, you have frequently seen the steps which lead up from the hall to this room."

"Frequently."

"How often?"

"Well, some hundreds of times."

"Then how many are there?"

"How many? I don't know."

"Quite so! You have not observed. And yet you have seen. That is just my point. Now, I know that there are seventeen steps, because I have both seen and observed. By the way, since you are interested in these little problems, and since you are good enough to chronicle one or two of my trifling experiences, you may be interested in this." He threw over a sheet of thick pink-tinted notepaper which had been lying open upon the table. "It came by the last post," said he. "Read it aloud."

The note was undated, and without either signature or address.

"There will call upon you to-night, at a quarter to eight o'clock," it said, "a gentleman who desires to consult you upon a matter of the very deepest moment. Your recent services to one of the Royal Houses of Europe have shown that you are one who may safely be trusted with matters which are of an importance which can hardly be exaggerated. This account of you we have from all quarters received. Be in your chamber then at that hour, and do not take it amiss if your visitor wear a mask."

"This is indeed a mystery," I remarked. "What do you imagine that it means?"

"I have no data yet. It is a capital mistake to theorise before one has data. Insensibly one begins to twist facts to suit theories, instead of theories to suit facts. But the note itself. What do you deduce from it?"

I carefully examined the writing, and the paper upon which it was written.

"The man who wrote it was presumably well to do," I remarked, endeavouring to imitate my companion's processes. "Such paper could not be bought under half a crown a packet. It is peculiarly strong and stiff."

"Peculiar — that is the very word," said Holmes. "It is not an English paper at all. Hold it up to the light."

I did so, and saw a large *E* with a small *g*, a *P*, and a large *G* with a small *t* woven into the texture of the paper.

"What do you make of that?" asked Holmes.

"The name of the maker, no doubt; or his monogram, rather."

"Not at all. The *G* with the small *t* stands for 'Gesellschaft,' which is the German for 'Company.' It is a customary contraction like our 'Co.' *P*, of course, stands for 'Papier.' Now for the *Eg*. Let us glance at our Continental Gazetteer."[1] He took down a heavy brown volume from his shelves. "Eglow, Eglonitz — here we are, Egria. It is in a German-speaking country — in Bohemia, not far from Carlsbad. 'Remarkable as being the scene of the death of Wallenstein,[2] and for its numerous glass factories and paper mills.' Ha, ha, my boy, what do you make of that?" His eyes sparkled, and he sent up a great blue triumphant cloud from his cigarette.

"The paper was made in Bohemia," I said.

"Precisely. And the man who wrote the note is a German. Do you note the peculiar construction of the sentence — 'This account of you we have from all quarters received.' A Frenchman or Russian could not have written that. It is the German who is so uncourteous to his verbs. It only remains, therefore, to discover what is wanted by this German who writes upon Bohemian paper, and prefers wearing a mask to showing his face. And here he comes, if I am not mistaken, to resolve all our doubts."

As he spoke there was the sharp sound of horses' hoofs and grating wheels against the curb, followed by a sharp pull at the bell. Holmes whistled.

"A pair, by the sound," said he. "Yes," he continued, glancing out of the window. "A nice little brougham and a pair of beauties. A hundred and fifty guineas apiece. There's money in this case, Watson, if there is nothing else."

"I think that I had better go, Holmes."

"Not a bit, Doctor. Stay where you are. I am lost without my Boswell.[3] And this promises to be interesting. It would be a pity to miss it."

"But your client —"

"Never mind him. I may want your help, and so may he. Here he comes. Sit down in that armchair, Doctor, and give us your best attention."

---

1   Probably an allusion to the *Gazetteer of the World* (1885), a standard reference text.

2   Albrecht Wenzel Eusebius von Waldstein (1583–1634), Duke of Friedland, Sagan and Mecklenburg, and a subject of a tragedy by Schiller.

3   James Boswell (1740–95), author of *The Life of Samuel Johnson*.

A slow and heavy step, which had been heard upon the stairs and in the passage, paused immediately outside the door. Then there was a loud and authoritative tap.

"Come in!" said Holmes.

A man entered who could hardly have been less than six feet six inches in height, with the chest and limbs of a Hercules. His dress was rich with a richness which would, in England, be looked upon as akin to bad taste. Heavy bands of Astrakhan[1] were slashed across the sleeves and fronts of his double-breasted coat, while the deep blue cloak which was thrown over his shoulders was lined with flame-coloured silk, and secured at the neck with a brooch which consisted of a single flaming beryl. Boots which extended half way up his calves, and which were trimmed at the tops with rich brown fur, completed the impression of barbaric opulence which was suggested by his whole appearance. He carried a broad-brimmed hat in his hand, while he wore across the upper part of his face, extending down past the cheek-bones, a black vizard mask, which he had apparently adjusted that very moment, for his hand was still raised to it as he entered. From the lower part of the face he appeared to be a man of strong character, with a thick, hanging lip, and a long straight chin, suggestive of resolution pushed to the length of obstinacy.

"You had my note?" he asked, with a deep harsh voice and a strongly marked German accent. "I told you that I would call." He looked from one to the other of us, as if uncertain which to address.

"Pray take a seat," said Holmes. "This is my friend and colleague, Dr. Watson, who is occasionally good enough to help me in my cases. Whom have I the honour to address?"

"You may address me as the Count Von Kramm, a Bohemian nobleman. I understand that this gentleman, your friend, is a man of honour and discretion, whom I may trust with a matter of the most extreme importance. If not, I should much prefer to communicate with you alone."

I rose to go, but Holmes caught me by the wrist and pushed me back into my chair. "It is both, or none," said he. "You may say before this gentleman anything which you may say to me."

The Count shrugged his broad shoulders. "Then I must begin," said he, "by binding you both to absolute secrecy for two years, at the end of that time the matter will be of no importance. At present it is not too much to say that it is of such weight that it may have an influence upon European history."

---

1 Type of wool from southwest Russia.

"I promise," said Holmes.

"And I."

"You will excuse this mask," continued our strange visitor. "The august person who employs me wishes his agent to be unknown to you, and I may confess at once that the title by which I have just called myself is not exactly my own."

"I was aware of it," said Holmes dryly.

"The circumstances are of great delicacy, and every precaution has to be taken to quench what might grow to be an immense scandal and seriously compromise one of the reigning families of Europe. To speak plainly, the matter implicates the great House of Ormstein, hereditary kings of Bohemia."

"I was also aware of that," murmured Holmes, settling himself down in his armchair, and closing his eyes.

Our visitor glanced with some apparent surprise at the languid, lounging figure of the man who had been no doubt depicted to him as the most incisive reasoner, and most energetic agent in Europe. Holmes slowly reopened his eyes, and looked impatiently at his gigantic client.

"If your Majesty would condescend to state your case," he remarked, "I should be better able to advise you."

The man sprang from his chair, and paced up and down the room in uncontrollable agitation. Then, with a gesture of desperation, he tore the mask from his face and hurled it upon the ground. "You are right," he cried, "I am the King. Why should I attempt to conceal it?"

"Why, indeed?" murmured Holmes. "Your Majesty had not spoken before I was aware that I was addressing Wilhelm Gottsreich Sigismond von Ormstein, Grand Duke of Cassel-Felstein, and hereditary King of Bohemia."

"But you can understand," said our strange visitor, sitting down once more and passing his hand over his high, white forehead, "you can understand that I am not accustomed to doing such business in my own person. Yet the matter was so delicate that I could not confide it to an agent without putting myself in his power. I have come *incognito* from Prague for the purpose of consulting you."

"Then, pray consult," said Holmes, shutting his eyes once more.

"The facts are briefly these: Some five years ago, during a lengthy visit to Warsaw, I made the acquaintance of the well-known adventuress, Irene Adler. The name is no doubt familiar to you."

"Kindly look her up in my index, Doctor," murmured Holmes, without opening his eyes. For many years he had adopted a system of docketing all paragraphs concerning men and things, so that it was difficult to name a subject or a person on which he could not at once furnish information. In this case I found her biography sandwiched in between that of a Hebrew Rabbi and that of a staff-commander who had written a monograph upon the deep sea fishes.

"Let me see?" said Holmes. "Hum! Born in New Jersey in the year 1858. Contralto — hum! La Scala,[1] hum! Prima donna Imperial Opera of Warsaw — Yes! Retired from operatic stage — ha! Living in London — quite so! Your Majesty, as I understand, became entangled with this young person, wrote her some compromising letters, and is now desirous of getting those letters back."

"Precisely so. But how —"

"Was there a secret marriage?"

"None."

"No legal papers or certificates?"

"None."

"Then I fail to follow your Majesty. If this young person should produce her letters for blackmailing or other purposes, how is she to prove their authenticity?"

"There is the writing."

"Pooh, pooh! Forgery."

"My private notepaper."

"Stolen."

"My own seal."

"Imitated."

"My photograph."

"Bought."

"We were both in the photograph."

"Oh dear! That is very bad! Your Majesty has indeed committed an indiscretion."

"I was mad — insane."

"You have compromised yourself seriously."

"I was only Crown Prince then. I was young. I am but thirty now."

"It must be recovered."

"We have tried and failed."

"Your Majesty must pay. It must be bought."

"She will not sell."

"Stolen, then."

---

1 Acclaimed opera house in Milan, built by Giuseppe Piermarini in 1775–78.

"Five attempts have been made. Twice burglars in my pay ransacked her house. Once we diverted her luggage when she travelled. Twice she has been waylaid. There has been no result."

"No sign of it?"

"Absolutely none."

Holmes laughed. "It is quite a pretty little problem," said he.

"But a very serious one to me," returned the King, reproachfully.

"Very, indeed. And what does she propose to do with the photograph?"

"To ruin me."

"But how?"

"I am about to be married."

"So I have heard."

"To Clotilde Lothman von Saxe-Meningen, second daughter of the King of Scandinavia. You may know the strict principles of her family. She is herself the very soul of delicacy. A shadow of a doubt as to my conduct would bring the matter to an end."

"And Irene Adler?"

"Threatens to send them the photograph. And she will do it. I know that she will do it. You do not know her, but she has a soul of steel. She has the face of the most beautiful of women, and the mind of the most resolute of men. Rather than I should marry another woman, there are no lengths to which she would not go — none."

"You are sure that she has not sent it yet?"

"I am sure."

"And why?"

"Because she has said that she would send it on the day when the betrothal was publicly proclaimed. That will be next Monday."

"Oh, then, we have three days yet," said Holmes, with a yawn. "That is very fortunate, as I have one or two matters of importance to look into just at present. Your Majesty will, of course, stay in London for the present?"

"Certainly. You will find me at the Langham, under the name of the Count Von Kramm."

"Then I shall drop you a line to let you know how we progress."

"Pray do so. I shall be all anxiety."

"Then, as to money?"

"You have *carte blanche*."

"Absolutely?"

"I tell you that I would give one of the provinces of my kingdom to have that photograph."

"And for present expenses?"

The king took a heavy chamois leather bag from under his cloak, and laid it on the table.

"There are three hundred pounds in gold, and seven hundred in notes," he said.

Holmes scribbled a receipt upon a sheet of his note-book, and handed it to him.

"And mademoiselle's address?" he asked.

"Is Briony Lodge, Serpentine-avenue, St. John's Wood."

Holmes took a note of it. "One other question," said he. "Was the photograph a cabinet?"[1]

"It was."

"Then, good night, your Majesty, and I trust that we shall soon have some good news for you. And good night, Watson," he added, as the wheels of the Royal brougham rolled down the street. "If you will be good enough to call tomorrow afternoon, at three o'clock, I should like to chat this little matter over with you."

II.

At three o'clock precisely I was at Baker-street, but Holmes had not yet returned. The landlady informed me that he had left the house shortly after eight o'clock in the morning. I sat down beside the fire, however, with the intention of awaiting him, however long he might be. I was already deeply interested in his inquiry, for, though it was surrounded by none of the grim and strange features which were associated with the two crimes which I have already recorded, still, the nature of the case and the exalted station of his client gave it a character of its own. Indeed, apart from the nature of the investigation which my friend had on hand, there was something in his masterly grasp of a situation, and his keen, incisive reasoning, which made it a pleasure to me to study his system of work, and to follow the quick, subtle methods by which he disentangled the most inextricable mysteries. So accustomed was I to his invariable success that the very possibility of his failing had ceased to enter into my head.

It was close upon four before the door opened, and a drunken-looking groom, ill-kempt and side-whiskered, with an inflamed face and disreputable clothes, walked into the room. Accustomed as I was to my friend's amazing powers in the use of disguises, I had to look three times

---

1 Photograph that is 3 7/8 inches by 5 1/2 inches.

before I was certain that it was indeed he. With a nod he vanished into the bedroom, whence he emerged in five minutes tweed-suited and respectable, as of old. Putting his hands into his pockets, he stretched out his legs in front of the fire, and laughed heartily for some minutes.

"Well, really!" he cried, and then he choked; and laughed again until he was obliged to lie back, limp and helpless, in the chair.

"What is it?"

"It's quite too funny. I am sure you could never guess how I employed my morning, or what I ended by doing."

"I can't imagine. I suppose that you have been watching the habits, and perhaps the house, of Miss Irene Adler."

"Quite so, but the sequel was rather unusual. I will tell you, however. I left the house a little after eight o'clock this morning, in the character of a groom out of work. There is a wonderful sympathy and freemasonry among horsey men. Be one of them, and you will know all that there is to know. I soon found Briony Lodge. It is a *bijou* villa,[1] with a garden at the back, but built out in front right up to the road, two stories. Chubb lock[2] to the door. Large sitting-room on the right side, well furnished, with long windows almost to the floor, and those preposterous English window fasteners which a child could open. Behind there was nothing remarkable, save that the passage window could be reached from the top of the coach-house. I walked round it and examined it closely from every point of view, but without noting anything else of interest.

"I then lounged down the street, and found, as I expected, that there was a mews in a lane which runs down by one wall of the garden. I lent the ostlers a hand in rubbing down their horses, and I received in exchange twopence, a glass of half-and-half,[3] two fills of shag tobacco, and as much information as I could desire about Miss Adler, to say nothing of half a dozen other people in the neighbourhood in whom I was not in the least interested, but whose biographies I was compelled to listen to."

"And what of Irene Adler?" I asked.

"Oh, she has turned all the men's heads down in that part. She is the daintiest thing under a bonnet on this planet. So say the Serpentine-mews,[4] to a man. She lives quietly, sings at concerts, drives out at five every

---

1   Charming, little house, "*bijou*" being French for jewel.

2   Lock patented by Charles Chubb.

3   Mixture of two malt liquors — usually porter and ale.

4   Those who live on Serpentine Avenue, a mews being a set of buildings around an open yard or lane.

day, and returns at seven sharp for dinner. Seldom goes out at other times, except when she sings. Has only one male visitor, but a good deal of him. He is dark, handsome, and dashing; never calls less than once a day, and often twice. He is a Mr. Godfrey Norton, of the Inner Temple.[1] See the advantages of a cabman as a confidant. They had driven him home a dozen times from Serpentine-mews, and knew all about him. When I had listened to all they had to tell, I began to walk up and down near Briony Lodge once more, and to think over my plan of campaign.

"This Godfrey Norton was evidently an important factor in the matter. He was a lawyer. That sounded ominous. What was the relation between them, and what the object of his repeated visits? Was she his client, his friend, or his mistress? If the former, she had probably transferred the photograph to his keeping. If the latter, it was less likely. On the issue of this question depended whether I should continue my work at Briony Lodge, or turn my attention to the gentleman's chambers in the Temple. It was a delicate point, and it widened the field of my inquiry. I fear that I bore you with these details, but I have to let you see my little difficulties, if you are to understand the situation."

"I am following you closely," I answered.

"I was still balancing the matter in my mind, when a hansom cab drove up to Briony Lodge, and a gentleman sprang out. He was a remarkably handsome man, dark, aquiline, and moustached — evidently the man of whom I had heard. He appeared to be in a great hurry, shouted to the cabman to wait, and brushed past the maid who opened the door with the air of a man who was thoroughly at home.

"He was in the house about half an hour, and I could catch glimpses of him, in the windows of the sitting-room, pacing up and down, talking excitedly and waving his arms. Of her I could see nothing. Presently he emerged, looking even more flurried than before. As he stepped up to the cab, he pulled a gold watch from his pocket and looked at it earnestly. 'Drive like the devil,' he shouted, 'first to Gross & Hankey's[2] in Regent-street, and then to the church of St. Monica in the Edgware-road. Half a guinea if you do it in twenty minutes!'

"Away they went, and I was just wondering whether I should not do well to follow them, when up the lane came a neat little landau,[3] the

---

1 One of four institutions called the Inns of Court that offered food, housing, and office space to barristers.

2 Jewellery establishment.

3 Two-seated, covered vehicle.

coachman with his coat only half buttoned, and his tie under his ear, while all the tags of his harness were sticking out of the buckles. It hadn't pulled up before she shot out of the hall door and into it. I only caught a glimpse of her at the moment, but she was a lovely woman, with a face that a man might die for.

"'The Church of St. Monica, John,' she cried, 'and half a sovereign if you reach it in twenty minutes.'

"This was quite too good to lose, Watson. I was just balancing whether I should run for it, or whether I should perch behind her landau, when a cab came through the street. The driver looked twice at such a shabby fare; but I jumped in before he could object. 'The Church of St. Monica,' said I, 'and half a sovereign if you reach it in twenty minutes.' It was twenty-five minutes to twelve, and of course it was clear enough what was in the wind.

"My cabby drove fast. I don't think I ever drove faster, but the others were there before us. The cab and the landau with their steaming horses were in front of the door when I arrived. I paid the man, and hurried into the church. There was not a soul there save the two whom I had followed and a surpliced clergyman, who seemed to be expostulating with them. They were all three standing in a knot in front of the altar. I lounged up the side aisle like any other idler who has dropped into a church. Suddenly, to my surprise, the three at the altar faced round to me, and Godfrey Norton came running as hard as he could towards me."

"Thank God!" he cried. "You'll do. Come! Come!"

"What then?" I asked.

"Come man, come, only three minutes, or it won't be legal."

"I was half dragged up to the altar, and, before I knew where I was, I found myself mumbling responses which were whispered in my ear, and vouching for things of which I knew nothing, and generally assisting in the secure tying up of Irene Adler, spinster, to Godfrey Norton, bachelor. It was all done in an instant, and there was the gentleman thanking me on the one side and the lady on the other, while the clergyman beamed on me in front. It was the most preposterous position in which I ever found myself in my life, and it was the thought of it that started me laughing just now. It seems that there had been some informality about their license, that the clergyman absolutely refused to marry them without a witness of some sort, and that my lucky appearance saved the bridegroom from having to sally out into the streets in search of a best man. The bride gave me a sovereign, and I mean to wear it on my watch chain in memory of the occasion."

"This is a very unexpected turn of affairs," said I; "and what then?"

"Well, I found my plans very seriously menaced. It looked as if the pair might take an immediate departure, and so necessitate very prompt and energetic measures on my part. At the church door, however, they separated, he driving back to the Temple, and she to her own house. 'I shall drive out in the Park at five as usual,' she said as she left him. I heard no more. They drove away in different directions, and I went off to make my own arrangements."

"Which are?"

"Some cold beef and a glass of beer," he answered, ringing the bell. "I have been too busy to think of food, and I am likely to be busier still this evening. By the way, Doctor, I shall want your co-operation."

"I shall be delighted."

"You don't mind breaking the law?"

"Not in the least."

"Nor running a chance of arrest?"

"Not in a good cause."

"Oh, the cause is excellent!"

"Then I am your man."

"I was sure that I might rely on you."

"But what is it you wish?"

"When Mrs. Turner has brought in the tray I will make it clear to you. Now," he said, as he turned hungrily on the simple fare that our landlady had provided, "I must discuss it while I eat, for I have not much time. It is nearly five now. In two hours we must be on the scene of action. Miss Irene, or Madame, rather, returns from her drive at seven. We must be at Briony Lodge to meet her."

"And what then?"

"You must leave that to me. I have already arranged what is to occur. There is only one point on which I must insist. You must not interfere, come what may. You understand?"

"I am to be neutral?"

"To do nothing whatever. There will probably be some small unpleasantness. Do not join in it. It will end in my being conveyed into the house. Four or five minutes afterwards the sitting-room window will open. You are to station yourself close to that open window."

"Yes."

"You are to watch me, for I will be visible to you."

"Yes."

"And when I raise my hand — so — you will throw into the room what I give you to throw, and will, at the same time, raise the cry of fire. You quite follow me?"

"Entirely."

"It is nothing very formidable," he said, taking a long cigar-shaped roll from his pocket. "It is an ordinary plumber's smoke rocket, fitted with a cap at either end to make it self-lighting. Your task is confined to that. When you raise your cry of fire, it will be taken up by quite a number of people. You may then walk to the end of the street, and I will rejoin you in ten minutes. I hope that I have made myself clear?"

"I am to remain neutral, to get near the window, to watch you, and, at the signal, to throw in this object, then to raise the cry of fire, and to wait you at the corner of the street."

"Precisely."

"Then you may entirely rely on me."

"That is excellent. I think perhaps it is almost time that I prepared for the new *rôle* I have to play."

He disappeared into his bedroom, and returned in a few minutes in the character of an amiable and simple-minded Nonconformist[1] clergyman. His broad black hat, his baggy trousers, his white tie, his sympathetic smile, and general look of peering and benevolent curiosity were such as Mr. John Hare[2] alone could have equaled. It was not merely that Holmes changed his costume. His expression, his manner, his very soul seemed to vary with every fresh part that he assumed. The stage lost a fine actor, even as science lost an acute reasoner, when he became a specialist in crime.

It was a quarter past six when we left Baker-street, and it still wanted ten minutes to the hour when we found ourselves in Serpentine-avenue. It was already dusk, and the lamps were just being lighted as we paced up and down in front of Briony Lodge, waiting for the coming of its occupant. The house was just such as I had pictured it from Sherlock Holmes' succinct description, but the locality appeared to be less private than I expected. On the contrary, for a small street in a quiet neighbourhood, it was remarkably animated. There was a group of shabbily-dressed men smoking and laughing in a corner, a scissors grinder with his wheel, two guardsmen who were flirting with a nurse-girl, and several well-dressed young men who were lounging up and down with cigars in their mouths.

---

1   Non-Anglican.

2   Eminent English actor and manager (1844–1921).

"You see," remarked Holmes, as we paced to and fro in front of the house, "this marriage rather simplifies matters. The photograph becomes a double-edged weapon now. The chances are that she would be as averse to its being seen by Mr. Godfrey Norton, as our client is to its coming to the eyes of his Princess. Now the question is — Where are we to find the photograph?"

"Where, indeed?"

"It is most unlikely that she carries it about with her. It is cabinet size. Too large for easy concealment about a woman's dress. She knows that the King is capable of having her waylaid and searched. Two attempts of the sort have already been made. We may take it then that she does not carry it about with her."

"Where, then?"

"Her banker or her lawyer. There is that double possibility. But I am inclined to think neither. Women are naturally secretive, and they like to do their own secreting. Why should she hand it over to anyone else? She could trust her own guardianship, but she could not tell what indirect or political influence might be brought to bear upon a business man. Besides, remember that she had resolved to use it within a few days. It must be where she can lay her hands upon it. It must be in her own house."

"But it has twice been burgled."

"Pshaw! They did not know how to look."

"But how will you look?"

"I will not look."

"What then?"

"I will get her to show me."

"But she will refuse."

"She will not be able to. But I hear the rumble of wheels. It is her carriage. Now carry out my orders to the letter."

As he spoke the gleam of the sidelights of a carriage came round the curve of the avenue. It was a smart little landau which rattled up to the door of Briony Lodge. As it pulled up one of the loafing men at the corner dashed forward to open the door in the hope of earning a copper, but was elbowed away by another loafer who had rushed up with the same intention. A fierce quarrel broke out, which was increased by the two guardsmen, who took sides with one of the loungers, and by the scissors grinder, who was equally hot upon the other side. A blow was struck, and in an instant the lady, who had stepped from her carriage, was the centre of a little knot of flushed and struggling men who struck savagely at each other with their fists and sticks. Holmes dashed into the crowd to protect the lady; but, just as he reached her, he gave a cry and dropped to the ground, with the blood running freely down his face. At his fall the guardsmen took to their heels in one direction and the loungers in the other, while a number of better dressed people who had watched the scuffle without taking part in it, crowded in to help the lady and to attend to the injured man. Irene Adler, as I will still call her, had hurried up the steps; but she stood at the top with her superb figure outlined against the lights of the hall, looking back into the street.

"Is the poor gentleman much hurt?" she asked.

"He is dead," cried several voices.

"No, no, there's life in him," shouted another. "But he'll be gone before you can get him to hospital."

"He's a brave fellow," said a woman. "They would have had the lady's purse and watch if it hadn't been for him. They were a gang, and a rough one too. Ah, he's breathing now."

"He can't lie in the street. May we bring him in, marm?"

"Surely. Bring him into the sitting-room. There is a comfortable sofa. This way, please!"

Slowly and solemnly he was borne into Briony Lodge, and laid out in the principal room, while I still observed the proceedings from my post by the window. The lamps had been lit, but the blinds had not been drawn, so that I could see Holmes as he lay upon the couch. I do not know whether he was seized with compunction at that moment for the part he was playing, but I know that I never felt more heartily ashamed of myself in my life than when I saw the beautiful creature against whom I was conspiring, or the grace and kindliness with which she waited upon the injured man. And yet it would be the blackest treachery to Holmes to draw back now from the part which he had entrusted to me. I hardened my heart, and took the smoke-rocket from under my ulster.[1] After all, I thought, we are not injuring her. We are but preventing her from injuring another.

Holmes had sat up upon the couch, and I saw him motion like a man who is in need of air. A maid rushed across and threw open the window. At the same instant I saw him raise his hand, and at the signal I tossed my rocket into the room with a cry of "Fire." The word was no sooner out of my mouth than the whole crowd of spectators, well dressed and ill — gentlemen, ostlers, and servant maids — joined in a general shriek of

---

1   Loose type of overcoat.

"Fire." Thick clouds of smoke curled through the room, and out at the open window. I caught a glimpse of rushing figures, and a moment later the voice of Holmes from within, assuring them that it was a false alarm. Slipping through the shouting crowd I made my way to the corner of the street, and in ten minutes was rejoiced to find my friend's arm in mine, and to get away from the scene of uproar. He walked swiftly and in silence for some few minutes, until we had turned down one of the quiet streets which lead towards the Edgware-road.

"You did it very nicely, Doctor," he remarked. "Nothing could have been better. It is all right."

"You have the photograph!"

"I know where it is."

"And how did you find out?"

"She showed me, as I told you that she would."

"I am still in the dark."

"I do not wish to make a mystery," said he laughing. "The matter was perfectly simple. You, of course, saw that everyone in the street was an accomplice. They were all engaged for the evening."

"I guessed as much."

"Then, when the row broke out, I had a little moist red paint in the palm of my hand. I rushed forward, fell down, clapped my hand to my face, and became a piteous spectacle. It is an old trick."

"That also I could fathom."

"Then they carried me in. She was bound to have me in. What else could she do? And into her sitting-room, which was the very room which I suspected. It lay between that and her bedroom, and I was determined to see which. They laid me on a couch, I motioned for air, they were compelled to open the window, and you had your chance."

"How did that help you?"

"It was all-important. When a woman thinks that her house is on fire, her instinct is at once to rush to the thing which she values most. It is a perfectly overpowering impulse, and I have more than once taken advantage of it. In the case of the Darlington Substitution Scandal it was of use to me, and also in the Arnsworth Castle business. A married woman grabs at her baby — an unmarried one reaches for her jewel box. Now it was clear to me that our lady of to-day had nothing in the house more precious to her than what we are in quest of. She would rush to secure it. The alarm of fire was admirably done. The smoke and shouting were enough to shake nerves of steel. She responded beautifully. The photograph is in a recess behind a sliding panel just above the right bell pull. She was there in an instant, and I caught a glimpse of it as she half drew it out. When I cried out that it was a false alarm, she replaced it, glanced at the rocket, rushed from the room, and I have not seen her since. I rose, and, making my excuses, escaped from the house. I hesitated whether to attempt to secure the photograph at once; but the coachman had come in, and, as he was watching me narrowly, it seemed safer to wait. A little over-precipitance may ruin all."

"And now?" I asked.

"Our quest is practically finished. I shall call with the King to-morrow, and with you, if you care to come with us. We will be shown into the sitting-room to wait for the lady, but it is probable that when she comes she may find neither us nor the photograph. It might be a satisfaction to His Majesty to regain it with his own hands."

"And when will you call?"

"At eight in the morning. She will not be up, so that we shall have a clear field. Besides, we must be prompt, for this marriage may mean a complete change in her life and habits. I must wire to the King without delay."

We had reached Baker-street, and had stopped at the door. He was searching his pockets for the key, when someone passing said: —

"Good-night, Mister Sherlock Holmes."

There were several people on the pavement at the time, but the greeting appeared to come from a slim youth in an ulster who had hurried by.

"I've heard that voice before," said Holmes, staring down the dimly lit street. "Now, I wonder who the deuce that could have been."

III.

I slept at Baker-street that night, and we were engaged upon our toast and coffee in the morning when the King of Bohemia rushed into the room.

"You have really got it!" he cried, grasping Sherlock Holmes by either shoulder, and looking eagerly into his face.

"Not yet."

"But you have hopes?"

"I have hopes."

"Then, come. I am all impatience to be gone."

"We must have a cab."

"No, my brougham is waiting."

"Then that will simplify matters." We descended, and started off once more for Briony Lodge.

"Irene Adler is married," remarked Holmes.

"Married! When?"

"Yesterday."

"But to whom?"

"To an English lawyer named Norton."

"But she could not love him?"

"I am in hopes that she does."

"And why in hopes?"

"Because it would spare your Majesty all fear of future annoyance. If the lady loves her husband, she does not love your Majesty. If she does not love your Majesty, there is no reason why she should interfere with your Majesty's plan."

"It is true. And yet —! Well! I wish she had been of my own station! What a queen she would have made!" He relapsed into a moody silence which was not broken, until we drew up in Serpentine-avenue.

The door of Briony Lodge was open, and an elderly woman stood upon the steps. She watched us with a sardonic eye as we stepped from the brougham.

"Mr. Sherlock Holmes, I believe?" said she.

"I am Mr. Holmes," answered my companion, looking at her with a questioning and rather startled gaze.

"Indeed! My mistress told me that you were likely to call. She left this morning with her husband, by the 5:15 train from Charing-cross, for the Continent."

"What!" Sherlock Holmes staggered back, white with chagrin and surprise. "Do you mean that she has left England?"

"Never to return."

"And the papers?" asked the King, hoarsely. "All is lost."

"We shall see." He pushed past the servant, and rushed into the drawing-room, followed by the King and myself. The furniture was scattered about in every direction, with dismantled shelves, and open drawers, as if the lady had hurriedly ransacked them before her flight. Holmes rushed at the bell-pull, tore back a small sliding shutter, and, plunging in his hand, pulled out a photograph and a letter. The photograph was of Irene Adler herself in evening dress, the letter was superscribed to "Sherlock Holmes, Esq. To be left till called for." My friend tore it open, and we all three read it together. It was dated at midnight of the preceding night, and ran in this way: —

"My Dear Mr. Sherlock Holmes, — You really did it very well. You took me in completely. Until after the alarm of fire, I had not a suspicion. But then, when I found how I had betrayed myself, I began to think. I had been warned against you months ago. I had been told that, if the King employed an agent, it would certainly be you. And your address had been given me. Yet, with all this, you made me reveal what you wanted to know. Even after I became suspicious, I found it hard to think evil of such a dear, kind old clergyman. But, you know, I have been trained as an actress myself. Male costume is nothing new to me. I often take advantage of the freedom which it gives. I sent John, the coachman, to watch you, ran upstairs, got into my walking clothes, as I call them, and came down just as you departed.

"Well, I followed you to your door, and so made sure that I was really an object of interest to the celebrated Mr. Sherlock Holmes. Then I, rather imprudently, wished you good night, and started for the Temple to see my husband.

"We both thought the best resource was flight, when pursued by so formidable an antagonist; so you will find the nest empty when you call tomorrow. As to the photograph, your client may rest in peace. I love and am loved by a better man than he. The King may do what he will without hindrance from one whom he has cruelly wronged. I keep it only to safeguard myself, and to preserve a weapon which will always secure me from any steps which he might take in the future. I leave a photograph which he might care to possess; and I remain, dear Mr. Sherlock Holmes, very truly yours,

"Irene Norton, *née* Adler."

"What a woman — oh, what a woman!" cried the King of Bohemia, when we had all three read this epistle. "Did I not tell you how quick and resolute she was? Would she not have made an admirable queen? Is it not a pity that she was not on my level?"

"From what I have seen of the lady, she seems, indeed, to be on a very different level to your Majesty," said Holmes, coldly. "I am sorry that I have not been able to bring your Majesty's business to a more successful conclusion."

"On the contrary, my dear sir," cried the King. "Nothing could be more successful. I know that her word is inviolate. The photograph is now as safe as if it were in the fire."

"I am glad to hear your Majesty say so."

"I am immensely indebted to you. Pray tell me in what way I can reward you. This ring —." He slipped an emerald snake ring from his finger, and held it out upon the palm of his hand.

"Your Majesty has something which I should value even more highly," said Holmes.

"You have but to name it."

"This photograph!"

The King stared at him in amazement.

"Irene's photograph!" he cried. "Certainly, if you wish it."

"I thank your Majesty. Then there is no more to be done in the matter. I have the honour to wish you a very good morning." He bowed, and, turning away without observing the hand which the King had stretched out to him, he set off in my company for his chambers.

And that was how a great scandal threatened to affect the kingdom of Bohemia, and how the best plans of Mr. Sherlock Holmes were beaten by a woman's wit. He used to make merry over the cleverness of women, but I have not heard him do it of late. And when he speaks of Irene Adler, or when he refers to her photograph, it is always under the honourable title of *the* woman.

George Egerton

"The Spell of the White Elf" (1893)

[The daughter of a Welsh mother and Irish father, George Egerton
(1859–1945; pseud. of Mary Chavelita Bright, neé Dunne) was borne in
Melbourne, Australia. She also lived in Norway, Ireland, and England.
Her collection of short stories *Keynotes* (1893), which includes the piece
anthologized here, was immensely popular and has come to be known as
a central text of feminist literature from the time. *Keynotes* was published
by John Lane, also the publisher of *The Yellow Book*, the Decadent magazine of Britain's *fin de siècle*, and it sported a cover by Aubrey Beardsley.
With the stories' impressionistic, moody style and their discussion of
misogyny and women's sense of isolation, the collection had a defining
impact on what became known as "New Woman" fiction. It was followed by other collections, including *Discords* (1894), *Symphonies* (1897) and
Fantasies (1898). "The Spell of the White Elf," like most of Egerton's stories, works against over-simplifying the collection of concerns facing
women who wanted greater responsibility and freedom within a culture
that encouraged their subordination and self-sacrifice.]

Have you ever read out a joke that seemed excruciatingly funny, or
repeated a line of poetry that struck you as being inexpressibly tender, and
found that your listener was not impressed as you were? I have, and so it
may be that this will bore you, though it was momentous enough to me.

I had been up in Norway to receive a little legacy that fell to me, and
though my summer visits were not infrequent, I had never been up there
in mid-winter, at least not since I was a little child tobogganing with Hans
Jörgen (Hans Jörgen Dahl is his full name), and that was long ago. We
are connected. Hans Jörgen and I were both orphans, and a cousin — we
called her aunt — was one of our guardians. He was her favourite; and
when an uncle on my mother's side — she was Cornish born; my father,
a ship captain, met her at Dartmouth — offered to take me, I think she
was glad to let me go. I was a lanky girl of eleven, and Hans Jörgen and

I were sweethearts. We were to be married some day, we had arranged all that, and he reminded me of it when I was going away, and gave me a silver perfume box, with a gilt crown on top, that had belonged to his mother. And later when he was going to America he came to see me first; he was a long freckled hobbledehoy,[1] with just the same true eyes and shock head. I was, I thought, quite grown up, I had passed my 'intermediate' and was condescending as girls are. But I don't think it impressed Hans Jörgen much, for he gave me a little ring, turquoise forget-me-nots with enamelled leaves and a motto inside — a quaint old thing that belonged to a sainted aunt — they keep things a long time in Norway — and said he would send for me; but of course I laughed at that. He has grown to be a great man out in Cincinnati and waits always. I wrote later and told him I thought marriage a vocation and I hadn't one for it; but Hans Jörgen took no notice; just said he'd wait. He understands waiting, I'll say that for Hans Jörgen.

I have been alone now for five years, working away, though I was left enough to keep me before. Somehow I have not the same gladness in my work of late years. Working for one's-self seems a poor end even if one puts by money. But this has little or nothing to do with the white elf, has it?

Christiania[2] is a singular city if one knows how to see under the surface, and I enjoyed my stay there greatly. The Hull boat was to sail at 4.30, and I had sent my things down early, for I was to dine at the Grand at two with a cousin, a typical Christiania man. It was a fine clear day, and Karl Johann[3] was thronged with folks. The band was playing in the park, and pretty girls and laughing students walked up and down. Every one who is anybody may generally be seen about that time. Henrik Ibsen[4] — if you did not know him from his portrait, you would take him to be a prosperous merchant — was going home to dine; but Björnstjerne Björnson,[5] in town just then, with his grand leonine head, and the kind, keen eyes behind his glasses, was standing near the Storthing House with a group of politicians, probably discussing the vexed question of separate consulship. In no city does one see such characteristic odd faces and such queerly cut clothes. The streets are full of students. The farmers' sons

---

1   A clumsy or awkward youth.

2   City, now called Oslo.

3   Karl Johann Street, main boulevard in Oslo.

4   Norwegian playwright (1828–1906), a founder of modern drama.

5   Norwegian writer (1832–1910), editor and theatre director, won the Nobel Prize in 1903.

amongst them are easily recognised by their homespun, sometimes home-made suits, their clever heads and intelligent faces; from them come the writers, and brain carriers of Norway. The Finns, too, have a distinctive type of head and a something elusive in the expression of their change-ful eyes. But all, the town students, too, of easier manners and slangier tongues — all alike are going, as finances permit, to dine in restaurant or steam-kitchen. I saw the *menu* for to-day posted up outside the door of the latter as I passed — 'Rice porridge and salt meat soup, 6d.,'[1] and Hans Jörgen came back with a vivid picture of childhood days, when every family in the little coast-town where we lived had a fixed *menu* for every day in the week; and it was quite a distinction to have meat balls on pickled herring day, or ale soup when all the folks in town were cooking omelettes with bacon. How he used to eat rice porridge in those days! I can see him now put his heels together and give his awkward bow as he said, 'Tak for Maden tante!'[2] Well, we are sitting in the Grand *Café* after dinner, at a little table near the door, watching the people pass in and out. An ubiquitous 'sample-count'[3] from Berlin is measuring his wits with a young Norwegian merchant; he is standing green chartreuse;[4] it pays to be generous even for a German, when you can oust honest Leeds cloth with German shoddy.[5] At least so my cousin says. He knows every one by sight, and points out all the celebrities to me. Suddenly he bows pro-foundly. I look round. A tall woman with very square shoulders, and gold-rimmed spectacles is passing us with two gentlemen. She is English by her tailor-made gown and little shirt-front, and noticeable anywhere.

'That lady,' says my cousin, 'is a compatriot of yours. She is a very fine person, a very learned lady; she has been looking up referats in the uni-versity bibliothek. Professor Sturm — he is a good friend of me — did tell me. I forget her name; she is married. I suppose her husband he stay at home and keep the house!'

My cousin has just been refused by a young lady dentist, who says she is too comfortably off to change for a small housekeeping business, so I excuse his sarcasm. We leave as the time draws on and sleigh down to the steamer. I like the jingle of the bells, and I feel a little sad. There is a

---

1   Six pence.

2   (Danish) Thank you aunt Maden!

3   Person imitating a count.

4   Buying everybody some chartreuse, a pale green brandy liqueur.

5   Metaphor for disguising his cheapness (in this case, by buying drinks).

witchery about the country that creeps into one and works like a love-philter, and if one has once lived up there, one never gets it out of one's blood again. I go on board and lean over and watch the people. There are a good many for winter-time. The bell rings. Two sleighs drive up and my compatriot and her friends appear. She shakes hands with them and comes leisurely up the gangway. The thought flits through me that she would cross it in just that cool way if she were facing death; it is foolish, but most of our passing thoughts are just as inconsequent. She calls down a remembrance to some one in such pretty Norwegian, much prettier than mine, and then we swing round. Handkerchiefs wave in every hand, never have I seen such persistent handkerchief-waving as at the departure of a boat in Norway. It is a national characteristic. If you live at the mouth of a fjord, and go to the market town at the head of it for your weekly supply of coffee beans, the population give you a 'send off' with fluttering kerchiefs. It is as universal as the 'Thanks.' Hans Jörgen says I am anglicised and only see the ridiculous side, forgetting the kind feelings that prompt it. I find a strange pleasure in watching the rocks peep out under the snow, the children dragging their hand-sleds along the ice. All the little bits of winter life of which I get flying glimpses as we pass, bring back scenes grown dim in the years between. There is a mist ahead; and when we pass Dröbak cuddled like a dormouse for winter's sleep I go below. A bright coal fire burns in the open grate of the stove, and the *Rollo* saloon[1] looks very cosy. My compatriot is stretched in a big arm-chair reading. She is sitting comfortably with one leg crossed over the other, in the manner called 'shockingly unladylike' of my early lessons in deportment. The flame flickers over the patent leather of her neat low-heeled boot, and strikes a spark from the pin in her tie. There is something manlike about her. I don't know where it lies, but it is there. Her hair curls in grey flecked rings about her head; it has not a cut look, seems rather to grow short naturally. She has a charming tubbed look. Of course every lady is alike clean, but some men and women have an individual look of sweet cleanness that is a beauty of itself. She feels my gaze and looks up and smiles. She has a rare smile, it shows her white teeth and softens her features:

'The fire is cosy, isn't it? I hope we shall have an easy passage, so that it can be kept in.'

I answer something in English.

She has a trick of wrinkling her brows, she does it now as she says:

---

1   A large cabin for use by all passengers.

'A-ah, I should have said you were Norsk. Are you not really? Surely you have a typical head, or eyes and hair at the least?'

'Half of me is Norsk, but I have lived a long time in England.'

'Father of course; case of "there was a sailor loved a lass," was it not?'

I smile an assent and add: 'I lost them both when I was very young.'

A reflective look steals over her face. It is stern in repose; and as she seems lost in some train of thought of her own I go to my cabin and lie down; the rattling noises and the smell of paint makes me feel ill. I do not go out again. I wake next morning with a sense of fear at the stillness. There is no sound but a lapping wash of water at the side of the steamer, but it is delicious to lie quietly after the vibration of the screw[1] and the sickening swing. I look at my watch; seven o'clock. I cannot make out why there is such a silence, as we only stop at Christiansand long enough to take cargo and passengers. I dress and go out. The saloon is empty but the fire is burning brightly. I go to the pantry and ask the stewardess when we arrived? Early, she says; all the passengers for here are already gone on shore; and there is a thick fog outside, goodness knows how long we'll be kept. I go to the top of the stairs and look out; the prospect is uninviting and I come down again and turn over some books on the table; in Russian, I think. I feel sure they are hers.

'Good-morning!' comes her pleasant voice. How alert and bright-eyed she is! It is a pick-me-up to look at her.

'You did not appear last night? Not given in already, I hope!'

She is kneeling on one knee before the fire, holding her palms to the glow, and with her figure hidden in her loose, fur-lined coat and the light showing up her strong face under the little tweed cap, she seems so like a clever-faced slight man, that I feel I am conventionally guilty in talking so freely to her. She looks at me with a deliberate critical air, and then springs up.

'Let me give you something for your head! Stewardess, a wine-glass!'

I should not dream of remonstrance — not if she were to command me to drink sea-water; and I am not complaisant as a rule.

When she comes back I swallow it bravely, but I leave some powder in the glass; she shakes her head, and I finish this too. We sat and talked, or at least she talked and I listened. I don't remember what she said, I only know that she was making clear to me most of the things that had puzzled me for a long time; questions that arise in silent hours; that one speculates over, and to which one finds no answer in text-books. How she

---

1 Ship's propeller.

knew just the subjects that worked in me I knew not; some subtle intuitive sympathy, I suppose, enabled her to find it out. It was the same at breakfast, she talked down to the level of the men present (of course they did not see that it might be possible for a woman to do that), and made it a very pleasant meal.

It was in the evening — we had the saloon to ourselves — when she told me about the white elf. I had been talking of myself and of Hans Jörgen.

'I like your Mr. Hans Jörgen,' she said, 'he has a strong nature and knows what he wants; there is reliability in him. They are rarer qualities than one thinks in men, I have found through life that the average man is weaker than we are. It must be a good thing to have a stronger nature to lean to. I have never had that.'

There is a want in the tone of her voice as she ends, and I feel inclined to put out my hand and stroke hers — she has beautiful long hands — but I am afraid to do so. I query shyly —

'Have you no little ones?'

'Children, you mean? No, I am one of the barren ones; they are less rare than they used to be. But I have a white elf at home and that makes up for it. Shall I tell you how the elf came? Well, its mother is a connection of mine, and she hates me with an honest hatred. It is the only honest feeling I ever discovered in her. It was about the time that she found the elf was to come that it broke out openly, but that was mere coincidence. How she detested me! Those narrow, poor natures are capable of an intensity of feeling concentrated on one object that larger natures can scarcely measure. Now I shall tell you something strange. I do not pretend to understand it, I may have my theory, but that is of no physiological value, I only tell it to you. Well, all the time she was carrying the elf she was full of simmering hatred and she wished me evil often enough. One feels those things in an odd way. Why did she? Oh, that … that was a family affair, with perhaps a thread of jealousy mixed up in the knot. Well, one day the climax came, and much was said, and I went away and married and got ill and the doctors said I would be childless. And in the meantime the little human soul — I thought about it so often — had fought its way out of the darkness. We childless women weave more fancies into the "mithering o' bairns"[1] than the actual mothers themselves. The poetry of it is not spoilt by nettle-rash or chincough any more than our figures. I am a writer by profession — oh, you knew! No, hardly celebrated, but I put my little chips into the great

---

1 Mothering of babies.

mosaic as best I can. Positions are reversed, they often are now-a-days. My husband stays at home and grows good things to eat, and pretty things to look at, and I go out and win bread and butter. It is a matter not of who has most brains, but whose brains are most saleable. Fit in with the housekeeping? Oh yes. I have a treasure, too, in Belinda. She is one of those women who must have something to love. She used to love cats, birds, dogs, anything. She is one bump of philo-progenitiveness,[1] but she hates men. She says: 'If one could only have a child, ma'm, without a husband or the disgrace; ugh, the disgusting men!' Do you know I think that is not an uncommon feeling amongst a certain number of women. I have often drawn her out on the subject. It struck me, because I have often found it in other women. I have known many, particularly older women, who would give anything in God's world to have a child of "their own" if it could be got just as Belinda says, "without the horrid man or the shame." It seems congenital with some women to have deeply rooted in their innermost nature a smouldering enmity, ay, sometimes a physical disgust to men, it is a kind of kin-feeling to the race dislike of white men to black. Perhaps it explains why woman, where her own feelings are not concerned, will always make common cause with woman against him. I have often thought about it. You should hear Belinda's "serve him right" when some fellow comes to grief. I have a little of it myself (meditatively), but in a broader way, you know. I like to cut them out in their own province. Well, the elf was born, and now comes the singular part of it. It was a wretched, frail little being with a startling likeness to me. It was as if the evil the mother had wished me had worked on the child, and the constant thought of me stamped my features on its little face. I was working then on a Finland saga, and I do not know why it was, but the thought of that little being kept disturbing my work. It was worst in the afternoon time when the house seemed quietest; there is always a lull then outside and inside. Have you ever noticed that? The birds hush their singing and the work is done. Belinda used to sit sewing in the kitchen, and the words of a hymn she used to lilt in half tones, something about 'joy bells ringing, children singing,' floated in to me, and the very tick-tock of the old clock sounded like the rocking of wooden cradles. It made me think sometimes that it would be pleasant to hear small pattering feet and the call of voices through the silent house. And I suppose it acted as an irritant on my imaginative faculty, for the whole room seemed filled with the spirits of little children. They

---

1 Love of children.

seemed to dance round me with uncertain, lightsome steps, waving tiny pink dimpled hands, shaking sunny flossy curls, and haunting me with their great innocent child-eyes; filled with the unconscious sadness and the infinite questioning that is oftenest seen in the gaze of children. I used to fancy something stirred in me, and the spirits of unborn little ones never to come to life in me troubled me. I was probably overworked at the time. How we women digress! I am telling you more about myself than my white elf. Well, trouble came to their home, and I went and offered to take it. It was an odd little thing, and when I looked at it I could see how like we were. My glasses dimmed somehow, and a lump kept rising in my throat, when it smiled up out of its great eyes and held out two bits of hands like shriveled white rose leaves. Such a tiny scrap it was; it was not bigger, she said, than a baby of eleven months. I suppose they can tell that as I can the date of a dialect; but I am getting wiser,' with an emotional softening of her face and quite a proud look. 'A child is like one of those wonderful runic alphabets; the signs are simple but the lore they contain is marvelous. "She is very like you," said the mother. "Hold her." She was only beginning to walk. I did. You never saw such elfin ears with strands of silk floss ringing round them, and the quaintest, darlingest wrinkles in its forehead, two long, and one short, just as I have,' putting her head forward for me to see. 'The other children were strong, and the one on the road she hoped would be healthy. So I took it there and then, "clothes and baby, cradle and all." Yes, I have a collection of nursery rhymes from many nations; I was going to put them in a book, but I say them to the elf now. I wired to my husband. You should have seen me going home. I was so nervous, I was not half as nervous when I read my paper — it was rather a celebrated paper, perhaps you heard of it — to the Royal Geographical Society. It was on Esquimaux marriage songs, and the analogy between them and the Song of Solomon.[1] She was so light, and so wrapped up, and my *pince-nez* kept dropping off when I stooped over her — I got spectacles after that — and I used to fancy I had dropped her out of the wrappings, and peep under the shawl to make sure' — with a sick shiver — 'to find her sucking her thumb. And I nearly passed my station. And then a valuable book — indeed, it is really a case of MSS.,[2] and almost unique — I had borrowed for reference with some trouble, could not be found, and my husband roared with laughter when it turned up in the cradle. Belinda was at the

---

1   Book of the Old Testament.

2   Abbreviation for "manuscripts."

gate anxious to take her, and he said I did not know how to hold her, that I was holding her like a book of notes at a lecture, and so I gave her to Belinda. I think the poor little thing found it all strange, and when she puckered up her face, and thrust out her under lip, and two great tears jumped off her lashes, we all felt ready for hanging. But Belinda, though she doesn't know one language, not even her own, for she sows her h's broadcast and picks them up at hazard, she *can* talk to a baby. I am so glad for that reason she is bigger now; I couldn't manage it, I could not reason out any system they go on in baby talk. I tried mixing up the tenses, but somehow it wasn't right. My husband says it is not more odd than salmon taking a fly that is certainly like nothing they ever see in nature. Anyway it answered splendidly. Belinda used to say — I made a note of some of them — "Did-sum was denn? Oo did! Was ums de prettiest itta sweetums denn? oo was. An' did um put 'em in a nasty shawl an' joggle 'em in an ole puff-puff, um did, was a shame! Hitchy cum, hitchy cum, hitchy cum hi, Chinaman no likey me!" This always made her laugh, though in what connection the Chinaman came in I never *could* fathom. I was a little jealous of Belinda, but she knew how to undress her. George, that's my husband's name, said the bath water was too hot, and that the proper way to test it was to put one's elbow in. Belinda laughed, but I must confess it did feel too hot when I tried it that way; but how did he know? I got her such pretty clothes, I was going to buy a pragtbind[1] of Nietzsche,[2] but that must wait. George made her a cot with her name carved on the head of it, such a pretty one.'

'Did you find she made a change in your lives?' I asked.

'Oh, didn't she! Children are such funny things. I stole away to have a look at her later on, and did not hear him come after me. She looked so sweet, and she was smiling in her sleep. I believe the Irish peasantry say that an angel is whispering when a baby does that. I had given up all belief myself, except the belief in a Creator who is working out some system that is too infinite for our finite minds to grasp. If one looks round with seeing eyes one can't help thinking that after a run of 1893 years, Christianity is not very consoling in its results. But at that moment, kneeling next the cradle, I felt a strange, solemn feeling stealing over me; one is conscious of the same effect in a grand cathedral filled with the peal of organ music and soaring voices. It was as if all the old, sweet, untroubled child-belief came back for a spell, and I wondered if far back in the Nazarene village

---

1 (Danish) edition.

2 Friedrich Wilhelm Nietzsche (1844–1900), German philosopher and poet.

Mary ever knelt and watched the Christ-child sleep; and the legend of how he was often seen to weep but never to smile came back to me, and I think the sorrow I felt as I thought was an act of contrition and faith. I could not teach a child scepticism, so I remembered my husband prayed, and I resolved to ask him to teach her. You see (half hesitatingly) I have more brains, or at least more intellectuality than my husband, and in that case one is apt to undervalue simpler, perhaps greater, qualities. That came home to me, and I began to cry, I don't know why, and he lifted me up, and I think I said something of the kind to him.... We got nearer to one another someway. He said it was unlucky to cry over a child.

'It made such a difference in the evenings. I used to hurry home — I was on the staff of the *World's Review* just then — and it was so jolly to see the quaint little phiz[1] smile up when I went in.

'Belinda was quite jealous of George. She said "Master worritted in an' out, an' interfered with everything, she never seen a man as knew so much about babies, not for one as never 'ad none of 'is own. Wot if he didn't go to Parkins hisself, an' say as how she was to have the milk of one cow, an' mind not mix it." I wish you could have seen the insinuating distrust on Belinda's face. I laughed. I believe we were all getting too serious, I know I felt years younger. I told George that it was really suspicious; how did he acquire such a stock of baby lore? *I* hadn't any. It was all very well to say Aunt Mary's kids. I should never be surprised if I saw a Zwazi[2] woman appear with a lot of tawny pickaninnies[3] in tow. George was shocked — I often shock him.

'She began to walk as soon as she got stronger. I never saw such an inquisitive mite. I had to rearrange all my bookshelves, change Le Nu de Rabelais, after Garnier,[4] you know, and several others from the lower shelves to the top ones. One can't be so Bohemian when there is a little white soul like that playing about, can one? When we are alone she always comes in to say her prayers, and good-night. Larry Moore of the *Vulture* — he is one of the most wickedly amusing of men, prides himself on being *fin de siècle*[5] — don't you detest that word? — or nothing,

---

1   Contraction of "physiognomy," meaning "the face or visage."

2   Member of the African Swasi.

3   Derogatory slang for "black children."

4   *Le Nu de Rabelais, d'après Garnier*, an illustrated book of art criticism by the French writer Armand Silvestre (1837–1901).

5   (French) end of the century; in the late-Victorian era, the term signified a feeling of decadence, boredom, and world-weariness.

raves about Dégas,[1] and is a worshipper of the decadent school of verse,[2] quotes Verlaine,[3] you know — well, he came in one evening on his way to some music hall. She's a whimsical little thing, not without incipient coquetry either; well, she would say them to him. If you can imagine a masher[4] of the Jan van Beer[5] type bending his head to hear a child in a white "nighty" lisping prayers, you have an idea of the picture. She kissed him good-night too; she never would before; and he must have forgotten his engagement, for he stayed with us to supper. She rules us all with a touch of her little hands, and I fancy we are all the better for it. Would you like to see her?' She hands me a medallion, with a beautifully painted head in it. I can't say she is a pretty child, a weird, elf-like thing, with questioning, wistful eyes, and masses of dark hair; and yet as I look the little face draws me to it, and makes a kind of yearning in me; strikes me with a 'fairy blast' perhaps.

The journey was all too short, and when we got to Hull she saw me to my train. It was odd to see the quiet way in which she got everything she wanted. She put me into the carriage, got me a footwarmer and a magazine, kissed me and said as she held my hand, 'The world is small, we run in circles, perhaps we shall meet again, in any case I wish you a white elf.' I was sorry to part with her; I felt richer than before I knew her; I fancy she goes about the world giving graciously from her richer nature to the poorer-endowed folks she meets on her way.

Often since that night I have rounded my arm and bowed down my face and fancied I had a little human elf cuddled to my breast.

*　　*　　*　　*

I am very busy just now getting everything ready; I had so much to buy. I don't like confessing it even to myself, but down in the bottom of my deepest trunk I have laid a parcel of things, such pretty tiny things. I saw them at a sale, I couldn't resist them, they were so cheap; even if one doesn't want the things, it seems a sin to let them go. Besides, there may

---

1　Edgar Degas (1834–1917), French Impressionist painter.

2　School of poetry popular at the end of the Victorian era; see note on page 394.

3　Paul Verlaine (1844–96), French poet associated with the decadents. See note 2 above.

4　Affected "lady's man."

5　Belgian artist (1852–1927) whose paintings were critiqued by some as cloying and anecdotal.

be some poor woman out in Cincinnati. I wrote to Hans Jörgen, you know, back in spring, and ... Du störer Gud![1] There is Hans Jörgen coming across the street.

---

[1] (Norwegian) Great God.

Evelyn Sharp

"In Dull Brown" (1896)

[Evelyn Sharp (1869–1955) was born the ninth of eleven children. A move to London precipitated her writing career, resulting in the production of numerous short stories, novels, and journalism articles. Her interest in women's rights places her squarely in the context of the "New Woman" writers, as do her journalistic works and her membership in the National Union of Women's Suffrage Society, the Women's Social and Political Union, and Women Writers Suffrage League. She was imprisoned for her part as a member of the WSPU. She is perhaps now best remembered for her militant acts on behalf of women's suffrage primarily during the early twentieth century. Like a number of Sharp's short stories, "In Dull Brown" offers tantalizing insights into the perspective behind this major movement. Moreover, it evokes a frustration and sense of cultural restriction that contrasts tellingly with the action found in the popular adventure and detective literature written by men at the time.]

"All the same," said Nancy, who was lazily sipping her coffee in bed, "brown doesn't suit you a bit."

"No," said Jean sadly, "and I should not be wearing it at all if my other skirt did not want brushing. Nevertheless, a russet-brown frock demands adventures. The girls in novels always wear russet-brown, whatever their complexion is, and they always have adventures. Now —"

"Isn't it time you started?" asked the gentle voice of her sister. Jean glanced at the clock and said something in English that was not classical.

"I shall have to take an omnibus. Bother!" she said, and the heroine of the russet-brown frock made an abrupt and undignified exit.

It was a fine warm morning in November, the sort of day that follows a week of stormy wet weather as though to cheat the unwary into imagining that the spring instead of the winter is on its way. The pavements were still wet from yesterday's rain, the trees in the park stood stripped by yesterday's gale; only the sun and the sparrows kept up the illusion that it was never going to rain any more. But the caprices of the atmosphere make no impression on the people who cannot help being out; and Jean, as she made the fourteenth passenger on the top of an omnibus, had a vague feeling of contempt for the other thirteen who were engrossed in their morning papers.

"Just imagine missing that glorious effect," she thought to herself, as they rumbled along the edge of the Green Park where the mist was slowly yielding to the warmth of the sun and allowing itself to be coaxed out of growing into a fog. And almost simultaneously she became as material as the rest, in her annoyance with her neighbour for taking more than his share of the seat.

"Nice morning!" he said at that moment, and folded up his *Telegraph*.

"Yes," said Jean, in a tone that was not encouraging. That the morning was "nice" would never have occurred to her; and it seemed unfair to sacrifice the effect over the Green Park, even for conversational purposes. Then she caught sight of his face, which was a harmless one, and in an ordinary way good-looking, and she accused herself of priggishness, and stared at the unconscious passenger in front, preparatory to cultivating the one at her side.

"We deserve some compensation for yesterday," she continued, more graciously.

"Yesterday? Oh, it was beastly wet, wasn't it? I suppose you don't like wet weather, eh?" said the man, with a suspicion of familiarity in his tone. Jean frowned a little.

"That comes of the simple russet gown," she thought; "of course he thinks I am a little shop-girl." But the sun was shining, and life had been very dull lately, and she would be getting down at Piccadilly Circus.[1] Besides, he was little more than a boy, and she liked boys, and there would be no harm in having five minutes' conversation with this one.

"I suppose no one does. I wasn't trying to be particularly original," she replied carelessly.

He smiled and glanced at her with more interest. Her identity was beginning to puzzle him.

"Going to business?" he asked tentatively.

"Well, yes, I suppose so. At least, I am going to teach three children all sorts of things they don't want to learn a bit."

"How awfully clever of you!"

---

1   Circular street in the West-end of London.

The little obvious remark made her laugh. In spite of the humble brown dress that did not suit her, she looked very pretty when she threw back her head and laughed.

"That is because you have never taught," she said; "to be a really good teacher you must systematically forget quite half of what you do know. For instance, I can teach German better than anything else in the world, because I know less about it. Perhaps that is why I always won the German prizes at school," she added reflectively.

"You are very paradoxical — or very cynical, which is it?" asked her neighbour, smiling.

"Oh, I don't know. Am I? But did you ever try to teach?"

"Not I. Gives one the hump,[1] doesn't it? I should just whack the little beasts when they didn't work. Don't you feel like that sometimes?"

"Clearly you never tried to teach," she said, and laughed again.

"Those are lucky pupils of yours," he observed.

"Why?" she asked abruptly, and flashed a stern look at him sideways.

"Oh, because you — seem right on it, don't you know," he answered hastily. The adroitness of his answer pleased her, and she put him down as a gentleman, and felt justified in going a little further.

"I like teaching, yes," she went on gravely. "But all the same I am glad that I only teach for my living and can draw for my pleasure. Now whatever made me tell you that I wonder?"

"It was awfully decent of you to tell me," he said; "I suppose you thought I should be interested, eh?"

"I suppose I did," she assented, and this time she laughed for no reason whatever.

"Will you let me say something very personal?" he asked, waxing bolder. But his tone was still humble, and she felt more kindly towards him now that he evidently knew she was not to be patronised. Besides, she was curious. So she said nothing to dissuade him, and he went on.

"Why do you look so beastly happy, and all that, don't you know? Is it because you work so hard?"

"I look happy!" she exclaimed. "I suppose it is the sun, then, or the jolly day, or — or the *feel* of everything after the rain. Yes, I suppose it must be that."

"I don't, then. Lots of girls might feel all that and not look as you do. I think it is because you have such a bally[2] lot to do."

---

1 State of depression.

2 Euphemism for "bloody."

"I should stop thinking that, if I were you," said Jean a little bitterly; "I know that is the usual idea about women who work — among those who don't. They should try it for a time, and see."

"I believe you are cynical after all," observed her companion. "Don't you like being called happy?"

"Oh, yes, I like it. But I hate humbug, and it is all nonsense to pretend that working hard for one's living is rather an amusing thing to do. Because it isn't, and if it has never been so for a man, why should it be for a woman? If anything, it is worse for women. For one happy hour it gives us two sad ones; it makes us hard — what you call cynical. It builds up our characters at the expense of our hearts. It makes heroines of us and spoils the woman in us. We learn to look the world in the face, and it teaches us to be prigs. We probe into its realities for the first time, and the disclosure is too much for us. Working hard to get enough bread and butter to eat is a sordid, demoralising thing, and the people who talk cant about it never had to do it themselves. *You* don't like the kind of woman who works, you know you don't!"

The omnibus was slowing at the Circus. Jean stopped suddenly and glanced up at her companion with an amused, half shamefaced look.

"I am so sorry. You see how objectionable it has made *me*. Aren't you glad you will never see me again?"

And before he had time to speak she had slipped away, and the omnibus was turning ruthlessly down Waterloo Place.

"What deuced odd things women are," he reflected, by way of deluding himself into the belief that amusement and not interest was the predominant sensation in his mind. But the next morning saw him waiting carefully in West Kensington for the same City omnibus as before; and when it rumbled on its way to Piccadilly Circus and no one in russet-brown got up to relieve the monotony of black coats and umbrellas round him, he was quite unreasonably disappointed, though he told himself savagely at the same time that of course he had never expected to see her at all.

"And if I had, she would have avoided me at once. Women are always like that," he thought, and just as the reflection shaped itself in his mind he caught a glimpse of Air Street that sent his usual composure to the winds and brought him down the steps at a pace that upset the descent of all the other passengers who had no similar desire to rush in the direction of Air Street.

"Did yer expect us to take yer to Timbuctoo?" scoffed the conductor, with the usual contempt of his kind for the passenger who gets into the wrong omnibus. But the victim of his scorn was as regardless of it as of the pink ticket he was grinding into pulp in his hand; and he stood on the pavement with his underlip drawn tightly inwards, until he had regained his customary air of gentlemanly indifference. Then he turned up into Regent Street and made a cross cut through the slums that lie on the borders of Soho.

And as Jean was hastening along Oxford Street, ten minutes later, she met him coming towards her with a superb expression of pleased surprise on his face, which deceived her so completely that she bowed at once and held out her hand to him, although, as she said afterwards to Nancy, "he was being most dreadfully unconventional, and I couldn't help wondering if he would have spoken to me again, if I had worn my new tailor-made gown and looked ordinary." At the time she only felt that Oxford Street, even on a damp and muggy morning, was quite a nice place for a walk.

"Beastly day for you to be out," he began, taking away her umbrella and holding his own over her head. To be looked after was a novel experience to Jean, and she found herself half resenting his air of protection.

"Oh, it's all right. You get used to it when you have to," she said with a short laugh. It was not at all what she wanted to say to him, but the perversity of her nature was uppermost and she had to say it.

"All the same, it is beastly rough on you," he persisted.

"Why? Some one must do the work," she said defiantly.

"Is it so important, then?" he asked with a smile that was half a sneer. Jean blushed hotly.

"It means my living to me," she said; and he winced at her unpleasant frankness.

"You were quite different yesterday, weren't you?" he complained gently.

"You speak as though my being one thing or another ought to depend on your pleasure," she retorted; "of course, you think like everybody else that a woman is only to be tolerated as long as she is cheerful. How can you be cheerful when the weather is dreary, and you are tired out with yesterday's work? You don't know what it is like. You should keep to the women who don't work; they will always look pretty, and smile sweetly and behave in a domesticated manner."

"I don't think I said anything to provoke all that, did I?"

"Yes, you did," she answered unreasonably. "I said — I mean *you* said, oh never mind! But you do like domesticated women best, don't you? On your honour now?"

There was no doubt that he did, especially at that moment. But he lied, smilingly, and well.

"I like all women. But most of all, women like you. Didn't I tell you yesterday how happy you looked? You are such a rum[1] little girl — oh hang, please forgive me. But without any rotting,[2] I wish you'd tell me what you do want me to say. When I said how jolly you looked, you were offended; and now I pity you for being out in the rain, you don't like that any better. What am I to do?"

"I don't see why you should do anything," she said curtly. They had reached the corner of Berners Street, and she came to a standstill. "I am glad I met you again," she added very quickly, without meeting his eyes. And then she ran down the street, and disappeared inside a doorway.

Tom Unwin stepped into a hansom with two umbrellas and an unsatisfactory impression of the last quarter of an hour. And for the next two mornings he went to the City by train. But the third saw him again in Oxford Street shortly before nine o'clock, and he held a small and elegant umbrella in his hand, although it was a cloudless day, and there was hoar frost beneath the gravel on the wood pavement.

"How very odd that we should meet again," she exclaimed, blushing in spite of the self-possession on which she prided herself.

"Not so very odd," he replied; "I believe I am responsible for this meeting."

"I feel sure there is a suitable reply to that, but you mustn't expect me to make it. I am never any good at making suitable replies," said Jean; and she laughed as she had done the first time they met.

"I don't want suitable replies from you," he rejoined, just as lightly; "tell me what you really think instead."

"That it was quite charming of you to come this particular way to the City on this particular morning," said Jean demurely. "Now, do you know, I should have thought it was ever so much quicker to go along the Strand."

"On the contrary, I find it very much quicker when I come along Oxford Street."

"At all events, *you* know how to make suitable replies."

"Then you thought that was a suitable reply? Got you there, didn't I?" and he laughed, which pleased her immensely, although she pretended to be hurt.

---

1   Fine.

2   Speaking nonsense.

"Isn't it queer how one can live two perfectly different lives at the same time?" she said irrelevantly.

"Two? I live half a dozen. But let's hear yours first."

"I was only thinking," continued Jean, "that if the mother of my pupils knew I was walking along Oxford Street with some one I had never been introduced to —"

"Well?" he said, as she paused.

"Oh, well, it isn't exactly an ordinary thing to do, is it?"

"Why not?"

"Well, it isn't, is it?"

"But must one be ordinary?"

"People won't forgive you for being anything else, unless you are in a history book, where you can't do any harm."

"People be hanged! When shall I see you again?"

"Next time you take a short cut to the City, I suppose. Good-bye."

"Stop!" he cried. And when she did stop, with an air of innocent inquiry on her face, he found he had nothing whatever to say.

"You — you haven't told me your name," he stammered lamely.

"Is that all? You needn't make me any later just for *that*," she exclaimed, turning away again. "Besides, you haven't told me yours," she added, over her shoulder.

"Do you want to know it?"

"Why, no; it doesn't matter to me. But I thought you wanted to make some more conversation. Good-bye, again."

"Well, I'm hanged! Look here, if I tell you mine, will you tell me yours?"

"But I don't mind a bit if you *don't* tell me yours."

"Will you, though?"

"Oh, make haste, or else I can't wait to hear it."

"Here you are, then. It is — Tom."

She faced him sternly.

"Why don't you go on?"

"Unwin," he added, hastily. "Now yours, please."

But the only answer he got was a mocking smile; and he was again left at the corner of Berners Street with a lady's umbrella in his hand.

The next morning there was a dull yellow fog, and Jean was in a perverse mood.

"I think you are very mistaken to walk to business on a day like this, when you might go by train," she said, as she reluctantly gave up her books to be carried by him. The fog was making her eyes smart, and she felt cross.

"But I shall get my reward," he said, with elaborate courtesy.

"Oh, please don't. The fog is bad enough without allusions to the hymn-book. Besides, I can't stand being used as a means for somebody else to get into heaven. It is very selfish of me, I suppose, but I don't like it."

"I am afraid you mistake me. I never for a moment associated you with my chances of salvation."

"Then why didn't you?" she cried indignantly. "I should like to know why you come and bother me every morning like this if you think I am as hopelessly bad as all that! I didn't ask you to come, did I? Please give me my books and let me go."

"I think you hopelessly bad? Why, I assure you —"

"Give me my books. Can't you see how late I am?" she said, stamping her foot impetuously. And she seized Bright's English History and Cornwall's Geography[1] out of his hand, and left him precipitately, without another word.

"You are a most unreasonable little girl," he exclaimed hotly; and the policeman to whom he said it smiled patiently.

He started with the intention of going by train on the following morning; then he changed his mind, and ran back to take an omnibus. After that he found it was getting late, so he took a cab to Oxford Circus, and then strolled on towards Holborn as though nothing but chance or necessity had brought him there. But, although he walked as far as Berners Street and back again to the Circus, he met no one in a dull brown frock. And he was just as unsuccessful the next morning, and the one after, and at the end of a week he found himself the sad possessor of a slender silk umbrella, a regretful remembrance, and a fresh store of cynicism.

"She is like all the others," he told himself, with a shrug of his shoulders; "they play the very devil with you until they begin to get frightened of the consequences, and then they fight shy. And I'm hanged if I even know her name!"

And the days wore on, and the autumn grew into winter, and Oxford Street no longer saw the playing of a comedy at nine o'clock in the morning. And Tom Unwin found other interests in life, and if a chance occurrence reminded him of a determined little figure in russet brown, the passing thought brought nothing but an amused smile to his lips.

Then the spring came, suddenly and completely, on the heels of a six weeks' frost; and chance took him down Piccadilly one morning in March, where the budding freshness of the trees drew him into the Green Park. The impression of spring met him everywhere, in the fragrance of the

---

1   Common textbooks of the period.

almond-trees, and the quarrelling of the sparrows, and the transparency of the blue haze over Westminster; and, indifferent though he was to such things, there was a note of familiarity in it all that affected him strangely, and left him with a lazy sensation of pleasure. What that something was he did not realise until his eyes fell on one of the chairs under the trees, and then, as he stood quite still and wondered whether she would know him again, he discovered what there was in the air that had seemed to him so familiar and so pleasant.

"I was just thinking about you," he said deliberately, when she had shown very decidedly that she did mean to know him. He spoke with an easy indifference that she showed no signs of sharing.

"Oh, I have been wondering —" she began, in a voice that trembled with eagerness.

"Yes? Supposing we sit down. That's better. You have been wondering —?"

She leaned back in her chair, and looked up through the branches at the pale blue sky beyond. There was an odd little look of defiance on her face.

"So, after all, you did find that the Strand was the quickest way," she said abruptly.

"Possibly. And you?" he asked, with his customary smile.

"How often did you go down Oxford Street after — the last time I saw you?"

"As far as I can remember, the measure of my endurance was a week. And how much longer did you take the precaution of avoiding such a dangerous person as myself?"

She turned round and stared at him with great wondering eyes, into which a look of comprehension was slowly creeping.

"You actually thought I did that? And all the time I was ill, I was having visions of you —"

"Ill? You never told me you had been ill," he interrupted.

"You didn't exactly give me the chance, did you? It was the fog, I suppose. I am all right now. They thought I should never go down Oxford Street again. But I take a good deal of killing, and so here I am again." She ended with a cynical smile. He was making holes in the soft turf with his walking-stick. She went on speaking to the pale blue sky and the network of branches above her.

"And the odd part is that I did not mind the illness so much as —" And she paused again.

"Yes?" he said, in a voice that had lost some of its jauntiness.

"I think it won't interest you."

"How can you say that unless you tell me?"

"I am sure it won't," she said decidedly. "And I couldn't possibly tell you, really."

"Go on, please," he said, looking round at her; and she went on meekly.

"The thing that bothered me was my having been cross the last time we met. You see, it was not the being cross that I minded exactly; *that* wouldn't have mattered a bit if I had seen you again the next day, but — "

"I quite understand. Bad temper is a luxury we keep for our most familiar friends. I am honoured by the distinction," he said, and his smile was not a sneer.

"I wish you wouldn't laugh at me," she said, a little wistfully.

"I am not laughing at you, child," he hastened to assure her, and he took one of her hands in his. "I have missed you, too," he went on, in a low tone that he strove to make natural.

"Did you *really*? I thought you would at first, perhaps, and then I thought you would just laugh, and forget. And you really did think of me sometimes? I am so glad."

He had a twinge of conscience. But a reputation once acquired is a tender thing, and must be handled with delicacy.

"I have not forgotten," he said, and tried to change the conversation. "And you never even told me your name, you perverse little person," he added playfully.

"You told me yours," she said, and laughed triumphantly.

"And yours, please?"

"It will quite spoil it all," she objected.

"Is it so bad as that, then? Never mind, I can bear a good deal. What is it — Susan, Jemima, Emmelina?"

There was a little pause, and then she nodded at the pale blue sky above and said "Jean" in a hurried whisper. And he was less exigent than she had been, for he did not ask for any more.

When he left her on her own doorstep she lingered for a moment in the sunlight before she went in to Nancy.

"And he really is coming to see me to-morrow," she said out loud with a joyous laugh; "I wonder, shall I tell Nancy or not?" After mature consideration she decided not to tell Nancy, though if Nancy had been less unsuspicious she would certainly have noticed something unusual in the manner of her practical little eldest sister, when she started for Berners Street on the following morning, and twice repeated that she would be back to tea should any one call and ask for her.

"Nobody is likely to ask for you," said Nancy with sisterly frankness, "nobody ever does. You needn't bother to be back to tea unless you like," she added with a self-conscious smile. "Jimmy said he might look in."

"So much the better," thought Jean; "I can bring in a cake without exciting suspicion." And she started gaily on her way, and wondered ingenuously why all the people in the street seemed so indifferent to her happiness. At Berners Street, a shock was awaiting her. Would Miss Moreen kindly stay till five to-day as the children's mother was obliged to go out, and nurse had a holiday? And as the children's mother had already gone out and nurse's holiday had begun before breakfast, there was no appeal left to poor Jean, and she settled down to her day's work with a sense of injustice in her mind and a queer feeling in her throat that had to be overcome during an arithmetic lesson. But as the day wore on her spirits rose to an unnatural pitch; she spent the afternoon in romping furiously with her pupils; and when five o'clock came, she was standing outside in the street counting the coins in her little purse.

"I can just do it, and I shall!" she cried, and a passing cabby pulled up in answer to her graphic appeal and carried her away westwards. He whistled when she paid him an extravagant fare, and watched her with a chuckle as she flew up the steps and fumbled nervously at the keyhole before she was able to unlock the door. He would have wondered more, or perhaps less, had he seen her standing on the mat outside the front room on the first floor, giving her hat and hair certain touches which did not affect their appearance in the least, and listening breathlessly to the sound of voices that came from within. Then she turned the handle suddenly and went in.

The lamp was not yet lighted and the daylight was waning. The room was in partial darkness, but the fire was burning brightly, and it shone on the face of a man as he leaned forward in a low chair, and talked to the beautiful girl who lay on the sofa, smiling up at him in a gentle deprecating manner, as if his homage were new and overwhelming to her.

The man was not the expected Jimmy, and Jean took two swift little steps into the room. The spell was broken and they looked round with a start.

"Oh, here you are," cried Nancy, gliding off the sofa and putting her arms round her in her pretty affectionate manner. "Poor Mr. Unwin has been waiting quite an hour for you. Whatever made you so late?"

Jean disengaged herself a little roughly, and held out her hand to Tom.

"Have you been very bored?" she asked him with a slight curl of her lip.

"That could hardly be the case in Miss Nancy's company," he replied in his best manner; "but if she had not been so kind to me your tardiness in coming would certainly have been harder to bear."

The carefully picked words did not come naturally from the boyish fellow who had talked slang to her on the top of the omnibus, but Tom Unwin never talked slang when there was a situation of any kind. Jean was bitterly conscious of being the only one of the three who was not behaving in a picturesque manner. The other two vied with each other in showing her little attentions, a fact that entirely failed to deceive her.

"Do they think I am a fool?" she thought scornfully. "Why should they suppose that I need propitiating?"

And she insisted curtly on pouring out her own cup of tea, and sat down obstinately on a high chair, without noticing the low one he was pulling forward for her.

"Don't let me disturb you," she said calmly; "you made such a charming picture when I came in."

They only seemed to her to be making a ridiculous picture now. She was conscious of nothing but the satirical view of the situation, and she had a mad desire to point at them and scream with laughter at their fatuity in supposing that she did not see through their discomfiture.

"We thought you were never coming," began Nancy in her gentle tired voice; "I was afraid you had been taken ill or something."

"Yes, indeed," added Tom with strained jocularity; "it was all I could do to restrain Miss Nancy from sending a telegram to somebody about you. She only gave up the idea when I got her to acknowledge that she didn't even know where to send it."

"Now, that is really too bad of you," exclaimed Nancy with a carefully studied pout; "you know quite well —"

"Indeed, I appeal to you, Miss Moreen —"

"Don't listen to him, Jean."

"It doesn't seem to me to matter very much," said Jean with much composure; "I am very glad that I gave you so much to talk about."

They made another attempt to conciliate her.

"Do have some cake. It isn't bad," said Nancy invitingly.

"Or some more tea?" added Tom anxiously. "You must be so played out with your long day's work. Have the little brats been very trying?"

"Oh, you needn't worry about the little brats, thanks," said Jean, eating bread and butter voraciously for the sake of an occupation.

"Come nearer the fire," said Nancy coaxingly; "Mr. Unwin will move up that other chair."

"Of course," said Mr. Unwin with alacrity, glad of any excuse that removed him for a moment from the unpleasant scrutiny of her large cold eyes.

"You are both very kind to bother about me like this. I am really not used to it," said Jean with a hard little laugh. "Won't you go on with your conversation while I write a postcard?"

She made a place for her cup on the tea-tray, strolled across the room to the bureau, and sat down to look vacantly at a blank postcard. The other two seated themselves stiffly at opposite ends of the hearthrug, and manufactured stilted phrases for the ears of Jean.

"Your sister draws, I believe?"

"Oh, yes. Jean is fearfully clever, you know. She used to win prizes and things. I never won a prize in my life. Oh, yes; Jean is certainly very clever indeed."

"I am sure of it. It must be charming to be so clever."

"Yes. Nothing else matters if you are as clever as all that. It doesn't affect Jean in the least if things happen to go wrong, because she always has her cleverness to console her, don't you see."

"Brains are a perennial consolation," said Tom solemnly; "I always knew, Miss Nancy, that your sister was very exceptional."

"Exceptional! Yes, I suppose I am that," thought Jean with a curious feeling of dissatisfaction. The burden of her own cleverness was almost too much for her, and she would have given worlds, just then, to have been as ordinary as Nancy — and as beautiful.

"Will you forgive me if I go upstairs and finish a drawing?" she said, coming forward into the firelight again. They uttered some conventional regrets, and Tom held the door open for her. "Good-bye," she said, smiling, "I am sorry my drawing won't wait. It has to go in to-morrow morning."

"I envy you your charming talent," he said with a sigh that was a little overdone.

"Do you? It prevents me from being domesticated, you know, and that is always a pity, isn't it?" she said, and drew her hand away quickly.

Upstairs with her head on an old brown cloak she lay and listened to the hum of voices below.

"Why wasn't I born a fool with a pretty face?" she murmured. "Fools are the only really happy people in the world, for they are the only people the rest of us have the capacity to understand. And to be understood by the majority of people is the whole secret of happiness. No one would take the trouble to understand *me*. Of course, it is unbearably conceited to say so, but there is no one to hear."

When Nancy came up to bed, she found her sister working away steadily at her drawing.

"It was very mean of you to leave me so long with that man, Jean; he stayed quite an hour after you left," she said, suppressing a yawn.

"Oh, I thought you wouldn't mind; I don't get on with him half so well as you do. Stand out of the light, will you?"

"He thinks you're immensely clever," said Nancy; "he says he never met any one so determined and plucky in his life. Of course you will get on, he says."

"Yes," said Jean with a strange smile, as she nibbled the top of her pencil; "I suppose I shall get on. And to the end of my days people will admire me from a distance, and talk about my talent and my determination, just as they talk about your beauty and your womanly ways. That is so like the world; it always associates us with a certain atmosphere and never admits the possibility of any other."

Nancy was perched on the end of the bed in her white peignoir, with her knees up to her chin and a puzzled expression on her face.

"How queer you are to-night, Jean," she said; "I don't think I understand."

"My atmosphere," continued Jean in the same passionless tone, "is the clever and capable one. It is the one that is always reserved for the unattractive people who have understanding, the sort of people who know all there is to know, from observation, and never get the chance of experiencing one jot of it. They are the people who learn about life from the outside, and remain half alive themselves to the end of time. Nobody would think of falling in love with them, and they don't even know how to be lovable. It is a very clinging atmosphere," she added sadly; "I shall never shake it off."

Nancy stopped making a becoming wreck of her coils of hair, and looked more bewildered than before.

"I don't understand, Jean," she said again.

Jean looked at her for a moment with eyes full of admiration.

"Don't worry about it, child," she said slowly; "you will never have to understand."

Ada Leverson

"The Quest of Sorrow" (1896)

["The wittiest woman in the world" — the title was bestowed upon London-born Ada Leverson (1862–1933) by none other than Oscar Wilde, the late-Victorian master of wit. The compliment gives us a sense of how respected Leverson was in her time. The daughter of Jewish parents, Leverson was well educated and became a central member of the aestheticist community of the 1890s. From 1907 to 1916, she dictated six novels from the comfort of her bed and her light camp tone found a new audience during the mid-twentieth century. She is now best known for her participation in the "yellow nineties" and her production of numerous witty stories, sketches, and essays that appeared in periodicals such as *Punch* and the *Yellow Book*. Like "The Quest of Sorrow," these works often poke fun at the pretensions of the dandy-aesthetes who dominated the scene. That said, the works also incorporate a sense of sympathy that reflect her positive relationships within the writing community of the day.]

I

It is rather strange, in a man of my temperament, that I did not discover the void in my life until I was eighteen years old. And then I found out that I had missed a beautiful and wonderful experience.

I had never known grief. Sadness had shunned me, pain had left me untouched; I could hardly imagine the sensation of being unhappy. And the desire arose in me to have this experience; without which, it seemed to me, that I was not complete. I wanted to be miserable, despairing: a Pessimist! I craved to feel that gnawing fox, Anxiety, at my heart; I wanted my friends (most of whom had been, at some time or other, more or less heartbroken) to press my hand with sympathetic looks, to avoid the subject of my trouble, from delicacy; or, better still, to have long, hopeless talks with me about it, at midnight. I thirsted for salt tears; I longed to clasp Sorrow in my arms and press her pale lips to mine.

Now this wish was not so easily fulfilled as might be supposed, for I was born with those natural and accidental advantages that militate most against failure and depression. There was my appearance. I have a face that rarely passes unnoticed (I suppose a man may admit, without conceit, that he is not repulsive), and the exclamation, "What a beautiful boy!" is one that I have been accustomed to hear from my earliest childhood to the present time.

I might, indeed, have known the sordid and wearing cares connected with financial matters, for my father was morbidly economical with regard to me. But, when I was only seventeen, my uncle died, leaving me all his property, when I instantly left my father's house (I am bound to say, in justice to him, that he made not the smallest objection) and took the rooms I now occupy, which I was able to arrange in harmony with my temperament. In their resolute effort to be neither uninterestingly commonplace nor conventionally bizarre (I detest — do not you? — the ready-made exotic) but at once simple and elaborate, severe and florid, they are an interesting result of my complex aspirations, and the astonishing patience of a bewildered decorator. (I think everything in a room should not be entirely correct; and I had some trouble to get a marble mantel-piece of a sufficiently debased design.) Here I was able to lead that life of leisure and contemplation for which I was formed and had those successes — social and artistic — that now began to pall upon me.

The religious doubts, from which I am told the youth of the middle classes often suffers, were, again, denied me. I might have had some mental conflicts, have revelled in the sense of rebellion, have shed bitter tears when my faiths crumbled to ashes. But I can never be insensible to incense; and there must, I feel, be something organically wrong about the man who is not impressed by the organ. I love religious rites and ceremonies, and on the other hand, I was an agnostic at five years old. Also, I don't think it matters. So here there is no chance for me.

To be miserable one must desire the unattainable. And of the fair women who, from time to time, have appealed to my heart, my imagination, etc., every one, *without a single exception*, has been kindness itself to me. Many others, indeed, for whom I have no time, or perhaps no inclination, write me those letters which are so difficult to answer. How can one sit down and write, "My dear lady — I am so sorry, but I am really too busy?"

And with, perhaps, two appointments in one day — a light comedy one, say, in the Park, and serious sentiment coming to see one at one's rooms — to say nothing of the thread of a flirtation to be taken up at dinner and having perhaps to make a jealous scene of reproaches to some one of whom one has grown tired, in the evening — you must admit I had a sufficiently occupied life.

I had heard much of the pangs of disappointed ambition, and I now turned my thoughts in that direction. A failure in literature would be excellent. I had no time to write a play bad enough to be refused by every manager in London, or to be hissed off the stage; but I sometimes wrote verses. If I arranged to have a poem rejected I might get a glimpse of the feelings of the unsuccessful. So I wrote a poem. It was beautiful, but that I couldn't help, and I carefully refrained from sending it to any of the more literary reviews or magazines, for there it would have stood no chance of rejection. I therefore sent it to a commonplace, barbarous periodical, that appealed only to the masses; feeling sure it would not be understood, and that I should taste the bitterness of Philistine scorn.

Here is the little poem — if you care to look at it. I called it

FOAM-FLOWERS

Among the blue of Hyacinth's golden bells
(Sad is the Spring, more sad the new-mown hay),
Thou art most surely less than least divine,
Like a white Poppy, or a Sea-shell grey.
I dream in joy that thou art nearly mine;
Love's gift and grace, pale as this golden day,
Outlasting Hollyhocks, and Heliotrope
(Sad is the Spring, bitter the new-mown hay).
The wandering wild west wind, in salt-sweet hope,
With glad red roses, gems the woodland way.

Envoi
A bird sings, twittering in the dim air's shine,
Amid the mad Mimosa's scented spray,
Among the Asphodel, and Eglantine,
"Sad is the Spring, but sweet the new-mown hay."

I had not heard from the editor, and was anticipating the return of my poem, accompanied by some expressions of ignorant contempt that would harrow my feelings, when it happened that I took up the frivolous periodical. Fancy my surprise when there, on the front page, was my poem–

signed, as my things are always signed, "*Lys de la Vallée.*"[1] Of course I could not repress the immediate exhilaration produced by seeing oneself in print; and when I went home I found a letter, thanking me for the *amusing parody on a certain modern school of verse* — and enclosing ten-and-six!

A parody! And I had written it in all seriousness!

Evidently literary failure was not for me. After all, what I wanted most was an affair of the heart, a disappointment in love, an unrequited affection. And these, for some reason or other, never seemed to come my way.

One morning I was engaged with Collins, my servant, in putting some slight final touches to my toilette, when my two friends, Freddy Thompson and Claude de Verney, walked into my room.

They were at school with me, and I am fond of them both, for different reasons. Freddy is in the Army; he is two-and-twenty, brusque, slangy, tender-hearted, and devoted to me. De Verney has nothing to do with this story at all, but I may mention that he was noted for his rosy cheeks, his collection of jewels, his reputation for having formerly taken morphia, his epicurism, his passion for private theatricals, and his extraordinary touchiness. One never knew what he would take offence at. He was always being hurt, and writing letters beginning: "Dear Mr. Carington" or "Dear Sir" — (he usually called me Cecil), "I believe it is customary when a gentleman dines at your table," etc.

I never took the slightest notice, and then he would apologise. He was always begging my pardon and always thanking me, though I never did anything at all to deserve either his anger or gratitude.

"Hallo, old chap," Freddy exclaimed, "you look rather down in the mouth. What's the row?"

"I am enamoured of Sorrow," I said, with a sigh.

"Got the hump[2] — eh? Poor old boy. Well, I can't help being cheery, all the same. I've got some ripping news to tell you."

"Collins," I said, "take away this eau-de-cologne. It's corked. Now, Freddy," as the servant left the room, "your news."

"I'm engaged to Miss Sinclair. Her governor has given in at last. What price that? ... I'm tremendously pleased, don't you know, because it's been going on for some time, and I'm awfully mashed, and all that."

Miss Sinclair! I remembered her — a romantic, fluffy blonde, improbably pretty, with dreamy eyes and golden hair, all poetry and idealism.

---

1 (French) "Lily of the Valley."

2 State of depression.

Such a contrast to Freddy! One associated her with pink chiffon, Chopin's[1] nocturnes, and photographs by Mendelssohn.[2]

"I congratulate you, my dear child," I was just saying, when an idea occurred to me. Why shouldn't I fall in love with Miss Sinclair? What could be more tragic than a hopeless attachment to the woman who was engaged to my dearest friend? It seemed the very thing I had been waiting for.

"I have met her. You must take me to see her, to offer my congratulations," I said.

Freddy accepted with enthusiasm.

A day or two after, we called. Alice Sinclair was looking perfectly charming, and it seemed no difficult task that I had set myself. She was sweet to me as Freddy's great friend — and we spoke of him while Freddy talked to her mother.

"How fortunate some men are!" I said, with a deep sigh.

"Why do you say that?"

"Because you're so beautiful," I answered, in a low voice, and in my *earlier manner* — that is to say, as though the exclamation had broken from me involuntarily.

She laughed, blushed, I think, and turned to Freddy. The rest of the visit I sat silent and as though abstracted, gazing at her. Her mother tried, with well-meaning platitudes, to rouse me from what she supposed to be my boyish shyness ...

II

What happened in the next few weeks is rather difficult to describe. I saw Miss Sinclair again and again, and lost no opportunity of expressing my admiration; for I have a theory that if you make love to a woman long enough, and ardently enough, you are sure to get rather fond of her at last. I was progressing splendidly; I often felt almost sad, and very nearly succeeded at times in being a little jealous of Freddy.

On one occasion — it was a warm day at the end of the season, I remember — we had gone to skate at that absurd modern place where the ice is as artificial as the people, and much more polished. Freddy, who was an excellent skater, had undertaken to teach Alice's little sister, and

---

1   Fryderyk Franciszek Chopin (1810–49), Polish composer of the Romantic movement in music.

2   Hayman Mendelssohn (?–1908), Polish-born London portrait photographer.

I was guiding her own graceful movements. She had just remarked that I seemed very fond of skating, and I had answered that I was — on thin ice — when she stumbled and fell.... She hurt her ankle a little — a very little, she said.

"Oh, Miss Sinclair — 'Alice' — I am sure you are hurt!" I cried, with tears of anxiety in my voice. "You ought to rest — I am sure you ought to go home and rest."

Freddy came up, there was some discussion, some demur, and finally it was decided that, as the injury was indeed very slight, Freddy should remain and finish his lesson. And I was allowed to take her home.

We were in a little brougham; delightfully near together. She leaned her pretty head, I thought, a little on one side — *my* side. I was wearing violets in my button-hole. Perhaps she was tired, or faint.

"How are you feeling now, dear Miss Sinclair?"

"Much better — thanks!"

"I am afraid you are suffering ... I shall never forget what I felt when you fell! — My heart ceased beating!"

"It's very sweet of you. But, it's really nothing."

"How precious these few moments with you are! I should like to drive with you for ever! Through life — to eternity!"

"Really! What a funny boy you are!" she said softly.

"Ah, if you only knew, Miss Sinclair, how — how I envy Freddy."

"Oh, Mr. Carington!"

"Don't call me Mr. Carington. It's so cold — so ceremonious. Call me Cecil. Won't you?"

"Very well, Cecil."

"Do you think it treacherous to Freddy for me to envy him — to tell you so?"

"Yes, I am afraid it is; a little."

"Oh no. I don't think it is. — How are you feeling now, Alice?"

"Much better, thanks very much." ...

Suddenly, to my own surprise and entirely without pre-meditation, I kissed her — as it were, accidentally. It seemed so shocking, that we both pretended I hadn't, and entirely ignored the fact: continuing to argue as to whether or not it was treacherous to say I envied Freddy.... I insisted on treating her as an invalid, and lifted her out of the carriage, while she laughed nervously. It struck me that I was not unhappy yet. But that would come.

The next evening we met at a dance. She was wearing flowers that Freddy had sent her; but among them she had fastened one or two of the violets I had worn in my button-hole. I smiled, amused at the coquetry. No doubt she would laugh at me when she thought she had completely turned my head. She fancied me a child! Perhaps, on her wedding-day, I should be miserable at last.

... "How tragic, how terrible it is to long for the impossible!"

We were sitting out, on the balcony. Freddy was in the ballroom, dancing. He was an excellent dancer.

"*Impossible!*" she said; and I thought she looked at me rather strangely. "But you don't really, really —"

"Love you?" I exclaimed, lyrically. "But with all my soul! My life is blighted for ever, but don't think of me. It doesn't matter in the least. It may kill me, of course; but never mind. Sometimes, I believe, people *do* live on with a broken heart, and —"

"My dance, I think," and a tiresome partner claimed her.

Even that night, I couldn't believe, try as I would, that life held for me no further possibilities of joy....

About half-past one the next day, just as I was getting up, I received a thunderbolt in the form of a letter from Alice.

Would it be believed that this absurd, romantic, literal, beautiful person wrote to say she had actually broken off her engagement with Freddy? She could not bear to blight my young life; she returned my affection; she was waiting to hear from me.

Much agitated, I hid my face in my hands. What! was I never to get away from success — never to know the luxury of an unrequited attachment? Of course, I realised, now, that I had been deceiving myself; that I had only liked her enough to wish to make her care for me; that I had striven, unconsciously, to that end. The instant I knew she loved me all my interest was gone. My passion had been entirely imaginary. I cared nothing, absolutely nothing, for her. It was impossible to exceed my indifference. And Freddy! Because *I* yearned for sorrow, was that a reason that I should plunge others into it? Because I wished to weep, were my friends not to rejoice? How terrible to have wrecked Freddy's life, by taking away from him something that I didn't want myself!

The only course was to tell her the whole truth, and implore her to make it up with poor Freddy. It was extremely complicated. How was I to make her see that I had been *trying* for a broken heart; that I *wanted* my life blighted?

I wrote, endeavouring to explain, and be frank. It was a most touching letter, but the inevitable, uncontrollable desire for the *beau rôle*[1] crept, I fear, into it and I fancy I represented myself, in my firm resolve not to marry her whatever happened — as rather generous and self-denying. It was a heart-breaking letter, and moved me to tears when I read it.

This is how it ended:

.... "You have my fervent prayers for your happiness, and it may be that some day you and Freddy, walking in the daisied fields together, under God's beautiful sunlight, may speak not unkindly of the lonely exile.

"Yes, exile. For to-morrow I leave England. To-morrow I go to bury myself in some remote spot — perhaps to Trouville[2] — where I can hide my heart and pray unceasingly for your welfare and that of the dear, dear friend of my youth and manhood.

"Yours and his, devotedly, till death and after,

"Cecil Carington."

It was not a bit like my style. But how difficult it is not to fall into the tone that accords best with the temperament of the person to whom one is writing!

I was rather dreading an interview with poor Freddy. To be misunderstood by him would have been really rather tragic. But even here, good fortune pursued me. Alice's letter breaking off the engagement had been written in such mysterious terms, that it was quite impossible for the simple Freddy to make head or tail of it. So that when he appeared, just after my letter (which had infuriated her) — Alice threw herself into his arms, begging him to forgive her; pretending — women have these subtleties — that it had been a *boutade*[3] about some trifle.

But I think Freddy had a suspicion that I had been "mashed," as he would say, on his *fiancée,* and thought vaguely that I had done something rather splendid in going away.

If he had only stopped to think, he would have realised that there was nothing very extraordinary in "leaving England" in the beginning of

---

1   Romantic role, or role of boyfriend.

2   Popular beach resort in France.

3   (French) outburst.

August; and he knew I had arranged to spend the summer holidays in France with De Verney. Still, he fancies I acted nobly. Alice doesn't.

And so I resigned myself, seeing, indeed, that Grief was the one thing life meant to deny me. And on the golden sands, with the gay striped bathers of Trouville, I was content to linger with laughter on my lips, seeking for Sorrow no more.

H.G. Wells

"The Star" (1897)

[H(erbert) G(eorge) Wells's (1866–46) literary recognition began with his early, scientific romances, which ranged from short stories to longer works such as *The Time Machine* (1895), *The Island of Dr. Moreau* (1896), and *The War of the Worlds* (1898). While venturing into imaginative and philosophic realms of possibility, the scientific pieces such as "The Star" — one of the most anthologized science fiction stories ever — frequently take as their subject the individual's sense of self within a world whose instability is found to be both attractive and frightening. Wells's focus on the "average man," meanwhile, reflects his socialist interests. He was for a short while a member of the Fabian Society and his first science fiction novel, *The Time Machine*, explores the relationship in the future between the seemingly privileged Elois and working-class Morlocks. In other works, he satirizes scientific egotism and his society's willingness to sacrifice values and beliefs for the sake of innovation or novelty.]

It was on the first day of the new year that the announcement was made, almost simultaneously from three observatories, that the motion of the planet Neptune, the outermost of all the planets that wheel about the sun, had become very erratic. Ogilvy had already called attention to a suspected retardation in its velocity in December. Such a piece of news was scarcely calculated to interest a world the greater portion of whose inhabitants were unaware of the existence of the planet Neptune, nor outside the astronomical profession did the subsequent discovery of a faint remote speck of life in the region of the perturbed planet cause any very great excitement. Scientific people, however, found the intelligence remarkable enough, even before it became known that the new body was rapidly growing larger and brighter, that its motion was quite different from the orderly progress of the planets, and that the deflection of Neptune and its satellite was becoming now of an unprecedented kind.

Few people without a training in science can realise the huge isolation of the solar system. The sun with its specks of planets, its dust of plane-toids, and its impalpable comets, swims in a vacant immensity that almost defeats the imagination. Beyond the orbit of Neptune there is space, vacant so far as human observation has penetrated, without warmth or light or sound, blank emptiness, for twenty million times a million miles. That is the smallest estimate of the distance to be traversed before the very nearest of the stars is attained. And, saving a few comets more unsub-stantial than the thinnest flame, no matter had ever to human knowledge crossed this gulf of space, until early in the twentieth century this strange wanderer appeared, a vast mass of matter, bulky, heavy, rushing without warning out of the black mystery of the sky into the radiance of the sun. By the second day it was clearly visible to any decent instrument, as a speck with a barely sensible diameter, in the constellation Leo near Regulus. In a little while an opera glass could attain it.

On the third day of the new year the newspaper readers of two hemi-spheres were made aware for the first time of the real importance of this unusual apparition in the heavens. "A Planetary Collision," one London paper headed the news, and proclaimed Duchaine's opinion that this strange new planet would probably collide with Neptune. The leader writers enlarged upon the topic. So that in most of the large capitals of the world, on January 3rd, there was an expectation, however vague, of some imminent phenomenon in the sky; and as the night followed the sunset round the globe, thousands of men turned their eyes skyward to see — the old familiar stars just as they had always been.

Until it was dawn in London and Pollux[1] setting and the stars overhead grown pale. The Winter's dawn it was, a sickly filtering accumulation of daylight, and the light of gas and candles shone yellow in the windows to show where people were astir. But the yawning policeman saw the thing, the busy crowds in the markets stopped agape, workmen going to their work betimes, milkmen, the drivers of news-carts, dissipation going home jaded and pale, homeless wanderers, sentinels on their beats, and in the country, labourers trudging afield, poachers slinking home, all over the dusky quickening country it could he seen — and out at sea by seamen watching for the day — a great white star, come suddenly into the westward sky!

Brighter it was than any star in our skies; brighter than the evening star at its brightest. It still glowed out white and large, no mere twinkling spot

---

1   Bright star in the constellation Gemini.

of light, but a small, round, clear shining disc, an hour after the day had come. And where science has not reached, men stared and feared, telling one another of the wars and pestilences that are foreshadowed by these fiery signs in the Heavens. Sturdy Boers,[1] dusky Hottentots,[2] Gold Coast negroes, Frenchmen, Spaniards, Portuguese, stood in the warmth of the sunrise watching the setting of this strange new star.

And in a hundred observatories there had been suppressed excitement, rising almost to shouting pitch, as the two remote bodies had hurried together, and a hurrying to and fro, to gather photographic apparatus and spectroscope, and this appliance and that, to record this novel astonishing sight, the destruction of a world. For it was a world, a sister planet of our earth, far greater than our earth, indeed, that had so suddenly flashed into flaming death. Neptune it was, had been struck, fairly and squarely, by the strange planet from outer space and the heat of the concussion had incontinently turned two solid globes into one vast mass of incandescence. Round the world that day, two hours before the dawn, went the pallid great white star, fading only as it sank westward and the sun mounted above it. Everywhere men marvelled at it, but of all those who saw it none could have marvelled more than those sailors, habitual watchers of the stars, who far away at sea had heard nothing of its advent and saw it now rise like a pigmy moon and climb zenithward and hang overhead and sink westward with the passing of the night.

And when next it rose over Europe everywhere were crowds of watchers on hilly slopes, on house-roofs, in open spaces, staring eastward for the rising of the great new star. It rose with a white glow in front of it, like the glare of a white fire, and those who had seen it come into existence the night before cried out at the sight of it. "It is larger," they cried. "It is brighter!" And, indeed the moon a quarter full and sinking in the west was in its apparent size, indeed, beyond comparison, but scarcely in all its breadth had it as much brightness now as the little circle of the strange new star.

"It is brighter!" cried the people clustering in the streets. But in the dim observatories the watchers held their breath and peered at one another. "*It is nearer*," they said. "*Nearer!*"

And voice after voice repeated, "It is nearer," and the clicking telegraph took that up, and it trembled along telephone wires, and in a thousand cities grimy compositors fingered the type. "It is nearer." Men writing in offices, struck with a strange realisation, flung down their pens, men

---

1   Dutch colonists in South Africa.

2   Race of people from Southwestern Africa.

talking in a thousand places suddenly came upon a grotesque possibility in those words, "It is nearer." It hurried along awakening streets, it was shouted down the frost-stilled ways of quiet villages, men who had read these things from the throbbing tape stood in yellow-lit doorways shouting the news to the passers-by. "It is nearer." Pretty women, flushed and glittering, heard the news told jestingly between the dances, and feigned an intelligent interest they did not feel. "Nearer! Indeed. How curious! How very, very clever people must be to find out things like that!"

Lonely tramps faring through the wintry night murmured those words to comfort themselves — looking skyward. "It has need to be nearer, for the night's as cold as charity. Don't seem much warmth from it if it *is* nearer, all the same."

"What is a new star to me?" cried the weeping woman kneeling beside the dead.

The schoolboy, rising early for his examination work, puzzled it out for himself — with the great white star, shining broad and bright through the frost-flowers of his window. "Centrifugal, centripetal," he said, with his chin on his fist. "Stop a planet in its flight, rob it of its centrifugal force, what then? Centripetal has it, and down it falls into the sun! And this —!"

"Do *we* come in the way? I wonder —"

The light of that day went the way of its brethren, and with the later watches of the frosty darkness rose the strange star again. And it was now so bright that the waxing moon seemed but a pale yellow ghost of itself, hanging huge in the sunset. In a South African city a great man had married, and the streets were alight to welcome his return with his bride. "Even the skies have illuminated," said the flatterer. Under Capricorn, two negro lovers, daring the wild beasts and evil spirits, for love of one another, crouched together in a cane brake where the fire-flies hovered. "That is our star," they whispered, and felt strangely comforted by the sweet brilliance of its light.

The master mathematician sat in his private room and pushed the papers from him. His calculations were already finished. In a small white phial there still remained a little of the drug that had kept him awake and active for four long nights. Each day, serene, explicit, patient as ever, he had given his lecture to his students, and then had come back at once to this momentous calculation. His face was grave, a little drawn and hectic from his drugged activity. For some time he seemed lost in thought. Then he stood up, went to the window, and the blind went up with a click. Half way up the sky, over the clustering roofs, chimneys and steeples of the city, hung the star.

He looked at it as one might look into the eyes of a brave enemy. "You may kill me," he said after a silence. "But I can hold you — and all the universe for that matter — in the grip of this little brain. I would not change. Even now."

He looked at the little phial. "There will be no need of sleep again," he said. The next day at noon, punctual to the minute, he entered his lecture theatre, put his hat on the end of the table as his habit was, and carefully selected a large piece of chalk. It was a joke among his students that he could not lecture without that piece of chalk to fumble in his fingers, and once he had been stricken to impotence by their hiding his supply. He came and looked under his grey eyebrows at the rising tiers of young fresh faces, and spoke with his accustomed studied commonness of phrasing. "Circumstances have arisen — circumstances beyond my control," he said and paused, "which will debar me from completing the course I had designed. It would seem, gentlemen, if I may put the thing clearly and briefly, that — Man has lived in vain."

The students glanced at one another. Had they heard aright? Mad? Raised eyebrows and grinning lips there were, but one or two faces remained intent upon his calm grey-fringed face. "It will be interesting," he was saying, "to devote this morning to an exposition, so far as I can make it clear to you, of the calculations that have led me to this conclusion. Let us assume —"

He turned towards the blackboard, meditating a diagram in the way that was usual to him. "What was that about lived in vain?" whispered one student to another. "Listen," said the other, nodding towards the lecturer.

And presently they began to understand.

That night the star rose later, for its proper eastward motion had carried it some way across Leo towards Virgo, and its brightness was so great that the sky became a luminous blue as it rose, and every star was hidden in its turn, save only Jupiter near the zenith, Capella, Aldebaran, Sirius and the pointers of the Bear.[1] It was very white and beautiful. In many parts of the world that night a pallid halo encircled it about. It was perceptibly larger; in the clear refractive sky of the tropics it seemed as if it were nearly a quarter the size of the moon. The frost was still on the ground in England, but the world was as brightly lit as if it were midsummer moonlight. One could see to read quite ordinary print by that cold, clear light, and in the cities the lamps burnt yellow and wan.

---

1   Capella is the brightest star in the constellation Auriga; Aldebaran is the double-star in the constellation Taurus; Sirius is a star in the constellation Canis Major; the Bear refers to the constellations Great Bear and Little Bear.

And everywhere the world was awake that night, and throughout Christendom a sombre murmur hung in the keen air over the country-side like the belling of bees in the heather, and this murmurous tumult grew to a clangour in the cities. It was the tolling of the bells in a million belfry towers and steeples, summoning the people to sleep no more, to sin no more, but to gather in their churches and pray. And overhead, growing larger and brighter, as the earth rolled on its way and the night passed, rose the dazzling star.

And the streets and houses were alight in all the cities, the shipyards glared, and whatever roads led to high country were lit and crowded all night long. And in all the seas about the civilised lands, ships with throbbing engines, and ships with bellying sails, crowded with men and living creatures, were standing out to ocean and the north. For already the warning of the master mathematician had been telegraphed all over the world, and translated into a hundred tongues. The new planet and Neptune, locked in a fiery embrace, were whirling headlong, ever faster and faster towards the sun. Already every second this blazing mass flew a hundred miles, and every second its terrific velocity increased. As it flew now, indeed, it must pass a hundred million of miles wide of the earth and scarcely affect it. But near its destined path, as yet only slightly perturbed, spun the mighty planet Jupiter and his moons sweeping splendid round the sun. Every moment now the attraction between the fiery star and the greatest of the planets grew stronger. And the result of that attraction? Inevitably Jupiter would be deflected from its orbit into an elliptical path, and the burning star, swung by his attraction wide of its sunward rush, would "describe a curved path" and perhaps collide with, and certainly pass very close to, our earth. "Earthquakes, volcanic outbreaks, cyclones, sea waves, floods, and a steady rise in temperature to I know not what limit" — so prophesied the master mathematician.

And overhead, to carry out his words, lonely and cold and livid, blazed the star of the coming doom.

To many who stared at it that night until their eyes ached, it seemed that it was visibly approaching. And that night, too, the weather changed, and the frost that had gripped all Central Europe and France and England softened towards a thaw.

But you must not imagine because I have spoken of people praying through the night and people going aboard ships and people fleeing towards mountainous country that the whole world was already in a terror because of the star. As a matter of fact, use and wont still ruled the world, and save for the talk of idle moments and the splendour of the night, nine human beings out of ten were still busy at their common occupations. In all the cities the shops, save one here and there, opened and closed at their proper hours, the doctor and the undertaker plied their trades, the workers gathered in the factories, soldiers drilled, scholars studied, lovers sought one another, thieves lurked and fled, politicians planned their schemes. The presses of the newspapers roared through the nights, and many a priest of this church and that would not open his holy building to further what he considered a foolish panic. The newspapers insisted on the lesson of the year 1000 — for then, too, people had anticipated the end. The star was no star — mere gas — a comet; and were it a star it could not possibly strike the earth, there was no precedent for such a thing. Common sense was sturdy everywhere, scornful, jesting, a little inclined to persecute the obdurate fearful. That night, at seven-fifteen by Greenwich time,[1] the star would be at its nearest to Jupiter. Then the world would see the turn things would take. The master mathematician's grim warnings were treated by many as so much mere elaborate self-advertisement. Common sense at last, a little heated by argument, signified its unalterable convictions by going to bed. So, too, barbarism and savagery, already tired of the novelty, went about their nightly business, and save for a howling dog here and there, the beast world left the star unheeded.

And yet, when at last the watchers in the European States saw the star rise, an hour later it is true, but no larger than it had been the night before, there were still plenty awake to laugh at the master mathematician — to take the danger as if it had passed.

But thereafter the laughter ceased. The star grew — it grew with a terrible steadiness hour after hour, a little larger each hour, a little nearer the midnight zenith, and brighter and brighter, until it had turned night into a second day. Had it come straight to the earth instead of in a curved path, had it lost no velocity to Jupiter, it must have leapt the intervening gulf in a day, but as it was it took five days altogether to come by our planet. The next night it had become a third the size of the moon before it set to English eyes, and the thaw was assured. It rose over America near the size of the moon, but blinding white to look at, and *hot*; and a breath of hot wind blew now with its rising and gathering strength, and in Virginia, and Brazil, and down the St. Lawrence valley, it shone intermittently through a driving reek of thunder-clouds, flickering violet light-

---

1   Mean time based on the meridian running through Greenwich, near London, and adopted internationally as the basis for calculating time.

ning, and hail unprecedented. In Manitoba was a thaw and devastating floods. And upon all the mountains of the earth the snow and ice began to melt that night, and all the rivers coming out of high country flowed thick and turbid, and soon — in their upper reaches — with swirling trees and the bodies of beasts and men. They rose steadily, steadily in the ghostly brilliance, and came trickling over their banks at last, behind the flying population of their valleys.

And along the coast of Argentina and up the South Atlantic the tides were higher than had ever been in the memory of man, and the storms drove the waters in many cases scores of miles inland, drowning whole cities. And so great grew the heat during the night that the rising of the sun was like the coming of a shadow. The earthquakes began and grew until all down America from the Arctic Circle to Cape Horn, hillsides were sliding, fissures were opening, and houses and walls crumbling to destruction. The whole side of Cotopaxi[1] slipped out in one vast convulsion, and a tumult of lava poured out so high and broad and swift and liquid that in one day it reached the sea.

So the star, with the wan moon in its wake, marched across the Pacific, trailed the thunderstorms like the hem of a robe, and the growing tidal wave that toiled behind it, frothing and eager, poured over island and island and swept them clear of men. Until that wave came at last — in a blinding light and with the breath of a furnace, swift and terrible it came — a wall of water, fifty feet high, roaring hungrily, upon the long coasts of Asia, and swept inland across the plains of China. For a space the star, hotter now and larger and brighter than the sun in its strength, showed with pitiless brilliance the wide and populous country; towns and villages with their pagodas and trees, roads, wide cultivated fields, millions of sleepless people staring in helpless terror at the incandescent sky; and then, low and growing, came the murmur of the flood. And thus it was with millions of men that night — a flight nowhither, with limbs heavy with heat and breath fierce and scant, and the flood like a wall swift and white behind. And then death.

China was lit glowing white, but over Japan and Java and all the islands of Eastern Asia the great star was a ball of dull red fire because of the steam and smoke and ashes the volcanoes were spouting forth to salute its coming. Above was the lava flood, hot gases and ash, and below the seething floods, and the whole earth swayed and rumbled with the earthquake shocks. Soon the immemorial snows of Thibet and the Himalaya

---

1   Volcano in central Ecuador.

were melting and pouring down by ten million deepening converging channels upon the plains of Burmah and Hindostan. The tangled summits of the Indian jungles were aflame in a thousand places, and below the hurrying waters around the stems were dark objects that still struggled feebly and reflected the blood-red tongues of fire. And in a rudderless confusion a multitude of men and women fled down the broad river-ways to the one last hope of men — the sea.

Larger grew the star, and larger, hotter, and brighter with a terrible swiftness now. The tropical ocean had lost its phosphorescence, and the whirling steam rose in ghostly wreaths from the black waves that plunged incessantly about the storm-tossed ships.

And then came a wonder. It seemed to those who in Europe watched for the rising of the star that the world must have ceased its rotation. In a thousand open spaces of down and upland the people who had fled thither from the floods and the falling houses and sliding slopes of hill watched for that rising in vain. Hour followed hour through a terrible suspense, and the star rose not. Once again men set their eyes upon the old constellations they had counted lost to them forever. In England it was hot and clear overhead, though the ground quivered perpetually, but in the tropics Sirius and Capella and Aldebaran showed through a veil of steam. And when at last the great star rose near ten hours late, the sun rose close upon it, and in the centre of its white heart was a disc of black.

Over Asia it was the star had begun to fall behind the movement of the sky, and then suddenly, as it hung over India, its light had been veiled. All the plain of India from the mouth of the Indus to the mouths of the Ganges was a shallow waste of shining water that night, out of which rose temples and palaces, mounds and hills, black with people. Every minaret was a clustering mass of people, who fell one by one into the turbid waters, as heat and terror overcame them. The whole land seemed a-wailing. And suddenly there swept a shadow across that furnace of despair, and a breath of cold wind, and a gathering of clouds, out of the cooling air. Men looking up, near blinded, at the star, saw that a black disc was creeping across the light. It was the moon, coming between the star and the earth. And even as men cried to God at this respite, out of the East with a strange inexplicable swiftness sprang the sun. And then, with a sickening swiftness, star, sun and moon rushed together across the heavens.

So it was that presently, to the European watchers, star and sun rose close upon each other, drove headlong for a space and then slower, and at last came to rest, star and sun merged into one glare of flame at the zenith of the sky. The moon no longer eclipsed the star but was lost to sight in the brilliance of the sky. And though those who were still alive regarded it for the most part with that dull stupidity that hunger, fatigue, heat and despair engender, there were still men who could perceive the meaning of these signs. Star and earth had been at their nearest, had swung about one another, and the star had passed. Already it was receding, swifter and swifter, in the last stage of its headlong journey downward into the sun.

And then the clouds gathered, blotting out the vision of the sky, the thunder and lightning wove a garment round the world; all over the earth was such a downpour of rain as men had never before seen, and where the volcanoes flared red against the cloud canopy there descended torrents of mud. Everywhere the waters were pouring off the land, leaving mud-silted ruins, and the earth littered like a storm-worn beach with all that had floated, and the dead bodies of the men and brutes, its children. For days the waters streamed off the land, sweeping away soil and trees and houses in the way, and piling huge dykes and scooping out Titanic gullies over the countryside. Those were the days of darkness that followed the star and the heat. All through them, and for many weeks and months, the earthquakes continued.

But the star had passed, and so men, hunger-driven and gathering courage only slowly, might creep back to their ruined cities, buried granaries, and sodden fields. Such few ships as had escaped the storms of that time came stunned and shattered and sounding their way cautiously through the new marks and shoals of once familiar ports. And as the storms subsided men perceived that everywhere the days were hotter than of yore, and the sun larger, and that the moon, shrunk to a third of its former size, took now four score days between new and new.

But of the new brotherhood that grew presently among men, of the saving of laws and books and machines, of the strange change that had come over Iceland and Greenland and the shores of Baffin's Bay, so that the sailors coming there presently found them green and gracious, and could scarce believe their eyes, this story does not tell. Nor of the movement of mankind now that the earth was hotter, northward and southward towards the poles of the earth. It concerns itself only with the coming and the passing of the Star.

The Martian astronomers — for there are astronomers on Mars, although they are very different beings from men — were naturally profoundly interested by these things. They saw things from their own standpoint of course. "Considering the mass and temperature of the missile that was flung through our solar system into the sun," one wrote, "it is astonishing what a little damage the earth, which it missed so narrowly, has sustained. All the familiar continental markings and the masses of the seas remain intact, and indeed the only difference seems to be a shrinkage of the white discoloration (supposed to be frozen water) round either pole." Which only shows how small the vastest of human catastrophes may seem, at a distance of a few million miles.

Israel Zangwill

"To Die in Jerusalem" (1899)

[Israel Zangwill (1864–1926) is best known for his gently satiric depictions of the relationship between Jews and gentiles in England and the intra-generational conflicts within the Jewish community, both themes demonstrated in his short story "To Die in Jerusalem." The son of a Russian father and Polish mother, Zangwill was born and educated in England. Specializing in Languages and Philosophy, he graduated with top honours from London University. Zangwill felt that the main purpose of fiction — and art in general — was to address the politics of contemporary society. His first major literary success was *Children of the Ghetto, Being Pictures of a Peculiar People* (1892), a book about London's poor Jews that he wrote upon the encouragement of the Jewish Publication Society of America. It was quickly followed by the highly successful collection *Ghetto Tragedies* (1893), to which the following story was added in a later edition.]

I

The older Isaac Levinsky grew, and the more he saw of the world after business hours, the more ashamed he grew of the Russian Rabbi whom Heaven had curiously chosen for his father. At first it seemed natural enough to shout and dance prayers in the stuffy little Spitalfields synagogue, and to receive reflected glory as the son and heir of the illustrious Maggid (preacher) whose four hour expositions of Scripture drew even West End pietists[1] under the spell of their celestial crookedness. But early in Isaac's English school-life — for cocksure philanthropists dragged the younger generation to anglicization — he discovered that other fathers did not make themselves ridiculously noticeable by retaining the

---

1 The West End was a fashionable part of London far from the main Jewish community in the East End. The implication is that their image of piety — or religious devotion — was not sincere.

gabardine,[1] the fur cap, and the ear-locks[2] of Eastern Europe: nay, that a few — O, enviable sons! — could scarcely be distinguished from the teachers themselves.

When the guardian angels of the Ghetto apprenticed him, in view of his talent for drawing, to a lithographic printer, he suffered agonies at the thought of his grotesque parent coming to sign the indentures.

"You might put on a coat to-morrow," he begged in Yiddish.

The Maggid's long black beard lifted itself slowly from the worm-eaten folio of the Babylonian Talmud,[3] in which he was studying the tractate[4] anent[5] the payment of the half-shekel[6] head-tax in ancient Palestine. "If he took the money from the second tithes[7] or from the Sabbatical year[8] fruit," he was humming in his quaint sing-song, "he must eat the full value of the same in the city of Jerusalem." As he encountered his boy's querulous face his dream city vanished, the glittering temple of Solomon[9] crumbled to dust, and he remembered he was in exile.

"Put on a coat?" he repeated gently. "Nay, thou knowest 'tis against our holy religion to appear like the heathen. I emigrated to England to be free to wear the Jewish dress, and God hath not failed to bless me."

Isaac suppressed a precocious "Damn!" He had often heard the story of how the cruel Czar Nicholas[10] had tried to make his Jews dress like Christians, so as insidiously to assimilate them away; how the police had even pulled off the unsightly cloth-coverings of the shaven polls[11] of the married women, to the secret delight of the pretty ones, who then let their hair grow in godless charm. And, mixed up with this story, were vaguer legends of raw recruits forced by their sergeants to kneel on little broken stones till they perceived the superiority of Christianity.

---

1 Long, loose smock.

2 Locks of curled hair that hang in front of the ears.

3 Sacred writings of Orthodox Judaism from Babylon.

4 Writings.

5 Concerning.

6 Ancient Jewish currency.

7 1/10th of one's production from land or labour taken annually as tax by one's religious institution.

8 According to Mosaic law, every seventh year the land is to remain untilled. The word "fruit" refers to the resources put aside for that year.

9 Temple of Babylon, which fell when King Solomon became corrupt.

10 Russian ruler, Czar Nicholas II (1868–1918).

11 Heads.

How the Maggid would have been stricken to the heart to know that Isaac now heard these legends with inverted sympathies!

"The blind fools!" thought the boy, with ever growing bitterness. "To fancy that religion can lie in clothes, almost as if it was something you could carry in your pockets! But that's where most of their religion does lie — in their pocket." And he shuddered with a vision of greasy, huckstering fanatics. "And just imagine if I was sweet on a girl, having to see all her pretty hair cut off! As for those recruits, it served them right for not turning Christians. As if Judaism was any truer! And the old man never thinks of how he is torturing *me* — all the sharp little stones he makes *me* kneel on." And, looking into the future with the ambitious eye of conscious cleverness, he saw the paternal gabardine over-glooming his life.

II

One Friday evening — after Isaac had completed his 'prentice years — there was anxiety in the Maggid's household in lieu of the Sabbath peace. Isaac's seat at the board was vacant. The twisted loaves seemed without salt, the wine of the consecration cup without savour.

The mother was full of ominous explanations.

"Perturb not the Sabbath," reproved the gabardined saint gently, and quoted the Talmud: "No man has a finger maimed but 'tis decreed from above."

"Isaac has gone to supper somewhere else," suggested his little sister, Miriam.

"Children and fools speak the truth," said the Maggid, pinching her cheek.

But they had to go to bed without seeing him, as though this were only a profane evening, and he amusing himself with the vague friends of his lithographic life. They waited till the candles flared out, and there seemed something symbolic in the gloom in which they groped their way upstairs. They were all shivering, too, for the fire had become gray ashes long since, the Sabbath Fire-Woman having made her last round at nine o'clock and they themselves being forbidden to touch even a candlestick or a poker.

The sunrise revealed to the unclosed eyes of the mother that her boy's bed was empty. It also showed — what she might have discovered the night before had religion permitted her to enter his room with a light — that the room was empty, too: empty of his scattered belongings, of his books and sketches.

"God in Heaven!" she cried.

Her boy had run away.

She began to wring her hands and wail with oriental amplitude, and would have torn her hair had it not been piously replaced by a black wig, neatly parted in the middle and now grotesquely placid amid her agonized agitation.

The Maggid preserved more outward calm. "Perhaps we shall find him in synagogue," he said, trembling.

"He has gone away, he will never come back. Woe is me!"

"He has never missed the Sabbath service!" the Maggid urged. But inwardly his heart was sick with the fear that she prophesied truly. This England, which had seduced many of his own congregants to Christian costume, had often seemed to him to be stealing away his son, though he had never let himself dwell upon the dread. His sermon that morning was acutely exegetical: with no more relation to his own trouble than to the rest of contemporary reality. His soul dwelt in old Jerusalem, and dreamed of Israel's return thither in some vague millennium. When he got home he found that the postman had left a letter. His wife hastened to snatch it.

"What dost thou?" he cried, "Not to-day. When Sabbath is out."

"I cannot wait. It is from him — it is from Isaac."

"Wait at least till the Fire-Woman comes to open it."

For answer the mother tore open the envelope. It was the boldest act of her life — her first breach with the traditions. The Rabbi stood paralyzed by it, listening, as without conscious will, to her sobbing delivery of its contents.

The letter was in Hebrew (for neither parent could read English), and commenced abruptly, without date, address, or affectionate formality. "This is the last time I shall write the holy tongue. My soul is wearied to death of Jews, a blind and ungrateful people, who linger on when the world no longer hath need of them, without country of their own, nor will they enter into the blood of the countries that stretch out their hands to them. Seek not to find me, for I go to a new world. Blot out my name even as I shall blot out yours. Let it be as though I was never begotten."

The mother dropped the letter and began to scream hysterically. "I who bore him! I who bore him!"

"Hold thy peace!" said the father, his limbs shaking but his voice firm. "He is dead. 'The Lord giveth and the Lord taketh away. Blessed be the name of the Lord.' To-night we will begin to sit the seven days' mourning. But to-day is the Sabbath."

"My Sabbath is over for aye. Thou hast driven my boy away with thy long prayers."

"Nay, God hath taken him away for thy sins, thou godless Sabbath-breaker! Peace while I make the Consecration."

"My Isaac, my only son! We shall say *Kaddish* (mourning-prayer) for him, but who will say *Kaddish* for us?"

"Peace while I make the Consecration!"

He got through with the prayer over the wine, but his breakfast remained untasted.

III

Re-reading the letter, the poor parents agreed that the worst had happened. The allusions to "blood" and "the new world" seemed unmistakable. Isaac had fallen under the spell of a beautiful heathen female; he was marrying her in a church and emigrating with her to America. Willy-nilly, they must blot him out of their lives.

And so the years went by, over-brooded by this shadow of living death. The only gleam of happiness came when Miriam was wooed and led under the canopy by the President of the congregation, who sold haberdashery. True, he spoke English well and dressed like a clerk, but in these degenerate days one must be thankful to get a son-in-law who shuts his shop on the Sabbath.

One evening, some ten years after Isaac's disappearance, Miriam sat reading the weekly paper — which alone connected her with the world and the fulness thereof — when she gave a sudden cry.

"What is it?" said the haberdasher.

"Nothing — I thought —" And she stared again at the rough cut of a head embedded in the reading matter.

But no, it could not be!

"Mr. Ethelred P. Wyndhurst, whose versatile talents have brought him such social popularity, is rumoured to have budded out in a new direction. He is said to be writing a comedy for Mrs. Donald O'Neill, who, it will be remembered, sat to him recently for the portrait now on view at the Azure Art Club. The dashing *comédienne* will, it is stated, produce the play in the autumn season. Mr. Wyndhurst's smart sayings have often passed from mouth to mouth, but it remains to be seen whether he can make them come naturally from the mouths of his characters."

What had these far-away splendours to do with Isaac Levinsky? With Isaac and his heathen female across the Atlantic?

And yet — and yet Ethelred P. Wyndhurst *was* like Isaac — that characteristic curve of the nose, those thick eyebrows! And perhaps Isaac *had* worked himself up into a portrait-painter. Why not? Did not his old sketch of herself give distinction to her parlour? Her heart swelled proudly at the idea. But no! more probably the face in print was roughly drawn — was only accidentally like her brother. She sighed and dropped the paper.

But she could not drop the thought. It clung to her, wistful and demanding satisfaction. The name of Ethelred P. Wyndhurst, whenever it appeared in the paper — and it was surprising how often she saw it now, though she had never noticed it before — made her heart beat with the prospect of clews. She bought other papers, merely in the hope of seeing it, and was not unfrequently rewarded. Involuntarily, her imagination built up a picture of a brilliant romantic career that only needed to be signed "Isaac." She began to read theatrical and society journals on the sly, and developed a hidden life of imaginative participation in fashionable gatherings. And from all this mass of print the name Ethelred P. Wyndhurst disengaged itself with lurid brilliancy. The rumours of his comedy thickened. It was christened *The Sins of Society*. It was to be put on soon. It was not written yet. Another manager had bid for it. It was already in rehearsal. It was called *The Bohemian Boy*. It would not come on this season. Miriam followed feverishly its contradictory career. And one day there was a large picture of Isaac! Isaac to the life! She soared skywards. But it adorned an interview, and the interview dropped her from the clouds. Ethelred was born in Brazil of an English engineer and a Spanish beauty, who performed brilliantly on the violin. He had shot big game in the Rocky Mountains, and studied painting in Rome.

The image of her mother playing the violin, in her preternaturally placid wig, brought a bitter smile to Miriam's lips. And yet it was hard to give up Ethelred now. It seemed like losing Isaac a second time. And presently she reflected shrewdly that the wig and the gabardine wouldn't have shown up well in print, that indeed Isaac in his farewell letter had formally renounced them, and it was therefore open to him to invent new parental accessories. Of course — fool that she was! — how could Ethelred P. Wyndhurst acknowledge the same childhood as Isaac Levinsky! Yes, it might still be her Isaac.

Well, she would set the doubt at rest. She knew, from the wide reading to which Ethelred had stimulated her, that authors appeared before the curtain on first nights. She would go to the first night of *The Whirligig* (that was the final name), and win either joy or mental rest.

She made her expedition to the West End on the pretext of a sick friend in Bow,[1] and waited many hours to gain a good point of view in the first row of the gallery, being too economical to risk more than a shilling on the possibility of relationship to the dramatist.

As the play progressed, her heart sank. Though she understood little of the conversational paradoxes, it seemed to her — now she saw with her physical eye this brilliant Belgravian world,[2] in the stalls as well as on the stage — that it was impossible her Isaac could be of it, still less that it could be Isaac's spirit which marshalled so masterfully these fashionable personages through dazzling drawing-rooms; and an undercurrent of satire against Jews who tried to get into society by bribing the fashionables, contributed doubly to chill her. She shared in the general laughter, but her laugh was one of hysterical excitement.

But when at last amid tumultuous cries of "Author!" Isaac Levinsky really appeared, — Isaac, transformed almost to a fairy prince, as noble a figure as any in his piece, Isaac, the proved master-spirit of the show, the unchallenged treader of all these radiant circles, — then all Miriam's effervescing emotion found vent in a sobbing cry of joy.

"Isaac!" she cried, stretching out her arms across the gallery bar.

But her cry was lost in the applause of the house.

IV

She wrote to him, care of the theatre. The first envelope she had to tear up because it was inadvertently addressed to Isaac Levinsky.

Her letter was a gush of joy at finding her dear Isaac, of pride in his wonderful position. Who would have dreamed a lithographer's apprentice would arrive at leading the fashions among the nobility and gentry? But she had always believed in his talents; she had always treasured the watercolour he had made of her, and it hung in the parlour behind the haberdasher's shop into which she had married. He, too, was married, they had imagined, and gone to America. But perhaps he *was* married, although in England. Would he not tell her? Of course, his parents had cast him out of their hearts, though she had heard mother call out his

---

1   Major street in London.

2   Belgravia was a fashionable, wealthy neighbourhood of London.

name in her sleep. But she herself thought of him very often, and perhaps he would let her come to see him. She would come very quietly when the grand people were not there, nor would she ever let out that he was a Jew, or not born in Brazil. Father was still pretty strong, thank God, but mother was rather ailing. Hoping to see him soon, she remained his loving Miriam.

She waited eagerly for his answer. Day followed day, but none came.

When the days passed into weeks, she began to lose hope; but it was not till *The Whirligig*, which she followed in the advertisement columns, was taken off after a briefer run than the first night seemed to augur, that she felt with curious conclusiveness that her letter would go unanswered. Perhaps even it had miscarried. But it was now not difficult to hunt out Ethelred P. Wyndhurst's address, and she wrote him anew.

Still the same wounding silence. After the lapse of a month, she understood that what he had written in Hebrew was final; that he had cut himself free once and forever from the swaddling coils of gabardine, and would not be dragged back even within touch of its hem. She wept over her second loss of him, but the persistent thought of him had brought back many tender childish images, and it seemed incredible that she would never really creep into his life again. He had permanently enlarged her horizon, and she continued to follow his career in the papers, worshipping it as it loomed grandiose through her haze of ignorance. Gradually she began to boast of it in her more English circles, and so in course of time it became known to all but the parents that the lost Isaac was a shining light in high heathendom, and a vast secret admiration mingled with the contempt of the Ghetto for Ethelred P. Wyndhurst.

V

In high heathendom a vast secret contempt mingled with the admiration for Ethelred P. Wyndhurst. He had, it is true, a certain vogue, but behind his back he was called a Jew. He did not deserve the stigma in so far as it might have implied financial prosperity. His numerous talents had only availed to prevent one another from being seriously cultivated. He had had a little success at first with flamboyant pictures, badly drawn, and well paragraphed; he had written tender verses for music, and made quiet love to ugly and unhappy society ladies; he was an assiduous first-nighter, and was suspected of writing dramatic criticisms, even of his own comedy. And in that undefined social segment where Kensington and Bohemia intersect,[1] he was a familiar figure (a too familiar figure, old fogies grumbled) with an unenviable reputation as a diner-out — for the sake of the dinner.

Yet some of the people who called him "sponge" were not averse from imbibing his own liquids when he himself played the gracious host. He was appearing in that rôle one Sunday evening before a motley assembly in his dramatically furnished studio, nay, he was in the very act of biting into a sandwich scrupulously compounded with ham, when a telegram was handed to him.

"Another of those blessed actresses crying off," he said. "I wonder how they ever manage to take up their cues!"

Then his face changed as he hurriedly crumpled up the pinkish paper.

"Mother is dying. No hope. She cries to see you. Have told her you are in London. Father consents. Come at once. — MIRIAM."

He put the crumpled paper to the gas and lit a new cigarette with it.

"As I thought," he said, smiling. "When a woman is an actress as well as a woman —"

VI

After his wife died — vainly calling for her Isaac — the old Maggid was left heart-broken. It was as if his emotions ran in obedient harmony with the dictum of the Talmud: "Whoso sees his first wife's death is as one who in his own day saw the Temple destroyed."

What was there for him in life now but the ruins of the literal Temple? He must die soon, and the dream that had always haunted the background of his life began to come now into the empty foreground. If he could but die in Jerusalem!

There was nothing of consequence for him to do in England. His Miriam was married and had grown too English for any real communion. True, his congregation was dear to him, but he felt his powers waning: other Maggidim were arising who could speak longer.

To see and kiss the sacred soil, to fall prostrate where once the Temple had stood, to die in an ecstasy that was already Gan-Iden (Paradise) — could life, indeed, hold such bliss for him, life that had hitherto proved a cup of such bitters?

Life was not worth living, he agreed with his long-vanished brother-Rabbis in ancient Babylon, it was only a burden to be borne nobly. But

---

1   I.e., where the upper-class and the artistic types interact.

if life was not worth living, death — in Jerusalem — was worth dying. Jerusalem! to which he had turned three times a day in praying, whose name was written on his heart, as on that of the mediæval Spanish singer, with whom he cried: —

"Who will make to me wings that I may fly ever Eastward,
Until my ruined heart shall dwell in the ruins of thee?
Then will I bend my face to thy sacred soil and hold precious
Thy very stones, yea e'en to thy dust shall I tender be.

"Life of the soul is the air of thy land, and myrrh of the purest
Each grain of thy dust, thy waters sweetest honey of the comb.
Joyous my soul would be, could I even naked and barefoot,
Amid the holy ruins of thine ancient Temple roam,
Where the Ark was shrined, and the Cherubim in the Oracle
        had their home."

To die in Jerusalem! — that were success in life.

Here he was lonely. In Jerusalem he would be surrounded by a glorious host. Patriarchs, prophets, kings, priests, rabbonim — they all hovered lovingly over its desolation, whispering heavenly words of comfort.

But now a curious difficulty arose. The Maggid knew from correspondence with Jerusalem Rabbis that a Russian subject would have great difficulty in slipping in at Jaffa or Beyrout, even aided by *bakhshish*.[1] The only safe way was to enter as a British subject. Grotesque irony of the fates! For nigh half a century the old man had lived in England in his gabardine, and now that he was departing to die in gabardine lands, he was compelled to seek naturalization as a voluntary Englishman! He was even compelled to account mendaciously for his sudden desire to identify himself with John Bull's[2] institutions and patriotic prejudices, and to live as a free-born Englishman. By the aid of a rich but pious West End Jew, who had sometimes been drawn Eastwards by the Maggid's exegetical eloquence, all difficulties were overcome. Armed with a passport, signed floridly as with a lion's tail rampant, the Maggid — after a quasi-death-bed blessing to Miriam by imposition of hands from the railway-carriage window upon her best bonnet — was whirled away toward his holy dying-place.

---

1   (Persian) gratuity, tip. In the present context, perhaps a bribe.

2   England or the typical English person, from John Arbuthnot's (1667–1735) satire *The History of John Bull* (1712).

VII

Such disappointment as often befalls the visionary when he sees the land of his dreams was spared to the Maggid, who remained a visionary even in the presence of the real; beholding with spiritual eye the refuse-laden alleys and the rapacious *Schnorrers* (beggars). He lived enswathed as with heavenly love, waiting for the moment of transition to the shining World-To-Come, and his supplications at the Wailing Wall[1] for the restoration of Zion's[2] glory had, despite their sympathetic fervour, the peaceful impersonality of one who looks forward to no worldly kingdom. To outward view he lived — in the rare intervals when he was not at a synagogue or a house-of-learning — somewhere up a dusky staircase in a bleak, narrow court, in one tiny room supplemented by a kitchen in the shape of a stove on the landing, itself a centre of pilgrimage to *Schnorrers* innumerable, for whom the rich English Maggid was an unexpected windfall. Rich and English were synonymous in hungry Jerusalem, but these beggars' notion of charity was so modest, and the coin of the realm so divisible, that the Maggid managed to gratify them at a penny a dozen. At uncertain intervals he received a letter from Miriam, written in English. The daughter had not carried on the learned tradition of the mother, and so the Maggid was wont to have recourse to the head of the philanthropic technical school for the translation of her news into Hebrew. There was, however, not much of interest; Miriam's world had grown too alien: she could scrape together little to appeal to the dying man. And so his last ties with the past grew frailer and frailer, even as his body grew feebler and feebler, until at last, bent with great age and infirmity, so that his white beard swept the stones, he tottered about the sacred city like an incarnation of its holy ruin. He seemed like one bent over the verge of eternity, peering wistfully into its soundless depths. Surely God would send his Death-Angel now.

Then one day a letter from Miriam wrenched him back violently from his beatific vision, jerked him back to that other eternity of the dead past.

Isaac, Isaac had come home! Had come home to find desolation. Had then sought his sister, and was now being nursed by her through his dying hours. His life had come to utter bankruptcy: his possessions — by a cruel coincidence — had been sold up at the very moment that the doctors announced to him that he was a doomed man. And his death-bed was

---

1   Remnant of the wall of the Second Temple of Jerusalem (destroyed in 70 BC), now a site of prayer.

2   Name of a hill in Jerusalem, but also used to refer to ancient Jerusalem itself, the Jewish religion, and the kingdom of Heaven.

a premature hell of torture and remorse. He raved incessantly for his father. Would he not annul the curse, grant him his blessing, promise to say *Kaddish* for his soul, that he might be saved from utter damnation? Would he not send his forgiveness by return, for Isaac's days were numbered, and he could not linger on more than a month or so?

The Maggid was terribly shaken. He recalled bitterly the years of suffering, crowned by Isaac's brutal heedlessness to the cry of his dying mother: but the more grievous the boy's sin, the more awful the anger of God in store for him.

And the mother — would not her own Gan-Iden be spoilt by her boy's agonizing in hell? For her sake he must forgive his froward offspring; perhaps God would be more merciful, then. The merits of the father counted: he himself was blessed beyond his deserts by the merits of the Fathers — of Abraham, Isaac, and Jacob. He had made the pilgrimage to Jerusalem; perhaps his prayers would be heard at the Mercy-Seat.

With shaking hand the old man wrote a letter to his son, granting him a full pardon for the sin against himself, but begging him to entreat God day and night. And therewith an anthology of consoling Talmudical texts: "A man should pray for Mercy even till the last clod is thrown upon his grave ... For Repentance and Prayer and Charity avert the Evil Decree." The Charity he was himself distributing to the startled *Schnorrers*.

The schoolmaster wrote out the envelope, as usual, but the Maggid did not post the letter. The image of his son's death-bed was haunting him. Isaac called to him in the old boyish tones. Could he let his boy die there without giving him the comfort of his presence, the visible assurance of his forgiveness, the touch of his hands upon his head in farewell blessing? No, he must go to him.

But to leave Jerusalem at his age? Who knew if he would ever get back to die there? If he should miss the hope of his life! But Isaac kept calling to him — and Isaac's mother. Yes, he had strength for the journey. It seemed to come to him miraculously, like a gift from Heaven and a pledge of its mercy.

He journeyed to Beyrout, and after a few days took ship for Marseilles.

VIII

Meantime in the London Ghetto the unhappy Ethelred P. Wyndhurst found each day a year. He was in a rapid consumption: a disorderly life had told as ruinously upon his physique as upon his finances. And with

this double collapse had come a strange irresistible resurgence of early feelings and forgotten superstitions. The avenging hand was heavy upon
him in life, — what horrors yet awaited him when he should be laid in the
cold grave? The shadow of death and judgment over-brooded him, cloud-
ing his brain almost to insanity.

There would be no forgiveness for him — his father's remoteness had
killed his hope of that. It was the nemesis, he felt, of his refusal to come
to his dying mother. God had removed his father from his pleadings, had
wrapped him in an atmosphere holy and aloof. How should Miriam's
letter penetrate through the walls of Jerusalem, pierce through the stonier
heart hardened by twenty years of desertion!

And so the day after she had sent it, the spring sunshine giving him a
spurt of strength and courage, a desperate idea came to him. If he could
go to Jerusalem himself! If he could fall upon his father's neck, and extort
his blessing!

And then, too, he would die in Jerusalem!

Some half-obliterated text sounded in his ears: "And the land shall forgive sin."

He managed to rise — his betaking himself to bed, he found, as the sunshine warmed him, had been mere hopelessness and self-pity. Let him meet
Death standing, aye, journeying to the sun-lands. Nay, when Miriam,
getting over the alarm of his uprising, began to dream of the Palestine climate curing him, he caught a last flicker of optimism, spoke artistically of
the glow and colour of the East, which he had never seen, but which he
might yet live to render on canvas, winning a new reputation. Yes, he would
start that very day. Miriam pledged her jewellery to supply him with
funds, for she dared not ask her husband to do more for the stranger.

But long before Ethelred P. Wyndhurst reached Jaffa he knew that only
the hope of his father's blessing was keeping him alive.

Somewhere at sea the ships must have passed each other.

IX

When the gabardined Maggid reached Miriam's house, his remains of
strength undermined by the long journey, he was nigh stricken dead on the
doorstep by the news that his journey was vain.

"It is the will of God," he said hopelessly. The sinner was beyond
mercy. He burst into sobs and tears ran down his pallid cheeks and
dripped from his sweeping white beard.

"Thou shouldst have let us know," said Miriam gently. "We never dreamed it was possible for thee to come."

"I came as quickly as a letter could have announced me."

"But thou shouldst have cabled."

"Cabled?" The process had never come within his ken. "But how should I dream he could travel? Thy letter said he was on his death-bed. I prayed God I might but arrive in time."

He was for going back at once, but Miriam put him to bed — the bed Isaac should have died in.

"Thou canst cable thy forgiveness, at least," she said, and so, without understanding this new miracle, he bade her ask the schoolmaster to convey his forgiveness to his son.

"Isaac will inquire for me, if he arrives alive," he said. "The schoolmaster will hear of him. It is a very small place, alas! for God hath taken away its glory by reason of our sins."

The answer came the same afternoon. "Message just in time. Son died peacefully."

The Maggid rent his bed-garment. "Thank God!" he cried. "He died in Jerusalem. Better he than I! Isaac died in Jerusalem! God will have mercy on his soul."

Tears of joy sprang to his bleared eyes. "He died in Jerusalem," he kept murmuring happily at intervals. "My Isaac died in Jerusalem."

Three days later the Maggid died in London.

Appendix A

Edgar Allan Poe, from a review of Nathaniel Hawthorne's[1]
Twice-told Tales *(1842)*

[American author Edgar Allan Poe (1809–49) is still recognized as one of the best short-story writers of all time. He had a notable influence on British and French literature of the nineteenth century. The following review is one of the earliest attempts to establish criteria by which short prose works can be generically categorized.]

… The tale proper, in our opinion, affords unquestionably the fairest field for the exercise of the loftiest talent, which can be afforded by the wide domains of mere prose. Were we bidden to say how the highest genius could be most advantageously employed for the best display of its own powers, we should answer, without hesitation — in the composition of a rhymed poem, not to exceed in length what might be perused in an hour. Within this limit alone can the highest order of true poetry exist. We need only here say, upon this topic, that, in almost all classes of composition, the unity of effect or impression is a point of the greatest importance. It is clear, moreover, that this unity cannot be thoroughly preserved in productions whose perusal cannot be completed at one sitting. We may continue the reading of a prose composition, from the very nature of prose itself, much longer than we can persevere, to any good purpose, in the perusal of a poem. This latter, if truly fulfilling the demands of the poetic sentiment, induces an exaltation of the soul which cannot be long sustained. All high excitements are necessarily transient. Thus a long poem is a paradox. And, without unity of impression, the deepest effects cannot be brought about. Epics were the offspring of an imperfect sense of Art, and their reign is no more. A poem *too* brief may produce a vivid, but never an intense or enduring impression. Without a certain continuity of effort — without a certain duration or repetition of purpose — the soul is never deeply moved. There must be the dropping of the water upon the

---

1   (1804–64) hugely influential American writer of short stories and novels.

rock. De Beranger[1] has wrought brilliant things — pungent and spirit-stirring — but, like all immassive bodies, they lack *momentum*, and thus fail to satisfy the Poetic Sentiment. They sparkle and excite, but, from want of continuity, fail deeply to impress. Extreme brevity will degenerate into epigrammatism; but the sin of extreme length is even more unpardonable. In *medio tutissimus ibis.*[2]

Were we called upon, however, to designate that class of composition which, next to such a poem as we have suggested, should best fulfil the demands of high genius — should offer it the most advantageous field of exertion — we should unhesitatingly speak of the prose tale, as Mr. Hawthorne has here exemplified it. We allude to the short prose narrative, requiring from a half-hour to one or two hours in its perusal. The ordinary novel is objectionable, from its length, for reasons already stated in substance. As it cannot be read at one sitting, it deprives itself, of course, of the immense force derivable from *totality*. Worldly interests intervening during the pauses of perusal, modify, annul, or counteract, in a greater or less degree, the impressions of the book. But simple cessation in reading, would, of itself, be sufficient to destroy the true unity. In the brief tale, however, the author is enabled to carry out the fulness of his intention, be it what it may. During the hour of perusal the soul of the reader is at the writer's control. There are no external or extrinsic influences — resulting from weariness or interruption.

A skilful literary artist has constructed a tale. If wise, he has not fashioned his thoughts to accommodate his incidents; but having conceived, with deliberate care, a certain unique or single *effect* to be wrought out, he then invents such incidents — he then combines such events as may best aid him in establishing this preconceived effect. If his very initial sentence tend not to the outbringing of this effect, then he has failed in his first step. In the whole composition there should be no word written, of which the tendency, direct or indirect, is not to the one pre-established design. And by such means, with such care and skill, a picture is at length painted which leaves in the mind of him who contemplates it with a kindred art, a sense of the fullest satisfaction. The idea of the tale has been presented unblemished, because undisturbed; and this is an end unattainable by the novel. Undue brevity is just as exceptionable here as in the poem; but undue length is yet more to be avoided.

---

1   Pierre-Jean de Béranger (1780–1857), French poet.

2   (Latin) You will go most safely in the middle (from the *Metamorphoses*, by the Roman writer Ovid [43 BC–AD 18]).

We have said that the tale has a point of superiority even over the poem. In fact, while the *rhythm* of this latter is an essential aid in the development of the poem's highest idea — the idea of the Beautiful — the artificialities of this rhythm are an inseparable bar to the development of all points of thought or expression which have their basis in *Truth*. But Truth is often, and in very great degree, the aim of the tale. Some of the finest tales are tales of ratiocination. Thus the field of this species of composition, if not in so elevated a region on the mountain of Mind, is a table-land of far vaster extent than the domain of the mere poem. Its products are never so rich, but infinitely more numerous, and more appreciable by the mass of mankind. The writer of the prose tale, in short, may bring to his theme a vast variety of modes or inflections of thought and expression — (the ratiocinative, for example, the sarcastic or the humorous) which are not only antagonistical to the nature of the poem, but absolutely forbidden by one of its most peculiar and indispensable adjuncts; we allude, of course, to rhythm. It may be added, here, *par parenthese*, that the author who aims at the purely beautiful in a prose tale is laboring at great disadvantage. For Beauty can be better treated in the poem. Not so with terror, or passion, or horror, or a multitude of such other points. And here it will be seen how full of prejudice are the usual animadversions against those *tales of effect*, many fine examples of which were found in the earlier numbers of Blackwood.[1] The impressions produced were wrought in a legitimate sphere of action, and constituted a legitimate although sometimes an exaggerated interest. They were relished by every man of genius: although there were found many men of genius who condemned them without just ground. The true critic will but demand that that the design intended be accomplished, to the fullest extent, by the means most advantageously applicable.

We have very few American tales of real merit — we may say, indeed, none, with the exception of "The Tales of a Traveller" of Washington Irving,[2] and these "Twice-Told Tales" of Mr. Hawthorne. Some of the pieces of Mr. John Neal[3] abound in vigor and originality; but in general his compositions of this class are excessively diffuse, extravagant, and indicative of an imperfect sentiment of Art. Articles at random are, now and then, met with in our periodicals which might be advantageously

---

1 *Blackwood's Edinburgh Magazine*, recognized as a major influence on Poe's own stories of terror.

2 (1783–1859) American author, now best known for his tales "Rip Van Winkle" and "The Legend of Sleepy Hollow."

3 American author (1793–1876).

compared with the best effusions of the British Magazines; but, upon the whole, we are far behind our progenitors in this department of literature.

Of Mr. Hawthorne's Tales we would say, emphatically, that they belong to the highest region of Art — and Art subservient to genius of a very lofty order. We had supposed, with good reason for so supposing, that he had been thrust into his present position by one of the impudent *cliques* which beset our literature, and whose pretensions it is our full purpose to expose at the earliest opportunity, but we have been most agreeably mistaken. We know of few compositions which the critic can more honestly commend than these "Twice-Told Tales." As Americans, we feel proud of the book.

Mr. Hawthorne's distinctive trait is invention, creation, imagination, originality — a trait which, in the literature of fiction, is positively worth all the rest. But the nature of originality, so far as regards its manifestation in letters, is but imperfectly understood. The inventive or original mind as frequently displays itself in novelty of *tone* as in novelty of matter. Mr. Hawthorne is original at *all* points....

Appendix B

Charles Dickens, from "Frauds on the Fairies" (1853)

[Charles Dickens (1812–70) is probably the best known short-story writer of the Victorian age. He was also a huge supporter of other writers of the same. In his well-known "Frauds on the Fairies," he critiques efforts by some people to impinge on the imagination and creativity of children's literature in the name of morality.]

We may assume that we are not singular in entertaining a very great tenderness for the fairy literature of our childhood. What enchanted us then, and is captivating a million of young fancies now, has, at the same blessed time of life, enchanted vast hosts of men and women who have done their long day's work, and laid their grey heads down to rest. It would be hard to estimate the amount of gentleness and mercy that has made its way among us through these slight channels. Forbearance, courtesy, consideration for the poor and aged, kind treatment of animals, the love of nature, abhorrence of tyranny and brute force — many such good things have been first nourished in the child's heart by this powerful aid. It has greatly helped to keep us, in some sense, ever young, by preserving through our worldly ways one slender track not overgrown with weeds, where we may walk with children, sharing their delights.

In an utilitarian age, of all other times, it is a matter of grave importance that Fairy tales should be respected. Our English red tape is too magnificently red ever to be employed in the tying up of such trifles, but every one who has considered the subject knows full well that a nation without fancy, without some romance, never did, never can, never will, hold a great place under the sun. The theatre, having done its worst to destroy these admirable fictions — and having in a most exemplary manner destroyed itself, its artists, and its audiences, in that perversion of its duty — it becomes doubly important that the little books themselves, nurseries of fancy as they are, should be preserved. To preserve them in their usefulness, they must be as much preserved in their simplicity, and purity, and innocent extravagance, as if they were actual fact. Whosoever alters them to suit his own opinions, whatever they are, is guilty, to our thinking, of an act of presumption, and appropriates to himself what does not belong to him.

We have lately observed, with pain, the intrusion of a Whole Hog of unwieldy dimensions into the fairy flower garden. The rooting of the animal among the roses would in itself have awakened in us nothing but indignation; our pain arises from his being violently driven in by a man of genius, our own beloved friend, Mr. George Cruikshank.[1] That incomparable artist is, of all men, the last who should lay his exquisite hand on fairy text. In his own art he understands it so perfectly, and illustrates it so beautifully, so humorously, so wisely, that he should never lay down his etching needle to "edit" the Ogre, to whom with that little instrument he can render such extraordinary justice. But, to "editing" Ogres, and Hop-o'-my-thumbs, and their families, our dear moralist has in a rash moment taken, as a means of propagating the doctrines of Total Abstinence, Prohibition of the sale of spirituous liquors, Free Trade, and Popular Education. For the introduction of these topics, he has altered the text of a fairy story; and against his right to do any such thing we protest with all our might and main....

Now, it makes not the least differences to our objection whether we agree or disagree with our worthy friend, Mr. Cruikshank, in the opinions he interpolates upon an old fairy story. Whether good or bad in themselves, they are, in that relation, like the famous definition of a weed; a thing growing up in a wrong place. He had no greater moral justification in altering the harmless little books than we should have in altering his best etchings. If such a precedent were followed we must soon become disgusted with the old stories into which modern personages so obtruded themselves, and the stories themselves must soon be lost. With seven Blue Beards[2] in the field, each coming at a gallop from his own platform mounted on a foaming hobby,[3] a generation or two hence would not know which was which, and the great original Blue Beard would be confounded with the counterfeits. Imagine a Total abstinence edition of

---

1   (1792–1878), political caricaturist and illustrator of books, including the Brothers Grimm's *Popular Stories* (1824–26); Daniel Defoe's *Robinson Crusoe* (first published in 1719) in 1831; and Dickens's own *Sketches by Boz* in 1836 and *Oliver Twist* in 1837.

2   "Blue Beard" was a popular tale, the oldest written version being in Charles Perrault's (1628–1703) *Histoiries et contes du temps passé* (1697), translated into English by Robert Samber as *Mother Goose Tales* (1729).

3   Hobby horse.

Robinson Crusoe, with the rum left out. Imagine a Peace edition, with the gunpowder left out, and the rum left in. Imagine a Vegetarian edition, with the goat's flesh left out. Imagine a Kentucky edition, to introduce a flogging of that 'tarnal old nigger Friday, twice a week. Imagine an Aborigines Protection Society edition, to deny the cannibalism and make Robinson embrace the amiable savages whenever they landed. Robinson Crusoe would be "edited" out of his island in a hundred years, and the island would be swallowed up in the editorial ocean....

Appendix C

*Margaret Oliphant, from "The ByWays of Literature:
Reading for the Million" (1858)*

[The Scottish writer Margaret Oliphant (1828–97) produced over 100 books over a number of decades. In the following essay, she argues that increased literacy had not resulted in increased morality, as many had hoped. The working class's "love of stories," she argues, reflects a preference for adventure and excitement over useful knowledge and moral instruction.]

… It is a fine thing to talk of the spread of education, the diffusion of knowledge, the constantly increasing extent of "reading for the million." If reading of itself were a virtuous and improving exercise, as innocent people once considered it, we too might echo the exultation with which a superficial sentiment regards the extending bulk of literature; but when we regard the matter with eyes less arbitrary, we are obliged to confess that it impresses us with a very doubtful satisfaction. True, these gifts of reading and writing are more likely to justify Dogberry's[1] conclusion in respect to them nowadays than ever before. True, every kind of publication has increased tenfold; and there is scarcely a house or a room in the country, down to the very boundary-line where poverty subsides into want, or rather where want meets destitution, in which something readable is not to be found. This is no small thing to say; and it is not wonderful that theorists, who take this simple fact for a foundation, should grow eloquent upon the diffusion of literature, and all its humanising influences. But reading is not always a humaniser; and it will scarcely do to pat our public on the head, as the old wives used to pat the cottage student of ten who scorched his flaxen hair by the fire o' nights, bent double over Captain Cook's *Voyages* or *Robinson Crusoe*.[2] Perhaps, after all, to be "fond of its

---

1   Character in Shakespeare's play *Much Ado about Nothing*. He makes the false assumption that, because Seacole can read and write, he will make a competent watchman.

2   James Cook (1728–79) wrote journals from which were compiled *An Account of a Voyage round the World* (1773) and other works. Daniel Defoe (1660–1731) wrote the popular *Robinson Crusoe* (1719).

book" is no such astonishing recommendation to our many-headed *pro-tegé* as one might suppose at the first glance — perhaps even a peep into the book which this big reader loves might not be inappropriate, before we give full course to our raptures. In the days when books were ponderous and readers few, it was only just to give the student credit for mental powers more active and more clear than those of his neighbours, who knew no intellectual appetite. Now, however, a stricter standard is necessary. There is abundance of reading in these days which requires no intellect: nay, we may go farther; to require no intellect is merely a negative; there are publications popular in this enlightened nineteenth century which reject the aid of mind more distinctly still — wastes of print, which nothing possessing intellect could venture on — wildernesses of words, where everything resembling sense is lost beyond description or recovery. Let us give the masses all credit for their gift of reading; but before we glorify ourselves over the march of intelligence, let us pause first to look into their books.

These unfortunate masses! When first the schoolmaster began to be abroad, how tenderly we took care of the improvement of their minds, and how zealously exerted ourselves to make literature a universal dominie,[1] graciously enlightening the neophyte on every subject under heaven! Does anybody remember now the Societies for the Diffusion of Knowledge — the Penny Magazines and Cyclopædias through which the streams of *useful* information fell benignly upon the lower orders? — how we laboured to bring ourselves down to the capacity of that unknown intelligence, the working man! — how we benevolently volunteered to amuse him in a profitable and edifying way, by histories and descriptions of the ingenious crafts, and nice accounts of how they make pins, and laces, and china, or how a steam-engine is put together! What a delightful ideal dwelt then in our inexperienced thoughts! Would any one have supposed that this intellectual creation, austerely brought up upon facts and figures, could ever own a guilty longing for stories, or verses, or other such amusements of a frivolous race? The idea was insulting to all our hopes and exertions; and when, by-and-by, the horrid numerals of a statistical account disclosed to us the fatal certainty that the multitude, like ourselves, loved amusement better than instruction — that working men, too, preferred *Guy Mannering*[2] to the *Novum Organum*,[3] and that

---

1   Schoolmaster, instructor.

2   Historical adventure novel (1815) by Sir Walter Scott (1771–1832).

3   (Latin) "New Instrument"; philosophical treatise (1620) by Francis Bacon (1561–1626).

Byron[1] was more to the purpose than Bacon[2] even in the library of a mechanics' institute — the chill of disappointed expectation consequent upon the discovery is not to be described. So the penny cyclopædias dropped one by one into oblivion, and nobody missed them; and lo, rushing into the empty space, the mushroom growth of a sudden impulse, rapid and multitudinous to meet the occasion, came springing up a host of penny magazines — spontaneous and natural publications, which professed no artificial mission, and aimed at no class-improvement, but were the simple supply of an existing demand — wares such as the customer wanted, and the market was suitable for. The Society for the Diffusion of Knowledge placed a wooden image of the most severe and edifying demeanour as the representative of literature to the multitude; but the multitude has avenged itself — here is the flesh and blood which has mounted upon the pedestal of useful information. Let us look at this natural index of the taste of the masses, and learn by their own assistance what that is which satisfies them best.

There are few words so difficult to define as that term literature, which is in everybody's mouth. To confine its meaning to that which we call literature, is about as exclusive and limited a notion as it is to confine that other term society to the fashionable world, which claims the name in sublime disdain of all competitors. Almost as numerous as the distinct "circles" which, upward to the highest *haut monde*,[3] and downwards to the genteelest coterie of a village, each calls itself by the all-comprehending name, are the widespread oligarchies and democracies of that Republic of Letters, which, like most other republics, claims throughout its ranks a noisy equality, pleasantly varied by the arrogance of individual despotisms. Let us not delude ourselves with the idea that literature is fully represented by that small central body of its forces of whom everybody knows every individual name. Nay, not everybody — only everybody who is anybody — not the everybody who reads the *London Journal* and the *Family Herald*. That eminent group, with which we at least do ourselves the credit to claim acquaintance, are only the chance oligarchs who stand up head and shoulders above the mass of their co-aspirants — whom, by virtue of that accident of stature, other countries see over our cliffs and channels, whom above a certain level of society it is impossible to avoid seeing — nay, even necessary and inevitable to know something of — and

---

1   George Gordon, Lord Byron (1788–1824), Romantic poet.

2   Francis Bacon (1561–1626), philosopher and politician.

3   (French) upper class.

whose works are forming the last ring in that big old tree called English literature. But it matters very little to the people in the valley whether a man stands on the top of the hill or only on the side of it — nay, for all their purposes, the lowest slope, being nearest, is the best; and so in the underground, quite out of sight and ken of the heroes, spreads thick and darkly an undiscriminated multitude — undiscriminated by the critics, by the authorities, by the general vision, but widely visible to individual eyes, to admiring coteries, and multitudinous lower classes, who buy, and read, and praise, and encourage, and, under the veil of their own obscurity, bestow a certain singular low-lying Jack-o'-lantern[1] celebrity, which nobody out of these regions is aware of, and which is the oddest travestie and paraphrase of fame. Some of these are religious writers, who perhaps of all others address the largest and most mixed community; some are eccentrics, moving in queer corners of their own, with a snug little audience close about them, and a little set of doctrines, arguments, and quarrels, "haill o' my ain, and nane o' my neighbours," which grow into the most magnificent grandiloquence of proportions by dint of being contemplated without intermission and very close at hand; and some are neither eccentric nor religious, neither witty nor eloquent, neither political nor philanthropical, but simply and solely the weekly amusers of that multitudinous public which opens its own mind to us, all unawares and unconsciously, by means of those penny papers — not one of which says a syllable about the manners or likings of its audience, in the way of description, but which, every one, help us to the geography of that strange region where such things as themselves can grow and flourish.

Perhaps for mere amusement, the periodical eccentrics of literature, the writers, vehemently inspired with "an object," and continually straining their eyes upon that to the exclusion of all the world beside, are the most inviting; but we will not be tempted aside, in the first place at least, even by the virtuous earnestness of *Notes and Queries*,[2] or the sublime and absorbed devotion of the *Ecclesiologist*.[3] These illustrate a very patent and unquestionable truth — which is, that a very small matter, placed close before an average pair of human eyes, and gazed at zealously and without intermission, will very soon eclipse the very mountains and seas in magnitude, and throw its shadow upon both earth and heaven. But we find a larger, a less comprehensible, and a more important field

---

1   Mischievous, momentary.

2   Periodical, founded in 1849, focussing on literature, art, and science.

3   Christian periodical, founded in 1841.

in the periodicals printed and published for the amusement of the many, without either object or mission separate from this. We should be afraid to pretend to know even the titles of all these distinguished serials — still less could we presumptuously venture to assume an acquaintance with the gifted contributors who secure their popularity; but the general aspect of these publications is certainly as different as can be conceived from the penny cyclopædias. *Their* useful information is like Falstaff's[1] halfpennyworth of bread; the amount of sack[2] — which, however, is not sack, but that poor creature small-beer[3] — is quite preposterous and intolerable. There are stories to begin with, stories to end with, and stories in the middle. Two serial tales, continued from week to week, is a moderate allowance for one of those twelve-page broadsheets; and even the little make-weights of history with which some of them ballast their lighter wares, have to be enlivened by an anecdote or a melodramatic scene. One can perceive pretty well at a glance that it is not instruction which the multitude demands most loudly, and that the popular mind does not by nature incline towards philosophy, even should it be the philosophy of the steam-engine, for the relaxation of its leisure hours. No; one genuine natural appetite, at least, if nothing more, displays itself most prominently in this "reading for the million." It is that love of stories which distinguishes all primitive minds, and which has its strongest development in savages and children. No disparagement to our friends of the multitude. They, too, share with the children and the savages a certain absolute and first-hand contact with things and facts, which throws out philosophy. Events great and grievous come upon them as upon their social superiors; but necessity thrusts them on without the lingering which we have time to make over our graves and shipwrecks. They have to gulp down their sob in the midst of the common work, which, by the compensation of Providence, is the best practical consoler; and with always the first absolute need of nature before them — the necessity to earn their daily bread — live, and are constrained to live a life outside of themselves — not of contemplation, but of activity. So it comes about that these labouring multitudes stand somewhat in the same position as, perhaps, the very knights of romance held four or five hundred years ago. It is not that they differ in natural intelligence from the classes above them; it is

---

1   Character in Shakespeare's *Henry IV*, *Henry V*, and *Merry Wives of Windsor*, characterized by poor quality and disorder.

2   Worthy material (but also a type of wine; thus the reference to "small-beer").

3   Something insignificant.

not that the delf[1] is duller than the porcelain; it is only that we have got so many centuries ahead by dint of our exemption from manual labours and necessities. They are still among the dragons and the giants, where hard hands and strength of arm are more in demand than thoughts and fancies. We have gained the thoughtful ways of civilisation, when we smile at Archimage,[2] and find St. George's hideous adversary a fabulous creation. Our leisure accordingly plays with all fancies, all inventions — all matters of thought and reason; whereas their leisure, brief and rapid, and sharpened with the day's fatigue, loves, above all things, a story, and finds in that just the amount of mental excitation which makes it somehow a semi-intellectual pleasure. For it is a story, for the story's sake; not a story because it is a good story — a work of genius — a revelation of nature. The simple practical mind is a great deal more absolute than that. Merit is quite a secondary consideration; it is the narrative which is the thing. What does a child care for the probabilities of fiction, for the wit of dialogue, or the grace of style? It is likely they bore him, detaining as they do the current of events with which his interest is linked; and though we will not say quite so much as this for the liking of the multitude, yet the principle is the same. It is the tale which is wanted; give but that, and the qualities of mind concerned in its production are quite a secondary consideration. The characters may be the merest puppets of wood; the springs of the machinery may betray themselves at every movement; the language may be absurd, the invention miserable; yet if it is a story, it will give a certain amount of pleasure to the dormant intelligences: nay, intelligences not dormant, bright enough in their own fashion, possibly a great deal cleverer than the story-teller, answer to the natural fascination.

This principle of mind is just what the societies for the diffusion of knowledge did not find out, and which we fear even the philanthropist of the day, who does popular lectures, persists in ignoring. People working face to face with the primitive powers — people in whose understanding poverty does not mean a smaller house, or fewer servants, or a difficulty about one's butcher's bill, but means real hunger, cold, and nakedness, are not people to be amused with abstractions. And it has often occurred to ourselves, that were all these benevolent, noble, right honourable, and dis-

---

1 Delftware, pottery made in Delft, Holland.

2 In Edmund Spenser's (c. 1552–99) *The Faerie Queene* (1590–96), the character Archimago symbolizes hypocrisy and is defeated in combat by the Redcrosse Knight (St. George, the patron saint of England).

tinguished lecturers to be replaced by so many minstrels of the antique
strain, yet of a modern fashion — men with stories on their lips, fresh,
new, and living — not stories written in books which anybody can read
who has a mind — that the effect would be something quite beyond our
modern calm and even level of interest. It has pleased one of our great novelists in recent days to read certain stories of his own to an elegant and
refined public, most of whom had read them before, and went to look at
the author with purely unexcited and philosophical minds. We presume
the audience had what they wanted, and were satisfied; and so probably
had the distinguished writer, reader, and actor, who made this entertainment for their benefit; yet after all, though it is becoming common,
it is not the most dignified meeting this between the story-teller and his
auditory. The relations between them are changed for the time, and not
agreeably changed. Somehow it seems a sin against good taste and the ret-
icence of genius, that the writer, with his own voice, should bring out and
emphasize those "points" already singled out by popular approbation,
which are sure to "bring down the house." It is altogether different with
the actor, whose personal triumph has a certain generous admixture of satisfaction in the growth of another's fame. One cannot but feel a certain
pleasure in knowing that Shakespeare was no more fit for the part of
Hamlet than we are, and could only do an awkward ghost when necessity urged him; and we confess we do not see what advantage, save the satisfaction of a perfectly unelevated curiosity, is to be gained by hearing from
the lips of its author a well-known tale which we have all read already, and
can read again to-morrow without trouble to anybody. But let the story-
teller bring us a tale fresh from his own conception, and unfamiliar to the
world, and the circumstances are changed. It is possible even that this
might be the "something new" after which this fatigued capital toils with
perseverance so praiseworthy. Suppose Mr. Thackeray[1] and Mr. Dickens,[2]
instead of monthly numbers yellow and green, had a monthly assembly,
and gave forth the story to a visible public, moved by all the visible emotions over which these magicians exercise their subtle power, — would not
that be an experiment sufficient to reinvigorate with all its pristine force
the flagging serial — possibly even by the prompt criticism of the audience to bestow a certain benefit upon the tale? And even if an attempt on
such a great scale were impracticable, what should hinder us from getting
our Christmas stories at first hand, before print had yet made them

---

1   William Makepeace Thackeray (1811–63), author of short stories and novels.

2   Charles Dickens (1812–70), author. See headnote to his short story in this collection.

common, or criticism breathed upon their virginal fair fame? But however that may be, there can be little question that the most practicable mental agent upon the masses, in their present condition of superficial intelligence, is the art of story-telling — whether true lives of true men, or simple fiction, matters little. A genuine story, rapid, clear, and intelligible, something in modern guise like the old ballad-stories which are the true beginning everywhere of literature for the people, would tell a hundred times better than the prettiest essay ever delivered — better, too, than even an old story of the highest fame, read to the humble audience by their volunteer teacher; for our friends are touchy — as ready to take offence as any knight of the middle ages, and might suspect a covert imputation upon their own knowledge and discrimination, if some one offered to read to them a book which they could read for themselves. No; give the people stories if you love them — narratives fresh, original, and unprinted — and the people will listen once more as their ancestors listened to "Chevy Chase"[1] and "Otterbourne."[2]

Every single page of our sixpenny-worth of periodicals proves more strongly this natural taste; and now it is about time that we should see what the manner of these stories is. In the first place, they have one particular and marked distinction — they are not of the class of those multitudinous tales which the art of criticism once patronised, and now extinguishes; the fiction feminine, which fills with mild domestic volumes the middle class of this species of literature. The lowest range, like the highest range, admits no women. We cannot take it upon us to say what this fact teaches, or if it teaches anything; but it is curious enough as a distinction. And if any one supposes that here, in this special branch of literature provided for the multitude, anything about the said multitude is to be found, a more entire mistake could not be imagined. It is only the higher classes who can find a hero in a tailor, or amuse themselves with the details of a workman's household and economy. An Alton Locke[3] may find a countess to fall in love with him, but is no hero for the sempstress, who makes her romance out of quite different materials; and whereas we can please ourselves with *Mary Barton*,[4] our poor neighbours share no such

---

1   "The Ballad of Chevy Chase," English ballad with versions as far back as the fifteenth century.

2   "The Battle of Otterbourne," English ballad included in Thomas Percy's (1729–1811) *Reliques of Ancient English Poetry* (1765).

3   Main character of Charles Kingsley's (1819–75) *Alton Locke* (1850), about the struggles and miseries of the working classes.

4   Novel (1848) by Elizabeth Gaskell (1810–65) about poverty and unemployment in contemporary England.

humble taste, but luxuriate in ineffable splendours of architecture and upholstery, and love to concern themselves with the romantic fortunes of a Gertrude de Brent and a Gerald St. Maur. No kindly cottage interior, or home of their own rank, opens to this class of readers that kind of gratification which we are so much disposed to accept as the chief charm of imaginative literature. It is not because their own trials are shadowed — their own sentiments expressed — their own life illustrated by the fictitious representation before them, that our humble friends love their weekly story-telling. When the future historian of this century seeks information about the life and manners of our poorer classes, he will find no kind of popular print so entirely destitute of the details he seeks as those penny miscellanies which are solely read by the poor, yet are full of tales about the rich....

... When you find instances of heroism, of self denial, of noble truth and virtue, among the poor, as, let us thank Heaven, such instances abound, tell them to the rich. But let your palette be splendid with all the colours of the rainbow, and fill the treasury of your imagination with the wealth of the Rothschilds[1] and the blood of the Howards,[2] when you wish to fix the interest and gain the attention of the crowd!

So, at least, says the crowd itself, in its unconscious testimony, through the publications it delights to honour.

The paper from which we have already quoted [*Cassell's Illustrated Paper*] has the orthodox allowance of two weekly stories — "to be continued" — and two others, complete in themselves, and professing to be incidents from history. The amount of ballast is greater than usual, and of a highly instructive character– beginning under the title of "Hopes and Helps for the Young," with a small prelection upon — of all subjects in the world — Public Speaking! and rules for the successful performance of the same. This is followed by French lessons, and lessons in Natural Philosophy — the art of oratory being, as it appears, as needful and instructive an exercise for the young of these latitudes, as it is to learn that *un homme* signifies a man, or what is the meaning of centrifugal force. Then there is an article upon the city and principles of Mormonism,[3] and another upon Ragged Schools,[4] where we are told that the name of the Earl of Shaftesbury[5]

---

1   Jewish, German family who became famous for their wealth arising, beginning in the late eighteenth century, from the business of international banking.

2   English family with a centuries-long lineage connected to royalty.

3   Religious doctrine of the Mormons, a Christian group founded in 1830.

4   Free schools intended for the poorest of children.

5   Anthony Shaftesbury, third earl of (1671–1713), philosopher of ethics and aesthetics.

> "Comes like the south wind o'er a bank of violets,
> Stealing and giving odours;"

by which means we get to the Facetiæ[1] at the end, and the page of Answers to Correspondents, which form so strange a feature in periodicals of this class. The *London Journal* is less edifying; but then it has the lofty purpose of acquainting its readers with works of higher character than are to be had nowadays; and so, besides the one superfine story with which its pages open, this serial dispenses in weekly portions the tale of *Kenilworth*[2] to its multitudinous readers; thus showing not only a praiseworthy desire to introduce into these regions the best literature, but a wise discrimination in the choice of its first venture — for Sir Walter is rarely so "thrilling" as in this beautiful romance. *Reynolds' Miscellany*, we are given to understand, is rather unorthodox and disrespectable, though we cannot say that we perceive any particular difference between it and its compeers, the stories being as fine, the personages as lofty, and the events as tragical as in other individuals of the fraternity. The *Home Magazine* is melodramatic and thrilling, dealing with dukes and lazzaroni[3] and Spanish cavaliers, with startling headings to its many chapters, such as the "Midnight Visitor," and the "Father's Fearful Vow!" The *Family Herald* is blandly narrative and story-telling, with a mixture of the fine, the thrilling, and, for a wonder, the domestic. Last of all comes a new experiment, which, perhaps, does not mean to address itself exclusively to the multitude — the *Welcome Guest* — a publication which propitiated many people who may never see its pages by a witty and clever prospectus, and which is, without doubt, quite above the level of its competitors. So much for our sixpenny-worth. For this small amount of capital we have eight complete original tales, and portions of eleven others — serial, and "to be continued" — not to speak of a couple of chapters of *Kenilworth*, and as many of the German novel *Debit and Credit*,[4] which is somewhat shabbily made the leading attraction of the *Welcome Guest*. Here is quantity at all events, if not quality; one-and-twenty stories, or parts of stories, for sixpence! Who would not expend that gracious minature[5] of her Majesty for such a budget of amusement? Who would not willingly encourage literature at so modest a cost?...

---

1   (Latin) amusing jest.

2   Novel (1821) by Sir Walter Scott (1771–1832).

3   Term (originating in Naples) referring both to those in dire poverty and to those who make their living by begging and occasional labour.

4   Extremely successful novel (1858) by Gustav Freytag (1816–95).

5   Miniature, referring to the small portrait of Queen Victoria on the sixpence coin.

We have not touched upon a half, or indeed a tenth part, of that reading for the million which has become so multitudinous. We have not even attempted to notice the countless swarms of serial stories, separate publications issued like the magazines in weekly numbers, printed on the worst paper, with the worst type and poorest illustrations of which the arts are capable, which, we believe, are about as popular as the periodicals themselves; — these are bought by the very poorest classes, but they are by no means *cheap* literature, though the weekly pennyworth, we presume, persuades these humble readers into supposing so — nor the penny papers, which, though bought by everybody, undoubtedly address themselves to the multitude. But, upon the whole, it is not with a very lofty opinion of the multitude that we turn from our inspection of their peculiar literature. The apologists and the assailants of this large portion of the community have equally ignored the fact, that it is a varied and fluctuating mass, as uncertain and changeable as any other class of the community, acted upon by peculiar and not very favourable circumstances, but acting with the same fickleness, short-sightedness, and inconsistency which rule over everybody else, that forms the lower order and basis of our commonweal.[1] They are not to be kept in perpetual lecturedom any more than we are; they are not inspired by a heroical antipathy to their betters, nor possessed with an incurable political fever like model Chartists[2] in novels; neither do they surpass their neighbours in honesty, sincerity, and single-mindedness, as some of us would have the world to suppose. Circumstances alone distinguish them, as it is circumstances which distinguish the other extreme of society. Some of these we have already pointed out. A life which has to be lived in the face of hard practical difficulties, and under the constant pressure of manual toil — an acquaintance with the world necessarily limited and narrow, and destitute of those experiences which force many men, no wiser by nature, into a more just estimate of themselves — education which, in most cases, cannot choose but be superficial, and which, striving with vain emulation over the widest area, drops the quality of depth altogether; all these accidents of their condition give colour to the character of the masses, and are faithfully reflected in the literature they patronise. For these reasons it is that political nostrums, warranted, by one arbitrary Act of Parliament, to cure everything, find ready acceptance among them. Their limited opportunities of observation have a constant effect of youth upon the whole class,

---

1   Commonwealth; the prosperity and well-being of a community.

2   Group of people in Britain working for social and electoral reform in the 1830s and 1840s.

and confer upon them all a certain class inconsequence and want of logic, which everybody must have perceived one time or another — a propensity to blame somebody for every grievance or hardship they experience, and to expect perfectly unreasonable results from every exercise of that power which they do not possess; — all these impatient qualities of mind forbid patient reading, or a modest complexion of literature; and we find, accordingly, that the merest and slightest amusement overbalances, to the most prodigious extent, everything else attempted by this reading for the million. As a general principle, they have no leisure to concern themselves with those problems of common life which all the philosophers in the world cannot solve, nor to consider those hard conditions of existence under which they and we and all the race labour on towards the restoration of all things. It is much easier to conclude that something arbitrary can mend all, and to escape out of the real difficulties into those fictitious regions of delight, where every difficulty is made to be smoothed away — those superlative and dazzling regions of wealth and eminence, where, to the hard-labouring and poverty-pinched, it is hard to explain where the shadows lie.

Whether the existing literature of the multitude is improbable, we will not take upon us to say; but certainly no one ever will improve it efficiently without taking into full account all the class-characteristics which have helped it into being. Once we were deeply impressed with the idea that to reach this class most effectually, one needed to enter into their own life, and make them aware of one's thorough acquaintance and familiarity not from a "superior" elevation, but on the same level with the everyday circumstances of their existence. Now our opinion is changed; we trust we have too much candour of mind to hold by our theory in the face of so many demonstrations to the contrary. No; let us change our tactics. The masses find no heroes among themselves; it is easy to do a little vapouring on the subject of aristocracy, and maintain against all the masters and all the rulers, natural antagonists of this perennial youth of civilisation, the innate superiority of the working man. But somehow a much more subtle evidence remains against him. No hero labouring with his own hands, no household maintaining its humble honour on the week's wages, no serving maiden, fair in her homely duties, conciliates in their own chosen medium of story-telling the favour of the multitude. The workman is no hero to the shop-girl, nor the poor seamstress to the workman — so the real hero dashes forward in his cab, and the true heroine tells her footman where the carriage is to meet her — and the one has five thousand a-year, and unlimited possibilities, while the other is troubled with the shadow of a coronet — and they talk of Shakespeare and the musical glasses, and see no end of fine society; and the penny magazine which contains their history circulates so widely that it has to go to press three weeks before the day of publication — and so, with a triumphant demonstration not to be disputed, we learn the likings of the multitude....

Appendix D

Frederick Wedmore, "The Short Story" (1898)

[Frederick Wedmore (1844–1921) was a short-story writer and reviewer. In the following piece, Wedmore's description of the short story demonstrates that what has often been seen as a modernist notion of the genre was a familiar model in nineteenth-century Britain. At the same time, he acknowledges a variety of other types of short prose worthy of attention.]

One of the most engaging of the wits of our day wrote lately in a weekly newspaper that it is, for the most part, only those who are not good enough actors to act successfully in life who are compelled to act at the theatre. Under the influence of such an amiable paradox it is possible that we may ask ourselves, in regard to story-writing, whether the people singled out to practise it are those, chiefly, to whose personal history Romance has been denied: so that the greatest qualification even for the production of a lady's love-tale, is — that the lady shall never have experienced a love-affair. Eminent precedents might be cited in support of the contention. A great editor once comfortably declared that the ideal journalist was a writer who did not know too much about his subject. The public did not want much knowledge, he said. The literary criticism in your paper would be perfect if you handed it over to the critic of Music; and the musical criticism would want for nothing if you assigned it to an expert in Art. And Mr. Thackeray,[1] speaking of love-tales, said something that pointed the same way. He protested, no one should write a love-story after he was fifty. And why? Because he knew too much about it.

But it was a personal application I was going to have given to the statement with which this paper begins. If the actor we see upon the boards be only there because more capable comedians fill the stage of the world, I am presumably invited by the editor of this Review to hold forth on the short story because I am not a popular writer. The editor, in the

---

1   William Makepeace Thackeray (1811–63), novelist and short-story writer.

gentle exercise of his humour, bids me to fill the place which should be filled by the man of countless editions. It is true that in the matter of short stories, such a writer is not easy to find; and this too at a time when, if one is correctly informed, full many a lady, not of necessity of any remarkable gifts, maintains an honourable independence by the annual production of an improper novel. Small as my personal claims might be, were they based only on my books — *Renunciations*, for example, or *Pastorals of France* — I may say my say as one who, with production somewhat scanty, has for twenty years been profoundly interested in the artistic treatment of the Short Story; who believes in the short story, not as a ready means of hitting the big public, but as a medium for the exercise of the finer art — as a medium, moreover, adapted peculiarly to that alert intelligence, on the part of the reader, which rebels sometimes at the *longueurs*[1] of the conventional novel: the old three volumes or the new fat book. Nothing is so mysterious, for nothing is so instinctive, as the method of a writer. I cannot communicate the incommunicable. But at all events I will not express opinions aimed at the approval of the moment: convictions based on the necessity for epigram.

In the first place, then, what is, and what is *not*, a short story? Many things a short story may be. It may be an episode, like Miss Ella Hepworth Dixon's or like Miss Bertha Thomas's; a fairy tale, like Miss Evelyn Sharp's; the presentation of a single character with the stage to himself (Mr. George Gissing); a tale of the uncanny (Mr. Rudyard Kipling); a dialogue of comedy (Mr. Pett Ridge);[2] a panorama of selected landscape, a vision of the sordid street, a record of heroism, a remote tradition or an old belief vitalised by its bearing on our lives to-day, an analysis of an obscure calling, a glimpse at a forgotten quarter. A short story — I mean a short imaginative work in the difficult medium of prose; for plot, or story proper, is no essential part of it, though in work like Conan Doyle's[3] or Rudyard Kipling's it may be a very delightful part — a short story may be any one of the things that have been named, or it may be something besides; but one thing it can never be — it can never be 'a novel in a nutshell.' That is a favourite definition, but not a definition that holds. It is a definition for the kind of public that asks for a convenient inexactness,

---

1   (French) long, tiresome sections of writing.

2   Late-Victorian writers of short stories, although they are also known for work in other genres. Works by Sharp and Kipling are included in this collection.

3   Arthur Conan Doyle (1859–1930), author best known for inventing "Sherlock Holmes." See headnote to his story in this anthology.

and resents the subtlety which is inseparable from precise truth. Writers and serious readers know that a good short story cannot possibly be a *précis*, a synopsis, a *scenario*, as it were, of a novel. It is a separate thing — as separate, almost, as the Sonnet is from the Epic — it involves the exercise almost of a different art.

That, perhaps, is one reason why it is generally — in spite of temporary vogue as pleasant pastime — a little underrated as an intellectual performance. That is why great novelists succeed in it so seldom — or at all events fail in it sometimes   even great novelists like Mr. Hardy,[1] the stretch of whose canvas has never led him into carelessness of detail. Yet with *him*, even, in his short stories, the inequality is greater than befits the work of such an artist, and greater than is to be accounted for wholly by mood; so that by the side of *The Three Strangers*, or, yet better, that delightful thing, the *Interlopers at the Knap*, you have short tales tossed off with momentary indifference — as you can imagine Sheridan,[2] with his braced language of comedy, stooping once to a charade. And if a *master* nods sometimes — a master like Hardy — does it not almost follow that, by the public at least, the conditions of the short story are not understood, and so, in the estimate of the criticism of the dinner-table, and by the criticism of the academic, the tale is made to suffer by its brevity? But if it is well done, it has done this amazing thing: it has become quintessence; it has eliminated the superfluous; and it has taken *time* to be brief. Then — amongst readers whose judgments are perfunctory — who have not thought the thing out — it is rewarded by being spoken of as an 'agreeable sketch,' 'a promising little effort,' an 'earnest of better things.' So — not to talk of any other instance — one imagines the big public rewarding the completed charm of *The Author of Beltraffio* and of *A Day of Days*, though pregnant *brevity* is not generally Mr. Henry James's[3] strength. And then Mr. James works away at the long novel, and, of course, is clever in it, because with him, *not* to be clever might require more than American passiveness. Very good; but I go back from the record of all that 'Maisie'[4] ought not to have known to *The Author of Beltraffio* and to *A Day of Days* — 'promising little efforts,' 'earnests of better things.'

---

1   Thomas Hardy (1840–1928), author. See headnote to his story in this collection.

2   Richard Sheridan (1751–1816), dramatist best known for his comic plays.

3   (1843–1916), American-born author who lived extensively in England and wrote a number of short stories and novels analysing English character.

4   Allusion to Henry James's novel *What Maisie Knew* (1897).

Well, then, the Short Story is wont to be estimated, not by its quality, but by its size, a mode of appraisement under which the passion of Schumann,[1] with his wistful questionings — in *Warum*, say or in *Der Dichter spricht* — would be esteemed less seriously than the amiable score of *Maritana!*[2] And a dry point by Mr. Whistler,[3] two dozen lines laid with the last refinement of charm, would be held inferior to a panorama by Phillopoteau,[4] or to the backgrounds of the contemporary theatre. One would have thought that this was obvious. But in our latest stage of civilisation it is sometimes only the obvious that requires to be pointed out.

While we are upon the subject of hindrances to the appreciation of this particular form of imaginative work, we may remind ourselves of one drawback in regard to which the short story must make common cause with the voluminous novel: I mean the inability of the mass of readers to do justice to the seriousness of any artistic, as opposed to any moral, or political, or pretentiously regenerative fiction. For the man in the street, for the inhabitant of Peckham Rye, for many prosperous people on the north side of the Park, perhaps even for the very cream of up-to-date persons whose duty it is to abide somewhere where Knightsbridge melts invisibly into Chelsea,[5] Fiction is but a *délassement*,[6] and the artists who practise it, in its higher forms, are a little apt to be estimated as contributors to public entertainment — like the Carangeot Troupe, and Alexia, at the Palace Theatre. The view is something of *this* nature — I read it so expressed only the other day: 'The tired clergyman, after a day's work; what book shall he take up? Fiction, perhaps, would seem too trivial; history, too solid.'

The serious writer of novel or short story brings no balm for the 'tired clergyman' — other than such balm as is afforded by the delight of serious Art. At high tension he has delivered himself of his performance, and if his work is to be properly enjoyed, it must be met by those only who are ready to receive it; it must be met by the alert, not the fatigued, reader; and with the short story in particular, with its omissions, with the

---

1 Robert Schumann (1810–56), German composer of the Romantic Movement.

2 Opera (1845) by William Vincent Wallace (1812–65).

3 James Abbott McNeill Whistler (1834–1903), American painter who worked extensively in London and Paris, known for his minimalist style and attention to form and line.

4 Paul Philippoteaux (1846–1923), French painter of panoramas and cycloramas (the latter being canvases arranged in a full circle with the viewer standing inside).

5 These locations are meant to describe a cross-section of the public from various classes.

6 (French) relaxation; pastime.

brevity of its allusiveness, it must be met half way. Do not let us expect it to be 'solid,' like Mill, or Lightfoot, or Westcott[1] — or even like A.B.C. Railway Guides. You must condone the 'triviality' which put its finger on the pulse of life and says, 'Thou ailest *here* and *here*' — which exposes, not a political movement, like the historian of the outward fact, but the secrets of the heart, rather, and human weakness, and the courage which in strait places comes somehow to the sons of men, and the beauty and the strength of affection — and which does this by intuition as much as by science.

But to go back to considerations not common in some degree to all Fiction, but proper more absolutely to the Short Story. I have suggested briefly what the short story may be; we have seen briefly the one thing it *cannot* be — which is, a novel told within restricted space. Let us ask what methods it may adopt — what are some of the varieties of its form.

The Short Story admits of greater variety of form than does the long novel, and the number of these forms will be found to be increasing — and we must not reject conventionally (as we are terribly apt to do) the new form because we are unfamiliar with it. The forms that are open to the novel are open to the short imaginative piece, and, to boot, very many besides. Common to both, of course, is the most customary form of all — that in which the writer narrates as from outside the drama, yet with internal knowledge of it — what is called the 'narrative form,' which includes within its compass, in a single work, narrative proper and a moderate share of dialogue. Common again to both short and long stories, obviously, is a form which, in skilled hands, and used only for those subjects to which it is most appropriate, may give strange reality to the matter presented — the form, I mean, in which the story is told in the first person, as the experience and the sentiment of one character who runs throughout the whole. The short story, though it should use this form very charily, adopts it more conveniently than does the long novel; for the novel has many more characters than the short story, and for the impartial presentation of many characters this form is a fetter. It gives of a large group a prejudiced and partial view. It commended itself once or twice only to Dickens.[2] *David Copperfield* is the conspicuous example. Never once, I think, did it commend itself to Balzac.[3] It is better adapted, no doubt, to

1   John Stuart Mill (1806–73), political philosopher; John Lightfoot (1602–75), biblical scholar; possibly Brooke Foss Westcott (1825–1901), Regius Professor of Divinity at Cambridge University as of 1870.

2   Charles Dickens (1812–70), author. See headnote to his story in this collection.

3   Honoré de Balzac (1799–1850), French novelist. His *Human Comedy* consisted of more than 90 novels and short stories that captured the realities of middle-class life in his time.

adventure, than to analysis, and better to the expression of humour than to the realisation of tragedy. As far as the presentation of *character* is concerned, what it is usual for it to achieve — in hands, I mean, much smaller than those of the great Dickens — is this: a life size, full length, generally too flattering portrait of the hero of the story — a personage who has the limelight all to himself — on whom no inconvenient shallows are ever thrown — the hero as beheld by Sant,[1] shall I say? rather than as beheld by Sargent[2] — and then a further graceful idealisation, an attractive pastel, you may call it, the lady he most frequently admired, and, of the remainder, two or three Kit-Cat portraits,[3] a head and shoulders here, and there a stray face.

The third and only other form that I can call to mind as common to both novel and short story, though not equally *convenient* to both, is the rare form of Letters. That again, like any other that will not bear a prolonged strain, is oftener available for short story than for big romance. The most consummate instance of its employment, in very lengthy work, is one in which with slow progression it serves above all things the purpose of minute and searching analysis — I have named the book in this line of description of it: I have named *Clarissa*.[4] For the short story it is used very happily by Balzac — who, though not at first a master of sentences, is an instinctive master of methods — it is used by him in the *Mémoires de Deux Jeunes Mariées*. And in a much lighter way, of bright portraiture, of neat characterisation, it is used by an ingenious, sometimes seductive, writer of our period, Marcel Prévost,[5] in *Lettres de Femmes*. It is possible, of course, to *mix* these different forms; but for such mixture we shall conclude, I fancy, that prolonged fiction offers the best opportunity. Such mixture has its dangers for the short story; you risk, perhaps, unity of effect. But there are short stories in which monotony is avoided, and the force of the narrative in reality emphasised, by some telling lines from a letter, whose end or whose beginning may be otherwise imparted to us.

I devote a few lines to but two or three of the forms which by common consent are for the short story only. One of them is simple dialogue. For

---

1   James Sant (1820–1916), popular portraitist.

2   John Singer Sargent (1856–1925), portrait painter known for his ability to capture his sitter's personality.

3   A portrait that is less than full length but includes the sitter's hands.

4   Eight-volume novel (1748–49) by Samuel Richardson (1689–1761).

5   (1862–1941), French novelist.

our generation, that has had the fascination of an experiment — an experiment made perhaps with best success after all in the candid and brilliant fragments of that genuine humorist, Mr. Pett Ridge. The method in most hands has the appearance of a difficult feat. It *is* one often — and so is walking on the slack-wire, and the back-spring in acrobatic dance. Of course a writer must enjoy grappling with difficulties. We understand that. But the more serious artist reflects, after a while, that the unnecessary difficulty is an inartistic encumbrance. 'Why,' he will ask, 'should the story-teller put on himself the fetters of the drama, to be denied the drama's opportunities?' Pure dialogue, we may be sure, is apt to be an inefficient means of telling a story; of presenting a character. There may be cited one great English Classic who has employed the method — the author of *Pericles and Aspasia*, of that little gem of conversation between Henry the Eighth and Anne Boleyn. But then, with Walter Savage Landor,[1] austere and perfect, the character existed already, and there was no story to tell. Pure dialogue, under the conditions of the modern writer, leaves almost necessarily the problem unsolved, the work a fragment. It can scarcely be a means to an end; though it may, if we like, be a permissible little end in itself, a little social chatter, pitched in a high key, in which one has known tartness to be mistaken for wit. Thus does 'Gyp'[2] skim airily over the deep, great sea of life. All are shallows to her vision. And as she skims you feel her lightness. I prefer the adventure of the diver, who knows what the depths *are*, who plunges, and who rescues the pearl.

Then, again, possible, though not often desirable for the short story, is the diary form — extracts from a diary, rather. Applied to work on an extensive scale, your result — since you would necessarily lack concentrated theme — your result would be a chronicle, not a story. Applied to the shorter fiction, it must be used charily, and may then, I should suppose, be used well. But I, who used the form in 'The New Marienbad Elegy' in *English Episodes*, what right have I to say that the form, in the hands of a master, allows a subtle presentation of the character of the diarist — allows, in self-revelation, an irony, along with earnestness, a wayward and involved humour, not excluding sympathy? It is a form not easily received, not suffered gladly. It is for the industrious, who read a good thing twice, and for the enlightened, who read it three times.

---

1   (1775–1864), English poet.

2   Pseudonym for Gabrielle de Mirabeau, Comtesse de Martel de Janville (1850–1932), French author.

I throw out these things only as hints; we may apply them where we will, as we think about stories. But something has yet to be said. Of the two forms already named as generally unfitted for the long novel, and fitted only now and again for the short story, one, it will be noticed, is all dialogue; the other, necessarily, a form in which there is no dialogue at all. And I think we find, upon reflection, the lighter work leans oftenest on the one form; the graver work leans oftenest on the other.

Indeed, from this we might go on to notice that as far as the short story is concerned, most of the finer and more lasting work, though cast in forms which quite *permit* of the dialogue, has, as a matter of fact, but little dialogue in it. Balzac's *La Grenadière* — it is years since I read it; but has it any dialogue at all? Balzac's *L'Interdiction* — an extraordinary presentation of a quaint functionary, fossiliferous and secluded, suddenly brought into contact with people of the world, and with the utmost ability baffling their financial intrigue — this is certainly the most remarkable short story ever written about money — *L'Interdiction* has not much dialogue. In the *Atheist's Mass*, again — the short story of such a nameless pathos — the piece which, more even than *Eugénie Grandet* itself, should be everybody's introduction, and especially every woman's introduction, to the genius of Balzac: *La Messe de l'Athée* has no dialogue. Coming to our actual *contemporaries* in France, of whom Zola[1] and Daudet[2] must still, it is possible, be accounted the foremost, it is natural that the more finished and minute worker — the worker lately lamented — should be the one who has made the most of the short story. And in this order of his work — thus leaving out his larger and most brilliant canvas, *Froment Jeune et Risler Aîné* — what do we more lastingly remember than the brief and sombre narrative of *Les Deux Auberges*? — a little piece that has no story at all; but a 'situation' depicted, and when depicted, *left*. There is an open country; leagues of Provence; a long stretching road; and on the roadside opposite each other, two inns. The older one is silent, melancholy; the other, noisy and prosperous. And the landlord of the older inn spends all his time in the newer: taking his pleasure there with guests who were once his own, and with a handsome landlady, who makes amends for his departed business. And in his own inn, opposite, a deserted woman sits solitary. That is all. But the art of the master!

Now this particular instance of a pregnant brevity reminds me that in descriptions of landscape the very obligations of the short story are an

---

1   Émile Zola (1840–1902), French novelist, leading figure of the naturalist school.

2   Alphonse Daudet (1840–97), French novelist.

advantage to its art. Nature in fiction requires to be seen not in endless detail, as a botanical or geographical study, but, as in Classic Landscape Composition, a noble glimpse of it, over a man's shoulder, under a man's arm. I know, of course, that is not the popular view. There are novels which have owed their popularity to landscape written by the ream. Coaches have been named after them: steamboats have been named after them. I am not sure that, in their honour, inaccessible heights have not been scaled and virgin forests broken in upon, so that somewhere in picturesque districts the front of a gigantic hotel shall have inscribed on it the title of a diffuse novel.

But that is not the great way. The great way, from Virgil's[1] to Browning's,[2] is the way of pregnant brevity. And where dialogue *is* employed in the finer short story, every line of it is bound to be significant. The short story has no room for the reply that is only *near* to being appropriate, and it deserves no pardon for the word that would not have been certainly employed. It is believed generally, and one can well suppose that it is true, that the average dialogue of the diffuse novel is written quickly. That is in part because so little of it is really dramatic — is really at all the inevitable word. But the limited sentences in which, when the narrator must narrate no more, the persons who have been described in the short story express themselves on their restricted stage, need, if I dare assert it, to be written slowly, or, what is better, re-read a score of times, and pruned, and looked at from without, and surveyed on every side.

But, indeed, of the *long* story, as well as of the short, may it not be agreed that on the whole the dialogue is apt to be the least successful thing? The ordinary reader, of course, will not be dramatic enough to notice its deficiencies. In humorous dialogue, these are seen least. Humorous dialogue has a legitimate license. You do not ask from it exactitude: you do not nail it down. But in serious dialogue, the dialogue of the critical moment, when the fire of a little word will kindle how great a matter, how needful then, and how *rare*, that the word be the true one! We do not want laxity, inappropriateness, on the one hand; nor, on the other, the tortured phraseology of a too resolute cleverness. And those of us who have a preference — derived, it may be, from the simpler generation of Dickens — for an unbending when it is a question of *little* matters, and, when it is a question of great ones, for 'a sincere large

---

1   (70–19 BC), author of the *Aeneid*, considered the greatest of the Latin poets.

2   Either Elizabeth Barrett Browning (1806–61) or husband Robert Browning (1812–89), both respected English poets.

accent, nobly plain' — well! there is much of modern finessing we are hardly privileged to understand. But if one wants an instance, in a long novel, in which the sentence now said at a white heat is the result, inevitable, burningly true to life, of the sentence that was said just before, one condones the obscurity that has had its imitators, and pays one's tribute of admiration to the insight of *Diana of the Crossways*.[1]

One of the difficulties of the short story, the short story shares with the acted drama, and that is the indispensableness of compression — the need that every sentence shall tell — the difference being, that in the acted drama it must tell for the moment, it must tell till it is found out, and in the short story it must tell for at least a *modest* eternity, and something more, if that be possible — for if a 'Fortnight is eternity' upon the Stock Exchange, a literary eternity is, perhaps, forty years.

Of course the short story, like all other fiction to be read, does not share the other difficulties of the acted drama — above all, the disadvantage which drags the acted drama down — the disadvantage of appealing to, at all events of having to give sops to, at one and the same moment, gallery and stalls: an audience so incongruous that it lies outside the power of Literature to weld it really together. In the contemporary theatre, in some of the very cleverest of our acted dramas, the characters are frequently doing, not what the man of intuition, and the man who remembers life, *knows* that they would do, but that which they must do to conciliate the Dress Circle, to entertain the Pit,[2] to defer not too long the gentle chuckle with which the 'average sensual man' receives the assurance that it is a delusion to suppose our world contains any soul, even a woman's soul, that is higher and purer than his. To such temptations the writer of the short story is not even exposed, if he be willing to conceive of his art upon exalted lines, to offer carefully the best of his reflection, in a form of durable and chosen grace, or, by a less conscious, perhaps, but not less fruitful, husbanding of his resources, to give us, sooner or later, some first-hand study of human emotion, 'gotten' as William Watson[3] says, 'of the immediate soul.' But again, contrasting his fortunes with those of his brother, the dramatist, the writer of short stories must, even at the best, know himself denied the dramatist's crowning advantage — which is the thrill of actual human presence.

---

1   Novel (1885) by George Meredith (1828–1909).

2   The "dress circle" refers to the first gallery in a theatre, where formal dress was once required. The "pit" is the main floor of a theatre, where less expensive general seating is available.

3   (1858–1935), English poet.

I have not presumed, except incidentally and by way of illustration, to sit in rapid judgment, and award impertinently blame or praise to the most or the least prominent of those who are writing short stories to-day. Even an occasional grappler with the difficulties of a task is not generally its best critic. He will criticise from the inside, now and then, and so, although you ought to have from him, now and again, at least — what I know, nevertheless, that *I* may not have given — illuminating commentary — you cannot have final judgment. Of the art of Painting, where skill of hand and sense of colour count for so much more than intellect, this is especially true. It is true, more or less, of Music — in spite of exceptions as notable as Schumann and Berlioz:[1] almost perfect critics of the very art that they produced. It is true — though in a less degree — of creative Literature. We leave this point, to write down, before stopping, one word about *tendencies*.

Among the better writers, one tendency of the day is to devote a greater care to the art of expression — to an unbroken continuity of excellent and varied style. The short story, much more than the long one, makes this thing possible to men who may not claim to be geniuses, but who, if we are to respect them at all, must claim to be artists. And yet, in face of the indifference of so much of our public here, to anything we can call Style — in face, actually, of a strange insensibility to it — the attempt, wherever made, is a courageous one. This insensibility — how does it come about?

It comes about, in honest truth, partly because that instrument of Art, our English tongue, in which the verse of Gray[2] was written, and the prose of Landor and Sterne,[3] is likewise the necessary vehicle in which, every morning of our lives, we ask for something at breakfast. If we all of us had to demand breakfast by making a rude drawing of a coffee-pot, we should understand, before long — the quickness of the French intelligence on that matter being unfortunately denied us — the man in the street would understand that Writing, as much as Painting, is an art to be acquired, and an art in whose technical processes one is bound to take pleasure. And, perhaps, another reason is the immense diffusion nowadays of superficial education; so that the election of a book to the honours of quick popularity is decided by those, precisely, whose minds are least trained for the exercise of that suffrage. What *is* elected is too often the

---

1   Hector Berlioz (1803–69), French composer.

2   Thomas Gray (1716–71), English poet.

3   Laurence Sterne (1713–68), English novelist.

work which presents at a first reading everything that it presents at all. I remember Mr. Browning once saying, à *propos* of such a matter, 'What has a cow to do with nutmegs?' He explained it was a German proverb. Is it? Or is it German only in the way of 'Sonnets from the Portuguese'?[1] Anyhow, things being as they are, all the more honour to such younger people as, in the face of indifference, remember that their instrument of English language is a quite unequalled instrument of art.

Against this happy tendency one has to set — in regard at least to some of them — tendencies less admirable. For, whilst the only kind of work that has a chance of engaging the attention of Sainte Beuve's[2] 'severe To-morrow' is work that is original, individual, sincere, is it not a pity, because of another's sudden success, to be unremittingly occupied with the exploitation of one particular world — to paint for ever, say, in violent and garish hue, or in deep shades through which no light can struggle, the life of the gutter? — to paint it, too, with that distorted 'realism' which witnesses upon the part of its practitioners to *one thing only*, a profound conviction of the ugly! I talk, of course, not of the short stories of the penetrating observer, but of those of the dyspeptic pessimist, whose pessimism, where it is not the *pose* of the contortionist — adopted with an eye to a sensational success of journalism, to a commercial effect — is hysteria, an imitative malady, a malady of the mind. The profession of the literary pessimist is already overcrowded; and if I name two writers who, though in different degrees, have avoided the temptation to join it — if I name one who knows familiarly the cheery as well as the more sombre side of Cockney character and life, Mr. Henry Nevinson,[3] the author of the remarkable short stories *Neighbours of Ours,* and then again a more accepted student of a sordid existence — Mr. George Gissing, in *Human Odds and Ends* especially — I name them but as such instances as I am privileged to *know,* of a profoundly observant and relatively an unbiassed treatment of the subjects with which they have elected to deal.

In France, in the short story, we may easily notice, the uglier forms of 'Realism' are wearing themselves out. 'Le soleil de France,' said Gluck[4] to Marie Antoinette, 'le soleil de France donne du génie.'[5] And the genius that it gives cannot long be hopeless and sombre. It leaves the obscure

---

1   Sonnet sequence (1850) by Elizabeth Barrett Browning (1806–61).

2   Charles-Augustin Sainte-Beuve (1804–69), French critic.

3   English writer (1856–1941) best known as a journalist and activist for women's rights.

4   Christoph Gluck (1714–87), Bohemian-German composer.

5   (French) "the French sun gives genius."

wood and tangled by-path; it makes for the open road: 'la route claire et droite' — the phrase is M. Poincarré's[1] — 'la route claire et droite où marche le génie Français.'[2] Straight and clear, generally, was the road followed — the road sometimes actually cut — by the unresting talent of Guy de Maupassant,[3] the writer of a hundred short stories, which, for the world of his day at least, went far beyond Charles Nodier's[4] earlier delicacy and Champfleury's[5] wit. But somehow, upon De Maupassant's whole nature and temperament the curse of pessimism lay. To deviate into cheeriness he must deal with the virtues of the *déclassées*[6] — undoubtedly an interesting theme — he must deal with them as in the famous *Maison Tellier*, an ebullition of scarcely cynical comedy, fuller much of real humanity than De Goncourt's[7] sordid document, *La Fille Elisa*. But that was an exception. De Maupassant was pessimist generally, because, master of an amazing talent, he refreshed himself never in any rarefied air; and the vista of the Spirit was denied him. His reputation he should more or less keep; but his school — the school in which a few even of our own juvenile and imitative writers prattled the accents of a hopeless materialism — his school, I fancy, will be crowded no more. For, with an observation scarcely less keen, and infinitely more judicial, M. René Bazin[8] treats, to-day, themes, we need not say more 'legitimate' — since much may be legitimate — but at least more acceptable. And then again with a style of which de Maupassant, direct and vigorous as was his own, must have envied even the clarity, and, of course, the subtler charm, a master draughtsman of ecclesiastic, and bookworm, of the neglected genius of the provincial town (some poor devil of a small professor), and of the soldier, and the shopkeeper, and the Sous-Préfet's wife — I hope I am describing M. Anatole France[9] — looks out on the contemporary

---

1   Either Henri Poincaré (1856–1912), French mathematician and savant whose scholarly works attracted a relatively large readership; or Raymond Poincaré (1860–1934), French politician and France's Minister of Education and Minister of Finance during the 1890s.

2   (French) "the straight and clear road where French genius travels."

3   (1850–93), French writer of short stories and novels.

4   French author (1780–1844).

5   Jules François Félix Husson, dit Fleury ou Champfleury (1821–89), French writer.

6   (French) those of a lower class.

7   Edmond and Jules de Goncourt (1822–96 and 1830–70), French brothers and authors who collaborated extensively in their writing.

8   French writer (1853–1932).

9   Pseud. Jacques-Anatole-François Thibault (1844–1922), French short story writer, novelist, and journalist, received the Nobel Prize for literature in 1921.

world with a vision humane and genial, sane and wide. Pessimism, as it seems to me, is only natural — can only be excusable — to those who are still bowed down by the immense responsibility of youth. It was a great poet[1] who, writing of one of his peers — a man of mature life — declared of him, *not* 'he mopes picturesquely,' but 'he knows the world, firm, quiet, and gay.' To such a writer — only to such a writer — is possible a happy comedy; and possible, besides, a true and an august vision of profounder things! And *that* is the spirit to which the Short Story, at its best, will certainly return.

---

49 Robert Browning (1812–89), English poet; the quotation is from "Dis Aliter Visum; or, Le Byron de Nos Jours" (c. 1862).

Appendix E

Laura Marholm Hansson, from "Neurotic Keynotes" (1896)

[Laura Marholm Hansson (1845–1928) was a well-known German author who wrote extensively on female authors and the impact that being a woman had on one's literary style, themes, and point of view. In "Neurotic Keynotes," she uses George Egerton's work to consider the ways in which female short-story writers can strike "the fundamental cord of women's nature."]

I.

Last year there was a book published in London with the extraordinary title of "Keynotes." Three thousand copies were sold in the course of a few months, and the unknown author became a celebrity. Soon afterwards the portrait of a lady appeared in "The Sketch."[1] She had a small, delicate face, with a pained and rather tired expression, and a curious, questioning look in the eyes; it was an attractive face, very gentle and womanly, and yet there was something disillusioned and unsatisfied about it. This lady wrote under the pseudonym of George Egerton,[2] and "Keynotes" was her first book.

It was a strange book! too good a book to become famous all at once. It burst upon the world like the opening buds in spring, like the cherry blossom after the first cold shower of rain. What can have made this book so popular in the England of to-day, which is as totally devoid of all true literature as Germany itself? Was it only the writer's strong individuality, which each successive page impressed upon the reader's nerves more vividly and more painfully than the last? The reader, did I say? Yes, but not the male reader. There are very few men who have a sufficiently keen

---

1 London periodical addressing arts and culture, notable for its heavy use of photographs.

2 Pseud. Mary Chavelita Dunne (1859–1945), English short-story writer. See headnote to her story in this collection.

appreciation for a woman's feelings to be able to put their own minds and souls into the swing of her confession, and to accord it their full sympathy. Yet there are such men. We may perhaps come across two or three of them in a lifetime, but they disappear from our sight, as we do from theirs. And they are not readers. Their sympathy is of a deeper, more personal character, and as far as the success of a book is concerned, it need not be taken into consideration at all.

"Keynotes" is not addressed to men, and it will not please them. It is not written in the style adopted by the other women Georges, — George Sand[1] and George Eliot,[2] — who wrote from a man's point of view, with the solemnity of a clergyman or the libertinism of a drawing-room hero. There is nothing of the man in this book, and no attempt is made to imitate him, even in the style, which springs backwards and forwards as restlessly as a nervous little woman at her toilet, when her hair will not curl and her stay-lace breaks. Neither is it a book which favors men; it is a book written against them, a book for our private use.

There have been such books before; old-maid literature is a lucrative branch of industry, both in England and Germany (the two most unliterary countries in Europe), and that is probably the reason why the majority of authoresses write as though they were old maids. But there are no signs of girlish prudery in "Keynotes;" it is a liberal book, indiscreet in respect of the intimacies of married life, and entirely without respect for the husband; it is a book with claws and teeth ready to scratch and bite when the occasion offers, — not the book of a woman who married for the sake of a livelihood, but the book of a devoted wife, who would be inseparable from her husband if only he were not so tiresome, and dull, and stupid, such a thorough man, insufferable at times, and yet indispensable as the husband always is to the wife.

And it is the book of a gentlewoman!

We have had tell-tale women before, but Heaven preserve us! Fru Skram[3] is a man in petticoats; she speaks her mind plainly enough, — rather too plainly to suit my taste. "Gyp,"[4] a distinguished Frenchwoman, has written "Autour du Mariage," and she cannot be said to mince matters either. But here we have something quite different; something which

---

1   Pseud. Amandine-Aurore Lucille Dupin (1804–76), French novelist.

2   Pseud. Mary Ann (later Marian) Evans (1819–80), English writer.

3   Amalie Skram (1846–1905), Norwegian writer.

4   Pseudonym for Gabrielle de Mirabeau, Comtesse de Martel de Janville (1850–1932), French author.

does not in the least resemble Gyp's frivolous worldliness or Amalie Skram's coarseness. Mrs. Egerton would shudder at the thought of washing dirty linen in public, and she could not, even if she were to force herself, treat the relationship between husband and wife with cynical irony, and she does not force herself in the very least.

She writes as she really is, because she cannot do otherwise. She has had an excellent education, and is a lady with refined tastes, with something of that innocence of the grown woman which is almost more touching than a girl's innocence, because it proves how little of his knowledge of life in general, and his sex in particular, the Teutonic husband confides to his wife. She stands watching him, — an eating, loving, smoking organism. Heavens! how wearisome! So loved, and yet so wearisome! It is unbearable! And she retreats into herself, and realizes that she is a woman.

It is almost universal amongst women, especially Germans, that they do not take man as seriously as he likes to imagine. They think him comical, — not only when they are married to him, but even before that, when they are in love with him. Men have no idea what a comical appearance they present, not only as individuals, but as a race. The comic part about a man is that he is so different from women, and that is just what he is proudest of. The more refined and fragile a woman is, the more ridiculous she is likely to find the clumsy great creature who takes such a roundabout way to gain his comical ends.

To young girls especially man offers a perpetual excuse for a laugh, and a secret shudder. When men find a group of women laughing among themselves, they never suspect that it is they who are the cause of it. And that again is so comic! The better a man is, the more he is in earnest when he makes his pathetic appeal for a great love; and woman, who takes a special delight in playing a little false, even when there is no necessity, becomes as earnest and solemn as he, when all the time she is only making fun of him. A woman wants amusement, wants change; a monotonous existence drives her to despair, whereas a man thrives on monotony, and the cleverer he is the more he wishes to retire into himself, that he may draw upon his own resources; a clever woman needs variety, that she may take her impressions from without.

... The early blossoms of the cherry-tree shudder beneath the cold rain which has burst their scales; this shudder is the deepest vibration in Mrs. Egerton's book. What is the subject? A little woman in every imaginable mood, who is placed in all kinds of likely and unlikely circumstances: in every story it is the same little woman with a difference, the same little woman, who is always loved by a big, clumsy, comic man, who is now good and well-behaved, now wild, drunk, and brutal; who some-times ill-treats her, sometimes fondles her, but never understands what it is that he ill-treats and fondles. And she sits like a true Englishwoman with her fishing-rod, and while she is waiting for a bite, "her thoughts go to other women she has known, women good and bad, school friends, casual acquaintances, women-workers, — joyless machines for grinding daily corn, unwilling maids grown old in the endeavor to get settled, patient wives who bear little ones to indifferent husbands until they wear out, — a long array. She busies herself with questioning. Have they, too, this thirst for excitement, for change, this restless craving for sun and love and motion? Stray words, half confidences, glimpses through soul-chinks of suppressed fires, actual outbreaks, domestic catastrophes, — how the ghosts dance in the cells of her memory! And she laughs — laughs softly to herself because the denseness of man, his chivalrous conservative devo-tion to the female idea he has created, blinds him, perhaps happily, to the problems of her complex nature, ... and well it is that the workings of our hearts are closed to them, that we are cunning enough or *great* enough to seem to be what they would have us, rather than be what we are. But few of them have had the insight to find out the key to our seeming contra-dictions, — the why a refined, physically fragile woman will mate with a brute, a mere male animal with primitive passions, and love him; the why strength and beauty appeal more often than the more subtly fine qual-ities of mind or heart; the why women (and not the innocent ones) will condone sins that men find hard to forgive in their fellows. They have all overlooked the eternal wildness, the untamed primitive savage tempera-ment that lurks in the mildest, best woman. Deep in through ages of con-vention this primeval trait burns, an untamable quantity that may be concealed, but is never eradicated by culture, — the keynote of woman's witchcraft and woman's strength."

They are not stories which Mrs. Egerton tells us. She does not care for telling stories. They are keynotes which she strikes, and these keynotes met with an extraordinary and most unexpected response. They struck a sym-pathetic chord in women, which found expression in a multitude of let-ters, and also in the sale of the book. An author can hope for no happier fate than to receive letters which re-echo the tune that he has discovered in his own soul. Those who have received them know what pleasant feel-ings they call forth. We often do not know where they come from, we cannot answer them, nor should we wish to do so if we could. They give us a sudden insight into the hidden centre of a living soul, where we can gaze into the secret, yearning life, which is never lived in the sight of the world, but is generally the best part of a person's nature; we feel the sympathetic clasp of a friendly hand, and our own soul is filled with a thankfulness which will never find expression in words. The dark world seems filled with unknown friends, who surround us on every side like bright stars in the night.

Mrs. Egerton had struck the fundamental chord in woman's nature, and her book was received with applause by hundreds of women. The critic said: "The woman in 'Keynotes' is an exceptional type, and we can only deal with her as such." "Good heavens! How stupid they are!" laughed Mrs. Egerton. Numberless women wrote to her, women whom she did not know, and whose acquaintance she never made. "We are quite ordinary, every-day sort of people," they said; "we lead trivial, unimportant lives; but there is something in us which vibrates to your touch, for we, too, are such as you describe." "Keynotes" took like wildfire.

There is nothing tangible in the book to which it can be said to owe its significance. Notes are not tangible. The point on which it differs from all other well-known books by women is the intensity of its awakened consciousness as woman. It follows no pattern and is quite independent of any previous work; it is simply full of a woman's individuality. It is not written on a large scale, and it does not reveal a very expansive temperament. But, such as it is, it possesses an amount of nervous energy which carries us along with it, and we must read every page carefully until the last one is turned, not peep at the end to see what is going to happen, as we do when reading a story with a plot; we must read every page for its own sake, if we would feel the power of its different moods, varying from feverish haste to wearied rest....

III.

Another characteristic is beginning to make itself felt, which was bound to come at last. And that is an intense and morbid consciousness of the ego in women. This consciousness was unknown to our mothers and grandmothers; they may have had stronger characters than ours, as they undoubtedly had to overcome greater hindrances; but this consciousness of the ego is quite another thing, and they had not got it.

Neither of these women, whose books I have been reviewing [Egerton and Lemerre], are authors by profession. There is nothing they care for less than to write books, and nothing that they desire less than to hear their names on every one's lips. Both were able to write without having learned.

Other authoresses of whom we hear have either taught themselves to write, or have been taught by men. They began with an object, but without having anything to say; they chose their subjects from without.

Neither of these women have any object. They do not want to describe what they have seen. They do not want to teach the world, nor do they try to improve it. They have nothing to fight against. They merely put themselves into their books. They did not even begin with the intention of writing; they obeyed an impulse. There was no question of whether they wished or not; they were obliged. The moment came when they were forced to write, and they did not concern themselves with reasons or objects. Their ego burst forth with such power that it ignored all outer circumstances; it pressed forward and crystallized itself into an artistic shape. These women have not only a very pronounced style of their own, but are in fact artists; they became it as soon as they took up the pen. They had nothing to learn, it was theirs already.

This is not only a new phase in the work of literary production, it is also a new phase in woman's nature. Formerly, not only all great authoresses, but likewise all prominent women, were — or tried to be — intellectual. That also was an attempt to accommodate themselves to men's wishes. They were always trying to follow in the footsteps of the man. Man's ideas, interests, speculations, were to be understood and sympathized with. When philosophy was the fashion, great authoresses and intelligent women philosophized. Because Goethe[1] was wise, Rahel[2] was filled with the wisdom of life. George Eliot preached in all her books, and philosophized all her life long after the manner of Stuart Mill[3] and Herbert Spencer.[4] George Sand was the receptacle for ideas — men's ideas — of the most contradictory character, which she immediately reproduced in her novels. Good Ebner-Eschenbach[5] writes as sensibly, and with as much tolerance, as a right worthy old gentleman; and Fru Leffler[6] chose her subjects from among the problems which were being discussed by a few well-known men. None of their writings can be

---

1   Johan Wolfgang von Goethe (1749–1832), highly influential German author.

2   Rahel Varnhagen (1771–1833), Jewish-German author and hostess of an influential salon for the discussion of art, literature, and philosophy.

3   John Stuart Mill (1806–73), political philosopher and author of *Liberty* (1859), *Utilitarianism* (1861), and other works.

4   (1820–1903), founder of "evolutionary" philosophy.

5   Marie von Ebner-Eschenbach (1830–1916), German writer.

6   Anne Charlotte Leffler (1849–92), Swedish author.

considered as essentially characteristic of women. It was not an altogether unjust assertion when men declared that the women who wrote books were only half women.

Yet these were the best. Others, who wrote as women, had no connection with literature at all; they merely knitted literary stockings.

Mrs. Egerton and the author of "Dilettantes" [Lemerre] are not intellectual, not in the very least. The possibility of being it has never entered their brain. They had no ambition to imitate men. They are not in the least impressed by the speculations, ideas, theories, and philosophies of men. They are sceptics in all that concerns the mind; the man himself they can perceive.

They perceive his soul, his inner self, — when he has one, — and they are keenly sensitive when it is not there. The other women with the great names are quite thick-headed in comparison. They judge everything with the understanding; these perceive with the nerves, and that is an entirely different kind of understanding.

They understand man, but, at the same time, they perceive that he is quite different from themselves, that he is the contrast to themselves. The one is too highly cultured; the other has too sensitive a nervous system to permit the thought of any equality between man and woman. The idea makes them laugh. They are far too conscious of being refined, sensitive women. They do not concern themselves with the modern democratic tendencies regarding women, with its levelling of contrasts, its desire for equality. They live their own life, and if they find it unsatisfying, empty, disappointing, they cannot change it. But they do not make any compromise to do things by halves; their highly developed nerves are too sure a standard to allow of that. They are a new race of women, more resigned, more hopeless, and more sensitive than the former ones. They are women such as the new men require; they have risen up on the intellectual horizon as the forerunners of a generation who will be more sensitive, and who will have a keener power of enjoyment than the former ones. Among themselves these women exchange sympathetic glances, and are able to understand one another without need of confession. They, with their highly-developed nerves, can feel for each other with a sympathy such as formerly a woman only felt for man. In this way they go through life, without building castles in the air, or making any plans for the future; they live on day by day, and never look beyond. It might be said that they are waiting; but as each new day arrives, and the sand of time falls drop by drop upon their delicate nerves, even this imperceptible burden is more than they can bear; the strain of it is too much for them.

IV

I have before me a new book by Mrs. Egerton, and two new photographs. In the one she is sitting curled up in a chair, reading peacefully. She has a delicate, rather sharp-featured profile, with a long, somewhat prominent chin, that gives one an idea of yearning. The other is a full-length portrait. A slender, girlish figure, with narrow shoulders, and a waist, if anything, rather too small; a tired, worn face, without youth and full of disillusion; the hair looks as though restless fingers had been passed through it, and there is a bitter, hopeless expression about the lines of the mouth. In her letters — in which we never wholly possess her, but merely her *mood* — she comes to us in various guises, — now as a playful kitten, that is curled up cosily, and sometimes stretches out a soft little paw in playful, tender need of a caress; or else she is a worried, disappointed woman, with overwrought and excitable nerves, sceptical in the possibility of content, a seeker, for whom the charm lies in the seeking, not in the finding. She is a type of the modern woman, whose inmost being is the essence of disillusion.

When we examine the portraits of the four principal characters in this book — Sonia Kovalevsky,[1] Eleonora Duse,[2] Marie Bashkirtseff,[3] and George Egerton — we find that they all have one feature in common. It was not I who first noticed this, it was a man. Ola Hansson,[4] seeing them lying together one day, pointed it out to me, and he said: "The lips of all four speak the same language, — the young girl, the great tragedian, the woman of intellect, and the neurotic writer; each one has a something about the corners of the mouth that expresses a wearied satiety, mingled with an unsatisfied longing, as though she had as yet enjoyed nothing."

Why this wearied satiety mingled with an unsatisfied longing? Why should these four women, who are four opposites, as it were, have the same expression? The virgin in body and soul, the great creator of the rôles of the degenerates, the mathematical professor, and the neurotic writer? Is it something in themselves, something peculiar in the organic nature of their womanhood, or is it some influence from without? Is it because they have chosen a profession which excites, while it leaves them dissatisfied, for the simple reason that a profession can never wholly satisfy a woman? Yet these four have excelled in their profession. But can a woman ever

---

1   (1850–91), renowned Russian mathematician and first woman to receive a PhD in mathematics.

2   (1858–1924), Italian actress.

3   (1859–84), Russian artist and diarist.

4   (1860–1905), Swedish writer.

obtain satisfaction by means of her achievements? Is not her life as a woman — as a wife and as a mother — the true source of all her happiness? And this touch of disillusion in all of them — is it the disillusion they have experienced as *woman*; is it the expression of their bitter experiences in the gravest moment in a woman's life? Disappointment in man? *The* man that fate thrust across their path, who was their experience? And their yearning is now fruitless, for the flower of expectant realization withered before they plucked it.

Two of these women have carried the secret of their faces with them to the grave, but the others live and are not willing to reveal it. George Egerton would like to be as silent about it as they are; but her nerves speak, and her nerves have betrayed her secret in the book called "Discords."

When we read "Discords" we ask ourselves how is it possible that this frail little woman could write such a strong, brutal book? In "Keynotes" Mrs. Egerton was still a little coquette, with 5 3/4 gloves and 18-inch waist, who herself played a fascinating part. She had something of a midge's nature, dancing up and down, and turning nervous somersaults in the sunshine. "Discords" is certainly a continuation of "Keynotes," but it is quite another kind of woman who meets us here. The thrilling, nervous note of the former book has changed into a clashing, piercing sound, hard as metal; it is the voice of an accuser in whom all bitterness takes the form of reproaches which are unjust, and yet unanswerable. It is the voice of a woman who is conscious of being ill-treated and driven to despair, and who speaks in spite of herself in the name of thousands of ill-treated and despairing women. Who can tell us whether her nerves have ill-treated this woman and driven her to despair, or whether it is her outward fate, especially her fate with regard to the man? Women of this kind are not confidential. They take back to-morrow what they have confessed to-day, partly from a wish not to let themselves be understood, and partly because the aspect of their experiences varies with every change of mood, like the colors in a kaleidoscope.

But throughout these changes, one single note is maintained in "Discords," as it was in "Keynotes." In the latter it was a high, shrill treble, like the song of a bird in spring; in "Discords" it is a deep bass note, groaning in distress with the groan of a disappointed woman.

V

The tone of bitter disappointment which pervades "Discords" is the expression of woman's disappointment in man. Man and man's love are not a joy to her; they are a torment. He is inconsiderate in his demands, brutal in his caresses, and unsympathetic with those sides of her nature which are not there for his satisfaction. He is no longer the great comic animal of "Keynotes," whom the woman teases and plays with — he is a nightmare which smothers her during horrible nights, a hangman who tortures her body and soul during days and years for his pleasure; a despot who demands admiration, caresses, and devotion, while her every nerve quivers with an opposite emotion; a man born blind, whose clumsy fingers press the spot where the pain is, and when she moans, replies with coarse, unfeeling laughter, "Absurd nonsense!"

Although I believed myself to be acquainted with all the books which women have written against men, no book that I have ever read has impressed me with such a vivid sense of physical pain. Most women come with reasonings, moral sermons, and outbursts of temper: a man may allow himself much that is forbidden to others, that must be altered. Women are of no importance in his eyes; he has permitted himself to look down upon them. They intend to teach him their importance. They are determined that he shall look up to them. But here we have no trace of Xantippe-like[1] violence, only a woman who holds her trembling hands to the wounds which man has inflicted upon her, of which the pain is intensified each time that he draws near. A woman, driven to despair, who jumps upon him like a wild-cat, and seizes him by the throat; and if that does not answer, chooses for herself a death that is ten times more painful than life with him, *chooses* it in order that she may have her own way.

What is this? It is not the well-known domestic animal which we call woman. It is a wild creature belonging to a wild race, untamed and untamable, with the yellow gleam of a wild animal in its eyes. It is a nervous, sensitive creature, whose primitive wildness is awakened by a blow which it has received, which bursts forth, revengeful and pitiless as the lightning in the night.

That is what I like about this book. That a woman should have sprung up, who with her instinct can bore to the bottom layers of womanhood the quality that enables her to renew the race, her primæval quality, which man, with all his understanding, has never penetrated. A few years

---

1   Wife of Socrates, characterized as ill-tempered.

ago, in a study on Gottfried Keller's[1] women, I mentioned wildness as the basis of woman's nature; Mrs. Egerton has given utterance to the same opinion in "Keynotes," and has since tried to embody it in "Discords;" her best stories are those where the wild instinct breaks loose.

But why this terror of man, this physical repulsion, as in the story called "Virgin Soil"? The authoress says that it is because an ignorant girl in her complete innocence is handed over in marriage to an exacting husband. But that is not reason enough. The authoress's intellect is not as true as her instinct. There must be something more. The same may be said of "Wedlock," where the boarding-house cook marries an amorous working-man, who is in receipt of good wages, for the sake of having her illegitimate child to live with her; he refuses to allow it, and when the child dies of a childish ailment, she murders his two children by the first marriage.

Mrs. Egerton's stories are not invented; neither are they realistic studies copied from the notes in her diary. They are experiences. She has lived them all, because the people whom she portrays have impressed their characters or their fate upon her quivering nerves. The music of her nerves has sounded like the music of a stringed instrument beneath the touch of a strange hand, as in that masterpiece, "Gone Under," where the woman tells her story between the throes of sea-sickness and drunkenness. The man to whom she belongs has punished her unfaithfulness by the murder of her child, and she revenges herself by drunkenness; yet, in spite of it all, he remains the master whom she is powerless to punish, and in her despair she throws herself upon the streets.

Only one man has had sufficient instinct to bring to light this abyss in woman's nature, and that is Barbey d'Aurevilly,[2] the poet who was never understood. But in Mrs. Egerton's book there is one element which he had not discovered, and, although she does not express it in words, it shows itself in her description of men and women. Her men are Englishmen with bull-dog natures, but the women belong to another race; and is not this horror, this physical repulsion, this woman raging against the man, a true representation of the way that the Anglo-Saxon nature reacts upon the Celtic?

Two races stand opposed to one another in these sketches; perhaps the authoress herself is not quite conscious of it, but it is plainly visible in her descriptions of character, where we have the heavy, massive Englishman,

---

1   (1819–90), Swiss writer of short stories, novels, and poems.

2   Jules-Amédée Barbey-D'Aurevilly (1808–89), French writer and critic.

l'animal mâle, and the untamable woman who is prevented by race instinct from loving where she ought to love.

In "The Regeneration of Two," Mrs. Egerton has tried to describe a Celtic woman where she can love, but the attempt is most unsuccessful, for here we see plainly that she lacked the basis of experience. There are, however, many women who know what love is, although they have never experienced it. Men came, they married, but the man for them never came.

VI

There is a little story in this collection called "Her Share," where the style is full of tenderness, perhaps even a trifle too sweet. It affects one like a landscape on an evening in early autumn, when the sun has gone down and twilight reigns; it seems as though veiled in gray, for there is no color left, although everything is strangely clear. Mrs. Egerton has a peculiarly gentle touch and soft voice where she describes the lonely, independent working girl. Her little story is often nothing more than the fleeting shadow of a mood, but the style is sustained throughout in a warm stream of lyric; for this Celtic woman certainly has the lyrical faculty, a thing which a woman writer rarely has, if ever, possessed before. There is something in her writing which seems to express a desire to draw near to the lonely girl and say: "You have such a good time of it in your grayness. In Grayness your nerves find rest, your instincts slumber, no man ill-treats you with his love, you experience discontent in contentment, but you know nothing of the torture of unstrung nerves. Would I were like you; but I am a bundle of electric currents bursting forth in all directions into chaos."

Besides these two dainty twilight sketches, she has others like the description in "Gone Under," of the storm on that voyage from America to England where we imagine ourselves on board ship, and seem to feel the rolling sea, to hear the ship cracking and groaning, to smell the hundreds of fetid smells escaping from all corners, and the damp ship-biscuits and the taste of the bitter salt spray on the tongue. We owe this forcible and matter-of-fact method of reproducing the impressions received by the senses to the retentive power of her nerves, through which she is able to preserve her passing impressions and to reproduce them in their full intensity. She relies on her womanly receptive faculty, not on her brain.

George Egerton's life has been of the kind which affords ample material for literary purposes, and it is probable that she has more raw material ready for use at any time when she may require it; but at present she retains it in her nerves, as it were, under lock and key. She had intended from child-hood to become an artist, and writing is only an afterthought; yet, no sooner did she begin to write than the impressions and experiences of her life shaped themselves into the form of her two published works. Until the publication of "Discords," we had thought that she was one of those intensely individualistic writers who write one book because they must, but never write another, or, at any rate, not one that will bear comparison with the first; the publication of "Discords" has entirely dispelled this opinion, and has given us good reason to hope for many more works from her pen.